SIR RICHARD FRANCIS BURTON (1821–1890) was a gifted linguist, daring explorer, prolific author and one of the most flamboyant celebrities of his day. Forced to leave Oxford for unruly behavior, he joined the British Army in India, where he gained a remarkable knowledge of Arabic, Hindustani, and Persian, eventually acquiring 29 languages and many dialects. He led the famed expedition to discover the source of the Nile and, disguised as a Moslem, made a pilgrimage to the then-forbidden city of Mecca and penetrated the sacred city of Harar in unexplored East Africa. Burton translated unexpurgated versions of many Oriental texts, including the *Kama Sutra* (1883) and *Arabian Nights* (1885–88), which is perhaps his most celebrated achievement.

JACK ZIPES is a professor of German at the University of Minnesota. The author of several books on fairy tales, including *Don't Bet on the Prince, Fairy Tales and the Art of Subversion,* and *Breaking the Magic Spell,* he is the editor and translator of *The Complete Tales of the Brothers Grimm* and *Beauties, Beasts and Enchantment: Classic French Fairy Tales.* He is also the editor of Signet Classic editions of *The Complete Fairy Tales of Oscar Wilde* and *Fairy Tales of Frank Stockton.*

Arabian Nights

The Marvels and Wonders of the Thousand and One Nights

Adapted from Richard F. Burton's unexpurgated translation

By Jack Zipes

A SIGNET CLASSIC

SIGNET CLASSIC
Published by New American Library, a division of
Penguin Putnam Inc., 375 Hudson Street,
New York, New York 10014, U.S.A.
Penguin Books Ltd, 27 Wrights Lane,
London W8 5TZ, England
Penguin Books Australia Ltd, Ringwood,
Victoria, Australia
Penguin Books Canada Ltd, 10 Alcorn Avenue,
Toronto, Ontario, Canada M4V 3B2
Penguin Books (N.Z.) Ltd, 182–190 Wairau Road,
Auckland 10, New Zealand

Penguin Books Ltd, Registered Offices:
Harmondsworth, Middlesex, England

Published by Signet Classic, an imprint of New American Library,
a division of Penguin Putnam Inc.

First Signet Classic Printing, August 1991
20 19 18 17 16 15 14 13

Library of Congress Catalog Card Number: 90-64160

Printed in the United States of America

Contents

A Note on the Text and the Translator

This adaptation is based on Richard F. Burton's *The Book of the Thousand Nights and a Night. A Plain and Literal Translation of the Arabian Nights Entertainment*, 10 vols. (Benares: Kamashastra Society, 1885–86). Considered one of the greatest scholar-explorers of the nineteenth century, Burton (1821–90) was the son of a retired lieutenant colonel and was educated in France and Italy during his youth. By the time he enrolled at Trinity College, Oxford, in 1840, he could speak French and Italian fluently along with the Béarnais and Neapolitan dialects, and he had an excellent command of Greek and Latin. In fact, he had such an extraordinary gift as linguist that he eventually learned twenty-five other languages and fifteen dialects. Yet, this ability was not enough to help him adapt to life and the proscriptions at Oxford. He soon encountered difficulties with the Oxford administration and was expelled in 1842. His troubles there may have been due to the fact that he was raised on the Continent and never felt at home in England.

Following in his father's footsteps, Burton enlisted in the British army and served eight years in India as a subaltern officer. During his time there, he learned Arabic, Hindi, Marathi, Sindhi, Punjabi, Teugu, Pashto, and Miltani, which enabled him to carry out some important intelligence assignments, but he was eventually forced to resign from the army because some of his espionage work became too controversial. After a brief respite (1850–52) with his mother in Boulogne, France, during which time he published four books on India, Burton explored the Nile Valley and was the first westerner to visit forbidden

Moslem cities and shrines. In 1855 he participated in the Crimean War, then explored the Nile again (1857–58), and in 1860 he took a trip to Salt Lake City, Utah, to do research for a biography of Brigham Young. In 1861, Burton married Isabel Arundell, the daughter of an aristocratic family, and accepted a position as consul in Fernando Po, a Spanish island off the coast of West Africa, remaining until 1864. Thereafter, he was British consul in Santos, Brazil (1864–68), Damascus, Syria (1868–71), and finally Trieste, Italy, until his death in 1890. Wherever he went, Burton wrote informative anthropological and ethnological studies such as *Sindh, and the Races That Inhabit the Valley of the Indus* (1851) and *Pilgrimage to El-Medinah and Mecca* (1855–56), composed his own poetry such as *The Kasidah* (1880), and translated unusual works of erotica such as the *Kama Sutra* (1883) and significant collections of folk tales such as Basile's *The Pentamerone* (1893). Altogether he published forty-three volumes about his explorations and travels, over one hundred articles, and thirty volumes of translations.

Burton's *Nights* is generally recognized as one of the finest *unexpurgated* translations of William Hay Macnaghten's Calcutta II edition (1839–42). The fact is, however, that Burton plagiarized a good deal of his translation from John Payne's *The Book of the Thousand Nights and One Night* (1882–84) so that he could publish his book quickly and acquire the private subscribers to Payne's edition. Payne (1842–1916), a remarkable translator and scholar of independent means, had printed only five-hundred copies of his excellent unexpurgated edition, for he had not expected much of a demand for the expensive nine-volume set. However, there were a thousand more subscribers who wanted his work, and since Payne was indifferent with regard to publishing a second edition, Burton received Payne's permission to offer his "new" translation to these subscribers about a year after Payne's work had appeared. Moreover, Burton profited a great deal from Payne's spadework (apparently with Payne's knowledge).

This is not to say that Burton's translation (which has copious anthropological notes and an important "Terminal Essay") should not be considered his work. He did most of the translation by himself, and only toward the end of his ten volumes did he plagiarize, although he kept his own style and apparently referred to the original text with regard to questions of interpretation. In contrast to Payne, Burton was more meticulous in respecting word order and the exact phrasing of the original; he included the division into nights with the constant intervention of Scheherazade and was more competent in translating the verse. Moreover, he was more insistent on emphasizing the erotic and bawdy aspects of the *Nights*. As he remarked in his introduction, his object was "to show what *The Thousand Nights and a Night* really is. Not, however, for reasons to be more fully stated in the Terminal Essay, by straining *verbum reddere verbo*, but by writing as the Arab would have written in English."

The result was a quaint, even bizarre and somewhat stilted, English that makes for difficult reading today. Even in his own day his language was obsolete, archaic, and convoluted. Therefore, I have endeavored to rework Burton's accurate but difficult translation into a more modern English idiom while trying to retain the flavor of his original and some of his stock phrases and mannerisms. To make his translation flow more smoothly I have eliminated redundant elements and garrulous passages. In addition, I have discarded all the poetry, since most of the poems were inserted later into the tales, often without reason, and I have changed the spelling of some of the characters' names and place-names. My small selection of tales from Burton's comprehensive ten volumes and his publication of supplemental tales has been made with an eye toward representing the various types of narratives that are in the larger collection: the fairy tale, the parable, the didactic tale, the fable, the legend, the jest, the anecdote, the apocryphal tale, etc. The two famous tales "Aladdin and the Magic Lamp" and "Ali Baba and the Forty Thieves" did not appear in Burton's original collection of the *Nights* but in his supplementary edition. His translation of "Aladdin and the Magic Lamp" was based on the Arabic manuscript published first in France under the title *Histoire d' Alá al-Din ou La Lampe Merveilleuse, Texte Arabe* (1888), edited by Hermann Zotenberg; and the translation of "Ali Baba and the Forty Thieves" was based on a nineteenth-century Hindustani version of *Hazar Dastan* ("The Thousand

Tales") by Totaram Sháyán. Most of my selections are well-known; others have been, in my opinion, unduly neglected. They are all included within the framework of Scheherazade's narrative that lends the collection its special meaning and charm, which I hope, I have managed to convey.

I would like to express my gratitude to Susan Rogers, who initiated this project, and to Rosemary Ahern, who supervised its completion with great care and concern. I also benefited from the fine editing of the tales by Ted Johnson. Finally, I should like to thank the John Simon Guggenheim Foundation, which provided me with a grant in 1989–90 that enabled me to undertake and complete the research for this project.

Jack Zipes
Minneapolis, 1991

Prologue

In the name of Allah, the Compassionate, who bestows His mercy on all! Praise be to Allah, the Beneficent King, the Creator of the Universe, Lord of the Three Worlds, and grace and blessing be upon Our Lord Mohammed, Prince of the Apostles!

Verily the works and words of our ancestors have become signs and examples to people of our modern age so that they may view what happened to other folk and take heed; so that they may peruse the annals of ancient peoples and read about everything they have experienced and thereby be guided and restrained.

Praise, therefore, be to Him, who has made the histories of the past an admonition for our own time! Their legacy has been passed on to us in the tales called "The Arabian Nights," together with their renowned legends and wonders.

And among these tales, thanks to the Omniscient and Almighty Allah, we have been given

The Story of King Shahryar and His Brother

A long time ago there was a mighty king of the Banu Sasan in the lands of India and China, and when he died, he left only two sons, one in the prime of manhood and the other still a youth, both brave cavaliers. But the elder was an especially superb horseman, and he became the successor to the empire and ruled the kingdom with such justice that he was beloved by all the people of his realm. His name was Shahryar, and he appointed his younger brother, Shah Zaman, king of Samarcan. In the years that followed, each brother was content to remain in his own kingdom, and each ruled with such equity and fairness that their subjects were extremely happy. Everything continued like this for twenty years, but at the end of that time, Shahryar yearned to see his younger brother once more before he died.

So he asked his vizier whether he thought it would be a good idea to visit his brother, but the minister found such an undertaking inadvisable and recommended that he write his brother a letter of invitation and send him gifts under the vizier's charge. Therefore, the king immediately ordered generous gifts to be prepared, such as horses that had saddles lined with gold and jewels, mamelukes, beautiful maidens, high-breasted virgins, and splendid and expensive cloth. He then wrote a letter to Shah Zaman expressing his strong desire to see him, and he ended it with these words: "I, therefore, hope that my beloved brother will honor me with his visit, and I am sending my vizier to make arrangements for the journey. My one and only desire is to see you before I die. If you refuse my request, I shall not survive the blow. May peace be with you!" Then King Shahryar sealed the letter, gave it to the vizier, and urged him to do his utmost to return as soon as possible.

"Your wish is my command," said the vizier, who began making all the preparations without delay. All this work occupied him three days, and on the dawn of the fourth he took leave of his king and journeyed over hills, deserts, and pleasant valleys without stopping night or day. Of course, whenever he entered a realm whose lord was under the rule of King Shahryar, he would be greeted with magnificent gifts and all kinds of fair and rare presents, and he would be obliged to stay there for three days, the customary term for the ritual to honor guests. And when he left on the fourth, he would be honorably escorted for one whole day to speed him on his way.

As soon as the vizier drew near Shah Zaman's court in Samarcan, he sent one of his high officials ahead to announce his arrival. This courier presented himself before the king, kissed the ground, and delivered his message. Thereupon, the king commanded various nobles and lords of his realm to go forth and meet his brother's vizier a good day's journey from his court. After they encountered him, they greeted him respectfully and formed an escort party. When the vizier entered the city, he proceeded straight to the palace, where he kissed the ground and prayed for the king's health and happiness and for victory over his enemies. Then he informed the king that his brother was yearning to see him and presented the letter, which Shah Zaman took from his hand and read. When the king fully comprehended its import, he said, "I cannot refuse the wishes of my brother. However, we shall not depart until we have honored my brother's vizier with three days of hospitality."

Shah Zaman assigned suitable quarters in the palace for the minister, and he ordered tents pitched for the troops and gave them rations of meat, drink, and other necessities. On the fourth day he prepared himself for the trip, gathered together sumptuous presents befitting his elder brother's majesty, and appointed his chief vizier to be viceroy of the land during his absence. Then he ordered his tents, camels, and mules to be brought forth, and he set up camp with their bales and loads, attendants and guards within sight of the city in order to set out early the next morning for his brother's capital.

It so happened, however, that in the middle of the night he suddenly remembered he had forgotten a gift in his palace that he wanted to take to his brother. So he returned alone and entered his private chambers, where he found the queen, his wife, asleep on his own couch, and in her arms she held a black cook with crude features, smeared with kitchen grease and grime. When he saw this, the world turned dark before his eyes, and he said, "If this is what happens while I am still within sight of the city, what will this damned whore do during my long absence at my brother's court?"

So he drew his scimitar, cut the two in four pieces with a single blow, and left them on the couch. Soon thereafter he returned to his camp without letting anyone know what had happened. Then he gave orders for immediate departure and set out on his trip. Nevertheless, he could not help thinking about his wife's betrayal, and he kept saying to himself over and over, "How could she have done this to me? How could she have brought about her own death?" until excessive grief seized him. His color changed to yellow, his body grew weak, and he appeared to be on the verge of death. So the vizier had to shorten the stages of the journey and remain longer at the watering places in order to take care of the king.

Now, when Shah Zaman finally approached his brother's capital, he sent messengers to announce his arrival, and Shahryar came forth to meet him with the viziers, emirs, lords, and nobles of his realm. After saluting him, he was overcome with joy and ordered the city to be decorated in his honor. At the same time, however, Shahryar could not help but see how poor his brother's health was, and he asked him what had happened.

"It's due to the long, hard journey," replied Shah Zaman, "and I'll need some care, for I've suffered from the change of water and air. But Allah be praised for reuniting me with my beloved brother!"

Then the two entered the capital in all honor, and Shahryar lodged his brother in his palace overlooking the garden. After some time had passed, King Shahryar noticed that his brother's condition was still unchanged, and he attributed it to his separation from his country. So he let him do as he pleased and asked him no questions until one day when he said, "My brother, I can't help noticing that you've grown weaker and paler than you were before."

"I'm sick in my heart," he replied, but he would not tell Shahryar about his wife and all that he had seen.

Thereupon Shahryar summoned doctors and surgeons and asked them to treat his brother to the best of their ability, which they did for a whole month, but their potions had no effect, for he dwelled upon his wife's treachery. Indeed, he became more and more despondent, and even the use of leeches failed to change his mood.

One day his elder brother said to him, "I've decided to go on a hunting expedition. Perhaps you'd feel better if you joined me."

However, Shah Zaman declined and said, "I am not in the mood for anything like this, and I beseech you to let me stay quietly in the palace, for I can't seem to get over this sickness."

So, King Shah Zaman spent the night in the palace by himself. The next morning, after his brother had departed, he left his room and sat down at one of the lattice windows overlooking the garden. There he rested awhile and became steeped in sad thoughts about his wife's betrayal, occasionally uttering sighs of grief. Now, as he was moaning and torturing himself, a secret door to the garden swung open, and out came twenty slave girls surrounding his brother's wife, who was marvelously beautiful and moved about with the grace of a gazelle in search of a cool stream. Shah Zaman drew back from the window, but he kept the group in sight from a place where they could not spot him, even though they walked under the very window where he had stationed himself. As they advanced into the garden, they came to a jetting fountain amidst a great basin of water. Then they stripped off their clothes, and Shah Zaman suddenly realized that ten of them were women, concubines of the king, and the other ten were white slaves. After they had all paired off, the queen was left alone, but she soon cried out in a loud voice, "Come to me right now, my lord Saeed!" and all of a sudden a big slobbering blackamoor with rolling eyes leapt from one of the trees. It was truly a hideous sight. He rushed up to her and threw his arms around her neck, while she embraced him just as warmly. Then he mounted her, and winding his legs around hers, as a button loop clasps a button, he tossed her to the ground and enjoyed her. The other slaves did the same with the girls until they had all satisfied their passions, and they did not stop kissing, coupling, and carousing until the day began to wane. When the mamelukes rose from the bosoms of the maidens and the blackamoor slave let go of the queen, the men resumed their disguises, and all except the Negro, who climbed up the tree, left the garden via the secret door and reentered the palace.

Now, after Shah Zaman had witnessed this spectacle, he said to himself, "By Allah, my misfortune is nothing compared to my brother's! Though he may be a greater king among kings than I am, he doesn't even realize that this kind of perfidious behavior is going on in his very own palace, and his wife is in love with the filthiest of filthy slaves. This only proves that all women will make cuckolds out of their husbands when given the chance. Well, then, let the curse of Allah fall upon one and all and upon the fools who need the support of their wives or who place the reins of conduct in their hands!" So, he cast aside his melancholy and no longer had regrets about what he had done. Moreover, he constantly repeated his words to himself to minimize his sorrow and added, "No man in this world is safe from the malice of women!"

When suppertime arrived, the servants brought him the trays, and he ate with a voracious appetite, for he had refrained from eating a long time, no matter how delicious the food. Now he was able once again to give grateful thanks to Almighty Allah for the meal and for restoring his appetite, and he spent a most restful night, savoring the sweet food of sleep. The next day he ate his breakfast with a hearty appetite and began to regain his health and strength and was in excellent condition by the time his brother came back from the hunt ten days later. When Shah Zaman rode out to meet him, King Shahryar looked at him and was astonished by the remarkable change in his brother's appearance, but Shah Zaman did not say or disclose a thing to him. Instead, the two just embraced, exchanged greetings, and rode into the city.

Later when they were seated at their ease in the palace, the servants brought them food, and they ate to their heart's content. After the meal was removed and they had washed their hands, King Shahryar turned to his brother and said, "I am astonished by the change in your condition. I had hoped to take you with me on the hunt, but I realized that your mind was sorely troubled by something, and you looked so pale and sickly. But now—glory be to God!—your natural color has returned to your face, and you're in fine shape. I had believed that your sickness was due to the separation from your family, friends, and country, so I had refrained from bothering you with probing questions. But now I beseech you to explain the cause of your troubles and the reason for your recovery to such good health."

When Shah Zaman heard this, he bowed his head toward the ground, and after a while he raised it and said, "I shall tell you what caused my troubles and bad health, but you must pardon me if I don't tell you the reason for my complete recovery. Indeed, I beg you not to force me to explain everything that has happened."

Shahryar was much surprised by these words and replied, "Let me hear first what caused you to become so sick and pale."

"Well then," began Shah Zaman, "it was like this. When you sent the vizier with your invitation, I made all sorts of preparations for three days and camped before my city to begin the journey early the next day. But that night I remembered that I had left a string of jewels in the palace that I intended to give to you as a gift. I returned for it alone and found my wife on my couch in the arms of a hideous black cook. So I slew the two and came to you. However, I could not help grieving about this affair and regretting what I had done. That's why I lost my health and became weak. But you must excuse me if I refuse to tell you how I managed to regain my health."

Shahryar shook his head, completely astonished, and with the fire of wrath flaming in his heart, he cried, "Indeed, the malice of woman is mighty! My brother, you've escaped many an evil deed by putting your wife to death, and your rage and grief are quite understandable and excusable, especially since you had never suffered anything as terrible as this before. By Allah, had this been me, I would not have been satisfied until I had slain a thousand women and had gone mad! But praise be to Allah, who has eased your tribulations, and now you must tell me how you regained your health so suddenly, and you must explain to me why you are being so secretive."

"Oh brother, again I beg you to excuse me for refusing to talk about this!"

"But I insist."

"I'm afraid that my story may cause you more anger and sorrow than I myself have suffered."

"That's even a better reason for telling me the whole story," said Shahryar, "and in the name of Allah, I command you not to keep anything back from me!"

Thereupon Shah Zaman told him all he had seen from beginning to end, and he concluded his story by saying, "When I saw your misfortune, and your wife's betrayal, my own sorrow seemed slight in comparison, and I became sober and sound again. So, discarding melancholy and despondency, I was able to eat, drink, and sleep, and thus I quickly regained my health and strength. This is the truth and the whole truth."

After King Shahryar heard this tale, he became so furious that it seemed his rage might consume him. However, he quickly recovered his composure and said, "My brother, I don't mean to imply that you have lied to me, but I can't believe your story until I see everything with my own eyes."

"If you want to witness your misfortune," Shah Zaman responded, "rise at once and get ready for another hunting expedition. Then hide yourself with me, and you'll see everything with your own eyes and learn the truth."

"Good," said the king, whereupon he made it known that he was about to travel again, and the troops set up camp outside the city. Shahryar departed with them, and after commanding his slaves not to allow anyone to enter his tent, he summoned his vizier and said, "I want you to sit in my place, and let no one know of my absence until three days have passed."

Then the brothers disguised themselves and returned secretly to the palace, where they spent the rest of the night. At dawn they seated themselves at the window overlooking the garden, and soon the queen and the slaves came out as before and headed for the fountain.

There they stripped, ten men to ten women, and the king's wife cried out, "Where are you, oh Saeed?"

The hideous blackamoor dropped from the tree right away, and rushing into her arms without delay, he exclaimed, "I am Sa'ad al-Din Saood, the auspicious one!"

The lady laughed heartily, and they all began to satisfy their lust and continued to do so for a couple of hours. Then the white slaves rose from the maidens, and the blackamoor left the queen, and they went into the basin. After bathing themselves, they donned their robes and departed as they had done before.

When King Shahryar saw the perfidious behavior of his wife and concubines, he became distraught and cried out, "Only in utter solitude can man be safe from what goes on in this vile world! By Allah, life is nothing but one great wrong! Listen to what I propose, brother, and don't stop me."

"I won't," Shah Zaman responded.

So the king continued, "Let us get up just as we are and depart right away. There are other things more important than our kingdoms. Let us wander over Allah's earth, worshiping the Almighty, until we find someone who has suffered the same misfortune. And if it should turn out that we don't find anyone, then death will be more welcome to us than life."

So the two brothers left through a second secret door to the palace, and they journeyed day and night until they came to a large tree in the middle of a meadow right near a spring of fresh water not far from the seashore. Both drank from the spring and sat down to rest. After an hour had passed, they suddenly heard a mighty roar as though the heavens were falling upon the earth. The sea broke with tidal waves, and a towering black pillar arose from it. Indeed, the pillar of smoke grew and grew until it almost touched the sky. Then it began heading toward the meadow, and the two brothers became very frightened and climbed to the top of the tree, from where they hoped to see what the matter was.

To their amazement, the smoke turned into a jinnee, huge, broad-chested, and burly. His brow was wide, his skin black, and on his head was a crystal chest. He strode to the shore, wading through deep water, and came to the tree in which the two kings were hiding, and sat down beneath it. He then set the chest on its bottom and pulled from it a casket with seven padlocks of steel, which he unlocked with seven keys of steel hanging beside his thigh. Suddenly a young lady appeared from the casket, white-skinned and pleasant, fine and thin, and bright as the full moon or the glistening sun. Taking her by the hand, the jinnee seated her under the tree by his side and gazed at her.

"Oh choicest love of this heart of mine!" he began. "Oh lady of noblest line, whom I snatched away on your wedding night and whom none has loved or enjoyed except myself. Oh, my sweetheart, I must sleep a little while."

He then laid his head upon the lady's thighs, and stretching out his legs, which extended down to the sea, he fell asleep and snored like thunder. Soon the lady raised her head and noticed the two kings perched near the top of the tree. Then she softly lifted the jinnee's head off her lap and placed it upon the ground. Afterwards she stood up and signaled to the kings, "Come down, you two. You have nothing to fear from this ifrit."

They were terribly scared when they realized that she had seen them and answered her in whispers, "By Allah and by your modesty, oh lady, excuse us from coming down!"

"Allah upon you both," she replied, "I want you to come down right away, and if you don't come, I shall wake this jinnee, who will attack you, and you'll die the worst death imaginable!" And she continued making signs to them to come.

So, being afraid, they came down to her, and she rose before them and said, "I want you to mount me and show me how nicely you can sit on my saddle, or else I'll set this ifrit upon you, and he'll slay you in the wink of an eye!"

"Oh lady," they said to her, "we beseech you, by Allah, don't force us to do this. We've given up such things and are in extreme dread of your husband!"

"No more talk. This is the way it must be," she said and swore to them by Him who raised the skies on high without prop or pillar that they would be slain and cast into the sea if they did not perform her will. Consequently, out of fear, King Shahryar said to King Shah Zaman, "Brother, do what she wants you to do."

But Zaman responded, "I won't do anything until you do it first."

And they began quarreling about who was to mount her.

"Why are you two quarreling?" she intervened. "If you do not come forward like men and do the deed I ask you to perform, I'll wake the jinnee!"

Given their fear of the jinnee, they finally did what she asked them to do, one after the other, and after they had dismounted, she said, "Well done!" Next, she took a purse from her pocket and drew out a knotted strand of five hundred and seventy rings and asked, "Do you know what these are?"

"No," they answered.

"These are the signets of five hundred and seventy men," she said, "who have futtered me on the horns of this filthy, stupid ifrit. So, brothers, I also want your royal rings."

After they had taken off their rings and given them to her, she said, "It's true that this jinnee carried me off on my wedding night, put me into a casket, and placed the casket in a chest. After he attached seven strong padlocks to it, he deposited it at the bottom of the deep sea and guarded me so that I would remain chaste and honest, and so that none but himself could have any contact with me. But I have lain under as many men as I've desired, and this wretched jinnee doesn't realize that destiny cannot be averted or hindered by anything and that whatever a woman wants, she will get, no matter how much a man might try to prevent it."

Upon hearing her story, the brothers were left speechless and watched her as she went back to the ifrit, put his head on her lap, and told them softly, "Now get on your way, and put the sight of this malice way behind you!"

So they moved on and said to each other, "May Allah help us and save us from women's malice and cunning! It seems nothing can surpass their power!"

"Just think," said King Shahryar, "how this marvelous lady has managed to deceive a jinnee, who is much more powerful than we are! Indeed, his misfortune is much greater than ours, so it is time to return to our kingdoms.

But I propose that we both never stay married long enough for women to betray us and that we take the proper action to put them in their place!"

Shah Zaman agreed, and they rode back to King Shahryar's encampment, which they reached on the morning of the third day, and after gathering together his viziers, emirs, chamberlains, and high officials, Shahryar gave a robe of honor to his viceroy and issued orders for an immediate return to the city. As soon as he took his seat upon his throne, he sent for his chief minister and declared, "I command you to take my wife and execute her, for she has broken her marriage vows."

So, the minister brought her to the place of execution and carried out the king's orders. Then King Shahryar took his sword in hand and went to the seraglio, where he slew all the concubines and their mamelukes. He also swore a binding oath that whenever he married, he would take his new wife's maidenhead at night and slay her the next morning to make sure of his honor, for he was convinced that there never was or could be one chaste woman upon the face of this earth.

Soon after Shahryar took this oath, his brother, Shah Zaman, asked permission to return home, and he was provided an escort that accompanied him until he reached his own country. Meanwhile Shahryar commanded his vizier to bring him a bride for that night so that he might enjoy her. Accordingly, the vizier produced a most beautiful girl, the daughter of one of the emirs, and the king broke her maidenhead in the evening, and when morning arrived, he commanded his minister to strike off her head. And the vizier did as he was ordered for fear of the sultan. During the next three years the king continued to act accordingly: he married a maiden every night and had her killed the next morning, until his people raised a great outcry against him. Indeed, they cursed him and prayed to Allah that he be utterly destroyed and dethroned. Women began protesting, mothers wept, and parents fled with their daughters until there was not one virgin left in the city.

Nevertheless, the king ordered his chief vizier, the same man who was charged with carrying out the executions, to bring him a virgin as was his wont. When the minister went forth, however, and searched all over, he returned home in sorrow, fearing for his life because the king would be displeased that there were no more virgins left in the city. Now, he had two daughters, Scheherazade and Dunazade. The older one, Scheherazade, had read the books, annals, and legends of former kings, and the stories, lessons, and adventures of famous men. Indeed, it was said that she had collected a thousand history books about ancient peoples and rulers. She had perused the works of the poets and knew them by heart. She had studied philosophy and the sciences, arts, and practical things. And she was pleasant and polite, wise and witty, well read and well bred. Consequently, on that particular day, she said to her father, "Why are you so downcast? You seem to be troubled by something. Remember the words of the poet:

"Tell whoever has sorrow
Grief shall never last.
Just as joy has no tomorrow,
Woe is bound not to last."

When the vizier heard these words from his daughter, he told her from first to last about everything that had happened between him and the king. Thereupon, she said, "By Allah, oh my father, how long shall this slaughter of women last? Shall I tell you what I'm thinking about that would stop all this destruction?"

"Tell me, my daughter," he said.

"I would like you to give me in marriage to King Shahryar. If I should live, I'd become the ransom for the virgin daughters of Moslems and rescue them from his hands and yours."

"Oh Allah!" he cried in his fury. "Have you lost your mind? I won't let you expose yourself to such danger. How can you be so unwise and foolish? I want you to know that unless you have experience in worldly matters, you'll be prey to misfortune!"

"I must do this," she responded. "Come what may!"

Again the vizier became enraged and scolded and reproached her. "In truth, I fear that the same thing that happened to the ox and the donkey will happen to you."

"And just what did happen to them, Father?" she asked.

Whereupon the vizier began.

The Tale of the Ox and the Donkey

There was once a merchant who owned a great deal of money and men, and who had a large number of cattle and camels. He also had a wife and family and dwelt in the country, since he knew a great deal about farming and agriculture. Now Allah Almighty had endowed him with the ability to understand the language of birds and beasts of every kind. However, it was decreed that if he were to divulge the gift to anyone, he would be punished by death. So, out of fear, he kept his unusual gift a secret.

In his barn he had an ox and donkey, each tethered in his own stall next to one another. One day, when the merchant was sitting nearby with his servants and children playing around him, he heard the ox say to the ass, "Greetings, friend. I hope that you continue to enjoy your rest and good care. Everything under you is swept neatly and watered down. Men wait on you and feed you sifted barley, and give you pure spring water to drink. On the other hand, I (unhappy creature!) am led forth in the middle of the night when they set the plow and something called a yoke on my neck. I'm exhausted from cleaving the earth from dawn till dusk. I'm forced to do more than I can and to bear all kinds of mistreatment every night. And at the end of my work they take me back with my sides torn, my neck flayed, my legs aching, and my eyelids sore with tears. Then they shut me up in the barn and throw me beans and hay mixed with dirt and chaff. And I lie in dung and filth, and there is nothing but a foul stench throughout the night. But you are always in a clean place and are always able to relax, except when the master has some business in town, and that's very seldom. Then he just mounts you and rides to the town and returns right away. This is the way things are: I toil and have no rest, while you relax and have leisure time. You sleep while I am sleepless. I starve while you have all you want to eat."

When the ox stopped speaking, the donkey turned toward him and said, "Oh you lost soul! Whoever dubbed you bull-head did not lie, for you are denser than the simplest of simpletons! With all your zeal you foolishly toil for the master, and wear yourself out and kill yourself for the comfort of someone else. At the call of dawn you set out to work and don't return until sundown, and throughout the livelong day you endure all kinds of hardships such as beatings and cursing. Now listen to me, carefully. When you go into the fields and they lay that thing called the yoke on your neck, lie down and don't get up again, even though they hit you with the switch. And if you do have to rise, lie down a second time. And when they bring you home and offer you beans, fall backward and only sniff your food. Don't taste it. Withdraw and content yourself only with the hay and chaff. Pretend you are sick, and continue to do this for two or three days. This way you'll be able to gain some rest from all your hard work."

When the ox heard these words, he knew that the donkey was his friend and thanked him. "This is good advice," he said, and prayed that the ass would be blessed with a fine reward.

The next day, the driver took the ox, set the plow on his neck, and made him work as usual. But the ox took the donkey's advice and shirked the plowing. Consequently, the plowman drubbed him until the ox broke the yoke and made off. But the man caught up to him and tanned him until he thought he would die. Nevertheless, he did nothing but stand still and drop down until evening came. Then the plowman led him home and put him into his stall, but the ox drew back from his manger and neither stamped, nor butted, nor bellowed as he was accustomed to do. Such strange behavior puzzled the plowman. Then he brought the ox beans and husks, but the animal sniffed at them and lay down as far from them as he could and spent the whole night fasting. Next morning the plowman came and saw the manger full of beans, the hay untasted, and the ox lying on his back in a most sorry plight with his legs outstretched and a swollen belly. Of course, he was very worried about him and said to himself, "By Allah, he has certainly become sick, and this is why he wouldn't plow yesterday." Then he went to the merchant and reported, "Master, the ox is sick. He refused his fodder last night, and he hasn't tasted a scrap of it this morning."

Now the merchant understood what all this meant, because he had overheard the talk between the ox and the ass. So he said, "Take that rascal donkey, and set the yoke on his neck. Tie him to the plow and make him do the ox's work."

Accordingly, the plowman took the ass and made him do the ox's work the entire day long. And when the donkey let up out of weakness, the driver made him feel his stick until the animal's ribs were sore and his sides were sunken and his neck flayed by the yoke. When the ass returned home in the evening, he could hardly drag his limbs along. Meanwhile, the ox had spent the day lying at full length and had eaten his fodder with an excellent appetite. He continually heaped blessings on the donkey for his good advice, not knowing how the donkey had suffered and that it was on his account. So, when night set in and the donkey returned to the barn, the ox rose up before him in his honor and said, "May good tidings warm your heart, my friend! Because of you I have rested the entire day, and I have eaten my food in peace and quiet."

But the ass did not reply, because his heart was burning with rage, and he was exhausted from the beating he had gotten. Indeed, he regretted that he had given the ox such good advice and said to himself, "This is the result of your folly in giving good counsel. I was living in joy and happiness until I mixed into somebody else's business. So now I must think of something and trick the ox so that he'll return to his place. Otherwise, I'll die." Then he went wearily to his stall, while the ox continued to thank and bless him.

"And the same thing will happen to you, my daughter," said the vizier. "You will die for not having used your brains. Therefore, I want you to sit still, say nothing, and refrain from exposing yourself to danger. By Allah, I'm offering you the best advice that comes from my affection and great concern for you."

"Father," she answered. "I must marry the king, and you can't stop me."

"I don't want you to do this."

"But I must."

"If you're not silent and do as I say, I'll do to you just what the farmer did to his wife."

"And what did he do?" Scheherazade asked.

After the donkey returned to his stall, the farmer went out on the terrace of his house with his wife and family, for there was a full moon. Now the terrace overlooked the barn, and as the merchant was sitting there with his children playing around him, he soon heard the donkey say to the ox, "Tell me, friend, what do you propose to do tomorrow?"

"To continue to follow your advice, of course," said the ox. "Indeed, it was as good as it could be, and it has given me a good deal of rest. So when they bring me my food, I'll refuse it, blow up my belly, and pretend to be sick."

The ass shook his head and said, "You'd better not do this."

"Why?" the ox asked.

And the donkey answered, "I must warn you that I heard the merchant say to the plowman, 'If the ox doesn't get up from his place to do his work this morning and doesn't eat his fodder today, take him over to the butcher to be slaughtered. Then give his flesh to the poor and make some leather out of his hide.' You see now why I'm afraid for your life. So, take my advice before something terrible happens to you: when they bring you your fodder, eat it. Then get up, bellow, and paw the ground, or else our master will surely have you slain. May peace be with you!"

Thereupon the ox arose, bellowed aloud, and thanked the ass. "Tomorrow, I'll certainly go out into the fields with them," he said, and he ate up all his food and even licked his manger. (All this took place while the merchant was listening to their talk.)

Next morning the merchant and his wife went to the ox's stall and sat down, and the driver came and led the ox out. Upon seeing his owner, the beast whisked his tail, broke wind, and frisked about so merrily that the merchant laughed loudly and kept laughing until he fell over on his back.

"Why are you laughing like this so much?" his wife asked.

"I laughed at a secret, something that I heard and saw, but I can't reveal it to you. If I do, I'll die."

"Well, I insist!" replied his wife. "Tell me why you laughed so loudly and what your secret is! I don't care if you have to die."

"It has something to do with the language of birds and beasts, but I'm forbidden to tell it to you."

"By Allah, you're lying!" she exclaimed. "This is a mere pretext. You were laughing at nobody except me, and now you want to hide something from me. But, by the Lord of the Heavens, if you don't tell me the cause, I won't sleep with you anymore. I'll leave you at once!" And she sat down and cried.

"Why are you weeping?" the merchant responded. "Stop all this jabbering and crying!"

"Tell me why you laughed!"

"Listen, I'm telling you the truth. When Allah granted me the gift of understanding the language of the birds and beasts, I made a vow never to disclose the secret under pain of death."

"No matter," cried she. "Tell me what the ox and donkey were saying, and if you have to die, you have to die."

And she did not stop nagging him until he was worn out and totally distraught. So at last he said, "Summon your father and mother, our kith and kin, and some of our neighbors."

While she went about doing this, he sent for the lawyers and assessors, intending to make his will, reveal his secret to her, and die under the penalty of death, since his love for her was immense. She was his cousin, the daughter of his father's brother, and the mother of his children, and he had lived with her for a hundred and twenty years.

Now, after all the members of the family and the neighbors had gathered, the farmer said to them, "Something strange happened to me some time ago, but if I reveal my secret story to anyone, I am bound to die."

As a result of his remarks, everyone present began

saying to the woman, "May Allah be with you, stop being so shamefully obstinate and realize what the consequences are. Otherwise, your husband and father of your children will die."

"I refuse to change my mind until he tells me his secret," she replied, "even though he may have to die."

So they stopped trying to persuade her, and the farmer got up and withdrew to a small chicken house in order to be by himself and pray before his death. Afterward he was going to return to them, tell his secret, and die. Now, in this chicken house the farmer had some fifty hens under one cock, and while he was getting ready to say his farewell to his people, he heard one of his farm dogs talking to the cock, who was flapping his wings, crowing lustily, and jumping from one hen's back to another and treading all in turn.

"Oh Chanticleer!" the dog cried out. "How can you be so mean and shameless! Whoever brought you up should be burned at the stake! Aren't you ashamed of doing such things on a day such as this?"

"And just what is so special about today?" asked the rooster.

"Don't you know that our master is preparing for his death today?" the dog responded. "His wife is determined that he must reveal the secret taught to him by Allah, and the moment he does this he's bound to die. We dogs are all mourning already, but you, you flap your wings, crow as loud as you can, and tread hen after hen. Is this the time for having fun and taking your pleasure? Aren't you ashamed of yourself?"

"By Allah," retorted the cock, "is our master a nitwit? Why doesn't he come to his senses? If he can't manage matters with a single wife, his life is not worth prolonging. Now I have some fifty dame partlets, and I please this one and provoke the other and starve one and stuff another. And through my good governance, they are all well under my control. Our master claims that he is smart and wise, but he has only one wife and hasn't discovered yet how to deal with her."

"Well, what should our master do?" asked the dog.

"He should get up right away," answered the cock, "and take some twigs from that mulberry tree over there and give her a good beating until she cries: 'I repent, oh, my lord! I'll never ask you another question as long as I live!' Then let him beat her nice and hard once more, and after he does this, he will sleep soundly and enjoy life. But this master of ours does not appear to have an iota of good sense or judgment."

When the merchant heard the wise words spoken by the cock to the dog, he arose in haste, cut some mulberry twigs, and hid them in his wife's room. Then he called to her, "Come into your room so that I may tell you the secret and die without anyone looking on."

She entered the room, and he locked the door. All of a sudden he began to beat her back, shoulders, ribs, arms, and legs in a great fury. "Are you going to continue to ask questions about things that don't concern you?" And he kept beating her until she was almost unconscious.

Soon she cried out, "I repent! By Allah, I won't ask you any more questions. I mean it. I repent with all my heart and life!"

Then she kissed his hands and feet, and he led her out of the room, submissive as a wife should be. Her parents and the entire company rejoiced, and sadness and mourning were changed into joy and gladness. Thus the merchant learned family discipline from his cock, and he and his wife lived happily ever after until death.

"And the same thing will happen to you, too, my daughter!" continued the vizier. "Unless you give up pursuing this matter, I'll do what the merchant did to his wife."

But she answered him with firm resolution, "I won't give up, Father, nor shall this tale make me change my mind. So stop your talk and babbling. I won't listen to your words, and if you try to prevent me, I'll go to the king alone and say, 'I asked my father to allow me to marry you, but he refused, since he begrudged you the right to have a maiden like me.' "

"Must it be this way?" her father asked.

"Indeed, it must."

Since the vizier was now weary of contending with his daughter and realized he could not dissuade her from doing what she wanted, he went to King Shahryar, and after blessing him and kissing the ground before him, told him all about his dispute with his daughter and how he now intended to bring her to him that night.

The king was most astonished, since he had made a special exception of the vizier's daughter, and he said to him, "Oh most faithful of counselors, how has this come about? You know that I have sworn by Almighty Allah that after I enter her this night, I shall say to you tomorrow morning: 'Take her and slay her!' And if you don't do this, I'll slay you in her place."

"May Allah guide you to glory and give you long life, your majesty," answered the vizier. "It was she who made this decision. I have told her what is to happen and more, but she won't listen to me, and she insists on spending this coming night with your highness."

So Shahryar rejoiced greatly and said, "So be it. Go get her ready and bring her to me this night."

The vizier returned to his daughter and informed her of the king's command. "By Allah, please don't make your father do this. I'm sure to lose you."

But Scheherazade rejoiced and got everything ready that she needed. Then she said to her younger sister, Dunazade, "Pay attention to what I tell you! After I have entered the king's private chamber, I'll send for you, and when you come and see that he has had his carnal pleasure with me, you're to say to me: 'Oh sister, since you're not sleepy, tell me some new delightful story to entertain us while we are still awake.' And I'll tell you a tale that will be our salvation, if it pleases Allah, for I'm going to tell a tale that will, I hope, divert the king from his bloodthirsty custom."

"I'll do whatever you say," Dunazade replied, "with all my heart."

So when it was night, their father led Scheherazade to the king, who was glad to see her and asked, "Have you brought me what I need?"

"I have," the vizier said.

But when the king took her to his bed, began toying with her, and was about to penetrate her, she wept, and consequently he asked, "What's wrong with you?"

"Your majesty," she replied, "I have a younger sister, and I would like very much to take leave of her tonight before dawn comes."

So he sent at once for Dunazade, and she came and

kissed the ground, and he permitted her to take a seat near the foot of the couch. Then the king arose and did away with his bride's maidenhead, and the three fell asleep. But when midnight arrived, Scheherazade awoke and signaled to her sister, Dunazade, who sat up and said, "May Allah be with you, my sister, please tell us some delightful story to while away the waking hours before dawn."

"I'd be most happy and willing to do this," answered Scheherazade, "if this pious and auspicious king will permit me."

"Permission granted," said the king, who happened to be sleepless and restless and was therefore pleased by the prospect of hearing her story. So Scheherazade rejoiced, and on the first night of many nights to come, she began telling the tales that were to fill the volumes of *The Arabian Nights*.

The Tale of the Merchant and the Jinnee

There was once a very wealthy merchant who had a great deal of business in various cities. Now, one day he mounted his horse and went forth to collect debts that were owed to him in certain towns. The heat was so terrible along the way that he dismounted and sat down beneath a tree. He put his hand into his saddlebags, took out some bread and dry dates, and began to break his fast. When he had finished eating the dates, he threw away the pits with all his might, and suddenly a huge jinnee appeared brandishing a drawn sword. As he approached the merchant, he said, "Stand up so I can slay you just as you've slain my son!"

"How have I slain your son?" asked the merchant.

"When you ate the dates and threw away the pits, they struck my son in the breast as he was walking by, and he died right on the spot."

"By Allah, if I slew your son," the merchant responded, "I slew him by chance. Therefore, I beg your pardon."

"There's nothing you can do," asserted the jinnee. "You must die." Then he seized the merchant, threw him down on the ground, and raised his sword to strike him. But the merchant wept and cried out, "May Allah take pity on me and hear my plea!"

"Cut your words short," the jinnee answered. "You must die."

But the merchant pleaded with him, "Listen to me. There's a great deal of money that's owed to me. I'm very wealthy and have a wife and children and many pledges in hand. So, permit me to go home and take care of all my claims, and I shall come back to you at the beginning of the new year. Allah be my witness that I'll return to you, and then you can do what you want with me."

The jinnee accepted his promise and let him go. So the merchant returned to his city and completed all his transactions. He gave all people their due, and after informing his wife and children what had happened to him, he appointed a guardian and lived with his family for a full year. At the end of that time, he performed the Wuzu ablution to purify himself before death, took his shroud under his arm, said farewell to family, friends, and neighbors, and went forth against his own will. As he left, they began weeping, wailing, and beating their breasts, but he traveled until he arrived at the same garden where he had encountered the jinnee. The day of his arrival was the beginning of the new year, and as he sat weeping over what had happened to him, a very old and honorable sheikh approached, leading a gazelle on a chain. After saluting the merchant and wishing him a long life, he asked, "Why are you sitting all alone in this place? Don't you know that it's the abode of evil spirits?"

The merchant related to him what had happened with the jinnee, and the old man was astounded and said, "By Allah, I've never seen such fidelity, nor have I ever heard such a strange story. If it were engraved for all to see, it would serve as a warning for all those who need to be warned." Then, seating himself near the merchant, he said. "My brother, I won't leave you until I see what is going to happen between you and this ifrit."

And after he sat down and the two were talking, the merchant became extremely anxious, terrified, and depressed. Just then a second sheikh approached them, and with him were two dogs, both black greyhounds. After the second man greeted them with the salaam, he asked them, "Why are you sitting in this place? Don't you know that it is the abode of the demon jinnees?"

So they told him the tale from beginning to end, and they had not been conversing very long before a third sheikh arrived, and with him was a she-mule with a bright bay coat. He saluted them and asked them why they were seated in that place, and they told him the entire story, and he too sat down with them. Just then a dust cloud advanced, and a mighty sand devil appeared amidst the waste. Soon the cloud opened, revealing the jinnee with a drawn sword and eyes shooting fire-sparks of rage, and he stepped forward, grabbed hold of the merchant, and separated him from the rest of the men.

"Stand up so I can slay you just as you slew my son, the soul of my life," the jinnee bellowed.

The merchant wailed and wept, and the three old men began sighing and crying with their companion. Soon the first man, the owner of the gazelle, approached the ifrit and kissed his hand. "Oh jinnee, crown of the kings of the jinn, if I were to tell you a story about me and this gazelle, and if you were to consider it wondrous, would you give me a third of this merchant's blood?"

"If you tell me your tale, oh sheikh, and it is indeed marvelous," the jinnee replied, "I'll give you a third of his blood."

Thereupon the old man began to tell

The First Sheikh's Story

I'll have you know, oh jinnee, that this gazelle is the daughter of my paternal uncle, my own flesh and blood, and I married her when she was a young maid. I lived with her for close to thirty years, but I was not blessed with any offspring. So I took me a concubine, who gave birth to a boy, fair as the full moon with glistening eyes, straight eyebrows, and perfect limbs. Little by little he grew to be a tall young man, and when he was fifteen, it became necessary for me to journey to certain cities with a large amount of goods. But my wife had learned the art of witchcraft, and she turned my son into a calf and his mother into a cow and placed them under the care of the herdsman. So, after a long time had passed and I returned from my journey, I asked for my son and his mother, and she answered me by saying, "Your slave girl is dead, and your son has fled, and I don't know where he's gone."

So my heart grieved for an entire year, and my eyes

did not stop weeping until the time came for the Great Festival of Allah. Then I sent for my herdsman and asked him to choose a fat cow for me. He brought me the one which had been my handmaid, whom this gazelle had bewitched. I tucked up my sleeves, put on an apron, and taking a knife, I began to cut her throat, but she bellowed so loudly and wept such bitter tears that I was astonished. Out of pity, I dropped the knife and said to the herdsman, "Bring me a different cow."

Then my wife cried out, "Slay her! There's none fatter or fairer."

Once more I made a move to sacrifice her, but again the cow bellowed loudly, and I could not bring myself to kill her. Instead, I commanded the herdsman to slay her and flay her. So, he performed the sacrifice and skinned her, but could not find fat or flesh, only hide and bone. I repented when it was much too late, and I gave her to the herdsman and said to him, "Fetch me a fat calf."

So he brought me my bewitched son. When the calf saw me, he broke his tether, ran to me, fawned upon me, and shed tears. Consequently, I took pity on him and said to the herdsman, "Bring me a cow, and let this calf go."

But my wife cried out, "You must kill this calf. It is a holy and blessed day, and nothing is to be slain except what is pure and perfect. And there is nothing among our calves that is fatter or fairer than this one!"

"Look at the cow that I have just had slaughtered at your request and how disappointed we are by the results," I said. "There was no benefit from her at all, and I'm extremely sorry for having killed her. So this time I'm not going to listen to you, and the calf will not be sacrificed."

"By Allah, you have no choice. You must kill him on this holy day, and if you don't kill him, you're no man for me, and I shall not be your wife."

Now, when I heard those hard words, I went up to the calf with knife in hand, unaware of my wife's real purpose. However, when I looked at the calf, I commanded the herdsman to take it away, and he did as I ordered him to do. On the next day as I was sitting in my own house, the herdsman came up to me and said, "Master, I want to tell you something that will make your soul rejoice and enable me to be the bearer of good tidings."

"I'm listening," I said.

"I have a daughter," he began, "and she learned magic in her childhood from an old woman who lived with us. Yesterday, when you gave me the calf, I went into the house with it, and she looked at it and veiled her face. Then she kept laughing and weeping and at last said to me, 'Oh father, has my honor become so cheap that you're now bringing strange men into the house for me?' I asked her, 'Where are these strange men and why are you laughing and crying?' She answered, 'To tell you the truth, the calf that you have with you is the son of our master, the merchant, but his wife bewitched him and his mother. That's why I laughed, and I wept because of his mother, whom the merchant slew unaware that it was she.' Of course, I was most astonished by this revelation, and I could hardly wait until the break of day to come and tell all this to you."

When I heard my herdsman's words, I went with him to his house and was drunk with joy without having the least bit of wine. His daughter welcomed me and kissed my hand, and the calf came right away and fawned all over me as before. "Is it true," I asked the herdsman's daughter, "all that you've said about this calf?"

"Yes, oh master," she said. "He's your son, your very own flesh and blood."

I rejoiced and said to her, "If you can release him from this spell, you can have whatever property and cattle I have."

"Master," she smiled, "I don't desire such goods, and I shall take them only under two conditions: the first, that you marry me to your son, and the second, that you allow me to bewitch your wife and imprison her. Otherwise, I won't be safe from her malice."

Now when I heard these words, I replied, "Not only do I grant you your wish, but you may have all the cattle and the household stuff in your father's charge, and as for my wife, anything you do to her is all right with me."

After I had spoken, she took a cup and filled it with water. Then she recited a spell over it and sprinkled it on the calf, saying, "If Almighty Allah created you as a calf, then remain as you are and don't change. But if you are enchanted, return to your rightful form!"

All of a sudden, the calf trembled and became a man, and I embraced him and said, "By Allah, tell me all that the daughter of my uncle did to you and your mother." And when he told me how everything had happened, I said, "My son, Allah blessed you by enabling someone to restore you to your real form, and you may now receive your rightful due."

Then I married him to the herdsman's daughter, and she transformed my wife into this gazelle by giving her a shape that is by no means loathsome. After this the herdsman's daughter lived with us day and night until she died. Then my son journeyed forth to the cities of Hind and also to the city of this man who has offended you. And I also took this gazelle and wandered with her from town to town seeking news of my son until destiny drove me to this place where I saw the merchant sitting and weeping. Such is my tale!

"This story is indeed strange," said the jinnee, "and thus I shall grant you a third of the merchant's blood."

Thereupon the second old man, who owned two greyhounds, came up and said, "Oh jinnee, if I relate to you what my brothers, these two hounds, did to me, and if you admit that it is more wondrous and marvelous than the tale that you've just heard, will you grant me a third of the merchant's blood as well?"

"I give you my word," said the jinnee, "but only if your adventures are truly more marvelous."

Thereupon the old man began

The Second Sheikh's Story

Let me begin by telling you, oh lord of the kings of the jinn, that these two dogs are my brothers, and I am the third. When our father died and left us a capital of three thousand gold pieces, I opened a shop with my share, and my brothers did the same. However, I had been in business just for a short time when my elder brother sold his stock for a thousand dinars, and after buying equipment and merchandise, he journeyed to foreign lands. He had been gone with his caravan for one whole year when, one day, as I was sitting in my shop, a beggar stood before me asking for alms, and I said to him, "Go try somewhere else!"

In response, the beggar began weeping, "Have I changed so much that you don't recognize me anymore?"

Then I looked at him more closely, and I realized it was my brother. So I stood up and welcomed him, and after seating him in my shop, I asked him what had happened.

"Don't ask me," he replied. "My wealth is all gone, and so is my health."

So I took him to the public bath, dressed him in a suit of my own, and gave him a room in my house. Moreover, after looking over the accounts of my stock in trade and my business profits, I found that my hard work had enabled me to earn one thousand dinars while my principal amounted to two thousand. So I shared the whole thing with him and said, "Just assume that you didn't make a journey abroad but remained at home. There's no reason now for you to be dejected about your bad luck."

He took the share gleefully and opened up his own shop. Things went well for some days, but soon my second brother, that dog over there, also set his heart on traveling. He sold whatever goods and stock in trade that he had, and although we tried to prevent him from leaving, he would not listen to us. He equipped himself for the journey and joined a group of travelers. After an absence of one year, he came back to me just as my elder brother had, and I said to him, "Didn't I try to dissuade you from traveling?"

"Destiny decreed it this way!" he wept and cried out. "Now I am a mere beggar without a penny to my name or a shirt on my back."

So I led him to the bath and dressed him in my own new clothes. Then I went with him to my shop, where I gave him something to eat and drink. Furthermore, I told him, "Brother, I generally draw up the accounts of my shop at the beginning of every year, and I intend to share the surplus with you."

Thus, some time later, when I found a profit of two thousand dinars, I praised the Lord and gave my brother one half and kept the other for myself. Thereupon, he set up his own shop, and we lived peacefully for many days. After a while, however, my brothers began to urge me to travel with them, but I refused and argued, "What did you two gain from all your voyages that would make me want to travel?"

Since I would not listen to them, we each returned to our own shops, where we bought and sold as usual. They kept urging me to travel for a whole year, but I continued to refuse. Finally, after six years had passed, I consented and said, "All right, my brothers, I shall be your companion and am ready to travel. Now, let me see what money you intend to bring with you."

I found, however, that they did not have anything, for they had squandered their funds on rich food, drink, and carnal pleasure. Still, I did not reproach them. Far from it. Instead, I looked over my shop accounts once more, sold what goods and stock in trade were mine, and came out with a profit of six thousand ducats, which I divided into half. After doing this, I went to my brothers and said, "These three thousand gold pieces are for me and you to conduct our trade during our travels. Let's bury the other three thousand in the ground in case anything should happen to us. And if something does, each shall take a thousand to open new shops."

Since they both agreed, I gave each one a thousand gold pieces and kept the same sum for myself. Then we prepared some goods for trading and hired a ship to carry our merchandise and proceeded on our voyage. After a month at sea, we reached a city, where we sold our goods, and for every piece of gold that we had invested we gained ten. And when we were about to resume our voyage, we found a maiden on the seashore clad in worn and ragged clothes. She kissed my hand and said, "Oh master, are you a man of charity and kindness? If so, I am prepared to repay you for your aid."

"You may find me benevolent and a man of good works," I said. "But I don't want any return for my deeds."

Then she said, "Please have me as your wife, oh master, and take me to your city, for I'm giving myself to you. Be kind, for I am one of those on whom charity and good works will not be lost. I can make you a fitting return for them, and you will not be shamed by my condition."

When I heard her words, my heart went out to her as though Allah had willed it. Therefore, I took her, clothed her, gave her a comfortable place in the vessel, and treated her with honor. So we continued our voyage, and I became more and more attached to her so that I could not bear to be separated from her day or night. Indeed, I paid more attention to her than to my brothers, with the result that they grew apart from me and became jealous of my wealth and the large amount of merchandise that I had acquired. So they planned to murder me and seize my wealth, and Satan made this seem right in their eyes.

They waited one night and found me sleeping by my wife's side, whereupon they carried us up to the deck of the ship and threw us overboard. My wife awoke startled from her sleep, and immediately she changed into a jinnee, whereupon she lifted me up, carried me to an island, and disappeared for a short time. When she returned in the morning, she said, "Here I am, your faithful slave, who has duly repaid you for your kindness, for I have saved you from death in the deep waters. I am a jinniyah, and when I first saw you, my heart went out to you by the will of the Lord, for I am a believer in Allah. So I went to you in the condition you saw me, and you married me. But I'm angry at your brothers, and I must certainly slay them."

When I heard her story, I was surprised and thanked her for all she had done. "But," I said, "when it comes to slaying my brothers, you must not do this."

Then I told her the tale of our lives from the beginning to the end, and on hearing it, she said, "Tonight I shall fly like a bird over their ship and sink it, causing them to die."

"By Allah," I responded, "don't do this! Remember the proverb: Whoever helps an evildoer should let the evildoer do his own evil deeds."

"Nothing can help them," the jinniyah replied. "By Allah, I must slay them."

I humbled myself before her and begged that she pardon them, whereupon she picked me up and flew away with me until she set me down on the terrace of my own house. Then I took what I had hidden in the ground, bought new merchandise, greeted various people, and reopened the doors of my shop. When night came, I went home, and there I saw these two hounds tied up. Upon seeing me, they arose, whined, and fawned upon me, and before I knew what was happening, my wife said, "These two dogs are your brothers!"

"Who has done this to them?" I asked.

"I sent a message to my sister, and it was she who transformed them into dogs. And they will not be released from their present shape until ten years have passed."

You find me now, oh jinnee, on my way to my wife's sister, because the time has come to release my brothers from their condition. I stopped at this place when I saw this young man, who told me all that had occurred to him, and I decided not to leave here until I saw what would happen between you and him. Such is my tale!

"This is certainly a remarkable story," said the jinnee. "Therefore, I'll give you a third of this man's blood."

Now the third sheikh, the master of the she-mule, approached the jinnee and said, "If I can tell you a tale more wondrous than these two, will you grant me the remainder of the merchant's blood?"

"You have my word!" the jinnee answered.

Then the old man began

The Third Sheikh's Story

I'll have you know, oh jinnee, that this mule was my wife. Now, it so happened that I had to leave home for one year, and when I returned from my journey, it was night, and I found my wife lying with a black slave on my couch. They were talking, laughing, kissing, and playing the close-buttock game. When she saw me, she stood up and rushed over to me with a jug of water. As she ran toward me, she muttered spells over the water and sprinkled me with it. "Change your shape," she exclaimed, "and become a dog!"

All of a sudden, I was a dog, and she drove me out of the house. I ran through the doorway and did not stop running until I came to a butcher's stall, where I rested and began to eat what bones were there. When the butcher saw me, he grabbed me and carried me into his house, but as soon as his daughter caught sight of me, she veiled her face and cried out, "What are you doing? Why are you bringing men to me?"

"Where's the man?" he father asked.

"This dog is a man, and his wife has enchanted him," she replied. "If you want, I can release him from the spell."

When her father heard her words, he said, "May Allah be with you, my daughter, release him."

So she took a jug of water, and after uttering words over it, she sprinkled a few drops on me and said, "Leave that shape and return to your former one."

And I returned to my natural shape. Then I kissed her hand and said, "I wish you'd transform my wife the same way you just changed me."

Thereupon she gave me some water and said, "As soon as you see her asleep, sprinkle this liquid on her and say the words you heard me utter. Then she'll become whatever you desire."

I returned to my house and found my wife fast asleep, and as I sprinkled the water on her, I said, "Leave that shape and change into a mule."

Within seconds she became a mule, and you are looking at her now, oh jinnee, with your own eyes!

Then the jinnee turned toward her and asked, "Is this true?"

And she nodded her head and replied by signs, "Indeed, it's the truth, for such is my tale."

The jinnee was very pleased by the old man's extraordinary story, and he gave him a third of the merchant's blood. Shaking with delight, he told the three sheikhs, "Thanks to you and your storytelling, the merchant is yours! You've saved him, and I now release him from his punishment."

Thereupon, the jinnee disappeared, while the merchant embraced the old men and thanked them. Then the sheikhs wished him happiness and continued their journeys, each one heading toward the city of his destination.

And Scheherazade noticed that dawn was approaching and stopped telling her tale. Thereupon Dunazade said, "Oh sister, your tale was most wonderful, pleasant, and delightful!"

"It is nothing compared to what I could tell you tomorrow night if the king would spare my life and let me live."

"By Allah," the king thought to himself, "I won't slay her until I hear some more of her wondrous tales."

So they continued to rest in mutual embrace until daylight finally arrived. After this the king got up to perform his official duties, but he did not call upon the vizier to perform the execution. Instead, he went to his assembly hall and began holding court. He judged, appointed, and deposed, forbidding this and permitting that, the rest of the day. After the divan was adjourned, King Shahryar returned to the palace. That night he had his will of Scheherazade, as was his wont, and afterward, as they were relaxing, Dunazade came to her sister and asked her to tell another tale.

"With the king's permission," she said.

And Shahryar replied, "You have my permission."

So Scheherazade resumed her storytelling.

The Fisherman and the Jinnee

There was once a poor old fisherman who had a wife and three children to support. When he went to work, he customarily cast his net four times a day, and no more than that. Now, one day he went to the seashore about noon and set his basket on the ground. After rolling up his shirt and plunging into the water, he cast his net and waited until it settled to the bottom. Then he gathered the cords together and tried to haul in the net. However, he found it too heavy, and no matter how hard he pulled, he could not bring the net up. So he carried the ends ashore, drove a stake into the ground, and tied the net to it. Afterward he stripped, dived into the water, and kept working until he had brought the net up. Filled with joy, he put on his clothes again and went to the net, in which he found a dead jackass that had torn the meshes. In his grief, he exclaimed, "By Allah, this is a strange way to earn a living!" Then he said to himself, "Up and at it! I'm sure that this must be some sort of blessing."

Once the fisherman got the dead ass free of the cords, he wrung out the net and spread it on the shore. Then he plunged into the sea, cast the net again, and cried out, "In Allah's name!" When he began pulling the net, it grew heavy and settled down more firmly than the first time. Now he thought that there were fish in it and tied the net to the stake again. He took off his clothes, dived into the water, and pushed and pulled until he got the net on dry land. Then he found a large clay pitcher filled with sand and mud and was very disappointed.

After throwing away the pitcher, he wrung his net, cleaned it, and cast it into the sea for a third time. Once

LOUIS RHEAD

it had sunk, he pulled at it and found potsherds and broken glass in it. Raising his eyes toward heaven, he cried out, "By Allah, don't You know that I cast my net only four times a day? The third is done, and thus far, You have granted me nothing. So, I beseech You, this time give me my daily bread."

Then he cast his net again and waited for it to sink and settle. When he tried to haul it in, he found that it had become entangled at the bottom. "By Allah!" he exclaimed as he stripped again and dived down into the sea. After freeing the net, he dragged it to land and found a copper jar in the shape of a cucumber. It was evidently filled with something. The mouth was sealed by a lead cap and stamped with the signet of our Lord Solomon, son of David. Seeing this, the fisherman rejoiced and said, "If I sell it in the brass bazaar, I should be able to get ten golden dinars for it." When he shook it, he found that it was heavy and remarked, "If only I knew what was inside! Well, I've got to open it, and then I'll store it in my bag and sell it at the brass market." Taking out his knife, he worked at the lead until he had loosened it from the jar. Then he laid the top on the ground and shook the jar, but he was astonished to find nothing in it. After a while, however, some smoke burst from the jar and soared like a spiral toward the heavens. Once the smoke reached its full height, the thick vapor condensed and became a huge jinnee, whose head touched the clouds while his feet were on the ground. His head was as large as a dome; his hands like pitchforks; his legs as long as masts; and his mouth as big as a cave. His teeth were like large stones; his nostrils, jars; his eyes, two lamps; and his look was fierce and threatening. Now, when the fisherman saw the ifrit, his entire body quivered; his teeth chattered; his spit dried up, and he was so terrified that he could not move or run away.

The ifrit gazed at him and cried, "There is no god but *the* God, and Solomon is the prophet of God." Immediately afterward, he added, "Oh Apostle of Allah, don't slay me. Never again will I slander you, or commit a sin against your laws."

"Oh jinnee," said the fisherman, "did you say, 'Solomon, the Apostle of Allah'? Solomon has been dead for some eighteen hundred years, and we are now approaching the end of the world! What happened to you? Tell me about yourself. How did you get into that jar?"

Now, when the evil spirit heard the words of the fisherman, he said, "There is no god but *the* God. Be of good cheer, fisherman!"

"Why should I be of good cheer?" asked the fisherman.

"Because you shall have to die this very hour."

"May heaven abandon you because of your good tidings!" replied the fisherman. "Why should you kill me? What have I done to deserve death? After all, it was I who freed you from the jar, saved you from the depths of the sea, and brought you up to dry land!"

"Ask me only how you will die, and how I shall slaughter you," the jinnee declared.

"What's my crime?" exclaimed the fisherman. "Why such retribution?"

"Hear my story, oh fisherman," answered the jinnee.

"Tell it to me," said the fisherman, "and be brief, for my heart is in my mouth."

"I'll have you know that I am one among the heretical jinn, and I sinned against Solomon. Consequently, the prophet sent his minister, Asaf son of Barkhiya, to seize me, and this vizier had me bound and brought me against my will to stand before the prophet as a suppliant. When Solomon saw me, he demanded that I embrace the true faith and obey his commands. But I refused, and he had me imprisoned in the jar, which was sealed by lead and stamped by his signet. After Solomon gave orders to a jinnee, I was carried off and cast into the middle of the ocean. I lived in the jar for a hundred years, during which time I said in my heart, 'I'll reward whoever releases me with great riches.' But a full century went by, and when no one set me free, I began the second and said, 'I'll open the hidden treasures of the earth for whoever releases me.' But still no one set me free, and four hundred years went by. Then I said, 'I'll grant three wishes to whoever releases me.' Yet no one set me free. Thereupon I became extremely furious and said, 'From this time on I promise to slay whoever releases me, and the only choice I'll give him will be the kind of death he'll die.' And now, since you've released me, I'll give you your choice of death."

Upon hearing the ifrit's words, the fisherman exclaimed,

"Oh Allah, why couldn't I have freed him before this! Spare my life, jinnee, and Allah will spare yours."

"Nothing can help you," replied the jinnee. "You must die! I'll only grant you your choice of death. So tell me how you want to die."

"I'd prefer that you pardon me for having freed you."

But the jinnee was resolute and said, "It's precisely because you've released me that I must slay you."

"Oh Chief of the Ifrits," said the fisherman, "I do you a good deed, and you return my good deed with evil."

"No more of this talk," the jinnee answered. "I must kill you."

Now the fisherman paused and thought to himself, "This is a jinnee, and I am a man whom Allah has blessed with cunning. So I must use my brains just as he has sought to make use of his malice." Then he said to the jinnee, "So you're really determined to kill me?"

"Indeed I am."

"But if I ask you a certain question, will you swear on the name engraved on the ring of Solomon that you will give me a truthful answer?"

The ifrit replied, "Yes." But hearing the holy name disturbed him, and he began to tremble. "Ask, but be brief."

"How did you fit into this bottle, which is not even large enough to hold your hand or even your foot? And how did it become large enough to contain you?"

"What?" exclaimed the jinnee. "You don't believe that all of me was in there?"

"No, I don't," responded the fisherman. "I'll never believe it until I see you inside with my own eyes."

And Scheherazade noticed that dawn was approaching and stopped telling her story. Then, when the next night arrived, her sister said to her, "Please finish the tale for us, since we're not sleepy."

The king nodded his approval, and so she resumed.

After the fisherman said to the ifrit that he would never believe him until he saw him inside the jar with his own eyes, the jinnee immediately shook and became a vapor, which condensed and gradually entered the jar until all of it was well inside. Right then and there the fisherman quickly took the lead cap with the seal, stopped the mouth of the jar, and cried out to the ifrit, "Ask me for a favor, and I'll grant you your choice of death! By Allah, I'll throw you into the sea right here, and I'll build a lodge on this spot. And I'll warn whoever comes not to fish here because a jinnee dwells in the waters, a jinnee who graciously rewards the person who saves him with a choice of death!"

Now, when the jinnee heard the fisherman's words and saw himself in limbo, he tried to escape, but he was prevented by Solomon's seal. So he knew that the fisherman had outwitted him, and he became submissive. "I was only jesting with you," he said in a humble manner.

"You're lying!" replied the fisherman. "You're the vilest, meanest, and filthiest of jinnees!" And he moved toward the sea with the ifrit crying out, "No! No!" and him responding with "Yes! Yes!"

Then the evil spirit softened his voice, sweetened his speech, and abased himself. "What are you going to do with me, fisherman?" he asked.

"I'm going to throw you back into the sea," he answered, "Where you were housed for eighteen hundred years. And I'm going to leave you there until Judgment Day. Didn't I say to you, spare me, and Allah will spare you, and don't slay me or Allah will slay you? But you spurned my pleas and intended only to treat me ungraciously. So now Allah has thrown you into my hands, for I am more cunning than you!"

"If you open the bottle, I'll make you a wealthy man," the jinnee replied.

"You're lying, you cursed jinnee," exclaimed the fisherman. "You and I are in exactly the same situation as King Yunan was with the Sage Duban."

"And who were King Yunan and the Sage Duban? What happened to them?" asked the jinnee.

Thereupon the fisherman began to tell

The Tale of King Yunan and the Sage Duban

A long time ago there lived a king called Yunan, who reigned over the city of Fars in the land of Persia. He was a wealthy and powerful ruler, who had massive armies and was allied with all nations of men. However, his body was afflicted with a leprosy that the doctors were unable to heal. He drank potions, swallowed pills, and used salves, but nothing would help. Finally, a mighty healer of men came to his city, the Sage Duban, who was extremely old and well versed in the works of the Greeks, Persians, Romans, Arabs, and Syrians. Moreover, he was skilled in astronomy and knew everything in theory and practice that could heal or harm a body. Indeed, he was familiar with the virtues of every plant, grass, and herb in the world and how they could benefit or damage a person, and he understood philosophy, medical science, and other branches of the tree of knowledge. Now, this physician had been in the city for only a few days when he heard about the king's malady and how he had been suffering from leprosy and how all the doctors and wise men had failed to heal him. As a result, he sat up the entire night and thought about the king's condition. When dawn broke, he put on his most becoming outfit and went to see King Yunan. After he kissed the ground before him, he wished the king long life and prosperity and introduced himself. "Your majesty, news has reached me that none of your physicians have been able to stop your sickness. However, you will see that I can cure you, and I shall have no need of potions or ointments."

When King Yunan heard these words, he responded with great surprise, "How are you going to do this? By Allah, if you heal me, I will make you and your grandchildren rich, and I will give you sumptuous gifts. Whatever you wish will be yours, and you will be my friend and boon companion." Then the king had him dressed in a robe of honor and asked him graciously, "Is it really possible for you to cure me without drugs and potions?"

"Yes!" he answered. "I'll heal you without the pains and drawbacks of medicine."

The king was astonished and said, "When will all this take place, and how soon? Let it be soon."

"As you wish," he replied. "The cure will begin tomorrow."

Upon saying this, the sage departed and rented a house in the city in order to store his books, scrolls, medicines, and aromatic roots in a better way. Then he set to work by choosing the most effective drugs and balsams. Afterward he carved a polo stick with a hollow inside and a wide end with which to hit a ball. All this was made with consummate art. On the next day when both the stick and ball were ready for use, he went to the king, and after kissing the ground, he asked the king to ride out onto the parade ground to play polo. He was accompanied by his emirs, chamberlains, viziers, and lords of the realm, and before he was seated, the Sage Duban went up to him, handed him the stick, and said, "Take this stick and grip it as I do. Good! Now lean over your horse and drive the ball with all your might until your palm is moist and your body perspires. Then the medicine will penetrate through your palm and will permeate your body. After you have finished playing and you feel the effects of the medicine, return to your palace and wash yourself in the Hammam bath. Then lie down to sleep, and you will be healed. Now, peace be with you!"

Thereupon King Yunan took the stick from the sage and grasped it firmly. After mounting his steed, he drove the ball before him and galloped after it until he reached it, and he did not stop hitting the ball until his hand became moist and his skin perspired so that he imbibed the medicine from the wood. Then the Sage Duban knew that the drugs had penetrated his body, and he told the king that it was time to return to the palace and enter the bath without delay. So King Yunan returned immediately and ordered them to prepare the bath for him. The carpet spreaders rushed about, and the slaves hurried and prepared a change of clothes for the king, who entered the bath and made the total ablution long and thorough. Then he put on his clothes within the Hammam and rode from there to his palace, where he lay down and slept.

Meanwhile, the Sage Duban returned home and slept as usual. When morning dawned, he went back to the palace and asked for an audience with the king. The king ordered him to be admitted, and after the Sage Duban sang a solemn song in honor of the king, the king rose to his feet quickly and embraced him. After giving him a seat by his side, the king had him clothed in a sumptuous robe, for it so happened that after the king had left the Hammam bath, he had looked at his body and had not been able to find a single trace of leprosy. Indeed, his skin had become as clean as pure silver, and he had rejoiced. Now the food trays carrying the most delicious viands were brought, and the physician ate with the king and remained with him all that day. Then at nightfall the king gave the Sage Duban two thousand gold pieces besides the usual robe of honor and other gifts galore. Finally, he sent him home on his own steed.

After the sage had departed, King Yunan again expressed his amazement at the doctor's art and said, "This man cured my body without the aid of ointments. Surely, this shows how great and consummate his skills are! I feel obliged to honor such a man with rewards and distinction and make him my friend and companion until the end of my days."

So King Yunan spent the night in joy and happiness because his body had been healed and had overcome such a pernicious malady. The next day the king left his seraglio and sat on his throne. The lords of estate stood around him, and the emirs and viziers sat on his right and on his left as was their custom. Then the king asked for the Sage Duban, who came in and kissed the ground before him. After the king rose to greet him and seated him by his side, he ate with him and wished him long life. Moreover, he gave him clothes and gifts and did not stop conversing with him until night approached. Then, as a kind of salary, the king gave him five robes of honor and a thousand dinars, whereupon the doctor returned to his own house full of gratitude to the king.

When the next morning dawned, the king went to his audience hall, and his lords, nobles, chamberlains, and ministers surrounded him just as the white encompasses the black of the eye. Now the king had a vizier among the nobility, unpleasant in appearance, sordid, ungenerous, full of envy and ill will. When this minister saw the king place the physician near him and give him all those gifts, he was jealous of him and planned to do him harm. So the minister went before the king and, kissing the ground between his hands, said, "Your majesty, I have some serious advice for you, and though you may not like it, I would be amiss in my duties as your minister if I did not speak my piece."

The king was troubled by the words of the minister and said, "What is this advice of yours?"

"Oh glorious monarch," he responded, "the wise men of former times have a saying which runs like this: whoever does not regard the end will not have Fortune as his friend. And indeed, I have recently seen the king heading in the wrong direction, for he has been bestowing lavish presents on his enemy, on one whose intention is to bring an end to your rule. You have favored this man and honored him unduly by making him an intimate friend. Consequently, I fear for the king's life."

The king, whose face changed color, was greatly disturbed and asked, "Whom do you suspect?"

"Oh king," the minister said, "if you are asleep, wake up! I am pointing at the physician Duban."

"You should be ashamed of yourself!" the king cried out. "He is a true friend, and I've favored him above all other men because he cured me of my leprosy, which had baffled all the physicians of my land. Indeed, there is no one like him to be found in these times—no, no one in the entire world from the far east to the far west! And this is the man whom you are accusing! Why, this very day I granted him a monthly salary and allowance of one thousand gold pieces, and were I to share my realm with him, it would be inconsequential. Therefore, I must assume that you are speaking about him out of mere envy and jealousy just as one spoke about King Sinbad."

And Scheherazade noticed that dawn was approaching and stopped her story. Then Dunazade said, "Oh my sister, your tale is delightful. How sweet and graceful!"

"This is nothing compared with what I could tell you tomorrow night if the king would spare my life," she replied.

Then the king said to himself, "By Allah, I won't slay her until I hear the rest of her tale, for it is truly wondrous."

So they rested that night in mutual embrace until dawn. Then the king went to his audience hall, and the vizier and the troops entered. The reception chamber was thronged, and the king judged, appointed, deposed, permitted, and prohibited during the rest of the day until the court was adjourned, whereupon King Shahryar returned to his palace. Later that night, Dunazade said to Scheherazade, "If you're not sleepy, will you please finish the story for us?"

"With the king's permission," she replied.

"You have my permission," said Shahryad.

And Scheherazade resumed:

If you recall, oh mighty monarch, King Yunan had said to his minister, "Oh vizier, the evil spirit of envy has contaminated you because of this physician, and you are trying to urge me to put him to death, after which I would sorely repent just as King Sinbad repented the killing of his falcon."

"Pardon me, your majesty, what was that about?" asked the vizier.

In reply the king began

The Tale of King Sinbad and His Falcon

There was once a king of Persia who enjoyed all the sporting life, especially hunting. He had raised a falcon which he carried all night on his fist, and he had a little gold cup made for it that was draped around its neck so it could drink at will. Of course, whenever he went hunting, he took this bird with him.

Now, one day as the king was sitting quietly in his palace, the high falconer of his household appeared before him and said, "Your majesty, this is just the right day for hunting."

So the king gave orders accordingly and set out with the falcon on his fist. They went merrily on their way until they found a ravine, where they laid their nets for the chase. Just then a gazelle came within sight, and the king cried, "I'll kill any man who allows that gazelle over there to jump over his head and get away!"

They closed in on the gazelle with the nets, driving it near the king's post. Then it squatted on its hindquarters and crossed its forehead over its breast, as if about to kiss the earth before the king. So unusual was this behavior that the king bowed his brow in acknowledgment to the gazelle, allowing the beast time to jump quickly over his head and disappear from sight. Thereupon, the king turned toward his troops and saw them pointing at him. "Oh vizier," he asked, "what are my men saying?"

"They say," the minister replied, "that you had proclaimed you would kill any man who allowed the gazelle to jump over his head."

"Well, by the life of my head, I shall pursue that gazelle until I bring it back!"

So he set off on his horse, galloping after the gazelle's trail, and he did not stop tracking the beast until he reached the foothills of a mountain chain where the quarry had made for a cave. Then the king set the falcon loose, and when the bird caught up with it, she swooped down, and drove her talons into its eyes, bewildering and blinding it. When he saw this, the king came up, drew his mace, and struck a blow that killed the beast. After that he dismounted, cut the antelope's throat, flayed the body, and hung it on the pommel of his saddle.

Now the time for siesta had arrived, and the surrounding land was parched and dry. There was no water to be found anywhere, and the king and his horse were thirsty. So he went searching until he found a tree moist with water on its boughs, as if butter were melting from its branches. Thereupon the king, who wore leather gauntlets to protect him against poison, took the cup from the hawk's neck, and after filling it with water, he set it before the bird, who suddenly struck it with her claws so that the liquid poured out. The king filled it a second time with the drops from the branches, thinking his falcon was thirsty, but the bird struck the cup again with her claws and knocked it over. Now the king became mad at the falcon and filled the cup a third time but offered it to his horse. Once more, the bird upset it with a flick of her wings.

"By Allah," said the king, "you miserable flying creature! You're keeping all of us from drinking."

So he struck the falcon with his sword and cut off her wing, but the bird raised her head and said by signs, "Look at what's hanging on the tree!"

The king lifted his eyes and caught sight of a brood of vipers, whose poison drops he had mistaken for water. Thereupon he repented for having lopped off the falcon's wing, and after mounting his horse, he moved on with the dead gazelle until he arrived at his camp. After throwing the quarry to the cook, he said, "Take it and broil it." Then he sat down on his chair to relax, but the falcon, still on his wrist, gasped and died. There was nothing left for the king to do but to cry in sorrow and remorse for having slain the falcon which had saved his life.

"Such was the sad story about King Sinbad, and I'm certain that if I were to do as you desire, I would regret it. In fact, I'd be in the same situation as the man who killed his parrot."

"And what happened to him?" the vizier asked.

In reply, the king began to tell

The Tale of the Husband and the Parrot

There was once a merchant who had married a perfectly beautiful wife, who was lovely and graceful. He was, however, so madly jealous of her that he would not leave her to conduct his business. At last an occasion arose that compelled him to travel. So he went to a bird market and bought a parrot for one hundred gold pieces. Then he placed the parrot in his house and expected it to act as a duenna and report to him everything that happened during his absence, for the bird was cunning and never forgot what it saw and heard.

Now the merchant's fair wife had fallen in love with a young Turk, who visited her during her husband's absence, and she treated him to a feast during the day and lay with him during the night. Soon the merchant completed his business, returned home, and began at once to question the parrot about the conduct of his wife while he was in foreign countries.

"Your wife has a male friend, who spent every night with her during your absence," the parrot declared.

Thereupon the husband went to his wife in a violent rage and gave her the beating of her life. Afterward, suspecting that one of the slave girls had been tattling to the master, the woman called them together and made them swear to tell her the truth. Indeed, they all swore that they had kept her secret, and they revealed to her that the parrot was the one who had squealed, insisting that they had heard it with their own ears.

As a result the woman ordered one of the girls to set a hand mill under the cage and to grind with it. Another girl was commanded to sprinkle water through the cage roof, and a third to run around flashing a mirror of bright steel throughout the night. Next morning when the husband returned home after being entertained by one of his friends, he ordered that the parrot be brought before him and asked what had taken place while he was away.

"Pardon me, oh master," said the bird, "I could neither hear nor see anything because of the thunder and lightning that lasted throughout the murky night."

Since it happened to be the height of summer, the master was astounded and cried, "But we're now in July, and there aren't any storms or rain."

"By Allah," replied the parrot, "I saw everything with my own eyes."

Thereupon the merchant, not suspecting his wife's plot, became extremely angry, for he now believed that he had wrongly accused his wife. So he reached out, pulled the parrot from its cage, and dashed it upon the ground with such force that he killed it on the spot.

Some days later one of the slave girls confessed to him the whole truth. But he would still not believe it until he saw the young Turk, his wife's lover, come out of her chamber. Consequently, he drew his sword and slew him by a blow on the back of the neck, and he killed his wife in the same way. Thus, the two of them, laden with mortal sin, went straight to hell. Despite the fact that the merchant now knew the parrot had told the truth, and despite the fact that he honored the bird with his mourning, his grief could not bring it back to life.

Upon hearing the words of King Yunan, the minister responded, "Your majesty, do you honestly think that I'm plotting against the Sage Duban? I'm only giving you my opinion and some advice. If you accept my advice, I think you'll be saved. Otherwise, you'll be destroyed just like that young prince who was treacherously betrayed by a certain vizier."

"And how did that come about?" asked the king.

In reply, the minister began

The Tale of the Prince and the Ogress

There was once a prince who was extremely fond of hunting, and consequently, his father commanded one of his viziers to accompany the prince wherever he went. One day the young prince went hunting and was accompanied by his father's minister. As they jogged on together, they caught sight of a big wild beast.

"Let's catch that noble beast!" cried the vizier to the prince.

So the prince followed it and soon disappeared from everyone's sight. Meanwhile, the beast got away from him in the woods, where he lost his way and could not decide which way to turn. All of a sudden a maiden appeared out of nowhere with tears streaming down her cheeks.

"Who are you?" the prince asked.

"I'm the daughter of a king among the kings of Hind," she responded, "and I was traveling with a caravan in the desert when drowsiness overcame me and I unwittingly fell from my horse. So now I'm cut off from my attendants and am quite bewildered."

After hearing these words, the prince took pity on her and helped her onto his horse. She sat on the horse's crupper, and they rode together until they came to an old ruin, where the maiden said to him, "Oh master, please stop. I must obey a call of nature."

After setting her down at the ruin, the prince waited and waited, but she took so long that he thought that she was wasting too much time. So, he followed her trail and was surprised to discover that she was a wicked ogress and had gone to tell her brood that she was going to bring them a fine fat youth for dinner.

They responded by crying out, "Bring him to us quickly, Mother, so we can fill our bellies!"

When the prince overheard their talk, it was clear that he would die, and his muscles quivered in fear. As he turned away to take flight, the ogress came out of the ruin and saw him trembling.

"Why are you so afraid?" she asked.

"I've encountered an enemy, whom I dread with all my might," he replied.

"Didn't you say that you are the son of a king?" asked the ogress.

"Indeed, I am," he said.

"Then why don't you give him some money?" she said. "That would satisfy him."

"He won't be satisfied with my money, only with my life," he stated. "And I'm petrified of him and fear for my life."

"If you're so distressed as you say," she said, "ask help from Allah, who will surely protect you from any harm or evil that threatens you."

Then the prince raised his eyes toward heaven and cried out, "May Allah help me in my need! Grant me victory over my foe. Protect me with all your might. Praise be to Allah!"

After hearing his prayer, the ogress decided to let him live, and the prince returned to his father and told him how the vizier had failed to protect him. Consequently, the king summoned the minister to him and slew him on the spot.

"Likewise, King Yunan, if you continue to trust this physician, you will die the worst kind of death. This man whom you have made your intimate companion and whom you treat with such great respect will work your destruction. Didn't you see how he healed your disease from the outside by something you grasped in your hand? Most assuredly he'll destroy you in the very same manner that he healed you!"

"You have spoken the truth," replied King Yunan. "It may be that this sage has indeed come as a spy with the intention of killing me, for certainly if he cured me by something held in my hand, he can kill me by something given me to smell. Well, minister, tell me what I should do with him."

"Have him summoned to you this very instant," replied the vizier, "and when he comes, have his head cut off, and you will be rid of him and his wickedness. Trick him before he tricks you."

"You have again spoken wisely, oh vizier," said the king, and he sent a servant to call the sage, who came in a joyful mood, for he did not know what was in store for him. When Duban entered, he gave thanks to the king for the generous gifts he had received and wished him well.

"Do you know why I have summoned you?" the king responded curtly.

"Only Allah Most Highest knows all there is to know!" the sage declared.

But the king retorted, "I have summoned you to take your life and to make sure that you are utterly destroyed."

Duban the Sage was puzzled and astonished by this strange statement, and he asked, "Oh king, why do you want to slay me? What harm have I done you?"

"Men tell me that you are a spy who has been sent to kill me," said the king, "and therefore I'm going to kill you before you kill me." Then he called his executioner and said, "Strike off the head of this traitor and deliver us from his evil practices."

"Spare me," said the sage, "and Allah will spare you. If you slay me, Allah will slay you."

And he repeated the very same words that I said to you, oh jinnee, and yet you wouldn't let me go because you were so bent on killing me. Likewise, King Yunan's only response was, "I shall not be safe without slaying you. You must understand that since you healed me by something that I held in my hand, I can't be safe from your killing me by something you might give to me to smell or other such things."

"So this is your reward!" remarked the sage. "You repay good only with evil."

"Nothing can help you," declared the king. "You must die and without delay."

Now when the physician was sure that the king would slay him without waiting, he wept and regretted the good that he had done for the king. The executioner stepped forward, bound Sage Duban's eyes, and drew out his sword. Then he turned to the king and said, "With your permission."

But the sage wept and cried, "Spare me, and Allah will spare you. If you slay me, Allah will slay you! Is this the reward that I deserve? It seems to me that you're giving me nothing but crocodile boon."

"What do you mean by crocodile boon? Tell me!" the king demanded.

"It's impossible for me to tell you anything in this state," countered the sage. "May Allah bless you if you spare me."

And he wept profusely until one of the king's favorites stood up and said, "Oh king, grant me the blood of this physician, for we have never seen him sin against you or do anything except heal you from a disease which baffled every doctor and scientist in your kingdom."

"You don't understand why I am putting this physician to death," announced the king. "Listen carefully! If I spare him, I shall be sentencing myself to certain death, for someone who healed me of such a malady by something held in my hand can slay me by something held to my nose. And I'm afraid that he may kill me for some price. Indeed, he might be a spy whose sole purpose in coming here was to plot my destruction. So nothing can help him: die he must, and only then shall I be sure of my own life."

"Spare me, and Allah shall spare you," Duban cried again. "If you slay me, Allah will slay you."

But it was in vain, and when the doctor knew for certain that the king would kill him, he said, "Oh king, if nothing will help me, grant me a small delay so that I may go to my house, take care of my obligations, and tell my people and neighbors where to bury me and distribute my books of medicine. Besides, among my books I have a most rare one that I would like you to keep as a treasure in your vaults."

"And what is in the book?" the king asked.

"Things beyond your imagination, and the most amazing secret is that if you turn three pages right after you cut off my head and read three lines of the page on your left, my head will speak and answer every question that you deign to ask it."

The king was most astonished, and, laughing with delight at the novelty, he said, "Do you really want me to believe that when I cut off your head, it will speak to me?"

"Yes, your majesty!"

"This is indeed a strange matter!" said the king, and he decided instantly to send him closely guarded to his house, where Duban settled all his obligations. The next day he went to the king's audience hall, where emirs, viziers, chamberlains, nabobs, nobles, and lords of estate were gathered together, making the chamber as colorful as a garden of flowers. The doctor went up to the king carrying an old worn book and a little metal can full of powder like the one that is used to protect the eyes. Then he sat down and said, "Give me a tray."

So they brought him one, and he poured the powder onto it, smoothed it down, and said, "Oh king, take this book, but do not open it until my head falls. Then place my head on this tray, press it down on the powder, and the blood will immediately stop flowing. That is the time to open the book."

Thereupon the king took the book and made a sign to the executioner, who arose and struck off the sage's head. Afterward he placed it on the middle of the tray and pressed it down on the powder. When the blood stopped flowing, Duban's eyes glistened again, and he said, "Now open the book, oh king!"

The king opened the book, and found the pages stuck together. So he put his finger to his mouth to moisten it, and he was then easily able to turn over the first six pages, but he found nothing written on them. So he cried out, "Doctor, there's nothing written here!"

"Turn the pages some more," Duban replied.

The king continued to turn the pages, but the book was poisoned, and before long the venom penetrated his system so that the king had strong convulsions and cried out, "The poison has done its work!"

And now the Sage Duban's head replied, "Fortune repays an ungrateful tyrant's oppressive ways with the just punishment he duly deserves!"

No sooner had the head stopped speaking than the king rolled over dead.

"Now I would like you to know, oh jinnee, that if King Yunan had spared the Sage Duban, Allah would have spared him, but he refused to do so, and thus Allah slew him. So, you see, ifrit, if you had spared me, Allah would have saved you."

And Scheherazade noticed that dawn was approaching, and she stopped telling her story.

"Oh my sister," said Dunazade, "how delightful, sweet, and graceful your tale is."

"That is nothing compared to what I could tell you this coming night if the king were to spare me and I could live."

"By Allah," the king said to himself, "I won't slay her until I hear the rest of the story, for it is truly wondrous."

They rested that night in mutual embrace until dawn finally came. Then the king went to his audience hall, where the viziers and troops came. So the king judged, appointed, deposed, commanded, and prohibited the rest of the day. When the court was adjourned, the king returned to the palace, and later that night Dunazade said to her sister, "Please finish the story for us."

And Scheherazade replied, "I shall, if the king gives his permission."

"Permission granted," said the king.

So Scheherazade resumed her tale.

Then the fisherman said to the ifrit, "If you had spared me, I would have spared you. But you wouldn't be content unless I died. So now I'll let you die by keeping you jailed up in this jar, and I'll hurl you into the sea."

Then the jinnee roared and cried out, "By Allah, fisherman, don't do this! Spare me, and pardon my past deeds. If I've been tyrannical, then you should be generous, for it is said that when good is done to him who has done evil, the evildoer will stop doing evil deeds. So do not deal with me as Umamah dealt with Atikah."

"And what was their story?" asked the fisherman.

"This is not the time for storytelling with me in this prison," said the jinnee. "But if you set me free, I'll tell you the tale."

"Enough talk," responded the fisherman. "Nothing can help you. I'm going to throw you back into the sea, and there's no way you'll ever be able to get out the bottle. When I humbled myself before you and wept, you sought only to slay me. I had done you absolutely no harm, and yet you repaid my kindness with evil. So now that I know just how evil you are, I shall warn whoever may fish you from the sea to toss you back again, and you'll remain under these waters until the end of time, when your own end will come."

"Set me free!" the jinnee cried. "This is a noble occasion for generosity, and I'll pledge never to do you any harm. In fact, I'll help you get whatever you need so you'll never be poor again."

The fisherman paused a moment and then finally accepted his promise on the condition that the jinnee would not harm him but would enter into his service. After making the jinnee swear a solemn oath by Almighty Allah, he opened the top, and the pillar of smoke rose up until it was completely out of the bottle. Then it thickened and became once more the hideous ifrit, who immediately kicked the bottle and sent it flying into the sea.

Upon seeing how badly the bottle was treated, the fisherman thought his turn would certainly come next, and he piddled in his pants. "This does not augur well for me," he said to himself, but he took heart and cried out, "Oh jinnee, keep your promise, for you will be judged later on how well you have kept your promises! You've made a vow to me and have sworn an oath not to deceive me. If you do, Allah will take His revenge, for He is a jealous God, who gives respite to the sinner but does not let him escape. So, let me remind you what the Sage Duban said to King Yunan, 'Spare me, and Allah will spare you!' "

The ifrit burst into laughter and stalked away, saying to the fisherman, "Follow me."

The man walked after him at a safe distance to make sure he might have a chance to escape, and they went around the suburbs of the city and entered some woods. After marching through the woods, they came to a vast wilderness, and in the middle of it stood a mountain lake. The jinnee waded into the middle of it and cried again, "Follow me!"

After the fisherman did this, the ifrit told him to cast his net and catch some fish. The fisherman looked into the water and was astonished to see all sorts of different-colored fish—white, red, blue, and yellow. When he cast his net and hauled it in, however, he saw that he had caught four fish, each with a different color. He rejoiced a great deal, and even more when the jinnee said to him, "Carry these to the sultan and offer them to him as a gift. In return he'll give you enough to make you a wealthy man. Now, you must pardon me, for I know of no other way of serving you. As you know, I have lain in the sea eighteen hundred years and have not seen the face of the world until just recently. Just remember not to fish here more than once a day." Then the ifrit wished the fisherman Godspeed and said, "May Allah grant that we meet once again." Thereupon the jinnee struck the earth with one foot and the ground parted and swallowed him up.

After his astonishment subsided, the fisherman took the fish and headed for the city. As soon as he reached home, he filled a clay bowl with water and threw the fish into it. Then he carried the bowl with the wriggling fish to the king's palace, as the ifrit had told him to do, and offered them to the king, who was amazed by the sight, for never in his life had he seen such marvelous fish as these.

"Give these fish to the slave girl who does our cooking," he said to his vizier, who carried the fish to the girl and told her to fry them.

After he had carried out his chore, the vizier returned to the king, who commanded him to give the fisherman four hundred dinars. After the fisherman received them, he ran home stumbling, falling, and jumping up, for he thought the whole thing was a dream. In reality, however, he bought everything his family wanted and was extremely joyful and happy to be with his wife once again.

In the meantime the sultan's cook cleaned the fish and set them in the frying pan. Then she basted them with oil until one side was dressed. When she turned them over, however, the kitchen wall split open, and there appeared a beautiful and graceful lady with an oval face and black eyelashes. She wore a silk dress lined in blue. Large earrings adorned her ears, a pair of bracelets her wrists, while rings with priceless gems were on her fingers. In one of her hands she held a long rod of rattan cane, which she thrust into the frying pan, and she said, "Oh fish! Oh fish! Are you keeping your pledge?"

When the cook saw this apparition, she gasped and fainted. The young lady repeated her words two more times, and at last the fish raised their heads from the pan and spoke in an articulate way, "Yes! Yes!"

After this the young lady upset the frying pan and went away the same way she had entered. The kitchen wall closed behind her, and when the cook recovered from her faint, she saw the four fish charred black as charcoal, and they cried out, "His staff broke in his first bout."

Once again the maiden fainted and fell to the ground. While she was in this condition, the vizier came for the fish, and when he saw her lying on the ground, completely dazed, he shoved her with his foot and said, "Bring the fish for the sultan!"

After recovering from her daze, she informed the vizier what had happened, and after getting over his astonishment, he sent for the fisherman. When the fisherman arrived, the vizier said to him, "I want you to fetch four more fish like those that you brought before."

Accordingly, the man returned to the lake and cast his net. When it settled, there were suddenly four fish in it just like the first. He carried them straight to the vizier, who took them to the cook and said, "Get up now and fry these fish in front of me so I can see what's going on here."

The maiden arose, cleaned the fish, and put them into the frying pan over the fire. After a few minutes the wall split into two, and the young lady appeared as before. In her hand was the wand, which she thrust into the frying pan again, and she said, "Oh fish! Oh fish! Are you keeping your pledge?"

Suddenly the fish lifted their heads and repeated, "Yes! Yes!"

* * *

And Scheherazade noticed that dawn was approaching and stopped telling her story. When the next night arrived, however, she received the king's permission to continue her tale and said,

When the fish spoke and the young lady upset the frying pan with her wand and left by the way she had come, the vizier cried out, "We must tell the king about this."

So he went and told the king what had happened, and the king responded by saying, "I must see this with my own eyes." The first thing he did was to send for the fisherman, whom he commanded to bring four other fish like the first. After the fisherman returned with the fish, the king rewarded him with four hundred gold pieces and turned to the vizier. "I want you to get up and fry the fish before me!" he commanded.

"To hear is to obey," the minister replied. He had the frying pan brought to him, cleaned the fish, and set the pan with the fish in it over the fire. Suddenly the wall split in two, and out burst a black slave like a huge rock carrying a green branch in his hand.

"Oh fish! Oh fish!" he cried in loud and terrible tones. "Are you keeping your old pledge?"

In turn the fish lifted their heads from the frying pan and said, "Yes! Yes! We're true to our word!"

Then the huge blackamoor approached the frying pan and upset it with the branch and left by the way he had come. After he had vanished from their sight, the king inspected the fish and found them all charred black as charcoal. Utterly bewildered, he said to the vizier, "This is truly a matter that should be made known to everyone, and as for the fish, there's certainly something marvelous connected to them."

So he summoned the fisherman and said to him, "You'd better fear for your life, fisherman, if you lie to me! Where did you catch these fish?"

"From a lake lying in a valley behind that mountain which you can see from your city," he replied.

"How many days' march is it from here?" the king asked.

"Your majesty, it's only a half hour from here."

The king was puzzled by this reply, but he quickly ordered his troops to get ready for an excursion. The fisherman had to lead the way as guide, and under his breath he began cursing the jinnee. They walked until they had climbed the mountain and descended into a great desert which they had never seen before in their lives. When they reached the valley set between four mountains and saw the lake with the red, white, yellow, and blue fish, they were even more astounded. The king stood fixed to the spot in amazement and asked everyone present, "Has any one of you ever seen this lake before?"

They all responded by saying that they had never seen the lake before, and they also questioned the oldest inhabitants they met, men well stricken in years, but each and every one of them responded that he had never seen such a lake in that place.

"By Allah," said the king, "I shall neither return to my capital nor sit upon the throne of my forebears until I learn the truth about this lake and these strange fish." He then ordered his men to dismount and set up camp all around the mountain. Then he summoned his vizier, a minister with a great deal of experience, sagacious, perceptive, and well versed in such affairs. "I've something in mind that I want to tell you about," the king said. "My heart tells me to travel forth tonight all alone and to search out the mystery of this lake and its fish. I want you to take my seat at the tent door and say to the emirs, viziers, nabobs, and chamberlains that the sultan is sick and has ordered you not to let anyone enter his tent. Be careful that you don't let anyone know my plans."

Since the vizier did not oppose his plan, the sultan changed his clothes, slung his sword over his shoulder, and left by a path which led up one of the mountains. He marched the entire night until dawn arrived, and he continued walking even then until the heat became too much for him. After resting for a while, he resumed his march and continued through the second night until dawn, when he suddenly noticed a black point in the far distance and said to himself, "Perhaps someone there will be able to tell me about the mystery of the lake and its fish!"

As he drew near the dark object, he realized that it was a palace built of dark stone plated with iron. One side of the gate was open, while the other was shut. The king's spirits rose high as he stood before the gate and rapped lightly. Hearing no answer, he knocked a few more times, yet nobody came. "Most likely it's empty," he said to himself. So he mustered up his courage and walked through the main gate into the large hall, where he cried out, "Holla, anyone here? I'm a stranger and traveler in need of food!" He repeated his cry two more times, but there was still no reply. So he made up his mind to explore the place, and he boldly strode through the vestibule into the very middle of the palace, but he did not find anyone.

The palace was furnished with silken materials that had gold stars on them, and there were hangings over the doorways. In the middle of the palace was a spacious court with four open salons set off on the sides. A canopy shaded the court, and in the center was a flowing fountain with four lion statues made of gold, spouting water from their mouths that was as clear as pearls. Birds were flying freely all around the place, and there was a net of golden wire set over the palace that prevented them from flying off. In short, there was everything imaginable in this palace except human beings.

The king was amazed by all this, but he felt sad that he had found no one who could reveal to him the mystery of the lake, the fish, the mountains, and the palace itself. When he sat down near the fountain to ponder the situation, however, he soon heard a mournful sigh that seemed to come from a grieving heart. The sultan sprang to his feet and followed the sound until he encountered a curtain draped over the entrance to a chamber. After raising it, he saw a young man sitting upon a couch about three feet above the ground. He was a handsome man and well-proportioned. His forehead was as white as a flower, and his cheeks were rosy. The king rejoiced and greeted him, while the young man, who was wearing a crown studded with gems, remained seated in his caftan of silken stuff lined with Egyptian gold. His face was sad with the traces of sorrow as he returned the royal greeting and said, "My lord, your dignity demands that I rise to greet you, but I can only beg your pardon for failing to do so."

"You have my pardon," the king said. "Please regard

me as your guest who has come here on a special mission. I would appreciate your telling me the secret of this lake and its fish and about this palace and your loneliness and why you are grieving."

When the young man heard these words, he began to weep so much that his bosom became drenched with tears. The king was astounded by such an outburst and asked him, "What's causing all these tears, young man?"

"Why shouldn't I weep when I am in the condition that I'm in?" responded the youth, who put out his hand and raised the skirt of his garment. Immediately the king realized that the youth's lower half was stone down to his feet, while his upper half was human and alive. Upon seeing this, the king was full of compassion and cried out, "Alas, young man, my heart goes out to you! In truth, you heap sorrow upon my sorrow. I had only wanted to ask you about the mystery of the fish. But now I am concerned to hear your story as well. Do not put me off, young man. I want you to tell me your entire tale right now."

"Lend me your ears, your sight, and your insight," he replied.

"All are at your service!" the king stated.

"My situation is highly extraordinary," the youth said, "and so is that of the fish. And if my tale could be engraved somewhere for all to see, it could serve as a wonderful warning."

"Why is that?" asked the king.

And the young man began to tell

The Tale of the Enchanted Prince

I'll have you know, my lord, that my sire was king of this city, and his name was Mahmud, lord of the Black Islands and ruler of what are now these four mountains. He reigned threescore and ten years, after which he died, and I was appointed sultan in his place. I took my cousin as my wife, the daughter of my paternal uncle, and she loved me with such abounding love that whenever I was absent she did not eat or drink until she saw me again. She had been living with me for five years when, on a certain day, she went to the Hammam bath and stayed there a long time. After asking the cook to get everything ready for our supper, I went into the palace and lay down on the bed where I was accustomed to sleep. Then I requested two maidens to fan my face, one sitting by my head and the other at my feet. But I was restless because my wife was absent, and I could not sleep. Though my eyes were closed, my mind and thoughts were wide awake. Soon I heard the slave girl at my head say to the one who was at my feet, "How I pity our poor master! His youth is being wasted, and it is all on account of our mistress, that cursed whore, who's betraying him!"

"Yes, you're right. May Allah curse all faithless women. Our talented master deserves something better than this harlot who sleeps with someone else every night."

"Is our master dumb and foolish?" asked the slave girl who sat by my head. "Why doesn't he question her?"

"Shame on you!" the other replied. "Our master doesn't know what she's doing, nor does he have a choice. She drugs his drink every night before he goes to bed. So he sleeps deeply and doesn't have an inkling about where she goes and what she does. But we know that after giving him the drugged wine, she puts on her richest clothes and perfumes. Then she goes away until the break of day, when she comes back to him and burns a pastille under his nose so he can awake from his deathlike sleep."

When I heard the slave girl's words, I was livid with rage, and I thought night would never fall. Soon, however, my wife returned from the bath, and we had dinner together. Afterward, as was our custom, we sat half an hour together and got ready to drink some wine. When she called for the particular wine I used to drink before sleeping and handed me the cup, I pretended to drink it but actually poured the contents into my bosom. Soon I lay down and let her think that I was asleep. Suddenly she cried out, "Sleep out the night, and never wake again. By Allah, I loathe you and your whole body. My soul is disgusted from living with you, and I can't wait for the day when Allah will snatch away your life!"

Then she rose and put on her most beautiful dress and

dowsed herself with perfume. Moreover, she slung my sword over her shoulder, opened the gates of the palace, and went on her evil way. So I got up and followed her as she threaded her way through the streets until she came to the city gate, where she said some words that I could not understand. All of a sudden the padlocks dropped by themselves as if broken, and the doors of the gate opened. She went through (and I after her without her noticing anything) and walked until she came to the garbage heaps and a reed fence built around a round-roofed hut of mud bricks. After she entered the door, I climbed onto the roof and managed to look inside without being seen. There I saw my wife approach a Negro slave with his upper lip like the cover of a pot, and his lower like an open pot—lips which could sweep up sand from the gravel floor of the cot. To boot, he was a leper and a paralytic, lying upon some sugar-cane trash and wrapped in an old blanket and dirty rags. She kissed the ground before him, and he raised his head so as to see her and said, "Woe to you! Why are you so late? Some of my black brethren were here with me for a while, and they drank their wine and had their young ladies. But I could not drink because you were absent."

"Oh my lord," she said, "my heart's love, don't you realize that I'm married to my cousin, whose very looks I loathe, and I hate myself when I am in his company? And if I were not afraid for your sake, I would not let a single sun rise before turning his city into a heap of rubble, and the ravens would croak, the owls hoot, and the jackals and wolves would run amok and loot. Indeed, I would have all the stones of the city removed to the back of the Caucasus."

"You're lying, damn you!" the slave responded. "Now I'm going to swear an oath by the valor and honor of blackamoor men (and don't think that our manliness is like the poor manliness of white men) that from this day forth, if you stay away from me until this hour, I will reject your company, nor will I glue my body to your body and strum and belly-bump. Do you think you can play fast and loose with us, you cracked pot, just so we can satisfy your dirty lust? You stink! Bitch! Vilest of the vile whites!"

When I heard his words and saw what was going on

between these two wretches, the world became dark all around me, and my soul no longer knew where it was. Meanwhile my wife stood up weeping humbly before the slave and said, "Oh my beloved, oh light of my eyes!" And she did not stop weeping and abasing herself until he deigned to accept her pleas. Then she was quite glad, stood up, took off her outer garments, and said, "Oh master, what do you have here for your slave to eat?"

"Take off the cover of the pot," he grumbled, "and you'll find some boiled bones of rats we dined on. Pick at them and then go to that slop pot, where you'll find the rest of some beer that you may drink."

So she ate, drank, and washed her hands. Afterward she went and lay down by the side of the slave on the cane trash, and after stripping herself stark naked, she crept in with him under his dirty cover and rags. When I saw my wife do this deed, I completely lost my head and climbed down from the roof. After I entered the hut, I grabbed the sword which she had with her and I was determined to slay them both. First I struck at the slave's neck and thought that death now beckoned him.

And Scheherazade noticed that dawn was approaching, and she stopped telling her story. When the next night arrived, however, she received the king's permission to continue her tale and said,

After striking the slave, I had thought that I had slain him, for he uttered a loud hissing groan, but I had only cut the skin and flesh of the gullet and two arteries! When these sounds awoke my wife, I sheathed the sword and rushed to the city. Then I entered the palace, lay down on my bed, and slept until morning. Later, when my wife aroused me, I saw that she had cut off her hair and had put on mourning garments.

"Oh, son of my uncle," she said, "don't blame me for what I'm doing. I have just learned that my mother is dead, and my father has been killed in a holy war. Moreover, one of my brothers has lost his life from a snake sting, and another has died by falling off a cliff. There is nothing I can or should do but weep and lament."

When I heard her words, I held back my reproaches

and only said, "Do what you think best. I certainly will not hinder you."

So she continued to grieve and mourn for one whole year, and when the full year had passed, she said to me, "I'd like to build a tomb with a cupola in your palace that I will set aside only for my mourning, and I'll call it the House of Lamentations."

"Do what you think best," I said again.

Then she built for herself a cenotaph in which she could mourn, and she also placed a dome on top of it under which there was a tomb like a Santon's sepulcher. It was to this place that she carried the slave and housed him, but he was exceedingly weak because of his wound and unable to make love to her. He could only drink wine, and from the day of his injury he could not speak a word, but he continued to live because his appointed hour for death had not yet arrived. Every day, morning and evening, my wife went to him and wept over him. She gave him wine and strong soups and kept doing this for one more year. I tolerated all this patiently and paid no heed to her. However, one day I went into her chamber without her noticing it, and I found her weeping, slapping her face, and crying, "Why are you so absent, my heart's delight? Speak to me, my life. Talk with me, my love!"

When she had stopped weeping, I said to her, "Cousin, let this mourning suffice, for there's nothing to gain from pouring forth tears!"

"Don't try to stop me," she answered, "or I'll do something violent to myself!"

So I kept my peace and let her go her own way. Indeed, she continued to indulge her affliction for yet another year. At the end of the third year I became tired of all this mourning, and one day, when I was annoyed and angry because of some frustrating matter, I happened to enter the cenotaph and heard her say, "Oh my lord, I never hear you say a single word to me! Why don't you answer me?"

All this caused me to become enraged, and I cried out, "That's enough! How long is this sorrow to last?"

When she heard my words, she sprang to her feet crying, "Shame on you, you cur! This is all your fault! You have wounded my heart's darling and have caused me a great deal of woe. Not only that, you've wasted his youth so that he has had to lay in bed these past three years more dead than alive!"

In my wrath I cried, "Oh you dirtiest of harlots and filthiest of whores, futtered by Negro slaves hired to have a go at you! Yes, indeed it was I who did this good deed," and snatching my sword, I drew it and tried to cut her down.

But she laughed at my words and ridiculed me by saying, "To heel, hound that you are! Alas for the past that cannot return to life, nor is it possible to bring the dead back to life. But Allah has indeed placed the person in my hands who did the deed that burns my heart with a fire which doesn't die and a flame which cannot be quenched!" Then she stood up, and pronouncing some unintelligible words, she said, "By virtue of my magic powers, you are to become half stone and half man!"

As a result, oh king, I have become what you see before you, unable to rise or to sit, neither dead nor alive. Moreover, she enchanted the city with all its streets and yards, and she used her magic to turn the four islands into four mountains around the lake about which you've been asking me. And the citizens, who were of four different faiths, Moslem, Nazarene, Jew, and Magian, she transformed into fish. The Moslems are the white, the Magians red, the Christians blue, and the Jews yellow. And every day she tortures me and gives me a hundred lashes, each of which draws floods of blood and cuts the skin of my shoulders to strips. Finally, she covers my upper half with a haircloth and throws these robes over them.

Upon saying all this, the young man began shedding tears, and the sultan turned toward him and said, "Prince, although you've relieved me of one concern, you've added another. Tell me, my friend, where is she? Where is the mausoleum in which the wounded slave is lying?"

"The slave is lying under that dome over there," the young man said, "and she's sitting in the chamber across from that door. Every day at sunrise, she comes to me and strips me. Then she gives me a hundred lashes with the leather whip. I weep and shriek, but there is no power in my legs to get away from her. After she finishes

tormenting me, she visits the slave and brings him wine and boiled meat. You can see for yourself, she'll be here tomorrow early in the morning."

"By Allah," the king declared, "I'm going to do you a favor, young man, and the world will take note of it. It will be such a bold deed that it will be chronicled long after I am dead."

Then the king sat down by the side of the young prince and talked till nightfall, when he lay down and fell asleep. But as soon as dawn approached, he arose, put on his shirt, drew out his sword, and rushed to the place where the slave was lying. He followed the light of the candles and lamps and the smell of the incenses and unguents that led him to the slave. With one stroke of his sword he killed him on the spot, after which he carried him out and threw him into a well that was in the palace. Soon thereafter he returned to the spot where the slave had lain and put on his garments. Finally, he lay down with his sword close by his side. After an hour or so the accursed witch arrived and went first to her husband, whom she stripped and flogged cruelly with a whip, while he cried out, "Ah! That's enough! Take pity on me, cousin!"

But she replied, "Did you take pity on me and spare the life of my true love, on whom I doted?" Then she drew the haircloth over his raw and bleeding skin and threw the robe over his entire body and went to the slave with a goblet of wine and a bowl of meat broth in her hands. She entered the dome weeping and wailing, "Oh my lord, say something to me! Oh my master, talk awhile with me!"

The king lowered his voice and, twisting his tongue, spoke the way that blackamoors speak. "Hear now, hear now, only Allah is all powerful and all glorious!"

Now when she heard these words, she shouted for joy and fainted. Upon recovering her senses, she asked, "My lord, can it be true that you've regained the power of speech?"

"You curse of my soul," the king replied in a small and faint voice, "do you deserve my talking to you?"

"Why shouldn't you?" she asked.

"Because you torment your husband the entire day," he responded, "and he keeps calling on heaven for aid so that I can't sleep from morning until evening. And he prays and curses us so much that I'm greatly disturbed. If things were different, I would have regained my health long ago, and it is this situation that prevents me from answering you."

"With your permission," she said, "I'll release him from the spell."

"Release him, and let's have some rest," the king declared.

"As you wish," the woman said, and she went to the palace, where she took a metal bowl, filled it with water, and said certain words over it that made the contents bubble and boil. Then she sprinkled some of the water over her husband, saying, "By virtue of the dread words that I have spoken, return to the form that is your own."

Suddenly, the young man shook and trembled, and finally he rose to his feet, and rejoicing at his salvation, he cried aloud, "I testify that there is no god but *the* God, and in truth, Mohammed is His Apostle, whom Allah blesses and keeps."

Then she said to him, "Go away and never return. If you do, I'll surely slay you!"

So he departed, and she returned to the dome and said, "My lord, come out so I can look at you and your godliness!"

The king replied in faint low words, "Why? What have you accomplished? You've gotten rid of the branch but not the root of my troubles!"

"Oh my darling," she asked, "what is the root?"

"Shame on you, curse of my soul!" he answered. "The people of this city and of the four islands lift their head every night in the lake in which you have turned them to fish, and they cry to heaven and call down its anger on me and you. And this is the reason why my body cannot return to health. Go at once and set them free. Then come to me and take my hand and raise me up, for I've already regained a little strength."

When she heard the king's words, still supposing him to be the slave, she cried out in joy, "Oh my master, your every word is my command!" So she sprang to her feet full of joy and ran down to the lake, where she took some of its water in the palm of her hand.

* * *

And Scheherazade noticed that dawn was approaching, and she stopped telling her story. When the next night arrived, however, she received the king's permission to continue, and she said,

Now the sorceress took the lake water and said some unintelligible words over it. Suddenly the fish lifted their heads and stood up like men. The spell on the people of the city had been removed. What was the lake became once again a crowded capital: the bazaars were thronged with folk who bought and sold; everyone became busy once again and began doing what they had normally done; and the four mountains became islands as they were before. Then the wicked sorceress returned to the king (still thinking he was the Negro) and said to him, "Oh my love, give me your honored hands so that I can help you stand up."

"Come nearer to me," said the king in a faint tone.

When she came close enough to embrace him, he grabbed his sword and struck her through the breast so that the point showed gleaming through her back. Then he struck her a second time and cut her in two, casting her to the ground in two halves. After doing this, he departed and found the young man, now freed from the spell, awaiting him. The king told him about his release, and the prince kissed his hand with abundant thanks.

"Do you want to continue to dwell in this city or come with me to my capital?" the king asked.

"Your majesty, do you know how far it is between your country and this city?"

"Two and a half days," said the king.

But the other replied, "You must be dreaming, my lord! It would take a good year for a sturdy walker to reach your country. You wouldn't have made it here in two and a half days if it weren't for the fact that my city had been enchanted. And now, my king, I shall never part from you. No, not even for the twinkling of an eye."

The king rejoiced at his words and said, "Thanks be to Allah, who has brought us together. From this hour on, you are my son and my only son, for until now I have not been blessed with offspring."

Thereupon they embraced and rejoiced. When they returned to the prince's palace, the prince informed his lords and nobles that he was about to visit holy places as a pilgrim, and he ordered them to get everything ready for the occasion. The preparations lasted ten days, after which time he set out with the sultan, whose heart yearned for his city, which he had not seen for a good year. They journeyed with an escort of mamelukes carrying all sorts of precious gifts and rare items, and it took them twelve months before they approached the sultan's capital. Messengers were sent in advance to announce their arrival, and the vizier and the entire army came out with great joy to meet their king, for they had given up hope of ever seeing him again. The troops kissed the ground before him and were glad to see him safe and sound. After he entered his palace and took his seat upon his throne and the minister came before him, the king told him what had happened to the young prince, and the vizier congratulated him on his narrow escape. After restoring order throughout the land, the king gave many generous gifts to his people and said to the vizier, "Bring me the fisherman who gave us the fish!"

So he sent for the fisherman, who had actually been responsible for bringing about the liberation of the prince's city, and when he came to the palace, the sultan bestowed on him a robe of honor, and asked him how he was doing and whether he had children. The fisherman told him that he had two daughters and a son. So the king sent for them and took one daughter for his wife and gave the other to the young prince, while he made the son his head treasurer. Furthermore, he appointed the vizier to be sultan of the city in the Black Islands that had once belonged to the young prince and sent him there with an escort of fifty armed slaves together with robes of honor for all the lords and nobles of that city. The vizier kissed his hands and went on his way, while the sultan and the prince dwelled at home in all the solace and the delight of life. Finally, the fisherman became the richest man of his age, and his daughters lived with the kings until death brought an end to their lives.

No sooner had Scheherazade concluded her tale than she said, "And yet, oh king, this tale is no more wondrous than the remarkable story of the ebony horse."

The Ebony Horse

Once upon a time there was a great and powerful king of Persia named Sabur, whose wealth and wisdom surpassed all other monarchs in his day and age. Moreover, he was generous, kind, and beneficent. He comforted those whose spirits were broken, and he treated those who fled to him for refuge with honor. He loved the poor and was hospitable to strangers, and he always sought to defend the oppressed against their oppressors.

King Sabur had three daughters as beautiful as flower gardens in full bloom and a son as handsome as the moon. And it was his custom to celebrate two holidays during the year, the Nau-Roz or New Year, and Mihgan or the Autumnal Equinox. On both occasions he threw open his palace, gave alms to the people, made proclamations of safety and security, and promoted his chamberlains and viceroys. The people of his realm came to him, saluted him, and celebrated these holy days with joy, and they also brought him gifts, servants, and eunuchs.

Now, King Sabur loved science and geometry, and on one holiday, as he sat on his throne, three wise men entered his palace and approached him. They were cunning inventors and masters of all sorts of crafts. Indeed, they could make things so unusual and rare that it was impossible to discern how they were invented. These men were versed in the knowledge of the occult and knew all about the mysteries of the world. Each one was from a different country and spoke a foreign language. The first was a Hindi or Indian, the second a Roumi or Greek, and the third a Farsi or Persian.

When the Indian stepped forward, he prostrated himself before the king, wished him a joyous holiday, and placed before him a gift befitting his dignity: it was a man of gold set with precious gems and jewels and holding a golden trumpet in his hand.

When Sabur saw this, he said, "Tell me, sage, what can this figure do?"

And the Indian answered, "My lord, if this figure is placed at the gate of your city, he will be a most powerful protector, for whenever an enemy tries to enter, the figure will blow this trumpet against him, and he will be seized with palsy and drop down dead."

The king was extremely astonished by this gift and declared, "By Allah, if you are telling the truth, I'll grant you anything you wish or desire."

Then the Greek stepped forward, and after prostrating himself before the king, he gave him a silver basin with a golden peacock and twenty-four golden chicks in the middle of it. Sabur looked at the basin and then inquired, "Tell me, sage, what can this peacock do?"

"My lord," he answered, "whenever an hour of the day or night elapses, it pecks one of its young, cries out, and flaps its wings every hour on the hour. Then, when the end of the mouth arrives, it will open its mouth, and you will see the crescent inside it."

And the king said, "If you're telling the truth, I'll grant anything you wish or desire."

Then the Persian sage stepped forward, and after prostrating himself before the king, he presented him with a horse made of the darkest ebony wood with a gold and jeweled inlay and with saddle, stirrups, and bridle suitable for the majesty of the king. When Sabur saw the horse, he was extremely astounded and admired the beauty of its form and style. So he asked, "What can this wooden horse do? Tell me its virtue and whether it can move."

"My lord," the Persian answered, "if one mounts this horse, it will carry him wherever he wants. It can ride through the air and cover the space of a year in a single day."

The king was amazed by these wonders, especially since they came all on the same day, and he turned to the Persian sage and said, "By Allah, if you are telling the truth, I'll certainly grant you whatever you desire."

Then he entertained the sages for three days so he

could try out their gifts. During that time each one demonstrated what his invention could do: the man of gold blew his trumpet; the peacock pecked its chicks; and the Persian sage mounted the ebony horse, which soared with him high in the air and descended again. When King Sabur saw all this, he was amazed and overcome with joy. Then he said to the three sages, "I'm now convinced of the truth of your words, and it behooves me to keep my promise. So, you may now ask for whatever you want, and I shall grant your wishes."

Well, news about the beauty of the king's three daughters had reached these sages, and thus they asked, "If the king is content with us and our gifts and allows us to make a request, we beg that he give us his three daughters in marriage so that we may become his sons-in-law."

"Your wish is granted," the king said and ordered the kazi to come right away so that he could marry his daughters to these sages.

Now it so happened that the princesses were behind a curtain and witnessed this entire scene. The youngest saw that her husband-to-be was at least a hundred years old. He had white hair, a drooping forehead, mangy eyebrows, cropped ears, a dyed mustache and beard, red eyes, bleached and hollow cheeks, a flabby nose, overlapping teeth, loose lips like camel's kidneys, and a face like a cobbler's apron. In short, he was a terror, a horror, a monster. Indeed, he was the most frightful sight of his time. In contrast, the girl was the fairest and most graceful of her time, more elegant than the finest gazelle, more tender than the gentlest breeze, and certainly more beautiful than the brightest full moon. She was made for love and walked with a graceful sway that captivated all those who saw her. In short, she was more beautiful and sweeter than her two sisters, who were splendid specimens themselves. So when she saw her suitor, she went to her room and strewed dust on her head, tore her clothes, slapped her face, and wept.

Now, her brother, Prince Kamar al-Akmar, had just returned from a journey, and when he heard her weeping like that he entered her chamber (for he loved her with more affection than his other sisters) and said, "What's wrong with you? What's happened to you? Tell me everything, and don't hide a thing."

"My brother," she responded, "I have nothing to hide. Our father has decided to do something atrocious, and I intend to leave the palace. And I'll do this even if he doesn't consent, for the Lord will provide for me."

"What's the meaning of this talk?" her brother responded. "What's caused all this trouble and disturbed your heart?"

And the princess answered, "Our father has promised me in marriage to a wicked magician who has brought him a horse of black wood as a gift. This magician has bewitched our father with his craft and sorcery, but as for me, I don't want to have anything to do with him, and I wish I had never been born because of him!"

After her brother comforted her, he went to his father and said, "Who is this wizard that you're going to wed to my youngest sister? What's so wonderful about his present that you don't care if your daughter is deeply distressed? Do you think what you're doing is right?"

Now the Persian was standing nearby and heard the prince's words, which filled him with rage. Meanwhile the king replied, "My son, if you saw this horse, you'd bc amazed." Then he ordered the slaves to bring the horse before him, and they did as he commanded. When the prince saw the horse, he was pleased, and being an accomplished cavalier, he mounted it right away and struck its sides with the stirrups. However, it did not move, and the king said to the sage, "Go and show him how it moves so that he may help you obtain your wish."

Of course, the Persian was still holding a grudge against the prince because the young man was opposed to his marriage with the princess. So he showed him the button on the right side of the horse that would make the horse take off and said, "Push this," and went away. Thereupon the prince pushed the button, and the horse soared with him high in the air as if it were a bird, and it kept on flying until it disappeared from everyone's sight. The king was extremely upset by this and said to the Persian, "See to it that you get him to descend."

"Oh lord," the Persian responded, "there's nothing I can do. You'll won't see him again until Resurrection Day, for he was too ignorant and too proud to ask me about the button for descending, and I forgot to tell him where it is."

When the king heard this, he became extremely angry and had the sage whipped and thrown in jail, while he himself discarded his crown, slapped his face, and pounded his breast. Moreover, he closed the doors of his palace, and he was joined by his wife, his daughters, and the rest of the people of the city in weeping and mourning for the prince. Thus, their joy was turned into sorrow and their happiness into sadness.

In the meantime, the horse kept soaring with the prince until it drew near the sun. As a result, the prince gave himself up for lost and repented for having mounted the horse. "Truly," he said, "the sage tricked me because of my youngest sister. By Allah, it seems I'm lost, but there must be a button for landing if there is one for taking off." Now, he was a smart and clever man, so he began to feel all the parts of the horse, but he saw nothing except buttons like cock's heads on the right and left shoulders of the horse. "That's all there is, it seems," he said to himself, "just these two buttons." Then he pushed the one on the right, and the horse increased its speed and flew higher. So he stopped and pushed the button on the left, and immediately the steed's upward motion slowed until it began to descend little by little toward the face of the earth.

And Scheherazade noticed that dawn was approaching, and she stopped telling her story. When the next night arrived, however, she received the king's permission to continue her tale and said,

When the prince saw what was happening and realized that he had learned to control the horse, he was filled with joy and thanked Almighty Allah, who had delivered him from certain death. Then he began to turn the horse's head wherever he wanted to go, and he made it soar and descend at his will until he attained complete mastery over it. Finally he made it descend, and this descent took the entire day, because the horse had carried him far from the earth. As he descended, he amused himself by viewing the different cities and countries that he had never seen before. Among them was a very beautiful city amidst a verdant countryside rich in trees and streams with gazelles gliding over the plains. Upon seeing this city he began musing to himself, "I wish I knew the name of that city and in what country it was!" And he began to circle and observe it.

By this time, the day had begun to decline, and it was near sunset. So he said to himself, "Certainly there's no better place to spend the night than in this fine city. I might as well stay here, and early tomorrow morning I'll return to my kith and kin and my kingdom. Then I'll tell my father and my family what happened and what I've seen." Now he began looking for a place where he might safely land, and where no one might catch sight of him. Soon he glimpsed a tall palace in the middle of the city. It was surrounded by a large wall with lofty towers and battlements and was guarded by forty black slaves clad in complete mail and armed with spears and swords and bows and arrows. "That's a good spot," he said, and he pushed the descent button, which made the horse fly down like a weary bird, and he landed gently on the terrace roof of the palace.

After the prince dismounted and gave his praise to Allah, he inspected the horse and said, "Whoever invented and built you so perfectly was a clever craftsman, and if the Almighty grants me a long life and reunites me with my father and family safe and sound, I'll certainly bestow on him all kinds of gifts and treat him with the utmost generosity." By this time, night had come, and he sat on the roof until he was certain that everyone in the palace was asleep. Indeed, he was extremely hungry and thirsty, for he had not eaten or drunk anything since he had been separated from his father. So he said to himself, "I'm sure that there's plenty to eat and drink in this palace."

So he left the horse above and went down into the palace in search of something to eat. Soon he came to a staircase, and after he went down to the bottom, he found himself in a court paved with white marble and alabaster, which shone in the light of the moon. He was astounded by the place and the fine architecture, but there was not a single sign of a living soul, and he was surprised and perplexed. After he looked to the right and the left, he could not decide which way to go and said to himself, "Perhaps it would be better if I returned to where I left my horse and spent the night by its side. Then, as soon as day dawns, I'll mount it and ride away."

* * *

And Scheherazade noticed that dawn was approaching, and she stopped telling her story. When the next night arrived, however, she received the king's permission to continue her tale and said,

As he was talking to himself, he spotted a light inside the palace, and after heading in that direction, he found that it came from a candle that stood in front of a door to the harem. Next to the candle was a huge eunuch, who was asleep. He looked like one of the ifrits of Solomon or a tribesman of the jinn, as long and as broad as a tree. As he lay on the floor, the pommel of his sword gleamed in the flame of the candle, and at his head was a bag of leather hanging from a granite column. When the prince saw the eunuch, he was frightened and said, "May Allah help me! Oh Holy One, just as you saved me in the sky, please let me escape safe and sound from this adventure!"

After saying this he reached for the leather bag, and after grabbing hold of it, he carried it to the side, opened it, and found some very good food. Thereupon, he ate his fill and refreshed himself. Afterward he returned the bag to its place and drew the eunuch's sword from its sheath while the slave kept sleeping.

Then the prince continued exploring the harem until he came to a second door with a curtain drawn before it. So, he lifted the curtain, and upon entering the room, he saw a couch of whitest ivory lined with pearls, jacinths, and jewels and four slave girls sleeping around it. He went up to the couch to see what was on it and found a young lady lying asleep. She looked like the full moon rising over the eastern horizon with her brow decorated by white flowers, her hair shining, her cheeks crimson and dotted by dainty moles. Indeed, he was amazed by her stunning beauty as she lay there, and he no longer was afraid of dying. So he went up to her, and trembling in every nerve and shuddering with pleasure, he kissed her on the right cheek, whereupon she awoke right away and opened her eyes. Seeing the prince standing before her, she said, "Who are you, and where have you come from?"

"I'm your slave and lover," he said.

"And who brought you here?" she asked.

"My Lord and my destiny," he replied.

"Then," said Shams al-Nahar, for that was her name, "perhaps you're the one who asked my father yesterday for my hand in marriage and was rejected by him because he thought you were atrocious. By Allah, if that's the case, my sire lied through his teeth when he said this, for you're quite handsome."

Now the son of the king of Hind had wanted to marry her, and her father had rejected him because he was indeed ugly and uncouth, and the princess thought the prince was the rejected suitor. So, when she saw how handsome and elegant he was (for he was clearly more radiant than the moon), she was ignited by the flaming fire of love, and they began to converse and talk. Suddenly, her waiting women awoke, and upon seeing the prince with their mistress, they said to her, "My lady, who is this man?"

"I don't know," she said. "I found him sitting by me when I woke up. Perhaps he's the prince who sought my hand in marriage from my father."

"By Allah," they cried out, "this man is not the one who sought your hand in marriage, for the other was hideous, and this one is handsome. Indeed, the other man is not even fit to be his servant."

Then the slave girls ran out to the eunuch, and after they waked him from his slumber, he jumped up in alarm.

"How is it that you're supposed to be on guard in the palace," they said, "and yet men come into our chamber when we are asleep?"

When the black heard this, he quickly grabbed for his sword but could not find it, and he was seized by fear. Totally confused by what was happening, he rushed to his mistress, and upon seeing the prince sitting and talking to her, he said, "My lord, are you a man or a jinnee?"

"Woe to you, you unluckiest of slaves!" the prince replied. "How dare you compare a son of the royal Chosroës with one of those pagan devils!" And he became like a raging lion, took the eunuch's sword in his hand, and said, "I am the king's son-in-law, and he's married me to his daughter and commanded me to go and see her."

When the eunuch heard these words, he replied, "My lord, if you are indeed the man you say you are, she's only fit for you, and you are worthier of her than anyone else."

Thereupon the eunuch ran to the king, shrieking aloud, tearing his garments, and tossing dust on his head. When the king heard this outcry, he said, "What's happened to you? Speak quickly, and be brief, for you've sent chills up my spine!"

"Oh king," answered the eunuch, "go and rescue your daughter, for a devil of the jinn, who's taken on the guise of a king's son, has got possession of her. Get up at once!"

When the king heard this, he would have liked to kill the eunuch for being so careless and letting a demon get hold of his daughter. Instead, he stood up and rushed to his daughter's chamber, where he found her slave women awaiting him.

"What's happened to my daughter?" he asked.

"Your majesty," they answered, "slumber overcame us, and when we awoke, we found a young man sitting on her couch in conversation with her. He looks like the full moon, and we've never seen a man as handsome as he is. So we asked him to explain everything, and he told us that you had given him your daughter in marriage. That's all we know, nor are we sure whether he's a man or jinnee. Whatever he is, he is certainly modest and well-bred and has done nothing disgraceful."

Now when the king heard these words, his wrath cooled, and he raised the curtain little by little, and as he looked in, he saw his daughter talking with a handsome prince whose face glistened like the moon. Yet he felt he must protect his daughter's honor and could not control his feelings. So he brushed the curtain aside, rushed in, and drew his sword like a furious ghoul.

When the prince saw him, he asked the princess, "Is this your sire?"

And she replied, "Yes."

And Scheherazade noticed that dawn was approaching and stopped telling her story. When the next night arrived,

however, she received the king's permission to continue her tale and said,

All at once, the prince sprang to his feet, seized his sword, and shouted at the king with such a terrible cry that the king became utterly confused. Indeed, the prince would have attacked the king with his sword, but the king realized that the young man was more stalwart than he was, so he sheathed his scimitar and dropped his arms until the prince came up to him. Then the king said, "Young man, are you a human or a jinnee?"

"If I did not respect your right as my host and cherish your daughter's honor," said the prince, "I'd seal your fate right here and now! How dare you associate me with devils, me, a prince of the royal Chosroës, who, if they wished to take your kingdom, could make you tremble, and you'd feel as if an earthquake had hit you and consumed your realm!"

Now, when the king heard his words, he was overcome with fear and awe, and he replied, "If you are indeed the son of kings, as you claim, how come you've entered my palace without my permission and besmirched my honor by making your way to my daughter and pretending that I've given her to you as your wife? I'll have you know that I've slain kings and sons of kings who sought her hand in marriage! Even now, who could save you from my might and majesty if I were to order my slaves and servants to put you to the vilest of deaths? Who could save you from my power?"

When the prince heard the king's speech, he answered, "Truly, I'm surprised by you and your lack of sense! Tell me, do you think you could possibly find a husband for your daughter more handsome than I am? Have you ever encountered a man with a stouter heart or one better suited for a sultan or more glorious in rank than I?"

"Nay, by Allah!" responded the king. "Still, you should have acted according to the custom of kings and asked me whether you could be her husband before witnesses so that I might have wed her to you in a public ceremony. Yet, even now, if I were to marry her to you in private, you've dishonored me in front of her."

"All this is true," the prince said, "but if you summon your slaves and soldiers, and they slay me, as you claim they can, you would but only make known your own disgrace, and the people wouldn't know whether to believe you or me. Therefore, it seems to me that you'd do well to listen to my advice."

"And what is that?" asked the king.

"I propose," the prince declared, "that either you meet me in personal combat, and whoever slays the other shall have complete claim to the kingdom; or else leave me alone this night, and when dawn arrives, call out your cavalry, infantrymen, and servants against me. But first tell me how many there are."

"There are forty thousand in the cavalry," said the king, "and just as many in my infantry."

"When day breaks," the prince said, "you can set them against me and say to them: 'This man is a suitor for my daughter's hand, and he may only have her if he fights you all alone and wins, for he claims that he can defeat you and put you to rout.' After you say this, let me fight them, and if they slay me, your secret and honor will be protected forever. If I overcome them, then a king could have no better son-in-law."

And Scheherazade noticed that dawn was approaching and stopped telling her story. When the next night arrived, however, she received the king's permission to continue her tale and said,

After hearing this proposal, the king agreed to it. Despite the fact that he was awed by the prince's bravery, the king was certain that he would perish in the fray, and therefore he would not have to fear being dishonored. So he called the eunuch and ordered him to go to his vizier right away and tell him to assemble the whole army and prepare for battle. The eunuch carried the king's order to the minister, who immediately summoned the captains of the army and lords of the realm and commanded them to prepare for battle. The king himself sat for a long while conversing with the young prince and was pleased by his wise talk, good sense, and fine breeding. When it was daybreak, the king returned to his throne, commanded his merry men to mount, and ordered them to saddle one of the best of the royal steeds with handsome trappings and to bring it to the prince.

But the young man said, "Your majesty, I won't mount a horse until I review your troops."

"As you wish," replied the king. Then the two went to the parade ground, where the troops were assembled, and the prince looked them over and noted their great number. At this point, the king declared to them, "Listen, all you men! This young man has come to ask for my daughter's hand in marriage. Quite truthfully, I've never met a finer lad, nor anyone with a stouter heart or a stronger arm, for he claims that he can overcome you single-handedly and put you to rout. Indeed, he's declared that even if you were a hundred thousand, he would prevail. Now, when he charges at you, I want you to greet him with your sharp pikes and sabers and show him that he's taken on much more than he can handle." Turning now to the prince, the king said, "Get on with it, my son. It's time to do your duty!"

"Your majesty," the prince replied, "you're not being fair with me. Am I to go against your men on foot while they are mounted?"

The king responded, "I asked you to mount before. Well then, choose any of my horses you like."

"None of your horses pleases me," the prince stated. "I'll only ride the horse that I came on."

"Well, where's your horse?" the king asked.

"On top of the palace," said the prince.

"In what part of my palace?"

"On the roof."

Now when the king heard these words, he cried, "Stop this nonsense! This is the first sign you've given that you're mad. How can the horse be on the roof? But we'll see at once if you're telling the truth." Then he turned to one of his chief officers and said, "Go to my palace and bring me whatever you find on the roof."

All the people gathered at the assembly were astounded by the prince's words, and they began murmuring, "How can a horse come down the steps from the roof? We've never heard of a thing like this before!" In the meantime the king's messenger returned to the palace, climbed the stairs to the roof, and found the horse standing there. Never had it looked more handsome, but when the officer drew near and examined it, he saw that it was made of ebony and ivory. Now this man was accompanied by other officers, who began laughing when they saw that the horse was wooden. "Was this the horse that the young man meant? He must be mad. Well, we'll soon see, no matter what."

And Scheherazade noticed that dawn was approaching and stopped telling her story. When the next night arrived, however, she received the king's permission to continue her tale and said,

Then they lifted the horse and carried it to the king. Once they set it down before him, all his lords flocked around it to marvel at its beauty and the rich saddle and bridle. The king, too, admired it and was astounded by it. Then he asked the prince, "Young man, is this your horse?"

"Yes," he responded, "this is my horse, and you'll soon see how wonderful it is."

"Then take it and mount it," commanded the king.

"I won't mount it until your troops withdraw a bit," he replied.

So the king ordered them to retreat a good bow's shot from the horse, and the prince cried out, "Now watch, my king, for I'm about to mount my horse and charge your army and scatter them left and right!" Then the prince mounted while the troops arranged themselves in rows before him, and one soldier said to another, "When he comes between the rows, we'll greet him with the points of our pikes and sabers."

"By Allah," said another, "this is unfortunate. I find it difficult to slay such a handsome youth."

And a third continued, "You'll have to work hard to get the better of him, for I'm sure he's not doing this without knowing his own strength and potential."

Meanwhile after the prince got settled in his saddle, he pushed the button to take off, and all the people strained their eyes to see what he would do. Just then the horse began to heave and rock and sway and make the strangest movements that a steed ever made. Soon its belly was filled with air, and it took off with its rider soaring high into the sky. When the king saw this, he cried out to his men, "Woe to you! Catch him, catch him before he escapes!"

But his viziers and viceroys yelled back, "Oh king, can a man overtake a flying bird? This man is surely some mighty magician or jinnee, and may Allah save you from him!"

After watching the prince's feat, the king returned to the palace, where he went straight to his daughter and told her what had happened on the parade ground. He found her very much distressed because of the prince's departure, and all at once she fell violently sick and took to bed. Now, when her father saw her in such a miserable state, he embraced her, kissed her on her forehead, and said, "My daughter, praise the Almighty Allah and thank Him for delivering us from this cunning enchanter, this villain, this thief, who thought only of seducing you!" And he repeated to her the story of the prince and how he had disappeared in the sky, and he cursed him, not knowing how dearly his daughter loved him. But she paid no attention to his words and kept on weeping and saying to herself, "By Allah, I'll neither eat nor drink until Allah reunites me with him!"

Consequently, her father became greatly concerned about her condition, and no matter how he tried to soothe her, her longing for the prince only increased.

And Scheherazade noticed that dawn was approaching and stopped telling her story. When the next night arrived, however, she received the king's permission to continue her tale and said,

Now when Prince Kamar al-Akmar had risen high in the sky, he turned his horse's head toward his native land, and all he could do was to think about the beauty of the lovely princess. Since he had asked some of the king's people what the name of the city was, he knew that the city was called Sana'a and kept its location in mind. Meanwhile, he journeyed as fast as he could to the capital of his own country, and after circling the city, he landed on the roof of his father's palace, where he left his horse. Then he descended into the palace, and upon seeing that the threshold was strewn with ashes, he thought that one of his family had died. As was his custom, he entered the large salon and found his father, mother, and sisters clad in black mourning garments, and all of them were haggard and had pale faces. When his father caught sight of him and was sure that it was his son, he uttered a great cry and fell down in a fit. After a while he came to himself and embraced the prince with great joy. Then they all began to ask him what had happened to him, and he told them everything from first to last.

"Praise be Allah for bringing you home safe and sound," the king said, and he ordered his servants to prepare a great festival while the good news spread throughout the city. Drums and cymbals proclaimed the event. The mourning clothes were discarded. The streets and markets were decorated. The people vied with one another as to who should be the first to make the king even more jubilant than he was. In the meantime the king announced a general amnesty and ordered all the prisoners to be released. Moreover, he had banquets prepared for the people of the city, and for seven days and seven nights everyone ate and drank all he wanted, while the king rode around on horseback with his son so that the people could see the prince and rejoice.

After a while, the prince asked his father, "What's happened to the man who made the ebony horse?"

And the king replied, "I rue the very day that I set eyes on him! He was the cause of your separation from us, my son, and he has been in jail ever since your disappearance." However, now the king ordered the sage to be released from prison, and after sending for him, he presented him with clothes befitting his dignity and treated him generously and kindly, but he would not allow him to wed his daughter. Consequently, the sage became furious and regretted that he had given the king the horse, especially since he knew that the prince had learned the secret of the steed and how to control its movements. Despite the fact that the prince had managed to operate the horse, his father said to him, "You'd do well not to go near the horse from here on, for you don't know all that it can do, and you may make a mistake if you mount it again."

Now the prince had told his father about his adventure with the king of Sana'a and his daughter, and his father remarked that if the king had intended to kill him, he would have done so, but his hour had not yet arrived. In the meantime, the celebrations had come to an end, and the king and his son returned to the palace, where they sat down to eat, drink, and make merry. While they were sitting there, one of the king's beauitful slave girls, who was skilled in playing the lute, began to sweep her fingers across the strings and sing a song about the separation of lovers. When the prince heard these verses, the sparks of longing flamed up in his heart, and he yearned for the daughter of the king of Sana'a. So he rose right away, and after eluding his father's sight, he went up to the roof of the palace, where he mounted the horse and pushed the takeoff button, and the horse soared toward the upper regions of the sky. Some time later his father wondered where he was, and after climbing to the roof of the palace, he saw his son high in the firmament and was greatly troubled and regretted that he had not taken the horse and hidden it. Then he said to himself, "By Allah, if my son returns to me, I'll destroy the horse so that he'll be forced to stay on the ground, where he belongs, and I won't have to worry about him anymore." And he began to weep and moan.

And Scheherazade noticed that dawn was approaching and stopped telling her story. When the next night arrived, however, she received the king's permission to continue her tale and said,

While the king was weeping, his son kept flying through the sky until he came to the city of Sana'a and landed on the roof as he had done before. Then he crept downstairs quietly and, finding the eunuch asleep as usual, he raised the curtain and entered the alcove of the princess's chamber. To be on the safe side, he stopped to listen and heard her shedding tears and reciting some verses, while her women slept soundly all around her. Soon, however, some of them woke up because of her weeping and said, "Mistress, why are you mourning for someone who doesn't mourn you?"

"You fools!" she replied, "Do you think he's the kind who forgets or who can be forgotten?" And she began to weep and wail again until sleep overcame her.

Upon hearing and seeing all this, the prince's heart melted. So he entered her chamber and saw that she was lying asleep without a cover and touched her hand, causing her to open her eyes and look at him.

"Why all this crying and mourning?" he asked.

And when she realized that it was he, she threw herself upon him, gave him a kiss, and said, "Because of you and because we were separated."

"My lady," he stated, "I, too, have been desolate because of our separation!"

"Then why did you leave me?" she asked. "If you had stayed away any longer, I would have died!"

"But think about my predicament with your father and how he treated me," he answered. "If it had not been for you, love of my life, I would have certainly slain him, but because I love you, I'll love him for your sake."

"But you still shouldn't have left me," she said. "Did you really believe that I could continue having a sweet life after meeting you?"

"Let us forget what's happened. That's all past," he declared. "Now I'm hungry and thirsty."

So she ordered her maidens to bring in something to eat and drink, and they began eating, drinking, and conversing until the night was almost over. When day broke, he rose to say goodbye to her before the eunuch would awake. But Shams al-Nahar asked him, "Where are you going?"

"To my father's house," he responded, "and I give you my word that I'll come to you once a week."

However, she wept and said, "I beg you, by Allah the Almighty, take me with you. I'll go wherever you go. Don't make me suffer the bitter separation again."

"Will you really go with me?" he asked.

"Yes."

"Then," said he, "let's rise and depart."

So she got up right away, went to a chest, and adorned herself in her richest and dearest trinkets and jewels. Then, without telling her maidens where she was going, she left the chamber with the prince, who took her up to the roof of the palace. After he mounted the ebony horse, he lifted her up behind him and tied her to him with some strong rope. When everything was set, he pushed the takeoff button, and the horse rose high in the air. When her slave girls saw this, they shrieked aloud and ran and told her father and mother, who rushed to

W. ORR

the rooftop only to see the magic horse fly away with the prince and princess. In his anguish, the king cried out, "Prince, I beg of you, by Allah, have mercy on us, and don't take away our daughter!"

The prince did not reply, but he thought to himself that the lady might regret being separated from her mother and father, and he asked her, "Oh beauty of the age, do you want me to take you back to your mother and father?"

"By Allah, my lord," she said, "my only wish is to be with you. I am so consumed by my love for you that I don't mind being separated from my mother and father."

Upon hearing these words, the prince rejoiced and made the horse fly carefully and gently so as not to disquiet her. Indeed, they kept flying until they caught sight of a green meadow with a spring of running water. Here they landed and ate and drank. Then they remounted and flew until they were in sight of his father's capital. The prince was filled with joy at seeing the city and thought that he would show to his beloved his father's dominions so that she would see that they were greater than those of her sire. So they landed in one of his father's gardens outside the city, and he carried her into a summerhouse with a dome. He left the ebony horse at the door and told the damsel to keep watch over it while he was away. "Sit here," he said, "until my messenger comes to you. I'm going to my father to ask him to prepare lodgings for you, and then I'll show you the royal estate."

She was delighted when she heard these words and said, "As you wish."

And Scheherazade noticed that dawn was approaching and stopped telling her story. When the next night arrived, however, she received the king's permission to continue her tale and said,

The prince's words indicated to her that he wanted to prepare everything for her so she could enter the city with due honor and respect according to her rank. So she was quite pleased. In the meantime, the prince went to the palace of his father, who rejoiced at his return. Then the prince said to him, "I've brought the king's daughter with me, the lovely damsel I told you about the other day. I've left her outside the city in the summer garden, and I'd like you to prepare a royal procession for her and go out to meet her in majestic array with all your troops and guards."

"I'm more than happy to do this," replied the king, and he immediately gave orders to have the town decorated. Then he went and mounted his horse and rode out in all splendor and majesty leading a host of high officers and servants followed by a band with drums, kettle-drums, fifes, trumpets, and all kinds of instruments. In the meantime, the prince went to his treasury and took out jewelry, rich apparel, and whatever else kings generally keep in a safe place, and he set up a splendid display of his wealth. Moreover, he ordered the servants to prepare a litter with a canopy of green, yellow, and red brocade, and he ordered Indian, Greek, and Abyssinian slave girls to sit inside. Then he left the litter and went to the pavilion where he had set the princess down. Yet, neither she nor the horse was there. When he saw this, he slapped his face, tore his garments, and began wandering around the garden as if he had lost his mind. Eventually, however, he came to his senses and asked himself, "How could she have discovered the secret of the horse? I didn't tell her anything. Maybe the Persian sage who made the horse happened to come upon her and flew off with her in revenge for the way my father treated him." Then he sought out the guards of the garden and asked them if they had seen anyone enter the grounds. "Tell me the truth and the whole truth, or I'll have your heads cut off right away!"

"No one has entered," they said, "except for the Persian sage, who came to gather some herbs for healing."

So the prince was sure that it was indeed the sage who had flown off with the maiden.

And Scheherazade noticed that dawn was approaching and stopped telling her story. When the next night arrived, however, she received the king's permission to continue her tale and said,

Confused and bewildered, the prince was ashamed when the king and his entourage arrived. Turning to his sire, he told him what had happened and said, "Take the troops and march back to the city with them. As for me, I'll never return until I've cleared up this affair."

When the king heard this he was distressed and wept. "My son," he said, "calm yourself. Try to get over your sorrow and come home with us. I can arrange a wedding with some other king's daughter."

But the prince paid no attention to his words, and after bidding his father farewell, he set out on a journey, while the king returned to the city, and their joy was changed into sadness.

Now, it was due to destiny that, after the prince had left the princess in the garden house and gone to his father's palace, the Persian entered the garden to gather some special herbs. But when he smelled the sweet aroma of musk and other perfumes that emanated from the princess and impregnated the whole place, he followed his nose until he came to the pavilion, where he saw the horse that he had made with his own hands. His heart was filled with joy, for he had bemoaned its loss a great deal since giving it away. So he went up to it, and after examining every part, he found it in perfectly good shape. Just as he was about to mount it and ride away, he said to himself, "Perhaps I should look at what the prince has brought here with the horse before I ride away." So he entered the pavilion, and when he saw the princess sitting there as though she were the sun shining serenely in the sky, he knew at first glance that she was some highborn lady and was certain that the prince had left her in the pavilion while he had gone to the city to prepare a splendid state procession for her. So he went up to her and kissed the ground before her. Startled, she looked at him and was taken aback by his atrocious appearance and manners.

"Who are you?" she asked.

"My lady," he answered, "I am a messenger sent by the prince who has asked me to bring you to another garden nearer the city, because the queen cannot walk this far and does not want to be robbed of the pleasure of welcoming you."

"Where's the prince?"

"He's in the city with his father," said the Persian, "and he will soon come to meet you in great state."

"Tell me, slave," said the princess, "couldn't he have found someone more handsome than you to bring this message to me?"

The sage laughed loudly when he heard this and replied, "To tell the truth, he doesn't even have a mameluke in his service uglier than I am. But don't let my ugly looks deceive you, my lady. He has benefited greatly from my services. Indeed, he chose me as his messenger to you because he is so jealously in love with you, and my loathsome and ugly looks don't threaten him. Otherwise, he has an enormous number of handsome mamelukes, Negro slaves, pages, eunuchs, and attendants."

When the princess heard this, it made sense, and she believed what the sage had told her. So she got up right away.

And Scheherazade noticed that dawn was approaching and stopped telling her story. When the next night arrived, however, she received the king's permission to continue her tale and said,

As the sage took her hand to help her, she asked, "What have you brought me to ride on?"

"My lady," he said, "you can ride the horse you came on."

"I can't ride it by myself," she said.

Her reply caused him to smile, for he now knew that he was in complete control of her. So he said, "I'll ride with you myself." So he mounted and then lifted her behind him and bound her to him as firmly as he could manage. Of course, she did not know what he was going to do with her. Then he pushed the takeoff button so that the belly of the horse became full of air, and it swayed back and forth like a wave of the sea. Soon the horse rose and soared into the sky until it was out of sight of the city. Now when Shams al-Nahar saw this, she asked him, "Hold on, you! What's going on? I thought the prince sent you to me!"

"May Allah damn the prince!" answered the Persian. "He is a mean miserly knave!"

"Woe to you!" she cried out. "How dare you disobey my lord's orders?"

"He's no lord of mine!" replied the sage. "Do you know who I am?"

"The only thing I know about you is what you've told me."

"What I told you was untrue," said the Persian. "It was a trick, for I've lamented the loss of this horse a long time. It was I who constructed it and learned how to master it. And now that I've regained control and have control over you as well, I'll scorch the prince's heart just as he's ravaged mine! I'll never let him have the horse again. Never! So don't fret and don't weep, for I can be of more use to you than he was. I'm just as generous as I am wealthy, and my servants and slaves will obey you as their mistress. I'll adorn you in the finest raiment and your every wish will be fulfilled."

When the princess heard this, she slapped her face and cried out, "I might as well die! Not only have I lost my mother and father, but I've lost my beloved as well!"

And she wept bitter tears over what had happened to her, while the sage kept the horse flying through the air until he came to the land of the Greeks and landed in a verdant meadow with streams and trees. Now this meadow was located near a city which was ruled by a powerful king, and it so happened that he had gone out hunting that day. As he passed by the meadow, he saw the Persian standing there with the damsel and the horse by his side. Before the Persian was aware of what was happening, the king's slaves seized him and took him, the lady, and the horse to their master. Since the sage's atrocious looks were such a striking contrast to the beauty of the girl, he asked, "My lady, what is your relationship to this old man?"

The Persian tried to intervene with a quick reply: "My lord, she's my wife and the daughter of my father's brother."

But the lady was quick to reveal his lie: "By Allah, I don't know this man, and he's certainly not my husband! No, he's a wicked magician who's abducted me by force and fraud."

On hearing these words, the king ordered his servants to give the Persian a beating, and they thrashed him until he was almost dead. Then the king commanded them to carry him to the city and throw him into jail. On the other hand, he kept the damsel with him and put her in his seraglio, while the horse was stored in his treasury, even though he did not know its secret and how valuable it was.

In the meantime, Prince Kamar al-Akmar journeyed from city to city and country to country asking the people he encountered whether they had seen the princess and the magic horse. Of course, everyone was amazed by his talk and thought he was somewhat touched in the head. Though he continued doing this for a long time, he did not obtain any news of her. At last he came to her native city of Sana'a, but nobody had any idea where she was, and her father was still mourning her loss. Therefore, he turned back and headed for the land of the Greeks and continued to make inquiries along the way.

And Scheherazade noticed that dawn was approaching and stopped telling her story. When the next night arrived, however, she received the king's permission to continue her tale and said,

As chance would have it, the prince stopped at a particular khan and saw a group of merchants sitting and talking. So he sat down near them and heard one of them say, "My friends, let me tell you about this marvelous thing that I recently witnessed."

"What was it?" they asked.

"I was visiting a district in the nearby city, and I heard the people talking about an event that had happened not too long ago. It so happened that their king went out hunting one day with his courtiers, and they came to a meadow where they found an old man with a woman and a wooden horse made out of ebony. The man was atrocious, but the woman was amazingly beautiful, elegant, and graceful. As for the wooden horse, it was miraculous. No one had ever seen anything as perfectly made as this horse was."

"And what did the king do with them?" they asked.

"Well," said the merchant, "the king questioned the man, who claimed to be the woman's husband, but she denied this right away and declared that he was a sorcerer and a villain. So the king took her from him and had him beaten and thrown into jail. As for the ebony horse, I don't know what happened to it."

When the prince heard the merchant's story, he drew closer to him and began questioning the merchant discreetly and asked him about the names of the king and the city. Once the prince found out all he wanted to know, he spent the night full of joy. As soon as it was dawn, he set forth until he reached the city, but just as he was about to enter it, the gatekeepers stopped him and intended to bring him before the king so his majesty could question him about the craft he practiced and the reason why he had come to the city. Such was the custom of their ruler. However, it was suppertime when he entered the city, and it was impossible to see the king or to ask for instructions as to what to do with the stranger. So the guards took him to jail, thinking that it would be best if he spent the night there. But when the wardens saw how handsome and dignified he was, they could not find it in their hearts to imprison him. Instead, they made him sit with them outside the walls, and when their food was brought to them, they allowed him to share their meal. As soon as they had finished eating, they turned to the prince and said, "What country do you come from?"

"I come from Persia," he answered, "the land of the Chosroës."

When they heard this, they laughed, and one of them said, "Oh Chosroan, I've heard men tell stories and have checked to see how much truth there was in them, but never have I seen or heard a bigger liar than the Chosroan who's in our jail right now."

"And never have I seen a face and figure as hideous as his," said another guard.

"What has he been lying about?" asked the prince.

"He claims that he's a sage!" one of the guards said. "The king found him one day when he was out hunting. The old man had a beautiful woman and a remarkable ebony horse with him. As for the damsel, she is with the king, who's fallen in love with her and wants to marry her. But she's mad, and if the old man were really so wise, he could heal her, but he can't, and the king has been doing his utmost to discover a cure for her disease. He's spent an enormous amount of money this past year for physicians and astrologers on her account, but nobody has found a way to cure her. As for the horse, it's in the royal treasury, and the ugly man is with us in prison. Every night, as soon as it gets dark, he begins to weep and won't let us sleep."

And Scheherazade noticed that dawn was approaching and stopped telling her story. When the next night arrived, however, she received the king's permission to continue her tale and said,

After listening to what the guards had to say about the Persian prisoner, the prince thought of a way to free the princess. In the meantime, the guards became tired, and since they wanted to sleep, they took the prince inside the jail and locked the door. Once there, the prince overheard the wails and moans of the Persian sage, who said in his own language, "Alas! How I repent my sins, for I've sinned against myself and the king's son. I should never have abducted the damsel! I haven't gained a single thing from it. Truly, I should know by now not to reach for things that are above my station in life!"

Now when the prince heard this, he approached the Persian and said, "How long will this weeping and wailing last? Tell me, do you think that what's happened to you has never happened to anyone else?"

Since the Persian did not recognize the prince, he made friends with him and began to tell him all about his misfortunes. And as soon as morning arrived, the guards took the prince to their king and informed him that he had entered the city on the previous night at a time when an audience was impossible.

"Where do you come from?" the king asked the prince. "What is your name and trade, and why have you traveled here?"

"As to my name," the prince answered, "I'm called Harjah in Persian, and I come from Persia. As to my profession, I practice the art of medicine and heal the sick and those whom the jinn drive mad. In order to learn all there is to know, I travel from country to country and try to learn more by healing new patients."

Now, when the king heard this, he was extremely glad

and said, "Oh excellent sage, you've come just at the right time." Then he told him about the princess and added, "If you cure her and she recovers from her madness, you may have anything you want from me."

"May Allah give his blessings to the king," said the prince. "Describe to me all the symptoms of her insanity, and tell me how long it's been since she had this malady. You must also recount how you found her, the horse, and the sage."

So the king told him the whole story from first to last, and he added, "Right now, the sage is in jail."

"And what have you done with the horse?" asked the prince.

"I still have it," he said. "I've put it in my treasury."

Hearing this, the prince said to himself, "I'd better see the horse first and make sure that it's in good condition. If it is, all will be well, and all will end well. But if its motor has been destroyed, I must find some other way of rescuing my beloved." So he turned to the king and said, "I must see the horse in question, for I may need it to help the damsel recover from her madness."

"With all my heart," said the king, and he took him by the hand and led him to the place where the horse was being kept. The prince went around it, examining its condition, and found it in perfect condition. Therefore, he was full of joy and said to the king, "May Allah bless you! Now I would like to go and examine the damsel to see what her condition is like, for I hope to heal her through the means of this horse."

Then he ordered them to take good care of the horse, and the king led him to the princess's chamber. While the king remained outside, the prince went in and found her wringing her hands, writhing, beating herself against the ground, and tearing her garments to tatters. But there was really no madness of the jinn in her, and she did this only to keep people away from her. When the prince saw her acting like this, he said, "Nobody's going to harm you, my beauty," and he went on to soothe her and speak sweetly to her until he could whisper, "I'm Kamar al-Akmar," whereupon she uttered a loud cry and fainted out of joy. The king thought this was epilepsy brought on by her fear of him. Then the prince put his mouth to her ear and said, "Oh Shams al-Nahar, be careful, for our lives are at stake. Be patient and on your guard. We must plan everything carefully to escape from this tyrannical king. My first move will be now to go out to him and tell him that you are possessed by a jinnee and hence your madness. Nevertheless, I'll tell him that I can heal you and drive the evil spirit away, but he must untie your bonds right away. Then, when he enters here, speak nicely to him so that he'll think that I've cured you. Then we'll be able to do whatever we want."

"Don't worry," she whispered, "I'll do just as you say."

So the prince went out to the king in a joyful mood and said, "Majesty, I've been fortunate to locate the root of her disease, and I've also managed to cure her for you. In fact, you may now go in to see her, but speak to her gently and treat her kindly. Make sure you promise her whatever she wants, and you will receive your just rewards."

And Scheherazade noticed that dawn was approaching and stopped telling her story. When the next night arrived, however, she received the king's permission to continue her tale and said,

So the king entered the chamber, and when she saw him, she rose and kissed the ground before him. Then she welcomed him by saying, "I'm grateful that you've come to visit your servant today."

The king was ecstatic and ordered the waiting women and eunuchs to attend her and take her to the Hammam and get various rich garments ready for her. So they, too, entered the chamber and saluted her, and she returned their salaams with the most polite language and pleasant comportment. Thereupon they clad her in royal apparel, and after putting a necklace of jewels around her neck, they took her to the bath and attended to her every need there. Then they brought her out, glistening like the radiant moon itself, and when she came into the king's presence, she saluted him and kissed the ground before him, whereupon he rejoiced and said to the prince, "Doctor, all this is due to your great gifts. May Allah enable us to profit even more from your healing spirit!"

"My king," the prince replied, "in order to complete the cure, it is necessary for you and your troops to return to the place where you found her, and you must bring the black wooden horse with her, for there is a devil in it, and unless I exorcise the satanic creature, he'll torment her at the beginning of every month."

"I'm only too happy to comply with your advice," said the king, "for you are the prince of all philosophers and the most learned of all who see the light of day."

Then the king ordered the ebony horse to be brought to the meadow and rode there with all his troops and the princess, nor did he have the slightest inkling about the prince's plans. Now, when they came to the appointed place, the prince, still dressed as a physician, ordered them to set the princess and the steed together and as far away from the king and his troops as possible. Once this was done, he turned to the king and said, "With your permission I'll now proceed to fumigate the enemy of mankind so that he'll never return to her again. After this I'll mount this wooden horse, which seems to be made of ebony, and set the damsel behind me. The horse will shake and sway back and will eventually head directly for you. At that point the affair will be at an end, and you'll be able to do with the damsel whatever you like."

When the king heard these words, he was ecstatic. So the prince left him and went to the horse. After mounting it and lifting the princess behind him, he tied her to him tightly, while the king and his troops observed. Then he pushed the takeoff button, and the horse sprang into the air and soared with them on high until they disappeared from sight. After this, the king stayed put for half the day expecting them to return, but they did not reappear. Eventually he gave up hope and regretted everything he had done and grieved over the loss of the damsel. Since there was nothing he could do, he went back to the city with his troops and sent for the Persian, who was in the prison, and said to him, "You traitor! You villain! Why did you hide the secret of the ebony horse from me? Now a swindler has come and stolen it from me along with your lady, whose ornaments are worth a mint, and I'll never see anything of them again!"

So the Persian related to the king everything that had happened to him in the past from the first to the last, and the king became so terribly furious that he almost died. He locked himself up in his palace for a while and kept mourning until his viziers came to him and comforted him. "Your majesty," they said, "truly, the man who took the damsel is an enchanter, and praise be to Allah, for He has rescued you from his sorcery!" And they did not stop talking to him in this way until he became reconciled to the fact that he had lost the princess forever.

In the meantime, the prince continued flying toward his father's capital in great joy until he landed on the terrace of the palace. After setting down the princess in safety, he went to his father and mother, saluted them, and told them that he had brought the princess back to the palace. Of course, they were extremely happy, and great banquets were prepared for the people of the city.

And Scheherazade noticed that dawn was approaching and stopped telling her tale. When the next night arrived, however, she received the king's permission to continue her tale and said,

The celebration of the prince's return lasted an entire month, and at the end of this time he married the princess, and they enjoyed each other with great delight on the wedding night. However, the king broke the ebony horse in pieces and destroyed the mechanism that enabled it to fly. Moreover, the prince wrote a letter to the princess's father telling him about everything that had happened to his daughter and informing him that she was now married to him and was safe and happy. This letter was sent by a messenger who carried valuable presents and rare articles for the king. When he arrived at the city of Sana'a and delivered the letter and presents, the king rejoiced and bestowed honors on the messenger. In addition, he sent rich gifts to his son-in-law via the same messenger, who returned to his master and reported everything that had happened, and the prince was glad. After this he wrote a letter every year to his father-in-law and sent him presents until, in the course of time, his own father, King Sabur, died, and he succeeded him to the throne. The new King Kamar al-Akmar was a just ruler, and he treated his lieges fairly and wisely so that his subjects became exceedingly loyal to him. Indeed, Kamar al-Akmar and his wife, Shams al-Nahar, led a life of joy and solace until they were finally visited by the Destroyer of delights and the Sunderer of societies.

No sooner had Scheherazade concluded her tale than she said, "And yet, oh king, this story is no more wondrous than the tale of Ali Baba and the Forty Thieves."

Ali Baba and the Forty Thieves

Once upon a time there were two brothers named Kasim and Ali Baba, who lived in a certain city of Persia. When their father died, they each received an equal share of his wealth and lost no time in spending and wasting it all. The elder brother, Kasim, however, married the daughter of a rich merchant, so that when his father-in-law passed away, he became the owner of a large shop that contained valuable merchandise and a storehouse of precious goods. Moreover, he inherited a great deal of gold buried in the ground. Thus, he became known throughout the town as a prosperous merchant.

Meanwhile, Ali Baba had married a poor and needy woman and lived with her in a dismal hovel. He eked out a scanty livelihood by gathering wood in a forest and selling it for fuel on his three asses in the bazaars around town.

Now, one day it so happened that Ali Baba had cut some dead branches and had placed the load on his donkeys when suddenly he perceived a cloud of dust high in the air and moving rapidly toward him from the right. When he took a closer look, he was able to distinguish a troop of horsemen, who would soon reach him, and this sight caused him great alarm, for he was afraid that they might be bandits who would slay him and drive off his donkeys. So he began to run, but since he could not possibly escape the forest in time to avoid them, he drove his donkeys into some nearby bushes and scampered up a huge tree, where he hid himself behind some leaves. Fortunately, he could observe everything beneath him without fear of being seen by the people below, and the

first thing he noticed was an immense rock that towered above the tree. When the horsemen finally arrived, it was right in front of this rock that they dismounted, and he could see that they were all young and strong. Moreover, it was clear from their looks and demeanor that they were a group of robbers, about forty in all, who had just attacked a caravan and had carried off the spoils and booty to this place with the intention of hiding it safely in some cache.

Indeed, the saddlebags which the men took from their horses proved to be full of gold and silver, and the men slung their bags over their shoulders. Then the robber who appeared to be their captain led the way and pushed through thorns and thickets until he came to a certain spot, where he uttered, "Open, Sesame!"

All at once a wide doorway appeared in the face of the rock, allowing the robbers to enter, and then the portal shut by itself. Although they were now inside the cave, Ali Baba remained perched on the tree, for he knew that the robbers could come out of the cave at any moment and slay him if they caught him descending the tree. Nevertheless, after waiting for a long time, he became tired and decided to mount one of their horses, herd his donkeys together, and then head toward the town. Just as hc reached his decision, the portal flew open and the chief emerged. Standing at the entrance, he counted his men as they came out, and finally he spoke the magic words "Shut, Sesame!" and the door closed by itself. After he inspected his men, they all slung their saddlebags onto their horses and bridled them. As soon as they were ready, they rode off, and their chief led them in the direction that they had come from.

However, Ali Baba did not budge from the tree until they were clean out of sight, for he was afraid that one of them might return and spot him. When he finally descended, he thought to himself, "Why not try those magic words and see if the door will open and close at my bidding?" So he called aloud, "Open, Sesame!" And no sooner had he said those words than the portal flew open, and he entered a large, vaulted cavern through the portal about the size of a man, and hewn in stone. There was also light that came though air holes and bull's-eyes in the upper surface of the rock that formed the ceiling.

He had expected to find nothing but a dark and gloomy den and therefore was surprised to see the whole cave filled with bales of all kinds of material, heaped from floor to ceiling with camel loads of silks, brocades, embroidered cloths, and mounds of different-colored carpets. In addition, he came across countless gold and silver coins, some piled on the ground and others bound in leather bags and sacks. Upon seeing such an abundance of goods and money, Ali Baba concluded that the thieves must have been storing their loot in this place for many decades and not just the last few years.

Although the door to the cave had closed once he had entered, Ali Baba was not dismayed, because he remembered the magic words, which he used to open the door once again so he could carry out some of the spoils. He paid no attention to the precious materials but rather concentrated on gathering as many sacks of coins as he thought his donkeys could carry. Then he loaded them on the beasts and covered his plunder with sticks and branches so that nobody would detect the bags. Finally, he cried out, "Close, Sesame!" and immediately the door shut, for the spell had been so conceived that if anyone entered the cave, its portal shut automatically behind him, and if he wanted to leave the cave, the door would not open again unless he uttered the words, "Open, Sesame!"

Now that Ali Baba had loaded his asses, he drove them toward the town as fast as he could, and after reaching his home, he led them into the yard and shut the outer door. Then he took off the sticks and branches from the donkeys and carried the bags of gold to his wife, who immediately began feeling what was inside. When she realized that they were full of coins, however, she suspected that Ali Baba had robbed some people and began reproaching him for having done such an evil thing.

And Scheherazade noticed that dawn was approaching and stopped telling her story. When the next night arrived, however, she received the king's permission to continue her tale and said,

Upset by his wife's reaction, Ali Baba told her that he

had not robbed anyone, and that instead of berating him, she should rejoice with him at their good fortune. Thereupon, he told her about his adventure and began to pour heaps of gold on the floor right before her eyes so that she was dazzled by the sight and delighted by his account of the events in the forest. Then she stooped down and began counting coin after coin until Ali Baba said, "Silly woman, how long are you going to do that? Let me dig a hole to hide this treasure so that nobody will know about it."

"That's a good idea," she replied. "But I'd still like to weigh the coins and get an idea of their worth."

"As you please," he said, "but make sure you tell nobody about the money."

So off she went in haste to Kasim's home to borrow a scale to weigh the coins and determine their value. When she could not find Kasim, she said to his wife, "I'd appreciate it if you could lend me a scale for a while."

"Do you need the bigger or smaller scale?" her sister-in-law replied.

"Just the smaller one," she answered.

"Stay here a moment while I try to find what you need."

It was under this pretext that Kasim's wife went off and secretly smeared wax and tallow on the pan of the scale so that she could discover what Ali Baba's wife intended to weigh. By doing this she could be certain that whatever it was, some little piece of it would stick to the wax and fat. Once she knew that her curiosity would be satisfied, she gave the scale to Ali Baba's wife, who carried it home and began to weigh the gold. In the meantime, Ali Baba kept digging, and when the money was weighed, they stored it in the hole, which they carefully covered with dirt. Then the good wife took the scale back to her sister-in-law, not realizing that a coin had stuck to the pan of the scale. So when Kasim's wife saw the gold coin, she fumed with envy and wrath and said to herself, "Well now, they've borrowed my scale to weigh coins!" And she was quite puzzled as to how such a poor man as Ali Baba had obtained so many coins that he had to weigh them with a scale. This matter occupied her thoughts for a long time, and when her husband returned home in the evening, she said to him, "You may consider yourself a prosperous man, but your brother, Ali Baba, is much richer than you are. In fact, he's an emir in comparison to you. He's got such heaps of gold that he has to weigh his money with scales, while you must content yourself with counting your coins."

"How do you know this?" Kasim asked.

Then his wife told him all about the scale and how she had found a gold coin stuck to it. To prove her point she showed him the gold coin, which bore the mark and inscription of some ancient king. Consequently, Kasim became so envious and jealous that he could not sleep that night, and early the next morning he arose, went to Ali Baba's house, and said, "Brother, it would seem that you are a poor and needy man, but in truth, you have so much wealth that you're compelled to weigh your gold with scales."

"What are you saying?" responded Ali Baba. "I don't understand you. Make your point clear."

"Don't pretend to be ignorant, and don't think you can fool me!" Kasim cried out angrily and extended the palm of his hand, revealing the ancient coin. "You must have thousands of these coins if you needed my scale. My wife found this one stuck to a pan."

Then Ali Baba understood how both Kasim and his wife knew that he had a great many coins and he realized that it would be to no avail to deny it, since his denial would only cause ill will and mischief. Therefore, he told his brother all about the bandits and also about the treasure in the cave. After hearing the story, Kasim exclaimed, "I want you to tell me exactly where you found the money and also the magic words to open and shut the door. And I warn you, if you don't tell me the whole truth, I'll inform the chief of police, and you'll have to give up all your gold and spend the rest of your days in jail."

Under such threats, Ali Baba revealed the magic words and the location of the cave. As a result, Kasim, who had noted everything carefully, set out for the cave the very next day with ten donkeys that he had hired. He had no difficulty in finding the place, and when he came to the rock, he cried out in great joy, "Open, Sesame!" Then all at once, the portal yawned wide, and Kasim entered and saw the piles of jewels and treasures lying all around

N. ORR-CO

him. As soon as he was fully inside the cave, the door shut after him as it was accustomed to do. Meanwhile, Kasim walked about in ecstasy, marveling at the treasures, and when he finally became tired of gaping, he gathered together enough bags of coins for his mules to carry and placed them by the entrance ready to take outside and load on his beasts. But by the will of Allah Almighty, he had clean forgotten the cabalistic words and cried out, "Open, oh Barley!" However, the door refused to budge. Astonished and confused, Kasim began calling out all the names that had something to do with grain except sesame, which had slipped from his memory as though he had never heard the word. In his distress, he neglected the gold coins that lay in heaps at the entrance. Instead, he paced back and forth inside the cave worrying about his predicament. The great treasures that had once filled his heart with joy and gladness were now the cause of bitter grief and sadness.

And Scheherazade noticed that dawn was approaching and stopped telling her story. When the next night arrived, however, she received the king's permission to continue her tale and said,

Kasim abandoned all hope for his life and regretted that he had risked his life out of greed and envy. Indeed, it so happened that the robbers returned to the rock by noon and saw the mules standing beside the entrance from afar. Unfortunately, Kasim had failed to tether them, and they had strayed about the forest, browsing here and there. Nevertheless, the thieves paid scant attention to the strays, nor did they bother to catch them and tie them to stakes. They were only puzzled as to how they had managed to wander so far from the town. After the robbers dismounted, the chief went up to the door and repeated the magic words, causing the door to fly open at once.

Now, Kasim had heard within the cave the sound of the horses drawing nearer and nearer, and he fell down on the ground in a fit of fear, never doubting that it was the clatter of the bandits, who would certainly slaughter him. Nevertheless, he summoned his courage, and when the door flew open, he rushed out, hoping to make good his escape. But the unfortunate man ran smack into the chief, who stood in front of the band and knocked Kasim to the ground. Immediately thereafter, one of the robbers drew his sword and cut Kasim in two with one slash. Then the bandits rushed into the cave and carried the bags of coins back to the spot where they had been before. Fortunately, they did not miss the ones that Ali Baba had taken, so stunned and amazed were they to discover that a stranger had gained entry to the cave. They all knew that it was impossible for anyone to drop through the skylights, because they were as tall and steep as the rock's face, which was too slippery to climb. They also knew that it was impossible to enter by the portal unless one knew the magic words to open it. Nevertheless, they decided to quarter Kasim's dead body and hang two parts on the right and two parts on the left of the door so that the sight would be a warning of doom to all those who might dare to enter the cave. After they finished this task, they left the cave, closed the door to the treasure hoard, and rode off to do their usual work.

Now, when night fell, and Kasim did not come home, his wife became uneasy. So she went to Ali Baba and said, "Your brother hasn't returned home. You know where he went, and I'm afraid that something terrible has happened to him."

Ali Baba also suspected that some accident had occurred to prevent his brother's return. Nonetheless, he tried to comfort his sister-in-law with words of cheer and said, "I'm sure that Kasim is just being cautious and has chosen a roundabout road to avoid the city. That's probably the reason why he's late. I'm sure he'll be here very soon."

After hearing these words, Kasim's wife felt comforted and went home, where she sat and awaited her husband's return. But when half the night had passed and he still had not come home, she was most distraught. She was afraid to cry aloud out of grief because the neighbors might hear her and come and learn the secret. So she wept in silence, scolded herself, and began thinking, "Why did I ever disclose the secret of the coins to him and make him jealous of Ali Baba? Now I've reaped nothing but disaster!" She spent the rest of the night in bitter tears, and early the next morning she rushed as fast as she could to Ali Baba and begged him to go and search for his brother. Again he comforted her and then set out right away with his asses for the forest. Once he reached the rock, he was startled to see fresh bloodstains, and since he could not find his brother or the ten donkeys, he was convinced something terrible had happened. So he went to the door and said, "Open, Sesame!" and when he entered, he saw Kasim's dead body, two parts hanging to the right, and the rest to the left of the entrance. To be sure, he was frightened beyond belief, but he wrapped the quarters in the two cloths and set them upon one of his asses, hiding them carefully with sticks and branches so that nobody could see them. Then he went in and took some more bags of gold, which he placed upon the other two animals, and covered them carefully as he had done before. When everything was ready, he closed the door to the cave with the magic words and set off for home with all due caution. Soon after his arrival, he told his wife to bury the bags of gold with utmost prudence, but he did not tell her about the condition in which he had found his brother. Then he took the other donkey with the corpse to the widow's house and knocked gently at the door.

Now, Kasim had a slave girl named Morgiana, who was extremely shrewd, and she quietly lifted the bolt and let Ali Baba and the ass into the courtyard. After he took the corpse from the beast's back, he said, "Quick, Morgiana, get everything ready to bury your lord. I'll return quickly to help you, but first I must go and tell the bad news to your mistress."

When Kasim's widow saw her brother-in-law, she exclaimed, "Oh, Ali Baba, what news do you have about my husband? Alas, I see grief written upon your face! Tell me quickly what's happened."

So he told her what had happened to her husband, how he had been slain by the robbers, and in what condition he had brought the dead body home.

"My lady," he said, "we cannot change what has happened, but we must keep this matter secret, for our lives depend upon it."

The widow wept bitter tears and then responded, "Fate dictated what was to become of my husband, and now for safety's sake, I give you my word that I won't reveal anything about this affair."

"There's nothing one can do when Allah decrees what is to happen," he stated. "Be patient until the days of your widowhood have expired. Then I'll take you as a wife, and you will live in comfort and happiness. And you don't have to worry that my first wife will be angry at you or jealous, for she is kind and tender."

"As you wish," she said.

While she continued weeping and mourning over her husband's death, Ali Baba said farewell and rejoined Morgiana. They discussed the best way to manage the burial of his brother, and he told her exactly what to do before he left the matter in her hands and went home. As soon as Ali Baba had departed, Morgiana went quickly to a druggist's shop, and in order to conceal the matter, she asked for a drug that was often administered to people with a dangerous distemper. The druggist gave it to her but said, "Who's become so ill at your house that he needs this medicine?"

"It's my master, Kasim, who's sick," she said. "He's not said a word or eaten anything for many days now, and we're afraid he may die."

The next day Morgiana went again and asked the druggist for more medicine given to the sick to help them rally when they may be on the brink of death. The man gave her the potion, and as she took it, she sighed loudly, wept a few tears, and said, "I fear that he may not even have the strength to drink this draught. I think it will be all over for him before I reach the house."

Early on the second day, Morgiana covered her face with a veil and went to a man named Baba Mustafa, an old tailor, who made shrouds and sewed cloths together, and as soon as she saw him open his shop, she gave him a gold coin and said, "I want you to let me bind a kerchief over your eyes and then to come along with me."

When Mustafa hesitated, she placed a second gold coin in his palm and pleaded with him to follow her. Since he was a greedy man, he finally agreed, and she tied a kerchief over his eyes and led him by the hand to the house in which the dead body of her master was lying. Then after taking off the kerchief in the darkened room, she told him to sew the quarters of the corpse, limb to limb, and after throwing a cloth over the body, she said, "Make haste and sew a shroud according to the size of this dead man, and I'll give you another ducat."

Baba Mustafa quickly made the cloth so that it fit the body, and Morgiana paid him the promised gold coin. Then she tied the kerchief around his eyes once more and led him back to his shop. After this she returned home as fast as she could, and with the help of Ali Baba, she washed the body in warm water and then covered the corpse with the shroud and placed it upon a clean place ready for burial. When all this was done, Morgiana went to the mosque and notified an imam, a leader of prayer, that a funeral was awaiting the mourners in a certain household, and she requested that he come and read the prayers for the dead. The imam consented and returned with her. Then four neighbors lifted the bier, carried it on their shoulders, and went forth with the imam and others, who customarily gave their assistance at such obsequies. After the funeral prayers had ended, four other men carried off the coffin, and Morgiana walked before it with a bare head, striking her breast and wailing loudly, while Ali Baba and the neighbors followed behind. Finally they entered the cemetery in this order, and buried him. Then, leaving him to Munkar and Nakir—the Questioners of the Dead—they all made their way to their homes.

According to the custom of the city, the women of the neighborhood soon gathered together in the house of mourning and sat with Kasim's widow, comforting her until she was somewhat resigned to her fate and felt better. Meanwhile, Ali Baba stayed forty days at home in ceremonial lamentation for the loss of his brother. So nobody in the town except himself, Kasim's widow, and Morgiana knew anything about the secret. When the forty days of mourning were over, Ali Baba moved all the property that had belonged to the deceased to his own house and publicly married the widow. Then he appointed his nephew, his brother's eldest son, to take charge of Kasim's shop and carry on the business, for he had lived with a wealthy merchant a long time and had learned all about matters concerned with trade, such as selling and buying.

And Scheherazade noticed that dawn was approaching and stopped telling her story. When the next night arrived, however, she received the king's permission to continue her tale and said,

* * *

Now, one day, the robbers happened to return to the cave and were extremely startled to find no sign or trace of Kasim's body, and they also noticed that much of the gold had been carried off.

"We must look into this matter right away," said the chief, "or else we'll suffer more losses, and our treasure that we and our forefathers have amassed over the course of many years will disappear."

All the robbers agreed, and they came to the conclusion that the man whom they had slain had known the magic words to open the door. Moreover, they believed that someone besides him had knowledge of the spell and had carried away the body and much of the gold as well. Therefore, they decided that they had to make discreet inquiries to find out who the man might be. To begin their search, they thought it best to choose one of the more cunning robbers among them to disguise himself in the dress of some merchant from a foreign country. He was to go into the city and move from quarter to quarter and from street to street to find out whether any townsman had recently died. If so, he was to learn where he lived, and with this clue they might be able to find the scoundrel they sought. When they had fully finished discussing their plans, one of the robbers said, "I'd like your permission to take on this task. I'll go into town and try to dig up all the information we need, and if I fail, you may take my life."

Thereupon, this bandit disguised himself as a foreigner and snuck into the city during the night. Early the next morning he went to the market square and saw that the only shop open was that of Baba Mustafa, the tailor, who sat upon his working stool with thread and needle in hand. The thief wished him a good morning and asked, "How can you see what you're sewing? It's still dark."

"Well, I can see that you're a stranger and don't know my reputation!" said the tailor. "Despite my years, my eyesight is so keen that only yesterday I sewed together a dead body while sitting in a very dark room."

The bandit immediately realized that he had stumbled onto something important, and in order to obtain some further clues, he said, "I think you're just joking with me. How could you possibly stitch a cerecloth for a corpse or sew shrouds?"

"I don't care whether you believe me," said the tailor. "And don't ask me any more questions."

Thereupon, the robber put a gold coin in his hand and continued, "I'm not interested in discovering what you're hiding. However, you can rest assured that my breast, like every honest man's, is the grave of secrets. The only thing I want to learn from you is the house in which you did your work. Can you direct me to it or lead me there?"

The tailor took the gold greedily and replied, "A certain slave girl led me to a place which I know quite well, and there she put a kerchief around my eyes and guided me to some tenement. After that she led me to a dark room where the dead body lay dismembered. Then she untied the kerchief and told me first to sew the corpse together and afterward the shroud. When I finished my job, she blindfolded me again and led me back to the place where she had brought me and left me there. So you see, I can't tell you the location of the house."

"Even though you don't know the dwelling," the robber said, "you can still take me to the place where you were blindfolded. Then I'll put a kerchief over your eyes and lead you. Perhaps in this way you may hit upon the house. And if you do this favor for me, I'll reward you with another gold ducat."

The bandit slipped another coin into the tailor's palm, and Baba Mustafa put it into his pocket. Then he left his shop and walked with the robber to the place where Morgiana had tied the kerchief around his eyes. Here he told the robber to blindfold him and to lead him by the hand. Since Baba Mustafa was exceedingly clever, he was soon able to find the street where he had walked before, and after counting step by step, he suddenly came to a halt and said, "This is as far as I came with her."

And the two of them stopped in front of Kasim's house, which had now become the dwelling of his brother, Ali Baba.

Quickly the robber made some marks with white chalk upon the door so that he could easily locate it again. Then he removed the kerchief from the tailor's eyes and said, "Baba Mustafa, I want to thank you for this favor, and may Almighty Allah reward you for your favor. Please tell me now who lives in that house over there."

"Quite honestly," he responded, "I don't know, for I'm not very familiar with this part of the city."

Since the robber realized that he would not be able to obtain any more valuable information from the tailor, he dismissed him and sent him back to his shop. In the meantime, the bandit went back to the meeting place in the forest where his comrades were waiting for him.

Not long after his departure, it so happened that Morgiana was struck by the white chalk marks on the door when she went out on some errand. She stood there awhile deep in thought and soon suspected that some enemy had made the signs so that he would be able to recognize the house and do some harm against her master. Therefore, she chalked the doors of all her neighbors in the same way and kept the matter secret, never revealing it either to her master or mistress. Meanwhile, the robber told his comrades about his adventure in the city and how he had found the clue. So the captain and the rest of the bandits went to the city and entered it one by one in different ways. The robber who had marked Ali Baba's door accompanied the chief to point out the place, and when they reached the house, he exclaimed, "This is the place where our culprit lives!"

But when the captain looked around him, he saw that all the dwellings were marked by chalk in the same fashion, and he replied in a baffled manner, "How do you know that this is the right house when all the houses here have similar chalk marks?"

The robber was completely confounded and could not reply. Then he swore an oath and said, "I assure you that I marked one of the doors, but I don't know where all the other marks have come from. And now, I can't really tell you which is the right one."

Thereupon the captain returned to the marketplace and told his men, "All our work was in vain, because we can't find the right house. Let's return to our meeting place in the forest, and I'll join you there."

The thieves marched off in different directions and gathered together again inside the cave. When they were all assembled, the captain decided to punish the robber who had led them astray by locking him up. Then he said, "I'll give a special reward to whoever goes to town and brings me information that will allow us to capture the man who's plundered our property."

So another one of the robbers came forward and said, "I will, and you can count on me to fulfill your wish this time."

After giving this robber presents and promises, the captain sent him on his way. As destiny would have it, this second robber went straight to the house of Baba Mustafa, just like the first one, and he, too, persuaded the greedy tailor with gold coins to let him lead him blindfolded in a certain quarter of the city. Once again, this thief was led to Ali Baba's door, which he marked with red chalk to distinguish it from the others, which were still marked with white. Then he stole back to the group of thieves in the forest. However, Morgiana also spotted the red signs on the entrance of the house, and with great foresight she marked all the other doors in the same way and did not tell a soul about what she had done. Meanwhile the bandit could not help boasting, "Captain, I've found the house, and I put a sign on it that will clearly distinguish it from all the others in the neighborhood."

And Scheherazade noticed that dawn was approaching and stopped telling her story. When the next night arrived, however, she received the king's permission to continue her tale and said,

Once again the captain and his men went into city, but this time they found all the houses marked with red chalk. So they returned disappointed to the cave, and the chief was extremely irritated and locked his spy in jail with the other robber. Then he said to himself, "Two men have failed to find the house and have been duly punished for leading us astray. Probably nobody else in my band will dare now to follow up their work. So I believe it's up to me to go and find the culprit's house." Therefore, he went back into the city, and with the help of the tailor Baba Mustafa, who had accumulated a good deal of gold coins by now, he hit upon the house of Ali Baba, but he did not mark it with a sign. Instead he memorized where it was and stamped it on the tablet of his heart. Soon afterward he returned to the forest and said to his men, "I know exactly where it is and have memorized the place. So now we won't have any trouble in finding it. Therefore, I want you to go right away and purchase nineteen mules, one large leather jar of mustard oil, and thirty-seven vessels of the same kind, but they must be empty. Without me and our two comrades locked up in our jail, you number thirty-seven, and I intend to hide you with your weapons in the jars. Then I'll load two of you on each mule. On the nineteenth mule there will be a man in one of the jars and oil in the other. I'll disguise myself as an oil merchant and drive the mules into the town. Since it will be nighttime, I'll ask the master of that house if I can stay there until morning. After this we'll look for an opportunity in the darkness to attack and slay him. When he's dead, we'll recover the gold treasure that he robbed from us and bring it back on the mules."

This plan pleased the robbers, who went off and purchased the mules and huge leather jars and did everything the captain had instructed them to do. After waiting three days, they arose shortly before dawn and hid themselves in the jars. The chief then disguised himself in some merchant's garments and loaded the jars onto the nineteen mules. When all this was done, he drove the beasts before him and reached Ali Baba's place by nightfall.

It so happened that the master of the house was strolling back and forth in front of his home after having enjoyed his supper. When the captain saw Ali Baba, he saluted him with the salaam and said, "I've come from a distant village with some oil, and unfortunately I've arrived too late and don't have lodgings for the night. Please have pity on me, my lord, and allow me to stay in your courtyard. I need to give my mules some rest from carrying the jars and to feed them."

To be sure, Ali Baba had heard the captain's voice when perched upon the tree, and he had seen him enter the cave. However, because of the disguise, he was not able to recognize the thief. So he gave him a hearty welcome and granted him permission to spend the night in his courtyard. He then led him to an empty shed where the mules could be tethered and ordered one of his slave boys to fetch grain and water. He also informed Morgiana that a guest had come to spend the night and said, "Make a supper for him as soon as possible and get the guest bed ready."

After the captain had unloaded all the jars and had fed and watered his mules, Ali Baba received him with courtesy and kindness. Summoning Morgiana, he said in her presence, "See to it that our stranger has everything he desires. Tomorrow morning I want to go to the Hammam and bathe. So give my slave boy Abdullah a suit of clean white clothes that I'll wear after my bath. Moreover, I want you to prepare a broth tonight that I'll be able to drink after I return home in the morning."

"I'll get everything ready for you as you wish," she replied.

So Ali Baba retired for the night, and the captain finished his supper, went to the shed, and made sure that all the mules had food and drink for the night. Then he whispered to his men who were hiding in the jars, "When you hear my voice at midnight, open the jars quickly with your knives and come out right away."

When he returned to the house, Morgiana led the chief through the kitchen to the guest room, where she had prepared a bed for him.

"If you need anything else, my lord," she said, "just call me, and I'll be at your service."

"There's nothing else I need," he answered, and after putting out the light, he lay down on the bed to relax and sleep until the time came to rouse his men and finish their work. Meanwhile, Morgiana did as her master had ordered her. First she took out a suit of clean white clothes and gave it to Abdullah, who had not gone to sleep yet. Then she placed the pipkin on the hearth to boil the broth and fanned the fire until it burned briskly. After a short wait she had to see if the broth was boiling, but by that time all the lamps had gone out, and she found that there was no more oil left and could not get a light, no matter where she looked. Abdullah noticed that she was irritated and said to her, "Why are you making such a fuss? There are many jars of oil in the courtyard shed. Why don't you just go and take as much as you need?"

Morgiana thanked him for his clever suggestion, and Abdullah, who was relaxing in the hall, went off to sleep so that he might awake on time and help Ali Baba with his bath. Meanwhile, Morgiana took an oil can and walked

to the shed, where the jars were arranged in rows. As she approached one of the vessels, the thief, who was hiding inside it, heard the footsteps and thought that it was his captain, whose command he was awaiting. So he whispered, "Is it time now for us to come out?"

Morgiana was startled and frightened by the voice, but since she was bold and alert, she replied in a disguised voice, "It's not time yet." Then she said to herself, "Something strange is going on here. These jars aren't filled with oil. I think the merchant is plotting something treacherous against my lord. May Allah the Compassionate protect us from his snare!" Once again she made her voice sound like the captain's and said to the robber in the jar, "Be patient. It's not time."

Then she went to the next jar and gave the same reply to the robber inside and so on until she had spoken to all the robbers in the vessels. "My God!" she said to herself. "My master extended his hospitality to this man because he thought he was an oil merchant, but he's actually taken in a band of robbers, who only await the signal to attack and kill him and plunder the place!" When she finally came to the last jar, she found it brimming with oil. So she filled her can, returned to the kitchen, trimmed the lamp, and lit the wicks. Next, she took out a large caldron and set it over the fire. After filling it with oil from the jar, she heaped wood on the hearth and fanned it to a fierce flame to make sure that it would boil its contents. When this was done, she bailed it out in potfuls and carried the boiling liquid into the courtyard, where she poured the seething-hot contents into the leathern jars one by one. Since the thieves were unable to escape, they were scalded to death, and every jar contained a corpse. Thus the clever Morgiana used her keen wit to make a clean end of everything without anyone in the house knowing what had happened.

Now, when she was certain that each and every man had been slain, she went back to the kitchen, shut the door, and continued brewing Ali Baba's broth. No more than an hour passed before the captain woke from his sleep, and after he opened his window, he saw that everything was dark and silent. So he clapped his hands as a signal for his men to come out of the jars, but not a sound was heard in return. After a while he clapped again and called out loud, but got no answer. And when he cried out a third time without a reply, he was perplexed and went out to the shed, where the jars were standing. He thought to himself that they might have all fallen asleep. But since the time for action was at hand, he felt he had to wake them without delay. So he approached the nearest jar and was startled by the smell of oil and seething flesh. Upon touching the outside of the vessel, he felt it reeking hot. Then he went to the others one by one and found them all in the same condition. It did not take him long to figure out what had happened to the members of his band, and fearing for his own safety, he climbed over the wall into a nearby garden and made his escape in high gear and with great disappointment.

Morgiana waited awhile for the captain to return from the shed, but he did not appear. Therefore, she realized that he had probably scaled the wall and had taken flight because the street door was double-locked. Since she knew the thieves could not cause any more trouble that night, Morgiana lay down to sleep in perfect contentment and with an easy mind.

Two hours before dawn, Ali Baba awoke and went to the Hammam, knowing nothing about the nocturnal adventure, for the gallant slave girl had not aroused him, nor had she deemed such action expedient. Indeed, if she had sought an opportunity to tell him about her plan, she most likely would have lost her chance, and the entire project would have been spoiled.

The sun was high above the horizon when Ali Baba walked back from the baths, and he was astounded to see the jars still standing under the shed. So he asked Morgiana, "How is it that my guest hasn't taken his jars of oil to the market?"

And Scheherazade noticed that dawn was approaching and stopped telling her story. When the next night arrived, however, she received the king's permission to continue her tale and said,

When Morgiana heard Ali Baba's question about his guest, she replied, "May Allah Almighty grant you threescore years and ten of safety! I'd like to have a private talk with you about this merchant."

So Ali Baba went off to the side with his slave girl, who took him into the courtyard and locked the door behind her. After showing him a jar, she said, "Please look inside, and tell me whether there's oil or something else."

After Ali Baba peered inside, he perceived a man, but the sight of the corpse scared him so much that he almost fled in fright.

"There's no need to fear this man," Morgiana said. "He's no longer capable of harming you. He's stone dead."

Upon hearing these comforting words, Ali Baba asked, "Morgiana, what evil things was he planning, and how did this wretch come to suffer this fate?"

"Praise be to Allah," she responded. "I'll tell you the whole story, but you must keep quiet and not speak so loud, or else the neighbors will learn about our secret. First, take a look into all the jars, one by one."

So Ali Baba examined them and found that they each contained a man, armed to the teeth, but scalded to death. To say the least, he was so amazed that he became speechless and could only stare at the jars. Soon, however, he recovered his composure and asked, "Where is the oil merchant?"

"That villain was not a trader," Morgiana replied, "but a lying crook whose sugar-coated words were intended to lead you into a trap. But before I tell you what he was and what has happened, you should drink some of this broth for your health and to sooth your stomach, since you've come fresh from the Hammam."

So Ali Baba went inside his house, and Morgiana served him the broth, whereupon he said, "I'd like to hear this wondrous story now. Please tell it to me, and set my heart at ease."

So the slave girl began by saying, "Master, when you told me to boil the broth and then retired for the evening, I obediently took out a suit of clean white clothes and gave it to Abdullah. After that I kindled the fire and set the broth on it. As soon as it was ready, I needed to light a lamp so that I could see to skim it, but all the oil was gone. When Abdullah heard me complaining, he advised me to take some of the oil from the jars that stood under the shed. Therefore, I took a can and went to the first vessel, when I suddenly heard a voice whisper cautiously, 'Is it time for us to come out?' I was amazed by this and suspected that the so-called merchant was plotting to kill you. So I replied, 'It's not time yet.' Then I went to the second jar and heard another voice, and I gave him the same answer. And so it went with the rest. I was now certain that these men were only waiting for some signal from their chief, who was the guest you had received into you house. Moreover, I was sure that he had brought these men to murder you and plunder your goods. But I gave him no opportunity to fulfill his wish. After taking some oil from the last jar, I lit the lamp and put a large caldron on the fire. Next I filled it up with oil which I brought from the jar and made a blazing fire underneath. When the contents were seething hot, I took out various cans, filled them with the liquid, and went to pour the boiling liquid on them one by one. After scalding them all to death, I returned to the kitchen, put out all the lamps, and watched how the traitorous merchant would act next. Not long after I had taken my place by the kitchen window, the robber captain awoke and signaled to his men. Since they did not reply, he went downstairs and into the courtyard. Finding that all his men were slain in the jars, he fled over the garden wall, and I don't know where he's gone. After I was sure that he had disappeared, I double-locked the door, and with my heart at rest, I slept."

After telling this story to her master, Morgiana added, "I've told you the complete truth, but I must say that I've had an inkling for some days that there was mischief in the air. However, I didn't say anything to you because I didn't want the neighbors to know anything. Now I must tell you why I was so concerned. One day, as I came to the house door, I spotted a white chalk mark on it, and the next day there was a red sign beside it. Although I didn't know how the marks had been made, I put others on the entrances of various neighbors' doors, for I felt that some enemy was plotting something evil against my master. And these other marks were just like the one on your door. I'm convinced that these thieves were the ones who marked our house so that they'd be able to recognize it again. Of the forty thieves there are two remaining, and I don't know where they are. So you had better beware of them, and of course, you'd best beware of their captain, who's the most dangerous of the lot. If you should fall into his hands, he'll definitely murder you. Of course, I'll do all I can within my powers to save you from harm and your property from damage. Indeed, you may depend on me to serve you as best I can."

Upon hearing these words, Ali Baba rejoiced and said to her, "I am most pleased by the way you acted. But now you must tell me what I can do in your behalf, for I'll never forget the brave deeds you've done for me as long as I live."

"Before we talk about this," Morgiana said, "we'd better bury these bodies in the ground so that we can keep everything secret."

Heeding her advice, Ali Baba took his slave boy Abdullah into the garden, and there they dug a deep pit for the corpses of the thieves, and after taking away their weapons, they dragged the bodies to the grave and threw them into it. Then they covered the remains of the thirty-seven robbers with dirt, and they made the ground appear just as level and clean as it used to be. They also hid the leather jars, the gear, and the weapons, and thereafter, Ali Baba sent the mules by ones and twos to the bazaar and sold them all with the capable aid of his slave boy Abdullah. Thus, the matter was hushed up and never reached the ears of any of his neighbors. However, Ali Baba remained ill at ease because he thought the captain or the two surviving robbers would seek revenge. He took pains to keep everything private and made sure that nobody learned anything of what had happened and how he had managed to obtain his wealth from the bandits' cave.

Meanwhile the captain of the thieves was living in the forest full of rage and extremely upset. He had great trouble controlling his feelings, and after thinking about the matter over and over again, he finally decided that he had to take Ali Baba's life, otherwise he would lose the entire treasure, because Ali Baba knew the magic words and could return and take anything he wanted. Furthermore, the captain was resolved to undertake this task alone, and once he had gotten rid of Ali Baba, he would assemble a new band of thieves and would pursue his career of brigandage as indeed his forebears had done for many generations. So he lay down to rest that night, and after rising early in the morning, he donned some garments of suitable appearance. When he arrived at the city, he stopped at a khan, thinking to himself, "I'm sure that the murder of so many men has reached the wali's ears and that Ali Baba has been imprisoned and brought to justice. His house must be leveled by now and his goods confiscated. The townsfolk must surely have heard all about this." So, without hesitating, he asked the keeper of the khan, "What strange things have been happening in the city during the last few days?"

And the other man told him all that he had seen and heard, but the captain did not learn a thing about what concerned him most. Thus, he realized that Ali Baba was very shrewd and wise, and that he had not only carried away a good deal of the treasure and destroyed many lives, but done all this without being scathed. Furthermore, the captain realized that he himself had better keep on his toes so as not to fall into the hands of his foe and perish.

With all this in mind, he rented a shop in the bazaar, to which he brought whole bales of the finest material and expensive merchandise from the cave in the forest. Soon he took his seat inside the store and began doing business as a merchant. By chance, his place was directly across from the booth of the deceased Kasim, where his son, Ali Baba's nephew, now conducted his business. The captain, who now called himself Khwajah Hasan, soon formed an acquaintance and friendship with the shopkeepers around him and treated everyone with profuse politeness, but he was especially gracious and cordial to the son of Kasim, a well-dressed, handsome youth. Sometimes he would sit and chat with him for hours.

A few days after the robber captain had set up his business, Ali Baba chanced to come by and visit his nephew, whom he found sitting in his shop. The captain recognized him right away, and one morning he asked the young man, "Please, tell me, who is that man who comes to visit you every now and then at your shop?"

"He's my uncle," responded the young man.

From then on the captain showed him even greater favor and affection in order to make use of him when the time came. Indeed, he gave the young man presents and had him dine with him and fed him with the most delicious dishes. Soon, Ali Baba's nephew thought it was only right and proper that he should invite the merchant to have supper with him. However, his own house was small, and since he could not make a show of splendor, as had Khwajah Hasan, he asked his uncle for some advice.

And Scheherazade noticed that dawn was approaching and stopped telling her tale. When the next night arrived, however, she received the king's permission to continue her tale and said,

So Ali Baba told his nephew, "It's best to treat your friend in the same splendid way that he's treated you. So, since tomorrow is Friday, shut your shop as all the distinguished merchants do. Then, after the early meal, take Khwajah for a stroll, and as you are walking, lead him to my house. Meanwhile, I'll tell Morgiana to get a meal ready for his arrival with the best of viands and everything else necessary for a feast. Don't worry about a thing. Just leave the matter in my hands."

Accordingly, on the next day, Ali Baba's nephew took Khwajah for a walk in the large park. And as they were returning, he led him to the street where his uncle lived. When they came to the house, the youth stopped at the door, and after knocking, said, "My lord, this is my second home, and since my uncle has heard me speak a great deal about you and the kindness you have shown me, he would like to meet you. Therefore, I'd appreciate it if you would agree to visit him with me."

To be sure, the robber captain rejoiced in his heart that he had now found a way to gain access to his enemy's house and carry out his treacherous plot. But he hesitated at that moment and tried to find some excuse to walk away. However, when the door was opened by the porter, Ali Baba's nephew took his companion's hand, and after a great deal of persuasion, he led him inside. So the robber chief acted as though he were very pleased and honored when the master of the house received him with respect and said, "My lord, I am grateful to you for showing favor to the son of my brother, and I can see that you regard him with even more affection that I myself do."

Khwajah Hasan replied with pleasant words, "Your nephew has caught my fancy, and I am very pleased with him. Although he is young, Allah Almighty has endowed him with a great deal of wisdom."

Thus the two had a friendly conversation, until the guest rose to depart and said, "My lord, I must bid you farewell right now. But on some future occasion, I hope to see you again."

However, Ali Baba would not let him leave and asked, "Where are you going, my friend? I'd like to invite you to enjoy a meal with us. Afterward you can go home in peace. Perhaps my dishes will not be as delicious as those which you are accustomed to eating, but I beg you to grant my request and have dinner with me."

"My lord," replied Khwajah Hasan, "I am obliged for your gracious invitation, and I'd like to accept your offer with pleasure. However, there is a special reason why I must refuse at this time. Therefore, please allow me to depart."

To this the host responded, "Please tell me, my lord, what is it that's so urgent and important that you can't dine with me."

And Khwajah Hasan answered, "The reason is this: my physician cured me of some malady and ordered me not to eat meat prepared with salt."

"If this is all it is," said Ali Baba, "do not deprive me of the pleasure and honor of your company. If the meat has not been cooked yet, I'll tell the cook not to use any salt. Just wait here a moment, and I'll return right away."

So Ali Baba went into the kitchen and told Morgiana not to put any salt in the dishes she was preparing. Puzzled by her master's instructions, she asked him, "Who is this person that doesn't eat meat with salt?"

"What does it matter to you who it is?" Ali Baba responded. "Just do as I say."

"As you wish," she said, but she still wondered who it was that had made such a strange request and wanted very much to get a look at him. Therefore, when all the meat was ready to be served, she helped the slave boy Abdullah to spread the table and set the meat on it. No sooner had she seen Khwajah Hasan than she knew who he was even though he had disguised himself in the dress of a foreign merchant. Furthermore, when she looked more closely at him, she noticed a dagger hidden under his robe. "So, that's it!" she said to herself. "This is the reason why the villain doesn't want to eat salt. He's looking for an opportunity to slay my master! Well, I'll beat him to the punch and take care of him before he has a chance to harm my master."

Now, Morgiana went back to the kitchen and began thinking of a way to get rid of the robber captain. Meanwhile, Ali Baba and Khwajah Hasan had eaten their fill of the meat, and Abdullah brought word to Morgiana to serve the dessert. Therefore, she cleared the table and set down fresh and dried fruit in trays. Then she placed a small tripod for three cups with a flagon of wine next to Ali Baba, and lastly, she went off with Abdullah into another room as though she wanted to eat her supper there. At this point, the robber captain thought the coast was clear and felt extremely good. "The time has come for me to take full vengeance," he said to himself. "With one thrust of the dagger I'll kill this wretch, and then I can make my escape through the garden. If his nephew tries to stop me, I'll stab him and settle his accounts on earth. However, I must still wait awhile until the slave boy and cook have eaten and gone to rest in the kitchen."

Unknown to him, Morgiana watched him carefully, and since she read his intentions, she said to herself, "I must not allow this villain to take advantage of my lord. There must be some way I can stop him and put an end to his life." Accordingly, the trusty slave girl quickly changed her dress and put on some clothes that dancers generally wear. She veiled her face with a costly kerchief, bound her head with a fine turban, and tied a sash embroidered with gold and silver around her waist, in which she stuck a dagger with a jeweled hilt. After disguising herself like this, she said to Abdullah, "Take your tambourine, and let us sing and dance in honor of our master's guest."

So he did as she requested, and the two of them went into the room, the young boy playing the tambourine followed by Morgiana. Making a low bow, they asked permission to perform, and Ali Baba granted it and said, "Do your best and dance so that our guest will enjoy himself."

"My lord," said Khwajah Hasan, "you are truly entertaining me in a most pleasant way."

LOUIS RHEAD

Then Abdullah began to strike the tambourine, while Morgiana performed with graceful steps and moves. Suddenly, she drew the dagger from her sash and paced from side to side, and this spectacle pleased them most of all. At times she stood before them, clapping the sharp-edged dagger under her armpit and then setting it against her breast. Finally, she took the tambourine from Abdullah, and while still holding the poniard in her right hand, she went around for gifts of money, as was the custom among entertainers. First she stood before Ali Baba, who threw a gold coin into the tambourine, and his nephew did likewise. As she approached Khwajah Hasan, he began to pull out his purse, and taking courage, she plunged the dagger into his heart quick as lightning, and the scoundrel fell back stone dead.

Ali Baba was dismayed and cried out angrily, "What have you done? This will be the ruin of me!"

But she replied, "No, my lord, I have slain this man to prevent him from harming you. Undo his garments and see what you will find there."

So Ali Baba searched the dead man's clothes and found a dagger concealed there. Then Morgiana said, "This wretch was your mortal enemy. Look at him carefully, for he is none other than the oil merchant and captain of the robbers. He came here to take your life, and when he would not eat your salt and you told me about this, I suspected something was wrong. After I got a look at him I was certain that he was the robber captain and that he had come to kill you. Praise be to Allah, for it was exactly as I thought it was."

Then Ali Baba lavished thanks upon her and said, "You have saved me from his hand two times, and now I grant you your freedom. And as a further reward for your fidelity, I am going to wed you to my nephew." Then, turning to the youth, he said, "Do as I bid you, and you will prosper. I want you to marry Morgiana, who is a model of duty and loyalty. You see now how this man only sought your friendship so that he could take my life, but this maiden, with her good sense and wisdom, has slain him and saved us."

Ali Baba's nephew consented to marry Morgiana on the spot. After reaching this agreement, the three of them lifted the dead body and carried it carefully into the garden, where they buried it as quickly as possible. For many years thereafter, nobody knew a thing about this.

In due time, Ali Baba married Morgiana to his nephew in great pomp and held a sumptuous wedding feast for his friends and neighbors. It was a joyful event with singing, dancing, and other entertainment. Thereafter, Ali Baba prospered in everything he undertook, and time smiled upon him as new sources of wealth were opened to him. For fear of the thieves, he did not return to the cave for a long time after his brother's death.

But one day, after some years had passed, he mounted his horse and journeyed there with care and caution. Since he did not find any signs of man or beast, he ventured to draw near the door. Then he got off his horse, tied it to a tree, and went to the entrance, where he pronounced the words, which he had not forgotten: "Open, Sesame!" As usual, the door flew open, and after entering, Ali Baba saw the goods and hoard of gold and silver untouched and lying exactly as he had left them. So he was convinced that none of the thieves remained alive, and with the exception of himself, there was not a soul who knew the secret of the place. Therefore, he carried a load of coins outside, put them in his saddlebags, and took the gold home with him. In the years that followed he showed the hoard to his sons and grandsons and taught them how the door could be opened and shut. Thus, Ali Baba and his family lived all their lives in wealth and joy in that city where he had once been a pauper. Thanks to the blessed secret treasure, he rose to a respectable position and became a dignified man.

No sooner had Scheherazade concluded her tale than she said, "And yet, oh king, this tale is no more wondrous than the remarkable story of 'Aladdin and the Magic Lamp.' "

Aladdin and the Magic Lamp

A long time ago in a city of China there lived a poor tailor with his only son, Aladdin. Now this boy had been obstinate and lazy ever since the day he was born, and when he became ten, his father wanted him to learn a proper trade, but since he lacked the money to pay for his son's apprenticeship in another craft, he had to take the boy into his own shop and teach him how to use a needle. However, since Aladdin was so stubborn and idle and preferred to play with the scamps in the neighborhood, he did not spend a single day in the shop. Instead, he would wait for his father to leave the shop for some reason or other, like paying a debt, and then he would run off at once to the gardens to be with some other little scoundrels. Such was his situation, and neither punishment nor good advice would help. He would not obey his parents or learn a trade. As a result his father became so sick due to his son's vicious personality and indolence that he died.

Despite his father's death, Aladdin continued to carry on as badly as he had done in the past, and when his mother saw that her son would not change, she sold the shop with all its contents and began spinning yarn to make a living. This work enabled her to feed herself and Aladdin, who became increasingly more lazy and wayward, especially when he no longer had to fear his father's stern reproaches. Indeed, the only time he came home was for his meals. Otherwise, his poor mother continued to toil for the both of them, while he persisted in his idle ways until he turned fifteen.

One day, while Aladdin was playing in the neighborhood with some of the other vagabonds, a dervish from Maghrib, the Land of the Setting Sun, came by and began gazing at the boys. However, he did not appear to notice anyone except Aladdin and kept staring at him. Now, this dervish, a Moor from the interior of Morocco, was a sorcerer whose magic powers were so powerful that he could turn mountains upside down. Moreover, he was adept in astrology, and after looking at Aladdin very closely, he said to himself, "This is the boy I've been searching for ever since I left my native land." So he took one of Aladdin's friends aside and began asking questions about him, such as who his father was. And he tried to learn all he could about Aladdin and the circumstances of his life. Once he was satisfied, the magician walked up to Aladdin, drew him aside, and asked, "My son, aren't you the son of the tailor Mustafa?"

"Yes, my lord," the boy answered, "but he died a long time ago."

Upon hearing these words, the Moor threw his arms around Aladdin, embraced him, and begin kissing him, while tears trickled down his cheeks. Of course, the boy was surprised by the magician's behavior, and he asked, "Why are you weeping, my lord? Did you know my father?"

"How can you ask me a question like that, my son?" replied the Moor. "Don't you realize how sad it makes me to learn that your father, who was my brother, is now dead? I was living in exile for many years and looked forward with joy to seeing him again and talking about the past, but now you've told me that he's passed away. But blood is thicker than water, and I had a feeling that you were my brother's son. I recognized you at once among all the boys. Of course, when I left the country your father had yet to marry. Unfortunately I've lost the joyous opportunity of seeing my brother again and have also missed the funeral services. But this was all due to the fact that I was far away and that Almighty Allah had decreed that this was the way it was to be—and there is no tinkering with fate. Now, my son, you are my only joy and comfort, and you are his replacement. As the saying goes, 'He who leaves an heir does not die.' "

After the Moor had spoken these words, he stuck his hand into his purse, pulled out ten gold pieces, and gave them to Aladdin. "My son, take this money and give it to your mother with greetings from me. Let her know that your uncle has returned from exile and that, God willing, I'll visit her tomorrow to see the house where my brother lived and also to have a look at his burial site."

Thereupon Aladdin kissed the Moor's hand, and after running at full speed and with great joy to his mother's house, he entered and surprised her, for he never came home except at mealtimes. "Mother!" he exclaimed in his delight. "I've come to bring you good news about my uncle, who's returned from his exile and has sent me to greet you."

"My son," she replied, "you're mocking me. Who is this uncle of yours? And since when have you ever had a living uncle?"

"How can you say that I don't have living uncles or relatives when this man is my father's brother?" Aladdin cried. "Indeed, he embraced and kissed me. And when he heard about my father's death, he wept bitter tears, and then he told me to inform you about his arrival."

"My son," she responded. "I know very well that you had an uncle once. But he's dead, and I was not aware that you had another."

The next morning the magician went looking for Aladdin, for his heart could not bear to be separated from him. As he wandered about the city, he finally encountered him, playing in the streets with other scamps and vagabonds, as he usually did. When the Moor approached him, he took Aladdin's hand, embraced him, and kissed him. Then he pulled two dinars from his pocket and said, "Go to your mother and give her these ducats. Tell her that your uncle intends to eat with you this evening and that she should prepare a delicious supper for us. But before you do this, show me the way to your house once more."

"Just follow me, uncle," said Aladdin, and he ran ahead, pointing out the street leading to the house.

Then the Moor left him and went his way, while Aladdin ran home and gave the ducats and the news to his mother. So she arose right away and went to the market, where she bought all that she needed. After returning to her dwelling, she borrowed pans and platters from her neighbors, and when the meal was cooked and suppertime came, she said to Aladdin, "My child, the meat is ready, but perhaps your uncle does not know the way to our dwelling. So go out and meet him on the road."

"As you wish," he replied, but before the two could finish their conversation, they heard a knock at the door, and when Aladdin opened it, the Moor stood there attended by a eunuch, who was carrying wine and fruit. So the boy let them in, and the slave went about his business. After entering, the Moor greeted his sister-in-law with a salaam, began to shed tears, and said, "Show me the place where my brother used to sit."

She pointed to the place, and the Moor went to it, prostrated himself in prayer, and kissed the floor. "How meager is my satisfaction!" he cried out. "How unfortunate I am, for I've lost you, brother, light of my eyes!"

And he continued weeping and wailing like this until he fainted. Consequently, Aladdin's mother was convinced that he was sincere and that he really was her husband's brother. She went over to him, and after lifting him up from the floor, she said, "Please stop, or else you'll kill yourself."

And Scheherazade noticed that dawn was approaching and stopped telling her story. When the next night arrived, however, she received the king's permission to continue her tale and said,

Aladdin's mother began consoling the Moor and led him to the couch. As soon as he was seated at his ease and was waiting for the food to be served, he began talking to her and said, "You must be wondering, my good sister-in-law, why you never saw me or knew anything about me while my late brother was alive. The reason for this is that I left this city forty years ago and wandered all over the lands of India, Sind, and Arabia and finally settled down in the magnificent city of Cairo in Egypt, which is one of the wonders of the world. Thereafter I traveled to the interior of Morocco, where I lived for thirty years. Then, one day, as I was sitting alone at home, I began thinking about my native land and my late brother, and my yearning to see him became so strong that I bemoaned my exile and the distance between my brother and myself. Finally, I decided to return to my birthplace and to see my brother once more, saying to myself, 'Oh you unhappy man, how long will you wander like a nomad from your birthplace and native land? You only have one brother and no more. So, rise and return to him before you die. Who knows what might happen to you and what changes might happen in the course of time? It would be most sad if you died without ever seeing your brother again. Allah has blessed you with ample wealth, and your brother might not be as fortunate as you are, whereby you might be able to help him in his distress.' So, I arose at once, prepared myself for the journey, and recited the Fatihah. After the Friday prayers ended, I mounted my steed and traveled to this city, suffering many hardships and encountering all sorts of dangers along the way, but I patiently endured them and was blessed by the Lord's protection, until I reached my goal. After I entered the city, I wandered about, and the day before yesterday I saw Aladdin playing with some boys on the street. By God, the moment I saw him, my heart went out to him, and I felt deep down that he was my nephew, for we are of the same blood. In fact, as soon as I spotted him, I forgot my trials and tribulations and became ecstatic. However, when he told me about his father's death, I fainted out of disappointment. Perhaps he has told you how sorrowful I was and how I reacted. Nevertheless, I'm somewhat consoled by the sight of Aladdin, my brother's son, for whoever leaves an heir does not die."

After hearing these words, Aladdin's mother began to weep, and the Moor now sought a way to complete his deception. So, while he comforted her, he turned to Aladdin and asked, "My son, what craft have you learned? What work do you do to support yourself and your mother?"

The boy was abashed and put to shame. He hung his head and lowered his eyes, but his mother spoke out, "What work? Indeed, he's never learned a thing. I've never seen such an ungrateful child as this one! Never! He wastes the entire day with the other scamps and vagabonds of the neighborhood like himself. He drove his father to his grave, and he'll do the same with me, too. I spin cotton and toil at the spinning wheel day and night so that I can earn a couple of scones of bread that we eat together. By the life of me, the only time I see my son is at mealtimes and none other. Indeed, I've been thinking about locking the house door and never opening it to him again. Then he'll have to go and seek a livelihood and earn a living. After all, I've gotten on in years and no longer have the strength to work the way I do. By Allah, I'm forced to provide him with his daily bread when I'm the one who should be provided for!"

Upon hearing this, the Moor turned to Aladdin and said, "Why are you doing this, nephew? Why are you so ungrateful? Your behavior is disgraceful and unworthy. You're a sensible young man, and the child of honest folk. Indeed, you should be ashamed that your mother at her age should have to struggle to support you. Now that you've reached manhood, it is incumbent upon you to learn some trade and to support yourself. Praise be to Allah, there are numerous craftsmen in this city, and there are many different trades. So choose something you would like to learn, and I'll help you get established. Later, when you're grown up, you'll be able to support yourself in your own business. Perhaps you didn't like your father's profession, and if that's the case, then choose some other craft that may suit you better. Then let me know, and I'll help you as best I can."

However, Aladdin kept silent, and the Moor realized that Aladdin preferred to continue living the life of a freeloader and vagabond. So he said to the boy, "I did not mean to be so harsh and severe, nephew. If you really don't want to learn a craft, despite all that I've said, I'll open a merchant's shop for you and furnish it with expensive stuffs. Then you can deal and trade with other merchants and become well known in the city."

Now, when Aladdin heard his uncle's words and his plan of making him a merchant and gentleman, he rejoiced, for he was quite aware of the fact that these people dressed in fine garments and had sumptuous meals. So he looked at the Moor, smiled, and nodded his head to show that he was content.

"Well now," said the Moor, "since you're willing to let me open a shop for you and make a gentleman out of you, then I'll take you to the bazaar first thing tomorrow morning, God willing, and I'll have a fine suit of clothes cut out for you like the one merchants wear. After that I'll look for a store for you, as I've promised."

Up to this point, Aladdin's mother still had some doubts as to whether the Moor was her brother-in-law, but when she heard his promise of opening up a merchant's shop for her son and providing him with stuffs and capital, she cast them to the wind and decided that the Moor was in truth her husband's brother, for a stranger would never do as much as he was doing for Aladdin. So she advised her son to mend his ways, get rid of his foolish ideas, and prove himself a man. Moreover, she told him to obey his excellent uncle as though he were the Moor's son and to make up for all the time he had wasted with his vagabond friends. After this she rose, set the table, and served the supper, whereupon they all sat down and began eating and drinking. During the meal, the Moor conversed with Aladdin about business matters and other similar topics so that later that night, after the Moor had departed and promised to return early the next morning, Aladdin could barely sleep for joy.

Indeed, as soon as dawn arrived, the Moor knocked at the door, and Aladdin's mother opened to let him in. However, the Moor would not enter. Instead, he asked permission to take the boy to the market, and Aladdin went straight to him, wished him good morning, and kissed his hand. Then the Moor took him to a clothier's shop at the bazaar and asked to look at expensive suits that were finely tailored and ready to wear. The merchant brought him what he desired, and the Moor said to the boy, "Choose whatever you like."

Aladdin was extremely happy about his uncle's generosity, and he picked out the suit that pleased him most, whereupon the Moor paid the merchant for the garments, and they left. Soon the Moor led the boy to the Hammam baths, and after they bathed, they drank sherbets together. Then Aladdin arose, put on his new garments with great joy, and went to his uncle, kissed his hand, and thanked him for all his favors.

When they left the Hammam, the Moor took Aladdin to the bazaar again and showed him how people traded at the market, buying and selling, and he said, "My son, it's important for you to become familiar with the people here, especially the merchants, so that you can learn their business, now that you are one of them." Then he showed Aladdin the city with its mosques and other interesting sights. Finally, they entered a cookery, where dinner was served to them on silver platters. After eating and drinking their fill, they continued on their walk, and the Moor took Aladdin to the parks, the magnificent buildings, and the sultan's palace, where they visited the grand and elegant apartments. Finally, they went to the khan of foreign merchants, where the Moor had taken his lodgings, and he invited various traders to have supper with them and told them that Aladdin was his nephew. By the time they had finished their meal, it was dark, and the Moor rose up and took the boy back to his mother, who mistook her son for a merchant but was extremely delighted when she recognized him. Immediately, she began expressing her gratitude toward her false brother-in-law for his kindness and said, "I can never thank you enough for your generosity. You're most kind."

"Please don't consider this mere kindness," said the Moor. "The boy is my own son, and it is incumbent on me to assume the role of my brother, his sire. So I hope you will be satisfied."

"May Allah bless you and grant you long life for my sake so that you may keep this orphan under your wing. And I hope that he will be obedient and do whatever you ask him to do."

"Aladdin has now become a man of good sense," the Moor replied. "I pray to Allah that he will follow in his father's footsteps and be a comfort to you in your old age. But I regret that tomorrow being Friday, I shall not be able to open his shop, since it is the day when all the merchants go to the parks and gardens after congregational prayer. On Saturday, however, we shall start his business, Allah willing. Meanwhile, tomorrow I'll come and take Aladdin for a pleasant stroll to see the parks and gardens outside the city that he has perhaps never seen before. He'll also be able to see the merchants and notables who go there and make their acquaintance."

After saying this, the Moor went away and spent the night at the khan.

* * *

And Scheherazade noticed that dawn was approaching and stopped telling her story. When the next night arrived, however, she received the king's permission to continue her tale and said,

Early the next morning the Moor arrived at Aladdin's house and knocked at the door. Now, after all the delights that the boy had experienced the day before, he had not been able to sleep a wink all night and could hardly wait until daybreak. So as soon as he heard the knock, he rushed to the door, opened it, and saw his uncle, the magician, who embraced and kissed him. Then, as they began walking, the Moor said to him, "Nephew, today I'm going to show you a sight that you've never seen before in your life." And he began to make the boy laugh and cheer him up with his pleasant talk.

Once they left the city gate, the Moor took him through the gardens and pointed out the fine buildings and marvelous pavilions. Whenever they stopped and stared at a mansion or palace, the Moor would ask Aladdin whether he liked it. Indeed, the boy was ecstatic and in seventh heaven because of the sights he had never seen in his entire life. Thus, they continued to stroll about and enjoy themselves until they became tired. Then they entered a huge wonderful garden that was nearby, a place that delighted their hearts and eyes, for it had a fountain that spouted water from the jaws of a golden lion, and the water flowed swiftly among an abundance of flowers. They found a nice place to sit down in the garden near a pond and rested a little while. Soon Aladdin began to jest with the magician and to have fun with him as though the Moor were really his father's brother. Then the Moor stood up, loosened his belt, and pulled out a bag full of dried fruits and other good things to eat.

"Perhaps you're hungry, nephew," he said. "Take whatever you'd like to eat."

Aladdin responded by sticking his hand into the bag, and the Moor ate with him. After they were refreshed and rested, the magician said, "Get up, nephew. If you're no longer tired, let's stroll onward and finish our walk."

Thereupon Aladdin arose, and the Moor accompanied him from garden to garden until they had left them all behind and reached the base of a huge and barren hill.

Since the boy had never gone beyond the city gates and had never taken such an extensive walk as this, he asked the Moor, "Where are we going, uncle? We've left the gardens behind us, and there's nothing but open country from here on. I'm tired and can't go on. So if there are no more gardens after this, let's return to the city."

"No, my son," said the magician. "This is the right way. You see, there are more gardens after this, and we're going to look at one that is more splendid than any royal garden in the world and beyond comparison with those you have just seen. So, pluck up your courage. You're a man now. Praise be to Allah!"

The Moor began to cajole the boy and to tell him wondrous tales, true stories as well as lies, until they reached the spot the magician had come all the way from Morocco to China to see. Upon arriving at their destination, the Moor said to Aladdin, "Nephew, sit down and take a rest, for this is the spot we've been looking for. If Allah is merciful, I'll soon be able to show you marvelous things that nobody in the whole world has ever seen before. Indeed, no one has ever had the pleasure of viewing that which you are about to see."

After they had relaxed awhile, the Moor spoke again. "Once you have rested, my son, I want you to get up and look for some wood chips and dry sticks so that we can start a fire. Then I'll show you things beyond your imagination."

Now, when Aladdin heard these words, he longed to see what his uncle intended to do, and forgetting how tired he was, he arose right away and began gathering small wood chips and dry sticks until the Moor cried to him, "Enough, nephew! Enough!"

Soon the magician took out a small box from his breast pocket, and after opening it, he took some incense, set fire to the wood, and sprinkled the incense on the fire. Then he conjured and uttered some strange words, and the sky darkened. Suddenly there was a burst of thunder, and the ground split open. Aladdin was so startled and frightened that he wanted to flee, but the Moor saw this and grew extremely angry, for without the boy his work would come to nothing. It was only with Aladdin's help that he would be able to obtain and open the hidden treasure. So he got up and gave the boy such a hard smack on the back of his head that his back teeth were almost knocked out, and Aladdin fell to the ground in a swoon. After a while the Moor revived him with some magic, and Aladdin wept and asked, "Uncle, what have I done to deserve such a beating?"

In response, the Moor began to comfort him and said, "My boy, it is my intention to make a man out of you. Therefore, don't contradict me, for I'm your uncle, and you are like a son to me. Obey everything that I tell you to do, and soon you'll forget all your hardships and become absorbed by all the marvels I'm about to show you."

Then the Moor looked down into the crack in the ground and showed Aladdin a marble slab that had a copper ring attached to it. After striking a geomantic table, he turned to Aladdin and said, "If you do everything I tell you, you'll become richer than all the kings of the world. That's why I struck you. There is a treasure down there in your name, and you were about to run away and abandon it. But now, pull yourself together."

And Scheherazade noticed that dawn was approaching and stopped telling her story. When the next night arrived, however, she received the king's permission to continue her tale and said,

"The treasure is under that marble slab," the Moor continued, "so place your hand on the ring and raise the slab. Nobody but yourself has the power to open it, and no mortal on this earth except yourself may set foot in this hidden place, for the treasure has been destined for you. But you must follow all my instructions carefully and remember every word I tell you. All this, my son, is for your own good. The treasure is of immense value, and it is worth more than any king on this earth has ever accumulated. Bear in mind that we shall share all this together."

So poor Aladdin forgot the slap on his head and his tears. Indeed, he was dumbfounded and overjoyed that he was fated to become richer than a sultan. Therefore, he cried out, "Uncle, tell me what to do, and I'll obey all your orders."

"Nephew," replied the magician, "you are like my

own child and even dearer to me because you are my brother's son. Since I have no other relatives, you will be my heir and successor." After saying this, he went over to Aladdin and kissed him. "Now you know why I have done all this work. It has been all for your sake, my son. You will become a rich and great man. So do exactly as I tell you, and go to the ring and lift it."

"But, uncle," Aladdin answered, "the ring is much too heavy for me. I can't lift it all by myself. You must come and help me, for you're stronger than I am."

"Nephew," the Moor replied, "if I help you, all our work will be in vain. You must place your hand on the ring and pull it, and the slab will rise right away. Remember, I told you that nobody can touch the ring but you. However, while you are raising it, you must pronounce your name and the names of your father and mother, and you'll see that you'll be able to lift the slab with ease."

Thereupon the boy mustered up his strength and set his mind to the task. He followed the Moor's instructions carefully, and before he knew it, he had lifted the slab and had cast it aside. Right below him was a stairway with twelve steps that led to a subterranean cave.

"Aladdin," the Moor said, "get a grip on yourself and do exactly what I tell you. I want you to descend the stairs to the vault as carefully as possible. Once you are at the bottom, you will find a space divided into four apartments, and in each one of these you will see four golden jars and other valuable articles made of gold and silver. Beware of all these things! Do not touch them or allow your garments to even brush the jars or the walls! Leave them where they are and continue walking forward until you reach the fourth apartment. If you don't do what I say, you'll be turned into a black stone. Now, when you reach the fourth apartment, you'll find a door, which you will open, and after pronouncing the words that you spoke over the slab, you're to enter and go through a garden adorned by fruit trees. The path that you're to take is about fifty yards long, and it leads to a terrace that has a ladder with some thirty rungs. And you will also see a lamp hanging from the ceiling of the terrace. You're to climb the ladder and take the lamp. After pouring out the contents, place it in your breast pocket. You don't have to worry about damaging your clothes, since the contents are not made of common oil. On your return, you may pluck whatever you want from the trees, for they are yours as long as the lamp is in your hands."

Now, when the Moor finished giving his instructions to Aladdin, he drew a ring from his finger, placed it on one of Aladdin's, and said, "My son, this ring will protect you from all harm and threat, but only on the condition that you bear in mind all that I've told you. So it's up to you now. Go to it, and be brave and determined. You're a man now and no longer a child. And very soon, you'll be the richest man in the world."

Eagerly, Aladdin descended into the cave, where he found the four apartments, each containing four jars of gold. He walked by them with utmost care and caution, just as the Moor had told him to do. From there, he entered the garden and walked down the path until he came upon the terrace, where he mounted the ladder and took the lamp, which he extinguished by pouring out the oil. After placing the lamp in his breast pocket, he descended the ladder and returned to the garden, where he began gazing at the trees and noticed that the birds were singing songs in praise of the Great Creator. Now, he had not realized upon entering that all the trees were covered with costly gems as their fruit, Moreover, each one had a different kind of jewel with various colors of green, white, yellow, and red. They all glistened, and their radiance made the rays of the sun in its midday brightness appear pale in comparison. Indeed, the size of each stone was beyond description, and it was evident that there was not a king in the world who owned a single gem equal to the larger sort or who could boast of even one that was half the size of a smaller kind.

Aladdin began walking among the trees and was surprised and bewildered by what he saw. In place of common fruit, there were all sorts of fine jewels and precious stones such as emeralds, diamonds, rubies, spinels, balasses, pearls, and other gems that were dazzling to the eyes. And since the boy had never seen anything like this in all his livelong days, and since he had no idea of the worth of such valuables (he being still but a boy), he thought that all these jewels were made of glass or crystal. So he gathered them and began filling his pockets, checking to see whether they were fruit such as grapes or figs. However, he found that they were all made of some glassy substance and said to himself, "They'll make wonderful playthings when I get home." He continued plucking numerous gems and crammed them in his pockets until they were stuffed full. After that he picked others and placed them in his belt and the folds of his garments. Then he hurried back along the path for fear that his uncle might become angry with him. As he went through the four apartments and passed by the four jars of gold, he did not touch them, even though he would have been allowed to take some of the contents on his way back. Finally, when he came to the stairs of the cave, he began climbing until he reached the last step. However, finding that this one was higher than all the others, he needed help to mount it. So he said to the Moor, "Oh uncle, lend me a hand so I can climb out."

But the magician answered, "First give me the lamp and lighten your load. It's probably weighing you down."

"It's not the lamp that's weighing me down," Aladdin responded. "Just lend me a hand, and as soon as I reach the ground, I'll give it to you."

Since the Moor's only goal was to obtain the lamp and none other, he began to insist that Aladdin give it to him at once. But the boy had placed it at the bottom of his breast pocket and his other pockets were bulging with gems. Therefore, he could not reach it with his fingers to hand it over, causing the magician to explode with rage. Indeed, the Moor persisted in demanding the lamp, while poor Aladdin could not get at it. Thinking that the boy wanted to keep the lamp for himself, the magician was now convinced that he would not be able to obtain it. In his fury he ran over to the fire, threw more incense on it, and uttered some magic words. Within seconds the power of the magic caused the marble slab to slide over the entrance to the cave, preventing Aladdin's escape.

Now, as I mentioned before, the sorcerer was really a stranger and was not related to Aladdin in any way. He had lied to the boy and had used him only so that he could obtain the treasure that had been intended for Aladdin. This Moor was an African, born in the interior of Morocco, and from his childhood on, he had been addicted to witchcraft and had studied and practiced ev-

LOVIS RHEAD

ery kind of occult science. Indeed, the city of Tunis itself is notorious for this unholy lore, and he continued to read and hear lectures there until he became a master in all kinds of sorcery and spells that he had acquired after forty years of study. Then one day he discovered through a satanic inspiration that there was a treasure hidden in one of the remote cities of China named Al-Kal'áas, a treasure that no king on earth could ever match. The most marvelous thing in this enchanted treasure was a wonderful lamp, and whoever possessed this magic lamp would become the richest man on earth and mightier than any king of the universe. However, the magician discovered that this treasure could only be opened by a poor boy named Aladdin, who lived in that Chinese city, and after he ascertained how easy it would be to obtain the lamp through the boy, he traveled to China and did what he did with Aladdin, thinking that he would become lord of the lamp. But when his attempt and hopes were thwarted and all his work went to waste, he decided to let the boy die there and heaped the soil on top of the entrance while saying to himself, "I have not touched a hand to him, and hence there is no murder." Once he was sure that it would be impossible for the boy to escape with the lamp, he made his way back to Africa, sad and dejected.

So much for the magician.

As for Aladdin, he began shouting to the Moor when he heard the earth being heaped on top of the marble slab, for he still believed that the magician was his uncle. He begged him to lend a hand so that he might get out of the cave, but no matter how loudly he yelled, there was no reply. Soon it became apparent to him that the Moor had deceived him, and that the man was no uncle but a liar and a wizard. Consequently, poor Aladdin became desperate, for he was certain there was no escape. After weeping awhile about his misfortune, he stood up and descended the stairs to see if Allah Almighty had somehow provided him with a way of escape. He turned to the right and to the left but saw nothing but darkness and four walls, for the sorcerer had locked all the doors through magic and had even cut him off from the garden to make sure that the boy would die. Then Aladdin's weeping became greater, and his wailing louder when he found all the doors shut tight, especially since he had hoped to find some solace in the garden. So there was nothing to do but to return and sit upon the stairs that led to the entrance of the cave.

And Scheherazade noticed that dawn was approaching and stopped telling her story. When the next night arrived, however, she received the king's permission to continue her tale and said,

As Aladdin sat on the stairs in utter misery and wept about his predicament, he began rubbing his hands together, as people who are in trouble generally do, and he raised them in prayer to Allah and begged for mercy. While he was thus imploring the Lord and chafing his hands, his fingers chanced to rub the ring that the sorcerer had given to him for his protection. All at once, there was some smoke and an enormous jinnee appeared before him and said, "I'm at your service, master! Your slave has come. Ask whatever you want, for I am the thrall of whoever wears my lord and master's ring."

Aladdin trembled at the sight of this ifrit, for he was as huge and terrifying as one of Solomon's jinn. However, when he recalled that the ifrit was to obey him because he was wearing the ring, he recovered his spirits. In fact, he was overjoyed and cried out boldly, "Slave of the ring, I want you to carry me to the face of the earth."

No sooner had he spoken than the ground split open, and he found himself outside at the entrance to the treasure in full view of the world. Since he had been sitting in the darkness of the cave for three whole days, the bright light of the sun hurt his eyes, and he was unable to keep them open. So he had to accustom himself to the light gradually to regain his vision. Astounded to be above earth once more, he thought at first that he was at some other place than the entrance to the cave. But then he saw the spot where they had lit the fire of wood chips and dried sticks and where the magician had uttered the magic spells over the incense. Then he turned right and left and caught sight of the gardens from afar, and his eyes recognized the road that they had taken. So he thanked Allah Almighty, who had brought him back to the face of the earth and had freed him from death after he had given up all hope of living. Soon he arose and walked toward the city until he reached the streets and made his way home. When he went into his apartment and saw his mother, he was so overcome by joy and so relieved to be at home again that he fainted right in front of her.

Now his mother had been very sad since he had left her and had rejoiced when he entered the apartment. However, when he sank to the ground in a swoon before her eyes, she was extremely upset and rushed to sprinkle some water on his face. Then she obtained some scents from the neighbors that she had him sniff. When he came around a little, he asked her to bring him some food and told her, "It's been three days since I've had anything to eat."

Thereupon she fetched him what she had on hand, set it before him, and said, "Come, my son, eat and refresh yourself. After you've rested, you can tell me what happened to you. At this point, I won't ask you any questions, for you seem quite exhausted to me."

After Aladdin had finished eating and drinking and had recovered his spirits, he began scolding his mother for leaving him in the hands of the magician. "I want you to know, Mother," he said, "that he intended to take my life. That man, who you said was my uncle, was a scoundrel, and if Almighty Allah had not rescued me from him, I would have been destroyed. Mother, the man was a sorcerer, liar, and hypocrite. I don't think there's a devil under the earth worse than he is. His only wish was to use me so he could obtain what he wanted, and then he planned to do away with me. His fondness for me was all show, and he wasn't interested in my welfare at all. Listen to what he did."

Then Aladdin told her about everything that had happened and wept as he related his adventures to her. At one point during his story he took out the lamp from his breast pocket to show it to her along with the gems and jewels he had brought from the garden, still unaware of their great value. When he finally concluded his story, he heaped abuse on the magician with a burning heart and in great anger.

"Truly," his mother said, "that man is a dangerous criminal and hypocrite who murders people with his magic.

Praise be to Allah, who saved you from the magician's treachery. I honestly thought he was your uncle."

Then, since the boy had not slept a wink for three days and found himself nodding, he went to sleep, and his mother did likewise. Indeed, he did not awake until about noon on the second day, and as soon as he shook off his slumber, he asked his mother for some food. However, she replied, "My son, I have nothing in the house, since you ate everything there was the day before. Be patient and wait until I finish spinning some yarn. Then I'll carry it to the market and buy some food for you with the money I earn from selling it."

"Mother," said he, "keep your yarn. Don't sell it. Just fetch me the lamp I brought with me. I'll go and sell it and buy some food with the money I earn. I'm sure that it will bring in more money than what you can get for your yarn."

So Aladdin's mother arose and fetched the lamp for her son. But while she was doing it, she saw that it was exceedingly dirty and said, "My son, here's the lamp, but it is filthy. I think that it will sell for more if we wash and polish it."

Then, taking a handful of sand, she began to rub the lamp with it. However, all of a sudden, a gigantic jinnee appeared, and he was just as horrifying as he was huge.

"Tell me what you want, mistress," the jinnee cried. "I am your slave and beholden to anyone who holds the lamp. Not only am I your slave, but so are all the other slaves of the lamp."

Aladdin's mother was so overcome with fright that she became tongue-tied and could not respond. Never in her life had she seen such an awesome figure, and she fell to the ground in a swoon. Now, Aladdin was standing at some distance, and he had already seen the jinnee of the ring that he had accidentally rubbed while he had been in the cave. Therefore, when he heard the slave talking to his mother, he rushed over and snatched the lamp from her hand.

"Oh, slave of the lamp," he said, "I am hungry, and I want you to fetch me something to eat. And let it be something delicious and sumptuous."

The jinnee disappeared for a split second and then returned with a vast silver tray loaded with twelve golden platters of different kinds of meat, delicious dainties, and bread whiter than snow. Moreover, there were two silver cups and many flasks of clear wine of the very best vintage. After setting all these things before Aladdin, he vanished from sight. Then Aladdin went and sprinkled rose water on his mother's face and revived her with some pure and pungent perfumes.

"Get up, Mother," he said, "and let us eat this food that Allah Almighty has provided for us."

But when she saw the vast silver tray, she was astounded and asked, "Who is this generous benefactor that has decided to help against our hunger and poverty? We are truly obliged to him. I think it may even be the sultan, who most likely heard about our dire need and misery and sent us this tray of food."

"Mother," Aladdin said, "this is no time for asking questions. Arise, and let us eat, for we are both famished."

Accordingly, they sat down to the tray and began eating, and Aladdin's mother tasted meat that she had never had the pleasure of tasting before. Indeed, they devoured the food in front of them with an appetite fit for kings. Neither one of them knew how valuable the tray was, for never in their born days had they seen the likes of it. As soon as they had finished the meal (leaving just enough for supper and the next day), they got up and washed their hands and chatted for a while. Then the mother turned to her son and said, "Tell me, Aladdin, now that we've eaten, what you did with the jinnee. You no longer have the excuse of saying, 'I'm hungry.' "

So Aladdin told her all that had taken place between him and the slave while she had been unconscious on the ground. His story caused her to be very surprised, and she said, "It's true that the jinnees do appear to humans, but I myself never saw one before this. He's probably the same one who rescued you while you were in the cave."

"It's not the same one, Mother," Aladdin replied. "The ifrit you saw is the slave of the lamp. The other was the slave of the ring and had a different shape."

When his mother heard these words, she cried, "You mean that accursed one who appeared before me and almost killed me is attached to the lamp?"

"Yes," he replied.

"Then, I beg you, my son," she said, "by the milk with

which I suckled you, throw away the lamp and the ring! They can only cause us a great deal of terror, and I couldn't bear to look at that jinnee a second time. Moreover, it is unlawful to have relations with them. Remember that the Prophet warned us against them, and may Allah bless and preserve him!"

"I shall take your concern to heart, Mother," Aladdin responded, "but it's impossible for me to part with the lamp or the ring. You yourself have seen how well the slave provided for us when we were famished. Moreover, that liar, the magician, sent me down into the cave not for the silver or the gold that filled the four apartments. Rather he wanted the lamp and nothing else, because he had learned about its priceless value. If he hadn't been sure about this, he would not have gone to so much trouble and suffered so much hardship, nor would he have traveled from his own country to ours in search of it. Indeed, he wouldn't have buried me in the cave after he had given up hope of obtaining the lamp from me. Therefore, we must keep this lamp and make certain not to disclose its secret powers to anyone. It is now the means of our livelihood and will make us rich. The same is true about the ring, which I shall never withdraw from my finger, since without it I would not be with you here today. Indeed, I would have died with the treasures in the cave. So how could you possibly ask me to remove it from my finger? And who knows what troubles and predicaments I may have in the future? I may need this ring to save my life again. However, since I know how you feel, I'll hide the lamp from your sight so that you'll never have to lay your eyes on it again."

When his mother heard his words and thought about them, she knew that he was right and said, "Do as you wish, my son. As far as I am concerned, I don't ever want anything to do with them, nor do I ever want to see that frightful sight again."

And Scheherazade noticed that dawn was approaching and stopped telling her story. When the next night arrived, however, she received the king's permission to continue her tale and said,

Aladdin and his mother continued eating the food that

the jinnee had brought them the next two days until it was all gone. Then Aladdin took one of the platters that the slave had brought upon the tray to the bazaar in order to sell it. He was still unaware that it was made of the finest gold imaginable, and he approached a Jew, who was shrewder than the devil himself to offer it for sale. When the Jew caught sight of it, he took the boy aside so that nobody might see him, and he examined the platter until he was certain that it was made of gold. However, since he did not know whether Aladdin realized its actual value or was naive, he asked him, "How much do you want for this platter?"

"You know what it's worth," replied the boy.

The Jew debated with himself as to how much he should offer, because Aladdin had given him a cunning reply. At first he thought of a small sum, but at the same time, he feared that the boy might be expecting a considerable amount. So he said to himself, "I had better make him a halfway decent offer even though he might be an ignoramus." So he pulled out a dinar from his pocket, and when Aladdin eyed the gold coin, he hastily took it from the Jew's palm and went his way. Thereupon the Jew realized that the boy had no idea of the platter's worth and regretted that he had not given him a copper carat instead of a gold dinar. In the meantime, Aladdin went straight to the baker's shop, where he bought bread and changed the ducat. Then he went to his mother and gave her the scones and the change from the ducat.

"Mother," he said, "take this money and buy whatever we need."

So she arose, walked to the bazaar, and brought back whatever they needed for the household. Afterward they had a fine meal and were refreshed. And whenever the food ran out, Aladdin would take another platter and carry it to the accursed Jew, who bought each and every one of them at the pitiful price of a dinar. He would even have tried to lower this price to next to nothing, but seeing how he had paid a dinar for the first platter, he feared to offer a lesser sum in case the boy might go to one of his rivals and he would lose his huge profits.

When all the golden platters had been sold, the silver tray was the only thing that remained. Because it was so large and heavy, Aladdin brought the Jew to his house and produced the article. When the buyer saw its size, he gave Aladdin ten dinars and went his way. Thereafter, the boy and his mother lived off this money for a while until it was fully spent. Consequently, Aladdin took out the lamp and rubbed it, and immediately the slave made his appearance once again.

"Ask, my lord, for whatever you want," the jinnee said. "I am your slave and the thrall of whoever possesses the lamp."

"Since I am famished, I want you to bring me a tray of food like the one you brought me before," the boy said.

In the wink of an eye the slave produced a similar tray carrying twelve platters of the most sumptuous food with pure white bread and various bottles of fine wine. Now, Aladdin's mother had gone out when she knew that he was about to rub the lamp so that she would not have to see the jinnee again. But after a while, when she returned and saw the tray covered with the gold platters and smelled the savory meat, she was astonished and pleased.

"Look, Mother!" cried Aladdin. "You wanted me to throw away the lamp, but look at its virtues."

"My son, may Allah reward the jinnee," she replied, "but I never want to see him again."

Then the boy sat down with his mother, and they ate and drank until they were satisfied. Then they put away the rest of the food for the next day. As soon as the food had been consumed again, Aladdin arose, hid a platter beneath his garments, and went off with the intention of selling it to the Jew. However, by chance, he passed the shop of an old jeweler, an honest and pious man who feared Allah. When the sheikh saw the boy, he asked him, "What are you doing here, my son? I've seen you pass by here many times. Moreover, I've seen you making deals with a Jewish man and exchanging various articles with him. It seems to me that you have something for sale and are looking for a buyer. But you probably don't know, my boy, that the Jews do not respect the laws of the Moslems and are always cheating them, especially this accursed Jew with whom you've been bartering. If you indeed have something to sell, you just have to show it to me. Never fear, by Allah, I'll pay you the true price."

Thereupon Aladdin took out the platter and gave it to the old goldsmith, who weighed it on his scales and asked the lad, "Did you sell something similar to this to the Jew?"

"Yes," Aladdin answered, "and others as well."

"What price did he pay you?"

"One dinar."

"What a thief that man is to rob Almighty Allah's servants in this way!" the goldsmith exclaimed. Then, looking at the boy, he remarked, "My son, that tricky Jew has cheated you! In truth, he's made a laughingstock out of you. This platter is pure gold, and it's worth seventy dinars. If you agree to this price, you may have the money."

Accordingly, the sheikh counted out seventy gold pieces, which Aladdin accepted and at the same time thanked him for exposing the Jew's treachery. And after this, whenever he needed to sell another platter, he would bring it to the goldsmith and so he and his mother were soon in better circumstances. Nevertheless, they did not stop living in their customary way as middle-class folk, for they did not squander or waste their money. Moreover, Aladdin had now changed his ways: he no longer associated with the scamps and vagabonds of the neighborhood, and he began to meet good honest men. He went to the market street every day, where he conversed with the merchants, both great and small, asking them about their trade and learning the price of investments and so forth. Likewise, he frequented the bazaars of the goldsmiths and jewelers, where he would sit and enjoy himself by examining their precious stones and noting how jewels were bought and sold. Soon he became aware that the fruit with which he had filled his pockets in the subterranean garden was neither glass nor crystal, but made up of rich and rare gems. Indeed, it dawned on him that he had acquired immense wealth that surpassed that of actual kings. This discovery became even more evident when he examined all the precious stones in the jewelers' quarter and found that their biggest gem could not even match his smallest.

Several years went by, and Aladdin kept frequenting the bazaars, where he became known and loved by most of the folk there. He bought and sold, traded the dear and the cheap, until one day, after rising at dawn and heading for the jewelers' bazaar as was his custom, he heard the town crier announcing something important in the streets: "By command of our magnificent master, the king of the time and the lord of the age and the tide, let all the people close their shops and stores and retire behind the doors of their houses. The Lady Badar al-Budur, the sultan's daughter, desires to visit the Hammam. Whoever does not respect this order will be punished by death and his blood will be upon his own head."

And Scheherazade noticed that dawn was approaching and stopped telling her story. When the next night arrived, however, she received the king's permission to continue her tale and said,

Since the Badar al-Budur's beauty and loveliness were the talk of the entire town, Aladdin began thinking of some way to catch a glimpse of the princess. At last, he decided that it would be best if he took a place behind the Hammam door, where he might see her face as she entered. With this plan in mind, he went straight to the baths before she was expected and stood behind the entrance, a place where none of the people happened to be looking. Now, when the sultan's daughter had made the rounds of the city and its main streets and had amused herself by sightseeing, she finally reached the Hammam, and upon entering, she raised her veil, and her face glittered like a bright sun or a pure white pearl.

After Aladdin saw how lovely she was, he muttered to himself, "Truly, she is a tribute to the Almighty Maker who has adorned her with such amazing beauty and loveliness." From the moment he saw her, he fell helplessly in love with her. His thoughts were distraught. His gaze was dazed. His entire heart was gripped by her. Later, when he returned home to his mother, he was in a state of ecstasy. His mother asked him why he was so delirious, but he would not respond. After she prepared the morning meal, he continued to act very strangely, and she asked again, "My son, what's happened to you? Tell me, is anything wrong? Let me know if something bad has happened to you, for it's not like you to remain silent when I speak to you."

Thereupon, Aladdin, who used to think that all women resembled his mother, and who did not know what "beauty" and "loveliness" meant, even though he had heard about the charms of the sultan's daughter, turned to his mother and shouted, "Let me be!"

However, she continued to plead with him at least to sit down and eat. So he did as she requested but hardly touched the food. After that he lay down on his bed and spent the night in deep thought until the next day. His condition remained the same that day, and his mother was distressed because she was not able to learn what was bothering her son. Since she thought he might be sick, she approached him and said, "My son, if you are feeling pain or something else, let me know so that I can go and fetch a doctor. In fact, the sultan summoned a doctor from the land of the Arabs, who has already arrived, and it is said that he is extremely skillful. If you want, I'll go and bring him to you."

"I'm feeling well, Mother," Aladdin replied. "I'm not in the least bit sick. The only thing is that until yesterday, I had always thought that all women resembled you. However, I've seen the Lady Badar al-Budur, the sultan's daughter, as she was going to the baths. And now I know differently." And he related to her everything that had happened to him and added, "You've probably heard the crier announce that no man was to open his shop or stand in the street so that the Lady Badar al-Budur could retire to the Hammam without anyone seeing her. But now you know that I have seen her as she is, for she raised her veil at the door. And when I caught sight of her and saw the noble work of the Creator, I became ecstatic and fell deeply in love with her. In fact, I'm now determined to win her hand, and I can't sleep a wink without trembling and thinking about her. Therefore, I intend to ask the sultan for permission to marry her in lawful wedlock."

When Aladdin's mother heard her son's words, she told him he was out of his mind and cried, "My child, may Allah protect you! It seems you've lost your head. You must try to regain your senses and stop acting like a madman."

"No, Mother," he responded, "I'm not out of my mind, nor am I a maniac. There is nothing that you have said or can say that will change how I feel and think. I can't rest until I've won the darling of my heart, the beautiful Lady Badar al-Budur. Believe me, I'm determined to seek her hand from her sire, the sultan."

"If you value my life," his mother replied, "don't talk this way! Somebody might hear you and declare you insane. Get rid of all these foolish ideas! Who would ever dare request such a thing from the king? Indeed, even if you persist, how would you go about making such a request? Who would represent you at the court?"

"Nobody else but you, Mother," Aladdin stated. "There's nobody fonder of me than you. And there's nobody whom I trust more than you. So my plan is that you will present my petition for me to the sultan."

"May Allah protect me and keep me from doing anything of the sort!" she exclaimed. "Do you think that I've lost my mind like you? Get that idea out of your head! Remember whose son you are, my child. You're the orphan boy of a tailor, the poorest of the tailors who toiled in this city. And I, your mother, also come from a poor family. How then can you dare to ask to marry the daughter of the sultan, who would never let his daughter marry anyone except a prince of the same rank and majesty? Even if a suitor were noble but a degree lower than his daughter, he would forbid a marriage!"

"Mother, everything you've told me is common knowledge," said Aladdin. "Moreover, I'm quite aware that I'm the child of poor parents. Despite all this, I'm not going to let myself be deterred. If you truly love me, I hope that you'll grant me this favor and present my petition. Otherwise, you'll destroy me. I shall die if I can't win the darling of my heart. Remember, Mother, I am your son."

Upon hearing these words, his mother wept and said, "Yes, indeed, I am your mother, and you are my only son. And my greatest desire is for you to marry. But even here, let us suppose that I would try to find a wife for you from a family that is our equal. Her parents would ask at once whether you have any property, merchandise, or trade to support their daughter. What can I reply then? I would be at a loss for words. And if I cannot possibly answer the poor like ourselves, how can I be so bold as to ask for the daughter of the sultan of China, who has no peer? Think about this. Who would ever dare ask the sultan to wed his daughter to the son of a tailor! If I ever did such a thing, our misfortunes would increase, and our lives would be in mortal danger from the sultan. It might even mean death for you and me. As far as I am concerned, how could I possibly gain access to the sultan? And even if I should succeed, what could I say when they ask me about your livelihood? The king would probably think that I'm a madwoman. And lastly, suppose that I obtain an audience with the sultan, what gift could I possibly bring to his majesty?"

And Scheherazade noticed that dawn was approaching and stopped telling her story. When the next night arrived, however, she received the king's permission to continue her tale and said,

After pausing a moment, Aladdin's mother continued trying to persuade her son to abandon his plan to marry the sultan's daughter, and she said, "It's true, my son, that the sultan is mild and merciful. He never rejects anyone who requests justice or protection from him, nor anyone who asks him for alms. He is most generous and kind and bestows favors on people near and far. But he grants favors only to those who deserve them, to men who have proved themselves in battle under his eyes or men who have rendered great service as civilians to his estate. But you haven't done anything! What deed have you performed before him or in public that merits his grace? Moreover, this favor that you intend to request from him cannot be granted to anyone of our rank. As I told you before, whoever goes to the sultan and asks for his daughter in marriage must offer him something that suits his exalted position."

"Mother, everything you've said thus far is true," Aladdin replied. "And it's a good thing that you've reminded me of all these things and made me think about them. However, my love for the Princess Badar al-Budur has inflamed my heart, and I can't rest unless I win her. When you brought up the subject of a gift, it was something I had not thought about, but it is this very thing that I can indeed offer the sultan. You see, Mother, I can offer the king something that no other monarch in the world has ever seen or possessed. If you remember, I brought back some glass and crystal from the cave that I thought was worth nothing. Well, it turns out that they are precious stones, and there is not a king in the world who can match even the smallest gem that I possess. Ever since I began associating with the jewelers, I've learned that they are priceless gems. So you don't have to worry whether we have an appropriate gift. There is a porcelain bowl in our house, and I'd like you to fetch it for me so that I may fill it with these jewels, which you will carry to the king as a gift. Then you will submit my petition to him, and I am sure that with such a gift as this, you will have no trouble. If you are unwilling to do this, Mother, I shall surely die. Just remember that this gift is one of the priceless gems, and in my many visits to the jewelers' bazaar, I observed the merchants selling jewels, whose beauty was not worth one quarter carat of what we possess. Therefore, I know for sure how priceless our gems are. Now, please bring me the bowl so that I can put some of them in there and arrange them in a splendid way."

So she stood up and fetched the bowl. As she was bringing it back to him, she said to herself, "I'll be able to know what to do after I see whether he was telling me the truth." Then she set the bowl before her son, who pulled some of the stones out of his pockets and put them into the bowl. He arranged all sorts of gems in the bowl until he had filled it, and his mother was astonished by the sight. Indeed, their radiance was so dazzling that she was bewildered. However, she was still not certain that they were indeed priceless, even though her son might have been telling the truth when he said that nothing like them could be found even among kings.

Then Aladdin turned to her and said, "You see how magnificent this present is for the sultan? I'm sure that it will enable you to be received with respect and honor by the king. Now you have no excuse. So, collect yourself and arise. Take this bowl, and bring it to the palace."

But his mother responded, "My son, it's true that the present is extremely valuable and precious, and that there is nothing like it in the world. But who can be so bold as to go and ask the sultan for his daughter? I can't imagine myself saying to him, 'I would like to request the hand of your daughter for my son.' I'd be tongue-tied in front of him. And even granting that Allah comes to my aid and gives me enough courage to say to him, 'I'd like to arrange a marriage between your daughter, the Lady Badar al-Budur, and my son, Aladdin,' they will surely think that I'm demented and cast me out in disgrace and disgust. Moreover, both you and I will be in danger of losing our lives from then on. Nevertheless, because I love you so much, I shall summon my courage and go to the court. Perhaps the king will receive me and honor me on account of the gift, but what shall I say when he asks me how much property you own and what you do for a living?"

"I don't think that the sultan will ask such questions when he gets a look at the jewels," Aladdin answered. "Don't worry yourself about things that may never happen. All you have to do is set this present of precious stones before him and ask his permission to wed me to his daughter. Don't make things difficult. Remember, I have the lamp that provides us with a stable income and whatever else I need. If indeed the sultan does ask you those questions, my hope is that the lamp will furnish me with the right answers."

Then Aladdin and his mother talked all night long about what she was to do, and when the next morning came, she arose and mustered up all her courage. Indeed, she felt somewhat better after Aladdin had explained to her how powerful the lamp was and that it could supply them with whatever they needed. However, now Aladdin was worried that his mother might tell people about the lamp and all its magical powers. So he said to her, "Mother, beware that you don't tell anyone about the powers of the lamp, since this is our most important possession. Be on your guard so that you don't tell anyone about it, no matter who it is. Otherwise, we shall probably lose it and lose the fortune and benefits that we expect from it."

"Have no fear," his mother said, and she arose and took the bowl full of jewels, which she wrapped up in a fine kerchief, and went straight to the divan before it became too crowded. When she entered the palace, she saw the viziers and various nobles go into the audience chamber, and after a short time, the divan was filled by the ministers, high officials, chieftains, and emirs. Finally, the sultan entered, and everyone bowed in respect. Then the king seated himself on the throne, and all who were present at the audience stood before him with crossed arms waiting for his command to sit down. When they received it, each man took his place according to his rank. Then the petitioners went before the sultan, and he judged each case according to its merits in his customary way until the divan came to an end. At this point the king arose and withdrew into the palace, and the people went their way.

And Scheherazade noticed that dawn was approaching and stopped telling her story. However, when the next night arrived, she received the king's permission to continue her tale and said,

Even though Aladdin's mother had been among the earliest to arrive at the sultan's court, she had not been able to find anyone to intercede for her before the king and was unfamiliar with the way the divan was held. Therefore, she was obliged to leave the palace and return home. As soon as Aladdin spotted her with the bowl in her hands, he thought that something unfortunate had happened, but he did not want to ask her until she came into the apartment and sat down. Thereupon, she told him what had occurred and said, "Praise be to Allah, my child, that I had enough courage to attend the audience today. And even though I was too scared to speak to the king today, I shall definitely do so tomorrow. There were many people like me today who could not get an audience with the sultan. Don't fret, my son, tomorrow I shall speak to him, and let come what may come."

When Aladdin heard his mother's words, he was relieved with joy, and although he had hoped the matter would be settled by then, he controlled himself with patience. They slept well that night, and early the next morning, Aladdin's mother went with the bowl to the king's court, which she found closed. So she asked the people what the matter was, and they told her that the sultan did not hold an audience every day but only three times a week. So she had to return home. After this, whenever the sultan held court, she appeared there and waited for someone to help her. However, nobody came to her assistance, and she continued to attend the audiences without success for one whole month.

Now, the king had noticed her presence at every audience, and on the last day of the month, when she took her usual place, her courage failed her, and she allowed the divan to come to a close without uttering a syllable. In the meantime, while the king was preparing himself to enter the harem accompanied by the grand vizier, he turned to him and said, "For the past few weeks I've noticed that old woman over there at every session, and she always seems to be carrying something under her mantilla. Do you know anything about her or what she wants?"

"My lord," the vizier responded, "women are very often petty-minded, and most likely this woman has come to make a complaint about her husband or one of her relatives and neighbors."

However, the sultan was not satisfied by this reply, and he told the vizier to bring the woman before him if she attended the next audience.

"As you command, your majesty," replied the vizier, placing his hand on his brow.

So the next time that Aladdin's mother attended the divan, the king caught sight of her and said to his grand vizier, "That's the woman we were talking about yesterday. Bring her to me so that I can find out what she wants and grant her request."

Accordingly, the minister brought her forward to be introduced to the sultan, and she kissed the ground before him in respect, wishing him glory, prosperity, and long life.

"Woman," said the king, "for some days now I've seen you at my audiences, and yet you've yet to say a word. So tell me now if there is a request that I may fulfill."

Aladdin's mother kissed the ground a second time, and, after blessing him, she said, "Truly, my lord, there is something I would like to request, but before I do this, I would like you to grant me immunity, because your highness may find my petition highly unusual."

Since the king wanted to know her request and was a man of exceptional mildness and clemency, he gave her his word that she would have immunity. Furthermore, he dismissed everyone at the court and allowed only his grand vizier to remain. Then he turned toward his petitioner and said, "Tell me your request, for you are under the protection of Allah Almighty."

"Your majesty, I also need your pardon," she said.

"May Allah pardon you as I myself do," he replied.

"Great king," she resumed, "I have a son named Aladdin, and one day some time ago, when he heard the town crier commanding all the people to close their shops and get off the streets because the Lady Badar al-Budur, the sultan's daughter, was going to the Hammam, he felt an uncontrollable urge to look at her and hid himself in a place behind the doors of the baths to catch sight of her. When she entered, he saw her, but it was too much for him. Ever since the time he looked at her, your majesty, he has not had a moment's peace. Moreover, he has demanded that I go and ask permission from your highness for him to wed your daughter. I tried to get him to drive this idea out of his head, but it was impossible. His love for your daughter has gripped him so deeply that he's told me he'll die if he cannot win your daughter for his bride. Therefore, I hope your highness will be merciful and mild and pardon my boldness and that of my son, and I beg you not to punish us."

After the sultan heard her tale, he regarded her with compassion, and laughing aloud, he asked her, "Tell me, what is that you've been carrying in your mantilla?"

Relieved that the sultan was laughing and was not angry at her, she immediately opened the mantilla and set the bowl of jewels before him. All at once, the audience hall was illuminated as though the chandeliers and torches had been lit. Indeed, the king was dazed and amazed by the radiance of the rare gems, and he marveled at their size, beauty, and quality.

"Never in my life have I seen anything as beautiful and superb as these jewels!" cried the king. "I don't think that I have a single one in my treasury like these." Then he turned to his minister and said, "What do you say? Have you ever seen such fine jewels as these before?"

"Never," replied the vizier. "I don't think you have anything in your treasury to match these."

"Indeed," resumed the king, "whoever makes a present like this to me deserves to become the bridegroom of my daughter. As far as I can see, nobody is more worthy than this man."

When the vizier heard the sultan's words, he was tongue-tied and highly distressed, for the sultan had promised to allow his son to marry the princess. So, after a while, he whispered, "Great king, your highness promised me that the Lady Badar al-Budur would wed my son. Therefore, I find it only just that your highness grant my son a delay of three months during which time he might find a gift more valuable than this."

Although the king knew that such a thing could not be done, not even by the vizier himself or any of his nobles, he granted him the desired delay out of kindness. Then he turned to Aladdin's mother and said, "Go to your son and tell him that I've pledged my word that my daughter shall marry him. First, however, he shall have to wait three months while I make the proper preparations for the wedding."

Aladdin's mother thanked the king and blessed him, and after leaving the palace, she rushed home in joy. When her son saw her enter the apartment with a smile on her face, he knew it was a sign of good news, especially since she had returned without the bowl.

"Allah willing, I hope you've brought me good news, Mother," he said. "Perhaps the jewels have done their job, and the king has received you with kindness and granted your request."

In response, she told him the whole story—how the sultan had treated her favorably and had marveled at the extraordinary size of the jewels and their superb quality, as had the vizier. Then she concluded by saying, "And he promised his daughter would be yours. However, I heard the vizier whisper something about a private contract made between him and the sultan. So the king granted him a delay of three months, and I am somewhat fearful that the vizier will not be kindly disposed toward you and will attempt to change the sultan's mind."

And Scheherazade noticed that dawn was approaching and stopped telling her story. When the next night arrived, however, she received the king's permission to continue her tale and said,

* * *

Despite the delay of three months, Aladdin was overjoyed by the news, and told his mother, "Inasmuch as the king has given his word, I am extremely pleased and want to thank you with all my heart. Before this, I felt as though I were dead, and now you've restored my life. Praise be to Allah, for there is no man on the face of this earth happier or more fortunate than I am!"

Aladdin showed great patience during the next two months and looked forward to the wedding. Then, one day toward sundown, his mother went to the bazaar to buy some oil, and she found all the shops shut and the whole city decorated. The people were hanging wax candles and flowers in their windows, and she saw soldiers and mounted troops in processions and carrying torches. Surprised by such a marvelous sight and glamorous scene, she went into a store that carried oil and that was still open, and as she was buying the supplies she needed, she asked why there was such a commotion.

"You must be a stranger in town," the shopkeeper replied.

"Not at all," she said.

"You're from this town, and you don't know that this is the wedding night of the sultan's daughter with the son of the grand vizier?" the shopkeeper asked. "How is that possible? Right now he's in the Hammam, and all these soldiers are standing guard and waiting for him to come out. Then they will escort him in the bridal procession to the palace, where the princess is expecting him."

When Aladdin's mother heard these words, she was extremely upset and also at a loss as to how to inform her son about this distressing news. She knew that the poor boy had been looking forward to his marriage with the princess, hour by hour, and could hardly wait until the three months would elapse. But she knew she had to tell him about this quickly, and when she returned home, she said, "My son, I must tell you some bad news that will cause you a great deal of suffering."

"Tell me right away," he said.

"The sultan has broken his promise to you," she said. "The grand vizier's son is to marry his daughter this very night. For some time I had suspected that the minister would change the king's mind, for I noticed how he whispered something to the sultan when your request was granted."

"And how did you learn that the vizier's son is to marry the princess tonight?" Aladdin asked.

Then she told him the whole story, how she had seen the closed shops, the decorations, the soldiers, and the processions, and Aladdin was overcome by grief and jealousy. However, after a short time, he remembered the lamp and recovered his spirits.

"Upon your life, Mother," he said resolutely, "I don't believe that the vizier's son will enjoy the princess tonight. But let's drop the subject. Please get up and serve me my supper. After that, I'm going to retire to my room. Don't worry, everything will turn out well."

After eating his meal, Aladdin locked himself in his room. Then he brought out the lamp and rubbed it. Immediately the jinnee appeared and said, "Ask whatever you want, for I am your slave and beholden to whoever holds the lamp, I and the other slaves of the lamp."

"Hear me!" Aladdin commanded. "I asked the sultan for his daughter's hand, and he gave his word that I could marry her after three months. But he has not kept his word and has given her to the vizier's son. Indeed, this very night the vizier's son is to enjoy her. Therefore, I order you, if you are indeed a trustworthy slave of the lamp, to carry the bride and bridegroom to this room tonight once they have gotten into bed. This is all I ask for the present."

Thereupon the slave disappeared, and Aladdin rejoined his mother to spend the rest of the evening with her. But at the hour when he knew that the slave would be coming, he arose and retired to his room. After a little while, the marid arrived and brought with him the newlyweds in their bridal bed. Aladdin rejoiced to see them and cried out to the slave, "Carry that scoundrel into the privy and put him to sleep!"

The jinnee did as he was commanded right away, but before leaving the vizier's son in the privy, he blew such a cold blast on him that the bridegroom shriveled and looked pitiful. Then the slave returned to Aladdin and said, "If you require anything else, just call me."

"Return to me in the morning," Aladdin said, "so that you can take them back to the palace."

"As you command," the jinnee said and vanished.

Soon Aladdin got up, hardly believing that the affair had been such a success, but when he looked at the Lady Badar al-Budur lying under his own roof, he knew everything had actually happened as he had planned it. However, he did not allow his burning desire to get the best of him and treated her with respect.

"Oh, most beautiful of princesses," he said, "don't think that I've brought you here to dishonor you. Heaven forbid! No, it was only to prevent the wrong man from enjoying you, for your sire, the sultan, promised you to me. Have no fear and rest in peace."

Now, when the Lady Badar al-Budur saw herself in that dark and dismal apartment and heard Aladdin's words, she began to tremble and was so petrified that she could not utter a reply. Soon the young man moved toward her, and after stripping off his outer dress, he placed a sword between them and lay down beside her. He did not come near the princess or do anything indecent, for all he wanted to do was to prevent the consummation of her nuptials with the vizier's son. On the other hand, the Lady Badar al-Budur spent a terrible night in bed and did not sleep a wink. The same was true of the vizier's son, who lay in the privy and did not dare to stir for fear that the jinnee might harm him.

As soon as it was morning, the slave appeared before Aladdin without the lamp being rubbed and said to him, "My lord, if you require anything, command me, and it will be done immediately."

"Go and return the bride and bridegroom to their apartment," said Aladdin.

So the slave carried out his order in the twinkle of an eye and carried the pair in their bed to the palace without their being able to see who was transporting them. Both were terribly frightened, and the marid had barely time to set them down again and disappear when the sultan came to visit and congratulate his daughter. Of course, as soon as the vizier's son heard the doors thrown open, he sprang quickly from the bed and got dressed, for he knew that it could only be the king who would enter at that hour. Nonetheless, it was extremely difficult for him to leave his bed, in which he would have preferred to warm himself after spending the night in the cold and damp privy.

And Scheherazade noticed that dawn was approaching and stopped telling her story. When the next night arrived, however, she received the king's permission to continue her tale and said,

After entering the apartment, the sultan kissed his daughter on her forehead, wished her good morning, and asked whether she was satisfied with the bridegroom. But her only reply was a scowl, which forced him to repeat his question a few times. However, she refused to answer. So the king left the room, and after going to the queen, he informed her of what had taken place between him and his daughter. Since the mother did not want her husband to stay mad at their daughter, she said, "This is just the way young married couples are nowadays, at least during the first few days of marriage. They're bashful and somewhat coy. So be patient and excuse her. After a while she'll become herself again and speak with people just as she did before. To be on the safe side, I'll go and see how she is."

So the queen arose and donned her dress. When she entered her daughter's room, she went over to her and gave her a kiss on her forehead. However, the princess did not respond, causing the queen to say to herself, "Something strange has definitely happened, otherwise she wouldn't be so troubled." Now she spoke directly to her daughter and said, "Tell me what's the matter. I've come to wish you a good morning, and all I get is silence for an answer."

Thereupon the Lady Badar al-Budur raised her head and said, "Pardon me, Mother, I've neglected my duty. I know I should have greeted you with respect, seeing that you have honored me by this visit. However, I want you to know the reason why I am in such a terrible mood, and how I have just experienced the most vile night of my life. You see, no sooner had we gotten into bed than some invisible creature came, lifted our bed, and transported it to some dark and dismal place." After that the princess related to her mother all that had happened that night: how the bridegroom had been taken away from her, how she had been left alone, and how another young man had come and lain down next to her after placing a sword between them. "In the morning," she resumed, "the creature who had carried us off came and returned us to the palace. But as soon as we arrived and he disappeared, my father entered, and I had neither the heart nor the tongue to speak to him, for I was still trying to get over my fright and terror. I'm sure that my poor behavior has made him angry. So I hope, Mother, that you will explain to him why I acted the way I did and that he will pardon me for not answering him the way I should have."

When the queen heard her daughter's story, she said to her, "My child, pull yourself together. If you tell this story, people will probably say that the sultan's daughter has lost her mind. And you've done the right thing by not recounting your adventure to your father. Beware, and again I say, beware of telling him anything about what happened last night."

"Mother," the princess replied, "I've told you the truth. I'm not crazy. This is what happened to me, and if you don't believe me, ask my husband."

"I want you to get up right away," the queen said, "and banish all such thoughts from your mind. Put on some clothes and go and watch the bridal festivities they've organized for you throughout the city. Listen to the drumming and the singing, and look at the decorations that were all created in your honor."

After saying this, the queen summoned the servants, who dressed and prepared the Lady Badar al-Budur. In the meantime she went to see the sultan and assured him that their daughter had suffered from some bad dreams and nightmares during the wedding night.

"Don't be severe with her for not answering you this morning," she said.

Thereafter she secretly sent for the vizier's son and asked him what had happened and whether what the Lady Badar al-Budur had said was true. However, since he feared losing his bride, he said, "My lady, I don't have the slightest clue about what you've just said."

The queen was now certain that her daughter had either hallucinated or was suffering from bad dreams.

The marriage festivities lasted the entire day, with professional dancers and singers performing to the accompaniment of all kinds of instruments with great mirth. Meanwhile the queen, the vizier, and the vizier's son did their very best to make sure that the princess would enjoy herself. That day they left nothing undone to increase her pleasure and make her forget everything that had been bothering her. Yet it was all in vain, for she watched the spectacles in silence. Indeed, for the most part she was downcast and brooded about everything that had happened to her during the past night. It is true that the vizier's son had suffered much more than she had, since he had spent the night in the privy. However, he had refused to tell the truth and repressed the incident for fear of losing his bride and the connection with the royal family that brought him so much honor. Moreover, everyone envied him because he had won such a lovely and beautiful young woman as the Lady Badar al-Budur.

In the meantime, Aladdin also went out that day to enjoy the festivities, which extended throughout the city as well as the palace. When he heard the people talk about the high honor that the vizier's son had gained and how he would prosper by becoming the son-in-law of the sultan, he began to laugh. And he said to himself, "Indeed, you poor wretches, you don't know what happened to him last night. Otherwise you wouldn't envy him the way you do."

When darkness fell and it was time for sleep, Aladdin arose in his room, rubbed the lamp, and the slave appeared in a flash. Once again Aladdin ordered him to bring the sultan's daughter, together with her bridegroom, just as he had done on the previous night, before the vizier's son could take her virginity. So the marid quickly vanished and at the appointed time returned with the Lady Badar al-Budur and the vizier's son in the bed. Once again he carried the bridegroom to the privy and left him there in fear and trembling. Meanwhile Aladdin arose and placed the sword between the princess and himself and lay down beside her. When day broke, the slave transported the pair back to the palace, leaving Aladdin filled with delight at the condition of the minister's son.

Now, when the sultan woke up in the morning, he decided to visit his daughter again and see if she would treat him as she had on the past day. So, shaking off his sleep, he jumped up, clothed himself, and went to the apartment of the princess. Upon hearing the knocking, the vizier's son jumped up and began donning his garments while his ribs were still freezing because the jinnee had just returned them to the palace. The sultan moved toward the wedding bed, raised the curtain, and wished his daughter good morning. Then he kissed her forehead and asked her how she felt. However, she looked sad and sullen, and instead of answering, she just scowled at him as though she were angry and suffering from a terrible plight. Thereupon the sultan became extremely angry at her for not replying, and he suspected that something bad had happened to her. So he drew his sword and cried out to her, "What's come over you? Either tell me what's happened, or I'll take your life this very moment! Is this the way to pay your respect to me, by not talking to me?"

When the Lady Badar al-Budur saw her father brandishing his sword at her and how furious he was, she felt somehow released from the past that was hanging over her and she managed to raise her head.

"Don't be angry with me, dear father," she cried out. "Please calm down, for I'm not responsible for the way I've been acting, as you will soon see. Please, if you listen to what happened to me during these past two nights, I'm sure you'll pardon me and have pity on me, for I'm still your loving child."

Then the princess told him all that had occurred during the past two nights and added, "If you don't believe me, ask my husband, and he'll tell your highness the whole story. I don't know what they did with him when they took him away from me or where they kept him."

When the sultan heard his daughter's words, he became sad, and his eyes brimmed with tears. Then he sheathed his sword and kissed her.

"My daughter," he said, "why didn't you tell me yesterday what had happened to you the night before? Then I could have protected you from the terror that you suffered this past night. But it doesn't matter now. Get up and forget about it all. Tonight I'll have guards posted around your room so that you'll never have to go through anything like this again."

Then the sultan returned to his palace and summoned the grand vizier right away. When he arrived, the king asked him, "How do you view this whole matter? I'm sure your son has told you what happened to him and my daughter."

The minister replied, "Great king, I haven't seen my son for two days."

Thereupon, the sultan told him what the princess had suffered and added, "I want you to find out what's happened to your son and all the facts pertaining to this case. Since my daughter has had such a great shock and appears to be terrified, she may not really know what happened to her, although I think she's told me the truth."

So the grand vizier arose, went out, and summoned his son. When the young man arrived, his father asked him whether the princess had been telling the truth.

"Father," he said, "heaven forbid that the Lady Badar al-Budur would ever lie. Indeed, she told the truth. These past two nights have been the most vile in my life when they should have been the most pleasurable. What happened to me was even worse than what happened to her because I was not allowed the pleasure of sleeping in a bed. Instead, I was stuck in a frightful black hole that had a horrible smell and was truly damnable. Moreover my ribs were frozen cold."

In short, the young man told his father the whole story and added, "I implore you, Father, speak to the sultan and ask him to release me from this marriage. I confess that it's a great honor for me to be the sultan's son-in-law, and I've fallen terribly in love with the princess. But I have no strength left to endure what I've suffered these past two nights."

When the vizier heard these words, he became exceedingly sad, for his most cherished wish had been to wed his son to the sultan's daughter and help him advance in life. He thought about the entire affair a long time and was in a quandary about what to do. Indeed, it upset him to break off the marriage and he was reluctant to do so especially since it had brought him such rare fortune. Consequently, he said, "Be patient, my son, until we see what happens tonight when we'll assign guards to protect your room. Don't be so quick to abandon the great distinction and honor that only you have achieved."

Then the vizier returned to the sultan and informed him that everything that the Lady Badar al-Budur had said was true. As a result, the king said, "Well then, given the situation, I must act immediately," and he commanded that all the festivities be stopped, and he annulled the marriage.

The people were stunned by this news, especially when they saw the grand vizier and his son leave the palace with miserable and angry faces. "Why was the marriage broken off?" They began to ask. "What happened?" Of course, nobody knew the truth except Aladdin, who claimed the princess's hand and laughed in secret joy. But even after the marriage was dissolved, the sultan forgot the promise that he had made to Aladdin's mother. The same was true with the grand vizier. Neither one of these men had an inkling of why and how everything had happened and did not link the incidents with Aladdin.

Aladdin waited patiently for the three months to elapse, and as soon as the term had expired, he sent his mother to the sultan to remind him of his promise. So she went to the palace, and when the king appeared in the divan and saw the old woman standing before him, he remembered his promise with regard to the marriage, and he turned to the minister and said, "That old woman over there is the one who gave me the jewels, and I gave her my word that when three months had elapsed, I would wed my daughter to her son."

The minister went over to her and brought her before the king, whom she saluted and blessed. In turn, the sultan asked her if there was anything he could do for her, and she answered, "Great king, the three months that you commanded me to wait have elapsed, and it is time to wed my son, Aladdin, with your daughter, the Lady Badar al-Badur."

The sultan was distraught at this request, especially since he saw that the woman was one of the poorest of his subjects. Nevertheless, the present she had brought him was magnificent and priceless. So he turned to the grand vizier and whispered, "What advice do you have for me? In truth, I did give my word. But it seems to me that they are poor and from the lower classes."

The vizier, who was mad with envy and bitter about what had happened to his son, said to himself, "How can someone like this wed the king's daughter and my son lose this high honor?" Therefore, he whispered to the king, "My lord, it will be easy to put off a poor devil like her son. He's certainly not worthy enough for your daughter, especially when you haven't even seen what he looks like."

"But how am I to do this?" the sultan asked. "I can't put off the man when I gave him my word. As you know, the word of kings is their bond."

"My lord," the vizier replied, "my advice is that you place another demand on him and ask for forty platters of pure gold filled with gems like the ones that this woman already brought you with forty white slave girls and forty black eunuch slaves to carry the platters."

"By Allah," the king answered, "that is good advice. It will be impossible for him to carry off such a feat, and then I'll be freed of my promise."

Then he turned to Aladdin's mother and addressed her loudly. "I want you to go and tell your son that I am a man of my word, but he can have my daughter only on the condition that he pay the dowry for my daughter. The settlement amounts to forty platters of pure gold, all brimful with gems, like those you've already brought me, with as many slave girls and black eunuchs to carry them. If your son can provide this dowry, then I'll marry him to my daughter."

Aladdin's mother departed, and on her way home she wagged her head and said to herself, "Where can my poor son procure these platters and jewels? Even if he were to return to the underground cave and pluck them from the trees, which I think is impossible anyway, how will he obtain the forty girls and black slaves?" Nor did she stop murmuring to herself until she reached her apartment, where she found Aladdin awaiting her, and she lost no time in saying, "My son, didn't I tell you to forget about the Lady Badar al-Budur and that people like us can't aspire to marriages with people of her rank?"

"Tell me what happened," Aladdin responded.

"The sultan received me with all due honor," she said,

"and it seems to me that his intentions toward us are noble. But your enemy is that accursed vizier, for after I addressed the king in your name as you requested, he turned to the minister, who spoke to him in a whisper. After that the sultan replied with a list of demands." Then she told her son the conditions for the marriage to take place and concluded by saying, "He expects you to give him a reply right away, but I suppose that we have no answer for him."

And Scheherazade noticed that dawn was approaching and stopped telling her story. When the next night arrived, however, she received the king's permission to continue her tale and said,

"Mother, calm down and collect yourself," Aladdin said. "Please bring me something to eat, and after we have dined, Allah willing, you'll see my reply. The sultan thinks, like you, that he has demanded such an extraordinary dowry that he can deter me from marrying his daughter. The fact is that he's demanded much less than I had expected. But do me a favor, and go out to purchase the food for dinner, and leave me alone to procure the reply."

So she went out to the bazaar to buy what was necessary for dinner while Aladdin retired to his room, where he took the lamp and rubbed it. Immediately the slave appeared to him and said, "Ask, my lord, whatever you want."

"I've asked permission from the sultan to marry his daughter," Aladdin said, "and he has demanded forty platters of purest gold each weighing ten pounds and all to be filled with gems that come from the garden in the underground cave. Furthermore, they are to be carried on the heads of forty white slave girls to be attended by forty black eunuchs. I want you to bring them to me at once."

"As you request, my lord," said the jinnee, who disappeared for an hour or so and then returned with the platters, jewels, slave girls, and eunuchs. After setting them down before Aladdin, he said, "Here is what you desired. If you would like anything else, just tell me."

"I don't need anything else right now," Aladdin replied, "but if I do, I'll summon you and let you know."

The slave now disappeared, and after a little while, Aladdin's mother returned home, and when she entered the apartment, she saw the slave girls and blacks and exclaimed with wonder, "All this has come from that marvelous lamp! May Allah preserve it for my boy!"

But before she could take off her mantilla, Aladdin said to her, "Mother, this is the time that the sultan usually goes to his seraglio palace. So take him what he's demanded at once so that he'll know that I'm prepared to provide him with all he wants and more. Also, he'll realize that the grand vizier has beguiled him, and that it is fruitless to try to deter me."

Then he arose right away and opened the door to the apartment so that the slave girls and eunuchs could depart. When the people of the neighborhood saw such a marvelous spectacle, they all stood to gaze at it, and they admired the slave girls, who were beautiful and lovely, for each one of them wore robes lined with gold and studded with jewels worth no less than a thousand dinars apiece. The people also stared at the platters, and although they were covered by brocades studded with gems, their glitter pierced the brocades, and their gleam surpassed the rays of the sun. As Aladdin's mother walked forward, the slave girls and the eunuchs followed her in a fine procession, and people from all quarters gathered to gaze at the beauty of the damsels, glorifying God Almighty, until the procession reached the palace and entered it. Now, when the high dignitaries, chamberlains, and commanders caught sight of Aladdin's mother and her company, they were all astonished, especially when they laid their eyes on the slave girls, for each and every one of them could ravish the reason of a monk. And although the chamberlains and officials were men from distinguished and wealthy families, the sons of grandees and emirs, they were dazzled by the costly dresses of the slave girls and the platters that they were carrying on their heads. In fact, they had to veil their eyes when they looked at the stunningly bright platters. Then the nabobs went in and reported to the king, who commanded them to enter his chamber right away, and Aladdin's mother went in with them. When they all stood before the sultan, they saluted him with every sign of respect and worship and prayed for his glory and prosperity. Then the slave girls removed the platters from their heads and placed them at his feet, and once they took off the brocade covers, they stood with their arms crossed behind them. The sultan was extremely astonished and captivated by the incomparable beauty and loveliness of the slave girls. Moreover, he was totally bedazzled by the golden platters filled with gems and so bewildered by this marvelous sight that he became dumbfounded and was unable to utter a syllable for quite some time. When he considered that all these treasures had been collected within an hour or so, he felt completely stupefied. Soon, however, he commanded the slave girls to carry the platters to his daughter's chamber. When they left his presence, Aladdin's mother stepped forward and said to the sultan, "My lord, this small token is the least we could do to honor the Lady Badar al-Budur. Actually, she really deserves much more than this."

Upon hearing this, the sultan turned to his minister and asked, "What do you say now? Isn't a man who can produce such great wealth in so short a time worthy of becoming the sultan's son-in-law?"

Although the minister was stunned by these riches, even more than the king, he was dying with envy and extremely frustrated because he saw that the king was satisfied with the dowry. Therefore, he replied with the intention of preventing the king from going through with the marriage, "It isn't worthy enough for her. Not even all the treasures of the universe could match your daughter's pinky. I believe that your highness is overestimating these things in comparison with your daughter."

When the king heard the vizier's words, he knew that they were prompted by great envy. So he turned to Aladdin's mother and said, "Go to your son and tell him that I've accepted his dowry and shall keep my word. My daughter shall be his bride, and he my son-in-law. Furthermore, tell him that I want him to appear before me at once so that I can become acquainted with him. He will be received with honor and consideration, and this night will be the beginning of the marriage festivities. Only he must come here without delay."

Aladdin's mother returned home faster than a cyclone

in order to congratulate her son, and she was in ecstasy at the thought that her boy was about to become the son-in-law of the sultan. After her departure from the palace, the king dismissed the divan and went to the princess's chamber, where he ordered the platters and slave girls brought before him so that he could inspect them with his daughter. When the Lady Badar al-Budur looked at the jewels, she was astonished and cried out, "I don't think that there are any jewels in the world that can compare to these!" Then she looked at the slave girls and admired their beauty and loveliness. Since she was aware that they had been sent to her by her new bridegroom, she was very pleased. To be sure, she had been distressed by what had happened to her former husband, the vizier's son, but now she was overjoyed when she gazed upon the damsels and their charms. Furthermore, her father was just as glad as she was and particularly happy when he saw that his daughter was no longer melancholy. Then he asked her, "Are you pleased with these things? Personally I think that your new bridegroom is more suitable for you than the vizier's son. And very soon, Allah willing, you'll find your happiness with him."

So much for the king.

In the meantime, as soon as Aladdin saw his mother enter the house with a great smile of joy on her face, he cried out, "May Allah be praised! All that I've ever desired has now been fulfilled!"

"You'll be glad once you hear my news," his mother said. "The sultan has accepted your offer, I mean, your dowry, and you are now engaged to the Lady Badar al-Budur. You are to be married to her this very night, my son. The king has given me his word and has proclaimed to the world that you will be his son-in-law. However, he also told me to send you to him right away so that he can become acquainted with you and receive you with honor and respect. So here I am, my son, my work is done. Let what may happen happen. The rest is up to you."

Aladdin arose and kissed his mother's hand and thanked her for her kind service. Then he left her, went into his room, took the lamp, and rubbed it. Immediately the jinnee appeared and cried out, "At your service, my lord. Ask whatever you want."

"I want you to take me to the finest Hammam in the world," Aladdin said. "Then fetch me the most expensive and regal garments that surpass anything ever worn by a king."

"As you command," the marid replied, and he carried Aladdin to baths that even the kings of the Chosroës had never seen. The building was made entirely of alabaster and carnelian, and it was lined with marvelous and captivating paintings. The great hall was studded with precious stones, and not a soul was there. But when Aladdin entered, a jinnee in human shape washed and bathed him as he wished. After Aladdin left the baths, he went into a large room, where he found a rich and princely suit. Then he was served with sherbets and coffee flavored with ambergris. Once he was done drinking, a group of black slaves approached him, sprayed him with perfume, and clothed him in the costliest of clothing.

As we know, Aladdin was the son of a poor tailor, but anyone who had seen him then would have said, "This young man is the greatest progeny of the kings. Praise be to Him who changes others and who does not change Himself!" Soon the jinnee arrived and transported him back to his home.

"My lord," the ifrit asked, "do you need me for anything else?"

"Yes," Aladdin replied. "I want you to bring me forty-eight mamelukes. Twenty-four are to precede me, and the other twenty-four are to follow me, and I want all of them equipped with the best suits of armor, weapons, and horses. Indeed, their outfits are to be the costliest in the world. Then fetch me a stallion fit for a king of the Chosroës, and let his trappings be studded with gold and the finest jewels. I also want forty-eight thousand dinars so that each white slave can carry a thousand gold pieces. Since I intend to visit the sultan right away, don't delay. Without all these men and equipment, it will be impossible to appear before him. Furthermore, I want you to produce a dozen slave girls, incomparably beautiful and magnificently dressed so that they can accompany my mother to the royal palace. Let each one of the slave girls be robed in raiment that would fit a queen."

"As you command," the jinnee replied, and after disappearing for a split second, he brought everything that he had been ordered to bring. In addition, he gave Aladdin a stallion unrivaled by the finest of Arabian steeds, and its saddle cloth was a splendid brocade lined with gold. Immediately, Aladdin sent for his mother and gave her the garments that she was to wear. In addition, he placed her in charge of the twelve slave girls, who formed her escort to the palace. Then he sent one of the mamelukes ahead to see if the sultan had left the seraglio or not. The white slave went and returned faster than lightning and reported, "My lord, the sultan is awaiting you!"

Thereupon, Aladdin arose and mounted his horse with his mamelukes riding behind and in front of him. They looked so splendid that all who saw them had to exclaim, "Praise the Lord who created them and endowed them with such magnificence and beauty!" And they scattered the gold coins among the crowds of people who came to watch them and their master, who surpassed not only his men but also the finest of princes in his splendor and glory. Praise be to the Bountiful Giver, the Lord Eternal! All this was due to the power of the magic lamp, which provided the person who possessed it with the fairest looks, enormous wealth, and great wisdom. The people appreciated Aladdin's generosity, and they were all captivated by his charm, elegance, comportment, and dignified manners. They praised the Creator for such a noble creation, and each and every person blessed Aladdin, for although they knew that he was the son of a poor tailor, nobody envied him, and they all felt that he deserved his good fortune.

And Scheherazade noticed that dawn was approaching and stopped telling her story. When the next night arrived, however, she received the king's permission to continue her tale and said,

Now the sultan had assembled the lords of the land and had informed them of the promise that he had made to Aladdin. Moreover, he ordered them to wait for Aladdin's approach and then to go forth, one and all, to meet and greet him. Therefore, the emirs, viziers, chamberlains, nabobs, and officers took their stations at the palace gate. Aladdin would have dismounted at the outer entrance, but one of the nobles, whom the king had assigned this duty, approached him and said, "My lord, your highness the sultan has commanded that you ride your steed up to the divan door, where you are to dismount."

Then they all accompanied him to the appointed place, where they helped him dismount. After this, all the emirs and nobles went ahead of him into the divan and led him up to the royal throne. Thereupon the sultan came down from his throne to prevent Aladdin from prostrating himself, and after embracing and kissing him, he seated him to his right. Aladdin did what was customary in greeting a king by blessing him and wishing him a long life and prosperity. Then he said, "My lord, thanks to your generosity, you have promised me the hand of your daughter the Lady Badar al-Budur, even though I do not deserve the greatness of such a gift, since I am but the humblest of your slaves. Indeed, I pray that Allah preserve you and keep you prosperous. In truth, great king, I do not have the words to thank you for the enormous favor that you have bestowed upon me. And I hope that you will grant me a plot of land where I can build a pavilion suitable for your daughter."

The sultan was struck with admiration when he saw Aladdin in his princely suit. He noted how handsome and attractive he looked and how remarkable the mamelukes were who served him. His astonishment grew even greater when Aladdin's mother approached him in a splendid and costly dress, clad as though she were a queen, and followed by twelve slave girls, who attended her with great respect and reverence. Finally, he was most impressed by Aladdin's eloquence and polite speech, and so was everyone else at this gathering. Of course, the grand vizier was so enraged with envy that he almost exploded, and he felt even worse when the sultan clasped Aladdin to his bosom and kissed him after listening to the youth's eloquent and respectful speech.

"Alas, my son," said the king, "that I have not had the pleasure of conversing with you until this day."

After making this remark, the sultan commanded the music to begin. Then he arose, and taking Aladdin by hand, he led him into the palace, where supper had been prepared, and the eunuchs at once laid the tables. Once the king had sat down and seated Aladdin on his right side, the viziers and other officials took their places, each according to his rank. Meanwhile, the bands played and a splendid marriage feast was displayed in the palace. The king started making friends with Aladdin and conversed with the youth, who answered the sultan politely and eloquently, as though he had been bred in the palaces of kings or had lived with them all his life. The more they conversed with each other, the more the sultan was delighted and pleased by his son-in-law's wit and elegance. After they had eaten and drunk and the trays were removed, the king summoned the kazis and witnesses, who wrote out the marriage contract between Aladdin and the Lady Badar al-Badur. Then the bridegroom arose and would have gone away if his father-in-law had not prevented him and asked, "Where are you going, my son? The wedding festivities have just begun. The marriage is made. The knot is tied. The contract written."

"My lord," Aladdin responded, "it is my desire to build a pavilion for the Lady Badar al-Budur suitable for her status and high rank. Until I do this, I cannot visit her. But, Allah willing, the building will be finished within the shortest amount of time, for your slave will do his utmost in regard for your highness. Although I long very much to be with the princess and to enjoy her company, it is incumbent upon me first to show my respect for her and to complete this task."

"Look around you, my son," replied the sultan, "and choose whatever ground you deem suitable for your plans. I'll leave it up to you. But I think the best place would be to build your pavilion on that broad ground over there facing my palace."

"I could wish for nothing better than to be near to your highness," said Aladdin.

After saying this, Aladdin bade farewell to the king, mounted his horse, and rode from the palace with his mamelukes following him. Along the way, crowds of people shouted their blessings until he reached his home. Once there, he entered his room, took the lamp, and rubbed it. Immediately the slave appeared and said, "Ask whatever you want, my lord."

"I have an important and urgent task for you," Aladdin replied. "I want you to build me a pavilion in front of the sultan's palace right away. It must be marvelous and furnished royally with every possible comfort."

"As you command," said the jinnee and vanished.

Before daybreak, the jinnee returned to Aladdin and said, "My lord, the pavilion is finished as you desired. If you would like to inspect it, please get up and come with me."

So Aladdin arose, and the slave carried him in a split second to the pavilion, which impressed him a great deal. The building was made out of jasper, alabaster, marble, and mosaics. The treasury was full of gold, silver, and costly gems, worth more than can be imagined. From there, the jinnee led him to another place where Aladdin saw tables, plates, dishes, spoons, ladles, basins, covers, cups, and saucers, all made out of precious metal. Next they went to the kitchen, where they found the cooks provided with all the utensils they needed, made out of gold and silver. After that they visited a warehouse filled with chests packed with royal garments, incredibly beautiful stuffs such as gold-lined brocades from India and China and velvet and silk materials. Then the jinnee led Aladdin on a tour of the numerous apartments, which contained marvelous things beyond description. When they went outside to the stables, Aladdin saw that they contained magnificent steeds that could not be found anywhere on the earth, even in the stables of kings, and even the harness rooms were hung with costly trappings, saddles, and bridles studded with pearls and precious stones. And all of this was the work of one night.

Aladdin was wonder-struck and astounded by the magnificent display of wealth, which not even the wealthiest monarch on earth could produce. He was even more astonished to see his pavilion fully provided with eunuchs and slave girls whose beauty could seduce a saint. Yet, the major attraction of the pavilion was the upper dome of twenty-four windows all made of emeralds, rubies, and other gems. And one window remained unfinished, at Aladdin's request, so that he could prevail upon the sultan to complete it.

After Aladdin had inspected the entire edifice, he was exceedingly happy and pleased. Then turning to the slave, he said, "I still need one thing more, which I forgot to ask."

"Ask whatever you want, my lord," the jinnee said.

"I want a carpet made of the finest brocade and woven with gold," he said. "When it is unrolled, I want it to extend to the sultan's palace so that the Lady Badar al-Budur can walk upon it without treading on common ground."

The slave departed momentarily, and upon his return, he said, "My lord, I've brought you what you wanted."

Then the jinnee took him and showed him a carpet which completely overwhelmed him by its splendor and extended from the pavilion to the palace. After this, the jinnee lifted Aladdin and transported him back to his home.

As the sun began to shine, the sultan rose from his sleep and went to his window, from which he saw a new grandiose pavilion opposite his palace. At first he could not believe his eyes and rubbed them to make sure that he was not dreaming. However, soon he was certain that the building was real, and he was amazed by its grandeur and by the carpet that was spread between his palace and the pavilion. The royal doorkeepers and all the members of his household were also astonished by the spectacle. Meanwhile, the vizier entered the palace, and when he caught sight of the newly built pavilion and the carpet, he was stupefied as well. He and the king began talking about this marvelous sight, and they finally agreed that no king in the universe could ever build such a pavilion. Addressing the minister, the sultan asked, "Do you agree now that Aladdin is worthy enough to be the husband of my daughter? You realize, of course, that no ordinary man could have built such an opulent and magnificent pavilion as this."

However, the vizier was still envious and replied, "Great king, I don't care how rich or adroit he may be. He must have used magic to build such a splendid pavilion in one night."

"I'm surprised to see that you continue to have a bad opinion of Aladdin," said the sultan. "I attribute it to your envy and jealousy. You were present when I gave him the ground to build a pavilion for my daughter. However that may be, I ask you, why would it be impossible for the man who gave me such remarkable gems for my daughter's dowry to build such an edifice as this?"

When the vizier heard the sultan speaking about Aladdin that way, he knew that his lord loved Aladdin a great deal, and thus his envy increased. It was only due to the fact that he could do nothing against the young man that he refrained from saying anything.

In the meantime it was broad daylight and the appointed time had arrived for Aladdin's return to the palace, where his wedding was being celebrated, and the emirs, viziers, and grandees had assembled to be present at the ceremony. So Aladdin arose and rubbed the lamp. Immediately the jinnee appeared and said, "Ask whatever you want, my lord. I am at your service."

"I want to go to the palace right away," Aladdin said. "Today is my wedding, and I want you to bring me ten thousand dinars."

The slave vanished, and in the twinkle of an eye he returned with the money. After Aladdin mounted with his mamelukes behind and in front of him, he headed for the palace, scattering gold pieces along the way, and the people praised him and held him in high esteem. When he drew near the palace, the emirs, officials, and officers, who were waiting for him, noticed his approach, and they hastened right away to inform the king. Thereupon the sultan rose and met his son-in-law. After embracing and kissing him, he led him into his own apartment, where he sat down and seated Aladdin on his right. The city was all decorated, and music rang throughout the palace. The singers sang, until the king commanded that the noon meal be served. Then the eunuchs and mamelukes spread the tables and trays fit for kings, and the sultan and Aladdin were joined by the lords of the realm, who took their seats and ate and drank until they were satisfied.

The wedding festivities in the palace and the city were glorious, and both nobles and commoners rejoiced and were glad, while the governors of the provinces and the nabobs of various districts flocked from far away to witness Aladdin's marriage with all its processions and festivities. Moreover, when the sultan looked at Aladdin's mother, he was astounded by the change that had come over her, for he recalled how she used to visit him as a poor woman even though Aladdin had such immense wealth.

When the spectators, who crowded the royal palace to

enjoy the wedding festivities, gazed upon Aladdin's pavilion and saw how beautiful it was, they were tremendously surprised that such a vast edifice as that could have been built in a single night. Therefore, they blessed Aladdin and cried out, "May Allah reward him and bless him with prosperity and long life!"

When dinner was over, Aladdin rose and said farewell to the sultan. He mounted his horse and rode with his mamelukes to his pavilion so that he could make the preparations to receive his bride there. And as he passed, the people shouted their good wishes and blessings, and immense crowds conducted him to his new home while he showered gold on them along the way. When he reached his pavilion, he dismounted, entered, and sat down on the divan, while his mamelukes stood before him with arms folded. After a short while they brought him sherbets, and when he had drunk them, he ordered his slave girls, eunuchs, and mamelukes to get everything ready for the Lady Badar al-Budur.

As soon as noon arrived and the great heat of the sun had abated, the sultan ordered his officers, emirs, and viziers to go down to the parade ground, where he joined them on horse. And Aladdin also assembled his mamelukes and mounted a stallion who surpassed all the steeds of Arabia to ride to the parade ground. There he displayed what an expert horseman he was by excelling in the various games that were played. Badar al-Badur watched him from her balcony and was so impressed by his good looks and equestrian skills that she fell head over heels in love with him and was ecstatic with joy. After the games were finished, the sultan and his nobles returned to the palace, and Aladdin went back to his pavilion with his mamelukes.

Toward evening the viziers and nobles took the bridegroom and escorted him to the royal Hammam, where he was bathed and sprayed with perfume. As soon as he came out, he donned a suit more magnificent than his previous one and rode with the emirs and officers in a grand cortege surrounded by the viziers with their swords drawn. All the people and troops marched before him in a throng carrying wax candles and kettledrums, pipes, and other musical instruments, and they led him to his pavilion. Here he dismounted, and after entering, he sat down and offered seats to the viziers and emirs who had escorted him. Meanwhile the mamelukes brought sherbets that they also passed around to the people who had followed in the procession. There was a huge crowd outside, impossible to count, and Aladdin ordered his mamelukes to go out and shower them with gold coins.

In the meantime, when the sultan returned from the parade ground, he ordered his household to form a cavalcade for his daughter according to ceremony and to take the Lady Badar al-Budur to her bridegroom's pavilion. So the nobles and officers, who had followed and escorted the bridegroom, now mounted at once, and the slave girls and eunuchs went out with wax candles and made a splendid procession for the Lady Badar al-Budur. They marched in front of her, and Aladdin's mother was by her side, until they entered the pavilion. There were also the wives of the viziers, emirs, grandees, and nobles in front of the princess, and she was also attended by the forty-eight slave girls whom Aladdin had given to her as a present. Each one of them held a huge torch of camphor and amber set in a gold candlestick studded with gems. Upon reaching Aladdin's pavilion, they led the princess to her chamber on the upper floor, changed her robes, and displayed her. Then they accompanied her to Aladdin's apartment, and soon he paid her his first visit.

Now his mother was with the bride, and when Aladdin came up to the princess and took off her veil, the old woman was greatly taken by Badar al-Budur's beauty and loveliness. Moreover, she looked around the pavilion entirely illuminated by gold and gems with a gold chandelier studded with precious gems like emeralds and jacinths. Awed by what she saw, she said to herself, "Once upon a time I thought the sultan's palace was splendid, but this pavilion surpasses everything. I don't think a single king of the Chosroës ever accomplished anything like this. I'm even positive that nobody in the world could build something like it."

Then the tables were spread, and they all ate, drank, and enjoyed themselves. At the end of the meal, forty damsels came before them, each holding a musical instrument in her hand, and they deftly moved their fingers, touched the strings, and broke into song. Their tunes were very melodic and also melancholy and captivated all the listeners. The princess was particularly enchanted by the music and said to herself, "Never in my life have I heard such songs as these." Indeed, she was so enraptured that she refrained from eating in order to pay closer attention to the music. At last, Aladdin poured out wine for her and gave it to her with his own hand. In sum, it was a magnificent night, and not even Alexander the Great had ever enjoyed a feast like this one. When they had finished eating and drinking, and the tables were removed, Aladdin stood up and took his bride to his apartment, where he enjoyed her.

The next morning, Aladdin arose, and his servant brought him sumptuous garments and helped him get dressed. After drinking coffee flavored with amber, he ordered the horses to be saddled. Then he mounted with his mamelukes behind and in front of him and rode to his father-in-law's palace. When the sultan's eunuchs saw him approaching, they went in and reported his coming to their lord.

And Scheherazade noticed that dawn was approaching and stopped telling her story. When the next night arrived, however, she received the king's permission to continue her tale and said,

Informed that Aladdin was approaching, the sultan got up to receive him, and he embraced and kissed him as though he were his own son. After seating him on his right side, he blessed him and prayed for him, as did the viziers, emirs, and grandees of the realm. Soon the king commanded the attendants to serve the morning meal, and all the nobles at the court broke their fast together. After they had eaten and drunk to their satisfaction and the tables were removed, Aladdin turned to the sultan and said, "My lord, would your highness deign to honor me at dinner in the house of Lady Badar al-Budur, your beloved daughter, and bring with him all the ministers and grandees of the realm?"

The king was delighted by the invitation and replied, "You are most generous, my son!"

Then the sultan gave orders to his nobles, and, with Aladdin at his side, they all rode over to the pavilion. As the king entered it and gazed at its construction, architecture, and masonry, all jasper and carnelian, he was bedazzled by the grandeur and opulence. Turning to his grand vizier, he asked, "What do you say now? Have you ever seen anything in your entire life, even among the mightiest of the earth's monarchs, that can compare to such wealth of gold and jewels?"

"As I told your majesty before," the vizier said, "this feat could not have been accomplished by mortals, whether they be kings or commoners. No builders in the universe could have constructed a pavilion like this. All this could only have been produced by sorcery!"

"That's enough," replied the sultan. "Don't say another word. I know exactly what's prompted you to say what you've said."

Aladdin preceded the sultan and conducted him to the upper dome, where he saw its skylights, windows, and lattices, which were made of emeralds, rubies, and other gems. Once more, the sultan was stunned and astonished by all that his eyes encountered. He strolled around the dome and enjoyed himself by looking at the various sights until he came to the window that Aladdin had purposely left undone. When the sultan noticed that it was not finished, he cried out, "It's a shame, poor window, that you've been left unfinished!" Then, turning to his minister, he asked, "Why do you think that this window was left incomplete?"

"I imagine," said the vizier, "that Aladdin felt rushed by you and was in such a hurry to get married that he was unable to finish it."

Meanwhile, Aladdin had gone to his bride and informed the princess of her father's presence. When he returned to the dome, the king asked him, "My son, why was this window here left unfinished?"

"Great king," responded Aladdin, "the wedding was so sudden that I failed to find the artists who could finish it on time."

"I have a mind to complete it myself," said the sultan.

"May Allah grant your majesty perpetual glory!" exclaimed Aladdin. "This way your memory will endure forever in your daughter's pavilion."

At once the sultan ordered that jewelers and goldsmiths be summoned, and he commanded that they should be provided with everything they might need, such as gold and gems from his treasury. When the craftsmen were all assembled, he told them how he wanted the work to be completed in the dome window. Meanwhile the princess came forth to meet her father, who noticed her smiling face as she approached. So he embraced and kissed her, and then led her down into the pavilion.

By this time it was noon, and one table had been spread for the sultan, his daughter, and Aladdin, and a second one for the viziers, lords, chief officers, chamberlains, and nabobs. The king took his seat between the princess and her husband, and when he reached out his hand and tasted the food, he was struck with surprise by the savory flavor of the dishes and the sumptuous cooking. Moreover, there were eighty damsels who stood before him, and they were all so beautiful and radiant that each and every one of them could have said to the moon, "Move on so that I may take your place!" They all held musical instruments, which they played with great expertise, and they sang melodic songs that touched the heart of everyone who listened. The sultan had a wonderful time, and at one point he exclaimed, "Truly, all this is beyond the compass of either king or emperor!"

Everyone partook in the delicious meal, and the wine flowed until they had drunk enough. Then the sweetmeats and other desserts were served in another room, and they all moved there and enjoyed their fill. Soon the sultan arose so that he could inspect the work of his jewelers and goldsmiths. However, he noted a great difference, for his men were incapable of making anything like the windows in Aladdin's pavilion. They informed him how all the gems stored in his minor treasury had been brought to them, and they had used them to the best of their ability. However, since they were insufficient, the sultan now ordered that the gems from his major treasury be delivered to them, but they only sufficed to finish half the window. Therefore, the king ordered that all the precious stones owned by the viziers and grandees of the realm be brought to them. Yet, even here, they fell far short of the supply the craftsmen needed.

The next morning Aladdin arose to look at their work and noticed that they had not finished even a half of what they needed to do to complete the window. As a result, he ordered them to undo all they had done and restore the jewels to their owners. Accordingly, they pulled out the precious stones and sent those that belonged to the sultan back to him and the others to the viziers and grandees. Then the craftsmen went to the sultan and told him what Aladdin had ordered them to do. So he asked them, "What did he say to you? Why wasn't he content with your work? And why did he make you undo everything?"

"We have no idea, your majesty," they replied. "He just made us to take everything apart."

At once the sultan called for his horse, and after mounting it, he rode over toward the pavilion.

In the meantime, after Aladdin had dismissed the workers, he retired to his room and rubbed the lamp. Immediately the jinnee appeared and said, "Ask what you want. Your slave is at your service."

"I want you to finish the window that was left unfinished," said Aladdin.

"As you command," said the marid and vanished. Within seconds he returned and said, "My lord, I have carried out your command."

When Aladdin went upstairs to the dome, he found that the entire window had been finished. While he was still inspecting it, one of his eunuchs came to him and said, "My lord, the sultan has come to visit you and is at the pavilion gate."

So Aladdin went at once to greet his father-in-law, who, upon seeing him approach, cried out, "Why didn't you allow the craftsmen complete their work?"

"Great king," Aladdin replied, "I had purposely left this window unfinished. Indeed, I was perfectly capable of completing it. Certainly I did not intend to invite your majesty to a pavilion that was still deficient. And since I want to show you that I capable of making everything perfect, I would like you to accompany me upstairs to inspect the window."

So the sultan went up with him, and after entering the dome, he looked all over but saw nothing missing in the windows. Indeed, they were all perfect. Astounded by the sight, he embraced Aladdin and said, "My son, how did you accomplish this? How is it that you can finish something in a single night that my workers need months to finish? By Allah, there's no one in the world who can rival you!"

"May Allah grant you long life and prosperity!" Aladdin replied. "Your slave does not deserve such a compliment."

"My son," the sultan asserted, "you deserve all the praise in the world for a feat that no craftsman could ever accomplish."

Then the sultan went downstairs with him to the apartment of his daughter, where he relaxed for some time with her. He was pleased to see how much she enjoyed the glory and grandeur of the pavilion, and after reposing awhile, he returned to his palace.

Now, Aladdin was accustomed to ride through the city street every day with his mamelukes in front and behind him, and he would scatter gold among the people. There was not a person, native or foreigner, who did not love him for his generosity and kindness. Moreover, he increased the payments to help the poor and needy, and he himself helped distribute alms to them. Because of his good deeds, he won high renown throughout the realm, and most of the lords and emirs of the realm ate at his table. Everyone wished him well.

Aside from helping those in need, Aladdin continued enjoying such pastimes as riding and hunting. He would often go to the parade ground in the presence of the sultan and display his equestrian skills. And whenever the Lady Badar al-Budur watched him riding his magnificent steeds, her love for him grew, and she thought to herself that Allah had been most beneficent to her by causing what happened to the vizier's son and preserving her virginity for her true bridegroom.

Day by day Aladdin's fame grew, and his reputation became so great that everyone loved and admired him. Moreover, it so happened at that time that certain enemies of the sultan began to wage war against him. Therefore, the sultan equipped an army and made Aladdin the commander in chief. Before long he marched out with his men until he drew near the hostile forces, which were vast. When the action began, he bared his sword and charged at the enemy. The battle was violent, but at last Aladdin broke through the enemy's lines and put the foe to flight. His troops destroyed a good part of their army, and plundered their cattle, property, and possessions.

Moreover, Aladdin confiscated countless goods. Then he returned victorious to the capital, which had been decorated in his honor. The sultan went forth to meet him and embraced him in joy. Following this, there were great festivities held throughout the kingdom, and the king and his son-in-law retired to the pavilion, where they were met by the Princess Badar al-Budur, who rejoiced when she saw her husband again. After kissing him on his forehead, she led him to her apartment. After a while the sultan joined them, and they sat down while the slave girls brought them sherbets and desserts, which they drank and ate. Then the sultan commanded that the whole kingdom be decorated to celebrate the victory of his son-in-law over the invader.

By this time, all the soldiers and people of the kingdom looked only to Allah in heaven and Aladdin on earth. They loved him more than ever because of his generosity and kindness, his noble horsemanship and his success in defeating the foes of their country. Such then was the great fortune of Aladdin.

Now let us return to the magician, that Moor, who had traveled back to his own country after he failed to obtain the lamp. Once he was there, he spent his days bemoaning all the hardships that he had suffered in his attempt to win the lamp. It had been most frustrating for him to lose the lamp just when he was about to taste victory. Whenever he thought about it, he became enraged, and at times he would exclaim, "My only satisfaction is that the little bastard has perished in the cave, and I can only hope that someday I may still obtain the lamp, since it is still safe underground."

One day, he cast a geomantic table of sand and noted their figures so that he could transfer them to paper. After this, he studied them carefully, because he wanted to make sure of Aladdin's death and determine the exact position of the lamp beneath the ground. Soon he established the sequence of the figures, their origins and destinations, but he could not see the lamp. The result made him furious, and he made another try with the sand to ascertain Aladdin's death, but he did not see him in the enchanted cave. Now he almost exploded with anger when he realized that the boy had escaped from the underground and was somewhere on the face of the earth, alive and well. Moreover, it became clear to him that Aladdin must be the possessor of the lamp for which he himself had endured more hardship than any other man could possibly have endured for such a great object. "I have suffered more pain than any other mortal could bear because of that lamp, and that miserable creature did not have to do a thing for it to fall into his hands. If he has learned the virtues of the lamp, he must be the richest man in the world. All the more reason why I must destroy him!"

Then the Moor struck another geomantic table and examined the figures, which revealed to him that Aladdin had become immensely rich and had married the sultan's daughter. Therefore, his envy was fired with the flame of wrath, and without delay, he arose and equipped himself for a journey to distant China, where he arrived in due time.

Now, when he reached the king's capital, he took lodgings at one of the khans. After he had rested from his long and exhausting journey, he donned his suit and wandered about the streets. Wherever he went, he continually heard people praising the pavilion and its grandeur and vaunting the handsome features of Aladdin, his kindness, generosity, fine manners, and good morals. Soon he entered a tavern where men were drinking a warm beverage, and after approaching one man who was lauding Aladdin, he said to him, "Young man, who is this man you've been praising?"

"Apparently, you're a stranger," the man said, "and you've come from far away. But even if this is true, how is it that you've never heard of the Emir Aladdin, whose renown, I would imagine, has spread all over the universe and whose pavilion is known to people far and wide as one of the wonders of the world? How come you've never heard of the name of Aladdin and his fame, may Allah increase his glory?"

"It would be my greatest wish to see his pavilion," the Moor said. "In fact, I would be very much obliged if you could show it to me, since I am a foreigner."

"As you wish," the man said, and after bringing him to the pavilion, he departed.

When the Moor saw it, he realized at once that it was the work of the lamp. So he cried, "Ah! Ah! I'm going to dig the grave of this son of a tailor, who was such a rotten egg that he couldn't even earn his own living! If the fates are with me, I'll destroy his life and send his mother back to her spinning wheel." After exclaiming this, he returned to the khan in a downcast and furious mood. Once he was alone in his room, he took out his astrological equipment and geomantic table to discover where the lamp was being kept, and he learned that it was in the pavilion and that Aladdin was not carrying it with him. This disclosure made him feel happy, and he exclaimed, "Now it will be an easy task to take the life of this miserable wretch and obtain the lamp."

Then he went to a coppersmith and said to him, "Make me a set of lamps, and if you do a fast job, I'll pay you more than they're worth."

"Your wish is my command," said the coppersmith, and he began work on the lamps immediately. When they were finished, the Moor gave him what he demanded. Then he took them to the khan and put them in a basket. Soon thereafter he began wandering through the streets and markets of the city crying aloud, "Ho! Who will exchange old lamps for new lamps!"

When the people heard him cry out like this, they derided him and said, "He's surely mad! Who would offer new lamps for old ones?" Many people began following him, and little scamps ran after him and laughed at him from place to place. But he did not mind their treatment and derision. He kept walking about the streets until he came to Aladdin's pavilion, where he shouted with his loudest voice, and the boys screamed at him, "Madman! Madman!"

Now, as destiny would have it, the Lady Badar al-Budur was sitting near a window of the dome, and she heard the cries of the Moor and the children bawling at him. Since she did not understand what was going on, she gave orders to one of her slave girls to find out who was crying and why. The girl went outside and came upon a man crying, "Ho! Who will exchange old lamps for new lamps?" And there were boys chasing after him and laughing at him. When she returned and told the princess what was going on, Lady Badar al-Budur laughed loudly. Now Aladdin had carelessly left the lamp in his apartment without hiding it and locking it up in his strong-

LOUIS RHEAD

box, and one of the slave girls, who had seen it, said, "I think I noticed an old lamp in the apartment of my lord Aladdin. So why don't we take it down to the old man and see if he is telling the truth and will exchange with us?"

"Bring me the old lamp which you've seen in my lord's apartment," the princess said.

Lady Badar al-Budur knew nothing about the lamp and its secret powers that had enabled Aladdin to marry her and achieve such grandeur. She was merely bemused by the old man in the street and wanted to find out whether he would really exchange a new lamp for an old one. So when the slave girl returned from Aladdin's apartment with the lamp, she ordered a chief eunuch to go down and exchange the old lamp for a new one, not suspecting how cunning the Moor really was. The eunuch did as he was commanded, and after taking a new lamp from the Moor, he returned and placed it before his lady, who broke into laughter about the demented state of the man when she saw that the lamp was brand-new.

However, as soon as the Moor held the lamp in his hands, he knew it was the magic one from the enchanted cave, and he immediately stuck it into his breast pocket, leaving all the other lamps to the crowd of people that had gathered around him. Then he ran through the streets until he was clear of the city and could slow down. Once he reached the open plains, he felt more relaxed and waited for nightfall. There in the desert he took out the lamp and rubbed it. Immediately the jinnee appeared and said, "I am at your service. Ask whatever you want."

"I want you to lift up Aladdin's pavilion from its present place with all the people and contents in it, and then transport it along with me to my own country in Africa," said the Moor. "You know my home city, and I want the building placed in the gardens that are right near it."

"As you command," the marid replied. "Close your eyes and open your eyes, and you will find yourself together with the pavilion in your own country."

The Moor did this, and in the twinkle of an eye, the magician and the pavilion with everything in it were transported to Africa. Such, then, was the work of the Moor. But now let us return to the sultan and his son-in-law.

* * *

And Scheherazade noticed that dawn was approaching and stopped telling her story. When the next night arrived, however, she received the king's permission to continue her tale and said,

Because of the affection that the king had for his daughter, it was his custom to look out his window every morning after he got out of bed and to gaze at her abode. So, that day, he arose and did what he usually did. But when the king drew near his window this time and looked out at Aladdin's pavilion, he saw nothing. In fact, the site was as smooth as a well-paved street and just as it had been before. There was no edifice, nothing. He was so astonished and bewildered that he rubbed his eyes to make sure his vision was not impaired, but he was finally certain that there was no trace or sign of the pavilion. Nor did he have the slightest idea about why and where it had gone. His astonishment quickly turned to grief, and he wrung his hands while tears trickled down his cheeks and over his beard, for he was worried about his daughter. Then he sent out officials right away and summoned the grand vizier, who came to him at once. When he saw the sultan in such a miserable state, he said, "Pardon, your majesty, may Allah keep you from evil. Why are you so downcast?"

"Don't you know why?" asked the sultan

"Not at all," said the minister. "By Allah, I don't know anything."

"Then it's quite clear that you haven't looked at Aladdin's pavilion today."

"True, my lord, it must still be shut."

"Since you have no inkling of what has happened," said the king, "I want you to go over to the window and look over at Aladdin's pavilion and tell me whether it is still shut."

The vizier did what the sultan commanded, but he could not see anything. There was no pavilion nor anything else. Completely baffled, he returned to his lord, who remarked, "Now you know why I'm so distressed."

"Great king," the vizier said, "I told you before that the pavilion and all those other feats were brought about through magic."

On hearing this, the sultan fumed with rage and cried out, "Where is Aladdin?"

"He's gone hunting," answered the vizier.

Immediately the king ordered some of his chief eunuchs and officers to find Aladdin and bring him back in chains and manacles. So they went in search of him, and when they found him, they said, "My lord, excuse us and don't be angry with us. The king has commanded that we take you to him in chains and manacles. Those were his royal orders, and we must obey them."

Aladdin was greatly surprised by their words and baffled by the king's orders. At first he did not know what to say, but once he recovered from the shock, he said to the officers, "Do you know why the king is doing this? I know that I'm innocent and that I've never sinned against the king or his kingdom."

"My lord," they answered, "we have no idea whatsoever why the king has issued his orders."

So Aladdin dismounted from his horse and said to them, "Do whatever the king ordered you to do, for you are obliged to carry out his commands."

After the officers had bound Aladdin with chains and manacled him, they brought him back to the city. But when the people saw him in bonds, they realized that the king intended to cut off his head, and since they loved and admired him so much, they took out their weapons, swarmed out of their houses, and followed the soldiers to see what they could do. When the troops arrived with Aladdin at the palace, they entered and informed the sultan that they had found Aladdin. Thereupon the king ordered the executioner right away to cut off his son-in-law's head.

Now, as soon as the crowds of people were aware of this order, they barricaded the gates, closed the doors of the palace, and sent a message announcing to the king that they would level his palace and everyone in it if Aladdin was harmed in the slightest way.

So the vizier went to the sultan and reported, "Great king, your order is also our death warrant. I think that it would be a better idea if you pardoned your son-in-law, or else we shall have to pay the price. Your subjects love him far more than they love us."

The executioner had already spread the carpet of blood

and had compelled Aladdin to take his place on it. After tying a blindfold around his eyes, he walked around him three times awaiting the king's final orders. However, the king looked out the window and saw that his subjects had already begun storming the palace and were climbing over the walls. So he immediately ordered the executioner to stay his hand and commanded the herald to go out to the crowds and announce that he had pardoned Aladdin. But when his son-in-law found himself free and saw the sultan seated on his throne, he went up to him and said, "My lord, until recently you had treated me with extreme favor. Therefore, I beg you, be gracious enough to tell me how and why I have sinned against you."

"Traitor!" cried the king. "Do you pretend not to know your own sin?" And turning to his vizier, he said, "Take him to the window and make him look out. After that, let him tell us where his pavilion is."

After Aladdin saw that the pavilion had disappeared and the site was as level as a paved road, he was astonished and bewildered, since he did not know what had happened. When he returned to the king, his father-in-law asked, "Where is your pavilion and where is my daughter, the darling of my heart, my only child?"

"Your majesty," Aladdin answered, "I don't know anything about it, nor do I know what's happened."

"Then you must find out," answered the king. "I have pardoned you only so that you can look into this affair and find out what has happened to my daughter. Do not ever show your face here again unless you bring her back with you, and if you don't bring her back, I swear that I'll cut off your head!"

"As you command," Aladdin replied. "My only request is that you grant me forty days to do this. If I don't produce her within forty days, you can cut off my head and do with me whatever you wish."

"I shall grant you a delay of forty days," said the king, "but don't think you can ever escape me. No matter where you go on this earth, and even if you hide in the clouds, I'll find you and bring you back."

"Your highness, I've given you my word," said Aladdin. "If I don't bring her back within forty days, I'll return, and you can cut off my head."

Now, when the people saw that Aladdin was free, they were overcome with joy. But the way he had been put to shame before his friends and the exultation of his envious foes made him hang his head. So he went into the city alone and wandered about, perplexed by what had happened. He lingered in the capital for two days in the most sorrowful state, not knowing what to do. Indeed, he did not have the slightest idea of how to find his wife and his pavilion, and during this time various friends brought him something to eat and drink. After the two days had passed, he left the city and drifted aimlessly about the fields and open plains. As he walked, he came upon a path that led him to a river, where, because of the stress and sorrow, he abandoned himself to despair and thought about throwing himself into the water. However, being a good Moslem, who believed in the unity of the Godhead, he feared Allah in his soul, and standing upon the river bank, he prepared himself to perform the Wuzu ablution. But just as he was scooping up the water in his right hand and rubbing his fingers, he also chanced to rub the ring. All at once its jinnee appeared and said to him, "At your service. Your thrall has come. Ask me whatever you want."

Upon seeing the marid, Aladdin rejoiced and cried out, "Slave, I want you to bring back my wife and pavilion and everything that was inside it."

"My lord," replied the jinnee, "you're demanding a service of me that is impossible for me to perform. Only the slave of the lamp can do this. I can't and won't even dare to attempt it."

"Well, since the matter is beyond your power," Aladdin responded, "I won't demand this of you, but at least transport me to my pavilion, wherever it may be."

"As you command, my lord," said the jinnee, and after lifting him high in the air, in a split second he set Aladdin down beside his pavilion in Africa on a spot facing his wife's apartment.

Despite the fact that it was nighttime, he took one look and recognized that it was his home. Now all his cares and worries disappeared, and he regained trust in Allah after abandoning all hope of ever finding his wife again. Then he began to ponder the secret and mysterious ways of the Lord (all glory to His omnipotence) and how Allah had deigned to bless him and how the ring had come to his rescue just as he had thought he had been overcome by despair. Happy and relieved, Aladdin was also exhausted, for he had spent four days without sleep because of the stress he had been under. So when he approached the pavilion, he found a spot beneath a tree and slept near the building that had been set down among the gardens outside the city.

Although his head was full of worries, he managed to sleep soundly until morning, when he was wakened by the warbling of small birds. So he arose and went down to the bank of the river that flowed into the city and washed his hands and face. After he had finished his Wuzu ablution, he said the dawn prayer and then returned to sit beneath the window of his wife's apartment.

Now, the Lady Badar al-Budur had become extremely sad at being separated from her husband and father, and she suffered greatly from the misfortune that she had experienced at the hands of the accursed Moor. Since she could not eat or drink and found it difficult to sleep, she had become accustomed to rising with the dawn and sitting in tears by her window. Her favorite slave girl would enter her chamber at the hour of morning prayer in order to dress her, and this time, as destiny would have it, when she threw open the window to let her lady comfort herself by looking at the trees and hills, she caught sight of her master sitting below and quickly informed the princess.

"My lady! My lady!" she cried out. "My lord Aladdin is sitting at the foot of the wall."

So the princess arose hurriedly and went to the window, where she saw Aladdin, who caught sight of her just as he was raising his head. Immediately they greeted each other, and their hearts soared with joy.

"Come up to me through the secret door," she called out to him. "The accursed magician is not here now."

And she gave orders to the slave girl, who went downstairs and opened the door for him. Once Aladdin entered, he was met by his wife, and they embraced and kept kissing each other with delight until they wept for joy. After this, they sat down, and Aladdin said, "My lady, before anything else, I must ask you a question. I used to keep an old copper lamp in my apartment. Could you tell me what happened to it?"

When the princess heard these words, she sighed and cried, "Oh my darling, it was that very lamp which caused this catastrophe."

"How did it happen?" Aladdin asked.

And she answered by recounting everything that had occurred from first to last, especially how they had exchanged the old lamp for a new one. Then she added, "The next day at dawn we suddenly found ourselves in this land, and the man who deceived us and took the lamp informed me that he had accomplished everything through the magic lamp. He is a Moor from Africa, and we are now in his native country."

"What does this wretched criminal intend to do with you?" asked Aladdin. "What has he said to you? What does he want from you?"

"Every day he comes to visit me, just once," she said. "He has been wooing me and wants me to forget you. In fact, he insists on replacing you and wants me to marry him. He told me that my father had cut off your head, and that it was he who made you so rich, for at one timc you were just the son of poor parents. Most of the times he has tried to use sweet talk with me, but he's only received tears and moans in reply. Not one kind word has passed through my lips."

"Tell me if you know where he keeps the lamp," Aladdin asked.

"He always keeps it on him," she answered. "It never leaves him. Once, when he was talking to me about it, he took it from his breast pocket and showed it to me."

When Aladdin heard these words, he was very pleased and said, "My lady, listen to me now. I intend to leave you right away, but I'll return after I change my clothes. So don't be alarmed when you see me in different garments. I want you to order one of your slave girls to stand by the secret door, and when she catches sight of me, she's to open it at once. Now I'm off to devise a plan to slay this damned madman."

Upon saying this, he arose and went through the secret door. Then he walked for a while until he met a peasant, to whom he said, "Friend, I would like to exchange clothes with you."

But the peasant refused, and Aladdin had to use force to strip him of his clothes, but he left the man with his own rich garments to wear. Then he followed the highway leading to the nearby city, and after entering it, he went to a bazaar where incense and drugs were sold. There he bought a rare and potent drug called bhang, and he returned by the same road in disguise until he reached the pavilion. Once the slave girl caught sight of him, she opened the secret door, and in he went to the Lady Badar al-Budur.

And Scheherazade noticed that dawn was approaching and stopped telling her story. When the next night arrived, however, she received the king's permission to continue her tale and said,

"Listen carefully," Aladdin said to his wife. "I want you to get dressed in your very best garments and cast off all show of melancholy. In addition, when the accursed Moor comes to visit you, you're to welcome him and greet him with a smiling face and invite him to dine with you. Make him think that you've forgotten Aladdin your beloved and your father as well, and that you've fallen tremendously in love with him. At one point, you're to ask for some wine. Make sure that it's red, and pledge yourself to him. After you've given him two or three cups full and he's grown careless, you're to drop this powder into his cup and fill it with wine. As soon as he drinks it, he'll fall down senseless as though he were dead."

"It will be very difficult for me to do all this," said the princess. "However, I know I must do it if we're to escape this vile magician who's tormented me by this abduction. It's both lawful and right to kill this villain."

Then Aladdin ate and drank with his wife to placate his hunger, and immediately afterward he left the pavilion. Then the Lady Badar al-Budur summoned her slave girls, who dressed her in her finest raiment, adorned her, and sprayed her with perfume. Just as they were finished, the Moor entered her apartment, and he was most pleased to see her in this condition, and even more when, contrary to her former behavior, she greeted him with a smiling face. All this made his love and lust for her increase. Then she took him by his hand, and seating him beside her, said, "My darling, if you are willing, I would like you to come and dine with me tonight. I have mourned long enough, and even if I continued to do so for a thousand or two thousand years, Aladdin could not return to me from the tomb, for I believe what you said yesterday, that my father had him slain in sorrow over the separation from me. So you needn't wonder why I've changed so much from one day to the next. I have thought about everything and decided to accept you as my friend and lover and as Aladdin's successor, especially since I have no other man except you. Therefore, I want you to dine with me tonight, and we can drink wine and enjoy each other's company. I'd particularly like to taste some of your African wine, since I've heard that it is much better than the wine we drink in China."

Although Lady Badar al-Budur's change was sudden, she managed to convince the Moor that she had abandoned all hope of seeing Aladdin, and in his ecstasy, he said, "Your wish is my command, my lady. I have a cask of our native wine at home that I've carefully kept stored deep in the ground for eight years, and I'll go now and fetch whatever we shall need and return to you as soon as I can."

But since the princess wanted to tease him and excite him even more, she said, "My darling, don't leave me alone. Send one of your eunuchs to fetch the wine. Remain seated next to me so that I may enjoy your company."

"My lady," he replied, "nobody knows where the cask is buried except me, and I won't be away too long."

After saying this, the Moor left, and after a short time, he brought back as much wine as they needed. Thereupon, the princess said to him, "You've gone to great pains to please me, my beloved, and I apologize."

"Not at all, my dearest," said the Moor. "It is an honor to serve you."

The Lady Badar al-Budur sat down at the table with him, and they began eating. Soon the princess requested the wine, and a slave girl filled her cup and then the Moor's. So she drank to his long life and his secret wishes, and he also drank to her life. Since the princess had a great gift in making eloquent speeches, she began to make all sorts of toasts to him and beguiled him by addressing him in the sweetest terms full of hidden meaning. Unable to see through her deception, the Moor thought that her actions resulted from her true inclination for him and did not suspect that she was setting a trap. So his longing for her increased, and out of love for her, his head began to swim, and the world seemed as if it were nothing in his eyes. When they came to the end of the dinner, and the wine had gotten the better of him, the princess realized that she had him at her mercy and said, "There is a custom in our country, but I don't know whether you do the same thing in yours."

"What is it?" asked the Moor.

So she said to him, "At the end of dinner, each lover takes the cup of the other beloved and drinks it."

Thereupon she took his cup and filled it with wine for herself. Then she poured the wine into hers, mixed with the drug, and asked a slave girl to give it to him. Now she had instructed the slave girl what she was to do, and all the slave girls and the eunuchs in the pavilion longed for the sorcerer's death and supported the princess's plan. Accordingly, the slave girl handed him the cup, and when he saw the princess drinking from his cup and was taken in by her show of love, he imagined he was Iskandar, Lord of the Two Horns. Then she leaned over to him, swaying to and fro, put her hand within his hand, and said, "Oh my life, your cup is with me, and mine with you, and this is the way that lovers drink from each other's cup."

Then she kissed the brim, drained his cup, and then kissed the brim of her own cup for him to drink. By now he was delirious, and he wanted to follow her example. He kissed the brim, raised the cup to her, and then drank the contents down, without worrying whether there was anything harmful in it. And immediately thereafter he rolled over on his back as though he were dead, and the cup dropped from his hand. Right then and there the slave girls ran hurriedly to the secret door and opened it for their lord Aladdin, who was still disguised as a peasant. He ran up to his wife's apartment and found her still sitting at the table and facing the drugged Moor. At once he approached her, kissed her, and thanked her for all that she had done. Overjoyed by what had taken place, he said, "Please withdraw with your slave girls to the inner chamber, and leave me alone for a while so that I may think about what I have to do."

The princess went away at once with her slave girls, and Aladdin locked the door behind them. Then he walked up to the Moor, stuck his hand into the magician's breast pocket, and drew out the lamp. After doing this, he unsheathed his sword and slew the villain. Then he rubbed the lamp, and immediately the jinnee appeared and said, "At your service, my lord. What is it you want?"

"I want you to take my pavilion and transport it to China," replied Aladdin. "You are to set it down on the spot where it was standing before."

"As you command, my lord," said the marid.

Then Aladdin went to his wife, and throwing his arms around her, he kissed her, and she kissed him, and they sat in conversation while the jinnee transported the pavilion and all its contents to the designated place. Soon Aladdin ordered the slave girls to set the table, and he and the Lady Badar al-Budur began eating and drinking with great joy until they had contented themselves. Thereafter, they withdrew to the drinking room, where they caroused and kissed each other. It had been a long time since they had been able to enjoy each other, and they continued to do so until the wine rose in their heads and sleep got the better of them.

Early the next morning, Aladdin awoke and woke his wife. Then the slave girls entered and helped her get dressed, while Aladdin donned his finest raiment. The two were ecstatic about their reunion, and the princess was especially joyous and glad that day because she expected to see her beloved father.

So much for Aladdin and his wife, the Lady Badar al-Budur. Now let us return to the sultan.

After he had driven away his son-in-law, he kept mourning the loss of his daughter, and every hour of every day he would sit and weep for her as women weep because she was his one and only child. And as soon as he shook off sleep morning after morning, he would rush to the window, throw it open, and peer in the direction of Aladdin's pavilion. Then tears would stream from his eyes until his lids were red and sore.

Now on that particular day he arose at dawn, and

according to his custom, he looked out and suddenly saw a building. So he rubbed his eyes and kept looking at it curiously until he was certain that it was his son-in-law's pavilion. So he called for a horse right away, and as soon as the steed was saddled, he mounted and headed for the pavilion.

When Aladdin saw his father-in-law approaching, he went down and met him halfway. Then, taking him by the hand, he helped the sultan upstairs to his daughter's apartment. Anxious to see her father, the princess had descended and greeted him at the door of the staircase facing the ground-floor hall. Thereupon the king hugged her in his arms and kissed her, shedding tears of joy, and she did likewise, until Aladdin finally led them to the upper salon, where they took seats, and the sultan began asking her all about what had happened.

"My father," she began, "I only regained my life yesterday when I saw my husband, and it was he who set me free from a vile magician. I don't believe that there is a more treacherous man on earth than this Moor. If it had not been for my beloved, I would never have escaped him, nor would you ever have seen me again. I had been deeply grieved because I had lost you and also my husband, to whom I shall be grateful for the rest of my life for freeing me from that wicked sorcerer."

Then the princess related everything that had happened to her, how the Moor had tricked her in the disguise of a lamp-seller, how she had given him the magic lamp, and how she had laughed at the Moor when she exchanged the old lamp for the new one, how she had been transported in the pavilion to Africa, and how Aladdin had freed them with the help of the potent drug. In turn, Aladdin recounted how he had slaughtered the wizard when he had found him dead drunk, how he had taken the lamp from the sorcerer's breast pocket, and how he had ordered the jinnee to transport the pavilion back to its proper site, ending his tale with, "And if your highness has any doubt about our story, come with me and take a look at the accursed magician."

Accordingly the king went with Aladdin, and after looking at the Moor, he ordered the corpse to be carried away and burned and its ashes scattered in the air. Then he embraced Aladdin and said, "Pardon me, my son.

Indeed I was on the verge of taking your life because of the foul deeds of this damned wizard, who put you in a dangerous situation. You must excuse me for what I did, because I was deeply upset about my daughter, my only child, who is dearer to me than my kingdom. You must know the great love parents bear for their offspring."

"Your majesty," Aladdin replied, "you did nothing that went against Holy Law, and likewise, I did not sin against you. The entire trouble was caused by that Moor, the unholy magician."

Thereupon the sultan ordered the city to be decorated and commanded the herald to announce, "This day is a great holiday. There will be public celebrations for one month in honor of the return of Lady Badar al-Budur and her husband Aladdin!"

And the people obeyed and held banquets and feasts throughout the city. And that was the end of Aladdin's troubles with the Moor.

However, even though the magician's body had been burned and his ashes scattered in the air, the villain had a brother even more vile than he was and even more adept in necromancy, geomancy, and astrology. As the saying goes, they were like two peas from the same pod, and when the pod was split, each dwelled in his own part of the globe and practiced sorcery, fraud, and treachery.

Now, one day it so happened that the Moor's brother learned what had happened to him through his geomantic sandboard. After grieving awhile, he cast the sand a second time to learn how his brother had died and where. This was how he discovered that the site was Africa and that his brother had been killed by a man called Aladdin, who was now living in China. Once this sorcerer had gathered all this information, he arose right away and equipped himself for the voyage to China. After he had traveled through wilderness and over mountains and plains for many months, he reached China and the city where he hoped to find his brother's murderer. He took lodgings at the inn for foreigners, and after resting in his room for a while, he went out and wandered about the streets contemplating a way to avenge his brother's death. Soon he entered a coffee house, a fine building which stood in the marketplace, and which attracted many people to play at dice, backgammon, chess, and other games.

There he sat down and listened to those seated next to him, and they happened to be speaking about a holy woman named Fatimah, who lived outside the town in a cell where she practiced her devotions. She entered the city only two days each month, and according to the people who were talking, she had performed many holy miracles to help those in need.

"This is exactly what I was looking for," said the Moorish sorcerer to himself. "God willing, I'll be able to carry out my plans with the help of this old woman." Then the magician turned to the people who were talking about the miracles performed by the devout old woman and said to one of them, "Friend, I heard you talking about the virtues of a certain holy woman named Fatimah. Could you tell me who she is and where she lives?"

"Remarkable!" exclaimed the man. "How come you've never heard about the miracles of the Lady Fatimah? Evidently you must be a stranger if you know nothing about her devout fasts, her asceticism, and her beautiful piety!"

"It's true, my lord," replied the Moor. "Yes, I am a stranger, and I arrived in your city only last night. And now I hope that you will tell me about the holy miracles of this virtuous woman and where she lives, for I've suffered a terrible calamity, and I'd like to visit her and request that she pray for me, so that Allah may deliver me from evil through her blessings."

In response, the man recounted the marvels of the Holy Fatimah, her piety and devout life. Then taking him by the hand, he led him outside the city and showed him the way to her abode, a cave on the top of a hill. The magician thanked him for showing him the place and returned to his khan. Now, as fate would have it, Fatimah came down to the city the very next day, and the Moor happened to leave his khan early the morning and encounter crowds of people. Since he was curious about what was going on, he went and saw the holy woman standing in the middle of a throng of people, and anyone who suffered from pain or sickness went up to her and solicited a blessing and prayer. Indeed, each and every one she touched was instantly cured from his illness. The sorcerer followed her about the city until she returned to her dwelling. Then he walked back to his khan and waited until evening, when he drank a cup of wine at a tavern. After this, he left the city and went straight to the holy woman's cave. After entering it, he saw her lying prostrate with her back on a strip of matting. So he moved forward, sat down on her stomach, drew his dagger, and began shouting at her. When she opened her eyes, she was terrified to find a Moor sitting on her belly with a dagger in his hand about to kill her. However, he said to her, "Don't utter a word! If you do, I'll slay you right this second. Now get up, and do everything I tell you to do."

Then he swore to her that if she obeyed his orders, no matter what they were, he would not kill her. After saying this, he got off her stomach and stood up, and Fatimah did likewise.

"Give me your dress," he said, "and take my garments."

So she gave him her headdress, veil, and mantilla. Then he said, "You must also use some ointment on me so that my face becomes the same color as yours."

Accordingly, she went to the back of the cave and brought out a jar of ointment, spread some of it on her palm, and smeared his face until it looked like hers. Then she hung her rosary around his neck, gave him her staff, and showed him how to walk and what to do when he entered the city. Finally, she handed him a mirror and said, "Now you look just like me."

When he gazed into the mirror, he appeared as though he were Fatimah herself. But when he had accomplished what he had wanted, he broke his word and asked for a piece of rope, which he used to strangle her. When she was dead, he hauled the corpse outside and threw it into a nearby pit. Then he went back to sleep in her cave, and when dawn arrived the next day, he went into the town and took a place under the walls of Aladdin's pavilion. Gradually the people began flocking to him, certain that he was the Holy Fatimah, and he did what she usually did. He placed his hands on those in pain and recited verses from the Koran. Soon the clamoring of the crowd was heard by the lady Badar al-Budur, who said to her slave girls, "Find out what's causing all that noise!"

So the chief eunuch went out to see what the matter was and soon returned to his mistress and said, "My lady, the commotion is being caused by the Lady Fatimah, and if you wish, I'll bring her to you so that you may obtain a blessing from her."

"Go and fetch her," said the princess. "I've heard about her miracles and virtues for some time now, and I'd very much like to meet her and get a blessing from her."

The eunuch went out and brought in the Moor disguised in Fatimah's clothing. When the magician stood before the Lady Badar al-Budur, he began to bless her right away with a string of prayers. Everyone was completely convinced that it was the holy woman herself. So the princess arose and saluted him and had him take a seat by her side.

"My lady Fatimah," she said, "It would be an honor if you would always stay here so that I could receive your blessings and learn how to follow your pious and good example."

Though this invitation was exactly what he had wanted, the sorcerer felt it would be best for the deception if he played hard to get. So he replied, "My lady, I'm a poor religious woman who dwells in a cave. People like myself are not fit to live in the palaces of kings."

But the princess replied, "Don't you worry in the least. I'll give you a separate apartment in the pavilion, and you'll be able to worship as you please. Nobody will disturb you, and it will be better place to pray to Allah than your cave."

"As you wish, my lady," said the Moor. "I'll accept your offer, for the commands of royalty are not to be opposed. My only wish is that I may be able to eat, drink, and sit in my own chamber that will be entirely private. I don't desire anything special except a bit of bread and some water that one of your slave girls could perhaps carry to me every day. If I happen to need food, I would prefer to eat it in my own room."

Of course, the reason the accursed magician said all this was to avert discovery at mealtimes, when he would have had to raise his kerchief, and his beard and moustache would have given him away.

"Oh Lady Fatimah," the princess replied. "There is nothing to worry about. Everything will be just as you desire. Now, please rise, so that I can show you the apartment."

Lady Badar al-Budur conducted the sorcerer to a separate apartment in the pavilion that she had kindly promised him for a home. Then she said, "Lady Fatimah, you can have your privacy here and live in comfort, and we shall name this place after you."

The Moor acknowledged her kindness and prayed for her. Then the princess showed him the jeweled dome with its twenty-four windows and asked him what he thought of the marvelous pavilion.

"By Allah, my daughter," said the magician, "it is wonderful, and there is probably nothing like it in the entire universe. However, it appears to be lacking one thing that would enhance its beauty."

"What is it?" asked the princess. "Please tell me, for I want it to be absolutely perfect."

"The only thing it needs," said the Moor, "is the egg of the bird Rukh hanging from the middle of the dome. If this were done, there would be absolutely nothing like this pavilion in the world."

"What is this bird?" the princess asked. "Where can we find her egg?"

"My lady, the Rukh is a gigantic bird," the sorcerer replied. "It is so powerful that it can carry off camels and elephants in its claws. It is found mainly on Mount Kaf, and the architect who built this pavilion is capable of bringing you one of its eggs."

Then they stopped their conversation, since it was noontime and when the servants set the table, the Lady Badar al-Budur invited the accursed Moor to eat with her, but he refused, and the princess had his meal carried to his room, where he ate by himself.

Now, when it turned evening, Aladdin returned from the hunt and greeted his wife by embracing and kissing her. However, when he looked her in the face, he noticed that she was somewhat sad and did not smile. So he asked her, "Has anything happened to you, my darling? Tell me what's troubling you."

"Nothing whatsoever," she replied. "But, my beloved, I had thought that our pavilion was absolutely perfect and did not lack a thing. But that is not entirely the case, Aladdin. I think that if there were a Rukh's egg that hung from the jeweled dome, there would be nothing like it in the universe."

"Is this all that's been bothering you?" Aladdin asked. "It's the easiest thing in the world for me to fix. So cheer up. All you have to do is to tell me when you want something, and I'll fetch it instantly, even if it's hidden in the bowels of the earth."

And Scheherazade noticed that dawn was approaching and stopped telling her story. When the next night arrived, however, she received the king's permission to continue her tale and said,

After making sure that his wife had regained her good spirits, Aladdin withdrew to his chamber, where he took the lamp and rubbed it. Immediately the jinnee appeared and said, "Ask whatever you want."

"I want you to fetch me the egg of the bird Rukh," Aladdin replied. "And I want you to hang it from the dome of my pavilion."

But when the marid heard these words, his face became fierce, and he shouted with a mighty and frightful voice, "You ungrateful soul! Isn't it enough that I and all the slaves of the lamp are always at your service? Yet now, you also demand that I bring you our mistress just for your pleasure and hang her up in the dome of the pavilion for the enjoyment of you and your wife. By Allah, you and she deserve to be reduced to ashes this very moment and to be scattered in the air. But since you two are not aware of the crime you have committed and its consequences, I'll pardon you. Innocent as you are, you can't help what you've done. The crime is due to that sorcerer, the brother of the Moorish magician, who is living here and pretending to be the Holy Fatimah. He put on her clothes and disguised himself as her after murdering her in her cave. Indeed, he came here to kill you out of revenge for his brother, and it is he who persuaded your wife to make this request to me."

After saying all this, the jinnee vanished. Yet, Aladdin was still trembling after hearing the marid shout at him, and he felt completely bewildered. But gradually he recovered his senses and went into his wife's apartment. There he pretended to have a headache, for he knew how famous Fatimah was for healing all sorts of pains like that. When the Lady Badar al-Budur saw him sitting with his hand on his head and complaining about the pain, she asked him what the matter was, and hc replied, "I don't know why, but I've got a terrible ache in my head."

Thereupon she ordered that the Holy Fatimah be summoned immediately so that she could put her hand on his head.

"Who is this Fatimah?" Aladdin asked.

So she informed him that it was the Holy Fatimah, for whom she had provided a home in the pavilion. Meanwhile a slave girl had gone to fetch the accursed Moor, and when the villain appeared, Aladdin stood up and, acting as though he knew nothing about the magician's decęption, he saluted him as though he were the real Fatimah. He kissed the hem of his sleeve, welcomed him, and treated him with honor.

"My Lady Fatimah," Aladdin said, "I would appreciate it if you would do me a favor. I am well aware that you are adept at curing pains, and I am now suffering from a terrible headache."

The accursed Moor could hardly believe his ears, since this was exactly what he had wanted. So he approached Aladdin to place his hand upon his head and heal his ache. As he did this, the other hand was under his gown holding a dagger and ready to kill him. But Aladdin was watching him carefully and waited patiently until the Moor revealed the dagger. Then, with a powerful grip, he wrenched the dagger from his grasp and plunged it deep into his heart. When the Lady Badar al-Budur saw him do this, she shrieked, "Why have you shed this holy woman's blood? Have you no fear of Allah? Don't you know that the Holy Fatimah's miracles are known throughout the world?"

"But I haven't killed Fatimah," Aladdin replied. "I've only killed Fatimah's murderer, the brother of that vile Moor who abducted you through his magic and transported my pavilion to Africa. His damned brother came to our city and planned our downfall. He murdered Fatimah and assumed her identity in order to avenge his brother's death. If you don't believe me, come over here and take a look at the person I have slain."

Thereupon Aladdin drew the Moor's veil aside, and the Lady Badar al-Budur saw a man with a full beard.

Realizing that her husband was telling the truth, she said, "My beloved, this is the second time that I've placed your life in danger!"

"No harm's been done," replied Aladdin. "Besides, your eyes are blessing enough for all the risks I've taken, and I'll joyfully take on anything that comes with being married to you."

Hearing these words, the princess embraced him and said, "My darling, I can't believe you've done all this out of your love for me! I never knew how much you loved me. But don't think that I take your affection for granted."

So Aladdin kissed her and held her close, and they could feel their love for each other grow stronger.

Now, just at that moment, the sultan appeared, and they told him about everything that had happened and showed him the corpse of the sorcerer. Consequently, the king commanded the body to be burned and the ashes to be scattered in the air, just as he had done with the wizard's brother.

Thereafter, Aladdin lived with his wife, the Lady Badar al-Budur, in happiness and joy, and he survived all the dangers that he later encountered. After a while, when the sultan died, Aladdin ascended the throne. During his reign he treated his subjects with justice and wisdom so that everyone loved him. And he lived with his wife in bliss and serenity until the Destroyer of delights and the Severer of societies came and visited him.

No sooner had Scheherazade concluded her tale than she said, "And yet, oh king, this tale is no more wondrous than the remarkable story of 'Julnar the Mermaid and her Son Badar Basim of Persia.' "

Julnar the Mermaid and Her Son Badar Basim of Persia

Many years ago there was once a mighty monarch in the land of Ajam called King Shahriman, who lived in Khorasan. He owned a hundred concubines, but none of them had blessed him by giving birth to a child. As time passed, he began to lament the fact that he was without an heir, and there would be nobody to inherit his kingdom as he had inherited it from his father and forebears. One day, as he was grieving about this, one of his mamelukes came to him and said, "My lord, there is a merchant at the door with a slave girl, who is more beautiful than any woman I've ever seen before."

"Send them in," the king said.

After they had entered, Shahriman saw that the girl had a marvelous figure and was wrapped in a silk veil lined with gold. When the merchant uncovered her face, the place was illuminated by her beauty, and her seven tresses hung down to her anklets in lovelocks. She had coal-black eyes, heavy lips, a slender waist, and luscious thighs. Just the sight of her could heal all maladies and quench the fire of hearts longing for love. Indeed, the king was amazed by her beauty and loveliness, and grace, and said to the merchant, "Oh sheikh, how much for this maiden?"

"My lord," answered the merchant, "I bought her for two thousand dinars from a merchant who owned her before I did. Since then I have traveled with her for three years, and she has cost me another three thousand gold pieces up to the time of my arrival here. Despite all these expenses, she is a gift from me to you."

As a reward for this gesture, the king presented him

with a splendid robe of honor and ten thousand ducats, whereupon the merchant kissed his hands, thanked him for his generosity, and went his way. Afterward the king gave the damsel to the slave girls and said, "Go and bathe her. Then adorn her and furnish her with a bower, where she is to reside." In addition, he ordered his chamberlains to bring her everything she requested and to shut her doors after they left.

And Scheherazade noticed that dawn was approaching and stopped telling her story. When the next night arrived, however, she received the king's permission to continue her tale and said,

Now, the king's capital was called the White City and was located on the seashore. Therefore, the chamber in which the damsel was installed had windows that overlooked the sea. When Shahriman eventually went to visit her there, she did not speak to him, nor did she take any notice of him.

"It would seem that she's been with people who never taught her any manners," he said. Then he looked at the damsel and marveled again at her beauty, loveliness, and grace. Indeed, she had a face like the rondure of the full moon or the radiant sun shining on a clear day. And he praised Almighty Allah for having produced such a splendid creature, and he walked up to her and sat down by her side. Then he pressed her to his bosom, and after seating her on his thighs, he sucked the dew of her lips, which he found sweeter than honey. Soon after this he called for trays spread with all kinds of the richest viands, and while he ate, he also fed her by mouthfuls until she had had enough. All the while she did not speak a single word. Even when the king began to talk to her and asked her name, she remained silent and did not utter a syllable or give him an answer. Only her incomparable beauty saved her from his majesty's wrath. "Glory be to God, the Creator of this girl!" he said to himself. "She would be perfectly charming if she would only speak! But perfection belongs only to Allah the Most High." And he asked the slave girls whether she had spoken, and they said, "From the time of her arrival until now she has not uttered one word, nor has she even addressed us."

Then he summoned some of his women and concubines and ordered them to sing to her and make merry so that perhaps she might speak. Accordingly they played all sorts of instruments and games before her so that all the people present enjoyed themselves except the damsel, who looked at them in silence and neither laughed nor spoke. The king became extremely distressed because of this, and he dismissed the women and the rest of the company. When everyone was gone, he took off his clothes and disrobed her with his own hand. When he looked at her body, he saw that it was as smooth as a silver ingot, and his love for her was aroused. So he lay down next to her and began making love. Soon he took her maidenhead and was pleased to find that she was a pure virgin. "By Allah," he said to himself, "it's a wonder that a girl so fair of form and face should have been left untouched and pure by the merchants!"

From then on he devoted himself entirely to her and gave up all his other concubines and favorites. Indeed, he spent one whole year with her as if it were a single day. Still, she did not speak one word, until one morning he said to her, "Oh love of my life, my passion for you is great, and I have forsaken all my slave girls, concubines, and favorites, and I have made you my entire world and had patience with you for one whole year. So I now beseech Almighty Allah to do me a favor and soften your heart so that you'll speak to me. Or, if you are mute, tell me by some sign so that I'll give up hope of ever hearing you speak. My only prayer is that the Lord will grant me a son through you so that there will be an heir to the kingdom after me. May Allah bless you, and if you love me, you'll now give me a reply."

The damsel bowed her head awhile in thought. Eventually she raised it and smiled at him, and it seemed to him as if the rays of the sun had filled the chamber. Then she said, "Oh magnanimous lord and valorous lion, Allah has answered your prayer, for I am with child by you, and the time of my delivery is near at hand, although I am not sure whether the baby will be a boy or girl. But one thing is certain: if I had not become pregnant by you, I would not have spoken one word to you."

When the king heard her talk, his face shone with joy and gladness, and he kissed her head and hands out of delight. "Praise the Lord!" he said. "Almighty Allah has granted all my wishes—your speech and a child!"

Then he got up, left her chamber, and seated himself on his throne. In his ecstasy he ordered his vizier to distribute a hundred thousand dinars to the poor and needy and widows as a way of showing his gratitude to Allah Almighty. The minister did as he was commanded, and then the king returned to the damsel, embraced her, and said, "Oh my lady, my queen, your slave desires to know why you were silent so long. You spent one whole year with me, and yet you did not speak to me until this day. Why?"

"Listen to me carefully, my lord," she replied, "for I want you to know that I am a wretched exile and broken-hearted. My mother, my family, and my brother are far away from me."

When the king heard her words, he knew how she felt and said, "There's no more need for you to feel so wretched, for I swear to you my kingdom and goods and all that I possess are at your service, and I have also become your husband. But as for your separation from your mother, brother, and family, I understand your sorrow, but just tell me where they are, and I will send for them and fetch them here."

"Gracious king, you must listen to the rest of my story," she answered. "First, let me tell you that my name is Julnar the Mermaid, and that my father was a descendant of the kings of the High Seas. When he died, he left us his realm, but while we were still upset and mourning him, one of the other kings arose against us and took over our realm. I have a brother called Salih, and my mother is also a woman of the sea. While all this was happening, I had a falling out with my brother and swore that I would throw myself into the hands of a man of the land. So I left the sea and sat down on the edge of an island in the moonshine, and a passerby found me. He took me to his house and tried to make love to me, but I struck him on the head so hard that he almost died. Once he recovered, he took me away and sold me to the merchant from whom you bought me. This merchant was a good man—virtuous, pious, loyal, and generous. If it were not for the fact that you fell in love with me and promoted me over all your concubines, I would not have remained with you a single hour. Rather, I would have sprung into the sea from this window and gone to my mother and family. Now, however, I've become ashamed to travel to them, since I am carrying your child. They would consider this to be sinful and would no longer regard me with esteem, even if I were to tell them that a king had bought me with his gold, given me his property, and preferred me over all his wives. —This then is my story."

And Scheherazade noticed that dawn was approaching and stopped telling her story. When the next night arrived, however, she received the king's permission to continue her tale and said,

Then the king thanked Julnar for telling him her story, kissed her on her forehead, and said, "By Allah, oh lady and light of my eyes, I can't bear to be separated from you for more than one hour. If you were ever to leave me, I would die immediately. What are we to do?"

"My lord," she replied, "the time of my delivery is near at hand, and my family must be present so that they can tend me. You see, the women of the land do not know how women of the sea give birth to children, nor do the daughters of the ocean know the ways of the daughters of the earth. When my people come, we will all be reconciled to one another."

"But how do people of the sea walk about in the water and breathe?" asked the king.

"We walk in the water and breathe as you do here on ground," she said, "thanks to the names engraved on the ring of Solomon David-son. But now, listen to me, when I call for my kith and kin to come here, I'll tell them how you bought me with gold and have treated me with kindness and benevolence. It will be important for you to show them that you have a magnificent realm and that you're a mighty king."

"My lady," he said, "do whatever you think is appropriate, and you can rely on me to carry out your commands."

Then the damsel continued telling him about her life. "Yes," she said, "we walk in the sea and perceive everything that is in the water. We even behold the sun, moon, stars, and sky, as though they were on the surface of the earth. But this does not bother us. There are many types of people in the high seas and various forms and creatures on land, but the differences are not all that great."

The king was astounded by her words, and then she pulled two small pieces of Comorin lign aloes from her bosom, and after kindling a fire in a chafing dish, she took some of the lign aloes and threw them into the fire. Right after that she whistled loudly and said something that the king could not understand. Suddenly a great deal of smoke arose, and she said to the king, "My lord, get up and hide yourself in a closet so that I may show you my brother, mother, and family without them seeing you. I have decided to bring them here, and you will soon see a wondrous thing and marvel at the strange creatures and forms that Allah Almighty has created."

So he quickly entered a closet and began watching what she would do. And indeed, she continued her incantations until the sea began to foam and froth, and all at once a handsome young man arose from it. He was as bright as the full moon with a handsome white brow, ruddy cheeks, and teeth like pearls. Moreover, he was very much like his sister in looks. After him came an ancient dame with speckled gray hair and five maidens, radiant moons, who resembled Julnar a great deal. The king watched them as they walked on the face of the water until they drew near Julnar's window and saw her. Once they recognized her, they entered the chamber through the window, and she rose to greet them with joy and gladness. Indeed, they embraced and wept profusely until one of them said, "Oh Julnar, how could you leave us four years and not tell us where you were? By Allah, we've been extremely upset since your separation, and we haven't been able to enjoy food or drink. No, not for one day. We have longed so much for you that we've not been able to stop weeping!"

Then Julnar began kissing the hands of her mother, brother, and relatives, and they sat with her awhile asking her to tell them what had happened to her and what she was doing there.

"When I left you," Julnar began, "I emerged from the sea and sat down on the shore of an island, where a man found me and sold me to a merchant, who brought me to this city and sold me for ten thousand dinars to the king of this country. Now, this king has treated me with great honor and given up all his concubines, women, and favorites for my sake. Moreover, he has devoted all this time and energy into looking after my welfare."

"Praise be to Allah, who has reunited us with you," said her brother. "But now, my sister, it's time for you to come back with us to our country and people."

When the king heard these words, he almost went out of his mind, fearing that Julnar might agree with her brother and he would not be able to stop her. He loved her passionately and was extremely afraid of losing her.

"By Allah," Julnar replied, "the mortal who bought me is the lord of this city, and he is a mighty king and a wise, good, and generous man. Moreover, he has a great deal of wealth and does not have an heir to his throne. He has treated me with honor, done all sorts of favors for me, and has never spoken one unkind word to me. He does nothing without my advice, and I have the best of all possible worlds with him. Furthermore, if I were to leave him, he would perish, for he cannot endure to be separated from me for more than one hour. Indccd, if I left him, I, too, would die because I love him so much. Even if my father were alive, I could not have a better life than the life I presently lead with this great and glorious monarch. And right now, to tell you the truth, I am carrying his child, and praise be to Allah, who has made me a daughter of the kings of the sea, and my husband the mightiest of kings of the land. Indeed, Allah has compensated me for whatever I lost."

And Scheherazade noticed that dawn was approaching and stopped telling her story. When the next night arrived, however, she received the king's permission to continue her tale and said,

Julnar paused for a moment and then continued explaining her situation to her brother and family. "As I mentioned before, this king does not have an heir, and so I have prayed to Allah to bless me with a son who would inherit everything that belonged to this mighty lord's realm."

Now, when her brother and family heard her speech, they understood her situation much better and responded, "Oh Julnar, you know how much we respect and love you. You are the dearest of creatures, and we only want you to lead a life without travail or trouble. Therefore, if you are suffering in any way, we want you to come with us to our land and folk. But if you are happy here and are honored the way you should be, we would not want to take you away or do anything against your wishes."

"By Allah," she said, "I have all the comfort, solace, and honor I need here."

When the king heard what she said, his heart was set at rest, and he thanked her silently for everything. His love for her grew immensely, and he now knew that she loved him as he loved her and desired to remain with him, and that he would get to see his child.

Then Julnar ordered her women to set the table with all sorts of viands, which had been cooked in the kitchen under her supervision, and fruit and sweetmeats. When that was done, she and her kinsfolk sat down and ate. But soon they said to her, "Julnar, we have never met your lord, and yet we have entered his house without his permission or knowledge. You have praised his excellent qualities and have set his food before us, which we have eaten. Yet, we have not enjoyed his company or seen him." So they all stopped eating and were angry with her. Suddenly fire spouted from their mouths, and the king was scared out of his wits.

But Julnar arose, and after calming them, she went to the closet where the king was hidden, she said, "My lord, have you seen and heard how I praised you to my people and have you noted that they would like to take me back to my land?"

"I heard and saw everything," he said. "May the Lord reward you for what you have said and done! By Allah, until this blessed moment I did not know how much you loved me!"

"My lord," she replied, "what is the best reward for kindness but kindness! You have been most generous with me and have treated me with love and respect. So, how could my heart be content to leave you, especially after you have been so good to me? But now I would like you to show how courteous you are. Please welcome my family and become friends with them. Thanks to my praise of you, my brother, mother, and cousins already love you and refuse to depart for their home until they have met you."

"As you wish," said the king. "Indeed, this has been my very own desire as well."

Upon saying this he arose, went over to them, and greeted them warmly. In turn, they stood up and received him with utmost respect. Then he sat down and ate with them, and he entertained them in his palace for the next thirty days, at which point they desired to return home. So they took leave of the king and queen, and after he showed them all possible honors, they departed for home. Some time after this Julnar gave birth to a boy, and he looked as radiant as the full moon. Of course, the king was beside himself with joy, for he had been longing to have an heir for many years. Soon they celebrated the event for seven days and decorated the entire city. Everyone was filled with joy, and on the seventh day Julnar's mother, Queen Farashah, her brother, and her cousins arrived, for they had learned about her giving birth to a son.

And Scheherazade noticed that dawn was approaching and stopped telling her story. When the next night arrived, however, she received the king's permission to continue her tale and said,

The king was most happy about their visit, and told them, "I promised not to give my son a name until you arrived and could know what he was to be called." So they named him Badar Basim, and all agreed that this was a fine name. Then they showed the child to his Uncle Salih, who took him in his arms and began to walk all around the room with him. Soon he left the palace with him and took him down to the ocean until he was hidden from the king's sight. Now, when Shahriman saw him take his son and disappear with him into the depths of the ocean, he gave the child up for lost and began weeping. But Julnar said to him, "Don't worry. There is no need to grieve for your son, for I love my child more than you, and he is with my brother. Therefore, you don't have to be afraid of the sea or of his drowning. If my brother had thought that the little one would be harmed, he would not have done this. Don't worry, he'll soon bring your son safely back to you."

After an hour went by and the ocean sea became turbulent, King Salih emerged and left the water. When he came up to them with the child lying quiet and his face as radiant as the full moon, he said to the king, "Perhaps you were afraid your son would be harmed when I plunged into the sea with him?"

"Yes," he said, "I was afraid and even thought that he wouldn't come back."

"My lord," Salih replied, "we penciled his eyes with an eye powder that we know and recited the names engraved on the ring of Solomon David-son over him, for this is what we generally do with our newborn children. Now you'll never have to fear his drowning or suffocation in all the oceans of the world. Just as you walk on land, we walk in the sea, and he, too, has our gift."

Then he pulled an engraved and sealed box from his pocket, and after he broke the seals and emptied it, all sorts of jacinths and other jewels fell out. In addition, there were three hundred emeralds and other gems as big as ostrich eggs that glistened more brightly than the sun and moon.

"Your majesty," said Salih, "these jewels and jacinths are a present from me to you. The reason we never brought you a gift before this is that we never knew where Julnar was residing, nor did we have any trace of her. But now that we know she is united with you and we have all become part of the same family, we have brought you this present, and every once in a while we shall bring you more of the same. These jewels and jacinths are like pebbles on the beach for us, and we know how good and bad they can be, and we know all about their power and where to find them."

When the king saw these jewels, he was completely amazed and dazzled. "By Allah," he said, "just one single gem of these jewels is worth my entire realm!" Then he thanked Salih the Merman, and turning toward Queen Julnar, he said, "I am abashed before your brother, for he has treated me most generously and bestowed this splendid gift on me."

So she, too, thanked him for his deed, and Salih replied to the king, "My lord, it is we who are obliged to you, for you have treated our sister with kindness, and we have entered your palace and eaten your food. Therefore, even if we stood on our heads in serving you, it would be nothing but a scant gesture for what you deserve."

The king thanked him warmly, and the merman and mermaids remained with him for forty days, at the end of which time Salih arose and kissed the ground before his brother-in-law, who asked, "What can I do for you, Salih?"

"Your majesty, you have done more than enough for us, and we only crave your permission to depart, for we long for our people and country. We shall never forget you, our sister, or our nephew and shall always be there to serve you. By Allah, it is not easy to part from you, because you have been so kind to us, but what can we do? We were reared in the sea, and we cannot get accustomed to the land."

When the king heard these words, he arose and said farewell to Salih, his mother, and his cousins, and they all wept together. Soon they said to him, "We must be off, but we won't forsake you, for we plan to visit you as often as possible."

Then they departed, and after descending into the sea, they disappeared from sight.

And Scheherazade noticed that dawn was approaching and stopped telling her story. When the next night arrived, however, she received the king's permission to continue her tale and said,

After this King Shahriman showed Julnar even more kindness and honored her with even more respect than before. Their son grew up and flourished, while his maternal uncle, grandma, and cousins visited the king whenever they could and stayed with him a month or two months at a time. The boy became more and more handsome and lovely as years went by, and when he reached the age of fifteen he had a grand physique. Moreover, he learned how to write and read the Koran and studied history, syntax, and lexicography. He became an expert in archery, spear-throwing, horsemanship, and whatever else it was fitting for the son of a king to learn. Everyone in the city, man, woman, and child, talked continually about the boy's charms, for he was perfectly handsome and pleasant. And, indeed, the king loved him more than anything else, and one day he summoned his vizier, emirs, chief officers of state, and grandees of his realm and made them take an oath that they would make Badar Basim their new king. In turn, they gladly pledged their loyalty, for the monarch was liberal to his lieges, diplomatic, and fair, and he always thought of his people first. The next day Shahriman mounted with his troops, emirs, and lords and went into the city to announce what they had done. Then they began their return to the palace, and as they approached it, the king dismounted to wait upon his son, who remained on his horse. The king and all the emirs and nobles carried the saddle cloth of honor before him, until they came to the vestibule of the palace, where the prince got off his horse, and his father and the emirs embraced him and seated him on the royal throne. While they stood before him, Badar Basim began to hold court and to judge the people, rewarding the just and punishing the unjust, and he continued doing so until noon, when he descended the throne and went to his mother, Julnar the Mermaid, with the crown on his head as if he were the moon. When she saw him with the king standing before him, she rose, and after kissing him, she rejoiced in his becoming sultan and wished him and his sire long lives and victory over their foes. Badar Basim sat with his mother and rested until the hour of midafternoon prayer, when he mounted his horse and went to the Maydan plain preceded by the emirs, and there he played at arms with his father and his lords until nightfall. After that he returned to the palace preceded by his entourage.

Badar Basim continued riding out every day to the tilting ground, and he continued judging the people in a just manner for one whole year. At the end of that time he went out hunting and made the rounds of the cities and countries under his rule, guaranteeing the people his protection and security as it was fitting for kings to do. Gradually he established a wonderful reputation among the people because of his valor and sense of justice.

Now one day it so happened that the old king fell ill, and when the sickness became worse and he knew that he was near death, he called his son and commended his mother and subjects to his care and ordered all the emirs and nobles once more to swear allegiance to the prince. After that he lingered a few days, and then Allah mercifully granted him his death. His son and widow and all the emirs, ministers, and lords mourned over him, and they built him a tomb and buried him in it. They continued mourning for one whole month until Salih, his mother, and cousins arrived and offered their condolences to the grieving young king. Then they said to Julnar, "Though the king is dead, he has left this noble and peerless youth, and he who has left such a valorous and radiant son is therefore still with us."

And Scheherazade noticed that dawn was approaching and stopped telling her tale. When the next night arrived, however, she received the king's permission to continue her tale and said,

So the nobles and ministers of the empire went to see King Badar Basim, and they said to him, "Your majesty, there is no harm in mourning for the late sovereign, but it is not fitting to mourn too long. Only women carry on like that, and we ask you not to occupy your heart and our hearts with mourning anymore. Remember, insofar as he has left you behind him, he is still with us."

Then they comforted him, provided him with distractions, and took him to the Hammam bath. When he came out of the bath, he donned a rich robe lined with gold and embroidered with jewels and jacinths. After placing the royal crown in his head, he sat down on his throne and regulated the affairs of the folk by ruling wisely and justly so that his people loved him and showed him great affection. He continued doing this for one whole year, while every now and then his kinsfolk of the sea visited him, and his life was pleasant, and he saw things clearly.

Now one night it so happened that his Uncle Salih came to visit Julnar, and after she greeted him, she asked, "How are you and my mother and cousins?"

"They are fine and doing well," he replied. "The only thing they lack is the sight of your face."

Then she set some food before him, and he ate. After

the meal they talked about King Badar Basim and all his remarkable charms and skills. Now Badar was lying on some pillows nearby, and since he heard that his mother and uncle were talking about him, he pretended to be asleep and listened to their conversation. Soon Salih said to his sister, "Your son is now seventeen years old and is unmarried, and I wouldn't want anything to happen to him without his having an heir to the throne. So I'd like him to marry soon, and indeed, I'd like him to marry a princess of the sea, who would be his match in beauty and loveliness."

"Whom do you have in mind?" she asked. "Tell me their names, for I know them all."

So Salih proceeded to name them to her, one by one, but as each princess was named, Julnar said, "I don't like her for my son. I'll only marry him to a princess who is his equal in beauty, wit, piety, good breeding, magnanimity, rank, and lineage."

"I've named all the daughters of the kings of the sea to you," said Salih, "and I don't know any more than the hundred I've mentioned. Of course, there is someone . . . But wait now, sister, and make sure that your son's asleep."

So she felt Badar to see if he was asleep, and he did not move. Consequently, she said to Salih, "Don't worry. I'm sure he's asleep. Now tell me what you have to say and why you wanted me to make sure that he was sleeping."

"Well, to tell the truth," he said, "There is a mermaid who would be a perfect match for your son. But I'm afraid to mention her name when he's awake. She is so remarkable, and if he were to fall in love with her and we were unable to win her, it would cause great trouble for us and the nobles of the realm."

When Julnar heard these words, she insisted, "Tell me all about her and her name. If I judge her worthy of Badar, I'll demand her in marriage from her father, even if I have to spend all that I possess for her. Tell me all about her, and don't worry, for my son's sound asleep."

So Salih said, "By Allah, my sister, no woman is worthy of your son except the Princess Jauharah, daughter of King Al-Samandal, for she is his match in beauty, loveliness, and brilliance. You won't find a sweeter gift on land or on sea than this princess, for she has rosy cheeks, a brow as white as a flower, sparkling teeth, dark black eyes, wide hips, a slender waist, and exquisite legs. When she moves about and turns, she puts the gazelles to shame. When she unveils her face, she outshines the sun and moon, and anyone who glances at her is immediately captivated. Ah, she has such sweet lips and such a soft manner!"

Now, when Julnar heard what Salih had to say, she replied, "All that you've said is true, my brother! By Allah, I've seen her many times, and she was my companion when we were little, but since then I've heard very little about her, nor have I set eyes on her for eighteen years. By Allah, none is worthy of my son but her!"

While they were talking, Badar heard everything from first to last, and he fell in love with the Princess Jauharah just on hearsay. Pretending to be asleep, he felt the fire of love being kindled in his heart because of her, and he was drowned in a sea without shore or bottom.

And Scheherazade noticed that dawn was approaching and stopped telling her story. When the next night arrived, however, she received the king's permission to continue her tale and said,

Then Salih said to his sister, "There is, however, one problem: there is no greater fool among the kings of sea than her father, nor one with a more violent temper than he! So don't tell your son the name of the girl until we demand her hand in marriage from her father. If he consents, we shall praise Allah Almighty, and if he refuses us, we won't say a word about it and seek some other match."

"That is sound advice," Julnar said, and they stopped talking, but Badar spent the night with a heart on fire for Princess Jauharah. However, he concealed his love and did not speak to his mother or uncle about it. Now, when morning came, the king and his uncle went to the Hammam bath and washed. Then they went back to the palace, drank wine, and ate. After the meal they washed their hands, and Salih rose and said to his nephew and sister, "With your permission, I would like to go to my mother and my folk, for I've been with you some days, and my kinfolk have been missing me."

But Badar Basim said to him, "Please spend the day with us and then depart." After Salih consented, the king continued, "Come, my uncle, let us go into the garden."

So they walked around the garden for a while until the king lay down under a shady tree with the intention of resting and sleeping, but he remembered his uncle's description of the beautiful Princess Jauharah and began shedding tears and sighing. When his uncle saw the tears, he smacked his hand on the ground and exclaimed, "By Allah, you heard your mother and me talking about Princess Jauharah last night!"

"Yes, my uncle," Badar Basim replied, "I fell in love with her through hearsay. Indeed, my heart has swollen with love, and I feel that I'm going to burst! I cannot live without her!"

"Let us return to your mother," Salih said, "and tell her how you feel. Then I'll ask her permission to take you with me and seek the princess's hand in marriage from her father. I'm afraid to take you without her leave, because she would be very angry with me. Indeed, she'd be right to be angry, because I'd be the cause of your departure. Moreover, the city would be left without a king, and there would be no one to govern the citizens and look after their affairs. Then the kingdom would be upset, and the people would no longer recognize you as their king."

But Badar Basim responded, "Uncle, if I return to my mother and ask for her advice in this matter, I know she won't grant me permission to depart. Therefore, I refuse to consult her." And he began weeping and added, "Let's just go, and we'll tell her everything when we return."

When Salih heard what his nephew wanted to do, he became confused and said, "May Allah help me!" However, he realized how determined his nephew was to go, whether his mother would grant him permission or not, and so he drew from his finger a ring with certain names of Allah the Most High engraved on it and gave it to him. "Put this on your finger," he said, "and it will keep you safe from drowning and other dangers, especially from the mischief of sea beasts and large fish."

So King Badar Basim took the ring and set it on his finger. Then they dove into the deep sea.

And Scheherazade noticed that dawn was approaching and stopped telling her story. When the next night arrived, however, she received the king's permission to continue her tale and said,

After diving into the deep, Salih and his nephew King Badar Basim journeyed until they came to Salih's palace, where they found Badar's grandmother seated with her kinsfolk. When the old queen saw Badar, she rose, embraced him, kissed him on his forehead, and said, "My blessings! And how is your mother?"

"She is well and happy," he replied, "and she sends you and her cousins her greetings."

Then Salih related to his mother what had happened between him and his sister and how Badar had fallen in love with the Princess Jauharah. He concluded his story by saying, "And Badar has come with the sole intention of marrying the princess."

Upon hearing this, the old queen was extremely angry with her son and most disturbed. "Oh Salih," she said, "it was wrong of you to name the princess in front of your nephew, especially since you know that her father is stupid and violent and is unwilling to give his daughter to anyone. All the monarchs of the high seas have sought her hand, and he has rejected every single one of them and argued, 'You are no match for her in beauty, loveliness, or anything else!' Therefore, I'm afraid to demand her hand in marriage from him. If he rejects us as he has rejected all the others, we shall be brokenhearted."

"Mother," Salih said, "what's there to do? The fact is that Badar is determined to marry her even if he has to give his whole kingdom for her. And he's also told me that if he cannot wed her, he'll die of love for her. To tell the truth, he is handsome and wealthier than she is. His father was king of all the Persians, and as his successor, no one is worthier of Jauharah than Badar. Therefore, I propose to carry a gift of jacinths and jewels to her father befitting his dignity and request her hand in marriage for Badar. If he objects and says that he is a king, I shall point out that our man is also a king and son of a king.

Or if he objects and says his daughter is beautiful, I shall point out that our man is more handsome than she is beautiful. Or if he objects and says his realm is vast, I shall point out that our man's realm is vaster and that he has many more troops and guards. I'll do anything I can to further the cause of my sister's son, even if it costs my life. In truth, I'm responsible for all this, and since I'm the one who plunged him into the ocean of her love, then with the help of Almighty Allah, I intend to help him marry her!"

"Do as you want," said his mother, "but beware of saying anything impolite to her father. You know how stupid and violent he is! I'm just afraid he might do you some mischief, for he has no respect for anyone."

"I'll remember your advice," Salih said, and he got up and left the room with his nephew. Then he took two bags full of gems such as rubies, emeralds, and other jewels and gave them to his servants to carry. Afterward he set out with Badar Basim for the palace of Al-Samandal. When they arrived there, he sought an audience with the king, and after being admitted, he kissed the ground before him and saluted him with a respectful salaam. The king rose and honored him with a seat, and after he was seated, the king said, "May you be blessed for visiting us. We have not had the pleasure of your company for a long time, Salih! What brings you to us? Tell me your errand, so I may help you fulfill it."

Thereupon Salih arose, kissed the ground a second time, and said, "I have come on an errand to you, my magnanimous liege lord and valiant lion, whose good qualities have been made known by caravans far and wide, and whose reputation for beneficence, clemency, graciousness, and generosity has been spread to all climes and countries." After making this address, Salih opened the bags of jewels, displayed their contents before Al-Samandal, and said, "I hope you will accept this gift and do me the favor of healing my heart."

And Scheherazade noticed that dawn was approaching and stopped telling her story. When the next night arrived, however, she received the king's permission to continue her tale and said,

* * *

Then King Al-Samandal asked, "Why have you given me this gift? Tell me your story and what is entailed. If it is within my power to help you accomplish your goal, I'll do what I must to save you toil and trouble. But if I'm unable to assist you, you will understand that Allah never compels anyone to exceed his power."

After listening to the king, Salih rose, kissed the ground three times, and said, "Your majesty, that which I desire is well within your power to grant. I do not intend to impose upon you, nor have I been demented by the jinn that I would ask the impossible of you. For as one of our sages has said, 'If you desire to have your wish granted, never ask what cannot be readily attained.' So, I have come to ask you, oh king, and may Allah bless you with long life, for something that is within your power to grant."

The king replied, "Ask what you would like and tell me what you are seeking."

Then Salih said, "Your majesty, I have come as a suitor, seeking that unique pearl the Princess Jauharah, daughter of our lord the king, and I beseech you not to disappoint me."

Now, when the king heard this, he laughed so hard that he fell over on his back. After mocking Salih like this, he stood up and said, "Oh Salih, I thought you were a young man with a good head on your shoulders. What's happened to your senses that you've been urged to seek this monstrous thing? Why are you endangering yourself by seeking to marry a daughter of kings, lords of cities and climates? Tell me, are you so lordly that you can aspire to such eminence? Have you lost your mind and thus feel free to offend me with this request?"

"By Allah," replied Salih, "I am not seeking her for myself, and even if I did, I am her match, and even more than her match, for you know that my father was king of the kings of sea despite the fact that you are king right now. No, I am seeking her for King Badar Basim, lord of the lands of the Persians and son of King Shahriman, whose power you know. If you maintain that you are a great and mighty king, well then, let me tell you that King Badar is greater. And if you maintain that your daughter's beauty is incomparable, well then, let me tell you that King Badar is more handsome and comes from a better rank and lineage. Indeed, he is the champion of the people of his day. Therefore, if you grant my request, your majesty, you will setting up a perfect match. But if you deal arrogantly with us, you'll pay for being unjust. Moreover, you know that the Princess Jauharah needs to be wedded and bedded one day, for the sage says, a girl's lot is either grace of marriage or the grave. Consequently, if you intend to marry her, my sister's son is more worthy of her than any man alive."

Now, when King Al-Samandal heard Salih's words, he became extremely furious. He almost lost his head, and his soul almost exploded from his body because of his rage. "Oh dog!" he cried. "How dare you name my daughter and address me as you have in front of my court assembled here? And how dare you say that the son of your sister Julnar is a match for her? Who are you and who is this sister of yours and her son and who was his father that you dare to speak to me this way? You're all nothing but dogs in comparison to my daughter!" Then he called out to his guards and barked, "Off with that scoundrel's head!"

So they drew their swords and approached Salih, but he fled and made for the palace gate, where he saw his kinsfolk and servants on horseback armed from head to foot in iron and close-knitted mail coats and carrying spears and glittering swords. And when they saw Salih come running out of the palace—they had been sent by his mother just in case—they asked him what had happened, and he told them what to do. Of course, they all knew that King Al-Samandal had a violent temper and was a fool to boot. So they dismounted, drew their swords, and entered the audience hall, where they found King Al-Samandal seated on his throne and unaware of their coming. He was still fuming because of Salih, and they caught him and his entourage unprepared. Then, when he saw them, he cried out, "Woe to you! Off with the heads of these dogs!" But before the hour had gone by, Al-Samandal's party was put to rout, and Salih and his kinsmen seized the king and bound him.

And Scheherazade noticed that dawn was approaching and stopped telling her story. When the next night arrived, however, she received the king's permission to continue her tale and said,

* * *

Right after the struggle began, Princess Jauharah awoke and discovered that her father had been taken captive and his guards slain. So she fled the palace to a certain island and climbed up a high tree and hid herself in the top. Now, when the two parties had clashed, Badar met some of King Al-Samandal's pages in flight and asked them what had happened. When he heard that the king was a prisoner, Badar became anxious, for he felt that he had caused all this turmoil, and that the guards would soon be after him. Therefore, he took to flight and ran without knowing where he was going. As destiny would have it, he landed on the very same island where the princess had taken refuge, and he came to the very tree which she had climbed. It was there that he threw himself down like a dead man, hoping to rest and not knowing that there is no rest for the pursued. Indeed, nobody knows what fate has in store for him. As he lay down, he raised his eyes, and his glance met the eyes of the princess in the treetop. As he gazed at her, he thought she was like the moon rising in the east, and he cried out, "Glory to Him who created that perfect form! By Allah, if my sentiments are true, it is Jauharah, daughter of King Al-Samandal! I believe that when she heard of our clash with her father, she fled to this island and hid herself in this treetop. But even if it isn't the princess herself, then it's a woman even more divine than she is." Then he reflected about his situation and said to himself, "I'll get up and seize her and ask her who she is. If she is indeed who I think she is, I'll ask her personally to marry me and win my wish."

So he stood up and called to her, "Oh end of all desire, who are you, and who brought you here?"

She looked at Badar Basim, and discovering that he was like the full moon when it shines through a black cloud, so slender in shape and so sweet a smile, she answered, "Oh fair one, I am Princess Jauharah, daughter of the King Al-Samandal, and I took refuge in this place because Salih and his host came to blows with my sire. They slew his troops and took him and some of his men prisoner. Therefore, I had to flee out of fear for my life, especially since I don't know what has happened to my father."

When King Badar Basim heard these words, he was astounded by this strange coincidence and thought to himself, "Undoubtedly I've won my wish, since her father is now a prisoner." Then he looked at Jauharah and said to her, "Come down, my lady, for I have fallen totally in love with you, and your eyes have captivated me. To tell you the truth, the battle that was fought today was because of me and you, for I am King Badar Basim, lord of the Persians, and Salih is my mother's brother, and it was he who came to request your hand in marriage for me. As for me, I left my kingdom for your sake, and our meeting here is a unique coincidence. Therefore, I beg you to come down to me, and let us two go to your father's palace so that I may beseech my Uncle Salih to release your father and so that I can make you my lawful wife."

When Jauharah heard these words, she said to herself, "It was because of this miserable scoundrel, then, that everything has happened! Because of him my father's been taken prisoner, his chamberlains and other officers have been slain, and I've been forced to flee the palace and take refuge on this island! And now, if I don't think of something fast to defend myself, he'll possess me and do what he wants with me. He's in love, and whenever a man's in love, anything he does is excusable." So she beguiled him with charming words and sweet speeches, while he was unaware that she was plotting something perfidious against him. And at one point she asked, "My lord and light of my eyes, tell me, are you truly King Badar Basim, son of Queen Julnar?"

And Scheherazade noticed that dawn was approaching and stopped telling her story. When the next night arrived, however, she received the king's permission to continue her tale and said,

When Badar heard her question, he replied, "Yes, my lady."

"Well, then," she replied, "may Allah turn His back on my father and take away his kingdom from him! May Allah let him suffer and drive him into exile! I say all this because he could not have found a more handsome or virtuous man to be my suitor. By Allah, he is not very smart or discerning!" Then she added, "Despite all this, oh king, please do not punish him for what he's done. If you have just a drop of the immense love I feel for you, then you'll do this for me. Indeed, I've fallen into the net of your love and have become your captive. The love that was in you has been transferred to me, and there is a little left in you and a vast amount in me!"

After saying all this, she slid down the tree and walked over to him. Then she drew him to her bosom and began kissing him, causing his passion and desire for her to increase and making him feel that she was definitely in love with him and he could trust her. Returning her kisses and caresses, he said to her, "By Allah, my uncle did not know the least thing about your charms!"

Then Jauharah pressed him even closer to her bosom, uttered some words that he did not understand, and suddenly spat on his face. "I command you to change your form! Change and become a bird! Yes, it's a bird you shall become!"

No sooner had she spoken than King Badar Basim found himself transformed into a beautiful white bird with a red bill and red legs, and he stood there in astonishment.

Now, Jauharah had one of her slave girls by the name of Marsinah with her, and she called her and said, "If it weren't for the fact that I fear for the life of my father, who is his uncle's prisoner, I would kill him! May Allah never reward him! He is the one who has caused all his misfortune. Yes, all this trouble is due to his stubbornness! So, I want you to bring him to the Thirsty Island and leave him there to die!"

So Marsinah left the island and brought him to another one with numerous trees, fruit, and streams, and after she deposited him there, she returned to her mistress and reported that she had left him on the Thirsty Island.

In the meantime, Salih had begun searching for Jauharah after capturing the king and killing his guards. However, since he could not find her, he returned to his palace and asked his mother, "Where is Badar?"

"By Allah," she replied, "I don't know where he is. When he learned that you and King Al-Samandal had come to blows and that the fighting had led to slaughter, he became frightened and fled."

When Salih heard this, he grieved for his nephew and said, "Mother, I've been too careless with King Badar, and I'm afraid that he might perish or meet one of King Al-Samandal's soldiers or his daughter, Jauharah. If that were to happen, Julnar would never forgive me, especially since I took her son without her permission."

Then he sent out his guards and scouts throughout the sea and other places to look for Badar, but they could not discover where he was. When they returned and told King Salih, his concern increased, and he was most distressed because of Badar.

Now, Julnar the Mermaid had been long expecting their return, but they had disappeared after going into the garden, and she had no news of them. Therefore, when many days of fruitless waiting had gone by, she arose, went down into the sea, and returned to her mother, who embraced her when she arrived. Then she asked her mother about King Badar Basim and her uncle, and the old queen replied, "To tell you the truth, he came here with his uncle, who took jewels and jacinths to King Al-Samandal and demanded his daughter for Badar. However, when the king did not consent, a violent battle ensued, and Allah helped your brother capture the king and slay his guards. Meanwhile, your son feared for his life and fled, and we have not had any news of him since then."

Then Julnar inquired about her brother, Salih, and her mother told her, "He has taken over King Al-Samandal's throne and has sent messengers and scouts in every direction to search for your son and Princess Jauharah."

When Julnar heard her mother's story, she mourned for her son and was extremely angry with her brother, Salih, for having taken her son and gone down into the sea without her permission. And she said, "Mother, I fear for our realm, for I came here without telling anyone, and I'm afraid that if I stay here too long, there will be chaos in the kingdom, and the throne will be usurped. Therefore, I think it's best if I return and govern the kingdom until my son's affair is settled here, if it pleases Allah. But I want you to look after him, for if he should be harmed in any way, I would die, since he is the joy of my life and the light of my world."

"I'll gladly do this, my daughter," she replied, "and

with love. We have already suffered a great deal because of his absence."

Then the old queen sent out messengers to search for her grandson, while Julnar returned to her kingdom, weeping and heavy-hearted, and indeed, she could no longer take delight in the world.

And Scheherazade noticed that dawn was approaching and stopped telling her story. When the next night arrived, however, she received the king's permission to continue her tale and said,

With regard to King Badar Basim, he dwelled as an enchanted bird on the island, eating its fruit and drinking its water, and did not know where to go or how to fly. Then one day, a fowler came to the island to catch some birds, for this was how he earned his living. When he caught sight of King Badar Basim in his form of a beautiful white bird with red bill and legs, he was captivated and said to himself, "What a wonderful bird! I've never seen anything as beautiful in my life." So he cast his net over Badar and took him to the town with the intention of selling him for a high price. On his way, one of the townspeople approached him and asked, "How much for that bird, fowler?"

"What will you do with him if you buy him?" responded the fowler.

"I'll cut his throat and eat him," said the man.

"Who could have the heart to kill this bird and eat him?" said the fowler. "I intend to give him to our king as a present, and he'll give me more than you would give me. Moreover, I'm sure he won't kill him but enjoy himself by gazing at the bird's beauty and grace. Honestly, in all my life, ever since I've been a fowler, I've never seen such a marvelous bird. In short, I won't sell him to you!"

Then he carried the bird to the king's palace, and when the king saw the bird from his window, he was pleased by his beauty and grace and by his unusual coloring. So he sent one of his eunuchs, who asked the fowler whether he would sell the bird.

"No," he replied. "The bird is a gift from me to the king."

So the eunuch carried the bird to the king and told him what the man had said. Thus the king took the bird and gave the fowler ten dinars, whereupon he kissed the ground and went his way. Then the eunuch carried the bird to a room in the palace and placed him in a fine cage with something to eat and drink and hung the cage up. When the king finished holding court, he said to the eunuch, "Where is the bird? Bring it to me so that I may gaze upon it. By Allah, it's the most beautiful bird I've ever seen!"

So the eunuch brought the cage and set it between the hands of the king, who looked and noticed that the food was untouched. "By Allah," the king said, "we must find the right food to nourish it!"

Then he called for food, and they set the table for the king to eat and let the bird out of the cage. Now, when the bird saw the meat, fruit, and sweetmeats, he began eating everything that was on the trays, while the sovereign and all the bystanders were amazed, and the king said to his attendants, "In all my life I've never seen a bird eat the way this one does!"

Then he sent a eunuch to fetch his wife so that she might enjoy watching the bird, and the eunuch said to her, "My lady, the king desires your presence so that you might enjoy watching a bird that he has bought. When we set it on the table, it ate everything that was on the trays. So please come and take pleasure in this wonderful sight!"

Upon hearing these words, she rushed to the king's chamber, but when she caught sight of the bird, she veiled her face and turned to leave. The king stood up immediately and asked her, "Why have you veiled your face when there is nobody in our presence except the women and eunuchs who wait on you and your husband?"

"Oh king," she said, "this bird is not a bird, but a man just like yourself."

"You're lying," he responded. "Or you're jesting. How can this bird be a man?"

"I'm not jesting," she contended. "I'm telling the truth. This bird is King Badar Basim, son of King Shahriman, lord of the land of the Persians, and his mother is Julnar the Mermaid."

* * *

And Scheherazade noticed that dawn was approaching and stopped telling her story. When the next night arrived, however, she received the king's permission to continue her tale and said,

"How was he turned into a bird?" the king asked.

"Princess Jauharah has enchanted him," she said and told him all that had happened to King Badar Basim from first to last.

The king was amazed by his wife's story and implored her to free Badar from this enchantment (for she was the most notable enchantress of her age) and to put an end to his torment. "May Almighty Allah cut off Jauharah's hand for doing this!" he said. "What a foul witch! She's nothing but a treacherous and cunning creature!"

Then the queen said, "You're to say to him, 'Oh Badar Basim, enter that closet over there!' "

So the king ordered him to enter the closet, and he went in obediently. After that the queen veiled her face, took a cup of water in her hand, and entered the closet, where she pronounced some incomprehensible words and ended with, "By virtue of these mighty names and holy verses and by the majesty of Allah Almighty, Creator of heaven and earth, you are to abandon this form and return to the shape in which the Lord created you!"

No sooner had she ended her words than the bird trembled once and became a man. Then he opened the closet door, and the king saw before him the most handsome youth on the face of the earth. And when King Badar Basim found himself restored to his own shape, he cried, "There is no god but *the* God. Glory be to the Creator of all creatures and the Provider of their provisions."

Then he kissed the king's hand and wished him long life, and the king kissed his head and said to him, "Oh Badar Basim, tell me your story from beginning to end."

So he told the king his entire tale and did not forget a thing, and the king was amazed by it and said, "Allah has saved you from the spell, but what do you intend to do now?"

"Your majesty," Badar replied, "I need your help and generosity, and I am requesting a ship with a company of your servants and all that is necessary for a voyage. I have been away from my kingdom a long time, and I'm worried that my kingdom might be usurped. Moreover, I fear that my mother may be dead from grief over my disappearance, for she does not know whether I am dead or alive."

"Your wish is my command," said the king after listening to this polite and touching speech. So he provided Badar with a ship and all that was needed for a voyage along with a company of his servants. After taking leave of the king, Badar Basim set sail, and for ten days he had a favorable wind, but on the eleventh, the ocean became turbulent. The ship rose and fell, and the sailors were unable to control it. So they drifted at the mercy of the waves, until the vessel came near a rock and crashed on it. All on board were drowned, except King Badar Basim, who got on one of the planks of the ship. For three whole days Badar was driven on the plank by the rough sea, and he had no notion about where he was going.

But on the fourth day, the plank drifted to a shore, where he sighted a white city built on a peninsula that jutted out into the sea. It was a magnificent city with high towers and lofty walls against which the waves beat. When Badar Basim saw this, he rejoiced, for he was almost dead of hunger and thirst. So he stood up and wanted to wade to the beach, but a herd of wild horses and mules came charging at him and prevented him from marching on the sand. So he swam around to the back of the city, where he waded to shore. After entering the place, he could not find a single soul and was astounded. "I wish I knew who ruled over this city," he said to himself. "And where did all those horses and mules come from that prevented me from landing?" He began walking and was pondering the situation when he came upon an old grocer. So he saluted him, and the grocer returned his salaam and asked him, "Where have you come from, my handsome youth, and what has brought you to this city?"

Badar told him his story, and the old man was amazed by it and said, "Did you see anything along the way?"

"To tell the truth," Badar replied, "I was astounded to find the city empty."

"My son," said the sheikh, "come into my shop or else you will perish from hunger."

So Badar went into his shop and sat down, whereupon

the old man brought him some food and said, "Glory be to Allah Almighty, who has preserved you from that she-devil!"

King Badar Basim was tremendously frightened by the grocer's words, but he ate his fill and washed his hands. Then he glanced at his host and said to him, "My lord, what is the meaning of your words? Truly, you've made me afraid of this city and its people."

"You must know, my son," replied the grocer, "that this is the City of the Magicians, and its queen is like a she-satan, a sorceress and a mighty enchantress. Oh, she is extremely crafty and treacherous! All those horses and mules you encountered were once sons of Adam, just like you and me. They were also strangers, for whoever enters this city, especially young men like yourself, this miscreant witch takes him and houses him for forty days. After that time is up, she enchants him, and he becomes a mule or a horse like those animals you saw on the seashore."

And Scheherazade noticed that dawn was approaching and stopped telling her story. When the next night arrived, however, she received the king's permission to continue her tale and said,

After the grocer paused for a moment, he continued his story by saying to Badar, "When you intended to land, they were worried that you would be transformed like themselves. So they tried to warn you by signs not to land, fearing that she would do the same thing to you that she's done to them. She took control of this city by sorcery, and her name is Queen Lab, which in Arabic means Almanac of the Sun."

When Badar Basim heard the old man's story, he was extremely frightened and trembled like a reed in the wind and said to himself, "No sooner am I freed from one enchantment than destiny sets another snare for me!" And he began reflecting about his predicament and everything that had happened to him. When the old man looked at him and realized how terrified he was, he said, "My son, come and sit at the threshold of the shop and look at the people and how they dress and act. Don't be afraid, for the queen and the entire city love me and will not annoy or trouble me."

So King Badar Basim went to the threshold and looked at the people who passed by the shop. When the people caught sight of him, they approached the grocer and said to him, "Is this young man your prisoner? Did you just capture him?"

"He is my brother's son," the old man replied. "I heard that his father had died, and so I sent for him so that I might comfort him."

"Truly, he is a handsome young man," they said, "but aren't you afraid that Queen Lab will turn on you and use some treacherous means to take him away from you? For she loves handsome young men."

"The queen will not go against my orders," the sheikh said, "for she loves me, and when she finds out that he is my brother's son, she will not molest him or trouble me on his account."

Then King Badar Basim stayed with the grocer for some months, and the old man became extremely fond of him. One day, as the grocer sat outside his shop, as was his custom, a thousand eunuchs with drawn swords and clad in various kinds of raiment with jeweled belts approached him on Arabian steeds. They saluted the grocer as they passed his shop, and soon they were followed by a thousand damsels like moons clad in silk and satin clothes lined with gold and embroidered with jewels of all kinds, and spears were slung over their shoulders. In their midst rode Queen Lab in all her majesty mounted on a marvelous mare with a golden saddle lined with jewels and jacinths. As the damsels rode by the shop, they, too, saluted the grocer, but Queen Lab came right up to him, because she had caught sight of King Badar Basim sitting in the shop as if he were a full moon. She was amazed by his handsome and lovely features and fell passionately in love with him. Her desire for him was so great that she dismounted and took a seat next to Badar and said to the old man, "Where does this handsome young man come from?"

"He's my brother's son," the sheikh replied, "and he's just arrived here."

"Let him stay with me tonight so that I may talk with him," she said.

"Only if you promise not to enchant him," he responded.

"But of course," she said.

"Swear it to me," he insisted.

So she swore to him that she would not do him any harm or enchant him. Then she commanded that a fine horse with a gold bridle and harness be brought over, and she gave the old man a thousand dinars and said, "These are for your daily expenses."

Then she led Badar Basim away on the horse, while all the people felt sorry for him and said, "By Allah, this handsome young man does not deserve to be bewitched by that wretched sorceress!"

Now King Badar Basim heard all they said, but he kept silent and left his fate in the hands of Allah Almighty.

And Scheherazade noticed that dawn was approaching and stopped telling her story. When the next night arrived, however, she received the king's permission to continue her tale and said,

When they arrived at the palace gate, the emirs, eunuchs, and noblemen dismounted, and the queen ordered her chamberlains to dismiss her officers and grandees, who kissed the ground and went away. Meanwhile she entered the palace with Badar Basim and her eunuchs and women. Never before in his life had he seen a place like that. The palace was built of gold, and in its midst was a large pond surrounded by a vast garden that had all kinds of birds warbling in sweet and melodious voices. Everywhere he looked he saw magnificent things and cried out, "Glory to God for providing such a marvelous estate!" The queen sat down at a latticed window overlooking the garden on an ivory couch next to a bed, and King Badar Basim seated himself by her side. She kissed him and pressed him to her breast, and soon thereafter she ordered her women to bring a tray of food. So they brought a gold tray lined with pearls and jewels, and on the tray were all kinds of viands.

Both the queen and Badar ate until they were satisfied, and then they washed their hands. Once again the waiting women came, and this time it was with gold and silver flagons and all kinds of flowers and dishes of dried fruit. Next the queen summoned the singing women, ten maidens as beautiful as the moon, and they all began playing different instruments. Queen Lab poured a cup to the brim, and after drinking off the top, she filled another and passed it to King Badar Basim, who took it and drank, and they kept drinking until they were satisfied. Then she ordered the damsels to sing, and they sang various kinds of songs until it seemed to Badar that the palace was dancing with joy. He was filled with ecstasy and felt so relieved that he forgot his outcast state and said to himself, "Truly, this queen is young and beautiful, and I'll never leave her, for her kingdom is vaster than my kingdom, and she is more beautiful than Princess Jauharah." So he resumed drinking until the evening, and they both became drunk, while the singers kept making music. Then Queen Lab, who was quite intoxicated, rose from her seat and lay down on a bed. After dismissing her women, she called to Badar Basim to come and sleep by her side. So he lay down beside her and enjoyed her till the morning.

And Scheherazade noticed that dawn was approaching and stopped telling her story. When the next night arrived, however, she received the king's permission to continue her tale and said,

When the queen awoke, she went to the Hammam bath in the palace with King Badar, and they bathed together and were purified. After that she clad him in the finest raiment and called for wine. After drinking the wine, the queen took Badar by the hand, and they sat down to eat and then washed their hands. Then the damsels fetched the fruit, flower, and confections, and they kept eating and drinking until the evening while the singing girls sang various songs. They continued this routine for forty days, at the end of which time the queen asked him, "Oh Badar Basim, tell me whether it is more pleasant to be at my place or at your uncle's shop."

"By Allah," he replied, "this is much more pleasant, for my uncle is but a poor man, who sells pots of herbs."

She laughed at his words, and the two of them lay together and enjoyed one another until the morning. Then Badar awoke from his sleep and did not find Queen Lab by his side. "If only I knew where she went!" he said to himself. And indeed he was troubled by her absence and puzzled by her disappearance, for she stayed away a long time and did not return. So he got dressed and went looking for her, and when he did not find her, he said to himself, "Perhaps she went to the garden." Thereupon he went into the garden and came to a stream, where he saw a white female bird, and on the bank of the stream was a tree full of birds of different colors, and Badar stood and watched the birds without them noticing him.

All of a sudden a black bird flew down upon the white female bird and began billing her in pigeon fashion. Then he leapt on her and trod her three consecutive times, after which the bird changed and became a woman, and Badar saw that it was Queen Lab! All at once it became clear to him that the black bird was a man, who had been transformed through magic. Moreover, it was clear that she was enamored of him and had transformed herself into a bird so that he could enjoy her. Consequently, Badar was overcome with jealousy and was angry with the queen because of the black bird.

Then he returned to his place and lay down on the couch, and after an hour or so she came back to him and began kissing and playing with him. However, since he was furious with her, he did not say a word to her. Nevertheless, she knew what he was feeling and was certain that he had witnessed what had happened to her when she had been a white bird, but she decided not to talk about it. After he had fulfilled her needs, he said to her, "Queen, I would like your permission to go to my uncle's shop, for I miss him and haven't seen him for forty days."

She replied, "You may go, but don't stay away very long from me, for I cannot stand to be parted from you more than an hour."

"As you wish," he said, and after mounting his steed, he rode to the shop of the grocer, who welcomed him with an embrace and asked him, "How are things going with the queen?"

"I was very happy until this past night," he replied, and he told him what had happened in the garden with the black bird.

Now, when the old man heard his story, he said, "Beware of her, for the birds on the trees were all young men and strangers whom she loved and turned into birds through magic. That black bird you saw was one of her mamelukes, whom she loved with great passion, until he cast his eyes upon one of her women. Consequently, she changed him into a black bird."

And Scheherazade noticed that dawn was approaching and stopped telling her tale. When the next night arrived, however, she received the king's permission to continue her tale and said,

Then the grocer added, "Whenever she lusts after him, she transforms herself into a bird so that he may enjoy her, for she still loves him with passion. Now that she has realized that you've discovered her relationship with the black bird, she will plot something evil against you, for she does not love you as much as she loves the mameluke. But no harm will come to you so long as I protect you. Therefore, you have nothing to fear, for I am a Moslem by the name of Abdallah, and there is no one who knows as much magic as I do in this day and age. However, I don't make use of my magical skills unless I am forced to do so. Many a time I have undermined the sorcery of that wicked queen and saved people from her, and I'm not worried about her, because she cannot harm me. In fact, she's even afraid of me, as are all the people of the city, who are magicians like her and serve the fire, but not the Omnipotent Sire. So I want you to come to me tomorrow and tell me all that she does, for tonight she will begin to look for a way to destroy you, and if you tell me all that you see tonight, I'll be able to tell you what mischief she's planning so that you'll be able to save yourself."

Then Badar said farewell to the sheikh and returned to the queen, who was awaiting him. When she saw him, she rose and welcomed him. Then she ordered the meal, and after they had had enough and washed their hands, they drank some wine until half the night was spent drinking and he was drunk and lost his head. When she saw him like this, she said, "By Allah and whatever you worship, if I ask you a question, will you answer me correctly and truthfully?"

And since he was drunk, he answered, "Yes, my lady."

"My lord and light of my eyes," she said, "when you awoke last night and did not find me, you kept looking for me until you saw me in the garden in the form of a white bird, and you also saw the black bird leap on me and tread me. Now I'll tell you the truth about this. That black bird was one of my mamelukes, whom I loved with a great passion. But one day he cast his eyes upon one of my slave girls, causing me to become jealous, and so I transformed him through a magic spell into a black bird and slew her. But now I cannot live without him for a single hour. So whenever I lust after him I change myself into a bird and go to him so that he can leap on top of me and enjoy me as you witnessed. Aren't you therefore furious with me because of this, even though I love you more than ever and have devoted myself to you?"

Being drunk, he answered, "You are right about my anger, for I am jealous of your love for the black bird."

After hearing this, she embraced him and kissed him and displayed a great deal of love for him. Then she lay down to sleep, and he was next to her. Soon, about midnight, she rose from the couch, and Badar Basim was awake, but he pretended he was asleep and watched stealthily to see what she would do. Indeed, she began taking something red out of a red bag, and she planted it in the middle of the chamber. Then it became like a running stream, and she took a handful of barley, strewed it on the ground, and watered it with water from the stream. All at once it became wheat, which she gathered and ground into flour. Finally, she set it aside, returned to bed, and lay down next to Badar.

The next morning he arose, washed his face, and asked her permission to visit the sheikh. She consented, and he went to Abdallah and told him what had happened. The old man laughed and said, "By Allah, this evil witch is plotting some mischief against you. But you have no need to be afraid of her!" Then he gave him a pound of parched corn and said to him, "Take this with you, and when she sees you with it, she'll ask what it is and what you intend to do with it. You're to answer, 'It's always good to have an abundant supply of good things.' Then eat it, and she'll bring out her own parched grain and say to you, 'Eat some of this sawik.' You are to pretend to eat some of it, but eat the parched corn instead. Be certain that you don't eat so much as a grain of hers, for if you do, her spells will have power over you, and she will enchant you and transform you into a bird or animal. If you don't eat her grains, her magic will be powerless, and nothing will happen to you. Once she realizes this, she will be exceedingly ashamed of herself and say to you, 'I really didn't want to enchant you. I was only jesting.' She'll make a great display of love and affection, but this will all be hypocritical. Nevertheless, you are also to make a great display of love and say to her, 'My lady and light of my eyes, eat some of this parched barley and see how delicious it is.' And if she eats some, even a grain, take some water in your hand and throw it in her face and say, 'Change your human form!' and give her whatever form you want. Then leave her and come to me, and I'll tell you what to do."

So Badar Basim took leave of him, and after returning to the palace, he went into see the queen, who said, "Welcome, and may you be in a good mood." And she rose and kissed him. "You've been away a long time, my lord."

"I've been with my uncle," he replied, "and he gave me some of this sawik to eat."

"We have better than that," she said. Then she placed his parched sawik in one plate and hers in another and said to him, "Eat this. It's better than yours."

So he pretended to eat it, and when she thought he had eaten it, she took some water in her hand, sprinkled him with it, and said, "Change your form, you miserable scoundrel, and become a stinking mule with one eye!"

But he did not change, and when she realized this, she went up to him, kissed him on the forehead, and said, "Oh my beloved, I was only jesting with you. Don't be angry with me because of it."

"Oh my lady," he said, "I'm not angry with you. No, I'm convinced that you love me, but why don't you eat some of my parched barley."

So she ate a mouthful of Abdallah's sawik, and no sooner had it settled in her stomach than she had convulsions, and King Badar Basim took some water in his hand, threw it at her, and said, "Change your form, and become a dapple mule!"

No sooner had he spoken than she found herself changed

into a mule, whereupon tears rolled down her cheeks, and she began to rub her muzzle against his feet. Then he wanted to bridle her, but she would not take the bit. So he left her, and after returning to the grocer, he told him what had happened. Abdallah brought out a bridle for him and told him to rein her with it. So he went back to the palace, and when she saw him, she came up to him, and he set the bit in her mouth, mounted her, and rode forth to the sheikh. When the old man saw her, he rose and said to her, "May Almighty Allah punish you for your sins, you wicked woman!" Then he said to Badar, "My son, there's no sense in your remaining in this city any longer. So ride her and travel wherever you want. But beware that you do not give the bridle to anyone else."

King Badar thanked him and said farewell. Then he journeyed for three days until he drew near another city, and there he met an old gray-headed man, who asked him, "Where are you coming from, my son?"

"From the city of this witch," replied Badar.

And the old man said, "Please be my guest tonight."

He consented and went with him along the way, until they met an old woman, who wept when she saw the mule, and said, "There is no god but *the* God! Truly, this mule resembles my son's dead mule, and his heart continues to long for this mule. So, please, my lord, sell it to me!"

"By Allah," he replied, "I cannot sell her."

But she cried, "Please don't refuse my request! My son will surely die if I don't buy this mule."

And she kept imploring him until he exclaimed, "I will only sell the mule for a thousand dinars," thinking to himself that this woman would never have a thousand dinars. However, she took out a purse containing a thousand ducats from her apron, and when Badar saw the purse, he said, "Mother, I was only jesting with you. I cannot sell the mule."

But the old man looked at him and said, "My son, in this city nobody may lie, and whoever lies they put to death."

And Scheherazade noticed that dawn was approaching and stopped telling her story. When the next night arrived,

however, she received the king's permission to continue her tale and said,

So King Badar Basim had to get off the mule, and when he delivered it to the old woman, she drew the bit from its mouth, took some water in her hand, sprinkled the mule, and said, "Oh daughter, change your form, and become what you were once before!"

All at once Queen Lab was restored to her original form, and the two women embraced and kissed each other. The old woman was no one else but the queen's mother, and Badar knew that he had been tricked and wanted to flee. But the old woman whistled loudly, and her call was obeyed by a jinnee as large as a mountain. Upon seeing this jinnee, Badar was terrified and could not budge from his spot. Then the old woman mounted the jinnee's back, placing her daughter behind her and Badar before her, and the ifrit flew off with them. Within an hour they were in the palace of Queen Lab, who sat down on her throne and said to Badar, "Now that I have returned to my palace, you are a dead man! I've gotten what I wanted, and soon I'll show you what I'm going to do with you and that old man the grocer! I've done numerous favors for him, and yet he offends me. Surely, you would not have been able to trick me without his help."

Then she took water, sprinkled him with it, and said, "Change your form and become a stinking bird, the foulest of all the birds," and she set him in a cage and deprived him of food and drink. However, one of her waiting women could not bear her cruelty and gave him food and water without her knowledge.

One day, this same woman slipped out of the palace without Queen Lab seeing this, and she went to the old grocer and told him, "Queen Lab intends to bring an end to your nephew's life," and she recounted everything that had happened.

The sheikh thanked her and said, "She leaves me no choice. Now I must take the city from her and make you the queen in her place." Then he whistled loudly, and a jinnee with four wings appeared before him. "Take this damsel," the sheikh said to the ifrit, "and carry her to the city of Julnar the Mermaid and her mother, Farashah, for the two are the most powerful magicians on the face of the earth." Then he turned to the damsel and said, "When you arrive there, tell them that King Badar Basim is Queen Lab's captive."

After he finished speaking, the ifrit picked up the damsel and flew with her to the terrace roof of Queen Julnar's palace, where he deposited her. Then she descended the stairs, and after entering the queen's chamber, she kissed the ground and told the queen what had happened to her son from first to last. Thereupon, Julnar arose, thanked her, and treated her with honor. Afterward she had the drums beat throughout the city and informed her lieges and lords about the good news about Badar. Then she and her mother, Farashah, and her brother, Salih, assembled all the tribes of the jinn and all the troops of the high sea, for the kings of the jinn obeyed them ever since Salih had taken King Al-Samandal prisoner. Soon they all flew up in the air, landed on the city of Queen Lab, sacked the town and palace, and slew all the unbelievers in the twinkling of an eye. Then Julnar said to the damsel, "Where is my son?"

And the slave girl brought the cage and pointed to the bird inside it. "This is your son," she declared.

So Julnar took him out of the cage, sprinkled some water on him, and said, "Return to your proper form!" No sooner had she spoken these words than Badar became a man as he was before. Upon seeing him as he once was, his mother embraced him and began weeping. Moreover, his Uncle Salih, his grandmother, and his cousins kissed his hands and feet. Then Julnar sent for Sheikh Abdallah and thanked him for the kindness that he had shown her son. Finally, Julnar married Abdallah to the damsel who had helped save Badar and made him king of the city. Moreover, she summoned the survivors of the city, who were all Moslems, and made them swear an oath of loyalty to Abdallah. Indeed, they all obeyed and pledged their allegiance. Afterward, Julnar and her company said farewell to Abdallah and returned to their own capital, where crowds of people came out to meet them with drums. Then they decorated the city, and for three days they celebrated the return of King Badar Basim with immense joy. After the celebration was over,

Badar said to his mother, "The only thing left is for me to marry."

"You're right, my son," Julnar replied, "but wait until we find the right princess for you."

And his grandmother Farashah and his cousins said, "Badar, we will help you fulfill your desire by searching for the damsel most suited for you."

Then each one of them arose and journeyed forth in foreign lands, while Julnar sent out her waiting women on the backs of jinnees, ordering them not to leave a city without looking at all the beautiful girls in it. But when Badar saw all the trouble they were taking in this matter, he said to Julnar, "Mother, please stop, for no one will satisfy me except Jauharah, daughter of King Al-Samandal. Indeed, like her name, she is a jewel!"

"I agree with you, my son," said Julnar, and she immediately ordered King Al-Samandal to be summoned to her. As soon as he was present, she sent for Badar Basim, and when Al-Samandal saw him, he stood up and saluted him. Thereupon, King Badar Basim requested his daughter's hand in marriage.

"You have my permission, and I shall place her at your disposal," said King Al-Samandal, and he sent some of his suite to search for her. When they found her, they told her that her sire was in the hands of King Badar Basim, and she returned with them through the air. As soon as the princess saw her father, she went up to him and threw her arms around his neck. Then, looking at her, he said, "My daughter, I want you to know that I have given you in wedlock to the magnanimous and valiant King Badar Basim, son of Queen Julnar the Mermaid. Indeed, he is the most beneficent of the people of his day, the most powerful, the most exalted, and the most noble. He is clearly your match, and you are clearly his."

"I shall not oppose you, my sire," she said. "Do as you wish, for sorrow and spite have come to an end, and I agree to be his wife."

So they summoned the kazi and the witnesses, who drew up the marriage contract between King Badar Basim and the Princess Jauharah, and the citizens decorated the city, rejoiced, and beat the drums. Amnesty was given to all the prisoners in the jails, while the king gave generously to the widows, orphans, and poor and bestowed robes of honor on the lords of the realm, the emirs, and the nobles. For ten days there were wedding feasts and banquets from morning until night, and at the end of that time they displayed the bride in nine different dresses before King Badar Basim, who bestowed an honorable robe on King Al-Samandal and sent him back to his country and people. And they did not stop leading a most pleasurable life nor enjoying fine food, drink, and luxury until the Destroyer of delights and the Sunderer of societies came upon them. This is the end of their story, and may Allah have mercy on them all!

No sooner had Scheherazade concluded her tale than she said, "And yet, oh king, this tale is no more wondrous than the tale about the thief of Alexandria and the police chief."

The Tale About the Thief of Alexandria and the Chief of Police

Once upon a time there was a chief of police in Alexandria called Husam al-Din, the sharp Scimitar of the Faith. Now one night, as he was sitting at his desk, a trooper came running into his office and said, "My lord, I entered your city this very night, and soon after I went to sleep at a certain khan, I awoke to find my saddlebags sliced open and a purse with a thousand gold pieces missing!"

No sooner had he finished speaking than the chief summoned all his officers and ordered them to seize all the people in the khan and throw them into jail. The next morning, he had rods and whips brought to his office, and after sending for the prisoners, he intended to have them flogged until someone confessed to the theft in the presence of the owner. Just then, however, a man broke through the crowd of people at his office and went straight to the chief.

"Stop!" he cried out. "Let these people go! They've been falsely accused. It was I who robbed this trooper. Look, here's the purse I stole from his saddlebags."

Upon saying this, he pulled out the purse from his sleeve and laid it before Husam al-Din, who said to the soldier, "Take your money, and put it away. You no longer have any grounds to lodge a complaint against these people of the khan."

Thereupon, the people of the khan and all those present began praising the thief and blessing him. However, he said, "Please stop. It doesn't take much skill to bring the purse to the chief in person. But it does take a great deal of skill to take it a second time from this trooper."

"And how did you manage to do that?" asked the chief.

And the robber replied, "My lord, I was standing in the money changer's shop at Cairo, when I saw this soldier receive the gold in change and put it into this purse. So I followed him from street to street but did not find the right opportunity to steal it. Then he left Cairo, and I followed from town to town, plotting along the way to rob him without avail, until I entered this city, where I dogged him to the khan. There I took my lodgings next to him and waited until he fell asleep. Then I went up to him quietly, and I slit open his saddlebags with this knife and took the purse just as I am taking it now."

No sooner had he spoken those words than he stretched out his hand and grabbed the purse from the trooper in front of the chief, and everyone thought that he was merely demonstrating how he had committed the theft. But, all at once, he broke into a run and sprang into a nearby river. The chief of police shouted to his officers, "Stop that thief!" And his men ran after him. But before they could doff their clothes and descend the steps of the river, he had made it to the other side. Of course, they continued searching for him, but there was no way they could find him, for he was able to escape through the back streets and lanes of Alexandria.

So the officers returned without the purse, and the chief of police said to the trooper, "I can't do anything for you now. The people are innocent, and your money was returned to you. But you weren't wise enough to protect it from the thief."

Consequently, the trooper was compelled to leave without his money, while the people were delivered from his hands and those of the chief of police. And all this had the blessing of Almighty Allah.

No sooner had Scheherazade concluded her story than she said, "And yet, oh king, this tale is no more wondrous than the tale of Prince Behram and the Princess Al-Datma."

Prince Behram and the Princess Al-Datma

There was once a king's daughter called Al-Datma who, in her time, had no equal in beauty and grace. In addition to her lovely looks, she was brilliant and feisty and took great pleasure in ravishing the wits of the male sex. In fact, she used to boast, "There is nobody who can match me in anything." And the fact is that she was most accomplished in horsemanship and martial exercises, and all those things a cavalier should know.

Given her qualities, numerous princes sought her hand in marriage, but she rejected them all. Instead, she proclaimed, "No man shall marry me unless he defeats me with his lance and sword in fair battle. He who succeeds I will gladly wed. But if I overcome him, I will take his horse, clothes, and arms and brand his head with the following words: 'This is the freedman of Al-Datma.' "

Now the sons of kings flocked to her from every quarter far and near, but she prevailed and put them to shame, stripping them of their arms and branding them with fire. Soon, a son of the king of Persia named Behram ibn Taji heard about her and journeyed from afar to her father's court. He brought men and horses with him and a great deal of wealth and royal treasures. When he drew near the city, he sent her father a rich present, and the king came out to meet him and bestowed great honors on him. Then the king's son sent a message to him through his vizier and requested his daughter's hand in marriage. However, the king answered, "With regard to my daughter Al-Datma, I have no power over her, for she has sworn by her soul to marry no one but him who defeats her in the listed field."

"I journeyed here from my father's court with no other purpose but this," the prince declared. "I came here to woo her and to form an alliance with you."

"Then you shall meet her tomorrow," said the king.

So the next day he sent for his daughter, who got ready for battle by donning her armor of war. Since the people of the kingdom had heard about the coming joust, they flocked from all sides to the field. Soon the princess rode into the lists, armed head to toe with her visor down, and the Persian king's son came out to meet her, equipped in the fairest of fashions. Then they charged at each other and fought a long time, wheeling and sparring, advancing and retreating, and the princess realized that he had more courage and skill than she had ever encountered before. Indeed, she began to fear that he might put her to shame before the bystanders and defeat her. Consequently, she decided to trick him, and raising her visor, she showed her face, which appeared more radiant than the full moon, and when he saw it, he was bewildered by her beauty. His strength failed, and his spirit faltered. When she perceived this moment of weakness, she attacked and knocked him from his saddle. Consequently, he became like a sparrow in the clutches of an eagle. Amazed and confused, he did not know what was happening to him when she took his steed, clothes, and armor. Then, after branding him with fire, she let him go his way.

When he recovered from his stupor, he spent several days without food, drink, or sleep. Indeed, love had gripped his heart. Finally, he decided to send a letter to his father via a messenger, informing him that he could not return home until he had won the princess or died for want of her. When his sire received the letter, he was extremely distressed about his son and wanted to rescue him by sending troops and soldiers. However, his ministers dissuaded him from this action and advised him to be patient. So he prayed to Almighty Allah for guidance.

In the meantime, the prince thought of different ways to attain his goal, and soon he decided to disguise himself as a decrepit old man. So he put a white beard over his own black one and went to the garden where the princess used to walk most of the days. Here he sought out the gardener and said to him, "I'm a stranger from a country far away, and from my youth onward I've been a gardener, and nobody is more skilled than I am in the grafting of trees and cultivating fruit, flowers, and vines."

When the gardener heard this, he was extremely pleased and led him into the garden, where he let him do his work. So the prince began to tend the garden and improved the Persian waterwheels and the irrigation channels. One day, as he was occupied with some work, he saw some slaves enter the garden leading mules and carrying carpets and vessels, and he asked them what they were doing there.

"The princess wants to spend an enjoyable afternoon here," they answered.

When he heard these words, he rushed to his lodging and fetched some jewels and ornaments he had brought with him from home. After returning to the garden, he sat down and spread some of the valuable items before him while shaking and pretending to be a very old man.

And Scheherazade noticed that dawn was approaching and stopped telling her story. When the next night arrived, however, she received the king's permission to continue her tale and said,

In fact, the prince made it seem as if he were extremely decrepit and senile. After an hour or so a company of damsels and eunuchs entered the garden with the princess, who looked just like the radiant moon among the stars. They ran about the garden, plucking fruits and enjoying themselves, until they caught sight of the prince disguised as an old man sitting under one of the trees. The man's hands and feet were trembling from old age, and he had spread a great many precious jewels and regal ornaments before him. Of course, they were astounded by this and asked him what he was doing there with the jewels.

"I want to use these trinkets," he said, "to buy me a wife from among the lot of you."

They all laughed at him and said, "If one of us marries you, what will you do with her?"

"I'll give her one kiss," he replied, "and then divorce her."

"If that's the case," said the princess, "I'll give this damsel to you for your wife."

So he rose, leaned on his staff, staggered toward the damsel, and gave her a kiss. Right after that he gave her the jewels and ornaments, whereupon she rejoiced and they all went on their way laughing at him.

The next day they came again to the garden, and they found him seated in the same place with more jewels and ornaments than before spread before him.

"Oh sheikh," they asked him, "what are you going to do with all this jewelry?"

"I want to wed one of you again," he answered, "just as I did yesterday."

So the princess said, "I'll marry you to this damsel."

And the prince went up to her, kissed her, and gave her the jewels, and they all went their way.

After seeing how generous the old man was to her slave girls, the princess said to herself, "I have more right to these fine things than my slaves, and there's surely no danger involved in this game." So when morning arrived, she went down by herself into the garden dressed as one of her own damsels, and she appeared all alone before the prince and said to him, "Old man, the king's daughter has sent me to you so that you can marry me."

When he looked at her, he knew who she was. So he answered, "With all my heart and love," and he gave her the finest and costliest of jewels and ornaments. Then he rose to kiss her, and since she was not on her guard and thought she had nothing to fear, he grabbed hold of her with his strong hands and threw her down on the ground, where he deprived her of her maidenhead. Then he pulled the beard from his face and said, "Do you recognize me?"

"Who are you?"

"I am Behram, The King of Persia's son," he replied. "I've changed myself and have become a stranger to my people, all for your sake. And I have lavished my treasures for your love."

She rose from him in silence and did not say a word to him. Indeed, she was dazed by what had happened and felt that it was best to be silent, especially since she did not want to be shamed. All the while she was thinking to herself, "If I kill myself, it will be senseless, and if I have him put to death, there's nothing that I'd really gain. The best thing for me to do is to elope with him to his own country."

So, after leaving him in the garden, she gathered together her money and treasures and sent him a message informing him what she intended to do and telling him to get ready to depart with his possessions and whatever else he needed. Then they set a rendezvous for their departure.

At the appointed time they mounted racehorses and set out under cover of darkness, and by the next morning they had traveled a great distance. They kept traveling at a fast pace until they drew near his father's capital in Persia, and when his father heard about his son's coming, he rode out to meet him with his troops and was full of joy.

After a few days went by, the king of Persia sent a splendid present to the princess's father along with a letter to the effect that his daughter was with him and requested her wedding outfit. Al-Datma's father greeted the messenger with a happy heart (for he thought he had lost his daughter and had been grieving for her). In response to the king's letter, he summoned the kazi and the witnesses and drew up a marriage contract between his daughter and the prince of Persia. In addition, he bestowed robes of honor on the envoys from the king of Persia and sent his daughter her marriage equipage. After the official wedding took place, Prince Behram lived with her until death came and sundered their union.

No sooner had Scheherazade concluded her tale than she said, "And yet, oh king, this tale is no more wondrous than the tale of the three apples."

The Tale of the Three Apples

One night the Caliph Harun al-Rashid summoned his vizier Ja'afar and said to him, "I want to go down into the city and question the common folk about the conduct of those charged with carrying out my laws. If the commoners complain about any of my officers, we will dismiss them, and those they praise, we will promote."

"As you wish," replied Ja'afar.

So the caliph went with Ja'afar and the eunuch Masrur to the town and walked about the streets and markets, and as they were passing through a narrow alley, they came upon a very old man with a fishing net and crate for carrying small fish on his head. In his hand he held a staff, and he walked at a leisurely pace and chanted a song about poor people.

When the caliph heard his verses, he said to Ja'afar, "I'm sure that this man's verses are about his own sorry state." Then he approached him and asked, "Tell me, oh sheikh, what do you do for a living?"

"My lord," he answered, "I'm a fisherman with a family to support, and I've been out between midday and this time, and Allah hasn't granted me a thing to feed my family. I can't even pawn myself to buy them a supper, and I hate and am disgusted by my life and I hanker after death."

"Listen to me," said the caliph. "If you return with us to the banks of the Tigris and cast your net, I'll pay you a hundred gold pieces for whatever turns up."

The man rejoiced when he heard these words and said, "Fine with me!"

Upon arriving at the river he cast his net and waited

awhile. Then he hauled in the rope and dragged the net ashore, and in it was a heavy chest with a padlock on it. The caliph examined the chest and found it to be very heavy. So he gave the fisherman two hundred dinars and sent him about his business.

In the meantime, Ja'afar and Masrur carried the chest to the palace, set it down, and lit some candles. Then the caliph told them to break it open, and they found a basket of palm leaves tied with red worsted. After cutting this open, they saw a piece of carpet, which they lifted out of the chest. Then they saw a woman's mantilla folded in four, which they also pulled out, and at the bottom of the chest they came upon a young lady, fair as a silver ingot, who had been slain and cut into nineteen pieces. When the caliph gazed upon her, he cried out, "Alas!" and soon tears ran down his cheeks as he turned to Ja'afar and said, "Can we allow folk to be murdered in my realm and cast into the river? This woman is our burden and responsibility! By Allah, we must avenge her, find the murderer, and make him die the worst of deaths!" After a brief pause, he added, "Now, as surely as we are descended from the sons of Abbas, if you don't bring me the murderer so I can bring him to justice, I'll hang you at the gate of my palace, you and forty of your kith and kin by your side."

Since the caliph was furious and fuming, Ja'afar requested three days to find the murderer, and the caliph granted his request. So Ja'afar returned to his own house, full of sorrow, and said to himself, "How shall I find the man who murdered this damsel? If I bring the caliph someone other than the murderer, the Lord will hold it against me. In truth, I don't know what to do."

Ja'afar stayed in his house for three days, and on the fourth the caliph sent one of the chamberlains for him, and when Ja'afar arrived before him, he asked, "Where is the murderer of the damsel?"

"Oh, Commander of the Faithful," Ja'afar replied, "I haven't been able to find the murderer. It's never been my duty to track down murderers, and I don't even know where to begin looking."

The caliph was furious at his answer and ordered his executioners to hang his minister in front of the palace gate. Before the hanging was to take place, however, he commanded that a crier be sent to announce the execution throughout the streets of Baghdad.

The people flocked from all quarters of the city to witness the hanging of Ja'afar and his kinsmen, even though they did not know why they were to be hung. After the gallows were erected, Ja'afar and the others were made to stand underneath to be ready for the execution, but while every eye looked for the caliph's signal and the crowd wept for Ja'afar and his cousins, a young man suddenly appeared and began pushing his way through the people until he stood immediately before the vizier. He had a fair face and dressed neatly and looked like the radiant moon with bright black eyes, white brow, rosy cheeks, fluff instead of a beard, and a mole like a grain of ambergris. As the vizier looked at him, the young man said, "I've come to rescue you, my lord, for I am the man who slew the woman you found in the chest! So hang me, and let justice be done in her name!"

When Ja'afar heard the youth's confession, he rejoiced, but he was sorry for the handsome young man. Just then, while they were still talking, another man, much older, pushed forward through the crowd of people until he came to Ja'afar and the youth. After saluting the vizier, he said, "Don't believe the words of this young man, my lord! I am the one who murdered the damsel. So take her vengeance out on me. I demand this before Almighty Allah!"

"Oh vizier," the youth intervened, "this old man has become senile, and he doesn't know what he's saying. I'm the one who murdered her. So take her vengeance out on me!"

"My son," said the old man, "you're young and can still appreciate the joys of the world. I'm old and weary and have had enough of the world. I want to offer my life as a ransom for you and for the vizier and his cousins. No one murdered the damsel but me. So, by Allah, I want you to hang me right away! There's no life left in me now that hers is gone."

The vizier was astonished by this strange exchange of words, and he brought the young man and the old man before the caliph. After kissing the ground seven times, he said, "Oh Commander of the Faithful, I bring you the murderer of the damsel!"

"Where is he?" asked the caliph.

"The young man says that he's the murderer," replied the vizier, "but this old man says that he's lying, and maintains that he's the murderer. So I have brought you both of them, and they are now standing before you."

The caliph looked at the old man and the young man and asked, "Which of you killed the girl?"

The young man responded, "No one slew her but me."

The old man answered, "The truth is that I'm the murderer."

Then the caliph said to Ja'afar, "Take the two, and hang them both."

But Ja'afar replied, "It would be an injustice to do that, my lord, since one of them is certainly the murderer."

"By Allah," cried the youth, "I'm the one who slew the damsel," and he went on to describe the way she was murdered and the basket, the mantilla and the bit of carpet, and, in fact, all that the caliph had found with her.

So the caliph was sure that the young man was the murderer, and he was puzzled why he had killed the maiden. "Tell me," he said, "why have you confessed without the bastinado? What brought you here to surrender your life, and what made you say, 'Take her vengeance out on me'?"

"My lord," the youth answered, "this woman was my wife and the mother of my children. She was also my first cousin and the daughter of this old man here, my paternal uncle. When I married her, she was a virgin, and Allah blessed me with three male children by her. She loved me and served me, and I saw no evil in her, for I also loved her with a great deal of affection. Now on the first day of this month, she fell ill with a terrible sickness, and after I had the physicians attend her, she recovered but very slowly. When I wanted her to go to the Hammam bath, she said, 'There is something I long for before I go to the bath, and I have a tremendous longing for it.' 'You only need to ask,' I responded. 'What is it?' Then she said, 'I have a great craving for an apple, to smell it, and to bite a bit of it.' 'Oh,' I replied, 'Even if you had a thousand longings, I'd try to satisfy them all.' So I went straight into the city and looked for apples, but I couldn't find any. Even if they had cost a gold piece each, I would have bought them. Naturally, I was extremely disturbed by this and went home and said, 'By Allah, I haven't been able to find any.' She was most distressed by this, and since she was still very weak, her sickness increased that night, and I felt anxious and alarmed about her condition. As soon as morning dawned, I went out again and made the rounds of the gardens, one by one, but found no apples anywhere. At last I encountered an old gardener, who said to me, 'My son, this is a rare fruit in these parts and can only be found in the garden of the Commander of the Faithful at Bassorah, where the gardener keeps the apples for the caliph's table.' Troubled by my lack of success, I returned home, and my love for my wife moved me to undertake the journey to Bassorah. So I got ready and traveled two weeks back and forth and brought her three apples, which I bought from the gardener for three dinars. But when I went to my wife and set them before her, she did not take any pleasure in them and let them sit by her side, for her fever had increased, and her malady lasted ten days without abating. After that time, she began to recover her health. Therefore, I left my house and began buying and selling again at my shop. About midday a great ugly black slave, long as a lance and broad as a bench, passed by my shop holding one of the three apples and playing with it. 'Oh my good slave,' I said, 'tell me where you got that apple so that I can get one like it.' He laughed and answered, 'I got it from my mistress, for I had been absent for some time, and on my return I found her lying ill with three apples by her side, and she told me that her horned nitwit of a husband had made a journey to Bassorah and had bought them for three dinars. So I ate and drank with her and took this one from her.' When I heard these words from the slave, my lord, the world darkened before my eyes, and I stood up, locked up my shop, and went home beside myself with rage. When I looked for the apples and found only two of the three, I asked my wife, 'Where is the third apple?' Raising her head languidly, she answered, 'I have no idea." This reply convinced me that the slave had spoken the truth. So I took a knife, approached her from behind, and slit her throat without saying a word. Then I hewed off her head and chopped her limbs into pieces. After wrapping her in her mantilla and a rag of carpet, I hurriedly sewed up the whole, which I set in a chest, which I locked up tight. Next I loaded the chest on my mule, brought it to the Tigris, and threw it in with my own hands. When I returned to my house, I found my eldest son crying, even though he didn't know what I had done to his mother. 'Why are you crying, my boy?' I asked him, and he answered, 'I took one of the three apples which were by my mommy and went down into the lane to play with my brothers, when all of a sudden a tall black slave snatched it from my hand and said, 'Where did you get this?' And I said, 'My father traveled to Bassorah for my mother, who was ill, and he bought it along with two other apples for three ducats.' He paid no attention to my words, and I repeatedly asked him to return the apple, but he cuffed me and kicked me and went off with it. I was afraid that my mother would give me a licking because of the apple. So, out of fear for her, I went with my brother outside the city and stayed there until evening came. And, truthfully, I'm afraid of her. So, please, Father, don't tell her anything about this, or it will make her more sick.' After I heard my son's story, I knew that the slave had slandered my wife and was sure that I had wrongfully slain her. So I wept profusely, and soon my uncle came, and I told him what had happened. He sat down by my side and wept with me, and we didn't stop weeping until midnight. We've been mourning for her these last five days, bemoaning her unjust death. If it weren't for the gratuitous lying of that slave, she'd still be alive today! So you now know how and why I killed her, and I beseech you, by the honor of your ancestors, kill me right away and let justice reign, for there is no life in me anyway after her death!"

The caliph was astounded by his words and said, "By Allah, this young man deserves to be pardoned. The only one I'll hang is that foul slave! It's the only way to do something which will comfort those who have suffered, and which will please the Almighty."

And Scheherazade noticed that dawn was approaching and stopped telling her story. When the next night arrived,

however, she received the king's permission to continue her tale and said,

Then the caliph turned to Ja'afar and said, "Fetch me the accursed slave, who was the sole cause of this catastrophe, and if you don't bring him to me within three days, you'll be slain in his stead."

So Ja'afar went away and began weeping, "I've already encountered death and survived, but if you fill a pitcher to the brim too often, it's bound to crack. Skill and cunning are no help here, and only He who saved my life the first time can save me again. By Allah, I won't leave my house during the next three days, and I'll let Him expose the truth as He desires." So Ja'afar stayed in his house for three days, and on the fourth day he summoned the kazi and legal witnesses, made his last will and testament, and began weeping as he took leave of his children. Soon a messenger from the caliph arrived and said to him, "The Commander of the Faithful is furious beyond belief, and he wants you to come to his palace right away. Moreover, he swears that you're sure to hang if you don't produce the slave who caused the damsel's murder."

When Ja'afar heard this, he wept even more, and his children, slaves, and friends wept with him. After he said adieu to everyone except his youngest daughter, he proceeded to bid farewell to her alone, for he loved this little one, who was a beautiful child, more than all his other children. When he pressed her to his breast and kissed her, he felt something round inside the bosom of her dress and asked her, "What are you carrying in your bosom, my dear?"

"It's an apple with the name of our lord the caliph written on it," she replied. "Rayhan, our slave, brought it to me four days ago and gave it to me, but only after I paid him two dinars for it."

When Ja'afar heard her speak of the slave and the apple, he was very happy and put his hand into the slit of his daughter's dress and drew out the apple. He recognized it immediately and cried with joy, "My trust in Allah is complete!" Then he ordered a servant to bring him the slave and said, "What a terrible thing you've done, Rayhan! Where did you get this apple?"

"By Allah, oh master," he replied, "it doesn't pay to tell lies, even if can get away with it once. Truth always pays. I didn't steal this apple from your palace, nor did I take it from the gardens of the Commander of the Faithful. The truth is that five days ago, as I was walking along one of the alleys of the city, I saw some little ones at play, and this apple was in the hand of one of them. So I snatched it from him and beat him, and he cried and said, 'Oh slave, this apple is my mother's, and she's ill. She told my father how she longed for an apple, and he traveled to Bassorah and bought her three apples for three gold pieces, and I took one of them to play with.' He wept again, but I paid no attention to what he said and brought it here, where my little lady bought it from me for two gold dinars. And this is the whole story."

When Ja'afar heard his words, he was astounded that the murder of the damsel and all the misery related to it could have been caused by his slave. He was sorry for the slave, with whom he had a good relationship, but he also rejoiced about his own escape from death. Then he took the slave's hand and led him to the caliph's palace, where he related the story from first to last, and the caliph was extremely astonished and then laughed until he fell on his back. Then he ordered that the story be recorded and made public among the people. But Ja'afar said, "You may find this adventure astonishing, Commander of the Faithful, but it is not as wondrous as the story of the Vizier Nur al-Din Ali of Egypt and his brother Shams al-Din Mohammed."

"What can be more marvelous than this adventure?" the caliph said. "Out with it!"

"My lord," Ja'afar answered, "I'll only tell it to you on the condition that you'll pardon my slave."

"If your story is indeed more wondrous than that of the three apples," the caliph said, "I'll grant you his blood, but if not, I'll definitely slay him."

So Ja'afar began in these words

The Tale of Nur al-Din Ali and His Son

In times gone by the land of Egypt was ruled by a generous and just sultan, one who loved the pious and the poor and who associated with the olema and learned men. Now, he had a vizier who was wise and experienced in the affairs and art of government. This minister, who was a very old man, had two sons like two moons, for no one had ever seen such handsome and graceful young men. The elder was called Shams al-Din Mohammed and the younger Nur al-Din Ali. Among the two, it was the younger who was more handsome and more pleasing, so that people heard about his fame in foreign countries and men flocked to Egypt just for the purpose of seeing him.

In the course of time their father, the vizier, died and was deeply missed and mourned by the sultan, who sent for his two sons, and after presenting them with robes of honor, he said to them, "Don't trouble yourselves, for you shall both replace your father and be joint ministers of Egypt."

Upon hearing this they rejoiced, kissed the ground before him, and performed the ceremonial mourning for their father one whole month. After that time was over, they became viziers, and their father's office passed into their hands, with each doing his duty for a week at a time. They lived under the same roof, and their word was one. Whenever the sultan desired to travel, they took turns attending him.

Now, it happened one night that the sultan decided to set out on a journey the next morning, and the elder, whose turn it was to accompany him, was sitting and conversing with his brother and said to him, "My brother, it's my wish that we both marry two sisters, and sleep with them on the same night, and they shall conceive on their wedding nights and bear children to us on the same day. And by Allah's will, your wife will bear you a son, and my wife will bear me a daughter. Then we'll wed them to each other, for they will be cousins."

"What dowry will you require from my son for your daughter?" Nur al-Din asked.

"I shall take three thousand dinars, three pleasure gardens, and three farms," said Shams al-Din. "It would not be fitting if the youth agreed to take less than this."

When Nur al-Din heard this demand, he replied, "Is this the kind of dowry that you would impose on my son? Don't you realize that we are brothers and both, by Allah's grace, vizers and equal in office? It's really your duty to offer your daughter to my son without a marriage settlement. Or, if one is necessary, then it should be nominal or a public gesture of some kind. Indeed, you know that the male is more valuable than the female, and our memory will be preserved by my son, not by your daughter."

"But what is she to have?" asked Shams al-Din.

"We won't be remembered among the lords of the earth through her," Nur a-Din stated. "But I see you'd like to treat me according to the saying—if you want to bluff off a buyer, keep asking him for a higher price. Or do as a man did who needed something and went to a friend for help and was answered, 'You're welcome to it, but come tomorrow and I'll give you what you need.' Whereupon the other replied in verse:

"When he who is asked a favor says 'tomorrow,'
The wise man knows 'tis vain to beg or borrow."

"Basta!" said Shams al-Din. "I see that you don't respect me, since you're placing more value on your son than on my daughter. And it's plain to see that you lack manners and understanding. Let me remind you, as your elder brother, that I decided to let you share the vizier's office out of pity, not wishing to mortify you, so that you could help me as a kind of assistant. But, by Allah, since you talk this way, I'll never marry my daughter to your son. Never, not for her weight in gold!"

When Nur al-Din heard his brother's words, he became angry and said, "And I, too, will never, never marry my son to your daughter, even if it would mean my death!"

Shams al-Din replied, "I wouldn't accept him as a husband, since he isn't even worth the tip of her toenail!

If I weren't about to travel, I would make an example of you. However, when I return, I'll show you how I can assert my dignity and vindicate my honor. But let Allah's will be done."

When Nur al-Din heard all this from his brother, he became furious and lost his head, but he hid what he felt and held his peace. The brothers spent the night far apart from one another, each fuming with anger at the other.

As soon as dawn arrived, the sultan journeyed forth in state and crossed over from Cairo to Jizah and headed for the Pyramids, accompanied by the vizier Shams al-Din, for it was his turn of duty. Meanwhile his brother, Nur al-Din, who had spent the night in rage, rose with the light and said the dawn prayer. Then he went to his treasury, took a small pair of saddlebags, and filled them with gold. All the while he recalled his brother's threats and the contempt that his brother had shown him, and he said to himself, "Travel, and you'll find new friends to replace the old ones left behind. There's no honor in staying at home." So he ordered one of his pages to saddle his Nubian mule. Now she was a dapple-gray mule with ears like reed pens and legs like columns and a back high and strong as a dome built on pillars. Her saddle was made of gold cloth and her stirrups of Indian steel. Indeed, she had trappings that could serve the Chosroës, and she was like a bride adorned for her wedding night. Moreover, Nur al-Din ordered a piece of silk to be laid on her back for a seat along with a prayer carpet, under which were his saddlebags. When this was done, he said to his pages and slaves, "I intend to go on a small trip outside the city on the road to Kalyub. I'll spend three nights away, and I don't want any of you to follow me, for there is something troubling my heart."

Then he took some provisions for the journey, mounted the mule in haste, and set out from Cairo into the open and wild countryside around it. About noon he reached the city of Bilbay, where he dismounted and stayed awhile to rest himself and his mule. After eating some of his victuals, he bought all that he needed for himself and his mule and continued on his journey. Toward nightfall he entered a town called Sa'adiyah, where he dismounted and ate some of his food. Then he spread his strip of silk on the sand and set the saddlebags under his head and slept in the open air, for he was still filled with anger. When morning arrived, he mounted and rode onward until he reached the Holy City of Jerusalem, and from there he went to Aleppo, where he dismounted at one of the caravan stops and stayed three days to rest himself and the mule and taste the air.

Determined to travel afar, he set out again, wandering without knowing where he was going. After having joined a group of couriers, he kept traveling until he reached Bassorah and did not even know what the place was. It was pitch-black when he arrived at the khan, so he spread out his prayer carpet, took down the saddlebags from the back of the mule, and told the doorkeeper to walk her about, and the porter did as he was requested to do.

Now it so happened that the vizier of Bassorah, a very old man, was sitting at the lattice window of his mansion opposite the khan, and he saw the porter walking the mule up and down. He was struck by her priceless trappings and thought her a nice beast suited for viziers or even for royalty. The more he looked, the more he was perplexed, and he finally said to one of his pages, "Bring me the porter over there."

The page went and returned with the porter, who kissed the ground, and the minister asked him, "Who is the owner of that mule you're walking, and what kind of man is he?"

"My lord," he answered, "the owner of this mule is a handsome young man, very pleasant but also grave and dignified. Undoubtedly he is one of the sons of the merchants."

When the vizier heard the porter's words, he arose right away, mounted his horse, rode over to the khan, and entered it to see Nur al-Din. As the minister advanced toward him, Nur al-Din stood up and greeted him. The vizier welcomed him to Bassorah, embraced him, made him sit by his side, and asked, "My son, where have you come from, and what are you doing here?"

"My lord," Nuir al-Din replied, "I've come from Cairo, where my father was the vizier, but he has died," and he continued to inform him of all that had happened to him from beginning to end, whereupon he added, "And now

I'm determined never to return home until I have seen all the cities and countries of the world."

When the vizier heard this, he said to him, "My son, don't let yourself be carried away by your emotions, or you'll become your own worst enemy. It makes no sense to wander aimlessly. Many regions are just wastelands, and I fear that fortune may turn against you." Then he had the saddlebags, the silk, and the prayer carpets loaded on the mule and brought Nur al-Din to his own house, where he lodged him in a pleasant place, treated him honorably, and indulged him, for he was extremely fond of him. After a while the vizier said to him, "Here I am, a man rich in years, but I have no sons. Fortunately, Allah has blessed me with a daughter who can match you in her beauty. Now, I've rejected all her suitors, men of rank and substance, but my affection for you has become deep, and I would like you to become her husband. If you accept, I'll go with you to the sultan of Bassorah and tell him that you are my nephew, the son of my brother. I'll arrange it so that you will be appointed vizier in my place so that I may keep the house, for I am stricken in years and have become weary."

When Nur al-Din heard the vizier's words, he bowed his head in modesty and said, "As you wish."

At this the vizier rejoiced and ordered his servants to prepare a feast and decorate the great assembly hall in which they were accustomed to celebrate the marriages of emirs and nobles. Then he assembled the notables of the realm, the merchants of Bassorah, and his friends, and when they all stood before him, he said, "I had a brother who was a vizier in the land of Egypt, and Allah Almighty blessed him with two sons, while to me, as you all well know, He gave a daughter. My brother requested that I wed my daughter to one of his sons, and I agreed. Since my daughter is now of the age to marry, he sent me one of his sons, the young man now present, to whom I intend to marry her. So I'm drawing up the contract and celebrating the night of unveiling with due ceremony, for he is nearer and dearer to me than a stranger. After the wedding, if it pleases him, he will dwell with me, or if he prefers, I will enable him to travel with his wife to his father's home."

Upon hearing this, everyone rejoiced and was pleased

by the vizier's choice of the bridegroom. Consequently, the vizier sent for the kazi and legal witnesses, and they wrote out the marriage contract, after which the slaves sprayed the guests with incense and served them with sherbet. Then they sprinkled them with rose water, and the people went their ways. Afterward the vizier ordered his servants to take Nur al-Din to the Hammam bath and sent him a suit of his own best raiment along with napkins, towels, bowls, perfume burners, and everything else that was necessary. When Nir al-Din came out of the bath and donned the garments, he was just like the full moon on the fourteenth night. Thereupon he mounted his mule and went straight to the vizier's palace, where he dismounted and went in to see the minister and kissed his hands, and the vizier bade him welcome.

And Scheherazade noticed that dawn was approaching and stopped telling her story. When the next night arrived, however, she received the king's permission to continue her tale and said,

After welcoming him, the vizier said, "Arise and go and see your wife tonight. Tomorrow I'll bring you to the sultan, and I pray that Allah will bless you and look after your welfare."

So Nur al-Din left him and went to his wife, the vizier's daughter. So much for Nur al-Din at present.

In the meantime, his elder brother, Shams al-Din, was absent with the sultan a long time, and when he returned from his journey, he did not find his brother, and he asked his servants and slaves where he was.

"On the day of your departure with the sultan," they replied, "your brother had his mule groomed and outfitted as if for a state procession. Then he mounted it and told us that he was going toward Kalyub and would be absent three days, for his heart was disturbed, and he didn't want any one of us to follow him. Well, ever since he left, we've had no news of him."

Shams al-Din was greatly troubled by the sudden disappearance of his brother and grieved at his loss. "This is only because I chided and upbraided him the night before my departure with the sultan," he said to himself.

"Most likely his feelings were hurt, and he decided to go off traveling, but I must send after him."

Then he went to the sultan and acquainted him with what had happened. Next he wrote letters and sent dispatches carried by couriers to his deputies in every province. But during the twenty days of Shams al-Din's absence, Nur al-Din had traveled far and had reached Bassorah. So after a diligent search the messengers failed to come up with any news of him and returned to Cairo. As a result, Shams al-Din despaired of finding his brother and said, "In truth, I exceeded the bounds of propriety in regard to the marriage of our children. If only I had not done that! All this comes from my carelessness and stupidity!"

Soon after this he sought the hand of the daughter of a Cairo merchant, drew up the marriage contract, and celebrated a splendid wedding with her. And so it happened that he slept with his wife on the very same night that Nur al-Din also slept with his wife, the daughter of the vizier of Bassorah. Of course, all this was in accordance with the will of Almighty Allah so that He might determine the destiny of His creatures. Furthermore, everything turned out as the brothers had said it would, for their two wives became pregnant by them on the same night, and both gave birth on the same day: the wife of Shams al-Din, vizier of Egypt, had a daughter, whose beauty was unmatched in Cairo; the wife of Nur al-Din had a handsome son, whose looks were incomparable in his time. They named the boy Badar al-Din Hasan, and his grandfather, the vizier of Bassorah, rejoiced when he was born, and on the seventh day after his birth, he held a banquet with entertainment that would have befitted the birth of a prince's son. Then he took Nur al-Din to the sultan, and his son-in-law kissed the ground in homage. In response, the sultan rose up to honor them and asked the vizier who the young man was. And the minister answered, "This is my brother's son," and related his tale from first to last.

"Well, how is it that he's your nephew," the sultan asked, "and we've never heard of him before this?"

"My lord," the vizier responded, "I had a brother who was a vizier in the land of Egypt, and he died and left behind two sons. The eldest took his father's place, and the younger, whom you see before you, came to me, for I had sworn that I would not marry my daughter to anyone but him. So, when he came, I married her to him. Now he is young, and I am old. My hearing has become weak, and my judgment is easily fooled. Therefore, I would like to request, my lord, that you let him take my place, for he is my brother's son and my daughter's wife. Moreover, he is fit to become a vizier, since he is a wise and cunning young man."

The sultan looked at Nur al-Din and took a liking to him. So he established him in the office of the vizier, and he presented him with a splendid robe of honor and a mule from his private stables. In addition, he gave him a salary, stipends, and supplies. Nur al-Din kissed the sultan's hand and went home with his father-in-law in a most joyous mood.

"All this follows on the heels of the boy Hasan's birth!" he said.

The next day he presented himself before the sultan and kissed the ground. Then the sultan asked him to sit down in the vizier's seat. So he sat down and began to address the business of his office. He went into the cases of the lieges and their suits, as is the custom of the ministers, while the sultan watched him and admired his wit, good sense, judgment, and insight. Indeed, he became deeply fond of him and took him into his confidence. When the divan was dismissed, Nur al-Din returned to his house and related what had happened to his father-in-law, who rejoiced. From then on Nur al-Din continued to serve as vizier, and the sultan sought his company day and night. Moreover, he increased his stipends and supplies until Nur al-Din's means were ample, and he became the owner of ships that made trading voyages at his command. He also possessed numerous mamelukes and blackamoor slaves, and he had many estates developed and set up Persian wheels and planted gardens. When his son, Hasan, was four, the old vizier died, and Nur al-Din arranged for a sumptuous funeral ceremony for his father-in-law before he was laid to dust. Then he concerned himself with the education of his son, and when the strong and healthy boy turned seven, he brought him a fakih, a doctor of law and religion, to teach him in his own house. Indeed, he charged the fakih to give him a good education and instruct him in politeness and good manners. So the tutor made the boy read and retain all kinds of useful knowledge as well as learn the Koran by heart. At the same time he continued to grow handsome and strong.

Over the years the professor brought him up in his father's palace teaching him reading, writing, and ciphering along with theology and belles lettres. Indeed, he never left the house and grounds, since he was fully occupied there. Then, on a certain day, his father clad him in his best clothes, mounted him on one of the finest mules, and went with him to the sultan. When the sultan gazed at Badar al-Din Hasan, he marveled at how handsome he was and took a great liking to him. As for the people in the city, they were so struck by his handsome features when he first passed before them that they sat down on the road to wait for his return so that they might gaze again at his graceful and lovely features. The sultan treated the lad with special favor and said to his father, "Oh vizier, you must bring him to me every day."

"As you wish," replied Nur al-Din.

Then the vizier returned home with his son and continued to bring him to court until he reached the age of twenty. At that time his father became sick and, after sending for Badar al-Din Hasan, he said, "I want you to know, my son, that the world of the present is but a house of mortality, while that of the future is a house of eternity. Before I die, I want to bequeath certain tasks to you, and I want you to pay attention to what I say and take my words to heart." Then he gave him last instructions about the best way to deal with his neighbors and his affairs. After all was said, he recalled his brother, his home, and his native land and wept over his separation from those he had first loved. As he wiped away his tears, he turned to his son and said to him, "Before I proceed to my last requests and commands, I want you to know that I have a brother, your uncle, who is called Shams al-Din, the vizier of Cairo. Many years ago I left him against his will. Now, take a sheet of paper and write down what I tell you."

Badar al-Din took a sheet of paper and did as his father requested, and he wrote down the full account of what had happened to his father from the day of his dispute with his brother twenty years ago to the very present. At the end, Nur al-Din added, "And this is written at my dictation, and may Almighty Allah be with him when I am gone!" Then he signed the paper, folded it, sealed it, and said, "My son, guard this paper with utmost care, for it will enable you to establish your origin, rank, and lineage, and if anything adverse happens to you, set out for Cairo, ask for your uncle, and show him this paper. Then tell him that I died a stranger far from my own people and full of yearning to see him and them."

So Badar al-Din Hasan took the document, and after wrapping it up in a piece of waxed cloth, he sewed it like a talisman between the inner and outer cloth of his skull-cap and wound his light turban around it. And he began to weep about his father and his untimely separation from him, for he was but a young man. Then Nur al-Din lapsed into a swoon that prefigured his death. Soon, however, he recovered a little and said, "Oh Hasan, my son, listen now to my five last commands. The first is that you should not be overly intimate with anyone or too familiar, otherwise you will not be safe from his mischief. Security lies in seclusion of thought and a certain distance from the company of your compatriots. The second command is that you should not deal harshly with anyone, otherwise fortune might deal harshly with you. In this world fortune is with you one day and against you the next. All worldly goods are but a loan to be repaid. The third command is that you should learn to be silent in society, and let the faults of others make you aware of your own faults. Safety dwells in silence. The fourth command, my son, is that you should be aware of indulging in too much wine, for wine is the head of all obstinance and a fine solvent of human brains. So shun, and again I say, shun mixing strong liquor. The fifth command is that you should take good care of your wealth, and if you do so, it will take good care of you. Guard your money, and it will guard you. Do not waste your capital, otherwise you might be forced to go begging from the meanest of mankind. Save your dirhams, and consider them the best salve for the wounds of the world."

Nur al-Din continued to advise his son in this way until his hour came, and sighing one last sob, he died. Then the voice of mourning rose high in his house, and the sultan and all the nobles grieved for him and buried him. However, his son did not stop lamenting his loss for two months, during which time he never mounted a horse, attended the divan, or presented himself before the sultan. At last the sultan became so furious with him that he replaced him as vizier with one of his chamblerlains and gave orders to seize and set seals on all Nur al-Din's houses, goods, and domains. So the new vizier went forth with a mighty posse of chamberlains, courtiers, watchmen, and a host of idlers to carry out the sultan's command and to seize Badar al-Din Hasan and bring him before the sultan, who would deal with him as he deemed fit.

Now, among the crowd of followers was a mameluke of the deceased vizier, and when he heard the sultan's order, he rode his horse full-speed to the house of Badar al-Din Hasan, for he could not endure to see the degradation of his old master's son. The mameluke found Badar al-Din Hasan sitting at the gate with his head hung down, mourning the loss of his father, as was his custom. So he dismounted, kissed his hand, and said, "My lord, hurry and get away before everything's laid to waste!"

When Hasan heard this, he trembled and asked, "What's the matter?"

"The sultan is angry at you," the man said, "and he's issued a warrant for your arrest. The evildoers are hard on my heels. So flee for your life!"

Upon hearing these words, Hasan's heart was ignited, his rosy cheeks turned pale, and he asked the slave, "Is there any time for me to get some of my things from the house that I may need during my exile?"

But the slave replied, "My lord, get up at once and save yourself! Leave this house while there's still time!"

So Badar al-Din covered his head with the skirt of his garment and went forth on foot until he stood outside the city where he heard the people saying, "The sultan's sent his new vizier to the house of the old one to seal his property and to seize his son, Badar al-Din Hasan, and bring him to the palace, where he's to be put to death."

"Alas! Such a handsome and lovely man!" they cried.

When he heard this, he fled at hazard and did not stop running until destiny drove him to the cemetery where his father was buried. So he entered and walked among the graves until he reached his father's sepulcher, where he sat down and let the skirt of his long robe fall from his head. While he was sitting by his father's tomb, a Jew suddenly came toward him, and he seemed to be a shroff with a pair of saddlebags containing a great deal of gold. After the Jew stopped and kissed his hand, he said, "Where are you going, my lord? It's late in the day. Indeed, you are lightly clad, and I read signs of trouble in your face."

"I had been asleep this past hour," answered Hasan, "when my father appeared to me and chided me for not having visited his tomb. So I awoke trembling and came straight here. Otherwise, the day would have gone by without my having visited him, and this would have been very grievous to me."

"Oh my lord," the Jew replied, "your father had many merchantmen at sea, and since some of them are now due to arrive, I would like to buy the cargo of the first ship that comes into port with this thousand dinars of gold."

"You have my consent," said Hasan, whereupon the Jew took out a bag full of gold and counted out a thousand sequins, which he gave to Hasan, the son of the vizier, and said, "Write a bill of sale for me and seal it."

So Hasan took a pen and paper and wrote these words in duplicate: "The writer, Hasan Badar al-Din, son of Vizier Nur al-Din, has sold to Isaac the Jew all the cargo of the first of his father's ships that comes into port for a thousand dinars, and he has received the payment for the goods in advance." And after the Jew took one copy, he put it into his pouch and went away. But Hasan began weeping as he thought of the dignity and prosperity that had once been his. Soon night fell, and he leaned his head against his father's grave and was overcome by sleep. He continued to slumber until the moon rose and his head slipped from the tomb so that he lay on his back with his limbs outstretched and his face shining bright in the moonlight. Now the cemetery was haunted day and night by jinnees who were of the true believers, and soon a jinniyah came out and saw Hasan asleep. She marveled at how handsome he was and cried, "Glory to God! This youth can be none other than one of the Wuldan of

Paradise." Then she flew high into the air, as was her custom, and she met an ifrit, who was also flying about. After he greeted her, she asked him, "Where are you coming from?"

"From Cairo," he replied.

"Do you want to come with me and gaze upon the beauty of a youth who is sleeping in that cemetery down there?" she inquired.

"Yes," he responded.

And so they flew until they landed at the tomb, where she showed him Hasan and remarked, "Did you ever in your born days see something like this?"

The jinnee looked at him and exclaimed, "Praise be to Him that has no equal! But, my sister, shall I tell you what I've seen this day?"

"What's that?" she replied.

"I have seen the counterpart of this youth in the land of Egypt," he said. "She is the daughter of the Vizier Shams al-Din, and she's a model of beauty and loveliness. When she reached the age of nineteen, the sultan of Egypt heard about her, and after sending for her father, he said to him, 'Hear me, oh vizier, I've been told that you have a daughter, and I want to request her hand in marriage.' The vizier replied, 'My lord, please accept my excuses and have compassion with me, for you know that my brother, who was my partner, disappeared from us many years ago, and we don't know where he is. He departed because of a quarrel we had while we were sitting together and talking of wives and children to come. Indeed, we had some sharp words with one another, and he went off extremely angry at me. But I swore that I would marry my daughter to no one but his son, and I took this oath on the day that my daughter was born nineteen years ago. Now, recently I've learned that my brother died at Bassorah, where he had married the daughter of the vizier, and she had given birth to a son. Consequently, I won't and can't marry my daughter to anyone but him in memory of my brother. I recorded the date of my marriage and the conception of my wife and the birth of my daughter, and from her horoscope I've found that her name is linked with that of her cousin. May I also remind my lord that he has the pick of numerous damsels in his kingdom.' Upon hearing his vizier's answer, the king became extremely furious and cried, 'When the likes of me asks for a damsel in marriage from the likes of you, it must be considered an honor! Yet you reject me and put me off with insipid excuses! Now by my life I intend to marry her to the most vile of my men to spite you!' In the palace was a horsegroom, a gobbo, with a hump on his breast and a hunch to his back, and the sultan sent for him and had him betrothed to the daughter of the vizier against his will. Then he arranged for a spectacular wedding procession for him. The hunchback is to sleep with his bride this very night. I have just now flown from Cairo, where I left the hunchback at the door of the Hammam bath among the sultan's white slaves, who were waving lit torches about him. As for the minister's daughter, she is sitting among her nurses and attendants, weeping and wailing, for they have forbidden her father to come near her. Never have I seen, my sister, a more hideous creature than this hunchback, while the young lady looks just like this young man. Indeed, she is even fairer than he."

And Scheherazade noticed that dawn was approaching and stopped telling her story. When the next night arrived, however, she received the king's permission to continue her tale and said,

After the jinnee had told the jinniyah how the sultan had caused the wedding contract to be drawn up between the hunchbacked groom and the lovely young lady, who was heartbroken out of sorrow, and how she was the fairest of Allah's creatures and even more beautiful than this youth, the jinniyah exclaimed, "You're lying! There's no one as handsome as this youth!"

But the ifrit insisted that he was telling the truth and added, "By Allah, this damsel is definitely fairer than this youth. Nevertheless, he's the only one who deserves her, for they resemble each other like brother and sister or at least like cousins. In any case, she's wasted on that hunchback!"

"Brother, I have an idea!" the jinniyah replied. "Let's lift him up and carry him to Cairo so that we can compare him with the damsel and determine which of the two is the fairer."

"Your idea is a good one," he answered. "This way we'll get right to the bottom of the matter, and I myself will carry him." So he raised Hasan from the ground and flew with him like a bird soaring through the air while the jinniyah kept close by his side at equal speed. Finally, they landed with him in Cairo, set him down on a stone bench, and woke him. Gradually he realized that he was no longer at his father's tomb in Bassorah, and after looking right and left he saw that he was in a strange place. Indeed, he would have cried out, but the ifrit gave him a cuff which persuaded him to keep quiet. Then he brought Hasan rich raiment with which he clothed him, and after giving him a lighted torch, he said, "I want you to know that I've brought you here with the intention of doing you a good turn for the love of Allah. So take this torch and mix with the people at the Hammam door. Then walk on with them without stopping until you reach the house of the wedding festivities. Then you're to go boldly forward and enter the great salon. Don't be afraid of anyone, but take a place at the right of the hunchback bridegroom. Whenever any of the nurses, maids, or singing girls come up to you, put your hand into your pocket, which you will find filled with gold. Take the gold out and throw it to them. You don't have to worry about losing your money, for your pouch will remain full. Give liberally and fear nothing, but place your trust in Him who created you, for this is not your own strength but that of Almighty Allah."

When Badar al-Din Hasan heard the ifrit's words, he said to himself, "If only I knew what all this means, and what's causing all this kindness!" Without further wondering, however, he began to mix with the people and moved on with the bridal procession until he came to the bath, where he found the hunchback already on horseback. Then he pushed his way into the crowd, and he was truthfully a handsome specimen of a man, dressed in the finest apparel with tarbush, turban, and a long-sleeved robe lined with gold. Whenever the singing girls stopped to receive money from people, he put his hand into his pocket, took out a handful of gold, and threw it on the tambourine until he filled it with gold pieces. The singers were amazed by his generosity, and the people were astounded by his handsome features, grace, and splendid dress. Now Hasan continued doing this until he reached the mansion of the vizier, who was his uncle. There the chamberlains drove the people back and forbade them to go any further. But the singing girls and maids said, "By Allah, we won't enter unless this young man is allowed to enter with us, for he has given us a long life with his generosity, and we won't display the bride unless he is present."

Consequently, Hasan was allowed to enter the bridal hall with them, and they made him sit down, defying the evil glances of the hunchbacked groom. The wives of the nobles, viziers, chamberlains, and courtiers stood in a double line, each holding a large torch. All of them wore thin face veils, and the two rows extended from the bride's throne to the head of the hall next to the chamber from where the bride was to come forth. When the ladies saw Badar al-Din Hasan and noticed his handsome features and lovely face that shone like the new moon, their hearts went out to him, and the singing girls said to all present, "That handsome man gave us nothing but gold coins. So don't hesitate to serve him and comply with his requests, no matter what he asks."

Then all the women crowded around Hasan with their torches, gazed at his handsome features, and admired his loveliness. One and all would gladly have lain on his bosom an hour if not a year. They were so excited that they let their veils fall from their faces and said, "Happy is she who belongs to this youth or to whom he belongs!" And they began cursing the crooked groom and the sultan, who was the cause of the hunchback's marriage to the vizier's beautiful daughter. As often as they blessed Badar al-Din Hasan, they damned the hunchback and said, "Truly, this youth and no one else deserves our bride. May Allah's curse land on the head of the hideous hunchback and on the sultan who commanded the marriage!" Then the singing girls beat their tambourines and announced the bride's appearance with joy.

The vizier's daughter entered with her attendants, who had made her look her best, for they had put perfume and incense on her and adorned her hair. Moreover, they had dressed her in raiment and ornaments that suited the mighty Chosroë kings. The most notable part of her dress was a loose robe worn over her other garments: it was embroidered with golden figures of wild beasts, birds whose eyes and beaks were made of gems, and claws of red rubies and green beryl. Her neck was graced with a necklace of Yamani work worth thousands of gold pieces, and the settings for the gems were great round jewels the like of which has never been owned by an emperor or Tobba king. Indeed, the bride resembled the full moon when at its fullest on the fourteenth night, and as she walked through the hall, she was like one of the houris of heaven!

Now the ladies surrounded her like clustering stars, and she shone among them like the moon when it eats up the clouds. When the bride emerged with her graceful swaying, Badar al-Din Hasan was sitting in full gaze of the people, and her hunchbacked bridegroom stood up to meet and receive her. However, she turned away from the horrid creature and walked forward until she stood before her cousin Hasan, the son of her uncle. Thereupon, the people laughed, but when they saw her attracted toward Badar al-Din, they made a mighty clamor, and the singing women shouted their loudest. Then he put his hand into his pocket, and after pulling out a handful of gold, he cast it into their tambourines, causing the girls to rejoice and say, "If we had our wish, this bride would be yours."

Upon hearing this, he smiled, and the people came around him, torches in hand, while the gobbo bridegroom was left sitting alone like a tailless baboon. Indeed, every time they lit a candle for him, it went out willy-nilly. So he was left in darkness and silence and could see nothing but himself. When Badar al-Din saw the bridegroom sitting alone in the dark and all the wedding guests with their torches and candles crowding around himself, he was bewildered, but he also rejoiced and felt an inner delight. He longed to greet the bride and gazed intently at her face, which was radiant with light. Then her attendants took off her veil and displayed her in the first bridal dress, which was made of scarlet satin. As Hasan looked at her, his eyes were dazzled, and his wits, dazed. She moved to and fro, swaying with graceful gait, and she turned the heads of all the guests, women as well as men. Then her attendants changed that dress and displayed her in a robe of azure. When she reappeared, it was like the full moon when it rises over the horizon. Her hair was coal-black; her cheeks, delicately fair; and her white teeth showed through her sweet smiles as her firm breasts rose and crowned her most soft sides and round waist. Next they changed her garments for some other dress. Veiling her face in her lush hair, they loosened her lovelocks that were so dark and long that their darkness and length outdid the darkest nights. After that her attendants displayed her in the fourth bridal dress, and she came forward shining like the rising sun and swayed to and fro with lovely grace and supple ease like a gazelle. And she struck all hearts with the arrows of her eyelashes. In her fifth dress she appeared as the very light of loveliness, like a wand of waving willow. Her locks which hung like scorpions along her cheeks were curled, and her neck was bowed in blandishment, and her lips quivered as she walked. Following this dress her attendants adorned her with a green one, and she shamed the brown spear in her slender straightness. Her radiant face dimmed the brightest beams of the full moon, and she outdid the bending branches in gentle movement and flexile grace. Her loveliness exalted the beauties of the earth's four quarters, and she broke men's hearts with her remarkable appearance. Finally, her attendants displayed her in the seventh dress with a color between safflower and saffron. Thus they showed the bride in her seven dresses before Badar al-Din, completely neglecting the gobbo, who sat moping alone. And when she opened her eyes, she said, "Oh Allah, make this man my bridegroom, and deliver me from the evil of this hunchbacked groom."

As soon as this part of the ceremony had come to an end, the wedding guests were dismissed, and everyone left with the exception of Hasan and the hunchback. Meanwhile the servants led the bride into an inner room to change her garb and get her ready for the bridegroom. Thereupon, the hunchback came up to Badar al-Din Hasan and said, "My lord, you have cheered us tonight with your good company and overwhelmed us with your kindness and courtesy, but now it's time to go."

"In Allah's name," he replied, "so be it!"

He rose and went to the door, where he was met by the jinnee, who said, "Stay right here, Badar al-Din, and when the hunchback leaves to go to the toilet, you're to go immediately to the alcove and sit down. When the bride comes, you're to say to her, 'It's me who is your husband, for the king devised this trick because he was afraid of the evil eye, and he whom you saw is only a syce, a groom, one of our stablemen.' Then walk boldly up to her and unveil her face."

While Hasan was still talking with the ifrit, the groom suddenly left the hall and entered the toilet, where he sat down on the stool. No sooner had he done this than the jinnee came out of the water tank in the form of a mouse and began to squeak.

"What's the matter with you?" asked the hunchback.

But the mouse grew until it became a pitch-black cat and let forth a "Meow! Meow!" Then it grew more and more until it became a dog and barked, "Bow-wow! Bow-wow!"

When the hunchback saw this, he became frightened and exclaimed, "Get out of here, you evil spirit!"

But the dog grew and swelled until it became an ass that brayed and snorted in his face, "Heehaw! Heehaw!"

Thereupon the hunchback quaked and cried, "Help! People, help!"

But the ass grew and became as big as a buffalo and wailed and spoke with the voice of the sons of Adam, "Woe to you, you hunchback, you stinkard, you filthiest of grooms!"

Upon hearing this, the groom was seized with a colic, and he sat down on the toilet bowl in his clothes with his teeth chattering.

"Is the world so tiny," asked the ifrit, "that the only person you can find to marry is my lady love?" Since the hunchback did not respond, the jinnee continued, "Answer me, or you'll become dust!"

"By Allah," said the gobbo, "Oh King of the Buffaloes, this is not my fault! They forced me to wed her, and honestly I didn't know that she had a lover among the buffaloes. So now I repent, first before Allah and then before you."

"I swear to you," said the jinnee, "that if you leave this place or utter a word before sunrise, I'll surely wring your neck. When the sun rises, I want you to go your way and never return to this house again." After saying this, the ifrit took the gobbo and set him head downward and feet upward in the slit of the privy. Then he declared, "I'm going to leave you here, but I'll be on the lookout for you until sunrise, and if you stir before then, I'll grab you by the feet and bash out your brains against the wall. So watch out for your life!"

In the meantime, Badar al-Din had made his way to the alcove and was sitting there when the bride came in. She was attended by a very old woman, who stood at the door and said, "My lord, arise and take what God has given to you."

Then the old woman went away, and the bride, Sitt al-Husan, otherwise called the Lady of Beauty, entered the inner part of the alcove brokenhearted and saying to herself, "By Allah, I'll never abandon myself to him. No, not even if he were to take my life!" But as she came to the far end of the alcove, she saw Badar al-Din Hasan, and she said, "My dear, are you still sitting here? By Allah, I had been wishing that you were my bridegroom, or at very least, that you and the hunchbacked horse groom were partners and shared me."

"Oh beautiful lady," he replied, "why should the syce have you, and why should he share you?"

"Who *is* my husband, you or he?"

"Sitt al-Husan," he answered, "we have not done this for mere fun, but only as a trick to ward off the evil eye. You see, when the attendants, singers, and wedding guests saw your beauty being displayed to me, they became afraid of fascination, and your father hired the horse groom for ten dinars to take the evil eye off us. And now the hunchback has received his pay, he has gone his way."

When the Lady of Beauty heard these words, she smiled and laughed pleasantly. Then she whispered to him, "By Allah, you have quenched a fire that was torturing me, and now, my dark-haired darling, take me to you and press me against your chest." Then she stripped off her outer garment, and she threw open her chemise from the neck downward and showed her womb and the rondure of her hips. When Badar al-Din saw this glorious sight, his desires were aroused, and he got up, took off his clothes, wrapped the purse of gold that contained the thousand dinars from the Jew in his bag trousers, and

N. ORR–CO.

laid them under the edge of the bed. Then he took off his turban, placed it on top of his clothes, and had nothing on except his skullcap and fine shirt of blue silk laced with gold. Thereupon, the Lady of Beauty embraced him, and he took her into his arms, set her legs around his waist, and aimed his cannon point-blank at the spot where it would batter down the bulwark of maidenhead and lay it to waste. And he found her a pearl unpierced and a filly unridden by men except himself. So he took her virginity and enjoyed her youth in his virility, and soon he withdrew sword from sheath. Then he returned to the fray right away, and when the battle and the siege were finished, there had been some fifteen assaults, and she conceived through him that very night. Afterward he placed his hand under her head, and she did the same, and they embraced and fell asleep in each other's arms.

As soon as the jinnee saw the two asleep, he said to the jinniyah, "Arise and slip under the youth, and let us carry him back to his place before dawn overtakes us, for day is near."

So she came forward and, after getting under him as he lay asleep, she lifted him, clad only in his fine blue shirt, and left the other garments under the bed. Once they were in the air, the jinnee joined them, and they kept flying until they realized that dawn was upon them, and they had only reached the halfway mark. Then Allah had his angelic host shoot the jinnee down with a shooting star, and he was consumed. But the jinniyah managed to escape, and she descended with Badar al-Din to the place where the jinnee was burned. After seeing what had happened to the jinnee, she decided not to carry Badar back to Bassorah, fearing that he might come to some harm.

Now, by the order of Him who determines all things, they arrived at Damascus in Syria, and the jinniyah set her burden down at one of the city gates and flew away. When the gates were opened, the people came forth and saw a handsome youth with no other clothes but his blue shirt of gold-embroidered silk and skullcap. He was lying on the ground drowned in sleep after his hard labor that night. So the people looked at him and said, "Oh lucky her who has spent the night with this young man! But he should have put on his garments afterward."

"They're a sorry lot, those sons of great families!" someone said. "Most likely he came out of a tavern and the wine went to his head. So he probably forgot where he was heading and strayed until he came to the gate of the city. Finding it shut, he lay down and went to bye-bye land!"

While the people were bandying guesses about him, the morning breeze suddenly blew upon Badar al-Din, and raising his shirt to his middle, it revealed a stomach and navel with something below it. His legs and thighs were as clear as crystal and smooth as cream, and the people cried, "By Allah, he's a pretty fellow!"

And as they cried out, Badar al-Din awoke and found himself lying at a city gate with a crowd gathered around him. Of course, he was greatly surprised by this and asked, "Where am I, good people? Why have you gathered around me?"

"We found you lying here asleep during the call to dawn prayer," they said, "and this is all we know. But where did you spend last night?"

"By Allah, good people," he replied, "I spent last night in Cairo."

"You've surely been eating hashish," said somebody.

"He's a fool," said another.

"He's a fathead," a third commented.

And a fourth asked him, "Are you out of your mind? How can you spend the night in Cairo and wake in the morning at the gate of Damascus?"

"By Allah, my good people," Hasan cried, "I'm not lying to you. Truthfully, I spent last night in Cairo, and before that, yesterday afternoon, I was in Bassorah."

"Well, well," remarked someone.

"Ho! Ho!" commented another.

"So! So!" said a third.

And a fourth exclaimed, "This young man is possessed by the jinnees!"

So they clapped their hands at him and said to one another, "Alas, such a pity, for he's so young. By Allah, he's a madman, and madness has no respect of anyone, no matter who the person is!"

Then they said to him, "Collect yourself, and be sensible! How could you have been in Bassorah yesterday and in Cairo last night, and wake up in Damascus this morning?"

But he persisted, "Indeed, I was a bridegroom in Cairo last night."

"Perhaps you were dreaming and saw all this in your sleep," they replied.

So Hasan pondered this for a while and said, "By Allah, this was no dream. Nor does it seem to have been a vision. I'm certain I was in Cairo. They displayed the bride before me in the presence of a third person, the hunchback groom, who was sitting nearby. By Allah, my brothers, this was not a dream, and if it were a dream, where is the bag of gold I was carrying with me, and where are my turban, my robe, and my trousers?"

Then he rose and entered the city meandering through the streets and bazaar, while the people followed him and jeered at him, "Madman! Madman!" until he was beside himself with rage and took refuge in a cook's shop. Now this cook was one of those who had been a trifle too cunning in his youth, that is, he was a rogue and a thief, but Allah had made him repent and turn from his evil ways. This is why he had opened a shop, and all the people of Damascus lived in fear of him because he could still be bold and mischievous. Consequently, when the crowd saw the youth enter his shop, they became afraid and went their ways. The cook looked at Badar al-Din, and, noting how handsome he was, he immediately took a great liking to him and asked, "Where have you come from, young man? Tell me your tale at once."

So Hasan told him all that had happened to him from beginning to end, and the cook said, "You undoubtedly realize how marvelous your story is. Therefore, I advise you to conceal what has happened to you until Allah takes care of the evil forces working against you. In the meantime, since I have no children, I'll adopt you."

"As you wish, uncle," Badar al-Din replied.

Accordingly, the cook went to the bazaar and bought a fine suit of clothes for him and made him put it on. Then he brought him to the kazi and formally declared that he was his son. So Badar al-Din Hasan became known in Damascus as the cook's son, and he stayed there for quite a long time.

With regard to his cousin, the Lady of Beauty, she

awoke in the morning and missed Badar al-Din Hasan, but she thought that he had gone to the privy and expected him to return in an hour or so. However, it was her father, Shams al-Din Mohammed, vizier of Egypt, who came to see her. Now, he was rather upset because of the harsh way that the sultan had treated him by forcing him to marry his daughter to the lowest of the sultan's menials, who, to boot, was a hunchback. Indeed, he said to himself, "I'll slay this daughter of mine if she yielded to that lump of a groom of her own free will." So he went to the door of the bride's private chamber and said, "Ho! Sitt al-Husan!"

She answered, "Here I am! Here I am, my lord!" and she came out unsteadily after the pains and pleasures of the night. She kissed her father's hands, her beautiful face glowing even brighter than usual for having lain in the arms of her cousin. When her father saw her in such condition, he asked, "You should be cursed for rejoicing after having slept with that horse groom!"

And Sitt al-Husan smiled sweetly and answered, "By Allah, don't mock me. I had enough of that yesterday when people laughed at me and joined me with that groom fellow, who is not even fit to carry my husband's shoes or slippers! My lord, never in my life have I spent a night so sweet as last night. So, don't mock me by reminding me of the gobbo!"

When her father heard her words, he was filled with anger, and his eyes glared at her so that only the whites showed, and he cried, "Shame upon you! What are you saying? It was the hunchbacked groom who spent the night with you!"

"By Allah," replied the Lady of Beauty, "don't trouble me about the gobbo. May Allah damn his father! And stop jesting with me! You know yourself that this groom was only hired for ten dinars and went his way after taking his wages. As for me, I entered the bridal chamber after the singers had displayed me to my true bridegroom, and I found him sitting there. It was the same young man who had crossed their hands with gold and had turned all the paupers at the wedding into rich people. And I spent the night on the breast of this lovely man, a most lively darling with his black eyes and full eyebrows."

When her father heard these words, the light before his face became night, and he cried out, "You whore! What's this you're telling me? Where are your brains?"

"Father," she responded, "you're breaking my heart! Why are you being so hard on me? Indeed, my husband, who took my virginity, has just gone to the privy, and I feel that he's made me pregnant."

The vizier was astounded by these words. So he turned from the door and went into the privy, where he found the hunchbacked horse groom with his head in the hole and his heels in the air. Confused by this sight, he said to himself, "Why it's none other than that rascal the hunchback!" So he called to him, "Ho, hunchback!"

The hunchback responded with a murmur and gulp, thinking it was the jinnee who was speaking to him. Therefore, the vizier shouted at him and said, "Speak out, or I'll cut off your head with this sword!"

"By Allah, oh Sheikh of the Jinnees," he replied, "ever since you put me in this place, I've not lifted my head. So take pity upon me, and treat me kindly!"

When the vizier heard these words, he asked, "What are you saying? I'm the bride's father, not a jinnee."

"Enough of this! You've practically been the death of me!" answered the hunchback. "Get out of here before he finds you here. Couldn't you have married me to someone else instead of the lady love of buffaloes and the beloved of jinnees? Allah curse her and curse him who married me to her and who has caused me such misery!"

And Scheherazade noticed that dawn was approaching and stopped telling her story. When the next night arrived, however, she received the king's permission to continue her tale and said,

Then the vizier said to him, "Get up and out of this place!"

"Do you think I'm crazy?" responded the hunchback. "I won't leave here without the permission of the ifrit, whose last words to me were: 'When the sun rises, get up and go your way.' So, has the sun risen or not? I won't budge from this place if it hasn't!"

"Who brought you here?" asked the vizier.

"I came here last night to answer a call of nature," said the hunchback, "and suddenly a mouse came out of the water and squeaked at me. The next thing I knew it swelled and grew until it was as big as a buffalo and uttered threats to me that I fully understood! Then he left me here and went away. May Allah curse the bride and him who married me to her!"

The vizier walked up to him and lifted his head out of the cesspool hole, and the hunchback ran out of the privy for dear life and did not bother to check whether the sun had risen or not. Indeed, he headed straight for the sultan and told him everything that had happened to him. In the meantime, the vizier returned to the door of the bride's private chamber, very worried about her, and he said to her, "Daughter, explain this strange matter to me!"

"It's simple," she answered. "The bridegroom to whom they displayed me last night lay with me all night and took my virginity, so that now I am with child by him. He is my husband, and if you don't believe me, his turban, dagger, and trousers are beneath the bed along with something wrapped up in them."

When her father heard this, he entered the private chamber and found the turban which had been left there by Badar al-Din Hasan, and he took it in his hand, turned it over, and said, "This is the turban worn by viziers. The only difference is that it's made of Mosul material." So he opened it, and, finding what seemed to be an amulet sewn up in the fez, he unsewed the lining and took it out. Then he lifted up the trousers that contained the purse of the thousand gold pieces. After opening the purse, he found the written receipt of the Jew made out to Badar al-Din Hasan, son of Nur al-Din, the Egyptian, and the thousand dinars were also there. No sooner had Shams al-Din read this than he uttered a loud cry and fell to the ground in a faint. As soon as he revived and understood the gist of the matter, he was astonished and said, "This must be the will of Allah the Almighty! Do you want to know, daughter, who it was who took your virginity?"

"Yes, of course," she replied.

"Truly, it was your cousin, the son of my brother, and this thousand dinars is your dowry. Praise be to Allah! If only I knew how all this has come about!" Then he opened the amulet that had been sewn in the lining of the turban and found a piece of paper in the handwriting of his deceased brother. When he saw the handwriting, he kissed it again and again, and he wept over his dead brother. Then he read the scroll and discovered the recorded dates of his brother's marriage with the daughter of the vizier of Bassorah, the night that he took her virginity, and the birth of Badar al-Din Hasan, and all his brother's doings up to the day of his death. He was greatly astounded by all this and shook with joy. Then he compared the dates with his own marriage, the taking of his wife's virginity, and the birth of their daughter, Sitt al-Husan, and he found that they matched perfectly with those of his brothers. Then he took the document, went with it to the sultan, and told him everything that had happened from first to last. Indeed, the sultan was so impressed by the wondrous events that he ordered them to be recorded at once.

Now the vizier stayed with his daughter expecting his brother's son to return, but he did not appear. So the vizier waited a second day, a third, and so on until the seventh day, but there was no news of him. So he said, "By Allah, I'm going to do something that's never been done before!" And he took pen and ink and drew a plan of the whole house on a sheet of paper. He showed the whereabouts of the private chamber with the curtain in such a place and the furniture in another and so on until he had noted everything that was in the room. Then he folded up the sketch and ordered all the furniture to be collected along with Badar al-Din's garments, the turban, robe, and purse. Afterward he had everything taken to his house, where he locked them up with a padlock on which he set his seal. Finally he declared that the lock was not to be opened until his nephew, Badar al-Din Hasan, returned.

After nine months passed, the vizier's daughter gave birth to a son as radiant as the full moon, the image of his father in beauty, loveliness, shape, and grace. Once the umbilical cord was cut and his eyelids penciled with charcoal to strengthen his eyes, they named him Ajib the Wonderful and gave him to the nurses and governesses. His early years passed rapidly, and when he became seven, his grandfather sent him to school and ordered the master to teach him the Koran and to educate him well. He remained at the school four years until he began to bully his schoolmates and abuse them.

"Who among you is like me?" he cried. "I'm the son of the vizier of Egypt!"

Finally, the other boys went to the assistant master to complain about how harshly Ajib had been treating them, and he said to them, "I'll tell you something you can do to him so that he'll stop coming to school. When he enters tomorrow, sit down around him, and one of you is to say to the other, 'By Allah, nobody is allowed to play this game unless he tells us the names of his mama and his papa, for he who doesn't know the names of his mother and father is a bastard, a son of adultery, and he won't be permitted to play with us."

When morning dawned, the boys went to school, and they flocked around Ajib and said, "Let's play a game, and no one can join unless he tells us the name of his mother and father." And everyone agreed. Then one of them cried out, "My name's Majid, and my mommy's name is Alawiyah, and my daddy's Izz al-Din." Another spoke up, followed by a third, until it was Ajib's turn, and he said, "My name's Ajib, and my mother's is Sitt al-Husan, and my father's Shams al-Din, the vizier of Cairo."

"By Allah," they cried out, "the vizier's not your true father!"

"Yes, the vizier is my father!" Ajib responded.

Then the boys all laughed and clapped their hands at him and cried out, "He doesn't know who his papa is! Get away from us! Nobody can play our game unless he knows his father's name."

Thereupon, they ran around him, laughed at him, and derided him. So he became choked up with tears, and his feelings were hurt. Then the assistant master said to him, "We know that the vizier is your grandfather, the father of your mother, Sitt al-Husan, and not your father. But neither you nor we know your father, for the sultan married your mother to the hunchbacked horse groom. Supposedly a jinnee came and slept with her, but nobody knows your father for sure. So stop bragging about yourself and mocking the little ones at the school until you know whether you have a legal father. Until then you'll pass among them as a child of adultery. Even a huckster's son knows his own father, but you only know your grandfather and not your father. So, be sensible and don't brag or exaggerate anymore!"

When Ajib heard these insulting words from the assistant master and the schoolboys and understood their reproach, he left the school at once and ran to his mother. But he was crying so bitterly that his tears prevented him from speaking for a while. When she heard his sobs and saw his tears, her heart felt as though it were on fire for him, and she said, "My son, why are you weeping? May Allah keep the tears from your eyes. Tell me what has happened to you."

So he told her all that he had heard from the boys and the assistant master and ended by asking, "And who is my father?"

"Your father is the vizier of Egypt," she replied.

"Don't lie to me!" he answered. "The vizier is your father, not mine! Who's my father? If you don't tell me the truth, I'll kill myself with this dagger."

When his mother heard him speak about his father, she recalled her cousin, the bridal night, and all that happened then, and she wept. Then she wailed and shrieked loudly, and her son did the same. All at once the vizier came in, and he was extremely upset by the way they were lamenting.

"Why are you crying?" he asked.

So the Lady of Beauty told him what had happened between her son and his schoolmates, and he also began to weep, since he recalled what had occurred between him and his brother and what had happened to his daughter and how he had failed to solve the mystery of her giving birth to Ajib. Then he got up and went straight to the sultan and told his tale, after which he asked his permission to travel to Bassorah and inquire about his brother's son. In addition, he requested that the sultan write him letters, authorizing him to take Badar al-Din into his custody, no matter where he might be. And he wept before the king, who took pity on him and wrote royal letters to his deputies in different cities and countries. So now the vizier rejoiced and prayed that Allah might help him. After taking leave of his sovereign, the vizier returned to his house, where he equipped himself, his daughter, and grandson Ajib with all the necessary things for a long journey. Then they set out and traveled three days until they arrived at Damascus, where the vizier set up camp on the open space called Al-Hasa. After pitching the tents, he said to his servants, "We'll stop here for two days."

So his servants went into town on several occasions to sell and buy this and that. They also went to the Hammam bath and visited the cathedral mosque of the Banu Umayyah, the Ommiades, which has nothing like it in the world. Ajib also went with his attendant eunuch to enjoy the city, and the servant followed with a staff of almond wood so heavy that if he struck a camel with it the beast would never rise again. When the people of Damascus saw Ajib's handsome features and perfect grace (for he was a marvel of comeliness and loveliness, softer than the cool breeze of the north, sweeter than the fresh water that the thirsty man drinks, and more pleasant than the good health that everyone desires), many followed him, while others ran on before him and sat alongside the road until he came by so that they could gaze at him. Then, as destiny had decreed, the eunuch stopped opposite the shop of Ajib's father, Badar al-Din Hasan, whose beard had grown long and thick and who had matured during the twelve years that had passed. During that time the cook had died, and Hasan of Bassorah had inherited his goods and shop, for he had been formally adopted before the kazi and witnesses. Now, when his son and the eunuch happened to stop near his shop, he gazed at Ajib with a throbbing heart and was drawn to him through blood and natural affection. Since he had just finished making a conserve of pomegranate grains with sugar, he called to his son, Ajib, and said, "My lord, you've overwhelmed my heart, and I would feel honored if you would grace my house and ease my soul by joining me in a repast of meat."

Then his eyes streamed with tears that he could not prevent, for he thought about all that he had gone through and all that he had become. When Ajib heard his father's words, his heart also yearned to be with him, and he looked at the eunuch and said, "To tell the truth, my good guard, my heart goes out to this cook. He is like one that has a son far away from him. So let us enter and warm his heart by accepting his hospitality. Perhaps, if we do so, Allah may reunite me with my father."

When the eunuch heard these words, he cried, "By Allah, what a thing to do! Shall the sons of viziers be seen eating in a common cook's shop? Indeed, I've kept the folk off you with my staff so they won't even dare look at you. And now I won't permit you to enter this shop at all."

When Hasan of Bassorah heard this speech, he was astounded and turned to the eunuch with tears pouring down his cheeks, and Ajib said, "Truly, my heart loves him!"

But the eunuch responded, "Stop this talk! I won't let you go in."

Thereupon, Hasan turned to the eunuch and said, "Worthy sir, why won't you warm my soul by entering my shop? Oh, you who are like a chestnut, dark but inside white of heart! Discreet and polite, angels would vie for your service."

The eunuch was pleased by these words, and so he took Ajib by the hand and went into the cook's shop. Then Hasan offered them saucers with pomegranate grains wonderfully coated with almonds and sugar and said, "You have honored me with your company. Please eat, and may you have good health and happiness!"

In response, Ajib said to his father, "Sit down and eat with us so that Allah might perhaps unite us with the man we long for."

"My son," said Hasan, "have you suffered the loss of a loved one in your tender years?"

"Indeed, I have," answered Ajib. "My heart burns for the loss of a beloved who is none other than my father. This is why I and my grandfather have gone out to search the world for him. It's such a pity that we haven't found him, for I long to meet him!" Then he wept a great deal, and his father also wept upon seeing him weep and also on account of his own bereavement, for he recalled his long separation from his mother and dear friends. And the eunuch was moved to compassion. Then they ate together until they were satisfied, and Ajib and the slave rose and left the shop. Immediately Hasan felt as though his soul had left his body and had gone with them, even though he did not know that Ajib was his son. Since he did not want to lose sight of the boy, he locked up his shop and hurried after them. And he walked so fast that he caught up with them before they had gone through the west gate. Now the eunuch turned toward him and said, "What's the matter with you?"

"When you left me," Badar al-Din replied, "it seemed as though my soul had gone with you, and since I had some business outside the city gate, I thought I might keep you company until I took care of my affairs."

The eunuch was angry and said to Ajib, "This is just what I had feared! We ate that unlucky mouthful (which we are bound to respect), and now this fellow is following us from place to place, for the vulgar can do nothing but vulgar things."

Upon seeing the cook behind them, Ajib's face reddened with anger, and he said to the servant, "Let him walk the highway of the Moslems, but when we turn off to go to our tents and he's still following us, we'll send him packing!" Then he bowed his head and moved on with the eunuch walking behind him. But Hasan was not daunted, and he followed them to the plain Al-Hasa, and as they drew near, Ajib became very angry, fearing that the eunuch might tell his grandfather what had happened. His indignation was particularly great because his grandfather might learn that the cook had followed them after they had entered the cook's shop. So he turned and looked at Hasan of Bassorah and found his eyes fixed on his own, for the father had become a body without a soul, and it seemed to Ajib that his eyes were treacherous or that he was some lewd fellow. So his rage increased and, stooping down, he picked up a stone weighing half a pound and threw it at his father. It struck him on the forehead, cutting it open from eyebrow to eyebrow and causing the blood to stream down. Then Hasan fell to the ground in a swoon while Ajib and the eunuch made for the tents. When Hasan came to himself, he wiped away the blood, tore off a strip from his turban, and bandaged his head. Then he began reprimanding himself and said, "I shouldn't have shut my shop and followed the boy! It wasn't right. Now he probably thinks that I'm some evil-minded fellow."

Then he returned to his place, where he opened up the

shop and proceeded to sell his sweetmeats as usual. However, he yearned to see his mother in Bassorah and wept when he thought about her. In the meantime, the vizier stayed in Damascus three days and then traveled to Emesa, making inquiries about Hasan along the way. From there he journeyed to Bassorah by way of Hamah, Aleppo, Diyar Bakr, Maridin, and Mosul. As soon as he secured lodgings there, he presented himself to the sultan, who treated him with high honor and respect due to his rank. When the sultan asked him the reason for his coming to Bassorah, the vizier told him all about his past and that the minister Nur al-Din was his brother. Upon hearing this, the sultan exclaimed, "May Allah have mercy on him!" Then he added, "My good sahib, he was my vizier for fifteen years, and I loved him very much. Then he died leaving a son who dwelled here for only one month after his father's death. Since that time, he's disappeared, and nobody has had any news of him. But his mother, who is the daughter of my former minister, is still with us."

When Shams al-Din heard that his nephew's mother was alive and well, he rejoiced and said, "Oh king, I would very much like to meet her."

The sultan gave him permission right away to visit her, and so he went to the mansion of his brother, Nur al-Din, where he cast sorrowful glances at all the things in and around it and kissed the threshold. Then he began weeping as he thought about his brother and how he had died in a strange land far away from kith and kin and friends. As he passed through the gate into a courtyard, he found a vaulted doorway built of hardest syenite with an inlay of different kinds of multicolored marble. After walking though this doorway, he wandered about the house and saw the name of his brother, Nur al-Din, written in gold upon the walls. So he went up to the inscription and kissed it and wept while thinking of how he had been separated from his brother and how he had now lost him forever. Then he walked on until he came to the apartment of the mother of Badar al-Din.

From the time of her son Badar al-Din's disappearance, his mother had never stopped weeping for him. And when the years grew long and lonely, she had a tomb of marble built in the middle of the salon, and she used to weep for him day and night and always slept close by. When the vizier drew near her apartment, he heard her voice and stood behind the door while she addressed the sepulcher. As she was talking, he entered and greeted her. Then he informed her that he was her husband's brother and told her the entire story of what had happened between them. In addition, he related to her how her son Badar al-Din Hasan had spent a whole night with his daughter ten years ago but had disappeared in the morning, and he ended by saying, "My daughter gave birth to a boy through your son, and your grandson is with me."

When she heard the news that her boy Badar al-Din was still alive, and when she saw her brother-in-law, she arose and threw herself at his feet and kissed them. Then the vizier sent for Ajib, and his grandmother stood up, embraced him, and wept. But Shams al-Din said, "This is no time for weeping. This is the time to get you ready for a journey to Eygpt. Let us hope that Allah will reunite you and me with your son and my nephew."

"As you wish," she said and immediately began to gather together her baggage, jewels, equipment, and slave girls for the trip while the vizier went to take his leave from the sultan of Bassorah, who requested that he carry presents and rare items from him to the sultan of Egypt. Then he set out at once on the homeward journey and came to Damascus, where he stayed at the same place. After pitching tents, he said to his company, "We'll stay here one week to buy presents and rare things for the sultan."

Now Ajib remembered what had happened before and said to the eunuch, "I want some amusement. Come, let us go down to the great bazaar of Damascus and see what's become of the cook whose sweetmeats we ate and whose head we broke, for he was indeed kind to us and we treated him badly."

"As you wish," the eunuch answered.

So they left the tents, and Ajib was drawn toward his father. After passing through the city gate, they walked through the streets until they reached the cook's shop, where they found Hasan of Bassorah standing at the door. It was near the time of the midafternoon prayer, and it so happened that he had just finished making a confection of pomegranate grains. When Ajib and the eunuch drew near him, Ajib's heart pounded with yearning, and when he noticed the scar from the stone that he had thrown had darkened on Hasan's brow, he said to him, "Peace be with you! I want you to know that my heart goes out to you!"

But when Badar al-Din looked at his son, his heart fluttered, and he bowed his head and remained speechless. Then he raised his head humbly toward the boy and said, "Heal my broken heart and eat some of my sweetmeats. By Allah, I cannot look at you without my heart fluttering. Indeed, I should not have followed you that other time, but I couldn't control myself."

"By Allah," answered Ajib, "you certainly do care for us! We ate a mouthful the last time we were in your house, and you made us repent it, for you almost disgraced us by following us. So now we won't eat here unless you promise us not to go out and trail us like a dog. Otherwise, we won't visit you again during our present stay. We'll be here one whole week, for my grandfather wants to buy certain presents for the sultan."

"I promise to do just as you wish," said Hasan.

So Ajib and the eunuch entered the shop, and his father set a saucer with pomegranate grains before them.

"Sit down and eat with us," Ajib said. "Let us hope that Allah will dispel our sorrows."

Hasan was exceedingly happy and sat down and ate with them, but his eyes kept gazing fixedly on Ajib's face. Finally, the boy said to him, "You're becoming a nuisance. Stop staring at my face!"

But Hasan kept feeding Ajib morsels of the pomegranate grains, as well as the eunuch, and they ate until they were satisfied and could eat no more. Then they all got up, and the cook poured water on their hands. After loosening a silken waist shawl, he dried their hands and sprinkled them with rose water from a bottle he had with him. Then he went out and soon returned with a goglet of sherbet flavored with rose water, scented with musk, and cooled with snow. He set this before them and said, "Complete your kindness to me!"

So Ajib took the goglet, drank from it, and passed it to the eunuch. And it went round until their stomachs were full, and they were content with a larger meal than they were accustomed to eat. Then they went away and walked hurriedly to their tents, and Ajib went in to see his grandmother, who kissed him, and thinking of her son, Badar al-Din Hasan, she groaned aloud and wept. Then she asked Ajib, "My son, where have you been?"

And he answered, "In the city of Damascus."

Thereupon she arose and set before him a bit of scone and a saucer with conserve of pomegranate grains, which was sweetened too much, and she said to the eunuch, "Sit down with your master!"

And the servant said to himself, "By Allah, we don't have any desire to eat right now. I can't stand the sight of food." But he sat down, and so did Ajib, although his stomach was full of what he had already eaten and drunk. Nevertheless, he took a bit of the bread and dipped it in the pomegranate conserve and started eating, but he found it too sweet and said, "Uggh! What's this terrible stuff?"

"Oh, my son," cried his grandmother, "don't you like my cooking? I made this myself, and no one can cook it as nicely as I can except for your father, Badar al-Din Hasan."

"By Allah, my lady," Ajib answered, "this dish tastes terrible, especially when you compare it to the pomegranate grains made by the cook in Bassorah. His dish has such a wonderful smell that it opens the way to your heart, and the taste makes a man want to eat it forever. Your dish can't match his in the least."

When his grandmother heard his words, she became extremely angry and looked at the servant.

And Scheherazade noticed that dawn was approaching and stopped telling her story. When the next night arrived, however, she received the king's permission to continue her tale and said,

"You will pay for this!" the grandmother said to the servant. "Do you think it's right to spoil my grandson and take him into common cook shops?"

The eunuch was frightened and denied taking Ajib there. "We didn't go into the shop," he said. "We only passed by it."

"By Allah," cried Ajib, "we *did* go in, and we ate till

it came out of our nostrils, and the dish was better than grandmother's dish!"

Then his grandmother rose and went to her brother-in-law, who was incensed by the eunuch's actions. Consequently, he sent for him and asked, "Why did you take my grandson into a common cook's shop?"

Since he was frightened, the eunuch answered, "We did not go in."

But Ajib said, "We *did* go inside and ate the pomegranate grains until we were full. And the cook also gave us iced and sugared sherbet to drink."

Upon hearing this, the vizier's indignation increased, and he continued questioning the castrato, who kept denying everything. Then the vizier said, "If you're speaking the truth, I want you to sit down and eat in front of us."

So the eunuch sat down and tried to eat. However, there was nothing he could do but throw away the mouthful.

"My lord," he cried, "I've been full since yesterday!"

Now the vizier knew that the eunuch had eaten at the cook's shop and ordered his slaves to give him a beating. So they began giving him a sound thrashing until he pleaded for mercy. "Master, please tell them to stop beating me, and I'll tell you the truth."

The vizier ordered his slaves to stop and said, "Now tell the truth!"

"Well," said the eunuch, "we really did enter the cook's shop, and he served us pomegranate grains. By Allah, I never ate anything as delicious as that in my life, and I must admit that this stuff before me has a nasty taste."

The eunuch's words made the grandmother very angry, and she said, "I've heard enough! Now you must go back to the cook and bring me a saucer of his pomegranate grains and show it to your master. Then he'll be able to judge which tastes better, mine or his."

"I'll do as you say," the eunuch replied.

The grandmother gave him a saucer and half a dinar, and he returned to the shop and said, "Oh sheikh of all cooks, we've made a wager in my lord's house concerning your abilities as a cook. Someone has made pomegranate grains there, too, and we want to compare it to half a dinar's worth of yours. So give me a saucerful and make sure it's your best, for I've already been given a full meal of a beating with sticks on account of your cooking, and I don't want them to make me eat more of that kind."

Hasan laughed and answered, "By Allah, no one can prepare this dish as it should be prepared except for me and my mother, and she's in a country quite far from here."

Then he ladled out a saucerful, and after finishing it off with musk and rose water, he sealed it in a cloth and gave it to the eunuch, who hurried back to his master. No sooner did Badar al-Din's mother taste it and examine the excellent way it had been cooked than she knew who it had prepared it. All at once she uttered a loud scream and fell down in a faint. The vizier was most startled by this and sprinkled rose water on her. After a while she recovered and said, "If my son is still alive, then it was he who prepared this conserve of pomegranate grains and nobody else! This cook must be my very own son, Badar al-Din Hasan. There is no doubt in my mind, nor can there be any mistake, for only he and I know how to prepare pomegranate grains this way, and I taught him."

When the vizier heard her words, he rejoiced and said, "How I long to see my brother's son! We've waited so long for this meeting, and only Allah can help us bring it about." Then he arose without delay, went to his servants, and said, "I want fifty of you to go to the cook's shop with sticks and staffs. You're to demolish it, tie his arms behind him with his own turban, and say, 'It was you who made that stinking mess of pomegranate grains!' and drag him here with force but without doing him any harm."

And they replied, "You can count on us to carry out your command."

Then the vizier rode off to the palace right away and met with the viceroy of Damascus and showed him the sultan's orders. After careful perusal, the viceroy kissed the letter and asked, "Who is this offender of yours?"

"A man who is a cook," said the vizier.

So the viceroy sent his guards to the shop at once, and they found it demolished and broken into pieces, for while the vizier had gone to the castle, his men had carried out his command. Then they waited for his return from the viceroy, and Hasan, who was their prisoner, kept saying to himself, "I wonder what they found in the conserve of pomegranate grains to do this to me!"

When the vizier returned from the viceroy, who had given him official permission to take his debtor and depart with him, he called for the cook. His servants brought him with his arms tied by his turban, and when Badar al-Din Hasan saw his uncle, he began to weep and said, "My lord, what have I done to offend you?"

"Are you the man who prepared the conserve of pomegranate grains?" asked the vizier.

"Yes," Hasan answered. "Did you find something in it that calls for the cutting off of my head?"

"You deserve even worse!" replied the vizier.

"Then tell me what my crime is, and what's wrong with the pomegranate grains!"

"Soon," responded the vizier, and he called aloud to his servants and said, "Bring the camels here."

So they pulled up the tents, and the vizier gave orders to his servants to put Badar al-Din Hassan in a chest, which they padlocked, and to place him on a camel. Then they departed and traveled until nightfall, when they halted and ate some food. Badar al-Din Hasan was allowed to come out of the chest to eat, but afterward he was locked up again. Then they set out once more and traveled until they reached Kimrah, where they took him out of the chest and brought him before the vizier, who asked, "Are you the one who prepared that conserve of pomegranate grains?"

"Yes, my lord," he answered.

And the vizier said, "Tie him up!"

And they tied him up and returned him to the chest and journeyed until they reached Cairo, where they stopped in the quarter called Al-Raydaniyah. Then the vizier gave orders to have Badar al-Din taken out of the chest, sent for a carpenter, and said to him, "Make me a cross of wood for this fellow!"

"And what will you do with it?" cried Badar al-Din Hasan.

And the vizier replied, "I intend to crucify you on it.

I'm going to have you nailed to the cross and paraded all about the city!"

"Why? Why are you punishing me like this?"

"Because of your vile cooking! How could you prepare conserved pomegranate grains without pepper and sell it to me that way?"

"Just because it lacked pepper you're doing all this to me! Wasn't it enough that you destroyed my shop, locked me in a chest, and fed me but once a day?"

"Too little pepper! Too little pepper! This is a crime that can only be expiated on the cross!"

Badar al-Din Hasan was astounded and began to mourn for his life. Thereupon the vizier asked him, "What are you thinking about now?"

"About dunceheads like you!" responded Hasan. "If you had just an ounce of any sense, you wouldn't be treating me like this!"

"It's our duty to punish you like this," said the vizier, "so that you'll never do it again."

"Your least punishment was already too much punishment for what I did!" Hasan replied. "May Allah damn all conserves of pomegranate grains and curse the hour when I cooked it! I wish I had died before this!"

But the vizier responded, "Nothing can help you. I must crucify a man who sells pomegranate grains that lack pepper."

All this time the carpenter was shaping the wood, and Badar al-Din looked on. At nightfall, his uncle had him locked up in the chest again and said, "Tomorrow the thing shall be done!" Then he waited until he was sure that Badar al-Din was asleep, whereupon he mounted his horse, entered the city, and had the chest brought to his own house. Then he entered his mansion and said to his daughter, Sitt al-Husan, "Praise be to Allah, who has reunited you with your husband! Get up now and arrange the house as if it were your bridal night!"

So the servants arose and lit the candles, and the vizier took out his plan of the nuptial chamber and told them what to do until they had put everything in its proper place so that whoever saw the chamber would have believed that it was exactly the same as it was on the very night of the marriage. Then he ordered them to put Badar al-Din Hasan's turban beneath the bed with his bag trousers and the purse. After this he told his daughter to undress herself and go to bed in the private chamber as on her wedding night, and he added, "When your uncle's son comes into the room, you're to say to him, 'You've certainly dallied in the privy a long time!' Then call him and have him lie by your side and talk to him until daybreak, when we will explain the whole matter to him."

Then he had Badar al-Din Hasan taken out of the chest. After untying the rope from his feet and arms, he had everything stripped off him except the fine shirt of blue silk in which he had slept on his wedding night so that he was practically naked. All this was done while he was utterly unconscious. Soon thereafter, as if decreed by destiny, Badar al-Din Hasan turned over and awoke, and finding himself in a vestibule bright with lights, he said to himself, "Surely I'm in the middle of some dream." So he arose and explored his surroundings until he came to an inner door and looked in. To his surprise he saw he was in the very chamber in which the bride had been displayed to him, and he saw the bridal alcove and the turban and all his clothes. He was so bewildered by what he saw that he kept advancing and retreating and said to himself, "Am I asleep or awake?" And he began rubbing his forehead and saying, "By Allah, this is definitely the chamber of the bride who was displayed to me! Where am I then? Moments ago I was in a chest!" While he was talking to himself, Sitt al-Husan suddenly lifted the corner of the chamber curtain and said, "Oh lord, don't you want to come in? Indeed, you've dallied a long time in the privy."

When he heard her words and saw her face, he burst out laughing and said, "Indeed, this is a very nightmare among dreams!" Then he sighed and went in, pondering what had happened, and he was perplexed by all that was happening. Everything became even more mysterious when he saw his turban and trousers and found the purse containing the thousand gold pieces. So he muttered, "By Allah, I'm surely having some sort of wild daydream!"

Then the Lady of Beauty said to him, "You look so puzzled and perplexed. What's the matter with you? You were a very different man at the beginning of the night."

He laughed and asked her, "How long have I been away from you?"

And she answered, "By Allah, you've only been gone an hour and have just returned. Have you gone clean out of your head?"

When Badar al-Din Hasan heard this, he laughed and said, "You're right, but when I left you, I became distracted in the privy and dreamed that I was a cook in Damascus and lived there ten years. And I met a boy who was the son of a great noble, and he was with a eunuch." As he was talking, he passed his hand over his forehead and, feeling the scar, he cried out, "By Allah, oh my lady! It must have been true, for he struck my forehead with a stone and cut it open from eyebrow to eyebrow. And here is the mark. So it must have happened." Then he added, "But perhaps I dreamed it when we fell asleep, you and I, in each other's arms. Yet, it seems to me that I traveled to Damascus without tarbush and trousers and worked as a cook." Then he was confused and thought awhile. "By Allah, I also imagined that I had prepared a conserve of pomegranates and put too little pepper in it. I must have slept in the privy and have seen all of this in a dream. But that dream was certainly long!"

"And what else did you see?" asked Sitt al-Husan.

So he told her everything and soon said, "By Allah, if I hadn't wakened, they would have nailed me to a cross of wood!"

"What for?" she asked.

"For putting too little pepper in the conserve of pomegranate grains," he replied. "And it seemed to me that they demolished my shop, destroyed all my equipment, and put me in a chest. Then they sent for a carpenter to make a cross for me, and they would have crucified me on it. Thanks to Allah, this happened to me in a dream, and not while I was awake!"

Sitt al-Husan laughed and clasped him to her bosom, and he embraced her. Then he thought again and said, "By Allah, it couldn't have happened while I was awake. Truly I don't know what to think of it all."

Then he lay down, and throughout the night he kept wondering about what had happened, sometimes saying, "I must have been dreaming," and then saying, "I was awake." When morning arrived, his uncle, Shams al-Din, came to him and greeted him. When Badar al-Din Hasan saw him, he said, "By Allah, aren't you the man who ordered that my hands be tied behind me and that my shop be smashed? Weren't you going to nail me to a cross because my dish of pomegranates lacked a sufficient amount of pepper?"

Thereupon the vizier said to him, "I must tell you, my son, that the truth has won out! All that was hidden has been revealed. You are the son of my brother, and I did all this to you to make sure that you were indeed the young man who slept with my daughter the night of her wedding. I couldn't be certain of this until I saw that you knew the chamber and the turban, trousers, and gold, for I had never seen you before, and I couldn't recognize you. With regard to your mother, I have prevailed upon her to come with me from Bassorah." After saying all this, he threw himself on his nephew's breast and wept for joy. After hearing these words from his uncle, Badar al-Din Hassan was astonished and also shed tears of delight. Then the vizier said to him, "All of this happened, my son, because your father and I once had a major quarrel." And he told him why they had separated, and why his father had journeyed to Bassorah. Finally, the vizier sent for Ajib, and when Badar saw him, he cried, "This is the one who struck me with the stone!"

"This is your son!" said the vizier.

And Badar al-Din Hasan embraced him and was extremely happy to be with his son. Just then his mother entered and threw herself into his arms. Then she wept and told him what had happened to her since his departure, while he related to her what he had suffered, and they thanked Allah Almighty for their reunion.

Two days after his arrival, the Vizier Shams al-Din went to see the sultan, and after kissing the ground, he greeted him in a manner suited for kings. The sultan rejoiced at his return, and after placing the vizier by his side, he asked him to tell him all that he had seen during his journey and all that had happened to him. So the vizier told him all that had occurred from first to last, and the sultan said, "Thanks be to Allah for your triumph, your reunion with your children, and your safe return to your people! And now I want to see your brother's son. So bring him to the audience hall tomorrow."

Shams al-Din replied, "He will stand in your presence tomorrow, if it be God's will."

Then the vizier saluted him and returned to his own house, where he informed his nephew of the sultan's desire to see him, whereupon Hasan consented. So the next day he accompanied his uncle to the divan, and after saluting the sultan, he showed him his respect with a courtly verse. The sultan smiled and signaled him to sit down. After Hasan took a seat close to his uncle, Shams al-Din, the sultan asked him his name.

"Your lowliest of slaves," said Badar al-Din Hasan, "is known as Hasan the Bassorite, who prays for you day and night."

The sultan was pleased by these words and began testing his learning and good breeding, and Hasan rose to the occasion with witty and polite verses.

"Hasan," said the sultan, "you've spoken extremely well and have proved yourself accomplished in every way. Now explain to me how many meanings there are in the Arabic language for the word *khál* or mole."

"May Allah keep the king," replied Hasan, "there are fifty-seven, but some say according to tradition that there are only fifty."

"You're correct," said the sultan. "Do you have any knowledge as to the points of excellence in beauty?"

"Yes," answered Badar al-Din Hasan. "Beauty consists in brightness of face, clearness of complexion, shapeliness of nose, gentleness of eyes, sweetness of mouth, cleverness of speech, slenderness of shape, and seemliness of all attributes. But the acme of beauty is in the hair."

The sultan was so captivated by the way Hasan spoke that he regarded him as a friend and asked, "What's the meaning of the saying 'Shurayh is foxier than the fox'?"

And Hasan answered, "Oh sultan, you must know that the lawyer Shurayh was accustomed to making visits to Al-Najaf during the days of the plague, and whenever he stood up to pray, a fox would come and plant himself in front of him. Then, by mimicking his movements, the fox would distract him from his devotions. Now, one day, when this became tiresome to him, he doffed his shirt and set it upon a cane and shook out the sleeves. Then, placing his turban on the top and making a belt with a shawl around the middle, he stuck it up in the place where he used to pray. Soon the fox trotted up as he was accustomed to do and stood across from the figure. Then Shurayh came from behind and grabbed the fox. Hence the saying 'Shurayh is foxier than the fox.' "

When the sultan heard Badar al-Din Hasan's explanation, he said to his uncle, Shams al-Din, "Truly, your brother's son is perfect in courtly breeding, and I'm convinced that there's no one like him anywhere in Cairo."

Upon hearing this, Hasan arose and kissed the ground before him and sat down again as a mameluke should sit before his master. When the sultan had thus assured himself of his courtly breeding and bearing and his knowledge of the liberal arts and belles lettres, he rejoiced and invested him with a splendid robe of honor and promoted him to an office that would help him advance his career. Then Badar al-Din Hasan arose and requested the king's permission to retire with his uncle. The sultan consented, and the two returned home, where food was set before them, and they ate what Allah had given them. After finishing his meal, Hasan went to the sitting chamber of his wife, the Lady of Beauty, and told her what had happened between him and the sultan, whereupon she said, "I'm sure that he will make you a boon companion and bestow favors on you. In this way, the rays of your perfection will spread on shore and on sea thanks to Allah's blessing."

"I propose to write a kasidah, an ode, in the sultan's praise," he said, "and perhaps his affection for me may increase."

"That's a good idea," she answered. "Weigh your words carefully, and I'm sure that the sultan will look upon your work with favor."

So Hasan shut himself up in his chamber and composed a remarkable poem. When he had finished transcribing the lines, he had one of his uncle's slaves carry them to the sultan, who read the poem and was very pleased by it. In fact, he read the ode to all those present, and they praised it with the highest praise. Thereupon, the sultan sent for the writer, and when Hasan entered his sitting chamber, he said, "From this day on you will be my boon companion, and I'm granting you a monthly salary of ten thousand dirhams over and above what I granted you before."

So Hasan arose and, after kissing the ground before the sultan several times, prayed for the king's glory, greatness, and long life. Thus Badar al-Din continued to gain great honor, and his fame spread to many regions. He lived in comfort and took great delight in life with his uncle and his own people until death overtook him.

After the Caliph Harun al-Rashid heard this story from the lips of his vizier, Ja'afar the Barmecide, he was extremely astounded and said, "These stories deserve to be written down in liquid gold." Then he granted the slave his freedom and endowed the young man who had slain his wife with a monthly stipend that would suffice to make his life easy. He also gave him a concubine from among his own slave girls, and the young man became one of his boon companions.

"Yet, this story," continued Scheherazade, "is in no way stranger than the tale of the hunchback."

"And what happened to him?" asked the king.

"Have patience," Scherherazade said, and she asked his permission to tell her tale the following night, and the king was most happy to grant her wish.

The Hunchback's Tale

Many years ago in a certain city of China there lived a tailor, a generous man, who loved pleasure and merry-making. From time to time he and his wife liked to relax by going to public entertainments. One time, after they had spent the entire day amusing themselves, they were returning home in the evening and encountered a hunch-back, whose features made one forget one's cares and banish despair. Delighted by his looks, they went up to him and invited him to go home with them to converse and carouse that night. He consented and accompanied them to their home, whereupon the tailor ran out to the bazaar and bought fried fish, bread, lemons, and dry sweetmeats for dessert. After setting the food before the hunchback, they all sat down to eat. The tailor's wife took a great piece of fish in her hand and stuffed it into the gobbo's mouth as a practical joke. "By Allah," she said, "you must down it in a single gulp, and I'm not going to give you time to chew it1"

So he bolted it down, but there was a hard bone that got stuck in his gullet, and apparently his time was up, and he died. When the tailor realized what had happened, he cried out, "Alas, why did this poor wretch have to die in such a foolish fashion at our hands!"

"Stop this idle talk," his wife responded. "Let's not waste our time in grief."

"Well, what should I do with him?" asked the husband.

"Get up and carry him in your arms with a silk ker-chief spread over his face. Then I'll walk ahead of you, and if we meet anyone, you're to say, 'This is my son,

and his mother and I are carrying him to the doctor so he can examine him.' "

So he rose, picked up the hunchback in his arms, and carried him through the streets preceded by his wife, who kept crying, "Oh my son, may Allah keep you! Where does it hurt? Where did the smallpox attack you?"

As a result, the people they encountered all thought that they were carrying a child sick with smallpox. And as the tailor and his wife went along, they asked for the way to a physician's house, and some folk directed them to the house of a doctor, who was a Jew. They knocked at the door, and a black slave girl opened it. When she saw that it was a man and his wife bearing a child, she said to them, "What's the matter?"

"We have a little one with us," answered the tailor's wife, "and we want to show him to the doctor. So take this dinar, and give it to your master, and ask him to come down and look at my son, who is very sick."

While the girl went up to tell her master, the tailor's wife walked into the vestibule and said to her husband, "Quick, leave the hunchback here, and let us run for our lives!"

So the tailor carried the dead man to the top of the stairs and propped him upright against the wall. Then he and his wife ran as fast as they could. Meanwhile the girl went to the Jew and said, "A man and a woman are at the door with a sick child, and they've given me a dinar for you to come down and look at the little one so that you'll prescribe something for him."

As soon as the Jew saw the dinar, he rejoiced and rose quickly. Since it was dark and he was hurrying, he had hardly reached the landing when he stumbled on the corpse and knocked it over so that it rolled to the bottom of the staircase. Immediately he called out to the girl to bring a light, and after she arrived, he went down, examined the hunchback, and found that he was stone dead. "Oh Moses!" he cried out. "I've killed the sick person! I must have stumbled against him, and now I'd better get rid of the body as soon as possible."

Then he picked up the body, carried it into his house, and told his wife what had happened, whereupon she responded, "Why are you sitting still? If you keep him here until daybreak, we'll both lose our lives. Let's carry him to the terrace roof and throw him over into the house of our neighbor, the Moslem. If the body stays there during the night, the dogs will come from the adjoining terraces and eat him up."

Now his neighbor was a steward, who was in charge of the sultan's kitchen, and he was accustomed to bringing back large quantities of oil, fat, and meat, but the cats and rats used to eat everything. Or if the dogs smelled a fat sheep's tail, they would come down from the nearest roofs and fight over it. So, generally speaking, the animals would always damage much of what he brought home. Knowing this, the Jew and his wife carried the hunchback up to their roof, and they let him down by his hands and feet through the wind shaft into the steward's house, where they propped him up against the wall and went their way.

No sooner had they done this than the steward, who had spent an evening with his friends hearing a recitation of the Koran, came home and opened the door. After lighting a candle, he glimpsed the hunchback standing in the corner under the ventilator. When he saw him, he cried out, "By Allah! It's a man who's been stealing the meat and fat after all! I had thought it was the cats and dogs, and I've been killing them and sinning against them. But all the while it was you who came into my house through the wind shaft, and now I'll get my revenge with my own hand!" So he snatched a heavy hammer, attacked the hunchback, and smashed him on the chest, causing him to fall down.

When he examined the hunchback, he found that he was dead, and he cried out in horror, thinking that he had killed him. "By Allah, what am I going to do?" And he feared for his life and said, "May Allah curse the oil, the meat, the fat, and the sheep's tail to boot! Why was I fated to kill this man?" Then he looked at the body, and seeing it was that of a gobbo, he said, "Wasn't it enough for you to be a hunchback? Why did you also have to be a thief and steal flesh and fat?" So he picked the hunchback up on his shoulders and left his house. It was now late at night, and he carried him to the nearest end of the bazaar, where he set him up on his feet against the wall of a shop at the head of a dark lane, left him there, and went away.

After a while a Christian came walking down the lane. He was the sultan's broker, who was feeling no pain from the liquor he had drunk and was heading for the Hammam bath as his drunkenness whispered in his ear, "It's almost time for vespers." He came staggering along until he came near the hunchback, and just then he had to relieve himself. As he got ready to pee, he happened to glance around and saw a man standing against the wall. Now some person had snatched the Christian's turban at the beginning of the night, so when he saw the hunchback nearby, he thought that he, too, would try to steal his headdress. Thereupon he clenched his fist, rushed over to the hunchback, and struck him on the neck, causing him to fall to the ground. Then he called aloud to the watchman of the bazaar while throttling the corpse in his drunken fury. Soon the watchman came, and finding a Christian kneeling on a Moslem and beating him, he asked, "What harm has this man done to you?"

"This fellow wanted to snatch my turban," the broker answered.

"Get off him," said the watchman.

So he arose, and the watchman went up to the hunchback, and finding him dead, he exclaimed, "By Allah! A Christian's killed a Moslem!" Then he seized the broker, and after tying his hands behind his back, he brought him to the governor's house, while the Christian kept saying to himself, "Oh Jesus! Oh Mary! How did I manage to kill this fellow? He must have been in a hurry to leave his life if he died from my simple blows!" As the Christian became more sober, he began to suffer from a hangover. So the broker and the body were kept in the governor's house until the morning, when the police chief came and sentenced the Christian to hang. He commanded one of his officers to announce the sentence, while the others began building a gallows under which they made the Christian stand. When the gallows was finished, the hangman threw a rope around his neck, passed one end through the pulley, and was about to hoist him up, when suddenly the steward, who was passing by, saw the Christian about to be hanged. Making his way through the crowd of people, he cried out to the executioner, "Stop! Stop! I'm the one who killed the hunchback!"

"What made you kill him?" asked the governor.

"When I went home last night," he answered, "I came upon this man, who had come down the ventilator to steal my property. So I hit him with a hammer on the breast, and he died right away. Then I picked him up, carried him to the bazaar, and set him up against the wall in a dark lane. It's enough for me to have killed a Moslem without also having a Christian on my conscience! So hang me, if you're going to hang anyone."

When the governor heard these words, he released the broker and said to the executioner, "Hang this man, since he's confessed."

So the hangman loosened the rope from the Christian's neck and threw it around the steward's. Then he made him stand under the gallows and was about to string him up when suddenly the Jewish physician pushed his way through the crowd of people and shouted to the executioner, "Stop! Stop! It was I and no one else who killed the hunchback! Last night I was sitting at home when a man and woman knocked at the door. They were carrying this gobbo, who was sick, and they gave my maid a dinar as a fee so that I would come down and look at him. While she went to fetch me, the man and woman brought him into the house, set him on the staircase, and went away. Soon I came down, and since I couldn't see him in the dark, I knocked him down, and he fell to the foot of the staircase and was dead on the spot. Then we picked him up, my wife and I, and we carried him to the top of our terrace. The house of the steward is next to mine, and we let the body down through the ventilator into his home. When he returned and found the hunchback in his house, he thought it was a thief and struck him with a hammer so that he fell to the ground, and our neighbor was certain that he had slain him. Now, it's enough for me to have killed one Moslem unwittingly without consciously causing the death of another one."

When the governor heard this, he said to the executioner, "Set the steward free, and hang the Jew."

Accordingly, the hangman took the Jew and slung the cord around his neck. Just then, however, the tailor pushed his way through the crowd of people and shouted to the executioner, "Stop! Stop! It was I and no one else who killed the hunchback, and this is the way it happened. I had been out enjoying myself yesterday, and on my way home for supper, I encountered this gobbo, who was drunk and drumming on his tambourine and singing merrily away. So I approached him and brought him to my house, and after I had bought a fish, we sat down to eat. Soon my wife took some of the fish, rolled it into a ball, and crammed it down his mouth. But some of it went down the wrong way or got stuck in his gullet, and he died on the spot. Then we lifted him up, my wife and I, and carried him to the Jew's house, where the slave girl came down and opened the door to us. After I said to her, 'Tell your master that there's a sick child that I want him to look at,' I gave her a dinar, and she went to fetch her master. While she was gone, I carried the hunchback to the head of the staircase and propped him up against the wall. Then my wife and I ran away as fast as we could. When the Jew came down, he stumbled over the hunchback and thought that he had killed him." Now, turning to the Jew, he asked, "Isn't this true?"

"Yes," the Jew answered.

Thereupon the tailor turned to the governor and said, "Let the Jew go, and hang me instead."

When the governor heard the tailor's tale, he was astonished by this case of the hunchback and exclaimed, "Truly, this is an adventure which should be recorded in books!" Then he said to the hangman, "Let the Jew go, and hang the tailor, since he's confessed."

The executioner took the tailor and put the rope around his neck and said, "I'm getting tired of such slow work. First we bring out this one, then we replace him with another and another. Soon no one will be hanged at all!"

Now, as it turned out, the hunchback in question was the jester to the sultan of China, who could not bear to be separated from him. So when the fellow got drunk and did not make his appearance that night or by noon of the next day, the sultan asked some of his courtiers where he was.

"Oh lord," they said, "the governor has found him dead and has ordered his murderer to be hanged. But when the executioner was about to hang him, three other men came and said that they were responsible for the hunchback's death. And each one gave a full and circumstantial account of how the jester was killed."

When the king heard this, he cried aloud to his chamberlain, "Go to the governor and bring me all four of these men!"

So the chamberlain went at once to the place of execution, where he found the executioner on the point of hanging the tailor, and he shouted to him, "Stop! Stop!" Then he gave the king's command to the governor, who took the tailor, the Jew, the Christian, and the steward and brought them to the king. In addition, he had the hunchback's body carried there on some men's shoulders. When the governor stood before the king, he kissed the ground and told the ruler the whole story, which is needless to relate, for, as they say, there is no avail in a thrice-told tale. Of course, the sultan was astounded when he heard it. Indeed, he was moved to mirth and ordered that the story be written down in letters of liquid gold. Then he said to all those present, "Have you ever heard of a more wondrous tale than that of my hunchback?"

Thereupon the Christian broker came forward and said, "Your majesty, with your permission, I'll tell you about something that happened to me, for it is more wondrous and delightful than the tale of the hunchback."

"Tell us what you have to say," said the king, "and if it is truly more wondrous, I'll pardon all your lives."

So he began in these words,

The Christian Broker's Tale

It was some time ago, your majesty, that I came to your country with my merchandise and intended simply to trade and then return home. However, I ended up by staying here. In actuality, my place of birth was Cairo in Egypt, where I was also brought up, for I am one of the Copts, and my father was a broker before me. It was when I reached manhood and after his death that I inherited his business.

Now, one day, as I was sitting in my shop in Cairo, a young man approached me. He was as handsome as could be and was wearing sumptuous clothes and riding a fine mule. When he saw me, he saluted me, and I stood up to greet him. Then he took out a kerchief containing a sample of sesame and asked, "How much is this worth per bushel?"

"A hundred dirhams," I answered.

"Take some porters tomorrow," he said, "and come to the Khan Al-Jawali near the Gate of Victory, where you will find me." Then he continued on his way, leaving me with the sample of sesame in this kerchief. Then I went around to my customers and ascertained that every bushel would fetch a hundred and twenty dirhams. So next day I took four porters and walked with them to the khan, where I found the young man awaiting me. As soon as he saw me, he rose and opened his shop. Then we measured the grain until the store was empty, and we found that there were fifty bushels that came to five thousand pieces of silver.

"Let ten dirhams for every bushel be your percentage as broker," he said. "After you sell everything, keep four thousand and five hundred dirhams for me in deposit. After I have sold some other merchandise from my warehouses, I'll come to you and collect my money."

"As you say," I answered, and after kissing his hand, I went away, having made a profit of a thousand dirhams that day.

He was absent a month, and at the end of that time, he came to me and asked, "Where are the dirhams?"

I arose, saluted him, and asked, "Won't you have something to eat at my house?"

But he refused and said, "Get my money ready, and I'll return in a short time to collect it."

Then he rode away, and I brought out the dirhams and sat down to wait for him, but he stayed away another month. When he came back, he said to me, "Where are my dirhams?"

I arose, saluted him, and asked, "Won't you have something to eat in my house?"

But again he refused and said, "Get my money ready, and I'll return in a short time to collect it."

Then he rode off. So I brought out the dirhams and sat down to await his return. But he stayed away again for a third month, and I said, "Truly, this young man is liberality incarnate."

At the end of the month he returned riding a mule and wearing a suit of sumptuous raiment. He looked like the splendid full moon, and it seemed as if he had come fresh from the baths with his rosy cheeks, flower-white brow, and a mole spot like a grain of ambergris. When I saw him, I rose, invoked blessings on him, and asked, "My lord, why won't you take your money?"

"Why the hurry?" he responded. "Wait until I have finished my business, and then I'll come and take it."

Again he rode away, and I said to myself, "By Allah, when he comes next time, I must make him my guest, for I have traded with his dirhams and have made a large profit from this."

At the end of the year he came again and was wearing a suit of clothes more sumptuous than the one he had worn before, and I begged him to stop at my house and eat some of my food, and he said, "I consent, provided that whatever you spend for the food comes from my money still in your hands."

"As you say," I answered and made him sit down while I got the food and drink ready for him. Then I set the tray down before him and invited him to eat. So he drew near the tray, put out his left hand, and ate with me. I wondered why he was not using his right hand, and when we had finished eating, I poured water on his hand and gave him something to wipe it off. After I set some sweetmeats before him, we began to converse, and I said to him, "Master, please relieve me of my curiosity and tell me why you eat with your left hand. Perhaps there's something wrong with your right hand?"

When he heard my words, he stuck out his right hand from his sleeve, and I saw that the hand was cut off, a wrist without a fist. I was astounded by this, but he said, "Don't be astonished, and don't think that I ate with my left hand out of insolence. It was out of necessity, for my right hand was cut off in a most strange adventure."

"Do tell me what happened," I asked.

I am from Baghdad, and my father was one of the notables of that city. When I reached manhood, I heard the pilgrims, travelers, and merchants talk about the land of Egypt, and their words made a deep impression on me. So when my father died, I took a large sum of money, bought merchandise for trading, and packed it all up in bales before beginning my journey. And Allah granted me a safe trip until I arrived at your city of Cairo. Then I stored my merchandise in the Khan Al-Masrur, and I gave a servant a few silver coins to buy me some food and lay down to sleep awhile. When I awoke, I went to the street called Bayn al-Kasrayn—Between the Two Palaces—and then returned and spent the rest of the night in the khan. At sunrise I opened a bale, took out some of my goods, and said to myself, "I'll go wandering through some of the bazaars and see what the markets are like." So I loaded the goods on some of my slaves and went to the Kaysariyah or Exchange of Jaharkas, where various brokers, who knew about my arrival, came to meet me. They took the goods and offered them for sale but could not get the prime cost. I was irritated by this, but the chief of the brokers said, "I'll tell you how you can make a profit off your goods. Do what the merchants do and sell your merchandise at credit for a fixed period with a contract drawn up by a notary with witnesses. Then hire a shroff to collect your payments every Monday and Thursday. This way you'll gain two dirhams and more for every one invested. In the meantime you'll be able to take it easy and enjoy yourself by seeing Cairo and the Nile."

I thought that this was good advice and brought the brokers to the khan. They took my goods, and I received bonds from them which I deposited with a shroff, a banker, who gave me a receipt, with which I returned to the khan, where I stayed a whole month. Each morning I broke my fast with a cup of wine and had meals of pigeon's meat, mutton, and sweetmeats, until the time came when my receipts were due. Every Monday and Thursday I used to go and sit in the shop of one of the merchants while the notary and shroff went around to collect money from the traders. Generally speaking, they would bring me the amount owed to me after the midafternoon prayer, and I would count it. After sealing the bags I would return with them to the khan.

One Monday, after going to the Hammam bath, I drank a cup of wine in my room and fell asleep. When I awoke, I ate a chicken, put on some lotion, and then went to the shop of a merchant called Badar al-Din

N. ORR—LO. SC.

al-Bostani, who welcomed me. We sat and talked awhile waiting for the bazaar to open. Soon we saw a lady wearing a splendid headdress. She had an aroma of the sweetest perfumes about her and walked with a graceful, swaying gait. Upon seeing me, she raised her mantilla and allowed me to glimpse her beautiful black eyes. Thereafter, she saluted Badar al-Din, who returned her greeting, stood up, and talked with her. The moment I heard her speak, I fell immediately in love with her. As she was talking to Badar al-Din, I heard her ask for a piece of stuff woven with thread of pure gold, and he showed her a piece from those he had bought from me and sold it to her for one thousand two hundred dirhams.

"If you don't mind," she said, "I'll take the piece home with me and send you the money."

"That is impossible, my lady," the merchant replied, "because the owner of this material is here, and I owe him a share of the profit."

"Shame upon you!" she cried. "Don't I regularly buy entire rolls of costly stuff from you and give you more profit than you expect and send you the money?"

"Yes," he answered, "but I'm in great need of the money today."

Thereupon she took the piece, threw it back on his lap, and said, "Get out of my sight! May Allah punish the whole tribe of you swindlers!"

As she turned to go, I felt my whole soul going with her. So I stood up and prevented her from parting. "I beg you, my lady," I said, "do me a favor, by Allah, and don't leave."

She turned back with a smile and said, "For your sake, I'll return," and she took a seat opposite me in the shop.

Then I said to Badar al-Din, "What is the price they asked you for this piece?"

"Eleven hundred dirhams." he said.

"The odd hundred shall be your profit," I replied. "Bring me a sheet of paper, and I'll write you a receipt for it." Then I wrote a receipt in my own handwriting and gave the piece to the lady. "Take it away with you, and if you want, bring me the payment next bazaar day. Or better still, accept it as my gift to you."

"May Allah bless you," she answered, "and make you my husband and lord and master over all that I have!"

And Allah granted her prayer, for I saw the Gates of Paradise swing open before me and said, "My lady, let this piece of stuff now be yours, and another like it is ready for you. Just let me have one look at your face."

So she raised her veil, and I saw a face that made me sigh a thousand sighs, and my heart was so captivated by her that I was no longer in command of my mind. Then she let the veil fall, and after taking my stuff, she said, "My lord, don't make me desolate by your absence!" and she turned away and disappeared from my sight.

I remained sitting there till it was past the hour of afternoon prayer, lost to the world by the love that had overwhelmed me. My passion was so strong that I began asking my friend the merchant about her, and he told me that she was a rich lady, the daughter of a certain emir, who had recently died and left her a large fortune. Then I took leave of him and returned home to the khan, where they set supper before me, but I could not eat because I kept thinking about her. Nor could I sleep. So I lay awake until morning, when I arose and donned fresh clothes and drank a cup of wine. After eating a small breakfast, I went to the merchant's shop, where I saluted him and sat down next to him.

Soon the lady came as usual, wearing a dress more sumptuous than before and followed by a slave girl. Then she saluted me without noticing Badar al-Din and said in a sweet and graceful voice (never had I heard a voice more mellifluous), "Send someone with me to get your thousand and two hundred dirhams."

"Why this hurry?" I asked.

"May heaven grant that I see you more often!" she answered and handed me the money.

Thereupon I sat and talked with her, and soon I indicated to her that I longed to enjoy her person, and she rose up in haste with a show of displeasure. Alas, my heart clung to her as she left the bazaar, and I was desolate.

Later as I was walking, a black slave girl suddenly stopped me and said, "Master, come and speak with my mistress."

I was surprised by her words and said to her, "There is nobody who knows me here."

But she responded, "My lord, how soon you've forgotten her! My lady is the same one who was at the merchant's shop just before."

Then I went with her to the shroff's, where I found the lady, who drew me to her side and said, "Oh my beloved, I can't get you out of my mind! From the moment I first saw you, I've been unable to eat, drink, or sleep!"

"I have suffered just as much as you," I replied, "but now I can't complain."

Then she said, "My beloved, at your house or mine?"

"I'm a stranger here," I answered, "and I have no place to receive you except the khan. So, if it pleases you, it shall be at your house."

"So be it," she said, "but this is Friday night, and nothing can be done till tomorrow after public prayers. Go to the mosque and pray. Then mount your mule, and ask for the Habbaniyah quarter, and when you get there, look for the mansion of Al-Nakib Barakat, commonly known as Abu Shamah the Syndic. That is where I live, and don't delay, for I'll be expecting you."

Upon hearing her words I was filled with joy. Then I took leave of her and returned to my khan, where I spent a sleepless night. After morning had dawned, I rose, changed my dress, put on some incense, took fifty dinars in a kerchief, and went from the Khan Al-Masrur to the Zuwaylah Gate, where I mounted an ass and said to its owner, "Take me to the Habbaniyah." So he set out with me and brought me in the twinkling of an eye to a street called Darb al-Munkari, where I said to him, "Go in and ask for the Syndic's mansion."

He was gone awhile, and when he came back, he said, "This is it."

"I want you to return here at dawn to bring me home," I said and gave him a quarter-dinar of gold. After taking it, he went his way. Then I knocked at the door, and out came two white slave girls, both young, high-bosomed virgins, pretty as moons, and they said to me, "Enter. Our mistress is expecting you, and she's been looking forward to seeing you with such delight that she couldn't sleep a wink last night."

I passed through the vestibule into a salon with seven doors. The floor was made of multicolored marble, and the room was furnished with curtains and hangings of colored silk. The ceiling was cloisonné with gold and corniced with inscriptions emblazoned in lapis lazuli. The walls were stuccoed with gypsum that reflected the onlooker's face. All around the salon were latticed windows overlooking a garden full of different kinds of fruit. The garden also had running streams and birds that were singing and trilling. In the heart of the hall was a jetting fountain, and at each corner was a bird made out of gold crusted with pearls and gems and sprouting crystal-clear water. After I entered this remarkable salon, I took a seat.

And Scheherazade noticed that dawn was approaching and stopped telling her story. When the next night arrived, however, she received the king's permission to continue her tale and said,

Once I was seated there, the lady came in at once. She was crowned with a diadem of pearls and jewels. Her face was dotted with artificial moles in indigo. Her eyebrows were penciled with charcoal, and her hands and feet reddened with henna. When she saw me, she smiled and embraced me. After clasping me to her breast, she put her mouth to my mouth, sucked my tongue (while I did the same), and said, "Can it be true, my little darkling, that you've come to me? You know you're welcome! By Allah, from the day I saw you, I haven't been able to eat or sleep."

"The same's been true with me," I said. "I'm your slave, your Negro slave."

Then we sat down to converse, and I hung my head out of shyness, but soon she set before me a tray of the most exquisite viands, marinated meats, fritters soaked in honey, chickens stuffed with sugar, and pistachio nuts, and we ate until we were satisfied. Soon thereafter her servants brought a basin, and I washed my hands. Then we scented ourselves with rose water and sat down again to converse. She told me all that had happened in her life, and I told her about mine. My love for her gripped my heart so strongly that all my wealth seemed nothing in comparison with her. Then we began playing and groping and kissing until nightfall, when the maidens set some meat and wine before us, and we sat carousing until midnight, when we lay down. Never in my life have I experienced a night like that night.

In the morning I arose and took leave of her, throwing the kerchief with the dinars under the carpet bed, whereupon she wept as I was leaving and said, "My lord, when shall I see your lovely face again?"

"I'll be with you at sunset," I replied, and when I was outside, I found the donkey boy, who had brought me there the day before, waiting for me at the door. So I mounted the ass and rode to the Khan al-Masrur. After dismounting I gave him a half-dinar and said, "Return at sunset." "I will," he responded.

Then I breakfasted and went out to inquire about the prices that my merchandise was fetching. Afterward I returned, bought a roast lamb and some sweetmeats, called a porter, and put the provisions in his crate, instructing him to bring everything to the lady. Finally I went back to my business until sunset, when the man with the donkey came to me. Once again I took fifty dinars in a kerchief and rode to her house, where I found the marble floor swept, the brasses burnished, and branch lights burning, the wax candles already lit, the meat served, and the wine poured.

When my lady saw me, she threw her arms around my neck and cried, "Your absence has made me desolate!"

Then she moved the table before me, and we ate until we were satisfied, when the slave girls carried away the trays and then served the wine. We did not stop drinking until half the night was gone, and since we were warmed up by the wine, we went to the sleeping chamber and lay there until morning. Then I arose and went away, leaving the fifty dinars with her as before. The donkey boy was at the door, and he took me to the khan, where I slept awhile. After that I went out to buy the evening meal, which consisted of a brace of geese with gravy on two platters of dressed and peppered rice, colocasia roots fried and soaked in honey, fruits, conserves, nuts, and almonds, and I sent all this to her along with some flowers. As soon as it was night, I again tied up fifty dinars in a kerchief and, mounting the ass as usual, rode to the mansion, where we ate and drank and lay together until morning, when I threw the kerchief and dinars to her and rode back to the khan.

I continued living like this until, after one sweet night, I awoke and found that I had become a beggar without dinars and dirhams. So I said to myself, "This is the work of Satan!" Then I left the khan and walked down the street until I came to the Zuwaylah Gate, where I found a crowd of people, and the gateway was blocked. As destiny would have it, I was pushed up against a trooper unintentionally so that my hand was next to his bosom pocket, and I felt a purse inside. I looked, and seeing a string of green silk hanging from the pocket, I knew it was attached to a purse. The crowd continued to push and knock me against the trooper, and just then, a camel laden with fuel happened to jostle the trooper on the other side, and he turned around to push it away so that it would not tear his clothes. It was at this point that Satan tempted me. So I pulled the string and drew out a little bag of blue silk containing some clinking coins. However, the soldier felt that something had happened, and when he put his hand to his pocket, he found it empty. Thereupon he turned to me, snatched his mace from his saddle, and struck me with it on the head. I fell to the ground while people gathered around us and seized the trooper's mare by the bridle and cried out, "Why did you strike this youth when he just pushed you?" "He's nothing but a cursed thief!" the trooper responded.

Just then I came to myself and stood up, and the people looked at me and said, "No, he's such a handsome youth. He wouldn't steal anything!"

Some of them took my side, and others were against me. The accusations and denials grew louder and louder. Some people pulled me and would have rescued me from his clutches, but as fate would have it, the governor, the chief of police, and the watchmen entered the Zuwaylah Gate at that moment, and seeing the people gathered around me and the soldier, the governor asked, "What's the matter?"

"By Allah, my lord," answered the trooper, "this man is a thief! I had a purse of blue silk with twenty good gold pieces in my pocket, and he took it while I was in the crowd."

"Was anyone with you at the time?" the governor asked.

"No," responded the soldier.

Thereupon the governor told the chief of police to seize me and strip me. And when they stripped me, they found the purse in my clothes. The governor took it, opened it, and counted it, and after finding the twenty dinars in it as the soldier had said, he became extremely angry and commanded his guard to bring me before him. Then he said to me, "Tell the truth, young man, did you steal this purse?"

I hung my head to the ground and said to myself, "If I deny having stolen it, I'll get myself into terrible trouble." So I raised my head and said, "Yes, I took it."

When the governor heard these words, he was surprised and summoned witnesses who came forward and testified against me. All this happened at the Zuwaylah Gate. Then the governor ordered one of his officers to cut off my right hand, and he did so. In fact, he would have cut off my left foot, too, but the soldier's heart softened. Out of pity for me he interceded with the governor, who consented not to chop it off and went away. Then some people gathered around me and gave me a cup of wine to drink. As for the trooper, he insisted on giving me the purse and said, "You're a handsome young man, and it doesn't suit you to be a thief."

After giving me the purse, the soldier departed, and I, too, went my way with my hand wrapped in a piece of rag and thrust in my bosom. Now my entire appearance changed. I grew yellow from the shame and pain that I had experienced. Yet, I went onward to my mistress's house, where, extremely disturbed, I threw myself down on the couch.

When the lady saw me in this state, she asked, "What's come over you? How come your looks have changed?"

"My head aches," I responded, "and I'm not feeling well."

On hearing this she became upset and was concerned about me. "My lord, don't let your woes consume you. Sit up, raise your head, and tell me what happened to you today, for your face tells me that you've got something to tell."

"Stop this chatter!" I said.

But she wept and said, "It seems you've become tired of me, for you're not your usual self."

Since I remained silent, she kept on talking to me until

nightfall. Then she set food before me, but I refused to eat it for fear that she would see me eating with my left hand. "I'm not hungry right now," I said.

"Tell me what happened to you today," she replied. "Why are you so broken in spirit and heart?"

"Wait awhile," I said, "and I'll tell you at my leisure."

Then she brought me some wine and said, "Down with it. This will help dispel your grief. You must drink and tell me what's happened."

"Must I really tell you?" I asked.

"Yes," she answered.

"If this is the way it must be," I said, "then give me a drink with your own hand." She filled the cup and drank it. Then she filled it again and gave me the cup, which I took from her with my left hand and began weeping.

"What's causing your tears?" she exclaimed. "You're tearing my heart to pieces. Why are you taking the cup in your left hand?"

"My right hand has a boil on it," I said.

"Stick it out, and I'll open it for you," she replied.

"No, it's not time yet to open it," I said. "So don't bother me about it, for I won't take it out of the bandage right now."

Then I drank out of the cup, and she kept giving me more and more wine until I was overcome with drink and fell asleep in the place where I was sitting. Then she looked at my right hand and saw a wrist without a fist. So she searched me thoroughly and found the purse of gold and my severed hand wrapped up in the bit of rag. As a result, she was overcome by sorrow and grief, and she did not stop lamenting for me until morning. When I awoke, I found that she had prepared a chicken broth, which she served to me with some wine. After I ate and drank, I put down the purse and would have left, but she said to me, "Where are you going?"

"I have some business to attend to." I answered.

"Sit down." she said. "I don't want you to go." So I sat down, and she continued speaking. "Has your love for me been so great that you've wasted all your money and lost your hand on my account? May Allah be my witness, I'll never part from you, and you'll soon see that my words are true."

Then she sent for the kazi and witnesses and said to

them, "Write up a marriage contract with this young man, and bear witness that I've received the marriage settlement." After they had drawn up the document, she said, "I want you all to certify that I'm giving to this young man out of my own free will all my money, which is in this chest, and all that I have in slaves and servants and other property."

So they took note of this statement that enabled me to assume possession of everything through the marriage, and after receiving their payment, they departed. Thereupon she took me by the hand, led me to a closet, opened a large chest, and said, "Look and see what's inside." And I looked and saw that it was full of kerchiefs. "This is the money that I received from you," she said. "Every kerchief that you gave me with the fifty dinars I wrapped up and threw into this chest. So, now take what belongs to you, and from this day on it is your property. Fortune and fate caused you to lose your right hand for my sake, and I can never pay you back. Indeed, even if I were to give my life for you, it would not be enough. I shall always remain in debt to you." Then she added, "Now take charge of your property."

So, I transferred the contents of her chest to mine and added my valuables to the money that I had given her, and my heart was eased, and my sorrow ceased. I stood up, kissed her, and thanked her, whereupon she said, "You've given your hand because of your love for me. How can I pay you back? By Allah, if I were to offer my life for your love, it would be but little and would not do justice to your claim on me."

Then she wrote up a deed that gave me all her clothes, gold, pearls, goods, farms, and chattel, and she would not go to sleep that night until I told her about everything that had happened to me. From then on, we began living together, but after a month, she became extremely sick, and her sickness was aggravated by her grief over the loss of my hand. Her illness lasted some fifty days, whereupon she passed away. So I laid her out and buried her body in mother earth and had a pious perfection of the Koran made for the sake of her soul. Moreover, I gave a great deal of money in alms for her and then turned from the grave and returned to the house. There I found that she had left a good deal of ready money, and among her storehouses was a granary of sesame seed. Part of this I sold to you, and I had neither time nor inclination to settle my accounts with you until I had sold the rest of the stock in store. Indeed, even now I don't feel inclined to concern myself with receipts. So I don't want you to protest what I'm about to say to you: twice I've eaten your food, and I want you to accept as a present the money that you have received for the sesame seed. And now you know why my right hand was cut off, and why I eat with my left.

"Indeed," I said, "you've explained everything to me with utmost kindness."

Then he asked me, "Why don't you travel with me to my native country? I'm about to return there with Cairene and Alexandrian stuff and materials. Please tell me that you'll accompany me."

"I will," I answered. So I agreed to go with him at the beginning of the month, and I sold all I had and bought other merchandise. Then we set out and traveled to your country, where he sold his goods and bought other materials from here and continued his journey to Egypt. But it was my destiny to stay here, and then all these strange things happened to me last night. So, tell me, your majesty, isn't this tale more wondrous and marvelous than the story of the hunchback?"

"No, it isn't," replied the king. "Certainly not. Nothing can help you now. Every one of you must be hanged."

And Scheherazade noticed that dawn was approaching and stopped telling her story. When the next night arrived, however, she received the king's permission to continue her tale and said,

Now the steward of the sultan's kitchen stepped forward and said, "If you permit me, your majesty, I'll tell you the tale of what happened to me before I found this gobbo, and if it proves to be more wondrous than the story of the hunchback, will you grant us our lives?"

"Yes," answered the king.

And he began to relate

The Steward's Tale

It so happened, your majesty, that last night I was at a party where they did a reading of the Koran and gathered together doctors of law and religion skilled in recitation. After the readers had ended, the table was spread, and among the many things they set before us was a marinated ragout flavored with cumin seed. So we sat down, but one of the members of our company held back and refused to touch it. We implored him to eat, but he was adamant in his refusal, and when we pressed him again, he said, "Don't be so insistent with me."

"But tell us your reason for refusing to eat the cumin ragout," we said.

"If it's necessary," he replied, "I'll eat it, but I won't do it unless I wash my hands forty times with soap, forty times with potash, and forty times with galingale."

Thereupon the host ordered his slaves to bring water and whatever else was required, and the young man washed his hands. Then he sat down, as if disgusted and frightened at the same time, and after dipping his hand in the ragout, he began eating and also showing signs of anger. Of course, we were puzzled by all this, for his hand trembled, and the morsel in it shook, and we saw that his thumb had been cut off and that he ate with only four fingers. So we asked him, "By Allah, what happened to your thumb? Were you born that way, or did you have some accident that caused you to lose your thumb?"

"Oh, my brothers," he answered, "it's not only this thumb that I've lost, but also my other thumb and both my great toes, as you shall see."

Upon saying this, he uncovered his left hand and his feet, and we saw that the left hand was just like the right, and that each of his feet lacked its great toe. When we saw him like this, we were all amazed, and we said to him, "We can hardly wait to hear your story. You must tell us how you lost your thumbs and toes and why you wash your hands one hundred and twenty times."

* * *

Let me begin by telling you that my father was chief of the merchants and the wealthiest of them all in Baghdad during the reign of the Caliph Harun al-Rashid, and he indulged himself so very much in drinking and listening to the lute and other instruments that when he died, he left nothing. I buried him and had perfections of the Koran made for him and mourned him days and nights. Then I opened his shop and found that he had very few goods left in it while he had many debts. So I reached agreements with his creditors, who granted me time to settle their demands, and I occupied myself with buying and selling merchandise and paid the creditors a percentage of my profits each week. Indeed, I did this until I had paid off all his debts in full and began adding to my principal. Then one day, as I sat in my shop, a young lady suddenly and unexpectedly appeared on the street. Never in my life had I seen a woman as beautiful as she was. Moreover, she was wearing the richest raiment and ornaments and was riding a mule with one Negro slave walking in front of her and one behind her. Then she stopped at the head of the exchange bazaar and entered it, followed by a eunuch, who said to her, "Come away from here and don't talk to anyone or else they'll light a fire that will burn us all up."

Indeed, he stood before her and guarded her from view while she looked at the shops. None were open at that time but mine. So she approached with the eunuch behind her, and after sitting down in my shop, she saluted me with a voice sweeter than I had ever heard before. Then she unveiled her face, and I saw that she was like the moon, and I stole a glance at her that caused me a thousand sighs, and my heart was captivated with love for her.

"Young man," she finally said to me, "do you have any fine cloth for sale?"

"My lady," I answered, "your slave is poor, but have patience until the merchants open their shops, and I will find something suitable for you."

Then we sat talking, and I was drowned in the sea of love and swept away by my passion for her. Eventually, the merchants opened their shops, and I rose and fetched everything she sought to the tune of five thousand dirhams. She gave the stuff to the eunuch, and after she mounted her mule, she went away without telling me where she came from, and I was too ashamed to speak of such a trifle. When the merchants demanded their five thousand dirhams, I guaranteed them payment and went home, drunken with love of her. When my servants set my supper for me, I ate a mouthful but could only think of her beauty and loveliness, and I sought to sleep, but sleep did not come to me. And this was how I was for one whole week until the merchants came and demanded payment from me. Fortunately, I persuaded them to have patience for another week, at the end of which time she appeared again mounted on a mule and attended by her eunuch and two slaves. After saluting me, she said, "Excuse the delay in bringing you the money for the material, master. But now we have it. So fetch the shroff, and take your payment."

So I sent for the money changer, and the eunuch counted out the coins before him and completed the payment. Then I sat there talking with the lady until the market opened, when she said to me, "Get me this and that."

So I got whatever she wanted from the merchants, and she took everything away without saying a word to me about the price. As soon as she was out of sight, I regretted what I had done, because the material that I had bought for her amounted to one thousand dinars, and I said in my soul, "What kind of love is this? She brought me five thousand dirhams and has now taken goods from me worth quite more, at least one thousand dinars." I was very much afraid that I might be reduced to a beggar if I had to pay the merchants their money, and I said to myself, "They only know me, and that's it. This lady is probably nothing but a cheat and a swindler, who has got the best of me because of her beauty and grace. She realized that I was a mere youth and laughed at me for not asking her address."

Since she did not return for a month, I was plagued by these fears and doubts, and then the merchants began to pester me for the money. In fact, they pressured me so much that I had to put my property up for sale and stood on the very brink of ruin. However, as I was sitting in my shop one day, drowned in melancholy, she suddenly rode up, and after dismounting at the bazaar gate, she came straight toward me. When I saw her, I forgot all my troubles and cares. After she greeted me with her sweet and pleasant voice, she said, "Fetch the shroff, and count your money."

So she gave me the price of the goods that I had purchased for her and even more, and then she began to talk so freely with me that I felt I would die from joy and delight. At one point she asked me, "Do you have a wife?"

"No," I answered. "In fact, I've never known a woman."

Thereupon I began to shed tears, and she said, "Why are you crying?"

"It's nothing!" I responded, but I gave the eunuch some of the gold pieces and asked him to act as a go-between in the matter.

But he laughed and said, "She's more in love with you than you are with her. She doesn't have any reason to buy the stuff that she's bought and did this only because she's in love with you. So ask her whatever you want. She'll do anything for you."

When she saw me giving the dinars to the eunuch, she returned and sat down again, and I said to her, "Be kind to your slave, and pardon him for what he is about to say."

Then I told her what was on my mind, and she consented and said to the eunuch, "You'll carry my message to him." And she turned to me, "And my message will tell you what to do."

Then she got up and went away, and I paid the merchants their money. Of course, they were happy with their profits, but I was sad because the lady had disappeared again, and I could not sleep that night. Many days passed before her eunuch came to me, and I asked after his mistress.

"Truly," he said, "she is desperately in love with you."

"Please tell me who and what she is," I responded.

"The Lady Zubaydah, queen consort of Harun al-Rashid, brought her up as a slave girl and promoted her to be stewardess of the harem," he said. "So she also has the right to move about as she pleases. Indeed, she spoke to the Lady Zubaydah about you and begged her to let her marry you, but the lady said that she would not allow this until she sees the young man in question. And if she thinks that you're worthy of her, the lady will allow the marriage to take place. So now we're looking for the right moment to smuggle you into the palace, and if you succeed, you'll have your wish and can wed her. But if anyone gets wind of the affair, the Lady Zubaydah will strike off your head. What do you say to this proposal?"

"I'll go with you," I answered, "and I'll take the risk."

"As soon as it is dark," he said, "you're to go to the mosque on the Tigris, say your evening prayers, and sleep there."

"Gladly," I responded.

So at nightfall I went to the mosque, where I prayed and spent the night. Early in the morning some eunuchs came in a skiff with a number of empty chests that they deposited in the mosque. Then all of them went their way except one, and after looking at him, I realized that he was our go-between. Soon my mistress entered and walked straight up to us. I rose and embraced her while she kissed me and shed tears. We talked awhile, and then she made me get into one of thc chests, which she locked. Soon the other eunuchs returned with a good deal of packages, and she began to put them into the chests and locked one after the other until they were all shut. When that was done, the eunuchs placed the chests in the boat and headed for Lady Zubaydah's palace. Just then I was plagued by fears, and I said to myself, "For sure, your lust and wantonness will be the death of you. And there's still a question as to whether you'll attain your wish." And I began to weep in the box and suffered from cramps. Moreover, I prayed to Allah to deliver me from the dangerous predicament that I was in, while the boat kept going until it reached the palace gate, wherc they lifted out all the chests, including the one in which I was locked. Then they carried them through a troop of eunuchs, guardians of the harem and the ladies behind the curtain, until they came to the post of the chief eunuch, who was startled from his slumber and shouted to the damsel, "What's in those chests?"

"They're full of merchandise for the Lady Zubaydah!"

"Open them, one by one, so that I can see what's in them."

"And why do you want to open them?"

"Don't speak back to me! These chests must and will be opened!"

Upon saying this, he sprang to his feet, and the first one that they brought to him was the trunk in which I was lodged. When I felt his hands upon it, I lost control of my body, and I began to wet in my pants so much that the water ran out of the box. Consequently, she said to the chief eunuch, "Look at what you've done! You're going to be the death of me, and you'll be put to death, too! You've damaged ten thousand dinars' worth of goods. This chest contains colored dresses and four gallon flasks of Zemzem water, and now one of them has become uncorked, and the water is running out over the clothes and will spoil their colors."

"Pick up your boxes," the eunuch answered, "and get out of here for God's sake!"

So the slaves carried off all the chests, including mine, and they rushed onward until I heard one of them cry out, "Oh no! It's the caliph! The caliph!"

When I heard that cry, I died a thousand deaths and said, "By Allah, I've only got myself to thank for this catastrophe!"

Soon I heard the caliph say to my mistress, "Curse you, what's in these boxes?"

"Dresses for the Lady Zubaydah," she answered.

Thereupon he declared, "Open them up right here and now!"

When I heard this, I said to myself, "By Allah, today is the very last of my days in this world. If I come out of this safely, I'll marry her, and there'll be no more words about it. But I'm about to be discovered, and my head is as good as chopped off." Then I professed my faith in Allah and said, "There is no god but *the* God, and Mohammed is the Apostle of God!"

And Scheherazade noticed that dawn was approaching and stopped telling her tale. When the next night arrived, however, she received the king's permission to continue her tale and said,

Just then I heard my mistress say to the caliph, "These chests were placed under my charge by the Lady Zubaydah, and she does not want their contents to be seen by anyone."

"No matter," said the caliph. "They must be opened, because *I* want to see what's in them," and he cried aloud to the eunuch, "Bring the chests before me."

Upon hearing this, I was sure that I was about to die and swooned away. Then the eunuchs brought the chests to him one after the other, and he began inspecting the contents. At first he saw only attars, fine dresses, and material in them, but he continued looking and found only such things as clothes and stuff until all the chests had been opened except mine. As the eunuchs went to open it, my mistress quickly said to the caliph, "This one you may only see in the presence of the Lady Zubaydah, for the contents are her secret."

When he heard this, he gave orders to carry in the chests. So they picked them up and carried them all into the harem, including the one in which I was boxed, and they set them down in the middle of the salon. In the meantime, my spittle had dried up out of fear. Then my mistress opened the chest, took me out, and said, "Don't be afraid. Nothing can harm you now. Just breathe easily, have courage, and sit down until the Lady Zubaydah comes, and then she'll certainly grant your wish to wed me."

So I sat down, and after a while ten maidens entered. They were as pretty as moons and arranged themselves in two rows, five facing five. After them came twenty other damsels surrounding the Lady Zubaydah, who could hardly walk because of the weight of her raiment and ornaments. As she drew near, the slave girls dispersed, and I advanced and kissed the ground. She signaled me to sit down, and after I did this, she began questioning me about my forebears, family, and present state of affairs, and my answers appeared to please her. Then she turned to my mistress and said, "Our education that we've given you has led to good results." Returning to me, she stated, "I want you to know that this maiden is like our own child, and we are giving her in trust to you, by Allah."

Again I kissed the ground before her, pleased that I could marry my mistress, and she ordered me to dwell in the palace for ten days. So I lived there ten days, during which time I did not see my mistress or anyone except one of the concubines, who brought me the morning and evening meals. In the meantime the Lady Zubaydah consulted with the caliph about the marriage of her favorite maiden, and he gave his permission and granted her a wedding dowry of ten thousand gold pieces. So the Lady Zubaydah sent for the kazi and witnesses, who wrote our marriage contract, after which the women prepared sweetmeats and rich viands and distributed them among all the concubines of the harem. They continued to do this for another ten days, at the end of which time my mistress went to the baths. Meanwhile, they placed a tray of food before me, and it had various meats that were enough to dazzle one's mind. Among other things there was a bowl of cumin ragout containing chickens' breasts flavored with sugar, pistachios, musk, and rose water.

On this occasion, gentlemen, I did not hesitate long but took my seat before the ragout and ate until I could eat no more. After this I wiped my hands but forgot to wash them. Then I sat till it grew dark. Afterward the wax candles were lit, and the singing women came in with their tambourines and began to display the bride in various dresses while carrying her in a procession from room to room all around the palace and having their palms crossed with gold. Finally, they brought her to me and disrobed her. When I found myself alone with her on the bed, I embraced her and could hardly believe that we were finally united. But she smelled the strong odors of the ragout on my hands and immediately uttered a loud cry, causing the slave girls to come running from all sides. I trembled with alarm, not knowing what the matter was, and the girls asked her, "What's troubling you, oh sister?"

Her response was: "Take this madman away from me! I thought he was a man with good sense!"

"What makes you think I'm mad?" I asked.

"You madman!" she responded. "What made you eat the cumin ragout and forget to wash your hands? By Allah, I'll make you pay for your misconduct. Do you think that the likes of you can come to bed with the likes of me with unclean hands?"

Then she took a whip from the side of her bed and began beating my back and rear until her arms were numb and I fainted from the whipping. After that she said to her maids, "Take him to the chief of police so that he may cut off the unwashed hand with which he ate of the cumin ragout."

I was just recovering when I heard her command. "By Allah!" I exclaimed. "Are you going to have my hand cut off just because I ate the cumin ragout and did not wash?"

The maids also interceded on my behalf and kissed her hand and implored, "Oh sister, this man is a simpleton. Don't punish him for such a meager incident."

But she responded, "By Allah, nothing can help him. I must dock him of something, especially the offending member."

Then she went away, and I saw no more of her for ten days, during which time she sent me meat and drink through a slave girl, who told me that she had fallen sick from the smell of the cumin ragout. After that time she came to me and said, "You blackguard! I'll teach you how to eat cumin ragout without washing your hands!"

Then she called to her maids, who held me tight, while she took a sharp razor and cut off my thumbs and large toes, just as you see, gentlemen. Thereupon I fainted, and she sprinkled some herbs on the stumps to heal them, and when the blood was stanched, I said, "Never again shall I eat cumin ragout without washing my hands forty times with potash and forty times with soap!"

And she made me swear an oath to that effect.

"Therefore, when you brought me the cumin ragout, my color changed, and I said to myself, 'It was this very dish that caused me to lose my thumbs and toes,' and when you forced me, I said, 'I must now keep the oath that I swore.' "

"And what happened to you after this incident?" asked the men who were present.

"When I swore to her," he replied, "she was appeased, and I slept with her that night. We lived there for a while until she said to me one day, 'Truly, the caliph's palace is not a pleasant place for us to live in, and no one has ever gained entrance to it except for you. But you were successful thanks only to the grace of Lady Zubaydah. Now she's recently given me fifty thousand dinars, and I want you to take this money and go out and buy us a fair house in which we can live.' So I left and bought a fine and spacious mansion, and she moved there with all her wealth while I transported all my property. So now you know the story, gentleman, of how my thumbs and toes came to be cut off."

As the steward finished his tale, he explained how he returned home after the supper and found the hunchback in his house and what happened. "Now, peace be with you, your majesty! What do you think of my story?"

"Your story," said the king, "is in no way more delightful or wondrous than that of the hunchback. In fact, it is even less so. Nothing will help you now. The whole lot of you must hang."

Then the Jewish physician came forward, kissed the ground, and said, "Your majesty, I'll tell you a story that is definitely more wonderful than that of the hunchback."

"Tell it, then," spoke the king of China.

So he began

The Jewish Doctor's Tale

During my youth I experienced something that was exceedingly marvelous. I was living in Damascus of Syria at that time, studying medicine, and one day, as I was sitting at home, a mameluke came from the household of the sahib and said to me, "My lord wants you to come and talk to him."

So I followed him to the viceroy's house, and after entering the great hall, I saw a gold-plated cedar couch at the other end, and on it lay a sickly youth more handsome than I had ever seen. I sat down by his head and prayed to heaven for a cure, and he made a sign to me with his eyes. So I said to him, "Oh my lord, give me your hands, and may the Lord heal you." Then he stuck out his left hand, and I wondered why such a handsome man, the son of a great house, should lack such good manners. Indeed, I thought that it could be nothing but pride and conceit. Nevertheless, I felt his pulse, wrote him a prescription, and continued to visit him for ten days, at the end of which time he recovered and went to the Hammam baths. Thereupon, the viceroy gave me a handsome dress of honor and appointed me superintendent of the hospital of Damascus. I accompanied the viceroy to the baths that were kept private for his visit, and the servants went in with him and took off his clothes. When he was stripped, I saw that his right hand had recently been cut off, and that this had been the cause of his malady and weakness. Of course, I was amazed by this and was sorry for him. Then, looking at his body, I saw the scars of whip lashes to which he had applied cream and salve. I was troubled by the sight, and my concern showed in my face. When the young man looked at me, he saw how upset I was and said, "Doctor, don't be so disturbed. I'll tell you my story as soon as we leave the baths."

Then we washed, and after returning to his house, we ate and rested awhile. Then he asked me, "What do you say to us relaxing some more in the dining room?"

"As you wish," I answered.

Accordingly he ordered his slaves to carry out the necessary carpets and cushions, a roast lamb, and some fruit. When they did as he requested, we ate together, and he used his left hand. After a while I said to him, "Now, tell me your tale."

Then listen, doctor, and you will learn what happened to me. First, let me tell you that I am from Mosul, where my grandfather died, leaving nine children, of whom my father was the eldest. All grew up and were married, but none of them were blessed with offspring except my father, whom Providence granted me. So I grew up among my uncles, who helped raise me until I reached manhood. One day, which happened to be a Friday, I went to the cathedral mosque of Mosul with my father and uncles, and after saying our prayers, everyone left except my father and uncles, who sat and talked about wonderful things and marvelous sights in foreign lands. At last they mentioned Egypt, and one of my uncles said, "Travelers tell us that there is no city fairer than Cairo on the face of the earth."

These words made me long to see Cairo, and then my father said, "Whoever hasn't seen Cairo hasn't seen the world. Its air is golden, and its Nile a miracle to behold. Its women are beautiful, and the houses unique. Its water is sweet and light, and its mud is a commodity and medicine beyond comparison. Moreover, the temperature is mild and with a fragrance that surpasses the smell of aloes wood. How should it be otherwise when Cairo is considered to be the Mother of the World? If your eyes ever see its soil, especially when it is in bloom, and the islands of the Nile and how rich and abundant they are, and if you view the Abyssinian Pond, you will never want to see anything else! Indeed, the two tributaries of the Nile embrace the most luxuriant verdure. And what is there to compare with the Rasad, the observatory, and its charms. And if you were to behold the garden at evening with its cool shade and slopes, you would marvel at the sight and become ecstatic. And if you were by Cairo's riverside, when the sun sinks, you would be invigorated with new life by its gentle breezes and encompassing shade."

So spoke my father and the rest of them as they were describing Egypt and the Nile. As I listened to their accounts, I was most impressed, and when we went our ways, and I lay down to sleep that night, I could not sleep because of my powerful longing for Egypt. From then on I could neither eat nor drink. Well, after a few days, my uncles equipped themselves to go trading in Egypt, and I wept in front of my father until he consented to my going with them. However, he said to them, "Don't let him enter Cairo. Let him stay in Damascus, where he is to sell his wares."

So I took leave of my father, and we traveled forth until we reached Aleppo, where we stopped for several days. Then we marched onward until we reached Damascus, and we found the city a paradise of trees, streams, birds, and all kinds of fruit. We stayed at one of the khans, where my uncles tarried awhile selling and buying. Moreover, they bought and sold for me, and each dirham turned a profit of five on prime cost, which pleased me greatly. After this they left me alone and headed toward Egypt while I remained in Damascus, where I hired a jeweler for two dinars a month and rented a beautiful house. So I proceeded to spend whatever money I had on eating, drinking, and enjoying the city, until one day as I was sitting at the door of my house a young lady came by. She was clad in the costliest raiment I had ever seen, and I winked at her. Without hesitating she stepped inside, and I shut the door behind her. Then she raised her veil and threw off her mantilla, and I found her like the picture of a rare moon. She was so marvelous and lovely that my heart was seized with love for her. So I went and brought her a tray of the most delicious food and fruit and whatever else befitted the occasion, and we ate and played, and after that we drank until the wine turned our heads. Then I spent the sweetest of nights with her, and in the morning I offered her ten gold pieces.

Suddenly her face lowered and her eyebrows wrinkled, and she cried out angrily, "Shame on you, my sweet companion! Do you think that I covet your money?" Then she took fifteen dinars out from the bosom of her shift, lay them before me, and said, "By Allah, if you don't take them, I'll never come back to you!"

So I accepted them, and she said to me, "My beloved, expect me back here in three days' time. In the meantime, take these dinars and prepare the same entertainment as we had yesterday."

Upon saying this, she took her leave and went away, and all my feelings went with her. On the third day she came again, clad in stuff woven with gold wire and wearing the finest raiment and ornaments. I had prepared the place for her before her arrival, and the repast was ready. So we ate and drank together till morning, as we had done before, and then she gave me another fifteen gold pieces and promised to come again in three days. Accordingly, I got everything ready for her, and at the appointed time, she appeared and was more richly dressed than on the other two occasions.

"My lord," she said to me, "do you find me beautiful?"

"By Allah, yes, you are!" I responded. "Would you allow me to bring with me next time a young lady who is younger and fairer than I am so that she may play with us?" she continued. "Indeed, you and she can laugh and have fun together, for she has been very sad for some time and has asked me to take her out and let her spend the night abroad with me."

"Of course!" I answered.

We drank till the wine turned our heads and slept till morning, when she gave me another fifteen dinars and said, "Add something to your usual provisions, because of the young lady who will come with me."

Then she went away, and on the fourth day I got the house ready as usual, and soon after sunset, she arrived and was accompanied by another damsel carefully wrapped in her mantilla. When they entered and sat down, I was glad to see them and lit the candles after expressing how happy I was to have them with me. When they took off their heavy outer dresses and the new damsel uncovered her face, I saw that she was like the full moon. Never have I seen a woman more beautiful. Then I rose and set food and drink before them, and we ate and drank, and I kept giving mouthfuls to the newcomer and drinking with her until the first damsel became jealous and asked "Isn't she more delicious than I am?"

"Yes," I answered. "Indeed, she is!"

"Well, it's my wish that you sleep with her tonight, for I'm your mistress, and she is our guest."

"You can count on me to do what you request," I replied, and I took the young lady and lay with her that night until morning.

When I awoke and found myself wet, I thought I was sweating. I sat up and tried to rouse the damsel, but when I touched her shoulders, my hand became crimson with blood, and her head rolled off her pillow. I lost control of myself and cried aloud, "Oh Almighty Allah, grant me your protection!" Finding that her head had been severed, I sprang up and looked for my former lover, but could not find her. So I knew that it was she who had murdered the damsel in her jealousy and said, "By Allah, what's to be done now?"

I thought for a while, and after putting on my clothes, I dug a hole in the middle of the courtyard in which I laid the murdered girl along with her jewelry and golden ornaments. Then I covered the grave with the dirt and replaced the slabs of marble pavement that I had lifted up before digging the whole. After this I performed the rites of ablution and put on clean clothes. Then I took whatever money I had left, locked up the house, summoned courage, and went to the owner, to whom I paid a year's rent. "I'm going to join my uncles in Cairo," I said and soon journeyed to Egypt, where my uncles rejoiced in seeing me. I found that they had completed selling their merchandise, and they asked me why I had come.

"I missed you," I replied and did not let them know that I had any money with me. I lived with them for one year and enjoyed the pleasures of Cairo and the Nile. While there I squandered the rest of my money in carousing until the time drew near for the departure of my uncles. Since I did not want to go with them, I fled and hid myself.

They made inquiries and searched for me, but when they did not obtain any news, they said, "He must have gone back to Damascus."

After they departed I came out of hiding and lived in Cairo another three years until nothing was left of my money. Now, every year I had been accustomed to sending the rent of the Damascus house to its owner. Since I had nothing left but one year's rent to pay him, I traveled to Damascus and arrived at the house, whose owner, the jeweler, was glad to see me, and I found everything locked up as I had left it. I opened the closets and took out my clothes and other necessary items and came upon a golden necklace set with ten remarkably beautiful gems. I found this necklace beneath the couch where I had spent the night with the girl who had been beheaded, and after cleaning the blood off it, I gazed at it and wept a while. I spent two more days in the house before I went to the Hammam baths on the third and changed my clothes. Since I had no money with me now, Satan whispered temptation in my ear so that the decree of destiny could be carried out. Consequently, the next day I took the necklace to the bazaar and handed it to a broker, who made me sit down in the shop of the jeweler, my landlord, and asked me to wait patiently until the market was full and active. Then he carried off the necklace and offered it for sale without my knowledge. The necklace was priced at two thousand dinars, but the broker returned to me and said, "The necklace is made of copper, and it's a European copy. I've been offered one thousand dirhams for it."

"I knew it was copper," I answered, "because we had it made to fool a certain person. But now my wife has inherited it, and we want to sell it. So, go and accept the thousand dirhams."

And Scheherazade noticed that dawn was approaching and stopped telling her story. When the next night arrived, however, she received the king's permission to continue her tale and said,

When the broker heard this, he knew the case was suspicious. So he took the necklace to the governor, who was also the chief of police, and told him the following lie: "This necklace was stolen from my house, and we've found the thief disguised as a trader."

So, before I knew what was happening, the guards came, seized me, and brought me to the governor, who questioned me about the necklace. I told him the tale that I had used with the broker, but he laughed and said, "These words are not true."

All at once, the guards stripped off my clothes and I was beaten by palm rods until my ribs were so sore that I confessed that I had stolen it. And I said to myself, "It's better for you to say that you stole it than to let them know that its owner was murdered in your house, for they would slay you to avenge her."

So they wrote down that I had stolen it, and they cut off my hand and scalded the stump in oil as I fainted because of the pain. Afterward they gave me wine to drink, and I recovered. As I picked up my hand and was about to go to my fine house, my landlord said to me, "Since you've been convicted of stealing, my son, you must leave my house and look for some other lodgings. You're a handsome young man, but who will pity you after this?"

"Master," I said, "bear with me for two or three days until I find another place."

"So be it," he replied and went away.

I returned to the house, where I sat weeping and said, "How shall I go back to my own people with my hand lopped off and without them knowing that I'm really innocent? Perhaps, despite what's happened, Allah may deign to help me." After I had grieved for two days, my landlord arrived suddenly, and with him were some of the guard and the syndic of the bazaar, who had falsely accused me of stealing the necklace. I went up to them and asked, "What's the matter?"

However, they grabbed me without saying a thing and threw a chain around my neck. "It turns out," they said, "that your necklace was the property of the vizier of Damascus, who is also the viceroy. It has been missing from his house for three years, ever since his younger daughter disappeared."

When I heard these words, my heart sank, and I said to myself, "Your life is certainly gone now! By Allah, I must tell the chief my story, and he'll either kill me or pardon me."

So they brought me to the vizier's house and made me stand before him. When he saw me, he glanced at me out of the corner of his eye and said to those present, "Why did you lop off his hand? This man is unfortunate, but he's done nothing wrong. Indeed, you've wronged him by cutting off his hand."

When I heard this, I took heart and said to him, "By Allah, my lord, I'm no thief, but they slandered me with a vile lie, and they whipped me in the middle of the market and made me confess because of the pain I experienced. I lied against myself and confessed to stealing. However, I'm not entirely innocent."

"Don't be afraid," said the viceroy. "No harm will come to you."

Then he ordered the syndic of the bazaar to be imprisoned and said to him, "Give this man the blood money for his hand, and if you delay, I'll hang you and seize all your property." Moreover, he called his guards, who dragged the syndic away, leaving me with the chief. Then he ordered his men to take the chain off my neck and untie my arms. After that he looked at me and said, "My son, tell me the truth. How did you get this necklace?"

"My lord," I answered, "I'll tell you nothing but the truth."

Then I related to him what had happened between me and the first lady, and how she had brought me the second and had slain her out of jealousy. And I furnished him with all the details to the very end. When he heard my story, he shook his head, made a gesture of regret, and putting his kerchief over his face, he wept awhile.

"I must tell you, my son," he turned to me, "that the elder damsel who first came to you was my daughter, whom I used to keep closely guarded. When she grew up, I sent her to Cairo and married her to her cousin, my brother's son. After a while he died, and she came back, but the people of Cairo had taught her to become wanton and carefree. So she visited you four times and brought her younger sister the last time. Now they were very attached to one another, and when her adventure with you had begun, she had disclosed her secret to her sister, who desired to go with her. So she asked your permission and brought her to you. After that incident, she returned home alone and was weeping. I asked her about her sister, but she said, 'I don't know anything about her.' However, she soon told her mother in private what had happened and how she had cut off her sister's head, and her mother told me. Then she began to weep and said, 'By Allah! I'll cry for her until I die.' And she did not stop mourning until her heart broke, and she died. So, you see, my son, this is the way everything happened, and now I don't want you to prevent me from doing what I am about to offer you. I intend to marry you to my youngest daughter. She is a virgin and born of another mother, and I'll demand no payment from you. On the contrary, I'm going to give you an allowance, and you're to live in my house as my son."

"So be it," I answered. "How could I ever have hoped for such good fortune?"

Then he sent at once for the kazi and witnesses, and he had a marriage contract drawn up, and I went to see his daughter. Moreover, he got a large sum of money for me from the syndic of the bazaar, and I soon became one of the viceroy's favorites. During that year I received news that my father had died, and the vizier sent a courier with letters bearing his royal insignia so that I could obtain the money that my father had left me. Now I am living in comfort, and now you know how my right hand was cut off.

I was astounded by his story [continued the Jew], and I lived with him for three days more. After that time he gave me a great deal of money, and I set out toward the east and traveled until I reached your city. In fact, I liked your city so much that I have lived here ever since up to this incident with the hunchback.

After hearing the Jewish doctor's tale, the king of China shook his head and said, "I'm sorry, but your story is not at all more marvelous or delightful than thc tale about my hunchback. I'm afraid you must all hang unless the tailor can help you. So, tailor, you're the one responsible for the entire series of crimes, and you're the last hope. Perhaps you can tell me something more wonderful than the story of the hunchback. If you succeed, I'll pardon all your offenses."

Thereupon the tailor came forward and began to tell

The Tailor's Tale

The most marvelous thing that ever happened to me, your majesty, was an incident that occurred yesterday before I encountered the hunchback. Earlier in the day I was at the marriage feast of one of my companions, who had gathered together some twenty of the craftsmen of this city in his house. Among them were tailors, silk spinners, carpenters, and many more. As soon as the sun had risen, they set food before us to eat, and just then the master of the house entered. He had a foreigner with him, a young man from Baghdad, who wore the most handsome clothes you ever saw. He himself was right comely, except that one leg was lame. He came and saluted us, and when he was about to sit down among us, he spotted a certain man, who was a barber, and suddenly he refused to join us and wanted to leave. However, we stopped him, and our host asked him why he did not want to sit down and enjoy himself. Thereupon he answered, "By Allah, my lord, don't stop me. The reason why I refuse to sit with you is that nasty barber over there, that blackguard, that ne'er-do-well!"

When the host heard these words, he was extremely

puzzled and asked, "Why are you so disturbed by that barber over there? After all, you're from Baghdad, and you can't really know him, can you?"

Then we looked at the stranger and said, "Tell us why you're so angry at that barber."

"Gentlemen," replied the stranger, "that barber is from Baghdad, and I was involved in a strange incident with him that I would like to forget. In fact, he caused me to break my leg and become lame, and I've sworn never to sit in the same place with him, nor even to spend time in the same town where he happens to dwell. Our meeting here is uncanny, for I said goodbye to Baghdad some time ago and traveled far to get away from him. But after arriving in your city and spending one night here, I find our paths have crossed again. However, you can be sure that I won't let another day go by before I leave."

"By Allah," we all said, "you must tell us your tale."

After calming himself somewhat, the young man began talking, and as he did, the barber changed color from brown to yellow. And this is what the youth had to say:

My father was one of the chief merchants of Baghdad, and Almighty Allah had blessed him with just one son, which was me. When I grew up and reached manhood, my father died and left me with a good deal of money, eunuchs, servants, and slaves, and I used to dress and eat well.

Now Allah had made me a hater of womankind, and one day, as I was walking along a street in Baghdad, I encountered a party of females face to face in the street. So I fled from them, and after entering an alley that was not a thoroughfare, I sat down on a stone bench. I had only been sitting there a short time when the latticed window of one of the houses opposite me was thrown open, and I saw a young woman who looked like the full moon at its fullest. Never in my life had I seen a woman as beautiful as she was. Then she began to water some flowers at the windowsill, and as she turned right and left, she saw me watching her and shut the window and went away. Suddenly my heart was afire. I was obsessed by her, and my hatred of women turned into love for this woman. I continued sitting there until sunset, lost to the world, and then the kazi of the city came riding up to the damsel's house with his slaves before him and his eunuchs behind him. After dismounting, he entered the house, and I realized that he was her father. So I went home in sorrow and threw myself on my bed in grief. Then my handmaids flocked in and sat around me, not knowing what was the matter with me. Since I did not tell them anything, they wept and wailed over me. Soon an old woman came in, and after looking at me, she saw with a glance what the matter with me was. So she sat down by my head and spoke to me softly. "My son," she said, "tell me all about it, and I'll bring about your union with her."

Consequently, I told her what had happened, and she remarked, "My son, this damsel is the daughter of the kazi of Baghdad, and he keeps her secluded and under tight guard. The window where you saw her is her floor, while her father occupies the large salon on the lower floor. She's often there alone, and since I'm used to visiting her house, you can win her through me. So be cheerful and set your wits to work." With these words, she went away, and I took heart at what she had said. Indeed, the next morning my servants rejoiced at seeing me rise in good health and humor. Bye and bye the old woman returned and looked downcast. "My son," she said, "don't ask how I did with her! When I told her about your interest, she yelled at me, 'If you don't hold your tongue, you old hag, and stop such talk, I'll treat you as you deserve, and you'll die the worst kind of death!' But I must have a second go at her."

When I heard this, I became sick again, and the neighbors visited me and thought that I was not long for this world. However, after some days, the old woman reappeared, and putting her mouth close to my ear, she whispered, "My son, I bring you good news."

Upon hearing this, my soul returned to me, and I said, "Whatever you want will be yours."

Thereupon she began, "Yesterday I went to the young lady, and since she saw that I was downcast and shedding tears, she asked, 'Old woman, what's the matter? Why are you so low in spirits?' And I answered her with bitter tears, 'My lady, I've just come from the house of a youth who loves you and is about to die for your sake.' Apparently her heart softened, and she asked, 'And who indeed is this youth?' 'He's like a son to me,' I said, 'the fruit of my vitals. He saw you some days ago at the window watering your flowers, and after gazing upon your face and hands, he fell in love with you at first sight. I let him know what happened to me the last time I was with you, whereupon he became desperately ill with love for you and took to bed. Now he is nothing but a dead man.' At this she turned pale and asked, 'All this for my sake?' And I answered, 'Yes, by Allah! Do you want me to do anything about it?' 'Go back to him,' she said, 'and greet him from me and tell him that I am just as much heartsick as he is. And on Friday, right before the hour of public prayer, tell him to come to the house, and I'll come down and open the door for him. Then I'll take him up to my chamber and spend some time with him. Afterward he can depart before my father returns from the mosque.' "

When I heard the old woman's words, my sickness suddenly vanished. My anguish ceased, and my heart was comforted. I took off what clothes were on me and gave them to her. As she turned to go, she said, "Keep a good heart!"

"There's no more sorrow left in me," I replied.

My household servants and companions rejoiced in my recovery, and I continued feeling well until Friday, when the old woman arrived and asked me how I was doing. I answered that I was well and in good shape. Then I dressed myself, put on some incense, and sat down to wait for the congregation to go to public prayer so that I might visit the damsel. But the old woman said to me, "You've got time to spare. So you'd do well to go to the Hammam baths and have your hair shaven off so as not to show any traces of your sickness."

"This is a good idea," I answered. "Although I've just finished bathing in hot water, I'll have my head shaved." Then I said to my page, "Go to the bazaar and bring me a barber, a discreet fellow, one not inclined to meddle or to be curious. Someone who's not an excessive talker."

The boy went out at once and brought back with him this wretched old man, this sheikh of ill omen. When the barber came in, he saluted me, and I returned his salutation. Then he said, "Well, I see that you're very thin."

"I've been sick," I said.

"May Allah drive away your woes and sorrow," he remarked.

"May Allah grant your prayer!" said I.

He continued, "I wish you happiness, my master. Indeed, you appear to have recovered. Do you wish to be polled or to be bled? Indeed, it was a tradition of Ibn Abbas, the Apostle, who said, 'The Lord shall prevent calamities from happening to whoever cuts his hair on a Friday.' And there is another saying attributed to him: 'Haircuts on Friday keep one from losing sight and contracting all sorts of diseases.' "

"Stop this idle talk!" I cried. "I can't stand it. Come and shave my head at once."

So he rose in a most leisurely way, stretched out his hand, took out a kerchief, and unfolded it. There I saw an astrolabe, a kind of sextant, with several parallel plates mounted in silver. Then he went to the middle of the court and raised his head and instrument toward the sun's rays and looked for a long time. When this was over, he came back to me and said, "I want to inform you that eight degrees and six minutes have elapsed on this day, which is Friday, and this Friday is the tenth of the month Safar in the six hundred and thirty-third year since the Hegira or Flight of the Apostle (and may He be blessed with peace!) and the seven thousand three hundred and twentieth of the era of Alexander. Furthermore, the ascendant of this day is, according to the most exact science of computation, the planet Mars. It so happens that Mercury is in conjunction with Mars, which denotes an auspicious moment for haircuts. Indeed, this also reveals to me that you desire a union with a certain person and that your intercourse will not be propitious. After this, I can see a sign indicating that something will happen to you, but I don't want to speak about this matter."

"By Allah!" I cried. "You're wearing me out and driving me crazy! What's more, you don't see much good in my future! I sent for you to cut my hair and nothing else. So get to it! Shave my head, and stop speaking!"

"By Allah," he replied, "if you knew what was about to happen to you, you'd do nothing this day, and I advise you to act as I tell you according to the computation of the constellations."

"Never have I met a barber like yourself who prides himself in his astrological skills!" I answered. "But I think and I know that you're more skilled in talking frivolously. Look, I sent for you only to shave my head, but you come and pester me with this trite prattle."

"What more could you desire?" he declared. "Allah has generously given you a barber who is an astrologer, one learned in alchemy and white magic; syntax, grammar, and lexicology; the arts of logic, rhetoric, and elocution; mathematics, arithmetic, and algebra; astronomy, astromancy, and geometry; theology, the Traditions of the Apostle, and the Commentaries on the Koran. Furthermore, I've read books galore and digested them and have had experience of affairs and have comprehended them. In short, I've learned the theory and practice of all the arts and sciences. I know them all by heart, and I am a past master *in tota re scribili*. Your father loved me for my lack of officiousness. Therefore, to serve you is a religious duty incumbent on me. I am not a busybody, as you may have supposed, and I am generally known as the Silent Man, also the Modest Man. Therefore, you should be thankful to Allah Almighty and not try to cross me, for I am your true counselor and inclined to be benevolent toward you. I wish I could serve you for one whole year so that you could do me justice! And I would ask no wages for my services."

After I heard this virtual storm of words, I said to him, "You're undoubtedly going to be the end of me this day!"

And Scheherazade noticed that dawn was approaching and stopped telling her story. When the next night arrived, however, she received the king's permission to continue her tale and said,

"Oh, my master," he replied, "I am called the Silent Man because I don't talk much, and my taciturn ways distinguish me from my six brothers. The eldest is called Al-Bakbuk, the Prattler; the second Al-Haddar, the Babbler; the third Al-Fakik, the Gabbler; the fourth, Al-Kuz al-aswani, the long-necked Goglet, because of his eternal chattering; the fifth, Al-Nashshar, the Tattler and Tale-teller; the sixth, Shakashik, or Many Clamors; and the seventh is famous as Al-Samit, the Silent Man, and this is my noble self!"

As his talk increased, I thought my gall bladder would burst. So I said to my servant, "Give him a quarter-dinar and dismiss him. For heaven's sake, get him away from me! I won't have my head shaved today."

"What are you saying, my lord?" he responded. "By Allah! I refuse to accept money from you until I've served you and have ministered to your wants. I couldn't care less about money! If you can't recognize my qualities, I can at least recognize yours. And I owe your father, an honest man (and may Allah have mercy on him!), many a kindness, for he had a liberal and generous soul. By Allah, he sent for me one day, just like this blessed day. and I went to him and found some of his friends around him. 'Let me bleed,' he said. So I pulled out my astrolabe, and after estimating the sun's altitude for him, I ascertained that his ascendant star was inauspicious and the hour unfavorable for bleeding. I informed him about this, and he listened to me and waited for a better opportunity. In the meantime I wrote some verses honoring your father. Well, your father was delighted, and he cried out to the servant, 'Give him a hundred and three gold pieces with a robe of honor!' The man obeyed his orders, and I waited for an auspicious moment, when I bled him. And he did not scold me. Rather he thanked me, and I was also thanked and praised by his friends. When the bloodletting was over, I could not keep silent and asked him, 'By Allah, why did you tell your servant to give me a hundred and *three* dinars?' And he answered, 'One dinar was for the astrological observation; another for your pleasant conversation; the third for the phlebotomization; and the remaining hundred and the dress were for your verses.' "

"May Allah show mercy to my father," I exclaimed, "for knowing the likes of you!"

He laughed and responded, "There is no god but *the* God, and Mohammed is the Apostle of God! Glory to Him who changes and is not changed! I took you for a man of sense, but I see that your illness makes you babble and blunder. Allah has said in the Blessed Book, 'Paradise is prepared for the good who know how to bridle their anger and forgive men,' and in any case, you're excused. Nevertheless, I can't understand why you are in such a hurry. You must know that your father and your grandfather did nothing without consulting me. And you must probably know the saying 'Let the adviser be esteemed,' or 'There is no vice in advice.' And there's also the proverb 'Whoever does not have an elder counselor will never be an elder himself.' Moreover, there's the poet who said, 'Whatever must be undertaken, consult the experienced and dare not oppose him.' And indeed, you'll never find a man better versed in the affairs of the world than I am, and here I am standing before you and ready to serve you. I'm not angry at you. So why should you be angry with me? Whatever happens I'll keep my patience with you in memory of the great kindness that your father showed me."

"By Allah!" I cried out. "You've got a tongue longer than that of a jackass, and you persist in pestering me with your babble! In fact, you're becoming even more tiring in your long speeches when all I want from you is to shave my head and go your way!"

Then he lathered my head and said, "I see that you're angry with me, but I won't hold this against you, for you're a bit weak in your head and you're still a young lad. It was only yesterday that I used to lift you onto my shoulders and carry you to school."

"For Allah's sake," I said, "do what I want, and be off." And I ripped my garments out of rage.

When he saw me do this, he took the razor and began sharpening it. However, he did not stop doing this until I was almost out of my head. Then he came up to me and shaved part of my head, whereupon he stopped and said, "My lord, haste is the way of Satan, while patience is practiced by Allah the Compassionate. In your case, master, I have a feeling that you don't know my rank. Honestly, my hand has touched the heads of kings, emirs, viziers, sages, and doctors learned in law."

"Will you *stop* talking about things that don't concern you!" I exclaimed. "You've managed to bother me and distract my mind."

"It seems to me that you're a hasty man," he replied.

"Yes, yes, yes!" I declared.

"I advise you to practice restraint," he said. "Haste is only Satan's way to profit, but men only repent it in the end. According to Almighty Allah, 'The best of works are those in which deliberation lurks.' Indeed, I have some doubt about your affair, and therefore, I'd like you to tell me what it is that you're in such a hurry to do. I fear that it will bring no good. There are only three hours until prayer time, and I must know everything exactly. For to tell you the truth, 'A guess shot in times of doubt often brings harm about.' This is particularly true of someone like me, a superior person, whose merits are famous among mankind at large. And it does not suit me to talk at random as the common sort of astrologers do." After saying this, he threw down the razor, picked up the astrolabe, and went out under the sun, where he stood a long time. Then he returned, counted on his fingers, and said, "There are still three full hours to prayer time, neither more nor less, according to the most learned astronomers and the wisest manufacturers of almanacs."

"By Allah," I cried. "hold your tongue! You're splitting my guts!"

So he took the razor, and after sharpening it as before and shaving two hairs off my head, he stopped again and said, "I'm concerned about your hastiness, and it would be much better if you told me the cause of it. It would be better for you, since neither your grandfather nor your father ever did a thing without my advice."

When I saw that there was no escaping him, I said to myself, "The time for prayer is drawing near, and I want to go to her before the people come out of the mosque. If I am delayed much longer, I don't know how I'll be able to reach her." Then I said aloud, "Be quick and stop this talk and impertinence. The reason I'm in a rush is that I have to go to a party at the house of some of my friends."

"Your day is a blessed day for me! You see, yesterday I invited a company of my friends, and just now I remembered that I've forgotten to provide anything for them to eat. Alas, I'll be disgraced in their eyes!"

"Don't be distressed," I answered. "Didn't I tell you that I'm entertaining my friends today? So, everything in my house, all there is to eat and drink, will be yours, if you will only get through with your work and shave my head!"

"May Allah bless you for your kindness!" he replied.

"But tell me specifically what you've ordered for your guests so that I'll know everything."

"Five dishes of meat," I said, "and ten chickens with reddened breasts and a roasted lamb."

"Set all this before me," he said, "so that I may see it all."

So I told my servants to buy, borrow, or steal the food and bring it in any way they could. When they accomplished their errand, I had it all set before him, but he cried out, "There's no wine!"

"I have a flagon or two of good old grape juice in the house," I responded.

"Have it brought out!" he said.

So I sent for it, and he exclaimed, "May Allah bless you for your kindness! But we still need essences and perfumes."

So I commanded my servants to set before him a box containing Nadd, the best of compound perfumes, together with fine lign aloes, ambergris, and musk unmixed, all worth fifty dinars. Now, the time was flying by, and I was very disturbed. So I said to him, "Take it all, and finish shaving my head!"

"By Allah," he responded, "I won't take any of this until I see what's inside."

So I ordered the page to open the box, and the barber put down the astrolabe, leaving the greater part of my head unshaven. As he sat on the ground he inspected the perfumes, aloes wood, and essences until I was almost completely distraught. Then he took his razor, came up to me, shaved off a few hairs, and recited these lines:

" 'Tis rare the father in the son we see:
He sometimes rises in the third degree."

Then he said, "By Allah, I don't know whether to thank you or your father. Indeed, thanks to your kindness and generosity, I'll be able to provide the proper entertainment for my friends. Although none of my company is worthy of such fine entertainment, they are still honorable men. For instance, I've invited Zantut the bathkeeper, Salia the corn chandler, Silat the bean seller, Akrashah the greengrocer, Humayd the scavenger, Said the camel man, Suwayd the porter, Abu Makarish the bathman,

Kasim the watchman, and Karim the groom. None among them is a bore or bully. Nor are they meddlers or misers. Each and every one knows a dance which he dances and a song which he sings. And best of all, they are all like me, your humble servant, who knows how to keep his tongue and is not at all pushy. The bathkeeper sings an enchanting song to the beating of a tom-tom. The corn chandler makes us laugh until we are about to split our guts. But the scavenger sings so beautifully that the birds stop to listen to him. Indeed, each one is perfect in whatever wit and charm he possesses. But hearing is not seeing, and if you were to decide to join us and put off going to your friends, it would be better for us and for you. I can still see traces of your illness in you, and you might be going to people who are mighty talkers, men who talk about things that don't concern them. Or there may be some insolent fellow there who will split your head, and you won't be able to defend yourself because of your sickness."

"Some other day," I replied and laughed with anger. "Finish your work now, and go to your friends, for they're expecting you."

"My lord," he answered, "I'd only like to introduce you to some fellows of infinite mirth. They are worthy men, and none of them are judgmental, inquisitive, or loquacious. Believe me, ever since I reached manhood, I've never been able to mix with men who ask questions about things that do not concern them. I prefer men like me, men of few words. I promise you that if you were to meet them just once, you would give up all your friends for them."

"I'm glad that you enjoy them so much," I replied. "You go and be with them. I'll meet them some other day."

"I wish it could be today," he insisted, "for I had my heart set on making you one of our company. But if you must be with your friends today, I'll take these good things that you have so honorably provided to my guests. Then I'll leave them there while they eat and drink and quickly return to you. There is nothing ceremonious between my friends and me that would prevent me from rejoining you. Fear not, I'll soon be back with you and accompany you wherever you go."

"Go to your friends and have a good time!" I shouted. "And *let* me go and be alone with my friends, for they're expecting me."

But the barber cried, "I won't let you go alone."

"The truth is," I declared, "nobody can enter where I am going except myself."

"I suspect," he rejoined, "that you have an assignation with some woman, or else you would take me with you. Even so, I am the right man to take with you, for I can help you achieve whatever you wish. But I fear that you're running after strange women and will lose your life. You realize, of course, that in Baghdad one cannot do anything along these lines, especially on a day like Friday. Our governor is a fearful man and a mighty sharp blade."

"Shame on you, you wicked, dirty old man!" I cried. "Be off! What are you saying to me?"

"You fool!" he responded. "You hide things and don't tell me the truth, but I know everything and am only doing my best today to help you."

I kept quiet a long time because I was afraid my servants or neighbors would hear the barber's talk. In the meantime he finished shaving my head, and the time for the hour of prayer had arrived. When he was done, I said to him, "Go to your friends with this food and drink, and I'll wait for your return. Then we'll go off together." I hoped that I might be able to trick the accursed loon and get rid of him this way.

But he replied, "You're trying to deceive me and would like to go to your appointment alone. But you'd be placing yourself in jeopardy, and there'll be no escape. By Allah, don't go until I return! It's important that I accompany you and keep an eye on your affair."

"So be it," I replied. "Don't be too long."

Then he took all the food and drink and all the rest of the articles I had given him and left my house. However, the crazy fellow gave everything to a porter and paid him to carry it all to his house. Then he hid himself in one of the alleys. As for me, I got up immediately, for the muezzins had already called the Dalam of Friday, the salutation to the Apostle, and I dressed in haste and went out alone. I hurried to the house where I had seen the young lady and found the old woman on guard at the door awaiting me. Then I went upstairs to the damsel's apartment, and no sooner had I reached it than the master of the house returned from prayers, entered the large salon, and closed the door. I looked down from the window and saw the barber (may Allah curse him!) sitting opposite the door of the house. "How did this devil find out where I was going?" I said to myself.

Suddenly, as Allah had decreed it, some slave girl in the house offended her master, and he began beating her. The blows were so hard that she shrieked, and the barber's slave ran in to intercede on her behalf, whereupon the kazi beat him as well, causing the slave also to roar and shriek. Now the damned barber thought that it was I who was being beaten. So he began to shout, tear his garments, and scatter dust on his head. "Help! Help!" he kept on yelling and crying. "My master is being murdered in the kazi's house!" Then he ran clamoring to my place with a crowd of people after him. There he told my servants and slaves what was happening, and they began to tear their clothes and let down their hair and shout. "Alas, our master!" And the barber led them out into the street with their clothes torn and in the sorriest plight. What was even worse was that the barber continued shouting like a madman, "Alas, our master's being murdered!" And they all returned to make an assault on the house in which I was hiding. Hearing the shouts and the uproar at his door, the kazi said to one of his servants, "See what's the matter outside."

The servant went out and then returned and said, "Master, there are more than ten thousand people, men and women, at the gate, and they're all crying out, 'Alas, our master's being murdered!' And they keep pointing to our house."

When the kazi heard this, he thought that the matter seemed serious and became angry. So he arose, opened the door, and saw a great crowd of people. Of course, he was very much surprised by this and cried out, "What's going on?"

"Oh, you accursed man! You dog! You hog!" my servants replied. "You've killed our master!"

"Good people," he responded, "why should I want to kill him? What's your master done to me?"

* * *

And Scheherazade noticed that dawn was approaching and stopped telling her tale. When the next night arrived, however, she received the king's permission to continue her tale and said,

Then the kazi continued, "This is my house, and it's open to you all."

"You beat him," said the barber, "and I heard him cry out."

"Why should I beat him?" asked the kazi. "And what brought him to my house? Where did he come from, and where has he gone?"

"Don't be such a wicked, perverse old man!" cried the barber. "For I know the whole story, and the long and short of it is that your daughter is in love with him, and he loves her. And when you found out that he had entered the house, you ordered your servants to beat him, and they carried out your command. By Allah, none other than the caliph will judge this case unless you bring out our master so that his people may take him. Otherwise, they'll go in and save him by force, and you'll be put to shame."

The kazi's tongue was tied, and his mouth was stopped by confusion. Finally, however, he said, "If you speak the truth, then come in and fetch him."

Thereupon, the barber pushed forward and entered the house. When I saw this, I looked around for a means of escape and flight, but saw no hiding place except a great chest in the upper chamber where I was. So I got into it and pulled the lid down and held my breath. No sooner was the barber in the room than he began looking around for me. He turned right and left and came straight to the place where I was. After stepping up to the chest, he lifted it on his head and made off with it as fast as he could. When this happened, I lost my head, for I knew that he would not let me be. Therefore, I summoned my courage, opened the chest, and threw myself to the ground. My leg was broken in the fall, and since the door was open, I saw a great crowd of people who were watching the entire incident. Now I was carrying a great deal of gold and silver in my sleeve in case I should have such a bad day as this. Consequently, I scattered it among the people to divert their attention from me, and while they were busy scrambling for the money, I set off, hopping as fast as I could through the bystreets of Baghdad, turning right and left.

But wherever I went, the damned barber followed me and cried out, "They wanted to take my master! They wanted to slay him, my benefactor! Praise be to Allah, who allowed me to prevail against them and who delivered my lord from their hands!" Then he yelled to me, "Where do you want to go now? You insisted in following an evil path, and so you brought this upon yourself. If Allah had not brought us together, you'd never have escaped this predicament. It would have been a total catastrophe! But I won't blame you. You just don't know how to use your brains and think things over carefully. No, you're too compulsive and hasty!"

"Haven't you done enough to me?" I responded. "Why must you now run after me and talk to me like this in the streets?"

I almost gave up the ghost, I was so enraged at him. Then I took refuge in a weaver's shop in the middle of the market and sought protection from the owner, who drove the barber away. Sitting in the back room, I said to myself, "If I return home, I'll never be able to get rid of this curse of a barber, who'll stay with me night and day. I can't endure the sight of him even for a second!" So I set out at once to look for witnesses. Then I made a will, dividing the greater part of my property among my people, and appointed a guardian over them who was also assigned the task of selling my houses and domains and looking after big and little matters. Then I set out on my travels so that I might free myself of this pimp, and I came to settle in your city, where I've lived for some time. When you invited me and I came here, the first thing I saw was this accursed pander seated in the place of honor. How then can I be glad and my stay be pleasant in the company of this fellow who brought all this upon me, and who caused me to break my leg and drove me into exile from home and native land?

So the young man refused to sit down and went away. After hearing his story, we were amazed and amused. Then we turned to the barber and asked, "Is it true what this young man has told us about you?"

"By Allah," he replied, "I used good sense, courtesy, and kindness in dealing with him. Had it not been for me he would have perished, and had it not been for me he would not have escaped. He's lucky that he only broke his leg and did not lose his life! If I had been a man of many words, a meddler, a busybody, I would not have acted in such a kind way. But now I'll tell you about something that happened to me, and I assure you that I am not long-winded or insolent. Indeed, I'm not at all like those six brothers of mine."

And he began to tell

The Barber's Tale of Himself

I lived in Baghdad during the time of the Caliph Al-Mustansir bi'llah, who loved the poor and needy and kept company with the learned and pious. Now, one day, the caliph became angry with ten highwaymen who were robbing people on his highway, and he ordered the prefect of Baghdad to bring them to him on the anniversary of the Great Pilgrimage Festival. So the prefect went searching for them, and after he had captured them, he intended to bring them back to Baghdad in a boat. I caught sight of them as they were embarking on the boat and said to myself, "These men are surely going to a marriage feast. It seems to me that they'll be spending their day in that boat eating and drinking, and I have a mind to join them."

So I rose and embarked with them. Soon I entered into conversation with the robbers, and after they were rowed to the opposite bank, the guardians of peace came up to them and put chains around their necks. To my surprise, they chained me along with the rest of them, and gentlemen, what more proof do you need of my polite manners and spareness of speech when I tell you that I held my peace and did not say anything?

Then they took us away in bilboes and brought us the next morning before Al-Mustansir, Commander of the

Faithful, who ordered that the ten robbers were to have their heads chopped off. So, after they were seated on the leather of blood, the executioner came forward and struck off their heads one after the other, but stopped when he reached me. The caliph was puzzled by this and asked the executioner, "What's the matter? Why have you struck off only nine heads?"

And he answered, "Allah forbid that I should have beheaded only nine when you ordered me to behead ten!"

"It seems to me," said the caliph, "that you have executed only nine, and this man before you is the tenth."

"By your beneficence!" replied the executioner. "I have beheaded ten."

"Count them!" cried the caliph. And when they counted the heads, they discovered there were ten. Then the caliph looked at me and asked, "What made you keep quiet at a time like this? Why were you with these robbers? Even though you're old, you don't seem to be very wise."

Now when I heard these words from the caliph, I sprang to my feet and replied, "I'll have you know, Prince of the Faithful, that I am the Silent Sheikh, and I was given this name to distinguish me from my six brothers. I'm a man of immense learning, and I have a profound capacity to understand things, use my wits, and keep quiet. My profession is that of a barber. Yesterday I went out early in the morning, and I saw these men heading for a skiff. Thinking that they were bound for a marriage feast, I joined them and kept their company. After a while, the guardians of the peace came up to them and put chains around their necks and mine as well. But because of my polite manners, I held my peace and did not say a word. I thought that this was the kind thing to do. When they brought us before you, and you gave the order to chop off their heads, I did not make myself known to you and remained silent in front of the executioner because of my great kindness and courtesy that led me to share their fate with them. Unfortunately, throughout my life I've dealt nobly with mankind, and they repay me in the worst ways!"

When the caliph heard my words and knew that I was a man of exceeding kindness and of very few words, one who is not insolent (as that young man would make me out to be, even though I rescued him from certain death and was paid back in such a scurvy way), he laughed so much that he fell on his back. Then he said to me, "Oh Silent Man, are your six brothers like you in wisdom and knowledge? Are they also men of few words?"

"They're not at all like me, your majesty!" I replied. "That would be an insult to compare them to me. You see, they all talk too much and lack wisdom and courtesy, and they've each been maimed in some way or another. One is a monocular, another palsied, a third stone-blind, a fourth cropped of ears and nose, a fifth shorn of both lips, while the sixth is a hunchback and a cripple. And don't think, Commander of the Faithful, that I'm being too loquacious now, but I must explain to you that I'm a man of greater importance and of fewer words than any of them. There's a tale that explains how each of my brothers obtained his bodily defect, and if you really want to know how different I am from them, you must listen to my tales."

So the caliph gave ear to

The Barber's Tale of His First Brother

My first brother, Al-Bakbuk, the Prattler, is a hunchback, who learned tailoring in Baghdad, and he used to sew in a shop that he leased from a wealthy man, who lived above the shop, and there was also a flour mill in the basement. One day, while my brother, the hunchback, was sitting and working in his shop, he happened to raise his head and see a lady above him at the balcony window of his landlord's house. She was as beautiful as the rising full moon and was looking at the passersby in the street. When my brother caught sight of her, he fell head over heels in love with her. In fact, he spent the whole day just gazing at her and neglected his tailoring.

The next morning he sat down to sew, but each time he stitched a stitch, he looked up at the window and saw her again, and his passion and infatuation for her increased. On the third day, as he was sitting in his usual place and gazing at her, she caught sight of him, and realizing that he had been captivated by her, she nodded favorably toward him while he smiled back at her. Then she disappeared and soon sent her slave girl to him with a bundle containing a piece of red silk with flowers on it. "My lady salutes you," the slave girl said, "and she requests that you put your skill to good work and make a shift for her out of this material."

"Her words are my command," he replied, and after he designed a chemise for her, he finished sewing it the same day. The next morning the slave girl came back to him and said, "My lady salutes you and asks how you spent the past night. She herself was unable to sleep because of her heart, which has been consumed by you." Then she laid before him a piece of yellow satin and said, "My lady requests that you cut her two pairs of yellow petticoat trousers out of this piece and sew them this very day."

"Her words are my command!" he replied and added, "Give her my best greetings and tell her that her slave will obey her orders. Moreover, she may command him to do whatever she wants." Then he worked diligently to cut out the trousers and sew them together. After an hour the lady appeared at the window and greeted him in various ways by lowering her eyes and then smiling at him. As a result, he was certain that he would soon make a conquest. However, she kept him working until he had finished the two pairs of trousers, whereupon she withdrew from the window and sent her handmaid, who picked up the garments and went her way.

That night he threw himself on his bed and tossed from side to side until morning, when he again sat down in front of his shop. Soon the slave girl came to him and said, "My master would like to see you."

Hearing these words, my brother became extremely fearful, but the slave girl saw how afraid he was and said, "Don't worry, no one intends to do you harm. On the contrary, you can expect good things. My mistress would just like you to make the acquaintance of my lord."

So my brother rejoiced and went with her, and when he came before the landlord, who was the lady's husband, he kissed the ground before him, and the master of the house returned his greeting, gave him a large piece of linen, and said, "Make me some shirts out of this stuff, and sew them well."

And my brother responded, "Your words are my command."

Thereupon, he began the work immediately in the landlord's house. He snipped, shaped, and sewed until he had finished twenty shirts by suppertime without stopping to eat.

When the house master came to pick them up, he asked my brother, "How much do I owe you?"

And he answered, "Twenty dirhams."

So the landlord cried out to the slave girl, "Bring me twenty dirhams."

My brother did not say a word, but his lady love was standing there, too, and signaled to him as if to say that he should not take anything from her husband. So he said, "By Allah, I won't accept anything from your hand."

Therefore, the landlord carried off the shirts while my brother took his tailor's gear and returned to his shop. Even though he was now destitute and did not have a red cent to his name, he continued making some shirts for them. In his zeal and diligence, he ate but a little bit of bread and drank only water, At the end of three days, the slave girl came again and asked him, "What have you done?"

"The new shirts are finished," he said, and he carried them to the lady's husband, who would have paid him for his work, but he said, "I won't accept anything," out of admiration for his lady love. And he returned to his shop and spent the night without sleep because of his hunger.

Now, without my brother's being aware of it, the lady had informed her husband about her little flirtation from the beginning. Moreover, the husband and wife had conceived a plan to make my brother sew their clothes for nothing just so they could have their fun with him and make him look ridiculous. So when the next morning arrived and he was sitting in his shop, the handmaid came and said, "My master would like to speak to you."

Once again my brother accompanied her to the husband, who said to him, "I want you to make five long-sleeved robes for me."

So he took the stuff away, designed the robes, and cut them out. After he had finished sewing them, he carried them to the gentleman, who praised his sewing and offered him a purse of silver. When he stuck out his hand to take it, the lady signaled to him from behind her husband not to do so, and he replied, "My lord, there's no hurry. We have plenty of time to settle our account." Then he left the house meaner and meeker than a donkey, for truly five things had accumulated within him: love, poverty, hunger, nakedness, and hard labor. Nevertheless, he kept his spirits up with the hope of gaining the lady's favors.

Finally, after he had completed all their jobs, they played another trick on him and married him to their slave girl. Then they convinced him it would be best to sleep with the maid only on a certain night. So the landlord told him, "Go to the mill in the cellar of my house tonight, and by tomorrow everything will be perfect."

My brother concluded that there was some good reason for this, but it turned out that he was to spend the night in the mill alone, for the maid did not show up. Instead, the husband had arranged with the miller to treat the tailor as though he were his bull and make him turn the mill. So when the night was half over, the miller came in and said to him, "What kind of a bull are you? You've become useless. You just stand and do nothing even though we have a great stock of corn to grind. However, I'll yoke you now and make you finish grinding everything before morning, since the people are waiting impatiently for their flour." So he filled the hoppers with grain, and after going up to my brother with a rope in his hand, he tied it around his neck and said to him, "Gee up! Around the mill you go! Do you think you can just grub, stale, and dung?" Then the miller took a whip and laid it on my brother's shoulders and calves so that he began to howl and bellow. But nobody came to help him, and he was forced to grind the wheat until dawn. Then the landlord entered, and when he saw my brother still tethered to the yoke and the man flogging him, he went away. Finally, as the sun began to shine, the miller returned home and left him there half dead.

Soon after, the slave girl came in and untied him while

saying, "My lady and I are quite sorry for what's happened to you. You can rest assured that we've shared in your suffering."

But he had no energy to answer her because of the beating and mill-turning. So he returned to his lodging, and suddenly the clerk who had drawn up the marriage contract entered his room, expecting a gift. After saluting him, the clerk said, "May Allah grant you a long life! May your wedding be blessed! Your exhausted face reveals that you must have had a pleasant time last night, kissing and clipping from dusk to dawn!"

"May Allah torment liars like you, you scoundrel!" My brother replied. "I did nothing but turn the mill in the place of the bull from night till morning!"

"Tell me your tale," he said, and my brother recounted what had happened to him, whereupon he responded, "Your star doesn't correspond well with hers, but if you want, I can alter the contract for you. But beware that you're not deceived again."

And my brother answered him, "Go ply your trade somewhere else!"

Then the clerk left, and he sat in the shop looking for someone to offer him work so that he could earn his daily bread. Soon the handmaid came to him and said, "My lady would like to speak to you."

"Begone, my good girl!" he replied. "There'll be no more dealings between me and your lady."

The handmaid returned to her mistress and told her what my brother had said, and soon she put her head out of the window and began weeping, "Why, my beloved, are there to be no more dealings between you and me?"

However, he refused to answer her. Then she wept and implored him and swore that the incident in the mill had not been sanctioned by her and that she was innocent of the entire matter. When he looked at her beautiful and lovely face and heard her sweet speech, the sorrow that had gripped him vanished all at once. He accepted her excuse and rejoiced at her sight. After saluting her, he talked with her while doing some work.

Later on the handmaid came to him and said, "My mistress sends greetings and wants you to know that her husband plans to spend the night in the house of one of his friends. So when he is gone, you're to come to us and spend the night with my lady and enjoy the pleasure of her company until morning."

Now, before the handmaid had delivered this message, the husband had asked his wife, "How shall we manage to keep his hands off you?"

And she answered, "Leave it to me. We'll play another trick on him, and he'll be the laughingstock of the entire town."

Unfortunately, my brother did not know how malicious women could be. As soon as it was dusk, the slave girl came to him and brought him to the house, and when the lady saw him, she said, "My lord, I've been longing for this moment!"

"By Allah," he cried, "kiss me quick before we do anything else."

No sooner had he spoken than the lady's husband came in from the next room, grabbed him, and said, "By Allah, I won't let you go until I deliver you to the town watch!"

My brother pleaded with him to let him go, but the husband would not listen and brought him to the prefect, who gave him a hundred lashes with a whip. Then he mounted him on a camel and had him promenaded around the city while the guards proclaimed loudly, "This is the reward for those who violate wives of honorable men!"

In addition to this humiliation, he fell off the camel and broke his leg, causing him to become lame. Then the prefect banished him from the city, and he left not knowing where to go. Yet, I heard about all this, and fearing that something worse might happen to him, I went after him and brought him back secretly to the city. There I restored him to health and let him stay in my house, where he's still living to the present day.

The caliph laughed at my story and said, "You've done well, oh Silent Man, oh man of few words!" and he offered me a present and said I could depart.

However, I replied, "I won't accept anything from you except your permission to let me tell you what happened to my other brothers. But I don't want my tales to lead you to believe that I'm a loquacious man. On the contrary, I want you to learn who you have before you."

So the caliph gave ear to

The Barber's Tale of His Second Brother

My second brother's name was Al-Haddar, otherwise known as the Babbler, and he was the paralytic. Now, one day, as he was going about his business, he encountered an old woman, who said, "Stop a moment, my good man. I'd like to ask you to do something for me, and if you do it, I'll pray to Allah to reward you in a goodly way." Since my brother stopped, she went on, "But you must not tell anyone about what you're to do."

"Well, out with it," he said.

"What would you say if I offered you splendid living quarters and a fair garden with flowing streams, flowers in bloom, ripe fruit, delicious wine, and a pretty girl whom you can embrace from morning until night? Indeed, if you do what I tell you, all this will be yours."

"Fine," my brother replied. "But tell me, is all this to be found in this world?"

"Yes," she answered, "it will be yours, if you stop talking so much and are sensible and do what I ask you to do."

"I will indeed, old woman," he said. "But how come you've chosen me to do this and not somebody else? What's there about me that's attracted you?"

"Didn't I tell you to stop talking so much?" she declared. "Now hold your tongue and follow me. Just remember that the young lady, whom you will soon meet, loves to have her own way and hates to be frustrated. So if you humor her, you'll be able to fulfill your desires."

So my brother said, "I won't cross her in anything."

Then the old woman continued walking, and my brother followed her, hungering after what she had described to him, and they entered a fine large house that was beautifully furnished. It was full of eunuchs and servants and showed signs of prosperity from top to bottom. As the old woman began leading him to the upper floor, the people of the house said to him, "What are you doing here?"

But the old woman answered them, "Hold your tongues,

and don't bother him. He's a workman, and we need him for something."

Then she brought him into a fine large pavilion with a garden in the middle. Never in his life had he seen such a garden as this one, and she made him sit down on a lovely couch. No sooner had he sat down than he heard a large noise, and in came a large group of slave girls surrounding a lady as beautiful as the moon at its fullest. When he saw her, he rose up and bowed to her, whereupon she welcomed him and asked him to be seated. So he sat down, and she said to him, "May Allah help you attain your honorable goals. Do you feel all right?"

"My lady," he said, "I feel fine."

Then she ordered food to be brought, and they set delicious viands before her. So she sat down to eat and showed signs of affection toward my brother, even though she jested with him and could not refrain from laughing at him. Meanwhile, whenever he looked at her, she made signs to her maidens, who mocked him behind his back. My brother, who was a real ass, understood nothing. Because of his ridiculous passion, he imagined that the lady was in love with him, and that she would soon grant him his desire.

When they were finished eating, the servants set wine before them, and ten maidens carrying lutes entered. They began singing with full voices, sweet and sad, whereupon my brother was seized with delight, and he took the cup from the lady's hands and drank it standing. "To your health," he said and bowed to her.

She handed him another cup, and when he drank this one, too, she slapped him hard on the nape of his neck. My brother reacted by leaving the pavilion in anger, and he would have departed if the old woman had not followed him and winked to him to return. So he came back, and the lady asked him to sit down, which he did without saying a word. Then she slapped him again on the nape of his neck, and this second slap was not enough for her. Indeed, she made all her maidens slap and cuff him as well, while he kept saying to the old woman, "What's going on here?"

In the meantime, the old woman exclaimed, "Enough, enough, I beg you, mistress!" But the lady slapped him until he almost swooned away. Soon my brother got up and went out to obey a call of nature, but the old woman overtook him and said, "Be patient a little longer, and you'll certainly win her."

"How much longer do I have to wait?" my brother replied. "All this slapping has made me feel dizzy."

"As soon as she's warm with wine," she answered, "your desire will be fulfilled."

So he returned to his place and sat down, whereupon all the maidens stood up, and the lady told them to spray him with pastilles and rose water. Then she said to him, "May Allah help you attain your honorable goals! You have entered my house and have endured the conditions. I'll have you know that I turn away whoever frustrates me, and I reward whoever is patient by fulfilling his desires."

"Oh mistress," said he, "I'm your slave, and I'll eat out of the hollow of your hand!"

"I also want you to know," she continued, "that Allah has made me passionately fond of frolic, and whoever complies with my humor gets whatever he wishes." Then she ordered her maidens to sing with loud voices until the whole company was delighted. After that, she said to one of them, "Take your lord, and do what is necessary. Then bring him back to me right away."

So the damsel came and took my brother's hand (and he was not aware what she would do with him). Meanwhile the old woman came up to him and said, "Be patient. There's not much left for you to do."

Upon hearing this, his face brightened, and he stood up before the lady while the old woman kept saying, "Be patient. You'll soon have your wish."

"Tell me what she wants the maiden to do with me," he said.

"Something good," she said. "Trust me. She only wants her to dye your eyebrows and pluck out your mustache."

"I don't mind the dyeing of my eyebrows, since that will come off when I wash them," he replied, "but as for the plucking out of my mustache, that's somewhat of a painful process."

"Be careful, and don't cross her," the old woman declared. "Remember, she has her heart set on you."

So my brother was patient and allowed the maiden to dye his eyebrows and to pluck out his mustache. After that the maiden returned to her mistress and told her what she had done. Thereupon she said, "There's only one thing left to be done. You must shave his beard and make his face smooth."

So the maiden went back and told him what her mistress had ordered her to do, and my brother (what a blockhead!) said to her, "How am I to do something that will be the disgrace of me before everyone?"

But the old woman said, "She wants you this way so that you'll be like a beardless youth that has no hair on his face to scratch and prick her delicate cheeks. Believe me, she's passionately in love with you. So be patient, and you'll attain your goal."

My brother *was* patient and did as he was requested and let the maiden shave off his beard. When he was finally brought back to the lady, his eyebrows were dyed red, his mustache was plucked off, his beard was missing, and his cheeks had rouge on them. At first she was frightened by him. Then she ridiculed him and laughed until she fell on her back. "My lord, you've indeed won my heart by your good nature!" Then she implored him to stand up and dance, and he rose and capered about while she threw every cushion that she could find in the house at his head. Likewise all her women kept pelting him with oranges, lemons, and citrons until he fell down unconscious from all the cuffing, the pillows, and the fruit.

"Now you've attained your wish," said the old woman when he came around. "There are no more blows in store for you, and there's only one thing left to do. It is her custom to let no one have her until she disrobes and is stark naked. Then she will ask you to take off your clothes and run. She will run before you as if she were fleeing from you, and you're to follow her from place to place until you have a full erection. That's exactly when she'll yield to you. So strip your clothes off at once."

Upon hearing this, he got up, and lost in ecstasy, he took of his clothes and stood there mother-naked.

And Scheherazade noticed that dawn was approaching and stopped telling her story. When the next night arrived, however, she received the king's permission to continue her tale and said,

* * *

Now the lady also stripped and said to my brother, "If you want anything, run after me until you catch me." Then she began running, and he ran after her. From room to room she rushed with my brother scampering after her in a rage of desire like a veritable madman. Indeed, he had reached full erection, and after she dashed into a dark place he plummeted after her until he suddenly felt something giving way under his weight. Before he was aware of where he was, he found himself in the middle of a crowded market, where the merchants sell leather goods, and they were yelling out the prices for their merchandise, when he suddenly burst upon them—naked with a full erection, shorn of beard and mustache, eyebrows dyed red, and cheeks painted with rouge. Horrified, the merchants shouted and clapped their hands at him. Then they began flogging him with their leather skins until he fainted. Finally, they threw him on the back of an ass and carried him to the chief of police.

"What's this?" asked the chief.

"This fellow suddenly appeared from the vizier's house," they said, "and this was the condition we found him in."

So the prefect gave him a hundred lashes and banished him from Baghdad. However, I went out after him and brought him back secretly into the city and gave him a daily allowance so he could support himself.

To tell you the truth, if it were not for my great sense of humor, I would not put up with the likes of him. And it is not much different with my third brother.

So, the caliph gave ear to

The Barber's Tale of His Third Brother

My third brother's name was Al-Fakik, the Gabbler, who was blind. Now, one day fate and fortune drove him to a fine large house, and he knocked at the door and asked to speak to the owner so that he might beg something from him.

"Who's at the door?" asked the master of the house.

But my brother did not utter a word, and soon he heard the master repeat, "Who's there?"

Again my brother did not say a word, and all at once he heard the master walk to the door, open it, and say, "What do you want?"

My brother answered, "Something for Allah Almighty's sake."

"Are you blind?" asked the man.

And my brother answered, "Yes."

"Stretch out your hand," the man said.

So my brother stretched out his hand, thinking that he would receive something, but the man took it, drew him into the house, and led him up the stairs until they reached the terrace on top of the house. All the while my brother kept thinking that he would surely receive some food or money. Finally, the man asked him, "What do you want, blind man?"

And he answered, "Something for the Almighty's sake."

"May Allah open some other door for you," replied the man.

"But why didn't you tell me this when we were downstairs?"

"You cadger, why didn't you answer me when I first called to you?"

"And what do you mean to do now?"

"There's nothing in the house to give you."

"Well, then, take me downstairs."

"The way is right before you."

So my brother rose and made his way downstairs until he came within twenty steps of the door. There his foot slipped, and he rolled to the bottom of the stairs and hurt his head. After leaving, he did not know where to turn and soon encountered two other blind men, companions of his, who asked him what he had earned that day.

So he told them what had happened to him and added, "My brothers, I need to take some of our common money and buy some provisions so I can eat."

Now, the master of the house had followed him and overheard their conversation. Of course, neither my brother nor his comrades were aware of this. So my brother went to their common lodgings and sat down to wait for his companions. The landlord entered after him

without being heard, and when the other blind men arrived, my brother said to them, "Bolt the door and search the house in case some stranger may have followed us."

Upon hearing this, the man grabbed hold of a rope that hung from the ceiling and clung to it, while they went around the house and searched but found no one. So they came back and sat down next to my brother, took out their money, which they counted, and there were twelve thousand dirhams. Each took what he needed, and they buried the rest in the corner of the room. Then they set some food before them and sat down to eat. Soon my brother heard an unfamiliar pair of jaws munching by his side, and he said to his friends, "There's a stranger among us," and he stretched out his hand and seized the house master, whereupon they all fell on top of him and beat him. When they got tired of pounding him, they shouted, "Oh Moslems! There's a thief here! He's trying to take our money!"

All at once a crowd of people gathered in their lodgings, but the intruder pretended to be one of the blind and complained and shut his eyes like them so that nobody would know whether he was blind or not. "Oh Moslems," he cried out, "May Allah save me! Take me to the governor, for I have some important information for him!"

Suddenly, the watch appeared, and they seized the whole lot of them (my brother included) and dragged them to the governor's house. Once there, the governor asked, "Tell me what's going on here!"

"Look and find out for yourself," said the intruder. "Not a word will be wrung from us unless you torture us. So begin by beating me, and after me, beat our leader." And he pointed to my brother.

So they threw the man down on the ground and gave him four hundred blows on his backside. The beating was so painful that he was forced to open one eye, and as they increased their blows, he opened the other. When the governor saw this, he said, "What do we have here, you scoundrel?"

"Pardon, oh governor!" he exclaimed. "All four of us have pretended to be blind so that we can enter houses, gaze upon the unveiled faces of the women, and bring about their corruption. By doing this we've gained a great deal of money, and our savings amount to twelve thousand dirhams. Well, when I insisted on having my share, which amounts to three thousand, my companions refused, took my money away, and beat me. So, by Allah, I need your protection. It's better that you have my share than they. And if you really want to find out if I'm speaking the truth, beat every one of my companions as you've beaten me, and they'll surely open their eyes."

The governor gave orders for the interrogation to begin with my brother, and they bound him to the whipping post. "Oh scum of the earth!" the governor exclaimed. "Have you been abusing the gracious gifts of Allah by pretending to be blind?"

"Allah! Allah!" cried my brother. "There's not one of us who can really see."

Then they beat him until he fainted, and the governor cried, "Leave him alone until he comes to. Then beat him again." After this the governor had each of the blind men receive three hundred blows, while the impostor kept saying to them, "Open your eyes, or they'll keep beating you." At last this man said to the governor, "Send someone with me to bring you the money, for these fellows refuse to open their eyes and be disgraced in front of all the people."

So the governor sent some guards with the impostor to fetch the money, and he gave this man his pretended share, or three thousand dirhams. Then he kept the rest for himself and banished the three blind men from the city. But I, oh Commander of the Faithful, went out and overtook my brother. After questioning him about what had happened, he told me the tale that I've told you, and I brought him secretly back into the city, where I gave him an allowance for food and drink.

The caliph laughed at my story and said, "Give him a gift and let him go."

But I said, "By Allah, I'll take nothing from you until I've told you what happened to the rest of my brothers. Truly, my lord, I am a man of few words and spare of speech."

Then the caliph gave ear to

The Barber's Tale of His Fourth Brother

My fourth brother was called Al-Kuz al-aswani, or the long-necked Goglet, because he was always brimming over with words. Blind in one eye, he became a butcher in Baghdad, and he sold flesh and fattened rams. Since many rich and great men bought their meat from him, he amassed a good deal of money and accumulated houses and cattle. Things continued to go well for him, until one day, as he was sitting in his shop, an old man with a long beard came in, laid down some silver, and said, "Give me some meat for this."

My brother gave him his money's worth, and the old man went his way. After examining the sheikh's silver and seeing that the dirhams were white and bright, he put them in a separate box. The old man continued to return to the shop regularly for five months, and my brother kept putting the coins he received from him in this separate box. Finally, Al-Kuz decided to take the money to buy some sheep, but when he opened the box, he found nothing in it except bits of white paper that were cut in circles to look like coins. So he cried aloud until people gathered around him, whereupon he told them his tale, and they were all astounded by it. Then, as was his custom, he rose, slaughtered a ram, and hung it up inside his shop. After that he cut off some of the meat and hung it outside the shop, saying to himself, "Oh Allah, I wish the old scoundrel would come again!"

Then, within that very same hour, the old man came with his silver, and immediately my brother rose, grabbed him, and cried out, "Come, help me, Moslems! Here's the thief!"

When the sheikh heard this, he said to him in a quiet voice, "What do you think will be better for you, to let me go, or to be disgraced by me before all the people gathering around us?"

"How can you disgrace me?"

"By showing that you're selling human flesh and not mutton."

"You're lying, you villain!"

"No! It's more villainous to have human flesh hanging in one's shop."

"If what you say is true," my brother declared, "you have my permission to take my money and my life!"

Then the old man shouted, "People, people, gather round! This man's selling human flesh! If you want to find out whether I'm telling the truth, enter this man's shop."

The people rushed in and found that the ram had become a dead man hung up for sale. So they attacked my brother and cried out, "Oh infidel! Villain!" And his best friends began cuffing and kicking him and accusing him, "Are you trying to make us eat human flesh?"

On top of it all, the old man struck him in the eye and poked it out. Then the people carried my brother and the dead body with its throat cut to the chief of police, and the old man said to him, "My lord, this fellow butchers humans and sells their flesh for mutton, and we've brought him to you to judge him."

My brother wanted to defend himself, but the chief refused to hear him. Instead, he sentenced him to receive five hundred lashes and to forfeit his entire property. And indeed, if it had not been for his extensive property that he spent in bribes, they would surely have slain him. Then the chief banished him from Baghdad, and my brother kept traveling until he came to a large town, where he set up shop as a cobbler and began earning a good living. One day, as he went out on some business, he heard the distant sound of horses and asked someone what was happening. He was told that the king was going out on a hunt. So my brother stopped to look at the fine entourage, and by chance, the king's eye met my brother's, whereupon the king lowered his head and said, "May Allah protect me from the evil of this day!" All of a sudden he turned the reins of his steed and returned home with his retinue. Then he gave orders to his guards, who seized my brother and beat him so badly that he almost died. Of course, my brother had no idea why he should be treated so harshly, and after he returned to his home, he went to one of the king's household and told him what had happened. The man laughed until he fell on his back and cried, "My friend, don't you know that the king cannot bear to look at a one-eyed person, especially if he is blind in the right eye? In fact, if the person is blind in his right eye, he usually has him executed."

When my brother heard this, he decided to flee that city. After his departure he traveled to a city where no one knew him, and he lived there a long time. One day, as he was steeped in melancholy thoughts about what had happened to him, he went out to try to comfort himself. Suddenly he heard the distant sound of trampling horses behind him and cried out, "The judgment of Allah is on me!" And he looked around for a hiding place but could not find anything. At last he saw a closed door, which he pushed until it gave way. Then he entered a long gallery in which he concealed himself, but no sooner had he done this than two men grabbed him and yelled, "Praise be to Allah for having delivered you into our hands, you infidel! For three nights you've robbed us of our rest and sleep, and you almost brought us to the brink of death!"

"What's wrong with you?" my brother asked.

And they answered, "Don't try to deceive us! We know that you've been plotting to kill the master of the house. Isn't it enough that you've brought him to poverty, you and your companions? But now give us the knife with which you've been threatening us every night!" Then they searched him and found his cobbler's knife stuck in his belt.

"Oh good people," my brother said, "please don't hurt me. Let me explain."

"You'd better be brief," they said.

So he told them his story with the hope that they would let him go. However, they paid no attention to what he said. Instead, they beat him and tore off his clothes. When they found the scars from his other beatings, they cried out, "You scoundrel! These marks are clearly signs of your guilt!" Then they took him to the governor, while he said to himself, "Now I'm going to be punished for my sins, and only Allah Almighty can save me!"

The governor began his interrogation right away by asking, "Why were you going to murder the master of that house, you villain?"

"By Allah," my brother answered, "I implore you to listen to my story and not to be hasty in condemning me!"

But the governor cried, "Why should I listen to a thief, who's driven these people to poverty and has the scars of a criminal on his back?"

So, without further ado, he sentenced my brother to receive a hundred lashes with a whip, and after this was done, they paraded my brother around the city and proclaimed, "This is what happens to all those robbers who break into people's homes!" Then they banished him from the city, and my brother wandered at random until I heard what had happened to him. Of course, I went in search for him, and when I found him, he told me all about his bad luck. After that I brought him secretly back to Baghdad and gave him an allowance for food and drink.

Then the caliph gave ear to

The Barber's Tale of His Fifth Brother

My fifth brother, Al-Nashshar, the Tattler, had both his ears lopped off, and he made his living as a beggar. Now, our father was a very old and sick man, and when he died, he left us seven hundred dirhams. So each son took his portion of one hundred, but my fifth brother did not know what he should do with his money. After a while he decided to invest it in all sorts of glassware and earn an honest penny by selling it. Therefore, he bought a hundred dirhams' worth of glassware, and after putting it all on a big tray, he sat down to sell it on a bench at the foot of a wall against which he leaned back.

As he sat with the tray before him, he began musing and said to himself, "Let's see now. I've invested a hundred dirhams in this glassware, and I'll certainly sell it for two hundred. Then I'll take the two hundred and double that until I've made at least four thousand. After I've accumulated all this money I'll buy merchandise, jewels, and attars and make a great profit, and, Allah willing, I'll build a capital of a hundred thousand dir-

hams. Then I'll purchase a fine house with white slaves, eunuchs, and horses, and I'll eat, drink, and enjoy myself. Moreover, I'll summon every singer and musician to my house and have them perform for me."

These were the thoughts that came to him while the tray of glassware, worth a hundred dirhams, stood on the bench before him, and after looking at it, he continued: "Once I've made a hundred thousand dirhams, I'll send out a matchmaker to arrange a marriage for me with the wife of the eldest daughter of the prime minister, for I've heard that she is perfectly beautiful and lovely and extremely talented. I'll offer her a marriage settlement of one thousand dinars, and if her father consents, all the better. If not, I'll take her by force from under his very nose. When she is safe at my house, I'll buy her ten little eunuchs, and for myself I'll buy a robe that only kings and sultans wear. Moreover, I'll purchase a saddle of gold and a bridle with valuable gems. After I mount the steed, my mamelukes will precede me, and I'll make the rounds of the city while the people salute and bless me. Finally, I'll go to the vizier, the father of my lady, with armed white slaves all around me, and when he sees me, he'll rise and offer me his place and sit down below me, for I'm to be his son-in-law. Now I'll have two eunuchs with me, and they'll be carrying purses, each containing two thousand dinars. One will be given to him as settlement for my marriage to his daughter, and the other as a gift to show him how generous I am. And for every ten words that he addresses to me, I'll answer him with two. Then back I'll go to my house, and whoever comes to me on the part of the bride, I'll give him a present of money and bestow a robe of honor on him. But if he brings me a gift, I'll refuse to accept it so that he may learn how proud I am and that nobody can denigrate me. In this way I'll establish my rank and status. After all the ceremonies are completed, I'll set a date for the wedding night and adorn my house in splendor. And when the time for displaying the bride arrives, I'll put on my finest clothes and sit down on a mattress of gold brocade. With my elbows propped up by pillows, I'll look just straight ahead of me to show how solemn and serious I am. And there before me will be my wife in her raiment and ornaments, lovely as the full moon. In my loftiness and majesty, I won't glance at her until those present say to me, 'Oh lord and master, your wife and slave is standing before you. Grant her one look, or else she'll be worn out by standing.' Then they'll kiss the ground before me many times, whereupon I'll raise my eyes and cast one single glance at her and quickly lower my eyes again. Then they'll carry her to the bride chamber, and I'll arise and change my clothes to put on even finer clothes. Then, when they bring in my bride a second time, I won't deign to throw her a look until they have begged me many times. Even then I'll only throw her a glance out of the corner of one eye and quickly lower my head. I'll continue to act this way until the displaying of the bride is finished."

And Scheherazade noticed that dawn was approaching and stopped telling her story. When the next night arrived, however, she received the king's permission to continue her tale and said,

Steeped in his daydreaming, my brother continued projecting into the future: "Upon the conclusion of this ceremony, I'll order one of my eunuchs to bring me a bag of five hundred dinars, which I'll give to the slave girls as a gift, and then I'll order them to lead me to the bride chamber. When they leave me alone with my bride, I'll neither look at her nor speak to her, but I'll lie down by her side with my face to the wall showing my contempt so that everyone will notice how high and mighty I am. Soon her mother will enter, and after kissing my hand, she'll say to me, 'Oh lord, look kindly upon your bride, who's longing for your favor. Please heal her broken spirit!' I'll refuse to answer, and when she sees this, she'll say, 'Oh my lord, my daughter is truly a beautiful maid, who has never been intimate with a man. If you continue to show her your aversion, her heart will break. So please turn toward her and speak to her and soothe her mind and spirit.' Then the mother will rise, fetch a cup of wine, and say to her daughter, 'Stand up and offer it to your lord.' But when she approaches me, I'll let her stand between my hands. First I'll prop my elbows on a round cushion lined with gold thread and lean back lazily without looking at her so that she may consider me like a

majestic sultan. Then she'll say to me, 'Oh my lord, may Allah bless you. Please don't refuse this cup from my hands, for I am bound to you.' However, I still won't speak to her, and she'll insist by saying, 'I won't take no for an answer. You must drink it!' And she'll put the cup to my lips, but I'll shake my fist at her and give her a good kick with my foot like this!"

And just then my brother gave a kick with his toe and kicked over the tray of glassware, which fell to the ground, and all that was on it was broken to bits. "Oh you stupid idiot!" cried my brother. "This is what you get for being so proud!" Then he began to beat himself, tear his clothes, and weep. The people who were flocking to their Friday prayers saw him, and some pitied him while others paid no attention to him. He wept for quite a long time until a beautiful lady came up to him. She had a lovely aroma of musk and was riding a mule with a gold saddle followed by several eunuchs. Indeed, she was on her way to Friday prayers, and when she saw the broken glass and my brother weeping, her kind heart was moved to pity for him. So she asked him what was wrong, and he told her how he had wanted to sell his tray full of glassware but that it had fallen and shattered all over the place. Thereupon, she called one of her eunuchs and said to him, "Give this poor fellow whatever money you're carrying with you." And he gave my brother a purse containing five hundred dinars, and he almost died for joy when he received it. Then he offered his blessings to her and returned to his abode a substantial man. As he sat in his room trying to make up his mind what he should do with the money, someone rapped at the door. So he rose, and after opening the door, he saw an old woman, whom he had never seen before. "My son," said she, "prayer time is approaching, and I haven't washed my hands and face yet. So please let me use your lodgings for this purpose."

"Of course," my brother responded, and he told her to follow him. So she entered, and he brought her a basin so she could wash herself, while he sat down to gaze with joy at his dinars, which he had tied up in his belt for a purse. When the old woman finished her ablution, she came up to my brother and blessed him with a holy benediction, and in his gratitude, he took out two dinars and gave them to her while he said to himself, "This will be my voluntary contribution to help the poor."

When she saw the gold, she cried, "By Allah, why do you treat me like a beggar? Take back your money. I don't need it. And if you don't want it, return it to the lady who gave it to you when your glassware was broken. But if you want to marry her, I can help you in the affair, for she is my mistress."

"Really?" my brother responded. "But how can I gain access to her?"

"My son," she said, "she's taken a liking to you, but she's married to a wealthy man. So take all of your money with you and follow me so that I can lead you to the object of your desire. And when you're in her company, do not stint in using fair words of persuasion but bring them all to bear upon her. This is the way that you'll be able to enjoy her beauty and wealth to your heart's content."

My brother took all his gold, got up, and followed the old woman, hardly believing in his luck. Eventually, they came to a tall gate at which she knocked, and a slave girl came out and opened up. Then the old woman led my brother into a large sitting room spread with marvelous carpets and hung with curtains. There he sat down with his gold before him and his turban on his knee. No sooner had he sat down than a young lady in sumptuous garments came to him. Never had he seen a woman more beautiful, and my brother rose to his feet. After smiling and welcoming him, she signaled him to be seated. Then she ordered the door to be shut, and after her order was carried out, she turned to my brother, took his hand, and led him to a private chamber furnished with various kinds of brocades and gold cloth. Here he sat down, and she sat by his side and toyed with him for a while. At one point she stood up and said, "Don't move from this spot. I'll come back to you soon." And she disappeared.

Meanwhile, as he was sitting there, a huge black slave holding a drawn sword entered and said to him, "Woe to you! Who brought you here, and what do you want?"

My brother was tongue-tied out of terror and could not reply. So the blackamoor seized him, stripped off his clothes, and bashed him with the flat of the sword's blade until he fainted to the ground. The horrendous Negro thought that he had done him in, and my brother heard him cry, "Where is the slave girl with the salt?"

All at once a maiden entered carrying a large tray of salt. Then she began rubbing it into my brother's wounds, but he did not stir, fearing that the slave would find out that he was not dead and kill him for sure. When the slave girl went away, the Negro cried out, "Where is the guardian of the vault?"

Thereupon the old woman came in and dragged my brother by his feet to a cellar and threw him upon a heap of dead bodies. He lay in this place for two whole days, and fortunately for him, the salt was what saved his life, because it stopped the flow of the blood. Once he felt able to move, Al-Nashshar rose and opened the trapdoor in fear and trembling and crept out into the open. He continued crawling in the darkness and hid himself in the vestibule until dawn, when he saw the cursed old woman leave the house in quest of another victim. He managed to follow her without her noticing it and soon found his own lodgings, where he dressed his wounds and doctored himself until he recovered from the beating. Meanwhile he continued to watch the old woman and trailed her constantly. Although he saw her accost one man after another, he did not utter a word. However, once he was hale and hearty, he took some material and made it into a bag, which he filled with broken glass and tied around his waist. In addition, he disguised himself as a Persian so that no one could recognize him, and he hid a sword under his clothes. Then he went out and purposely encountered the old woman, speaking Arabic to her with a Persian accent. "Venerable lady," he said, "I'm a stranger and have just arrived here today. Since I don't know anyone, could you tell me where I could find some scales to weigh eleven hundred dinars? I'd be glad to give some of them to you for your help."

"I have a son who's a money changer," she replied. "So come with me before he leaves his house, and he'll weigh your gold."

"Lead the way!" my brother answered.

She led him to the house to which he had been taken before, and the young lady herself came out and opened the gate. Then the old woman smiled to her and said, "I'm bringing some ripe fruit today."

Then the damsel took my brother by the hand and led him to the same chamber as before, and after sitting with him for a while, she rose and said, "Don't move from your seat until I come back."

Soon the cursed slave entered. His sword was drawn, and he cried out, "Get up, for your time has come!"

So he rose, and as the slave walked in front of him, he drew the sword from under his clothes and chopped his head off. Then he dragged the corpse by the feet to the cellar and shouted, "Where's the slave girl with the salt?"

When the girl entered carrying the tray of salt, she saw my brother with the sword in his hand. As she turned to flee, he followed her and struck off her head. Then he shouted, "Where's the guardian of the vault?"

When the old lady entered, he said, "Do you recognize me again, you old hag?"

"No, my lord," she replied.

And he told her, "I'm the owner of the five hundred gold pieces, and you entered my house to snare me!"

"May Allah save me!" she cried out, but he had no mercy on her and struck her with the sword until he had sliced her in four pieces. Then he went to look for the young lady, and when she saw him, she almost lost her mind and cried out piteously, "I surrender! Mercy!"

So he spared her and asked, "What made you take up with this blackamoor?"

And she answered, "I was once a merchant's slave, and the old woman used to visit me until I took a liking to her. One day she said to me, 'We're going to have a marriage celebration at our house the likes of which you've never seen before, and I'd like you to come and enjoy everything.' 'Of course, I will,' I said, and after I put on my finest clothes and ornaments, I took a purse with me that contained a hundred gold pieces. Then she brought me here, and no sooner had I entered the house than the black seized me, and they kept me this way for three whole years and forced me to participate in their perfidious game."

Then my brother asked, "What does he have in this house?"

"A huge amount of wealth," she answered. "And if you're able to take it away with you, do so, and may Allah let you enjoy it."

My brother went with her, and she opened various chests with so many bags of money that he was astounded. Then she said to him, "Go now and fetch some men to carry away the money."

So he went out and hired ten men, but when he returned, he found the door wide open, the damsel gone, and nothing left but a small amount of coins and household goods. Realizing that the girl had tricked him, he opened the storerooms and took whatever was in them, along with the rest of the money, and left nothing in the house. He spent the night rejoicing, but when morning dawned, he found twenty troopers at the door, and they immediately arrested him and said, "The governor wants to speak to you!"

My brother implored them to allow him to return to his home and even offered them a large sum of money. But they refused, and after binding him with a rope, they set off. On the way they met a friend of my brother, and my brother clung to his skirt and asked him to intercede for his protection. The man stopped and asked them what the matter was, and they answered, "The governor has asked us to bring this fellow before him, and we are just carrying out his command."

My brother's friend urged them to release him by offering them five hundred dinars to let him go and telling them, "When you return to the governor, say to him that you were unable to find him."

But they would not listen to him and dragged my brother along on his face and set him before the governor, who asked, "Where have you gotten all this money and these goods?"

And he answered, "I pray for mercy!"

So the governor granted him mercy, and my brother told him everything that had happened to him from first to last, and he ended by saying, "Take whatever you want from what I have. Just leave me enough to support myself."

But the governor took all the goods and all the money for himself, and since he was afraid that the sultan might get wind of the affair, he told my brother to leave the city or else he would hang him.

"Your words are my command," my brother responded, and he set out for another town. On the way he was robbed by thieves, who stripped him, beat him, and lopped off his ears. When I heard the news of his misfortunes, I went out in search of him, and then I brought him secretly back into the city and gave him an allowance for food and drink.

After hearing this story, the caliph now gave ear to

The Barber's Tale of His Sixth Brother

My sixth brother was called Shakashik, or Many Clamors, and he was shorn of both lips. At one time he had been a rich man, who was driven to poverty. So one day he went out to beg to keep himself alive. When he was on the road he suddenly caught sight of a large and magnificent mansion with a separate large building at the entrance, where various eunuchs were sitting. My brother asked one of them who owned the mansion, and the eunuch replied, "The palace belongs to a scion of the Barmaki house."

So my brother stepped up to the doorkeepers and asked them for some alms.

"Enter," they said. "You'll get what you want from the vizier, our master, by the large gate."

Accordingly, he went in and walked until he came to a mansion of great beauty and elegance. It was paved with marble and had splendid curtains on the walls and a flower garden the likes of which he had never seen before. My brother stood there awhile as though he were bewildered and did not know which way to turn. Then he saw a chamber at the far end of the garden, and he went over to it and found a handsome man with a comely beard. When this person caught sight of my brother, he stood up, welcomed him, and asked him about himself, whereupon Shakashik told him that he was a needy soul and asked him for some charity. Upon hearing these words, the nobleman showed great concern, and after placing his hand to his fine robe, he tore it and exclaimed, "What! Am I in this city and you're going hungry? I can't bear such disgrace!" Then he promised my brother all sorts of things that would cheer him up and said, "Of course, you must now stay with me and eat of my bread."

"Oh my lord," answered my brother, "I can't wait any longer, for I am indeed dying of hunger."

So the nobleman cried out, "Boy! Bring a basin and jug!" And turning to my brother, he said, "Come here, my guest, and wash your hands."

My brother rose to do so, but he saw neither jug nor basin. Yet his host kept washing his hands with invisible soap in imperceptible water and cried out, "Bring the table!"

But my brother again saw nothing. Then the host said, "Honor me by eating this meat and don't be ashamed." And he kept moving his hand back forth to his face as if he were eating, and he said to my brother, "I'm puzzled that you're eating so little. Don't stint yourself, for I'm sure that you're famished."

So my brother began to pretend as though he were eating while his host kept saying to him, "That's it! Have you noticed how excellent the bread is? It's so white!"

However, my brother still did not see anything, and he said to himself, "This man is obviously fond of poking fun at people." So he replied, "My lord, in all my days, I've never tasted bread whiter or sweeter than this here."

"This bread was baked by a slave girl of mine whom I bought for five hundred dinars," he commented and then called out, "Boy! Bring in the meat pudding, and make sure there's plenty of fat in it." And turning to Shakashik, he said, "By Allah, have you ever seen anything finer than this meat pudding? Now, eat and don't be shy!" Soon he called out again, "Boy! Serve the marinated stew with the grouse in it." And he said to my brother, "Go to it, my guest, for truly you must be hungry." So my brother began moving his jaws as if chopping and chewing, while the host continued to call for one dish after another and yet produced nothing but orders to eat. Soon he cried out, "Boy! Bring us the chickens stuffed with pistachio nuts," and he said to my brother, "I fattened these chickens with pistachios, and I'm sure you've never tasted anything like them in your life."

"Oh my lord," replied my brother, "they are indeed first-rate."

Then the host began motioning with his hand as though he were giving my brother a mouthful, and he kept extolling the various dishes to Shakashik, whose hunger became so great that his soul lusted after just a bit of bread or barley scone.

"Did you ever taste anything more delicious than the seasoning of these dishes?" asked the nobleman.

"Never, my lord!" replied my brother.

"Eat heartily, and don't be bashful," said the host.

And the guest answered, "I've eaten my fill of meat."

Then the nobleman cried out, "Boy! Take away the meat, and bring in the sweets." And turning to my brother, he said, "Eat some of this almond conserve, for it is prime, and take one of the honey fritters before the syrup runs out."

"How can I ever thank you, my lord?" said my brother, and he began to ask him about the abundance of musk in the fritters.

"That's my custom," he responded. "I have them put a spoonful of musk in every honey fritter and half that quantity of ambergris."

Meanwhile my brother kept moving his head and jaws until the master cried, "Enough of this. Let's have the dessert! Eat some of the almonds, walnuts, and raisins, and don't be shy!"

But my brother replied, "Oh lord, I'm full. I really can't eat any more."

"If you like these good things," the host responded, "then you must eat. By Allah, I don't want you to remain hungry!"

"My lord," Shakashik said, "how can I be hungry after eating all these dishes?" Then he thought a moment and said to himself, "I'll do something that will make him regret these pranks."

"Bring the wine!" the host cried out, and he moved his hands in the air as if the boy had set the wine before them, and he gave my brother a cup. "Take this cup, and let me know if you like it."

"My lord," my brother replied, "it certainly smells good, but I'm accustomed to drink wine that's been aged at least twenty years."

"Well then, this is the very thing for you," said the nobleman. "You can't drink anything better."

"To your health," my brother motioned as though he were drinking.

"And to yours," replied the host, who began drinking. Then he handed my brother another cup, which he drank and then pretended to be drunk. All of a sudden, however, he took the host by surprise and slapped him on the nape of his neck so hard that the palace echoed with the sound of the blow. Then he gave him a second cuff, and the host cried aloud, "What's going on here, you scum of the earth?"

"My lord," my brother declared, "you've shown your slave a great deal of kindness by taking him into your house and offering him a sumptuous meal. Then you offered him the best of wines that made him so drunk that he became boisterous and wild. But since you have shown how noble you are, my lord, I'm sure that you will pardon his offense."

When the host heard my brother's words, he burst out laughing and said, "It's been my custom for a long time now to have my fun with people by playing the madcap, but never have I come across a single person who had the patience and cleverness to play along with me as well as you have! So, I forgive you, and I want you to become one of my boon companions and never leave me."

Then he ordered his servants in earnest to set the table, and they brought out all the dishes about which the nobleman had spoken in sport. In turn he and my brother ate until they were satisfied. After that they went to a salon, where they found damsels as beautiful as the moon. The women sang all kinds of songs and played all kinds of instruments, while the two men drank until their wine got the better of them. The host treated my brother like a familiar friend, so Shakashik became like his brother and received a robe of honor and was treated with a great deal of affection. Next morning the two began to feast and carouse again, and they continued to lead this life for a period of twenty years, at the end of which time the nobleman died. Then the sultan took possession of all his wealth and squeezed all the money out of my brother until he was left a pauper without a penny to his name. So he left the city and wandered aimlessly for a while.

However, during his wanderings he was attacked by wild Arabs, who bound him and took him to their camp, where his captor proceeded to torture him. "Give me your money," the Arab said, "or else I'll kill you!"

"By Allah!" my brother wept and replied. "I have neither gold nor silver. So you may do with me as you wish."

Then the chief of the bedouin drew out a knife with a broad blade. It was so sharp that if it were plunged into a camel's throat it could sever its jugular with one clean cut. It was with this knife that the chief sliced off my brother's lips. Nor did he release him at this time, for he was sure my brother had money somewhere.

Now, the chief had a fair wife, who in her husband's absence used to make advances to my brother and offer him favors. However, he resisted her. Then, one day, as she began to tempt him, he gave in and began playing with her on his lap. All of a sudden, the chief arrived and saw what was going on. "You villain!" he cried out. "You think you can defile my wife!" Then he took out his knife and cut off my brother's penis. Afterward he bound him on the back of a camel, took him to a mountain, and left him there to perish. Eventually he was found by someone who recognized him and gave him something to eat and drink and informed me about his condition. Of course, I left the city immediately and brought him back to Baghdad, where I gave him an allowance so he could support himself.

The End of the Barber's Tale

"So now, oh Commander of the Faithful, you've heard the history of my six brothers, and the reason why I told you these tales is that I didn't want to leave you with the impression that I was like any one of them. And now you also know that I have six brothers on my hands, and since I am more upright than they, I'm compelled to support the entire family."

When the caliph heard my entire story, and I told him everything about my brothers, he laughed and said, "You speak the truth, oh Silent Man! You are indeed a man of few words, nor are you intrusive. But now I want you to leave this city and settle somewhere else."

And he banished me under edict. So I left Baghdad and traveled in foreign countries until I learned about his death and the succession of another caliph. Then I returned to Baghdad, where I found that all my brothers had died. It was at this point that I encountered this young man, whom I saved from certain death with my kind efforts. Yet he slanders me and accuses me of something that is not in my nature to do. Indeed, I am certainly not meddlesome, impudent, or intrusive, and it was only due to him that I had to leave Baghdad again and travel in foreign countries until I came to this city."

The End of the Hunchback's Tale

"After hearing the barber's tale," the tailor said to the king of China, "we realized how garrulous he was and how he had victimized this young man. So we grabbed him, made him shut his mouth, and locked him up in a nearby home. Then we sat down in peace to eat and drink all the good things at the marriage celebration. When midafternoon prayer arrived, I left the party and returned home. But my wife greeted me with a sour look and said, 'While you go out and have a good time with your friends, you leave me sitting here all alone with nothing to do! Well, let me tell you something, unless you take me out and let me amuse myself for the rest of the day, you're going to be a divorced man!'

"So I took her out, and we amused ourselves until suppertime. On our way home we encountered this hunchback, who was drunk and spewing out some songs. As you know, I invited him to have supper with us and went out to buy some fried fish. When we sat down to eat, my wife took a piece of bread and some fish and stuffed them into his mouth, and he choked. Though I slapped him long and hard on his back, I couldn't prevent his death. Then I carried him to the house of this Jewish physician, who in turn threw him into the steward's house, and the steward managed to place him in the path of this Christian broker. All this happened to me just yesterday, my lord. Now, don't you think that this adventure is more wondrous than the story of your hunchback?"

When the king of China heard the tailor's tale, he shook his head with pleasure and surprise and said, "The adventure of the young man and that busybody of a barber is indeed more delightful and wondrous than the story of my lying knave of a hunchback!" Then he ordered one of his chamberlains to go with the tailor and bring the barber to him. "I want to hear what this Silent Man has to say, for he's the reason that I'm allowing you all to keep your lives," the king proclaimed. "After that we'll bury the hunchback, for he's been dead since yesterday."

And Scheherazade noticed that dawn was approaching and stopped telling her story. When the next night arrived, however, she received the king's permission to continue her tale and said,

So the chamberlain and the tailor went to the place in which the barber had been locked up, and soon they returned with him to the king, who looked him over very carefully, and he was surprised to see an ancient man over ninety with a dark complexion, long white beard, gray eyebrows, long nose, and tiny ears. In addition, he had a conceited and silly expression on his face, and the king could not help but laugh at this ridiculous figure.

"Oh Silent Man," the king said, "I want you to tell me something about your life."

"Allow me, my lord, to ask you first," the barber replied, "what has happened to this Christian, Jew, and Moslem? Why are all these people gathered here, and why is the corpse of the hunchback lying here?"

"Why do you ask?" said the king.

"I'm asking," responded the barber, "so that the king may know that I'm not an insolent person, busybody, or impertinent meddler. Moreover, those who have accused

me of being garrulous have committed slander, for I am known as the Silent Man, a name that suits me well!"

Then the king said to those gathered around him, "Tell the barber the story of the hunchback and what happened to him at supper. Also, tell him the stories told by the Christian, the Jew, the steward, and the tailor."

After all the stories were told again, the barber shook his head and said, "By Allah, this is marvelous! Unveil the corpse of the hunchback lying over there, and let me look at it."

After they took off the sheet that covered the hunchback's body, the barber sat down, took the hunchback's head in his lap, looked at his face, and laughed until he fell over on his back and said, "There's a simple explanation for each and every death, but the death of this hunchback is so unusual that it should be recorded in letters of liquid gold!"

The entire company including the king was astonished by the barber's words, and the king asked him, "What do you mean by all this?"

"My lord," said the barber, "I swear by all that is holy that there's still life in this gobbo golightly!"

Thereupon, he pulled a tube of ointment from his barber's belt and began rubbing the hunchback's neck and arteries with the salve. Then he took a pair of iron tweezers, and after inserting them into the hunchback's throat, he drew out the fishbone covered with blood. Suddenly, the hunchback sneezed heartily and jumped up as if nothing had happened and rubbed his face with his hands. "There's no god," he said, "but *the* God, and Mohammed is the Apostle of God."

Everyone present was astounded by this sight, and the king of China laughed until he fainted, and so did everyone else. Then the sultan said, "By Allah, this is the most marvelous thing I've ever seen! Oh my good Moslems and my soldiers, have any of you ever seen a man die and come back to life again? Truly, had Allah not sent this barber to him, the hunchback would be a dead man!"

And they all agreed that it was the most miraculous thing they had ever seen. Then the king of China ordered that the tale be recorded and stored in one of his royal parchment rooms. Following this, he bestowed robes of honor on the Jew, the Christian, and the steward and allowed them to depart in his good grace. Then he gave the tailor a sumptuous garment and appointed him to the office of royal tailor with a suitable allowance. Moreover, he restored peace between the tailor and the hunchback, to whom he also gave a splendid garment and appropriate allowance. Finally, he was just as generous with the barber, who received a gift and a robe of honor. Moreover, he gave him a fine salary and made him barber-surgeon of state and one of his boon companions. Afterward they continued to lead the most pleasurable and delightful of lives, until the Destroyer of all earthly pleasure and the Sunderer of all societies arrived and ended their days.

No sooner had Scheherazade concluded her tale than she said, "And yet, oh king, this tale is no more wondrous than the story of the hedgehog and the pigeons."

The Hedgehog and the Pigeons

A hedgehog once came to a date tree on which a pigeon and his wife had built their nest, and it was plain to see that this couple was leading a comfortable life on this tree. So the hedgehog said to himself, "These pigeons are eating the fruit of the date tree, and I have no means of getting at the dates. Therefore, I'll have to find a way of tricking them to get my share." After saying this, he dug a hole at the foot of the palm tree and took up his lodging there with his wife. Moreover, he built a chapel beside the hole and went into retreat as though he were a devout monk renouncing the world. The male pigeon saw him praying and worshiping, and his heart softened toward him because of his pious ways.

"How many years have you been like that?" asked the pigeon.

"Thirty years," replied the hedgehog.

"What food do you eat?"

"Whatever falls from palm trees."

"What clothes do you wear?"

"Prickles," announced the hedgehog, "and I benefit from their roughness."

"And why have you chosen this place to dwell rather than some other location?" asked the pigeon.

"I prefer this place to all the others I've seen because it will allow me to guide those who are going astray down the right path and to teach the ignorant!"

"I thought you were much different," said the pigeon, "but now I wish I were more like you."

"I fear that you don't mean what you say," said the hedgehog. "You'll probably be like the farmer who, when it was time to plant seeds, neglected to do so with the excuse that he dreaded sowing seeds because they might not produce what he desired and cause him to lose his energy. When harvest time came, and he saw the people harvesting their crops, he regretted that he had failed to do what he should have done and died of sorrow."

"Well, tell me what I can do," replied the pigeon. "I'd like to free myself from all worldly things and obligations so that I can serve the Lord much better."

"You must begin preparing yourself for the next world," said the hedgehog, "Content yourself with a pittance of your provisions."

"How can I do this when I'm only a bird and unable to go beyond the date tree which provides me with my daily bread?" the pigeon responded. "And even if I could do so, I know of no other place where I could live."

"You can shake down enough fruit from the date tree to provide a whole year's supplies for you and your wife. Then you can set up your abode in a nest under the trunk so that you can pray and seek to be guided in the right way. After you've built your new nest, you can turn to the dates that you've shaken to the ground and carry them to your home, where you can store them and eat them whenever the need arises. After you run out of your provisions and time weighs heavily on your hands, you can observe total abstinence."

"May Allah bless you!" exclaimed the pigeon. "May He reward you for showing me the right path and reminding me of my duties."

Then he and his wife worked hard at knocking down the dates until nothing was left on the palm tree, while the hedgehog joyfully collected the dates and filled his den with the fruit, storing it up for the days to come. In his mind he kept thinking, "When the pigeon and his wife need some food to eat, they'll come to me, since they won't be able to live off their abstinence and devoutness. Since they've heeded my advice once, they'll draw near again, and I'll make a nice meal out of them. After that I'll have the place all to myself, and whatever drops from the date tree will be mine."

Once the pigeons had shaken all the dates from the palm tree, the pigeon and his wife descended and found that the hedgehog had removed all the dates to his own place.

"Hedgehog!" they cried out to him. "You pious preacher of good counsel, there's no sign of the dates, and we have nothing else to eat."

"The wind has probably carried them away," replied the hedgehog. "But turning from your provisions to the Provider is the essence of salvation, and He who has cleft the corners of the mouth has never left the mouth without nourishment." And he kept preaching to them in this way and making a show of piety. Indeed, he used such flowery speech that they eventually trusted him and entered his den without suspecting what might happen. Once they were inside, the hedgehog slammed the door shut and gnashed his teeth. Upon realizing how treacherous the hedgehog was, the pigeon said to him, "Do you know what tonight has to do with last night? Don't you know that there's a helper for the oppressed? Beware of treachery, or you'll suffer the same thing that happened to the two thieves who plotted against the merchant."

"What was that?" asked the hedgehog.

And the pigeon answered, "Let me tell you about

The Tale of the Merchant and the Two Thieves

In a city called Sindah there was once a very wealthy merchant who loaded his camels with goods and set out for a certain city with the purpose of selling his merchandise there. Now he was followed by two thieves, who had made bales out of whatever goods they could find, and pretending to be merchants themselves, they managed to join the merchant along the way. Beforehand they had agreed to trick the merchant at the first resting place they reached and to take all that he had. At the same time, each of the thieves had secretly planned to trick the other and thought that if he could cheat his comrade, he could have all the goods to himself, and everything would go well for him.

So, after planning their scheme, one of them took food and put poison in it and brought it to his comrade. Meanwhile the other had done the same, and they both ate poisoned food and died. Now, right before this they had been sitting with the merchant, and he began wondering why they were staying away so long. So he went in search of them and found the two lying dead. As a result, he knew the two were thieves who had plotted against him, but their rotten scheme had backfired. So the merchant was saved and took what they had.

"Oh Scheherazade," said the king, "these fables are not only edifying, they're delightful. Let me hear some more."

And when the next night arrived, Scheherazade began to relate

The Tale of the Thief and His Monkey

There was once a man who had a monkey, and this man was a thief who never entered any of the market streets of the city without walking off with some great profit. Now, it so happened that one day he saw a man offering worn clothes for sale in the market, but nobody desired to buy from him. Soon the thief who had the monkey saw the man with the old clothes place them in a wrapper and sit down to rest out of exhaustion. So the thief made the monkey play around in front of him to catch his eye, and while the man was busy gazing at the animal, he stole the parcel from him. Then he took the monkey and went off to a private place, where he opened the wrapper, took out the old clothes, and folded them neatly in a piece of costly stuff. Then he carried this bundle to another bazaar and offered the costly stuff and its contents for sale but only on the condition that the parcel not be opened at the market. Indeed, he tempted prospective buyers by setting a low price on the bundle. Some man was attracted by the beautiful wrapper and bought it under the condition set by the thief. When he took it home, he was certain that he had a bargain with him, and his wife asked him what he had bought.

"It's valuable stuff that I bought at an extremely low price, and I intend to sell it again and make a big profit," he boasted.

"You fool," she said, "would this stuff have been sold at such a low price unless it had been stolen? Don't you know that whoever buys something without examining it is bound to make a mistake, just as the weaver did?"

"And what happened to him?" the man asked.

And she related

The Tale of the Foolish Weaver

There was once a weaver who lived in a village, and despite the fact that he was very industrious, he could earn a living only by taking on additional work. Now it so happened that one of the rich men in the neighborhood held a wedding feast and invited all the people to attend. Everyone at the celebration was served delicious food, and the weaver saw that the master of the house made much ado about the guests who were wearing fine clothes. So the weaver said to himself, "If I change my craft for another that's more highly esteemed and better paid, I can amass a great deal of money and can buy splendid attire. Then I'll be able to rise in rank and be exalted in people's eyes just like these rich guests."

After a while he saw one of the mountebanks at the feast climb up a high wall and jump to the ground, where he landed on his feet. Impressed by this feat, the weaver said to himself, "I've got to show them that I can do what he did. It doesn't seem all that difficult." So he climbed the wall and proceeded to jump off it, whereupon he broke his neck and died.

* * *

"Now I've told you this tale," said the woman to her husband, "so that you'll try to earn money by doing what you know best and not be tempted by greed. Remember, it's hazardous to lust after things that are not within your reach."

"Not every wise man is saved by his wisdom," responded her husband, "nor is every fool lost by his folly. I have seen a skillful snake charmer bitten to death by the fangs of a snake, and I have watched others who know nothing whatsoever about serpents manage to tame them."

So he did not listen to his wife and continued to buy stolen goods below their value until he came under suspicion by the authorities and was sentenced to death.

No sooner had Scheherazade concluded her tale than she said, "And yet, oh king, this story is no more wondrous and edifying than the tale of the wily Dalilah and her daughter Zaynab."

The Wily Dalilah and Her Daughter Zaynab

During the time of Harun al-Rashid there were two men living in Baghdad who were former masters of fraud and stealth and were known to have done unusual things in their day. One was called Ahmad al-Danaf and the other Hasan Shuman, and the caliph decided at one point to bestow caftans of honor on them and make them captains of the watch for Baghdad. Moreover, they each received a salary of a thousand dinars a month and forty stalwart men under their command. So Ahmad and Hasan went forth in the company of the Emir Khalid, the chief of police, attended by their forty followers on horseback and preceded by the town crier, who proclaimed, "By order of the caliph, Ahmad al-Danaf and Hasan Shuman have been appointed captains of the watch, and both are to be obeyed and to be held in all honor and respect!"

Now there was an old woman called Dalilah the Wily who was living in the city at that time, and she had a daughter by the name of Zaynab the rabbit catcher. When they heard this proclamation about the new captains of the watch, Zaynab said to Dalilah, "You realize, don't you, Mother, that this fellow Ahmad al-Danaf came here from Cairo a fugitive and played the double-dealer in Baghdad until he wormed his way into the caliph's company? Now he's become a captain of the watch, while that mangy chap Hasan Shuman has also become a captain! Each one can count on a full meal every day and a monthly salary of a thousand dinars, whereas we're unemployed and have been discarded without rank and honor."

At one time Dalilah's husband had been town captain

of Baghdad with a monthly salary of one thousand dinars, but he had died, leaving two daughters, one married with a son named Ahmad al-Lakit, and the other called Zaynab, a spinster. And Dalilah herself had formerly been skilled in all kinds of trickery and double-dealing. Indeed, she could wile any dragon out of his den, and Iblis might have learned a thing or two about deception from her. Her father had also been governor of the caliph's carrier pigeons with a salary of one thousand dinars a month. He used to rear the birds to carry letters and messages, and in time of need each one of the pigeons had been dearer to the caliph than his own sons. So Zaynab said to her mother, "Let's get to work and make ourselves notorious with some clever scheme. Maybe that way we'll be able regain Father's salary for ourselves. It's the least we deserve."

And Scheherazade noticed that dawn was approaching and stopped telling her story. When the next night arrived, however, she received the king's permission to continue her tale and said,

"You can bet your life, daughter," Dalilah replied, "I'll show Baghdad some high-class tricks that will make Calamity Ahmad and Hasan the Pestilent look like mere amateurs."

After saying that, she rose and threw the Lisam veil over her face and donned clothes that the poorer Sufis generally wear: petticoat trousers falling over her heels and a gown of white wool with a broad belt. She also took a pitcher and filled it with water to the neck. After this she set three dinars in its mouth and stopped it up with a plug of palm fiber. Then she threw a rosary as big as a load of firewood around her shoulder, took a flag made of red, yellow, and green rags, and went out crying, "Allah! Allah!" As her tongue celebrated the praises of the Lord, her heart galloped in the devil's racecourse, seeking how she might play some sharp trick in the city. She walked from street to street until she came to an alley paved in marble and swept clean, where she saw a vaulted gateway with a threshold of alabaster and a porter standing at a door made of sandalwood, plated with brass, and furnished with a silver ring for a knocker. Now this house belonged to the chief of the caliph's sergeant-ushers, a man of great wealth who owned a great deal of property. He was called the Emir Hasan Sharr al-Tarik, or Evil of the Way, and he received this name because his sword preceded his word. He was married to a fair damsel called Khatun, whom he loved, and who had made him swear on the night that he took her virginity from her that he would take no other woman as a wife nor sleep away from home for one single night. And so things went that way until one day he went to the court and saw that each emir had a son or two with him. Then he entered the Hammam bath, looked at his face in the mirror, noted that the white hairs in his beard overlay the black, and said to himself, "By my father's death, I must have a son!"

So he went to his wife in an angry mood, and when she said good evening to him, he replied, "Get out of my sight! From the day you came into my life nothing good has happened to me."

"How so?" she asked.

"On the night I took your maidenhead," he said, "you made me swear that I wouldn't take another wife, and today I've seen each emir with a son and some even with two. So I realized I was getting older and closer to death and have yet to have a son or daughter. You know as well as I do that whoever leaves no male progeny behind him will not be remembered. This is the reason for my bad mood, for you are barren, and knowing you is like plowing a field full of rocks."

"By Allah!" she cried. "It's true that I've become a bit worn out with beating wool and pounding rugs, but I'm not to blame. You're the one who's barren, for you're a snub-nosed mule, and your sperm is weak and watery so that I can't get pregnant or have children."

"When I return from my journey," he declared, "I intend to take another wife!"

"Allah will decide our fates, not you!" she replied.

Then he left her, and both regretted the sharp words that they had spoken to each other. Now, as the emir's wife glanced out of her lattice window, she looked as beautiful as one of the fairy damsels who guard hidden treasures, for she was wearing a great deal of sparkling jewelry, and Dalilah caught sight of her from the street and admired her costly clothes and ornaments. "It would be a marvelous trick," she said to herself, "if I could entice that young lady from her house, strip her of all her jewels and clothes, and make off with the whole lot." So she took a position under the windows of the emir's house and began calling loudly, "Allah! Allah! Gather around me, you friends of the Lord! Come to me!"

Since she was crying so loudly, every woman in the street looked from her window, and seeing a woman clad in Sufi fashion with clothes of white wool as if she were a pavilion of light, they said, "Allah, bless and help this pious old person, whose face radiates light!"

And Khatun burst into tears and said to her slave girl, "Go down, oh Makbulah, and kiss the hand of Sheikh Abu Ali, the porter, and tell him to let that pious old lady enter our house so that I may get a blessing from her."

So the slave girl went down, and after kissing the porter's hand, she said, "My mistress tells you to let the pious old woman come in so that she may get a blessing from her, and perhaps her benediction will cover us as well."

And Scheherazade noticed that dawn was approaching and stopped telling her story. When the next night arrived, however, she received the king's permission to continue her tale and said,

The gatekeeper went up to Dalilah to kiss her hand, but she withdrew it and said, "Get away from me or else my ablution will be made null and void! You, too, are drawn to God and kindly regarded by Allah's saints and are under His special protection. May He deliver you from your servitude!"

Now the porter had not been paid for three months by the emir and was still having difficulty in obtaining his wages from his lord. Therefore he said to the old woman, "Oh mother, give me something to drink from your pitcher so that I may be blessed through you."

She took the pitcher from her shoulder and whirled it around in the air so that the plug flew out of its mouth and the three dinars fell to the ground. When the porter saw them, he picked them up and said to himself, "Glory to God! This old woman is one of the saints that have treasures at their command. She's discovered that I'm in need of money for my daily expenses and has conjured these three dinars out of the air for me." Then he said to her, "Mother, take these three dinars that fell from your pitcher."

And she replied, "Get them away from me! I don't concern myself with worldly things. No, never! Take them and use them for your own benefit in place of those that the emir owes you."

"May Allah bless you for your help!" he said. "This is straight out of the chapter of revelation!"

Thereupon the slave girl approached her, kissed her hand, and led her to her mistress. Dalilah found the lady looking like a treasure whose guardian talisman had been cut away, and Khatun welcomed her and kissed her hand.

"My daughter," said Dalilah, "I've come to save you, not because of your wealth but for the sake of Allah."

When Khatun had food set before her, she said, "My daughter, I eat nothing but the food of paradise, and except for five days in the year I fast most of the time. But, my child, I see that you are sad, and I want you to tell me the cause of your distress."

"Mother," replied Khatun, "I made my husband swear on our wedding night that he would take no other wives but me. However, he's seen other men with children and has said to me, 'You're nothing but a barren turf!' And I replied, 'You're a mule with dried-up sperm.' And now, just before he left on a trip, he became angry with me and said, 'When I come back from my journey, I'm going to take another wife!' Well, if he has children from another wife, they will get his money, and he has a great deal from the property and land he owns."

"My daughter," Dalilah said, "you evidently haven't heard of my master, Sheikh Abu al-Hamlat. Well, if anyone in debt visits him, the debt is canceled through Allah. More important for you, when a barren woman visits him, she conceives."

"Oh mother," Khatun replied, "ever since the day I married I've remained in this house. I've not even left it to pay condolence visits or to attend celebrations."

The old woman replied, "Have no fear, I'll take you to him, and you can reveal your sorrows and make a vow to him. Perhaps when your husband returns from his journey and sleeps with you, you'll conceive through him and give birth to a girl or a boy. But whether it be female or male, it will be a dervish of the Sheikh Abu al-Hamlat."

Thereupon Khatun rose and dressed herself in her richest raiment and put on all her jewelry. Turning to her maid, she said, "Keep an eye on the house."

"As you say," said the slave.

Then she went down the stairs with Dalilah, and the porter Abu Ali met her and asked, "Where are you going, mistress?"

"I'm going to visit the Sheikh Abu al-Hamlat," she answered.

"My lady," he said, "the old woman who is with you is truly one of Allah's holy saints. She has hidden treasures at her command and helped me without my asking her. She even knew that I was in need of money."

As Dalilah escorted Khatun beyond the gate, she said, "My daughter, after you have visited the Sheikh Abu al-Hamlat, your soul will be comforted, and with Allah's permission, you will conceive, and through the sheikh's blessings your husband will love you and never utter a spiteful word toward you again."

"Oh, let us go and visit him!" Khatun responded.

But Dalilah said to herself, "Where can I take her so I can strip her and steal her clothes and jewelry? There are too many people here." Then she turned to Khatun and said, "My daughter, walk behind me and keep within sight of me, for your mother is terribly burdened. Everyone who has a burden casts it on me, and all who have pious offerings to make give them to me and kiss my hand."

So the young lady followed her at a distance while her anklets tinkled and her braids clinked with their gold coins as she went. After they reached the bazaar, they came to the shop of a young merchant named Sidi Hasan, who was very handsome and had no hair on his face. When he saw the young lady approach, he began throwing stolen glances at her, and when Dalilah saw this, she beckoned Khatun and said, "Sit down in front of this shop until I return to you."

Khatun obeyed her and sat down in front of the young merchant, and each glance that he cast at her cost him a thousand sighs. Then Dalilah entered the shop and saluted him. "Tell me," she said, "isn't your name Sidi Hasan, son of the merchant Mohsin?"

"Yes," he replied, "Who told you my name?"

"Some reputable people directed me to you," she said. "The lady sitting in front of your shop is my daughter, and her father was a merchant who died and left her a great deal of money. Since she has come of marriageable age, the wise men have told me, 'Offer your daughter in marriage, and not your son.' Well, today is the first day she has left our house since she was born, and this is because I have finally received a secret and divine command that I should wed her to you. So, if you are poor, I'll give you enough capital so you can open two shops instead of one."

Upon hearing this, the young man said to himself, "I asked Allah for three things—coin, clothing, and conjugality." Then he turned to Dalilah and remarked, "Mother, your intentions are good, but I've always been told not to marry unless I see what I am getting into."

"Rise and follow me," Dalilah said, "and I'll show her to you without her veil."

So he got up and took a thousand dinars with him, for he thought to himself, "Perhaps I'll need to buy something or pay the fees for a marriage contract."

And Scheherazade noticed that dawn was approaching and stopped telling her story. When the next night arrived, however, she received the king's permission to continue her tale and said,

The old woman told him to walk behind the young lady at a distance but to keep her in sight, and she said to herself, "Where can I take the young lady and the merchant so I can strip them both while his shop is closed?"

Then she walked on followed by Khatun and the young merchant until she came to a dyer's shop owned by a man named Hajj Mohammed, a man with a bad reputation, who loved to eat both figs and pomegranates and cut the male and female leaves of the colocasia both ways. Well, he heard the tinkle of the anklets and, when he raised his head, he saw the lady and the young man. So the old woman came up to him and, after saluting him and sitting down opposite him, she asked, "Are you Hajj Mohammed the dyer?"

He answered, "Yes, I am. What do you want?"

"Some reputable people have directed me to you," she said. "Look at that beautiful girl, my daughter, and that handsome beardless youth, my son. I brought them both up and spent much money on both of them. Now, I'll have you know that I have a big old house that is in ruins. So I've had to shore it up with wood, and the builder told me to go and live in some other place or else it will collapse on me. Only when he has finished repairing it can I return. So I left the house to look for new lodgings, and these reputable people directed me to you, and I would like my son and daughter to live with you."

When the dyer heard all of this, he thought to himself, "Truly, this is like icing on some cake for me." Then he said to the woman, "It's true that I have a house with a salon and upper floor, but I can't spare any part of it because I need it all for my guests and clients."

"My son," she replied, "it will only be a month or two at the most until our house is repaired. You would be doing us a big favor, for we are strangers here. We can share the guest chamber, you and us, and by my life, if you desire your guests to be ours, we will welcome them and eat and sleep with them."

Upon hearing this, he gave her three keys and said, "The big one is for the house, the crooked one for the salon, and the little one for the upper floor."

So Dalilah took the keys and led the young lady and the merchant to the house that was in a nearby lane. She opened the door and invited the damsel to come inside. "My daughter," she said, pointing to the salon, "this is the lodging of the Sheikh Abu al-Hamlat. But first, go to the upper floor and take off your outer veil and wait until I come to you."

So she went upstairs and sat down. Soon the young merchant entered, and Dalilah took him into the salon and said, "Sit down, while I fetch my daughter and show her to you."

So he sat down, and the old woman went upstairs to Khatun, who said, "I would like to visit the sheikh before the people come."

"My daughter," Dalilah replied, "we are worried about you."

"How come?" she said.

"Because one of my sons lives here," she replied, "who believes in leading a totally natural life and can't tell summer from winter. He walks around naked all the time and is the sheikh's deputy, and if he were to see a woman like you come to visit his chief, he would snatch her earrings, tear her ears, and rip off her silken robes. So please take off your jewelry and clothes, and I'll keep them safe for you until you have finished your pious visit with the sheikh."

Accordingly, the damsel took off her outer dress and jewels and gave them to the old woman, who said, "I'll place them on the sheikh's curtain for you so that you'll be blessed."

Then she went out of the room, leaving the lady in her shift and petticoat trousers, and she hid the clothes and jewels in the staircase. After that she went to the young merchant, whom she found impatiently waiting for the girl, and he cried, "Where is your daughter? I want to see her!"

But she put her hand to her head and shook it as if very worried.

"What's the matter?" he asked.

"There are evil-minded and jealous neighbors here!" she exclaimed. "They saw you enter the house with me and asked about you. And I told them that this is the bridegroom I found for my daughter. Well, they were so jealous because of you that they said to my daughter, 'Has your mother become so tired of supporting you that she's going to marry you to a leper?' Because of this, I had to swear to her that she could see you naked, and indeed, she refuses to see you any other way."

"May Allah protect me from such jealous neighbors!" he said.

"Have no fear," Dalilah said, "for you'll see her just as naked as you will be."

So he said, "Well then, let her come and look at me."

Thereupon he took off his pelisse, sables, belt, dagger, and the rest of his raiment except for his shirt and bag trousers. He was about to place the purse with the thousand dinars with them, but Dalilah cried out, "You'd better give that to me. I'll put it in a safe place."

So she took the purse and left the room. After she fetched the girl's clothes and jewelry, she put everything together in a sack and made sure to lock the door to the house before she left it and went her way.

And Scheherazade noticed that dawn was approaching and stopped telling her tale. When the next night arrived, however, she received the king's permission to continue her tale and said,

Dalilah went straight to a druggist, who was a friend of hers, and she deposited her spoils with him. Then she returned to the dyer, whom she found sitting and awaiting her.

"Tell me," he said, "does the house please you?"

"It's a blessing for us," she said. "Now I have to go and hire porters to carry our goods and furniture there. But my children have asked me for a panade with meat, and I would appreciate it if you would take this dinar, buy a dish, and enjoy a meal with them."

"But who will guard the shop and the people's goods that are in it while I'm gone?" he asked.

"Your assistant," said the old woman.

"So be it," he replied and went out to do her bidding.

Meanwhile Dalilah ran and fetched the clothes and jewels she had left with the druggist, returned to the shop, and said to the assistant, "Run and bring back your master. I've got something important to tell him. I'll watch the place until you both return."

"As you wish," he answered and went away, leaving her time to collect all the customers' goods. Soon a mule driver appeared, a scavenger, who had been out of work a week, and who was a hashish eater to boot. Dalilah caught sight of him and called to him, "Come here, mule driver!" So he went over to her, and she asked to him, "Do you know my son, the dyer?"

And he replied, "Yes, I know him."

Then she said, "The poor fellow is loaded with debts and has become insolvent. Every time he's slapped in prison, I must set him free. Now I want to see him declared bankrupt, and I'm going to return the goods to their owners. So lend me your ass to carry the load, and you can have this dinar. When I'm gone, take the handsaw and empty out the vats and jars and break them so that if an officer from the kazi's court comes, he'll find nothing in the shop."

"Since I owe Hajj a favor," he replied, "I'll gladly repay him for Allah's sake, too."

So he loaded the things on the ass and set out for her house, where she arrived in safety and went inside to see her daughter, Zaynab, who said to her, "Mother, I was worried about you! What have you been up to? What trouble have you caused?"

"I've played four tricks on four poor souls," Dalilah replied. "The wife of the sergeant usher, a young merchant, a dyer, and a mule driver. And I've brought you all their spoils on the donkey."

"Oh Mother," Zaynab cried, "you'll never be able to go around town anymore. The sergeant usher is a man to be feared. Besides, you'll also have to worry about the merchant, dyer, and mule driver."

"Pooh, my girl!" Dalilah responded. "I'm not concerned about any one of them, except the mule driver, who knows me."

Meanwhile the dyer bought the meat panade and set out for the house followed by his servant with the food on his head. On the way there, he passed his shop, where he found the donkey boy breaking the vats and jars so that there was neither stuff nor liquids left in them and the dyery was a wreck.

"Stop! What are you doing!" yelled the dyer.

And the mule driver stopped and cried out, "Praise be to Allah that you're safe! Truly, my heart was with you."

"How so?" the dyer asked.

"Why, everyone knows that you've become bankrupt and that they've filed a docket concerning your insolvency."

"Who told you this?"

"Your mother told me, and she also told me to break the jars and empty the vats so that the kazi's officers would find nothing in the shop if they come."

"May Allah curse her living soul!" the dyer shouted. "My mother died a long time ago." And he beat his breast and shouted even louder, "Alas, all my goods are lost, and all the goods of my customers!"

The mule driver also exclaimed, "Alas, my ass is lost!" And he turned to the dyer and bawled, "Give me back my ass! Your mother stole it from me!"

But the dyer grabbed hold of him by the throat and began slapping him and said, "Bring me the old woman!" And the mule driver boy fought back and said, "Give me back my donkey."

So they beat and cursed each other until a large crowd of people gathered around them.

And Scheherazade noticed that dawn was approaching and stopped telling her story. When the next night arrived, however, she received the king's permission to continue her tale and said,

One of the people in the crowd intervened in the fight and asked, "What's the matter, Master Mohammed?"

"I'll tell you what the matter is," answered the mule driver, and he concluded his story by saying, "I thought I was doing the dyer a favor, but when he saw me, he beat his breast and said, 'My mother is dead!' And now I for one want my ass back from him, since he's the one who pulled this trick on me and caused me to lose my donkey."

Then the people began asking the dyer, "Master Mohammed, how long have you known this woman, and why did you trust her to look after your shop and all the goods in it?"

"I hardly know her," he replied, "but she took lodgings with me today, for herself and her son and daughter."

"In my judgment," one person said, "the dyer is bound to pay back the mule driver."

"Why so?" asked another.

"Because," replied the first, "the mule driver wouldn't have trusted her and given her his ass if he hadn't seen her watching over the dyer's shop."

And a third person said, "Master, since you've given her lodgings, I think you're obligated to get the man back his ass."

Then they all set out for the house to see what was going on there.

In the meantime the young merchant had been waiting

for the old woman to come to him with her daughter, but she did not come, nor did her daughter appear. At the same time the young lady in question had also been waiting for her to return with her son the sheikh's deputy, so that she could present herself to the holy one. Tired of waiting, she got up to visit the sheikh by herself and went down into the salon, where she found the young merchant, who said to her, "Come here! Where is your mother, who brought me here to marry you?"

"My mother is dead," she replied. "Are you the old woman's son, the deputy of Sheikh Abu al-Hamlat?"

"The swindling old trot is no mother of mine," he said. "She's cheated me and taken my clothes and a thousand dinars."

"And she's swindled me, too!" Khatun exclaimed. "She brought me here to see the Sheikh Abu al-Hamlat, and instead, she's stripped me of my clothes and jewelry."

Thereupon all at once he declared, "It's up to you to make good my clothes and my thousand dinars!"

"What?" she cried. "I look to you to make good my clothes and jewelry!"

Just at this moment the dyer barged into his house, and seeing them both stripped of their raiment, he demanded, "Tell me where your mother is!"

So the young lady related everything that had happened to her, and the young merchant told him everything that had happened to him, and the dyer exclaimed, "Alas, all my goods are gone, and those of my customers as well!"

And the mule driver cried out, "Alas, my ass is gone! Dyer, give me back my ass!"

Then the dyer said, "This old woman is surely a thief, and I want the two of you out of here right now so I can lock the door."

But the merchant said, "It would be a disgrace for you if we were to enter your house dressed and leave it undressed."

So the dyer clad him and the damsel and sent her back to her house. Then he went with the young merchant and the mule driver to his shop, and after shutting it, he said, "Come, let's go to the chief of police."

So they went to the chief of police and lodged a complaint against Dalilah, and he asked, "What do you want me to do?" And when they told him that they wanted him to arrest her, he replied, "Do you know how many old women there are in this city who fit her description? Get out of here! First you go and look for her, and when you find her, bring her back here, and I'll torture her for you and make her confess."

So they went off and began looking for her all over the city.

As for the wily Dalilah, she said to her daughter, "I'm in the mood to play another trick."

"Mother," Zaynab said, "I'm worried about you."

But the old woman laughed and said, "I'm like the bean husks that neither fire nor water can destroy." So she rose, put on a slave girl's dress, and went out to look for someone to swindle. Soon she came to a bystreet and saw a magnificent house that had carpets spread before it and bright lamps hanging from its walls, and she heard some women singing and the drumming of tambourines. While she was standing there, she saw a slave girl with a boy on her shoulder. He was clad in trousers laced with silver and was wearing a little Aba cloak of velvet with a pearl-embroidered tarbush cap on his head, and around his neck was a chain of gold set with jewels.

Now the house in which this celebration was taking place belonged to the provost of the merchants of Baghdad, and the boy was his son. In addition, he had a virgin daughter, who was soon to be married, and they were celebrating her betrothal that day. Her mother was surrounded by a company of noble women and singers, and whenever she went upstairs or downstairs, her son had clung to her. That is why she had called the slave girl and said, "Take the young master, and play with him until the company breaks up."

Upon seeing this, Dalilah approached the slave girl and asked her what was being celebrated in her mistress's house.

"Her daughter is being married today," she said, "and that is why she has singing women with her."

And so Dalilah said to herself, "The thing to do is to spirit this boy away from the maid!"

* * *

And Scheherazade noticed that dawn was approaching and stopped telling her tale. When the next night arrived, however, she received the king's permission to continue her tale and said,

All of a sudden, Dalilah began crying out, "Oh disgrace! Oh bad luck!" Thereupon, she pulled out a brass token resembling a dinar, and she said to the maid, who was a simpleton, "Take this ducat, and go inside to your mistress and tell her, 'Umm al-Kayr rejoices with you and is beholden to you for the favors that you have bestowed on her. On the day of the assembly she and her daughters will visit you and give the servant women the usual gifts.' "

"Oh mother," said the slave girl, "my young master here grabs hold of his mama whenever he sees her."

"Well," Dalilah replied, "give him to me while you run in and come back."

So she gave her the child, took the token, and ran inside the house, while Dalilah made off with the boy to a bylane, where she stripped him of his clothes and jewels. Then she thought to herself, "It would be indeed the finest of tricks to carry on the game and pawn the boy for a thousand dinars." So she went to a jewelry market, where she saw a Jewish goldsmith seated with a cage full of jewelry before him and said to herself, "It would be a rare trick to cheat this Jewish fellow and get some jewelry worth a thousand gold pieces from him by pawning this boy as my deposit for the jewels."

When the Jew looked up at them and saw the boy with the old woman, he recognized him as the son of the provost of the merchants. Now the Israelite was a man of great wealth, but he was always desirous of buying and selling, even though he did not have to. Therefore, when he caught sight of Dalilah, he said, "What are you looking for, mistress?"

Since she had already inquired about his name, she asked, "Are you Master Azariah, the Jew?"

"Yes," he answered.

"This boy's sister, daughter of the shahbandar of the merchants, is having her betrothal celebrated today," she said, "and she needs jewelry. So give me two pair of gold ankle rings, a brace of gold bracelets, pearl earrings, a belt, a poignard, and a regal ring."

He brought them out, and altogether she collected a thousand dinars' worth of jewelry. "I'll take these ornaments on approval, and the jewels that please them they will keep, and I'll bring you the money for them. In the meantime I'll leave the boy here with you until I return."

"As you wish," he said.

So she took the jewelry and set off for her own house, where her daughter asked whether she had pulled off another trick, and Dalilah told her how she had stripped the shahbandar's boy.

"You'll never be able to walk about the town again in broad daylight," Zaynab said.

In the meantime the slave girl had gone inside to her mistress and said, "My lady, Umm al-Khayr salutes you and rejoices with you, and on assembly day she will come with her daughters and give the customary presents."

"Where is your young master?" asked her mistress.

"I left him with her," she said. "I was afraid that he might cling to you, and she gave me this dinar as a token for the singing women."

So the lady passed on the money to the chief of the singers, who took it, and when she saw that it was a brass counter, she yelled at the maid, "Get out of here, you whore, and look after your young master!"

Frightened, the slave girl went outside, and when she could not find the boy or the old woman, she shrieked aloud and fell on her face. The joy at the celebration was turned to sorrow, and the provost came running to his wife. After he learned what had happened, he went out in search of the child, while the other merchants also went forth to help him. After looking everywhere, the shahbandar finally spotted his son sitting naked in the Jew's shop and said to the owner, "This is my son."

"That's right," answered the Jew.

So overjoyed was he in finding in his son that the merchant picked him up without asking for his clothes, but the Jew grabbed hold of him and said, "Why are you treating me like this? By Allah, I think you'd even harm the caliph!"

"What's wrong with you, Jew?"

And he replied, "A little while ago the old woman

took a thousand dinars' worth of jewelry for your daughter, and she left your son as a pledge for the jewels. I certainly would not have trusted her, but I recognized your son, and she offered to leave him here until she returned with the money."

"My daughter doesn't need any jewelry," said the provost. "Now give me the boy's clothes."

All at once the Jew shrieked, "Come and help me, good Moslems!"

But just at that moment, the dyer, the merchant, and the mule driver appeared on the scene in search of the old woman, and they asked the Jew and the provost why they were quarreling. So they told them what had happened, and the newcomers said, "The old woman is the same swindler who cheated us before you!"

Then they told the Jew and the provost what she had done to them, and the merchant said, "Since I've found my son, let his clothes be his ransom money! And if I ever meet that woman, I'll demand she pay me back." And he carried the child home to his mother, who was extremely happy that he was safe.

Then the Jew said to the three others, "Where are you going?"

"We're going to look for her," they said.

"Let me go with you," he said and added, "Do any of you know her?"

"I know her!" the mule driver cried out.

"If we all go looking for her together," said the Jew, "then we'll never catch her. She'll be able to spot us and escape. So let's each take a different path, and we'll all meet at the shop of Hajj Mas'ud, the barber."

They all agreed, and each set off in a different direction. Soon Dalilah went out again to play her tricks, and the mule driver bumped into her and recognized her immediately. So he grabbed hold of her and said, "Woe to you! Have you been up to this monkey business for a long time?"

"What's the matter with you?" she asked.

"Give me back my ass," he answered.

"If you look after yourself, Allah will look after you, my son," she replied. "Do you want your ass and all the other people's things as well?"

"I just want my ass," he said. "That's all."

"I saw that you were poor," she replied, "so I deposited your ass for you at the Moorish barber's shop. Stand here while I talk to him nicely so that he'll give you back your beast."

So she went up to the Moor, kissed his hand, and shed tears. Now, the barber was puzzled by this and asked her what the matter was, and she said, "Just look at my boy standing over there. He exposed himself to some foul air that's made him sick and disturbed his mind. He used to have a fine donkey, but he lost it, and now, if he stands, he says nothing but 'My ass!' and if he sits, he cries, 'My ass!' I brought him to a doctor, who told me that nothing will cure his sickness unless two of his molars are pulled out and he's cauterized on both temples. So please take this dinar and call him over to you. All you have to say is 'Your ass is with me.' "

"What a case!" said the barber. "May I fast for one whole year if I don't manage to make him stop worrying about his ass!"

Now the barber had two journeymen with him, and he told one of them to go and heat the irons, while the old woman went her way. Once the irons were hot, the barber called over to the mule driver, "Your ass is with me, good fellow! Come and get it. You won't have to worry about it anymore!"

So the mule driver came to him, and the barber led him into a dark room, where the journeymen knocked him down and bound him hand and foot. Then the barber pulled out two of his molars and cauterized him on both his temples. Then he let the mule driver get up, and he said, "Oh Moor, why have you done this to me?"

"Your mother told me that you lost your mind because of some illness," he said, "and she told me that all you could say was 'My ass!' and she asked me to fix you so that you'd stop worrying about it."

"May Allah pay you back for pulling out my teeth!" the mule driver said.

The barber kept trying to explain what had happened, and he left the shop arguing with the mule driver, who shouted, "May Allah torment her!" And they continued walking down the street and quarreling for some time. When the barber returned to his shop, he found it empty, for while he was gone, the old woman had taken all that was there to her daughter and told her what she had done.

Upon seeing his place plundered, the barber ran back to the mule driver, caught hold of him, and said, "Bring me your mother!"

But he answered, "I told you, she's not my mother! She's a thief who has swindled many people and has stolen my ass."

Just at this moment the dyer, the young merchant, and the Jew arrived, and when they saw the Moorish barber holding the mule driver, who had been cauterized on both temples, they asked, "What's happened to you?"

So he told them everything that had happened to him, and the barber did the same, and in turn the others told the Moor all about the tricks that the old woman had played on them. Then he shut his shop and went with them to the police chief's quarters, where they demanded that he look into their case and obtain recompensation for them.

"How many old women are there in Baghdad?" he asked again. "Tell me, do any of you know her?"

"I do," said the mule driver. "So give me ten of your officers."

So he gave them half a score of archers, and all five went out followed by the soldiers. Indeed, they patrolled the city until late at night. Finally, they captured her and took her to the police chief's house, where they waited under his office windows for him to come out. However, soon the guards fell asleep because they were tired of watching her, and Dalilah pretended to follow their example, while the mule driver and his comrades also nodded their heads in slumber. Upon seeing that they were all asleep, Dalilah crept away and went inside the chief's house and then into the harem, where she kissed the hand of the mistress of the house and asked her, "Where is the chief of police?"

The lady of the house answered, "He's asleep. What do you want from him?"

"My husband is a merchant of chattels," she said, "and he gave me five mamelukes to sell just before he departed on a journey. Well, the chief met me and bought them from me for a thousand dinars and two hundred commission for myself. And he told me to bring them to his house, and so I've brought them."

And Scheherazade noticed that dawn was approaching and stopped telling her story. When the next night arrived, however, she received the king's permission to continue her tale and said,

The lady of the house believed Dalilah's story and asked her, "Where are the slaves?"

"My lady," said Dalilah, "they are asleep under the window of your house."

When the lady looked out the window, she saw the Moorish barber clad in a mameluke habit while the young merchant looked like a drunken mameluke, and the Jew, the dyer, and the mule driver appeared to be shaven mamelukes. Indeed, the lady thought to herself, "Each of these white slaves is worth more than a thousand dinars." So she opened her chest and gave the old woman a thousand ducats and said, "You may go now, but come back later when my husband wakes up, and I'll give you the other two hundred dinars that he owes you as your commission."

"My lady," said Dalilah, "be so kind as to keep a hundred dinars for yourself, and the rest I'll procure when I return. Now, please let me out by the private door."

So the lady let her out, and Allah Almighty protected her, and she made her way home to her daughter and told her how she had obtained a thousand gold pieces and had sold her five pursuers into slavery. "Still," she concluded, "I'm worried about the mule driver, because he's the only one who knows me and can recognize me."

"Mother," Zaynab said, "why don't you stay put awhile and be content with what you've done. Remember, the crock won't always escape the shock."

Now, when the chief of police awoke, his wife said to him, "I'm very happy about the five slaves you bought from that old woman."

"What slaves?" he asked.

And she answered, "Stop toying with me. Allah willing, they'll suit our position very well."

"Upon my life," he said, "I haven't bought any slaves! Who told you this?"

"That woman," she said, "that merchant's wife from whom you bought them. Remember? You promised her a thousand dinars for them and two hundred for herself as a broker fee."

"Did you give her the money?" he asked.

"Yes," she replied. "After all, I saw the slaves with my own eyes, and each one of them is wearing a suit of clothes worth a thousand dinars. So I sent out the sergeants to look after them."

The chief of police got up and went outside, and when he saw the five plaintiffs, he asked the guards who were there, "Where are the five slaves we bought for a thousand dinars from the old woman?"

"There are no slaves here," they said. "Only these five men, who captured the old woman and brought her here. We fell asleep while waiting for you, and she crept away and entered the harem. Sometime later a maid came out and asked us, 'Are the five who came with the old woman with you?' and we answered, 'Yes.' "

"By Allah," cried the chief of police, "this is the worst of her swindles!"

And the five men said, "You're responsible for recovering our goods!"

"That old woman sold you to me for a thousand gold pieces," he said.

"That's not allowed," they declared. "We are freeborn men and aren't allowed to be sold. We'll appeal our case to the caliph!"

"Nobody showed her the way to the house except you," the chief said, "and I'm going to sell you to the galleys for two hundred dinars apiece."

Just then the Emir Hasan Sharr al-Tarik appeared. He had returned from his journey and had found his wife stripped of her clothes and jewelry and had learned about everything that had happened. Of course, he had responded by declaring, 'The chief of police will answer to me for all that's happened!' Therefore, when he showed up at the police chief's house, he said, "How can you allow old women to go around town and swindle people of their goods? You're not doing your duty, and I'm holding you responsible for my wife's property!"

Then he turned to the five men standing there and asked them, "What are you all doing here?"

So they told him their stories, and he said, "You've all been wronged." And turning to the chief of police, he asked, "Why are you arresting them?"

"These five men are responsible for bringing the old wretch to my house, and then she took a thousand dinars of my money and sold them to my wife."

Thereupon the five men cried out, "Oh Emir Hasan, please intercede for us!"

Then the chief of police said to the emir, "I'll assume responsibility for your wife's goods, and you have my pledge that I'll capture the old woman. But which one of you can recognize her?"

"We can all recognize her by now," they cried. "Just send ten officers with us, and we'll catch her."

So he gave them ten men, and the mule driver said, "Follow me. I could recognize her even if I were blindfolded."

So they went forth, and just as they were crossing a bystreet, they came upon old Dalilah and seized her once again. Then they brought her to the chief of police, who asked her, "Where are the people's goods?"

But she answered, "I've neither taken them nor seen them."

Thereupon he cried to the jailer, "Take her with you and lock her up in the jail until the morning."

But the jailer replied, "I won't take her, nor will I lock her up. If she plays one of her tricks on me, then I'll be held responsible, and I don't want that!"

So the chief of police mounted his horse and rode outside the city with Dalilah and the rest of the people to the bank of the Tigris, where he ordered the lamplighter to crucify her by her hair. So he drew her up by the pulley and bound her to the cross. After that the chief of police set ten men to guard her and went home.

Now, outside the city, a certain bedouin Arab was resting at a camp and heard one man say to a friend, "Praise be to Allah for your safe return! Where have you been all this time?"

"In Baghdad," replied the other, "where I broke my fast on honey fritters."

Then the Arab thought to himself, "I had better go to

Baghdad and eat honey fritters there," for he had never been to Baghdad nor seen fritters of this kind. So he mounted his stallion and rode toward Baghdad while saying to himself, "It must be a fine thing to eat honey fritters! Upon my honor as an Arab, I intend to have breakfast with honey fritters and nothing else!"

And Scheherazade noticed that dawn was approaching and stopped telling her story. When the next night arrived, however, she received the king's permission to continue her tale and said,

So the Arab continued riding until he came to the place where Dalilah was crucified, and she heard him utter his desire to eat honey fritters. When he saw her, he went up to her and asked her, "What are you doing here?"

"I ask for your protection, oh sheikh of the Arabs!" she said.

"May Allah indeed protect you!" he replied. "But why are you being crucified?"

"I have an enemy," she said. "He's an oilman, who fries fritters, and I stopped to buy some from him, but I happened to spit, and some of my spit fell on the fritters. So he complained to the governor, who ordered me to be crucified and said, 'I sentence you to be fed ten pounds of honey fritters on the cross. If you eat them, you may be set free. However, if you don't, you must continue to hang there until you die.' And surely I shall die, for my stomach can't stand sweet things."

"By the honor of the Arabs," cried the bedouin, "I left my camp just to taste honey fritters. You must let me eat them for you!"

"Nobody may eat them," she said, "except the person who is hanging here."

So he fell into her trap and untied her. Then he allowed her to bind him in her place, and after she had stripped him of his clothes and turban and put them on, she covered herself, mounted his horse, and rode to her house, where Zaynab asked her, "Why are you dressed up like that?"

"They crucified me," Dalilah said, and she told her about what had happened with the Arab.

Now, the watchmen at the crucifix woke up the next day and cried out, "Dalilah." But instead of Dalilah, they heard the Arab, who responded by saying, "By Allah, I haven't eaten all night! Have you brought the honey fritters?"

"This is a man and a bedouin!" they all exclaimed, and one of the guards asked him, "Where's Dalilah, and who released her?"

"It was I," he answered, "and she won't eat the honey fritters against her will, for she hates them."

When he said that, they knew that the Arab was an innocent fool and had been swindled by Dalilah. So they said to one another, "Shall we flee, or shall we face the fate that Allah has in store for us?"

As they were talking, the chief of police approached them with all the people whom the old woman had cheated and said to the guards, "Arise, and untie Dalilah."

"I haven't eaten all night," said the Arab. "Have you brought the honey fritters?"

On hearing this voice, the police chief raised his eyes to the cross, and when he saw the bedouin hung up there instead of the old woman, he asked the guards, "What's the meaning of this?"

"Pardon!" they cried. "We became tired guarding her and said, 'Dalilah is crucified, and nothing can happen,' so we went to sleep. When we awoke, we found the bedouin hanging in her place. We are at your mercy!"

"May Allah's mercy be with you, guards," said the chief. "She is indeed a clever cheat!"

Then he ordered the guards to untie the bedouin, who grabbed hold of the police chief and said, "May Allah protect the caliph against you! I hold you responsible for my horse and my clothes!"

So the chief questioned him, and he told him what had happened, and the magistrate was astounded and asked him, "Why did you release her?"

"I didn't know that she was a criminal," the Arab said.

Then the other men who had come with the wali said, "We hold you responsible for our goods now. Remember, we delivered the old woman into your hands, and she was in your custody when this happened. So we're going to bring charges against you at the caliph's court."

So off they went to the caliph's divan, and when they

arrived, they found the Emir Hasan, who had also gone to the caliph to prefer charges against the chief of police. Then they all began saying at once, "Truly we have all been cheated!"

"Who's cheated you?" asked the caliph.

Each one of the men came forward and told his story, and then the chief of police said, "Oh Commander of the Faithful, the old woman cheated me also and sold me these five men as slaves for a thousand dinars even though they are freeborn."

"I shall take the responsibility of compensating you for all that you have lost," said the caliph, and then he turned to the wali and said, "But I hold you responsible for capturing the old woman."

But the police chief shook his head and said, "She's not my responsibility! After I hung her on the cross, she tricked this bedouin, and when he untied her, she tied him up in her place and made off with his horse and clothes."

"Well then, whom shall I make responsible for this case?" asked the caliph.

"Make Ahmad al-Danaf responsible," said the wali. "After all, he has a salary of a thousand dinars a month and forty officers who earn a hundred dinars each."

So the caliph cried out, "Come here, Captain Ahmad!"

"At your service, Commander of the Faithful," he said.

"I'm making you responsible for capturing the old woman and bringing her to court," said the caliph.

"I accept the assignment," said the captain.

So the bedouin and the five wronged men stayed with the caliph while Calamity Ahmad went off in search of Dalilah.

And Scheherazade noticed that dawn was approaching and stopped telling her story. When the next night arrived, however, she received the king's permission to continue her tale and said,

Ahmad and his men went down to their mess hall, and there they said to one another, "How are we going to catch this old woman when there are so many that look like her in the city?"

So Ahmad turned to Hasan Shuman and asked him, "What do you advise?"

"Why are you asking Hasan Shuman?" said one of his officers named Ali Kitf al-Jamal. "Do you think that the Pestilent One knows more than we? He's nothing special!"

"Why are you disparaging me, Ali?" asked Hasan. "If that's the way things are, by Allah, I won't go along with you this time!" And he got up and left the hall in anger.

Then Ahmad said to his officers, "I want every sergeant to take ten men each to his own quarter and search for Dalilah."

They all agreed to do as he ordered, including Ali, and they said, "Before we depart, let's set a rendezvous in the Al-Kalkh quarter."

Now word got around that Calamity Ahmad had assumed the responsibility of capturing the wily Dalilah, and Zaynab said to her, "Mother, even if you are a great trickster, do you think you can fool Ahmad al-Danaf and his company?"

"I'm not afraid of anyone but Hasan Shuman," she said.

Then Zaynab said, "By my life, it's my turn now to help you strip those officers who are looking for you."

So she put on her veil and went to a certain druggist, who had a salon with two doors. After saluting him, she gave him an ashrafi and said, "Take this gold piece as rent for your salon, and let me have it until the end of the day."

So he gave her the keys, and she used the stolen ass to carry carpets and other things to furnish the place. Afterward she set a tray of meat and wine on each of the raised platforms. Then she went outside and stood at the door with her face unveiled. Just then Ali Kitf al-Jamal and his men came by. She kissed his hand, and since she was so beautiful, he fell in love with her and asked her, "What do you want?"

"Are you the Captain Ahmad al-Danad?" she asked.

"No," he said, "but I am one of his officers. My name is Ali Kitf al-Jamal."

"Where are you going?" she asked.

"We're looking for a sharkish old woman, who's stolen people's goods, and we're going to capture her," he said. "But who are you, and what are you doing here?"

"My father owned a tavern at Mosul," she replied, "and he died and left me a great deal of money. So I came here because I was afraid of the authorities, and I asked the people who could protect me the best. And they all replied, 'Nobody but Ahmad al-Danaf.' "

"From this day on," all the officers proclaimed, "consider yourself under his protection!"

"May Allah bless you," she said. "It would make me feel good if you would eat some of my food and have a cup of water."

The officers consented, and after entering they ate and drank until they were drunk, for she had drugged them with bhang. Then she stripped them of their clothes and arms, and she managed to trick the three other groups of officers searching for her mother in the same way. Finally, Calamity Ahmad went out to look for Dalilah, but he could not find her, nor could he find any of his officers. Still, he continued looking until he came to the door where Zaynab was standing, and when she kissed his hand, he fell in love with her.

"Are you the Captain Ahmad al-Danaf?" she asked.

"Yes," he replied, "and who are you?"

"I'm a stranger from Mosul," she said. "My father was a vintner there, and he died and left me a great deal of money. So I came to this city because I was afraid of the authorities there, and I opened up this tavern. The chief of police has imposed a tax on me, but I would prefer to place myself under your protection and pay you what the chief is taking from me, because you have more right to the money."

"Don't pay him anything," he said. "You are welcome to my protection."

"May Allah bless you," she said. "It would warm my heart, then, if you would eat some of my food."

After entering the salon, he ate and drank wine until he could not sit upright. So she drugged him and took his clothes and arms. Then she loaded her booty on the bedouin's horse and the mule driver's ass and made off with it.

When Ali Kitf al-Jamal awoke, he found himself naked and saw Ahmad and his men drugged and stripped. So he revived them with an antidote, and they awoke only to find themselves naked as well.

"What's going on here?" cried Calamity Ahmad. "We were out to catch that old thief, and now we've been snared by this strumpet! Hasan Shuman will certainly have a good laugh about this! But we'll wait until it's dark, and then we'll sneak away."

In the meantime, Hasan the Pestilent asked the man in charge of the mess hall where Ahmad's men were, and just as he was asking, up they came naked. Then he looked at them and asked, "Who managed to trick you and steal all your clothes?"

"We went searching for the old woman," they said, "and a pretty girl stripped us."

"She's done a good job," he said.

"Do you know her?" they asked.

"Yes, I know her," he replied, "and the old trot, too."

"What shall we tell the caliph?" they asked.

"When you go to him and he asks you why you haven't caught her yet, you're to say, 'We can't recognize her and want you to make Hasan Shuman responsible for her capture, because he knows her.' And if he places the responsibility on me, I'll capture her."

So they all went to sleep, and the next morning they went to the caliph's divan and kissed the ground before him.

"Where is the old woman, Captain Ahmad?" he asked.

But he shook his head, and the caliph asked him why he was doing this, whereupon he replied, "We can't recognize her and want you to make Hasan Shuman responsible for her capture, because he knows her and her daughter as well."

Then Hasan interceded on her behalf and told the caliph, "She hasn't played these tricks because she desired to have the goods she stole. On the contrary, she just wanted to show you how clever she and her daughter are so that you would continue paying their father's salary to her. Provided that you spare her life and her daughter's, I'll capture them for you."

"By the life of my ancestors," cried the caliph, "if she restores the people's property, I'll pardon her, thanks to your intercession."

But the Pestilent One said, "Give me your pledge, oh Prince of True Believers!"

Thereupon Al-Rashid gave him the kerchief of pardon. So Hasan went to Dalilah's house and called to her. However, her daughter Zaynab answered him instead, and he asked, "Where is your mother?"

"Upstairs," she answered.

"Tell her to take the people's property and come with me to the caliph," he said. "I've brought her the kerchief of pardon, and if she doesn't come with good grace, she has only herself to blame for the consequences."

So Dalilah came down, and after tying the kerchief around her neck, she gave him the people's goods on the mule driver's ass and the bedouin's horse.

"What about the clothes of Ahmad and his men?" he asked

"By Allah," she replied, "it wasn't I who stripped them."

"That's true," said Hasan, "it was your daughter, Zaynab, and she did you a big favor by doing that."

Then he took her to the divan, and after laying out all the people's goods and property before the caliph, he brought forth the old trot. As soon as he saw her, he ordered her to cast herself down on the carpet of blood, and she cried out, "I throw myself under your protection, oh Shuman!"

So he rose, kissed the hands of the caliph, and said, "Pardon, oh Commander of the Faithful! Remember, you gave me the kerchief of pardon."

"I shall pardon her for your sake," said the caliph. "Come here, old woman. What is your name?"

"My name is Wily Dalilah," she answered.

"Indeed, you are crafty and full of guile," the caliph said. "Why have you played all these tricks and worn us out?"

"I didn't do this because I lusted after their goods, your majesty, but because I had heard of the tricks that Ahmad al-Danaf and Hasan Shuman played in Baghdad and said to myself, 'Why not do the same thing?' But now I've returned the goods that I stole to their owners."

However, the donkey driver stood up and said, "I invoke Allah's holy law that she be punished, 'eye for eye, tooth for tooth.' It wasn't enough for her just to steal my ass, she egged on the Moorish barber to tear out my teeth and brand me on both temples."

* * *

And Scheherazade noticed that dawn was approaching and stopped telling her story. When the next night arrived, however, she received the king's permission to continue her tale and said,

Thereupon the caliph ordered that the mule driver be given a hundred dinars and that the dyer be given the same amount. And he said to the dyer, "Go and set up your shop again."

So the mule driver and the dyer asked Allah to bless him and went away. The bedouin also took his clothes and horse, and as he departed, he said, "From now on I'll never enter Baghdad and eat honey fritters."

Then the others took their goods and went their way. Finally, the caliph said to Dalilah, "Ask a boon of me, Dalilah!"

And she said, "Not long ago my father was governor of your carrier pigeons, and I know how to rear the birds. Moreover, my husband was town captain of Baghdad. Now I want to have the position my husband held, and my daughter would like to have that of her grandfather."

The caliph granted both their requests, and she said, "I would like to be the guardian of your khan."

Now it was well known that the caliph had built a khan of three stories for the merchants so that they would have a place to lodge. In order to keep the place in good condition he had assigned forty slaves and also forty dogs that he had brought from the king of the Sulaymanniyah, after he had deposed him. The khan also had a slave who cooked for the chattels and fed the hounds. So the caliph said, "Dalilah, I'll write a deed testifying that you are the new guardian of the khan, and if anything is ever lost from there, you'll be held responsible."

"That's fine with me," she said. "But please let my daughter live in the pavilion over the door of the khan, for it has terraced roofs, and that will be an ideal place for her to rear the carrier pigeons."

The caliph granted her this request as well, and Zaynab moved to the pavilion, where she hung up the forty-one robes of Calamity Ahmad and his officers. Moreover, she was given forty pigeons to carry the royal messages, while Dalilah set up her watch right behind the door of the khan, and every day she went to the caliph's divan to see if he would need a message sent by a pigeon. She would stay there until evening while the forty slaves under her charge stood on guard at the khan. When darkness descended, they released the forty dogs so that they could keep watch over the place during the night.

Thus ended the merry ways and deeds of Dalilah the Wily One in Baghdad.

No sooner had Scheherazade concluded her tale than she said, "And yet, oh king, this story is no more wondrous than the tale of Judar and his brothers."

The Tale of Judar and His Brothers

There was once a merchant named Omar, and he had three sons. The oldest was called Salim, the middle Seleem, and the youngest Judar. He raised them all until manhood, but he was most fond of the youngest. Because of this, the other two brothers became jealous of Judar and came to hate him.

Now, when their father, who was an extremely old man, saw that his two eldest sons hated Judar, he was afraid that something might happen to him. So he assembled a group of his relatives along with various learned men and property distributors of the kazi's court, and he ordered them to bring all his money and merchandise. "My friends," he said, "divide this money into four portions according to the law."

They did as he said, and he gave one part to each of his sons and kept the fourth for himself. "These were my goods, and I have divided them among my offspring during my lifetime. The portion that I have kept shall go to their mother so that she will be provided for after I am gone."

Not long after this he died, and neither of the two elder brothers was content with his share. So they demanded more from Judar and said, "Our father's wealth is in your hands."

But he appealed to the court, and the Moslems who had been present at the partition came and gave testimony so that the judge ruled in favor of Judar. Yet, during the proceedings Judar and his brothers wasted a good deal of money on bribes that they gave to the judge.

After this his brothers left him alone for a while. Soon, however, they began to plot against him again, and he appealed a second time to the magistrate, who once more decided in his favor, and all three brothers lost a good deal of money in bribes that went to the judge. Despite the loss of money, Salim and Seleem continued to prosecute their brother and took the case from court to court until the three of them had lost all their money. Then the two elder brothers went to their mother and flouted her and beat her. After this they took all her money and drove her away.

So she went to her son Judar and told him how his brothers had treated her and began cursing them.

"Mother," Judar said, "don't curse them, for Allah will repay them for their evil deeds. The fact is, I've become a poor man, and so have my brothers. We've quarreled and fought, and only the judges have profited from our quarrel. Indeed, we've wasted all the money that our father left us and have disgraced ourselves before everyone with our accusations against one another. Do you want me now to bring them to court on your account? Should we appeal to the judges? We can't do this! The best thing to do is for you to come live with me and share my food. Pray to Allah, and He will help us and punish my brothers for what they have done." And he continued to comfort his mother until she agreed to come and live with him. Then he took out a net and went fishing every day in the nearby river, or he would go to the riverbanks near Bulak and old Cairo, where there was water. Some days he would earn ten coppers, another twenty, and another thirty, and he would use this money for his mother and himself so they managed to eat and drink well.

As for his brothers, they did not work. Nor did they begin to trade. Therefore, misery and ruin overcame them, and they wasted all the money that they had taken from their mother and became part of the troop of wretched naked beggars in Cairo. At times they would come to their mother and humble themselves before her and complain about their hunger. Since she was indeed their mother, she could not help but feel pity for them and would give them some moldy bread, or if there was some meat that had been cooked the day before, she would say to them, "Eat it quick, and go your way before your brother comes, for it would be a disgrace if he saw me with you and he would be angry at me."

So they would eat hastily and go away. Now one day when they came to Judar's house, their mother set cooked meat and bread before them. All of a sudden, as they were eating, their brother entered, and their mother was put to shame and confused, for she was afraid that Judar would be furious with her. So she bowed her face abashed before him, but Judar smiled and said, "Welcome, brothers. This is a blessed day! How is it that you've graced me with your visit today?" Then he embraced them both, treated them with affection, and said, "I never thought that you would stay away from your mother and me."

"By Allah," they replied, "we've longed to visit you for some time, but we felt too ashamed about what happened between us. Indeed, we've regretted what we did and repented it all. It was Satan's doing, and may Allah Almighty curse him! And now we have nobody to turn to except you and our mother."

And Scheherazade noticed that dawn was approaching and stopped telling her story. When the next night arrived, however, she received the king's permission to continue her tale and said,

So Judar made peace with them, and they had supper with him and spent the night in his dwelling. The next morning, after breakfast, Judar picked up his net and went out to try his luck while his brothers went forth and were gone until noon, when they returned to have their midday meal. In the evening, Judar came home and brought with him some meat and vegetables. They all continued living like this for a good month. Judar would catch fish, sell it, and buy all the necessities for his mother and brothers so they could eat and enjoy themselves. However, one day, he went down to the river, and after throwing his net, it came back empty. He cast it a second time, but again it returned empty, and he said to himself, "No fish in this place!" So he went to another place and cast his net, but without luck. And he continued moving from place to place until evening, but he did not catch a single thing. "What's going on here?" he said to himself. "Have the fish fled the river or what?" Then he flung his net over his shoulder and headed for home, greatly disappointed and concerned for his mother and brothers, for he had no idea how he would be able to provide for them that night. As he passed the baker's shop, he saw a crowd of people with money in their hands lining up for bread. So he stood there sighing, and the baker called to him and said, "Welcome, Judar! Do you want some bread?"

When he did not respond, the baker continued, "Even though you don't have any dirhams, take what you need on credit."

"Give me ten coppers' worth of bread," Judar replied, "and take this net as a guarantee."

"No, my poor fellow," said the baker. "The net is the way you earn your living. If I were to take it from you, you'd have no way to subsist. Take this bread, and ten coppers as well, and tomorrow you can bring me fish for the twenty."

"You can count on me," said Judar, and he took the bread. "Tomorrow the Lord will help me and provide me with means to pay you back."

Then he bought meat and vegetables and carried them home to his mother, who cooked them. Afterward they had their supper and went to bed. The next morning Judar arose at daybreak and took his net, and his mother said to him, "Sit down and have some breakfast."

But he said, "No, you and my brothers should have some breakfast. I must be off."

So he went down to the river near Bulak, where he cast his net three times and moved about all day without catching anything. When the hour of midafternoon prayer arrived, he picked up his net and left the river very dejected. His way led him past the shop of the baker, who began counting out some money for him and gave him some more bread, for he saw that Judar was dejected. "Come, take it and go. If you don't pay me back today, then it'll be tomorrow."

Judar wanted to apologize, but the baker said, "Go! No apologies. If you had caught something, you'd have it with you. Tomorrow you'll have better luck. Come, take this bread, and don't be ashamed. You can have it all on credit."

So Judar took the bread and money and went home. On the third day he went out again and fished in all sorts of different places until the time of afternoon prayer. However, he caught nothing, and after going to the baker, he took bread and money from him as he had done before. He continued doing this for seven days until he became most disheartened and said to himself, "Today I'll go to Lake Karun."

Well, after walking there, he was about to cast his net when a Moor came riding up to him. He was clad in splendid attire and seated on a mule with a pair of gold-embroidered saddlebags. Upon dismounting, the Moor said to him, "Peace be with you, Judar, oh son of Omar."

"May peace be with you, too, my lord," replied the fisherman.

"Judar," the Moor said, "I am in great need of you, and if you obey me, you won't be sorry, for you'll become my companion, manage my affairs for me, and become well-to-do."

"My lord," answered Judar, "tell me what is on your mind, and I'll obey you as you wish."

"Repeat the Fatihah, the opening chapter of the Koran," the Moor requested.

So he recited it with him, and then the Moor took out a silken cord and said, "Tie my elbows behind me as tightly as you can, and throw me into the lake. Then wait awhile, and if you see me lift my hands out of the water before my body shows, cast your net over me and drag me out as quickly as possible. But if you see me come up feet first, you'll know that I'm dead. If that occurs, I want you to leave me and take the mule and saddlebags and carry them to the bazaar, where you'll find a Jew named Shamayah. Give him the mule, and he'll give you a hundred dinars, which you're to take and go your way. After that you're to keep the matter completely secret."

So Judar tied his arms tightly behind his back, and the Moor kept saying, "Tie tighter." And after he was bound, he said, "Now push me into the lake."

So he pushed him in, and the Moor sank. Judar stood waiting some time until he saw the Moor's feet appear above the water indicating that he was dead. So he left him and drove the mule to the bazaar, where he saw the

Jew seated on a stool at the door of his storehouse. When the Jew caught sight of the mule, he cried, "So, he's perished, and greed was his undoing." Then he took the mule from Judar, gave him a hundred dinars, and told him to keep the matter secret. In turn, Judar went and bought what bread he needed from the baker and said, "Take this gold piece."

After the baker figured out what Judar owed him, he said, "I still owe you two days' worth of bread."

And Scheherazade noticed that dawn was approaching and stopped telling her story. When the next night arrived, however, she received the king's permission to continue her tale and said,

Judar told the baker to keep what was left from the gold piece to pay for the bread the next two days, and he went on to the butcher, gave him a gold piece as well, and said, "Keep the rest of the dinar on account." Afterward he bought some vegetables, and when he arrived home, he found his brothers begging their mother for food, while she cried, "Have patience until your brother comes home. I have nothing right now."

So he entered the house and said, "Take this food and drink."

And his brothers fell on the food like cannibals, while Judar gave the rest of his gold to his mother and said, "If my brothers come to you, give them some money to buy food and eat while I'm gone."

That night he slept well, and the next morning, he took his net, went down to Lake Karun, and was about to cast the net when another Moor came riding toward him on a mule that was even more splendidly adorned than the one the day before, and it was carrying a pair of saddlebags with caskets in them.

"Peace be with you, Judar," said the Moor.

"And peace be with you, my lord," replied Judar.

"Did a Moor come riding by here yesterday on a mule like mine?" he asked.

When he heard this question, Judar was alarmed and answered, "No, not while I was here." Indeed, Judar was afraid that if he said yes the Moor would ask where he had gone and might accuse him of drowning the other Moor in the lake.

"Listen, you poor devil! The man who came by here yesterday was my brother!"

"I didn't see anyone," Judar insisted.

Then the Moor asked, "Didn't you bind his arms behind him and throw him into the lake, and didn't he say to you, 'If my hands appear above the water first, cast your net over me and drag me out as soon as possible. But if my feet show first, you'll know that I'm dead, and you're to take the mule to the Jew Shamayah, who'll give you a hundred dinars'?"

"Since you know all this," Judar replied, "why are you questioning me?"

"Because I want you to do the same thing with me as you did with my brother," said the Moor. Then he gave him a silken cord and said, "Tie my hands behind me and throw me in, and if my feet come up first as my brother's did, take the mule to the Jew, and he'll give you a hundred dinars."

So Judar bound him and pushed him into the lake, where he sank. After a while, the Moor's feet appeared above the water, and the fisherman said, "He's dead and damned! By Allah, let the Moors come to me every day, and I'll bind them and push them into the lake. I'll certainly be happy with a hundred dinars after they die."

Then he took the mule to the Jew, who waited for him to approach and then asked, "So, the other is dead, too?"

"May Allah bless you with a long life," said Judar.

"Now you see how the greedy have been rewarded," the Jew said, and he took the mule and gave Judar a hundred dinars, which he brought to his mother.

"Oh son," she asked, "where have you gotten this money?"

So he told her, and she said, "Don't go to Lake Karun again. I'm afraid that the Moors will do something to you!"

"But Mother," he replied, "I'm only doing what they want me to do. Besides, I'm earning a hundred dinars, and I always return safely. So I'm going to continue to go to Lake Karun and drown the Moors until they're all gone."

The following day Judar did indeed go to the lake and stood there until a third Moor came riding toward him in a mule with saddlebags and even more splendidly adorned than the one before. "Peace with you, Judar, oh son of Omar," said the Moor.

And Judar remarked to himself, "How is it that they all know me?" And he returned the Moor's salute.

"Have any other Moors passed by here?" asked the pilgrim.

"Two," answered Judar.

"Where did they go?"

"I bound their hands behind them and threw them into the lake, where they drowned, and the same fate is in store for you," Judar declared.

The Moor laughed and responded, "You miserable wretch, every life is predestined to run its own course."

Then he dismounted, gave the fisherman a silken cord, and said, "Do the same with me, Judar, that you did with them."

"Put your hands behind your back so I can tie you, for I'm in a rush, and time's flying," answered Judar.

So the Moor put his hands behind him, and Judar tied him up and threw him into the lake. Then he waited awhile, and soon the Moor thrust both hands out of the water and called out to him, "Ho, good fellow, cast your net!"

So Judar threw the net over him and dragged him ashore, and in each of his hands he held a fish as red as coral.

"Bring me the two caskets that are in the saddlebags," said the Moor, and after Judar brought them, he opened them and laid a fish in each casket and shut them. Then he pressed Judar to his bosom, kissed him on both cheeks, and said, "May Allah make your life comfortable! If you hadn't thrown your net over me and pulled me out, I certainly would have drowned."

"My lord," Judar answered, "may Allah bless you, and I beg of you now to tell me the true story about the two drowned men, the fish, and the Jew."

And Scheherazade noticed that dawn was approaching and stopped telling her story. When the next night arrived, however, she received the king's permission to continue her tale and said,

* * *

I want you to know, Judar [said the Moor], that these two men were my brothers, Abd al-Salam and Abd al-Ahad. My own name is Abd al-Samad, and the Jew is also our brother. His name is Abd al-Rahim, and he's not a Jew, but a true believer of the Maliki school. Our father, whose name was Abd al-Wadud, taught us magic and the art of solving mysteries and discovering hidden treasures, and we studied diligently until we were able to compel the ifrits and marids of the jinn to serve us. Eventually our sire died and left us a great deal of wealth. Then we divided his treasures and talismans among us until we came to his books, when we had an argument about a volume entitled *The Lore of the Ancients*, for there is nothing like it in the world, and it is worth more than its weight in gold and jewels. The reason it is so valuable is that it contains all the information about the hidden treasures of the earth and the solution to every secret. Our father often made use of this book, and we had learned some portions of it by heart. Consequently, each one of us wanted to possess it to learn everything that was in it. Now, when we began arguing with one another, there was an old man by the name of Cohen al-Abtan living with us, and it was he who had raised our sire and taught him divination and magic, and he said to us, "Bring me the book."

So we gave it to him, and he continued, "You are the sons of my sons, and thus I don't want to wrong any one of you. Therefore, whoever would like to have this book must first discover the treasure of Al-Shamardal and bring me the celestial orb, the vial of kohl, the royal ring, and the sword. The ring is served by a marid called Al-Ra'ad al-Kasif, and whoever has the ring will prevail against kings and sultans. In fact, if he desires, he can make himself master of the earth with it. As for the sword, its owner need only to draw it and wield it against an army, and the army will be put to rout. And if he says, 'Slay those troops over there,' lightning and fire will emanate from the sword and kill the enemy. As for the orb, its owner need only to turn his face toward any country he desires to see, and he will see the country and its people as if they were between his hands. And if he is angry with a city and wants to burn it, he need only point the orb toward the sun and say, 'Let such and such a city be burned,' and that city will be consumed with fire. As for the vial of kohl, whoever applies the kohl to his eyes will be able to see all the treasures of the earth. Now, I'm going to place one condition on all of you. Whoever fails to discover the treasure will forfeit his right to the book. Whoever finds the treasure and brings me the four precious things that are in it may claim the book."

Of course, we all agreed to this condition, and then the sage continued, "My sons, I want you to know that the treasure of Al-Shamardal is guarded by the sons of the Red King, and your father told me that he himself had tried to obtain the treasure but was unable to do so, for the sons of the Red King fled from him into the land of Egypt, where they took refuge in a lake called Lake Karun. He pursued them there, but he could not conquer them because they had escaped into the lake, which is protected by a spell."

And Scheherazade noticed that dawn was approaching and stopped telling her tale. When the next night arrived, however, she received the king's permission to continue her tale and said,

"So your father returned empty-handed, unable to attain his goal. Later on he told me about his unsuccessful venture, and I drew up an astrological chart and found that the treasure would be obtained only through a young fisherman of Cairo named Judar bin Omar at Lake Karun. Indeed, he would bring about the capture of the sons of the Red King, and this could only be achieved if he bound the hands of the treasure seeker behind him and threw him into the lake to do battle with the sons of the Red King. Whoever's destiny it was to succeed would conquer the sons. If not, he would perish and his feet would appear above water. As to the man who succeeded, his hands would show first, and Judar would be obligated to cast the net over him and drag him ashore."

So my brothers Abd al-Salam and Abd al-Ahad said, "Even though we may perish, we want to go."

Then I said, "I want to go, too."

But my brother Abd al-Rahim, the one you saw dressed as a Jew, stated, "I don't want to participate."

Thereupon we agreed that he should travel to Cairo in the disguise of a Jewish merchant so that if any of us perished in the lake, he would take his mule and saddlebags and give the bearer a hundred dinars. Now the sons of the Red King slew my first brother as well as the second, but they did not prevail against me, and I managed to overcome them.

"And where is your catch?" cried Judar.

"Didn't you see me put them in the caskets?" responded the Moor.

"Those were fish," said Judar.

"No," the Moor responded. "They are jinnees in the guise of fish. Whatever the case may be, Judar, you know that the treasure can only be obtained through your help. So, tell me, will you do as I request and go with me to the city of Fez-and-Meknes, where we will open the treasure? After that I'll give you whatever you desire, and you shall forever be my brother and return to your family with a joyful heart."

"My lord," Judar responded, "I've got my mother and two brothers to worry about."

And Scheherazade noticed that dawn was approaching and stopped telling her tale. When the next night arrived, however, she received the king's permission to continue her tale and said.

And Judar continued, "If I go with you, who will look after them? Who will provide them with food and drink?"

"This is a poor excuse!" the Moor said. "If it's a matter of money, I'll give you a thousand ducats so your mother can provide for herself, and you should return within four months."

When Judar heard the sum of a thousand dinars, he said, "If you give them to me right now, my good pilgrim, I'm your man."

Within seconds the Moor pulled out the money and gave it to him. In turn, he went to his mother and told her all that had happened. "Take these thousand dinars," he said, "and use them for yourself and my brothers while I journey to Morocco with the Moor. I'll be absent four months, and I'm bound to return with a fortune. So give me your blessings, Mother!"

"My son, you make me sad," she said. "And I'm afraid that something may happen to you."

"Mother," he replied, "nothing can happen to me if I'm protected by Allah, and the Moor is a man of integrity," and he went on to praise the Moor's virtues until she said, "May Allah favor you! Go with the Moor, my son. Perhaps he will reward you."

So he took leave of his mother and went back to Abd al-Samad, who asked him, "Have you consulted your mother?"

"Yes," Judar said, "and she gave me her blessings."

"Then mount behind me," said the Moor.

So Judar mounted the mule, and they rode on from noon until the time of midafternoon prayer, when the fisherman became hungry, and seeing no provisions with the Moor, he said, "My lord, have you perhaps forgotten to bring some food for the journey?"

"Are you hungry?" asked the Moor.

"Yes," Judar answered.

So they both dismounted, and Abd al-Samad took down the saddlebags and asked Judar, "What would you like to eat?"

"Anything," responded Judar.

"By Allah, tell me exactly what you'd like to have."

"Bread and cheese."

"My poor fellow, bread and cheese are too meager for you. Wish for something good."

"Anything would taste good to me right now."

"Would you like a nice roast chicken?"

"Yes!"

"Would you like rice and honey?"

"Yes!"

And the Moor went on to ask him if he would like this dish and that until he named twenty-four kinds of meat, and Judar thought to himself, "He must be daft! Where are all these delicious things to come from? He has neither cook nor kitchen. But I might as well say to him that it's enough already." So he cried out, "That will do! You make me crave all these delicious things, and there's nothing to see."

"You are welcome to it all, Judar," said the Moor,

who put his hand into the saddlebags and pulled out a golden dish containing two roast chickens. Then he put his hand in a second time and pulled out a golden dish full of kabobs, nor did he stint taking out other dishes from the saddlebags until he had brought out the twenty-four different kinds that he had mentioned before. While he was doing this, Judar looked on, and when he was finished, the Moor said, "Go to it, poor fellow."

"My lord," Judar replied, "you must have loads of cooks and kitchens in your saddlebags!"

The Moor laughed and replied, "These are magic saddlebags, and they contain a servant, who would bring us a thousand dishes an hour if we so desired."

"By Allah," said Judar, "that's a neat thing to have."

Then they ate their fill and threw away what was left. Afterward, the Moor put the empty dishes back into the saddlebags, from which he also withdrew a jug. Then they drank, washed themselves, and said the midafternoon prayer. Finally, Abd al-Samad put the jug back into the saddlebags along with the caskets, and after throwing the bags over the mule's back, he mounted and cried out to Judar, "Get up here, and let's be off. Now, do you know how far we've come since Cairo?"

"Not at all," he replied.

"We've traveled a whole month."

"How do you know that?"

"I'll have you know, Judar," the Moor said, "this mule under us is a marid of the jinn, who can cover an entire year in a day's journey. But, for your sake, it's gone at an easier pace."

Then they set out again and traveled westward until nightfall, when they stopped and the Moor brought out supper from the saddlebags, and he did the same for their breakfast the next morning. So they rode on four days, journeying until midnight and sleeping until morning, and whatever Judar desired, he asked the Moor, who brought it out of the saddlebags. On the fifth day they arrived at Fez-and-Meknes and entered the city, where all who met the Moor saluted and kissed his hands, and he continued riding through the streets until he came to a certain door, at which he knocked. When it was opened, a girl as beautiful as the moon came out, and he said to her, "Open the upper chamber for us, my daughter."

"As you wish, Father!" she replied, and as she walked before them, her hips swayed to and fro with a graceful gait like a gazelle's, and Judar was captivated by her and said, "She can be no other than a king's daughter."

After opening the upper chamber, the Moor took the saddlebags from the mule's back and said to his daughter, "Go, and may God bless you!"

All of a sudden the earth split, swallowed the mule, and closed so quickly that it became the way it had been before without appearing to have changed in the least. And Judar said, "Praise be to Allah, who kept us safe on the mule's back!"

"Don't be amazed, Judar," said the Moor. "I told you that the mule was a jinnee. Now, come with me to the upper chamber."

So they went to the chamber, and Judar was astounded by the rich furniture, pendants of gold and silver, jewels, and other rare and precious things that he saw there. As soon as they were seated, the Moor ordered his daughter, Rahmah, to bring him a bundle of garments, and after receiving it, he drew out a robe worth a thousand dinars, which he gave to Judar, and said, "Put on this robe, Judar, and be welcome here."

So Judar put the robe on and became like one of the fine kings of the West. Meanwhile the Moor placed the saddlebags before him, and after he reached inside, he pulled out dish after dish until they had forty different kinds of meat before them. Then he said to Judar, "Draw near and eat. Please excuse us if we don't know what meat you desire. But if you tell us what you desire, we'll set it before you without delay."

And Scheherazade noticed that dawn was approaching and stopped telling her story. When the next night arrived, however, she received the king's permission to continue her tale and said,

"By Allah," Judar said, "I love all kinds of meat. So you don't have to ask me. Just bring me whatever comes to your mind, and I'll just eat it."

After this he spent twenty days with the Moor, who

clad him in new clothes each day, and during this time they ate from the saddlebags, for the Moor did not buy any meat, bread, or anything else. Whatever they ate, whether it was fruit or meat, came from the saddlebags. On the twenty-first day the Moor said, "Judar, get up. This is the day assigned for opening the treasure of Al-Shamardal."

So Judar rose, and they walked outside the city, where they found two slaves, each holding a mule. The Moor mounted one beast and Judar the other, and they rode till noon, when they came to a river, where they dismounted. Then Abd al-Samad signaled to his slaves to take the mules away, and after they did this, they returned with tents that they began to set up. In addition, they spread carpets, mattresses, pillows, and cushions in the tents. Finally, one of them brought the caskets containing the two fish, and the other fetched the saddlebags. Once everything was finished, the Moor arose and said, "Come, Judar!"

So Judar followed him into the tent and sat down beside him, and the Moor bought out dishes of meat from the saddlebags, and they enjoyed a fine meal. Then the Moor took the two caskets and pronounced a magic incantation over them, whereupon voices from within cried out, "At your service, oh wizard of the world! Have mercy on us!"

The Moor repeated his incantations, and the voices kept begging for mercy until the two caskets burst into pieces, and out came two men with their hands tied. "Mercy! Mercy, oh wizard of the world! What do you want from us?"

"I intend to burn you both to ashes unless you agree to help me open the treasure of Al-Shamardal."

"We promise," they said. "We'll open the treasure if you produce Judar bin Omar, the fisherman, for the treasure can only be opened through his help, and nobody may enter the place of the treasure except Judar."

"I've brought Judar with me," said the Moor. "Indeed, he's right here listening and looking at you."

Thereupon, they agreed to open the treasure, and the Moor released them from the magic spell. Then he brought out a hollow wand and placed tablets of red carnelian on it. After this he took a chafing dish, put charcoal on it, and blew, and the charcoal ignited. Immediately thereafter he brought incense and said, "Judar, I'm about to begin the necessary incantations and fumigations, and after I've begun, I'm not allowed to speak, otherwise the charm will not work. So first I'll teach you what you must do to attain your goal."

"Teach me," said Judar.

"It's important for you to know," declared the Moor, "that after I've recited the spell and thrown the incense, the water will dry up in the river's bed, and you'll see a golden door as large as a city gate with two rings of metal on it. You're to go down to the door, knock lightly, and wait awhile. Then knock a second time a little louder than the first and wait another while. After that, knock three times in rapid succession, and you'll hear a voice ask, 'Who's knocking at the door of the treasure and does not know how to solve the secrets?' You're to answer, 'I am Judar the fisherman, son of Omar,' and the door will open, and a figure will emerge with a sword in hand, and he'll say to you, 'If you are that man, stretch forth your neck so that I may strike off your head.' Then you're to stretch forth your neck, but don't be afraid, for when he lifts his hand and hits you with the sword, he'll fall down before you, and in a little while he'll lose his soul. The blow will not hurt you, nor will you be harmed in any way. But if you oppose him, he'll kill you. After you've undone his enchantment with your obedience, enter and move on until you see another door. You're to knock there again, and a man will come out riding on a mare with a lance on his shoulder, and he'll say to you, 'Why have you come here? Don't you know that neither man nor jinnee may enter here?' And he'll threaten you with his lance. You're to bare your breast to him and he will strike you and then fall from his horse right away and lose his soul. But if you cross him, he'll kill you. Then you're to go on to the third door, where a man with a bow and arrows in his hand will come out and take aim at you. Again, you're to bare your breast to him, and after he shoots you, he'll fall down before you without a soul in his body. But if you oppose him, he'll kill you."

And Scheherazade noticed that dawn was approaching and stopped telling her story. When the next night arrived,

however, she received the king's permission to continue her tale and said,

"Then you're to go the a fourth door," the Moor continued telling Judar, "and knock. When it is opened, a huge lion will come out and rush at you with his mouth wide open. Don't be afraid, and don't flee. Just give him your hand, and he'll bite it, fall down dead, and you won't be hurt. Then walk to the fifth door, where you'll find a black slave, who'll ask, 'Who are you?' You're to answer, 'I am Judar!' And he will respond, 'If you are he, open the sixth door.' Then you're to go to that door and say, 'Oh Isa, tell Musa to open the door.' Thereupon the door will open, and you'll see two dragons, one on the left and the other on the right. They will open their jaws and fly at you, both at the same time. Stretch out your hands at them, and they will each bite a hand and fall down dead. But if you resist them, they'll kill you. Then go on to the seventh door and knock. Thereupon, your mother will come out and say, 'Welcome, my son, come in so I may welcome you!' But you are to reply, 'Keep away from me, and take off your dress!' And she'll answer, 'My son, I am your mother, and I have suckled and raised you. Why do you want me naked?' Then you are to say, 'Unless you take off your clothes, I'll kill you!' Then look to your right, and you'll see a sword hanging on the wall. Take the sword, draw it, and say, 'Strip!' In turn, she will try to wheedle herself out of the situation by pleading and humbling herself before you, but you must have no pity on her, and each time she takes off something, you're to cry, 'Keep on!' And you are to keep threatening to kill her until she has taken off everything that she is wearing. Then she'll fall to the ground, and the magic spell will be broken, the charms undone, and you will be safe. Then enter the hall of the treasure, where you'll see heaps of gold. But pay no attention to this gold. Instead, look for a closet at the upper end of the hall, where you'll see a drawn curtain. Pull back the curtain, and you will find the enchanter Al-Shamardal lying on a couch of gold with something round above his head shining like the moon. This is the orb. Next to him will be the sword. The ring will be on his finger, and the vial of kohl will be hanging from a chain around his neck.

Bring me the four talismans, and beware! If you forget anything that I've told you, you will regret it, and I'm afraid of what will happen to you!"

The Moor repeated his instructions four times until Judar said, "I know them by heart, but do you really think that I can withstand these magic creatures and endure these mighty terrors?"

"Judar," replied the Moor, "there's no need to be afraid. They are only phantoms." And he continued to bolster his courage until Judar placed his trust in Allah and agreed to undertake the venture. Then Abd al-Samad threw incense on the chafing dish and began reciting the incantations for a while. All of a sudden, the water disappeared and uncovered the riverbed, revealing the door of the treasure. So Judar went down to the door and knocked, whereupon he heard a voice that said, "Who's knocking at the door of the treasure and does not know how solve the secrets?"

"I am Judar, son of Omar," he replied.

The door opened, and a man holding a sword came forward and said, "Stretch out your neck."

Judar stretched out his neck, and when the man delivered the blow with his sword, the phantom fell down dead. Then Judar went to the second door and did the same thing, and he continued doing so until he had undone the enchantments of the first six doors. When he came to the seventh, his mother emerged and said, "Welcome, my son!"

"Who are you?" he asked.

"My son, I am your mother who carried you nine months and suckled and raised you," she answered.

"Take off your clothes," he said.

"You're my son," she said. "Why do you want me naked?"

But he said, "Strip, or I'll strike off your head with this sword." And he stretched out his hand for the sword and threatened her with it. "If you don't strip, I'll kill you." Then she tried to plead, beg, and argue with him, and he had to increase his threats by crying out, "Keep on!"

She removed each article slowly and kept saying, "My son, this is a disgrace!" But she was forced to keep undressing until she had nothing left on her but her petticoat pants. Then she said, "My son, is your heart made of stone? Why are you dishonoring me? This is against the law! My son, think of the shame!"

Finally, he answered, "You're right. Don't take off anything more."

As soon as he uttered these words, she cried out, "He's failed the test! Beat him!"

All at once the servants of the treasure fell upon him and dealt him blows that came at him like a storm of rain. Indeed, they gave him a thrashing that he never forgot, and afterward they threw him outside. When the door to the treasure closed, he lay on the bank of the river while the water returned to the river's bed.

And Scheherazade noticed that dawn was approaching and stopped telling her story. When the next night arrived, however, she received the king's permission to continue her tale and said,

While Judar lay on the riverbank, the Moor quickly ran over to him, picked him up, and recited a magic incantation so that Judar came to his senses. Though he was still dazed, the Moor asked him, "What have you done, you wretch?"

"My brother," said Judar, "I had broken all the spells until I came to my mother, who pleaded and argued with me for a long time. Nevertheless, I made her take off her clothes until nothing remained except her petticoat pants. Then she said, 'Don't dishonor me! Don't disgrace me with this shame!' So I told her to stop undressing out of pity, and suddenly she cried out, 'He's failed the test! Beat him!' Suddenly, some people came at me out of nowhere and beat the daylights out of me. Then they threw me out the door, and I don't know what happened after that."

"Didn't I warn you to obey all my instructions?" said the Moor. "To tell you the truth, you've done me harm and yourself as well. If you had made her take off all her clothes, we would have attained our goal. But now you must remain with me for one more year before we try again."

Then he commanded his two slaves to pull down the tent and load it on the mules. After that they brought the mules over to the Moor and Judar, who mounted and road back to the city of Fez, where Judar remained with the Moor, eating and drinking well and donning a grand robe every day until one year had passed. Then the Moor said to him, "Come with me, for this is the appointed day."

And Judar said, "As you wish."

So the Moor took him outside the city, where they found the two slaves with the mules, and then they mounted the mules and rode till they reached the river. There the slaves pitched the tent and furnished it with carpets, mattresses, and pillows. The Moor took out food and drink from the saddlebags, and they had a fine meal. After eating, Abd al-Samad brought out the wand and the tablets as he had done once before, and after kindling the fire in the chafing dish, he got the incense ready. Then he said, "Judar, I want to repeat my instructions to you."

"My lord," said Judar, "do you think I've forgotten them after the beating I received?"

"You're sure you've remembered them?" the Moor asked.

"Yes," said Judar.

"Keep your wits about you," the Moor admonished him. "And don't think the woman is your mother! She's only a phantom, and her only purpose is to make you fail. You got off alive the last time, but if you make a slip this time, they'll kill you."

"If I slip this time," Judar said, "I deserve to die."

Then Abd al-Samad cast the incense into the fire and recited the incantation until the river dried up, whereupon Judar descended and knocked. The door opened, and he entered and broke the six spells until he came to the seventh door. Now, however, his mother's phantom appeared before him and said, "Welcome, my son!"

"You cursed fiend!" he responded. "Since when am I your son? Strip!"

And she tried to wheedle out of the situation by pleading with him and taking off her garments very slowly until nothing remained except her petticoat pants.

"Strip, you fiend!" he cried out.

So she finally took off the petticoat pants and lost her soul. Then he entered the hall of treasures, where he saw gold lying in heaps on the ground, but he paid no attention to them and went straight to the closet at the upper end of the hall. There he saw the enchanter Al-Shamardal lying on a couch of gold with a sword by his side, the ring on his finger, the vial of kohl on his breast, and the orb hanging over his head. So he grabbed hold of the sword and took the ring, the vial of kohl, and the orb and left the hall. All at once, music burst forth in his praise, and the servants of the treasure cried out, "May you be happy with what you've gained, Judar!" The music continued until Judar came out of the riverbed and went to the Moor, who recited an incantation, rose up, and embraced him. Then Judar gave him the four talismans, and the Moor took them and called to the slaves, who carried the tent away and brought the mules. So they mounted and returned to the city of Fez, where the Moor fetched the saddlebags and brought forth dish after dish until the tray was full.

"Eat, my brother Judar," he said. "Eat!"

So he ate until he was satisfied, at which point the Moor threw away the rest of the meat and other dishes and put the golden platters back into the saddlebags. Then he said, "Judar, you left your home and native land on my account, and you accomplished what I desired. Therefore, I want to reward you, and you may now request whatever your heart desires. Don't be ashamed, for you deserve whatever you want."

"My lord," said Judar, "I would like to have those saddlebags."

So the Moor ordered his servants to give him the saddlebags and said, "Take them, for they are your due. And if you had asked something else of me, I would have complied with your wish. Eat from them, you and your family. But, my poor fellow, these bags will only supply you with food, and you have worn yourself out for me, and I promised to send you home full of joy. So I am going to add gold and gems to these saddlebags and return you to your native land as a gentleman and merchant. Then you will be able to provide for yourself and your family and never lack for money. Now here is how you are to use the bags. When you put your hand in, you're to say, 'Oh servant of these saddlebags, I command you by the mighty names that have power over you, bring me such and such a dish!' And he will provide you with whatever you ask, even if you should ask for a thousand different dishes a day."

After telling him this, the Moor filled a second pair of saddlebags with gold, gems, and precious stones. Then he sent for a slave and a mule and said, "Judar, mount this mule, and the slave will show you the way to the door of your house, where you are to take the two pairs of saddlebags and give him the mule so that he can bring it back to me. But remember, don't tell anyone about your secret! Go now, and may Allah bless you."

"May the Almighty increase your happiness and wealth!" replied Judar, and after putting the two saddlebags on the mule's back, he mounted and set out for his home. The slave walked in front of him, and the mule followed all that day and night. The next morning he entered Cairo through the Victory Gate, where he saw his mother seated and crying out, "Alms, for the love of Allah!"

Upon seeing his mother in this condition, he almost lost his mind, and he quickly dismounted and threw his arms around her. When she realized who it was, she burst into tears. Then he mounted her on the mule and brought her to the house, where he set her down, took the saddlebags, and left the mule to the slave, who returned the beast to his master.

Judar was distraught to have found his mother a beggar, and when he was inside the house, he asked her about his brothers.

"They are both well," she said.

"Well, why are you begging by the road?" Judar replied.

"Because I'm hungry," she said.

"Before I went away, I gave you more than a thousand dinars," he said. "What happened to this money?"

"My son," she answered, "they cheated me by saying they would buy some goods with it. Then they drove me away, and I had to begin begging out of hunger."

"Mother, nobody will harm you now that I've returned. You won't have to worry about a thing. These saddlebags are full of gold and gems, and things have gone well for me."

"Truly, you are blessed, my son! May Allah continue to reward you. Now, please go and fetch us something to eat, for I was unable to sleep last night because of my hunger."

"You're welcome to what I have," said Judar. "Just tell me what you want, and I'll set it before you right away. I have no need to go to the market or to cook."

"But, son, I see nothing with you."

"I have all kinds of meat in my saddlebags."

"Well," she said, "whatever's ready will be just the right thing to satisfy my empty stomach."

"It's true that when there's no choice, men are content with the smallest thing, but when there's plenty, they like to eat what's good. So since I have plenty in my saddlebags, I want you to ask for whatever you want."

"My son, just give me some fresh bread and a slice of cheese."

"That does not suit your present situation now, Mother."

"Then give me whatever you think befits my situation," she said.

"Mother," he replied, "you deserve roast meat and chicken, peppered rice, sausages, stuffed cucumbers and lamb, stuffed ribs of mutton, and vermicelli with sliced almonds and nuts and honey and sugar and fritters and almond cakes."

However, she thought he was mocking her and said, "Alas, what's come over you? Are you dreaming, or are you daft?"

"Why do you think that I'm mad?"

"Because you're talking to me about all these delicious dishes that we can't afford," she replied.

"By Allah," he said, "You're going to have all of these dishes that I've been talking about right now. Bring me the saddlebags."

So she fetched the bags, and when she picked them up, she felt them, and they were empty. Nevertheless, she set them before him, and he stuck his hand in one of them, and he pulled out dish after dish until he had placed every single one he had named before her. Thereupon, she asked, "My son, the saddlebags are small, and they were also empty. Yet you took out all these dishes. Where were they?"

"Mother, these saddlebags were given to me by the Moor, and they are enchanted. There is a servant in them, and I can have anything I want by saying, 'Oh servant of these saddlebags, by virtue of the mighty names that command you, bring me such-and-such a dish!' and he will bring it."

"May I stick my hand in, and ask for something?"

"Go ahead."

So she stuck her hand in one of the bags and said, "Oh servant of these saddlebags, by virtue of the mighty names that command you, bring me stuffed ribs." Then she took out a dish containing delicious stuffed ribs and called for bread and other things that came to her mind.

"Mother," said Judar, "after you're done eating, empty what is left onto other plates, and put the empty platters back into the saddlebags. Also make sure that the bags are kept safely hidden."

So she arose and put the bags in a safe place.

"One more thing, Mother," he said. "You must keep all this secret. You can take the saddlebags and give alms and feed my brothers, whether I am here or not. But don't tell them how you get the food."

Then he began eating with her, and while they were enjoying themselves, his two brothers entered, for one of the neighbors had run to them and said, "Your brother has returned, and he's riding a mule that's led by a slave. And his robe is more splendid than anything I've ever seen before."

So they said to each other, "If only we hadn't treated our mother so badly! She'll surely tell him how bad we've been, and we'll be disgraced."

"Our mother is softhearted," commented one of the two, "and even if she does tell Judar, he's even milder, and if we apologize, I'm sure he'll accept our apologies."

So they entered, and he rose, greeted them in the friendliest way, and asked them to sit down and join them in their meal. So they ate until they were satisfied, for they were weak with hunger. After the meal, Judar said to them, "Brothers, take what is left and distribute it to the poor and needy."

"No," they replied. "We'd better keep it for our next meal."

But he answered, "When suppertime comes, you'll have much more than this."

So they took the leftovers, went outside, and gave them to a poor man who was passing by. Then they brought back the empty platters, and Judar said to his mother, "Put them in the saddlebags."

And Scheherazade noticed that dawn was approaching and stopped telling her story. When the next night arrived, however, she received the king's permission to continue her tale and said,

When evening came, Judar entered the room where the saddlebags were kept hidden, took out forty dishes, and brought them to the kitchen. After sitting down with his brothers, he said to his mother, "Bring in the supper."

So she went into the kitchen, and finding the dishes ready, she brought them in to her sons, one after the other. Then they ate the evening meal, and when they were done, Judar said to his brothers, "Take the left-overs and feed the poor and needy."

So they took what was left and gave it to some beggars. Soon thereafter Judar brought them sweetmeats, which they ate, and then he ordered them to give the rest to the neighbors. The next morning they had their breakfast in the same way, and the meals continued to be produced like this for ten days until Salim said to Seleem, "How do you think that our brother provides us with feasts in the morning and at noon and in the evening and with sweetmeats at night? And why do you think he gives the leftovers to the poor? Truthfully, this is the way sultans live. Yet we never see him buy anything. He doesn't have a cook, and there's nothing in the kitchen. Where does he get this great supply of food? Don't you want to find out?"

"By Allah," Seleem replied, "I really don't know how he does it. Who do you think knows?"

"I'm sure our mother knows," said Salim.

So they conceived a plot to trick their mother, and one day, when their brother was not at home, they went to her and said, "Mother, we're hungry."

"Don't worry," she said. "I'll soon feed you."

So she went to the room where the saddlebags were kept, and she took out some hot meat dishes and brought them to her sons.

"Oh Mother," they cried, "this meat is hot, and yet you haven't been cooking, and we don't see a fire."

"The dishes come from the saddlebags," she said.

"What kind of saddlebags are they?" Salim asked.

"They're enchanted," she said, "and the food is produced by saying the magic words." And she proceeded to tell them all about the special powers of the bags and swore them to secrecy.

"You can rest assured, Mother," they said, "the secret will be safe with us. But tell us what one must say to get the food."

So she taught them the secret command, and they began to put their hands in the bags and take out whatever they desired. Later, when they were alone, Seleem said to Salim, "How long are we to put up with living with Judar like servants and eating his handouts? Don't you think we should try to get the saddlebags from him and take them away?"

"Yes," said Salim, "but how shall we do it?"

"Let's sell him to the galleys."

"How can we do that?"

"We'll go to the chief captain of Suez and invite him to our house with two of his men. Whatever I say to Judar, I want you to confirm, and by the end of the night you'll see how I'm going to handle it."

So after agreeing to sell their brother, they went to the captain's quarters and said, "Captain, we've come to you on an errand that will please you."

"Fine," he answered.

"We're brothers," they continued, "and we have a third brother, a lewd fellow and good-for-nothing. When our father died, he left us some money, which we shared among ourselves, and he took his part of the inheritance and wasted it in debauchery until he was reduced to poverty. Then he went to the courts and accused us of having taken his property and that of his father. Of course, we contested the matter, but we lost our money. Then he waited awhile and started a second proceeding and reduced us to beggary. Yet even now, he is not content and has continued to persecute us. In fact, we've become so exhausted by him that we want to sell him. Are you interested?"

"If you can manage to bring him here," said the captain, "I'll pack him off to sea right away."

"We can't manage that," they replied, "but if you

come to our house tonight for dinner and bring two of your men with you, we'll grab him after he goes to bed and gag him. Then you can take him from the house in the dark, and you can do whatever you want with him."

"That's a deal," said the captain. "Will you sell him for forty dinars?"

"Yes," they answered, and they gave him the directions to the house and told him they would be waiting for him.

"All right," the captain said. "Now, be off."

Then they returned to Judar, and after waiting awhile, Seleem went up to him and kissed his hand.

"What's the matter with you, brother?"

And Seleem said, "Well, I have a friend who invited me to his house many times during your absence, and he treated me very kindly. Indeed, I owe him a thousand favors, as my brother here can confirm. I met him today, and he invited me to his house, but I said to him, 'I can't leave my brother Judar.' Then he said, 'Bring him with you.' And I replied, 'He would not consent, but if you would be my guests, you and your brothers (for his brothers were sitting with him), my brother would be pleased.' And I invited them thinking that they would refuse. But he accepted my invitation for all of them and said, 'Look for me at the gate of the little mosque, and I'll come to you and your brothers.' Now I fear that they are coming, and I'm ashamed to ask you whether you can find it in your heart to entertain them this night. Indeed, you have more than enough to share, but if you don't consent, please let me invite them into the homes of the neighbors."

"Why should you take them to the neighbors' homes?" Judar asked. "Do you think that I'm all that stingy or that I wouldn't share the abundance that we have? Shame on you! You only have to ask for what you need, and you'll have rich viands, sweetmeats, and other things to spare. Whenever you bring home people in my absence, you only have to ask our mother, and she'll set more than enough food before you. So go and fetch your friends, for we will be blessed by their presence."

Seleem kissed his hand and went straight to the gate of the little mosque, where he sat and waited until sunset. When the captain and his men arrived, he led them to the house. Judar welcomed them, asked them to be seated, and made friends with them, unaware what the future had in store for him. Then he called to his mother to bring the supper, and she began taking dishes out of the saddlebags until she set forty different dishes before them. They ate their fill, and the sailors thought that Seleem was the one who had provided such a generous meal. When a third part of the night had passed, Judar took out sweetmeats from the bags and asked Seleem to serve them, while his two brothers sat with the guests. Finally, they all became tired and decided to sleep. Accordingly, Judar lay down, and the others with him. When they were certain he had fallen asleep, they fell upon him, gagged and tied him, and carried him out of the house under the cover of the night.

And Scheherazade noticed that dawn was approaching and stopped telling her tale. When the next night arrived, however, she received the king's permission to continue her tale and said,

After they packed Judar off to Suez, the captain had him shackled and put him to work as a galley slave, and Judar was compelled to work this way for one whole year.

As for his brothers, they went to their mother the next morning and asked her, "Mother, isn't Judar awake?"

"Go and wake him," she said.

"Where is he?"

"With the guests?"

"I think he went away with them while we slept," said Seleem. "It seemed that he was longing to travel in foreign lands and hunt for hidden treasures, for we heard him talk with the seamen, and they said to him, 'We'll take you with us and show you where the treasure lies.' "

"Has he been keeping company with seamen?" she asked.

"Weren't they our guests last night?" Salim answered.

"Most likely he's gone with them," she said. "But Allah will look after him, for he is blessed, and I'm sure he'll come back with a great deal of money."

Nevertheless, she wept, for it was distressful to be separated from her son.

Then they said to her, "You wretched woman, you love Judar with all your love, while you don't care anything about us! You never shed tears for us, nor are you happy with us. But aren't we your sons just as much as Judar?"

"Indeed, you are my sons," she replied, "but you are scoundrels, and you have no place in my heart! Ever since your father died, you've shown how rotten you are, while Judar has treated me with respect and affection. Therefore, my heart goes out to him and I weep for him because of the way he's been so kind to me and to you."

When they heard this, they abused her and beat her. Then they looked for the saddlebags until they found them. They held on to the magic saddlebags while emptying the other pair of the gold and jewels and declaring, "This was our father's property!"

"It's not true!" their mother cried. "All this belongs to your brother Judar, who brought it back from Morocco."

"You're lying," they said. "It was our father's property, and we'll dispose of it as we please." Then they divided the gold and jewels between them, but they began arguing over the enchanted saddlebags.

"They're mine!" said Salim.

"No!" responded Seleem. "They're mine!"

The exchange of words became extremely heated, and their mother said, "My sons, you've divided the gold and the jewels, but this cannot be divided, nor can its value be estimated in terms of money. If it's cut in two, the spell will dissolve. So leave it with me, and I'll give you food from it whenever you want and be content to eat a morsel whenever necessary. If you give me some clothes every now and then, that will be sufficient for me. In the meantime you can use the food to trade with other people. You are my sons, and I am your mother. So let us try to get along with one another. Otherwise, we'll be disgraced when your brother returns."

However, they did not listen to her and spent the night squabbling with each other. Now, it so happened that an officer of the king's guards was a guest in the house next to Judar's and heard them through the open window. So he looked out and heard their dispute and watched them divide the spoils. Consequently, the next morning he went to the king of Egypt, whose name was Shams al-

Daulah, and told him everything he had heard. As a result, the king sent for Judar's brothers and interrogated them until they confessed their crime. As punishment, the king took the saddlebags from them and had the brothers locked up in prison while he gave their mother a sufficient daily allowance that would enable her to subsist.

Now, with regard to Judar, he spent a whole year as a slave at Suez. Then one day while he was on a ship bound on a voyage over the sea, a wind arose and cast the vessel on some rocks of a nearby cliff, causing the ship to break into pieces. All on board were drowned with the exception of Judar, who managed to swim ashore. As soon as he was on land, he headed inland until he reached an encampment of bedouin Arabs, who asked him about himself, and he told them he had been a sailor. Now, in the camp was a merchant, a native of Jiddah, who took pity on him and said, "Would you like to enter my service, Egyptian? I'll provide you with clothes and take you with me to Jiddah."

Judar accepted the offer and accompanied him to Jiddah, where he treated Judar well. After a while the merchant set out on a pilgrimage to Meccah and took Judar with him. When they reached the city, Judar went to the Haram temple to join the Ka'abah procession. As he was occupied in the devotion, he suddenly saw his friend Abd al-Samad, the Moor, who was also participating in the procession.

And Scheherazade noticed that dawn was approaching and stopped telling her tale. When the next night arrived, however, she received the king's permission to continue her tale and said,

When the Moor caught sight of him, he saluted him and asked him how he was, whereupon Judar wept and told him about everything that had happened to him. So the Moor took him to his lodgings, treated him with honor, clad him in an incomparably rich robe, and said, "The bad times are over for you, Judar." Then he took out a geomantic figure that showed what had happened to Seleem and Salim. "Your brothers are now in the king of Egypt's prison, but you are welcome to stay with me and finish performing the ordinances of the pilgrimage. Everything will turn out well for you."

"My lord," Judar replied, "let me go first and take my leave of the merchant, and then I'll return to you."

"Do you owe him money?" asked the Moor.

"No."

"Then go and take your leave," said Abd al-Samad. "But come back right away, for even the righteous must eat at some time."

So Judar went to the merchant to bid him adieu and said, "I've met my brother here."

"Well, go and bring him here," said the merchant, "and we'll provide him with entertainment."

But Judar answered, "He doesn't need that, for he's a wealthy man with a great many servants."

Then the merchant gave Judar twenty ducats and said, "This should free me of all responsibility toward you."

Judar took the money, and as he was walking away from the merchant, he saw a poor man and gave him the twenty ducats. Soon he joined the Moor, with whom he stayed until they had both finished performing their pilgrimage rites. It was then that Abd al-Samad gave Judar the royal ring that he had taken from the treasure of Al-Shamardal. "This ring will grant your every wish," he said. "It is enchanted and has a servant by the name of al-Ra'ad al-Kasif. So, whenever you have the least desire, you rub this ring, and its servant will appear and do anything you request." Then he rubbed the ring in front of Judar, and the jinnee appeared and said, "At your service, my lord! Ask whatever you will, and I'll carry out your wish. Would you like me to restore a ruined city, or would you like me to ruin a populous one? Would you like me to slay a king or rout a whole army?"

"Oh Ra'ad," said Abd al-Samad, "you now have a new lord, and you're to serve him faithfully." Then he dismissed him and turned to Judar. "Whenever you rub the ring, the servant will appear as he did just now. Then command him to do whatever you like, and you needn't worry about his defying you. Now, go to your own country and take care of the ring, and use its power wisely, for you'll be able to prevail over all your enemies with it."

"Thank you, my lord," Judar said. "With your permission, I'll set out for my home."

"Summon the jinnee," the Moor said, "and mount his

back, and if you say, 'Bring me to my native city this very day,' he will carry out your command."

So Judar took leave of the Moor and rubbed the ring, whereupon Al-Ra'ad appeared and said, "At your service, my lord. Ask whatever you want, and I'll carry out your command."

"Carry me to Cairo today," said Judar.

"Your words are my command," said the jinnee, and he took Judar on his back and flew with him from noon until midnight. Then he set him down in the courtyard of his mother's house and disappeared. Judar went inside and found his mother weeping. When she saw him, she stood up and greeted him fondly and told him how the king had beaten his brothers, thrown them in jail, and taken the saddlebags. Judar was very much concerned about all this and said to his mother, "Don't grieve over the past. I'll show you what I can do, and I'll even have my brothers released right away."

So he rubbed the ring, and the jinnee appeared. "Here I am!" he said. "Ask, and it will be yours."

"I want you to bring my two brothers from the king's prison," Judar said.

So the jinnee sank into the ground and did not emerge until he was in the middle of the jail, where Seleem and Salim were suffering because of the miserable conditions of the prison. In fact, their plight was so severe that they wished they were dead, and one of them said to the other, "By Allah, I can't stand this affliction anymore! How long will it go on? For me, death would be a relief!"

As he was speaking, the earth suddenly split open, and out came Al-Ra'ad, who seized them both and plunged back into the ground. So scared were the brothers that they fainted, and when they recovered, they found themselves in their mother's house and saw Judar seated by her side.

"Welcome, my brothers!" he said. "Your presence warms my heart."

And they bowed their heads and burst into tears.

Then Judar said, "Don't weep, for it was Satan and greed that drove you to commit your crimes. How else could you sell me? But I comfort myself by thinking of Joseph, whose brothers did worse than you've done by casting him into the pit."

* * *

And Scheherazade noticed that dawn was approaching and stopped telling her story. When the next night arrived, however, she received the king's permission to continue her tale and said,

And Judar continued, saying to his brothers, "You need only to repent to Allah and beg His pardon, and He will forgive you both, for He is merciful. As for me, I pardon you and welcome you. Nor will you be harmed." Then he comforted them, put their hearts at ease, and told them what had happened to him until he had encountered the Sheikh Abd al-Samad. Moreover, he even told them about the powers of the royal ring.

"Oh brother," they replied, "forgive us this time, and if we return to our old ways, you may do whatever you want with us."

"Don't worry, I won't harm you," he replied. "But tell me what the king did to you."

"He beat us, threatened us with death, and took the saddlebags from us."

"He shall answer for this," said Judar and rubbed the ring, whereupon Al-Ra'ad appeared.

When his brothers saw him, they became frightened and thought Judar would order him to slay them. So they fled to their mother crying, "Mother, have pity on us and intercede for us!"

"Don't worry, my sons," she responded. "You have nothing to fear."

Then Judar said to the servant, "I command you to bring me everything that is in the king's treasury. Don't leave anything behind, and make sure that you fetch the two saddlebags that he took from my brothers."

"Your words are my command," replied Al-Ra'ad, and after disappearing, he went straight to the king's treasury, where he gathered everything he could see in the treasury, including the two saddlebags, and brought it all back to Judar. After depositing the goods at his feet, he said, "My lord, I've left nothing in the treasury."

Judar gave the treasure to his mother and told her to keep it in a safe place. After putting the saddlebags down before him, he summoned the jinnee and said, "Tonight I want you to build à lofty palace for me, gild it with gold, and furnish it with all sorts of magnificent things. All this is to be done before the break of dawn."

"Your wish will be carried out," said the jinnee, and he sank into the earth.

Then Judar brought food out of the saddlebags, and they ate, enjoyed themselves, and went to sleep. In the meantime, Al-Ra'ad called forth his attendants among the jinn and ordered them to build the palace. Immediately they set to work, and while some cut stones and built the structure, others plastered, painted, and provided furnishings. By dawn the palace was complete, and Al-Ra'ad went to Judar and said, "My lord, the palace is finished and in the best of condition. If it would please you, come and look at it."

So Judar went with his mother and brothers, and they saw the most magnificent palace in the world and were amazed by its splendid structure. Judar was delighted with the vast building that towered high on the major road, especially since it had cost him nothing. Then he asked his mother, "Would you like to make this palace your home?"

"Yes, indeed," she replied and called upon Allah to bless him.

Then he rubbed the ring and ordered the jinnee to bring him forty beautiful white slave girls, forty black slave girls, and just as many mamelukes and black slaves.

"As you wish," answered Al-Ra'ad, and he left with forty of his attendants among the jinn for India, Sind, and Persia, where they snatched every beautiful girl and boy they saw until they had acquired the necessary number. Moreover, Al-Ra'ad had forty black girls and forty black slave boys captured and taken to Judar, who was pleased with them and said, "Bring them each the finest clothes to wear."

"It will be done," replied his servant.

"I also want you to bring robes for my mother, brothers, and me."

So the jinnee fetched all that was needed, and after clothing the female slaves, he said to them, "This is your mistress. Kiss her hands, and obey her every wish."

The mamelukes also put on their garments and kissed Judar's hands while he and his brothers clad themselves in the robes that the jinnee had brought them. Indeed,

Judar became like a king and his brothers like viziers. Since his palace was spacious, he gave individual quarters with slave girls to Seleem and Salim, while he and his mother inhabited another part. Each was like a sultan in his own place.

Now, in the meantime, the king's treasurer needed something from the treasury, and when he went there, he found it empty. So he uttered a great cry and fell down in a fit. After he came to his senses, he went to King Shams al-Daulah and said, "Oh, Commander of the Faithful, I've come to inform you that the treasury has been cleaned out overnight."

"What have you done with my money?" asked the king.

"By Allah, I've done nothing with your money, nor do I know what's happened to all your wealth! I had been there just yesterday, and it was full. But today, when I went in, I found it completely empty even though the doors were locked, the walls still solid, and the bolts unbroken. I cannot imagine how a thief could have entered."

"Are the two pairs of saddlebags gone?" asked the king.

"Yes," replied the treasurer.

When the king heard this, he became enraged.

And Scheherazade noticed that dawn was approaching and stopped telling her story. When the next night arrived, however, she received the king's permission to continue her tale and said,

Now the king stood up and said, "Lead the way to the treasury!"

When they arrived there, the king saw that it was indeed empty and became extremely angry with the treasurer. Then he called together the members of the court and his soldiers and cried out, "My treasury has been plundered during the night! I don't know who did this deed or would dare to commit such an outrage."

"How did it happen?" they asked.

"Ask the treasurer," he responded.

So they questioned him, and he replied, "Yesterday I visited the treasury, and it was full, but this morning when I entered it, I found it empty, though the walls were still solid and the doors unbroken."

They were all astounded by this and were trying to figure out how it could have been done when in came the officer who had denounced Seleem and Salim and said, "Majesty, I've not been able to sleep a wink because of what I saw last night."

"Well, what did you see?" the king asked.

"My lord, all night long I amused myself by watching builders at work," the officer said. "Then, by sunrise, I saw the most magnificent palace in the world. When I asked whose palace it was, I was told that Judar had come back with great wealth and mamelukes and slaves and that he had freed his two brothers from prison. It was he who had this palace built, and he's living in it like a sultan."

"Go look in the prison," the king commanded.

So his officers ran to the prison and saw that Seleem and Salim had disappeared, and they rushed back to tell the king, who said, "It's plain now who the thief is: whoever helped Seleem and Salim escape from the prison is the same person who stole my money!"

"And who is that, my lord?" asked the vizier.

"It is their brother Judar, and he's also taken the two pairs of saddlebags. So, minister, I want you to send an officer with fifty men to seal up his property and seize Judar and his brothers and bring them to me so that I may hang them! Do it now!" the king yelled in anger. "I want them put to death as soon as possible!"

But the vizier said to him, "Your majesty, be merciful, for Allah is merciful and does not act rashly to punish His servants, even when they sin against Him. Besides, whoever can build a palace in a single night, as they say Judar has done, is a formidable person. Quite honestly, I fear that the officer will have a great deal of difficulty with Judar. Therefore, have patience, while I think of some way of getting at the truth of the matter that will enable you to punish those who have offended you."

"Well, what do you advise?" asked the king.

"Send an officer to him and invite him to come to see you. When he is here, I'll flatter him and treat him in a friendly way and ask him all about his estate. After that, we shall see. If we find him formidable, we'll have to think of some way to deceive and capture him. If he's weak, we'll seize him on the spot, and you can do whatever you want with him."

The king agreed to this plan and sent one of his officers called Othman to invite Judar to come and visit him. "Tell him that we are having a banquet," said the king, "and make sure that you return with him."

Now this Othman was a proud and conceited fool, and when he came to the gate of Judar's palace, he saw a eunuch seated on a chair of gold before the door, and this eunuch did not get up. On the contrary, though Othman had fifty soldiers with him, he pretended as if nobody were approaching the gate, for this eunuch was none other than Al-Ra'ad al-Kasif, whom Judar had commanded to sit in front of the gate in the disguise of a eunuch. When Othman finally rode up to him and asked him where his lord was, he answered bluntly, "In the palace," and did not stir.

Thereupon Othman became angry and said, "You filthy slave, you should be ashamed of yourself! When I speak to you, I want you to stand up and show me the respect I deserve!"

"Be off, and stop wasting your words!" said the eunuch.

As soon as he heard this, the officer became enraged, drew his mace, and would have struck the eunuch, unaware that he was a jinnee. But Al-Ra'ad leapt upon him, took the mace from him, and dealt him four blows. Now, when the fifty soldiers saw their lord being beaten, they were mortified and drew their swords and ran to slay the eunuch. However, he cried out to them, "You dogs! Do you think you can draw on me?" And he attacked them with the mace, breaking their bones and drowning them in blood. So they turned on their heels and retreated while he followed them and kept beating them until he had driven them far from the palace gate. After this he returned to the chair at the door and sat down as though nothing had happened.

And Scheherazade noticed that dawn was approaching and stopped telling her story. When the next night arrived, however, she received the king's permission to continue her tale and said,

* * *

When Othman returned to the palace, beaten and disarrayed, he told the king what had happened to him, and the king became furious and commanded a hundred men to seize the eunuch. Accordingly, a hundred soldiers went to attack him, but he arose and fell upon them with the mace and kept beating them until he put them to rout and then returned to his chair. In the meantime the soldiers returned to the king and told him what had occurred.

"Your majesty, when he started beating us, we had to flee in fear."

Then the king sent two hundred men against him, but he forced these soldiers to retreat as well. Finally, Shams al-Daulah said to his minister, "I command you to take five hundred men and bring this eunuch back to me along with his master Judar and his brothers."

"My king," he replied, "I don't need any soldiers. I'll go alone and unarmed."

"Go," said the king, "and do as you see fit."

So the vizier discarded his weapons, put on a white robe, took a rosary in his hand, and set out on foot and alone. When he came to Judar's gate, he saw the slave sitting there, went up to him, sat down by his side politely, and said to him, "Peace be with you, my lord!"

"Peace be with you, oh mortal!" replied the eunuch. "What do you want?"

When the vizier heard him say "oh mortal," he knew that he was a jinnee and quaked for fear. Then he asked him, "My lord, tell me, is your master Judar here?"

"Yes," answered the eunuch, "he's in the palace."

"Would you then go to him, my lord, and tell him that king Shams al-Daulah salutes him and requests his company at a banquet to be held in his honor."

"Wait here while I go ask him," said the eunuch.

So the vizier stood there respectfully, and the marid went to the palace and said to Judar, "My lord, the king sent an officer and fifty men to you, and I beat them and drove them away. Then he sent a hundred men, and I beat them, too. Next he sent two hundred men, and I put them to rout as well. Finally he has sent his vizier unarmed with an invitation to visit him and dine at a banquet in your honor. What do you say to this?"

"Go and bring the vizier here," said Judar.

"As you wish," said the eunuch.

When the vizier entered the palace, he found Judar seated on an incomparably beautiful couch and in greater array than any king he had ever seen. He was dazed and amazed by the architecture of the palace and its splendid decoration and furnishings that made it seem as if he were a beggar in comparison. So he kissed the ground before Judar and asked that Allah bless him.

"Why have you come here, oh vizier?" Judar asked.

"My lord, your friend King Shams al-Daulah salutes you and would like the honor of your company at a banquet. Therefore, I ask whether you will warm his heart and accept his invitation."

"If he is indeed my friend, salute him, and tell him to come to me," Judar said.

"You may count on me to extend your invitation," said the minister.

Then Judar rubbed his ring and ordered the jinnee to fetch him the very best of robes, which he gave to the vizier. "Don this robe, and go tell the king what I have said."

So the vizier donned the robe, thc likes of which he had never worn before, and he returned to the king and told him what had happened, praising the palace and everything in it and extending Judar's invitation.

So the king called out to his officers, "Get up, my men. Mount your horses and bring me my steed so that we may go to Judar's palace!"

Then he and his suite rode off to the palace. In the meantime, Judar summoned the jinnee and said to him, "I want you to bring some of the ifrits under your command in the guise of guards and station them in the open square in front of the palace so that the king may see them and be awed by them. Then his heart will tremble, and he will know that my power and majesty are greater than his."

Thereupon Al-Ra'ad brought him two hundrcd huge and mighty jinnees in the guise of guards, magnificently armed and equipped, and when the king came and saw these tall burly fellows, he was scared to death. Then he entered the palace and found Judar sitting in more glorious array than any king or sultan could ever do. So he saluted him with respect and humility, but Judar did not rise or do him honor or tell him to be seated. Rather, he left him standing there.

And Scheherazade noticed that dawn was approaching and stopped telling her story. When the next night arrived, however, she received the king's permission to continue her tale and said,

As the king stood there, he was paralyzed with fear and said to himself, "If he was afraid of me, he wouldn't let me stand here without paying me any attention. Perhaps he intends to harm me in some way because of what I did to his brothers."

Then said Judar, "Your majesty, it does not suit someone like you to wrong people and take away their property."

"My lord," the king said, "please excuse me, for I was tempted by greed, and fate had its way. But if people did not offend, there would be no forgiving." And he went on to apologize for his past actions and to beg Judar's pardon and indulgence. Indeed, he kept humbling himself until Judar said, "May Allah pardon you!" and told him to be seated. So he sat down, and Judar bestowed garments of pardon and immunity on him, and he ordered his brothers to spread the table. When they had eaten, he clad all of the king's company in robes of honor and gave them gifts. After that he told the king to depart, which he did. From then on the king came to visit Judar every day and did not dare to hold his divan except in Judar's palace. Gradually, they became intimate friends, until one day, when the king was alone with his vizier, he said to him, "I'm having dreadful thoughts that Judar will slay me and take the kingdom away from me."

"Majesty," said his minister, "I don't think you have to fear that Judar will take away your kingdom, for his present estate is greater than yours, and to take your kingdom would be beneath his dignity. But if you fear that he intends to kill you, why don't you offer your daughter to him as his wife, and you and he will be united through the marriage."

"This is a good idea," said the king, "and I want you to act as my intermediary."

"I advise you to invite him to an evening of entertainment in your palace and to spend the night in one of your salons," said the vizier. "Then tell your daughter to don her richest dress and ornaments and pass by the door of the salon. When he sees her, he will surely fall in love with her, and once we are certain of this, I shall turn to him and tell him that she is your daughter and gradually induce him to ask you for her hand in marriage. When you've wed her to him, you and he will be bound together, and you'll be safe from him. And if he dies, you'll inherit all his wealth."

"These are wise words," said the king, and he made a banquet and invited Judar. When he came, they enjoyed themselves immensely, and toward the end of the day they were seated in the salon. Now the king had ordered his wife to dress their daughter in the richest raiment and ornaments and to lead her by the door of the salon. Of course, she did as he had told her, and when Judar saw the princess, who was incomparably beautiful and graceful, he stared at her for a long time and said "Ah!" Indeed, he felt the pangs of love, and he was seized with longing and passion for her, so much so that he turned pale.

"Is something wrong, my lord?" asked the vizier. "Why have you suddenly turned pale? You seem to be suffering."

"Oh, vizier," Judar said, "whose daughter is that damsel? Truly, she has enthralled me, and I'm mad about her."

"She's the daughter of the king," said the vizier, "and if she pleases you, I'll speak to him and see if I can arrange a marriage."

"Do so, vizier," said Judar, "and upon my life, I'll give you whatever you want and will give the king whatever he wants, and we shall become kinsmen."

Then the vizier turned to the king and whispered, "Your majesty, your friend Judar seeks an alliance with you and wants me to ask you whether you will give him your daughter's hand in marriage. Please don't disappoint me, for he will give you whatever dowry you demand."

"I've already received the dowry," said the king, "and as for the girl, she is his, if he will do me the honor of accepting her."

* * *

And Scheherazade noticed that dawn was approaching and stopped telling her story. When the next night arrived, however, she received the king's permission to continue her tale and said,

So they spent the rest of the night together, and the next day the king summoned all the members of his court, great and small, along with the Sheikh al-Islan. Then Judar demanded Princess Asiyah in marriage, and the king said, "I've received the dowry." Consequently, they drew up the marriage contract, and Judar sent for the saddlebags containing the jewels and gave them to the king as a settlement for his daughter. The drums beat, and the pipes sounded, and after a grand wedding festival, Judar spent the night with his wife and took her virginity.

From then on Judar and the king were like blood brothers, and they lived like that for many months until Shams al-Daulah died. Then the king's troops proclaimed Judar the new sultan, but he refused. However, they insisted until he consented, and they made him king. Then he ordered them to build a mosque over the late king's tomb in the Bundukaniyah quarter and endowed it with a great deal of money. Now the quarter in which Judar had built his palace was called Yamaniyah, but when he became sultan, he built a congregational mosque there and other buildings so that the quarter was named after him and called the Judariyah quarter.

In the meantime, Judar appointed both Seleem and Salim his viziers, and they lived peacefully together for one year, but no more than that. At the end of that time Seleem said to Salim, "How long are we supposed to live like this? Are we to spend our whole lives as slaves of our brother Judar? We shall never be our own masters and enjoy our power as long as he lives. So, I ask you, how can we kill him and take possession of the saddlebags and the ring?"

"Since you are more cunning than I am," Salim replied, "you devise a plan for killing Judar, and I'll help you."

"If I do this," said Seleem, "will you agree that I am to be sultan and keep the ring, and you'll be my vizier and can keep the saddlebags?"

"I agree," said Salim.

Soon thereafter they made plans to slay Judar because of their desire for power and wealth. When they had set their snare, they went to Judar and said, "Brother, we would like to celebrate your glory and invite you to one of our houses for a banquet and entertainment."

"Of course," Judar said. "In whose house will the banquet be?"

"In mine," said Seleem. "And after you have eaten, we shall have the entertainment in Salim's house."

"Very good," said Judar, and he went with him to his house, where Seleem set poisoned food before him. After Judar had eaten some, his flesh rotted from his bones, and he died. Then Seleem went up to him and tried to pull the ring from his finger, but it would not come off. So he cut off the finger with a knife and rubbed the ring. When the jinnee appeared, he said, "At your service! What is your command?"

"Get my brother Salim, and put him to death," said Seleem. "Then carry the two bodies of my brothers and throw them down before the troops."

So the marid went and killed Salim. Afterward he carried the two corpses and threw them down before the chief officers of the army, who were sitting at a table in the parlor of Judar's palace. When they saw the murdered bodies of Judar and Salim, they stopped eating and were seized by fear. "Who's done this to the sultan and the vizier?" they asked.

"Their brother, Seleem," replied the jinnee.

Suddenly Seleem appeared before them and said, "Soldiers, eat and make merry, for Judar is dead, and I have taken the royal ring served by this marid. I ordered him to slay my brother Salim so that he would not try to take over the kingdom. He was a traitor, and I was afraid that he would try to scheme against me. So now I've become your sultan. If you don't accept me, I'll rub the ring and order the jinnee to slay you all, great and small."

And Scheherazade noticed that dawn was approaching and stopped telling her story. When the next night arrived, however, she received the king's permission to continue her tale and said,

* * *

The officers replied, "We accept you as our king."

Then he ordered them to bury his brothers and assembled his court. Some of the people followed the funeral procession, while others preceded him in a state procession to the audience hall of the palace, where he sat down on the throne, and they paid him homage as king. After this ceremony, he said, "It is my desire to marry my brother Judar's wife."

"Wait till the proper period of her widowhood is over," they said.

"I don't care about the proper days of widowhood or anything else," he said. "Upon my life, I want to have her and sleep with her this very night."

So they drew up the marriage contract and informed Princess Asiyah about this matter. In turn, she sent for him, and when he entered her chamber, she received him with a show of joy and welcome. However, at one point she poured some poison in his water and brought about his end. Then she took the ring and broke it so that no one might ever possess it again. She also tore up the saddlebags and then informed the Sheikh al-Islan and other great officers of state what had happened and told them to choose a new king to rule over them.

And this, then, is the story about Judar and his brothers that has been passed down to us.

No sooner had Scheherazade concluded her tale than she said, "And yet, oh king, this story is no more wondrous than the tale of Sinbad the Seaman and Sinbad the Landsman."

Sinbad the Seaman and Sinbad the Landsman

During the reign of the Commander of the Faithful, Harun al-Rashid, a poor man named Sinbad the Hammal lived in the city of Baghdad. He earned his living by carrying heavy loads on his head, and one very hot day he happened to be carrying such a tremendous load that he began to sweat profusely and was exhausted from the heat and the weight of the load. He needed to rest desperately, and as he passed the gate of a merchant's house, where the ground was watered and the air mild, he spotted a broad bench beside the door. So he placed his load on the bench to take a rest and smell the air. Indeed, a pleasant breeze and delicious fragrance came out of the court door, and he sat down on the edge of the bench. All of a sudden, he heard the melodious sound of lutes and other stringed instruments coming from inside the house, and there were also joyful and excited voices singing and reciting along with the songs of all sorts of warbling birds, doves, mockingbirds, merles, nightingales, cushats, and stone curlews. Sinbad was amazed by all this and felt cheerful and contented. Then he went up to the gate and saw a great flower garden, in which there were pages, black slaves, servants, attendants, and the like such as are usually found only in the homes of kings and sultans. As he was standing there, he began to smell the savory odors of all kinds of rich and delicious meats and splendid wine. So he raised his eyes toward heaven and said, "Glory to You, oh Lord! I beg You, please pardon me for all my sins and crimes. May Your will be done as You so choose, for You are almighty. Praise be to You, Most Perfect One. Whomever You desire, You make rich, whomever You desire, You make poor. Whomever You desire, You exalt. Whomever You desire, You debase. There is no God but You! You favor whomsoever You desire, whereby the owner of this place abides in the joy of life and delights himself with pleasant fragrances, delicious meats, and exquisite wines of all kinds. It is You who ordains all of this, wherefore some are weary and others lead lives of leisure; some enjoy fair fortune and affluence, while others suffer the extreme of travail and misery as I myself do."

When Sinbad the porter finished his recitation, he picked up his load and was about to move on when a handsome page in elegant garments came forth from the gate, caught him by the hand, and said, "Come in and talk to my lord, for he summons you."

The porter wanted to excuse himself, but the page was adamant that he come. So he left his load with the doorkeeper in the vestibule and followed the boy into the house, which was a good-sized mansion, radiant and full of majesty. The page led him to the grand sitting room, where Sinbad saw a group of nobles and great lords seated at tables garnished with all sorts of flowers and sweet-scented herbs along with plenty of dainty viands, dried and fresh fruit, and wines of the choicest vintages. There were also musical instruments, mirth, and lovely slave girls playing and singing. The entire company was arranged according to rank. In the highest place was a stately and noble man with a gray beard. His demeanor was pleasant and full of dignity and majesty. All of this astounded Sinbad, and he said to himself, "By Allah, this must be either a part of paradise or some king's palace!" Then he greeted the company with a great deal of respect, praying for their prosperity, and kissing the ground before them. His head was bowed in a humble attitude, and the master of the house requested that he draw near and be seated. His voice was kind, and he bid him welcome. Then he set various kinds of rich and delicious viands before him, and the porter began to eat his fill, after which he exclaimed, "Praised be Allah, no matter what our condition may be!" And after washing his hands, he thanked the company for the meal and entertainment.

"You are welcome," said the host, "and may your day

be blessed. But now, tell me, what is your name and your calling?"

"Oh my lord, my name is Sinbad the Hammal, and I carry folks' goods on my head for hire."

The master smiled and replied, "I want you to know, oh porter, that your name is just like mine, for I am Sinbad the Seaman, and now, oh porter, I want you to recite the words that you just said at the gate."

The porter was abashed and responded, "May Allah be with you, excuse me, for toil, travail, and lack of luck teach a man poor manners and boorish ways."

"Don't be ashamed. You have become my brother. So repeat the words you uttered at the gate."

So the porter repeated his words, and they delighted the merchant, who said to him, "I want you to know, oh Hammal, that my story is a wonderful one, and you will hear everything that happened to me and everything that I underwent before I rose to this state of prosperity and became the lord of this place. Indeed, I did not come to this high position without a great deal of travail and perils galore. You can't imagine how much toil and trouble I suffered in the past! I made seven voyages, and there are marvelous tales connected to each one, tales which baffled the mind, and it was fate and fortune that determined everything, for it is true that one cannot avoid one's destiny." The master paused and turned to his company. "Now I'll have you know, my lords, that I am about to recount

The First Voyage of Sinbad the Seaman

My father was a merchant, one of the notables of my native land, a man of wealth and ample means, who died while I was still a child, leaving me a great deal of money, land, and farmhouses. When I grew up, I was given the entire inheritance and ate the best, drank freely, wore rich clothes, and lived lavishly. I kept company with young men of my own age, and I thought that this way of life would continue forever. Thus, for a long time I lived a life of leisure, but at last I awoke from my carefree life and returned to my senses. Indeed, I found that my wealth had been depleted, and my condition was poor, and all that I had once owned was no longer my property. Stricken with dismay and confusion, I thought of a saying of our lord Solomon, son of David, which I had heard a long time ago from my father: "Three things are better than three others; the day of death is better than the day of birth, a live dog is better than a dead lion, and the grave is better than poverty."

Then I gathered together the remains of my estates and property and sold everything, even my clothes, for three thousand dirhams, with which I intended to travel to foreign lands. I bought goods, merchandise, and everything needed for a voyage. Impatient to take to sea, I embarked with a company of merchants on board a ship bound for Bassorah. There we again embarked and sailed many days and nights, and we went from island to island and sea to sea and shore to shore, buying, selling, and bartering everywhere the ship touched. We continued our course until we came to an island that seemed to be part of the gardens of paradise. Here the captain cast anchor and extended planks so that everyone could go ashore, where we lit fires and occupied ourselves in various ways, some cooking and some washing, while others walked around the island for pleasure. Meanwhile the crew began eating, drinking, and playing.

I was one of the walkers, but while I was on my way, I heard the captain suddenly cry out, "Ho there! Passengers, run for your lives! Return to the ship as fast as you can! Leave your gear and save yourselves from destruction, and may Allah preserve you! This island that you're standing on is not a real island, but a huge whale in the middle of the sea. The sand has settled on it and trees have grown on it over time so that it seemed like an island. But when you lit fires on it, the whale felt the heat and has moved. In a moment it will dive down into the sea, and you'll all be drowned. So leave your gear and seek safety before you die!"

* * *

And Scheherazade noticed that the dawn was approaching and stopped telling her story. When the next night arrived, however, she received the king's permission to continue her tale and said,

Now all those who heard the captain left their gear and goods, their washed and unwashed clothes, and their fire pots, and they fled back to the ship for their lives. Some reached it, while others—and I was among them—did not, for suddenly the island shook and sank into the depths of the sea with all that was on it, and the dashing sea surged over it with clashing waves. I sank with the others, down, down into the deep, but Almighty Allah preserved me from drowning and threw a great wooden tub in my way, one that had served the ship's company for washing. I grabbed onto it for dear life and mounted it as if I were riding a horse. I paddled with my feet as oars while the waves tossed me from right to left.

Meanwhile the captain made sail and departed with those who had reached the ship, regardless of the drowning and drowned. I kept following the vessel with my eyes until it disappeared from sight, and I was sure I would die. While I was in this plight, darkness descended on me, and the winds and waves drove me on all night and the next day, until the tub carried me to a lofty island with trees bowing over the inlet. I caught hold of a branch and swung myself onto the land with its help. But when I reached the shore, I found that my legs had cramps and were numb, and my feet bore traces of the nibbling of fish on their soles. In all, I felt nothing but anguish and fatigue and threw myself down on the ground like a dead man. Before I knew it, I fainted and did not recover my senses until the next morning, when the sun rose and revived me. But I found my feet were so swollen that I had to make do by crawling on my knees. Fortunately there was a lot of fruit and fresh water on that island, and the fruit helped me recover my strength. I continued to live from the fruit and water for days and nights until my life seemed to return and my spirits began to revive. When I was able to move about, I decided to explore the island and cut a staff from one of the trees to help me walk. Then I amused myself by looking at all the things that Almighty Allah had created there.

One day, as I was walking along the shore, I caught sight of some object in the distance and thought it was a wild beast or one of the monsters of the sea. But as I drew near it, constantly keeping it view, I realized that it was a noble mare tethered on the beach. When I went up to her, however, she neighed so loudly that I trembled with fear and turned to go away. Just then a man appeared from under the ground and followed me, crying out, "Who are you? Where have you come from? How come you're here?"

"Oh my lord," I answered, "I am in truth a waif, a stranger, and was left to drown with others from the ship we voyaged in. But Allah graciously sent me a wooden tub. So I saved myself on it and floated until the waves cast me upon this island."

When the man heard this, he took my hand and said, "Come with me." Then he led me into a great underground chamber, which was as spacious as a salon. He made me sit down at its upper end and brought me some food. Since I was hungry, I ate until I was satisfied and refreshed, and when he had put me at my ease, he began questioning me, and I told him everything that had happened to me from first to last. Since he seemed to wonder about my adventures, I said, "By Allah, excuse me, I've told you the truth about my situation and the accident. Now I'd appreciate it if you'd tell me who you are and why you're dwelling here under the ground and why you've tethered the mare on the shore."

"I'd be glad to answer all your questions," he responded. "Let me begin by telling you that I am one of several grooms of King Mihrjan stationed in different parts of this island, and all his horses are in our charge. Every month about the time of the new moon, we bring our best mares which have never been mated to this spot, and we picket them on the seashore and hide ourselves underground so that no one can see us. Soon the stallions of the sea smell the mares and come up out of the water. When they are sure that no one is near, they leap upon the mares and have their will with them. After they have mated with them, they try to drag them away but can't succeed because of the leg ropes. So they neigh at them, butt them, and kick them, and this tells us that they have dismounted. Then we run out and shout at them, and our cries and noise startle them so much that they return to the sea in fear. Some time later the mares bear colts and fillies worth a great deal of money, and there's nothing like them on the face of the earth. As you can see, you've arrived here at the very time that we usually bring our mares to mate with the sea stallions, and now I'll take you to King Mihrjan and show you our country. Let me tell you that if you hadn't stumbled upon us, you would have probably perished, and nobody would have found you. But I'll be glad to help you find a way to return to your native land."

I thanked him for his generosity and kindness, and while we were still talking, a stallion appeared suddenly out of the sea, and after uttering a great cry, he sprang upon the mare and mounted her. When he had had his will of her, he dismounted and tried to carry her away with him but was not able to do this because of the tether. She kicked and neighed at him, while the groom took a sword and shield and ran out of his hiding place. As he ran, he hit the shield with the blade and called to his company, who came up shouting and brandishing spears. Frightened, the stallion took flight and plunged into the sea, where he disappeared under the waves. After this we sat awhile until the rest of the grooms reached us, each leading a mare. When they saw me with their comrade, they asked me where I had come from, and I repeated my story to them. Afterward they spread a table and invited me to eat with them. So I ate with them, and then they gave me a horse and set out with me to the capital of King Mihrjan. Upon our arrival, they told him my story, and he sent for me. When I was presented to him and the salaams had been exchanged, he gave me a cordial welcome, wishing me a long life, and then requested that I tell him my tale. So I related to him all that I had seen and all that had happened to me from first to last.

The king was astounded by what he heard and said to me, "By Allah, my son, you have been miraculously saved. If you were not destined to live a long life, you would never have escaped from such peril. Praise be to Allah for your safety!"

Then he spoke cheerfully to me and treated me with kindness and consideration. Moreover, he made me his

agent for the port and registrar of all ships that entered the harbor. I visited him regularly to receive his commands, and he favored me by kind acts and by adorning me with costly and splendid robes. Indeed, my credit as an intermediary for the folk was high, and I often intervened for the people when they needed something.

I lived this way for a long time, and whenever I passed through the city on my way to the port, I asked merchants, travelers, and sailors about Baghdad on the chance that I might learn of some way to return to my native land, but I could not find anyone who knew Baghdad or who was planning a voyage there. I was disappointed by this, for I yearned for my home. My disappointment lasted for some time, until one day I visited King Mihrjan and found a company of Indians with him. I greeted them and they returned my salaam and politely asked me what my country was.

And Scheherazade noticed that dawn was approaching and stopped telling her story. When the next night arrived, however, she received the king's permission to continue her tale and said,

After I told them about my country, I asked them about theirs, and they told me they were of various castes, some called Shakiriyah, who are the noblest and do not oppress anyone or commit violent acts against other people; others called Brahmans, who abstain from wine, but live in delight and pleasure and own camels, horses, and cattle. Moreover, they told me that the people of India are divided into seventy-two castes, and I was most astonished by this.

Among other things that I saw in King Mihrjan's dominions was an island called Kasil, where the beating of drums and taborets was heard all night, but we were told by the people of the neighboring islands and by travelers that the inhabitants of Kasil were diligent and prudent. In the surrounding sea I also saw a fish two hundred feet long, and since the fishermen are afraid of it, they strike pieces of wood against each other and scare it away. I also saw another fish with a head like that of an owl, and there are many other wondrous things that I saw, but it would be tedious to recount all of them.

I spent a good deal of time visiting the islands until one day, while I was standing in the port with a staff in my hand, according to my custom, a large ship appeared on the horizon sailing for the harbor, and there were apparently many merchants on it. When it reached the inner port where the ships anchor, the captain furled his sails and put out the landing planks, while the crew began to unload the cargo. I stood there and wrote down the contents of the cargo, and it took a long time for them to bring the goods ashore. When I asked the captain, "Is there anything left on ship?" he answered, "My lord, there are various bales of merchandise in the hold, but the owner drowned at one of the islands along our way. So his goods remained in our charge by way of trust, and we intend to sell them and note their price so that we may take the money to the people in the city of Baghdad, the home of peace."

"What was the merchant's name?" I asked.

"Sinbad the Seaman," he responded.

Whereupon I looked at him more closely, and upon realizing that I knew him, I uttered a great cry. "Oh captain, I am that Sinbad the Seaman, who traveled with the other merchants, and when the whale heaved and you called to us, some saved themselves and others drowned. I was one of them who almost drowned, but Allah Almighty threw a great washing tub of wood in my way, and the winds and waves carried me to this island, where by Allah's grace, I encountered King Mihrjan's grooms, and they brought me here to their master. After I told the king my story, he bestowed his favor upon me and made me his harbormaster. Since then I have prospered in his service, and he has approved my work. These bales, therefore, are mine, the goods that God has given me."

"By Allah," the captain exclaimed, "there is neither conscience nor good faith left among men!"

"Captain," I responded, "what do you mean by those words? Haven't I told you my story?"

"Just because you heard me say that I have some goods with me and the owner of these goods has drowned, you think you can take them. But it is forbidden by law, for we saw him drown before our very own eyes along with some other passengers, who also drowned. So how can you pretend that you are the owner of these goods?"

"Oh captain," I said, "listen to my story and pay attention to my words, and the truth will become evident. I'm not a hypocrite, nor am I a liar."

Then I told him everything that had happened to me since I sailed from Baghdad on his ship until we came to the whale island, where we were nearly drowned. I also recalled certain matters that had gone on between us, and when he and the merchants were convinced that my story was true and had recognized me, they rejoiced at my salvation and cried out, "By Allah, we thought for sure that you had drowned! But the Lord has granted you new life."

Then they delivered my bales to me, and I found my name written on them, and nothing was missing. So I opened them and took out one of the finest and costliest items as a present for King Mihrjan and had the sailors carry it up to the palace. Then I went to the king and laid my present at his feet, telling him all about what had happened and how I had recovered my goods. Of course, he was most astounded, and he soon saw that everything I had told him was true. After that his affection for me increased, and he showed me even more honor and gave me a great present in return for the one I had given him. Then I sold my bales and other goods, making a great profit on them, and bought other homemade goods that came from the island.

When the merchants were about to start on their homeward voyage, I embarked on board the ship and took all my possessions with me. Before I left, I went to the king and thanked him for all his favors and friendship and asked his permission to return to my land and friends. He bid me farewell and gave me numerous articles made on his island. Then we set sail and traveled many days and nights until we arrived safely at the city of Bassorah, where I rejoiced at my return to my native soil. After a short stay I began my trip to Baghdad with all my valuable goods and commodities. Upon reaching the city I went straight to my house, where all my friends and kinsfolk came to greet me. Then I bought eunuchs, concubines, servants, and Negro slaves until I had a large establishment, and I bought houses, land, and gardens until I was richer and in a better situation than I had been before. So I began enjoying the company of my friends and comrades once again and even more intensively that I had done before, forgetting all my hardships, perils, and loneliness in a foreign land. I allowed myself all sorts of joys, pleasures, and delights, eating the most tender viands and drinking the most delicious wines. Thanks to my wealth, of course, I was able to do this for quite some time.

This, then, is the story of my first voyage, and tomorrow I shall tell you the tale of the second of my seven voyages.

After saying this, Sinbad the Seaman invited Sinbad the Landsman to have supper with him and ordered that he be given a hundred gold pieces. After supper he remarked, "You have cheered us with your company this day, and I want you to return tomorrow."

The porter thanked him, took his gift, and went his way, pondering all he had heard and wondering about the marvelous things that happen to people. He spent the night in his own place, and early the next morning he returned to the home of Sinbad the Seaman, who received him with honor and seated him by his side. As soon as the rest of the company was assembled, the host had meat and drink set before them, and when they had all eaten and drunk and were in a merry mood, he picked up the threads of his story and began telling them the tale of

The Second Voyage of Sinbad the Seaman

I was leading a most enjoyable life until one day I became obsessed by the thought of traveling about the world and visiting foreign cities and islands. I also had a longing to trade goods and make money. Consequently, I took a great deal of cash, bought some goods and traveling gear, and had them bound up in bales. Then I went down to the riverbank, where I found a brand-new and noble ship about to sail. Since it was equipped with sails of fine cloth and well manned, I booked passage with a number of other merchants, and after having our goods loaded on board, we embarked the same day. Our voyage was most pleasant, and we sailed from place to place and from island to island, and whenever we anchored, we met a crowd of merchants, notables, and customers and bought, sold, and bartered with them. At last, destiny brought us to a fair and verdant island that had an abundance of trees, ripe fruit, fragrant flowers, and warbling birds. There were also crystal and radiant streams but no sign of human life. The captain weighed anchor, and the merchants and sailors landed on the island, walking about and enjoying the shade of the trees and the song of the birds. I landed with the rest and sat down by a spring of fresh water and ate some food that I had with me. So sweet was the breeze and so fragrant were the flowers that I became drowsy and fell asleep.

When I awoke, I found myself all alone, for the ship had sailed and left me behind. Not a single one of the merchants or sailors had thought of me. So I searched all over the island but found neither man nor jinnee. As a result, I was extremely troubled, and my gall was about to burst because of my disappointment and anguish. There I was all alone without any gear, meat, or drink, weary and heartbroken. Indeed, I gave myself up for lost and said, "The crock can't always expect to escape the shock. I was saved the first time by finding someone who took me from a desolate spot to a port city, but now there is no hope for me."

Then I began to weep and wail and became angry at myself for having undertaken the dangers and hardships of voyaging when I had been comfortable in my own house in my own land, delighting in good meat, drink, and clothes and lacking nothing, neither money nor goods. And I repented of having left Baghdad, all the more so after all the travails I had undergone during my first voyage, when I had barely escaped with my life. Soon I got up and walked around the island, unable to sit still or remain in any one place. Then I climbed a tall tree and looked in various directions, but saw nothing except the sky, sea, birds, islands, and sand. However, after a while my eager glances caught sight of some great white thing far off in the interior of the island. So I climbed down from the tree and headed for the thing I had seen, which turned out to be a huge white dome rising high in the air. I walked all around its vast exterior but found no door to enter, nor could I muster enough strength to climb it, because it was exceeding smooth and slippery. So I marked the spot where I stood and went around the dome to measure its circumference, which I found to be fifty good paces. As I stood there trying to figure out how I could enter, the sun began to set, and the air became dull and dark. I thought a cloud had come over the sun, even though it was summer. While I was wondering about this, I lifted my head to look up at the sky, and suddenly I saw that the cloud was none other than an enormous bird of gigantic girth and wide wings. And as it flew through the air, it veiled the sun and hid it from the island. This sight made me even more astounded, and I remembered a story.

And Scheherazade noticed that dawn was approaching and stopped telling her story. When the next day arrived, however, she received the king's permission to continue her tale and said,

I had heard this story a long time ago from pilgrims and travelers. It was about a huge bird called the Rukh, that dwelled on an island, and it fed its young one elephants. Now I was sure that the dome which had caught my sight was none other than a Rukh's egg, and as I watched in wonder at the marvelous works of the Almighty, the bird landed on the dome and covered it with its wings, while its legs stretched out behind it on the ground. In this posture it fell asleep, and when I saw this, I got up and unwound my turban from my head. By doubling it, I twisted it into a rope with which I girt my middle and bound my waist tightly to the legs of the Rukh. "Perhaps," I said to myself, "this bird will carry me to a land with cities and people, and that will be better than dwelling on this deserted island."

I spent the night watching and afraid to sleep in case the bird caught me by surprise and flew away with me.

As soon as dawn broke and the sun began to shine, the Rukh rose from its egg, spread its wings with a great cry, and flew up into the air, dragging me with it. Nor did the bird stop soaring until I thought it had reached the outer limit of the firmament. Then it started to descend little by little until it landed on the top of a high hill. As soon as I found myself on firm ground, I quickly untied myself, quaking with fear of the bird, even though it did not pay any attention to me or even feel me. After loosening my turban from its feet, I made off as fast as I could. Soon thereafter I saw it catch something from the earth with its huge claws and fly high into the air with it. When I observed it more closely, I realized that the bird was carrying a gigantic serpent, and it soon flew away clean out of my sight.

Now I found myself on a peak overlooking a great and wide valley, bordered by vast mountains that shot high into the air. It was impossible to discern what was on top of the mountains because they were so high, nor could anyone climb them. When I realized this, I blamed myself for making a mistake and said, "If only I had stayed on the island! It was better than this wild place. At least I had fruit to eat and water to drink, while there's nothing but trees here. No fruit or streams. By Allah, it seems that as soon as I get myself out of one dangerous situation, I fall into one that is more perilous and distressing." However, I took courage and walked along the summit. I found that the soil was of diamond, and the valley swarmed with snakes and vipers, each big as a palm tree, and they could have swallowed an elephant with one gulp. They came out by night and hid during the day, when they were afraid the Rukhs and eagles might pounce on them and tear them to pieces as was their wont. Again I regretted the mistake I had made and said, "By Allah, I've only got myself to blame for falling into such a miserable predicament!"

The day began to wane as I walked along, and I looked around for a place where I could spend the night. Since I was more afraid of the serpents, I gave no consideration to my hunger and thirst but to my safety. Soon I caught sight of a cave nearby. It had a narrow doorway, and after I entered, I rolled a great stone up to the entrance and stopped it. "I'm safe here for the night," I said, "and as soon as it's day, I'll go out and see what destiny has in store for me." Then I looked around the cave and saw a great serpent at the upper end sitting on her eggs. My flesh quaked, and my hair stood on end, but I raised my eyes to heaven and placed my fate in God's hands. I remained there the entire night without sleeping, and when daybreak arrived, I rolled back the stone from the mouth of the cave and staggered forth like a drunken man, for I had become giddy from fear and hunger. It was in this sorry state that I walked along the valley, and suddenly a slaughtered beast fell down before me even though there was no one around me who could have killed it. I was most astonished, and then I recalled a story from traders, pilgrims, and travelers about the mountains that are full of diamonds. These mountains are treacherous and dangerous, and no one can travel through them. But the merchants who trade in diamonds have developed a means to obtain them. They slaughter a sheep, skin it, cut it into pieces, and throw them down from the mountaintops into the valley. Since the meat is fresh and bloody, some of the gems stick to it. By midday the eagles and vultures swoop down on the meat and carry it to the mountaintops, where the merchants rush toward them, shouting and scaring them away from the meat. Once the birds depart, the merchants take the diamonds that they find sticking to the meat. Then they go their way and leave the meat to the birds and beasts. This is the only way that one can obtain the diamonds.

So when I saw the slaughtered beast fall, I remembered this story and went and filled my pockets, belt, turban, and folds of my clothes with the choicest diamonds. As I was doing this, another piece of meat fell down next to me. Then I took my unrolled turban, lay on my back, and set the piece on my breast so that I was hidden by the meat, which was thus raised above the ground. Hardly had I gripped it when an eagle swooped down upon the flesh, seized it with its talons, and flew high into the air with me clinging to the meat. The eagle did not stop flying until it landed on the top of one of the mountains, where it dropped the carcass and began to tear at it. But all of a sudden there was a great deal of shouting and clattering of wood, causing the bird to take flight and disappear. Then I loosened myself from the

meat and stood up with my clothes soaked in blood. Just then the merchant who had shouted at the eagle came up and saw me standing there, but he did not speak to me because he was trembling with fright at my sight. However, he did go up to the carcass, and turning it over, he saw that there were no diamonds sticking to it. "By Allah, what a disappointment!" he exclaimed, and he moaned and beat his hands. "Alas, what a pity! How did this happen?"

Then I went up to him, and he asked me who I was and how I had managed to get to there.

"Don't be afraid," I replied. "I'm a man and a good man and merchant. My story is wondrous, my adventures are marvelous, and my arrival here is extraordinary. So don't worry, because I'm going to give something to you that will make you rejoice. I have plenty of diamonds with me, and I'll give you enough to make you happy. Indeed, these diamonds are better than you would otherwise get. So don't worry."

Upon hearing this the man rejoiced and blessed me. Then we talked together, until the other merchants from his group who heard us conversing came up and greeted me, for each one had thrown down his piece of meat. And as I went along with them, I told them my whole story, and I gave the owner of the meat a number of the stones I had with me. So they all rejoiced with me about my escape and said, "Fortune smiles upon you, for no one before you has ever reached that valley over there and come away alive. But praise Allah for your safety!"

We spent the night together in a safe and pleasant place and celebrated my deliverance from the Valley of Serpents and my arrival in a land with people. The next morning we set out and journeyed over the mighty range of mountains and saw many serpents in the valley. Then we came to a beautiful large island on which there was a garden of huge camphor trees that could shelter a good hundred men. When the folk want to get camphor, they bore into the upper part of the bole with a long iron, whereupon the liquid camphor, which is the sap of the tree, flows out, and they catch it in vessels. Then it becomes more solid, like gum. However, after this the tree dies and becomes used for firewood. Aside from the trees, there was a wild beast on the island called a rhinoceros, which grazes as the steers and buffaloes do with us. But it is a huge brute with a body bigger than a camel, and like the camel it feeds on leaves and twigs of trees. It is a remarkable animal with a great thick horn ten feet long in the middle of its head. If the horn is cut off, its head is like that of a man. Travelers and pilgrims declare that this beast can carry off a large elephant on its horn, then graze about the island and the seacoast with it on its horn, paying no attention to it. When the elephant dies and its fat melts in the sun and runs down into the rhinoceros's eyes and blinds it, it is forced to lie down on the shore. Then the Rukh arrives and carries off both the rhinoceros and the elephant to feed its young.

While on the island I saw many kinds of oxen and buffaloes, whose like cannot be found in our country. Here I sold some of the diamonds which I had with me for gold dinars and silver dirhams, and I traded others for the produce of the country. After that I loaded the goods on beasts of burden and traveled on with the merchants from valley to valley and town to town, buying and selling and visiting foreign countries until we came to Bassorah. After spending a few days there, I continued on to Baghdad. Soon after my arrival I gathered my friends and relatives together and offered them rare gifts. I also gave alms and then began eating and drinking, wearing fine clothes, and making merry with my friends. I forgot all my sufferings because of the pleasures and delights I enjoyed at home. And all who heard about my return came and asked me about my adventures and the foreign countries, and I told them about everything that had happened to me and all that I had suffered. They were astonished by my tale and wished me happiness after my safe return.

This, then, is the end of the story of my second voyage, and tomorrow I'll tell you what happened to me in my third voyage.

Once again the company marveled at this story and enjoyed dinner with him. Afterward Sinbad ordered a hundred dinars of gold to be given to the porter, who took the sum with many thanks and blessings, amazed by what he had heard. Next morning when day came in all its glory, he rose, said the dawn prayer, and returned to the house of Sinbad the Seaman, just as he had been requested to do. After entering, the merchant welcomed him and made him sit with him until the rest of the company arrived. When they had all eaten and drunk and were merry, their host began by saying, "Listen, my brothers, to what I am about to tell you, for it is even more wondrous than what you have already heard. Listen to

The Third Voyage of Sinbad the Seaman

As I told you yesterday, I came back from my second voyage overjoyed at my safe return and with a great deal more wealth than I had before, thanks to Allah, who had compensated me for all that I had lost. For a while I dwelled in Baghdad savoring my comfort and prosperous condition, until I was once again seized by a longing for travel and adventure. Moreover, I yearned for trade, lucre, and profit, for the human heart is weak and prone to evil. So I gathered together plenty of goods suitable for a sea voyage and traveled to Bassorah, where I went down to the shore and found a fine ship ready to sail with a full crew and many merchants, men of worth and substance and of faith, piety, and kindness. After embarking with them, we congratulated one another on our good fortune and bon voyage as we sailed from sea to sea and island to island and city to city, enjoying ourselves, buying and selling wherever we touched shore, until one day the dashing sea became swollen with clashing billows, and the captain, who stood on the gunwale examining the ocean, cried out to his men to furl the sail and cast the anchors. As the sea buffeted his face, plucked his beard, and soaked his clothes, we called to him, "Oh captain, what's the matter?"

"May Allah preserve you, my brethren! The wind has gotten the better of us and has driven us off course into the middle of the ocean. As fate would have it, we are bound for the Mountain of the Zughb, a hairy folk like apes, and no man who has encountered them has ever come away alive. I have the awful feeling that we will all be dead men soon!"

No sooner had the captain ended his speech than the apes descended on us. They surrounded the ship on all sides, swarming like locusts and crowding the shore. They were the most frightful of wild creatures, covered with black hair like felt, ugly and small, about four feet high, with yellow eyes and black faces. Nobody knows their language, nor what they are, and they shun the company of men. We were afraid to slay them, strike at them, or drive them away because there were hordes of them there. If we had hurt one of them, the rest would have attacked us and killed us, for numbers prevail over courage. So we let them do what they wanted, even though we feared they would plunder our goods and our gear.

They swarmed up the cables and gnawed them to pieces, and they did the same with all the ropes of the ship so that it became stranded on the mountainous coast and could not be propelled by the wind. Then they seized all the merchants and the crew and set us on the island. In the meantime they made off with the ship and its cargo, and we had no idea where they went. Thus we were left on the island, where we ate fruit and herbs and drank the fresh water, until one day we caught sight of what seemed to be an inhabited house in the middle of the island. We headed for it as fast as our feet could carry us, and it turned out to be a strong and tall castle, encircled by a lofty wall with a two-door gate of ebony wood that stood open.

We entered and found a large open space like a great square. Around it were many open doors, and at the far end there was a long bench of stone and braziers with cooking gear hanging on it and bones strewn about it. But we did not see anyone and were astounded by our surroundings. Then we sat down in the courtyard for a little while and soon fell asleep. In fact, we slept from noon until sundown, when suddenly the earth trembled under our feet and the air rumbled with a terrible noise. From the top of the castle a huge creature that resembled a man came down upon us. He was black, tall, and husky, with eyes like coals of fire, teeth like boar's tusks, and a vast mouth like the size of a well. To boot, he had long loose lips like a camel's hanging down upon his chest, and ears like two mortars falling over his shoulder blades, and the nails of his hands were like the claws of a lion. When we saw this frightful giant, we felt like fainting, and every moment increased our fear and terror. In fact, given our horror and fright, we thought we were already dead.

And Scheherazade noticed that dawn was approaching and stopped telling her story. When the next night arrived, however, she received the king's permission to continue her tale and said,

After trampling upon the earth, the giant sat awhile on the bench. Then he got up, and as he approached us, he grabbed me by the arm and lifted me in the air, separating me from the other merchants. As he turned me over with his hands, he felt me with his fingers as a butcher feels a sheep that he is about to slaughter—and I but a little mouthful in his hands! Fortunately, he found me too lean because of the stress and troubles I had experienced, and he let me go and picked up another, whom he likewise turned over and felt and let go. So he continued to feel and turn over the rest of us, one after another until he came to the captain of the ship. Now he was a sturdy, stout, broad-shouldered man, fat and in full vigor. So he pleased the giant, who grabbed him, as a butcher would grab hold of a beast, and throwing him down, he set his foot on his neck and broke it. After that he fetched a long spit, thrust it up his backside, and brought it through the top of his head. Next he lit a huge fire, set the spit with the captain on it over the fire, and turned the coals until the flesh was roasted. When he finally took the spit off the fire and set it like a kebab stick in front of him, he tore the body from limb to limb as though it were a chicken, tearing the flesh from the bones with his nails. After he had gnawed the bones, there was nothing left, and he threw some of the bones to a side of the wall. Now that he was done, he sat for a while until he decided to lie down on the stone bench and fell asleep, snoring like a gurgling cow with its throat cut.

It was morning by the time he awoke, got up, and went his way.

As soon as we were sure that he was gone, we began talking with one another, weeping and bemoaning our fate. "If we had only been drowned in the sea!" we cried. "If only the apes had eaten us! That would have been better than to be roasted over coals. By Allah, this is a vile, foul death! Yet who dares question the will of the Lord, for He is all almighty and glorious! We shall certainly die a miserable death, since there's no escape from this place."

Then we arose and roamed around the island, hoping that we might by chance find a place to hide or some way of escape. It was not so much death we feared, but being roasted over the fire and being eaten. However, we could not find a hiding place, and we were overtaken by darkness. So we returned to the castle and sat down awhile. Soon the earth trembled under our feet, and the black ogre came up to us. Then he began turning us over, one by one, until he found a man to his liking, whom he grabbed and roasted as he had done the captain. After that he lay down on the bench and slept all night, snarling and snoring like a beast with its throat cut, until daybreak, when he arose and went as he had done the day before.

Then we gathered together and said to one another, "By Allah, we had better throw ourselves into the sea and drown than be roasted, for this is an abominable death!"

"Listen to me!" one of the merchants said. "Let's look for a way to kill him and do away with the grief we are suffering. We must rid Moslems of his barbarity and tyranny!"

Then I said, "Hear me, my brothers, if we are going to slay him, let us carry some of this firewood and planks down to the seashore and build a boat. So if we succeed in slaughtering him, we can either embark and let the sea carry us where Allah wills, or else we can stay here until some ship passes by and we can board it. If we fail to kill him, we can still embark in the boat and put out to sea. Then, even if we drown, we shall at least escape being roasted over a kitchen fire. In short, if we escape, we escape. If we drown, we die as martyrs."

"By Allah," they all said, "you're right!"

After agreeing about what we were going to do, we set about carrying out our plans. So we dragged the pieces of wood that were lying around the bench down to the beach. There we made a boat, moored it to the strand, and stowed some food in it, and then we returned to the castle. As soon as evening arrived, the earth trembled under our feet, and the blackamoor descended upon us, snarling like a dog about to bite. He came up to us and turned us over one by one until he grabbed a merchant and roasted him over the fire as he had done with the others. After he had finished eating him, he lay down on the bench and snored and snorted like thunder.

As soon as we were certain that he was asleep, we arose and took two iron spits and heated them in the furious fire until they were as hot as burning coals. Then we grabbed hold of them, went up to the snoring giant, and thrust them into his eyes. We all pressed down on the spits with all our might so that his eyeballs burst, and he became stone blind. In his anguish he roared a great cry so that our hearts trembled. As he sprang up from the bench, he began blindly to grope after us, but we fled from him right and left. Although he could not see us, we were terribly frightened and certain that our end was near and we would never escape. Then he found the door, feeling for it with his hands, and went out roaring aloud. Indeed, his roars were so tremendous that the ground shook, and we quaked with fear.

When he left the castle, we followed him and then headed for the place where we had moored our boat, saying to one another, "If this cursed ogre doesn't return to the castle at sunset, we will know that he is dead. If he comes back, we will embark in the boat and paddle until we escape and leave our fate in the hands of Allah."

While we were talking, however, the blackamoor suddenly appeared with two others, who looked like ghouls. They were more vile and frightful than he was and had eyes like red-hot coals. When we saw them, we hurried into the boat, cast off the moorings, paddled away, and pushed out to sea. As soon as the ogres caught sight of us, they cried out at us and ran along the seashore pelting us with rocks. Some hit us, and others fell into the sea. We paddled with all our might until we were beyond their reach, but most of us were killed by their rocks. Meanwhile the winds and waves had their sport with us and carried us into the midst of the dashing sea with clashing waves. We had no idea where we were heading, and my comrades died one after another until only three of us remained alive.

And Scheherazade noticed dawn was approaching and stopped telling her story. When the next night arrived, however, she received the king's permission to continue her tale and said,

We had thrown all those who had died into the sea, and we were now terribly exhausted because of hunger, but we encouraged one another and took heart. Working for dear life, we paddled with all our might until the winds cast us onto an island. Hungry, afraid, and exhausted, we were like dead men, but we walked around the island for a while and found that it had an abundance of trees, streams, and birds. We ate some fruit and celebrated our escape from the black ogre and our deliverance from the perils of the sea. When night came, we lay down and fell asleep out of fatigue. No sooner had we closed our eyes, however, than we were aroused by a hissing sound like the whizzing of the wind, and we saw a serpent the size of a dragon. It was a sight seldom seen: a monstrous snake with an enormous belly that lay in a circle around us. Soon it reared its head, and seizing one of my companions, it swallowed him up to his shoulders. Then it gulped down the rest of him, and we heard his ribs crack in its belly. Afterward it went its way, and we remained there petrified and grieved over our comrade. Indeed, we were now in mortal fear for our lives and said, "By Allah, this is astonishing! Each death that threatens us is worse than the last. We were celebrating our escape from the black ogre and our deliverance from the perils of the sea, but now we have encountered something more terrible. By the Almighty, how shall we escape from this abominable and vile monster?"

Then we walked about the island, eating some fruit and drinking fresh water from the streams until dusk, when we climbed up high into a tree and went to sleep there with me resting on the highest bough. As soon as it was pitch-black, the serpent arrived looking right and left. Then it headed for the tree, where we were, and climbed up to my comrade and swallowed him down to his shoulders. Then it coiled around the trunk of the tree with him while I, who could not take my eyes off the sight, heard my friend's bones crack in the serpent's belly, and it swallowed him whole and slid down the tree.

When the day broke and the light showed me that the serpent was gone, I came down feeling that I was bound to die. I thought about throwing myself into the sea to forget the woes of the world, but I could not bring myself to do this, for truly life is dear. So I took five pieces of long and wide wood and tied one crosswise to the soles of my feet and did likewise with some others on my right and left sides and over my chest. The largest I tied across my head and pulled them tight with ropes. Then I lay down on the ground on my back so that I was completely fenced in by the pieces of wood that enclosed me like a closet.

As soon as it was dark, the serpent came as usual and headed toward me, but it could not get at me or swallow me because of the wood. It wriggled around me on all sides while I looked on terrified to death. Every now and then the serpent would glide away and come back, but each time it tried to get at me, the wood prevented it. The serpent kept trying from sundown till dawn, but when the light of day shone upon the beast, it departed in total fury and extreme disappointment. Then I put out my head and untied myself more dead than alive from the fright and pain. I went down to the seashore, and suddenly I saw a ship far off in the middle of the waves. I quickly tore off a great branch of a tree and made signs with it to the crew while shouting all the time. When the ship's company saw the branch, they said to one another, "We must sail closer and see what this is. It could be a man."

So they made for the island and soon heard my cries, whereupon they took me on board and asked me to explain how I had got there. Of course, I responded by telling them all my adventures from first to last. In turn, they were amazed and covered my body with some of their clothes. Moreover, they gave me some food to eat, and I ate my fill and drank fresh cold water until I was completely refreshed. And Allah Almighty helped me recover so that it soon seemed to me that all I had suffered had been something I had dreamed. In the meantime we sailed on a fair wind until we came to an island called Al-Salahitah that was known for its sandalwood, and the captain cast anchor.

And Scheherazade noticed dawn was approaching and stopped telling her story. When the next night arrived, however, she received the king's permission to continue her tale and said,

When the merchants and sailors landed to sell and buy goods, the captain turned to me and said, "Listen to me, you are a stranger and a pauper, and you've told us that you've undergone terrible hardship. So I intend to help you with something that might enable you to regain your native land. And if I do this, I hope that you will always bless me and pray for me."

"So be it," I answered. "My prayers will go with you."

"Then I must tell you," the captain replied, "that there was a traveler with us, and I suspect we lost him along the way. We don't know whether he's alive or dead, since we haven't heard from him. I propose to give you his bale of goods so you can sell them on this island. We'll give you a part of the proceeds as compensation for your pains and service, and the rest we will keep until we return to Baghdad, where we will inquire about his family and deliver it to them, together with the unsold goods. Tell me, then, will you undertake the charge and sell the goods as the other merchants are doing?"

"I'll do this most obediently, my lord," I answered. "Your kindness is great."

As I thanked him, the captain ordered the sailors and porters to carry the bales in question ashore and place them under my command. The ship's clerk asked him, "Oh master, what are these bales, and what merchant's name shall I write on them?"

"Write the name of Sinbad the Seaman," the captain responded, "for it was he whom we lost at the Rukh's island and haven't heard from since. I want this stranger to sell them, and we'll give him part of the profits for his pains and keep the rest until we return to Baghdad, where, if we find the owner, we'll hand it over to him, and if not, to his family."

And the clerk said, "Your words are well-spoken, and you are certainly doing the right thing."

"By Allah, I am Sinbad the Seaman!" I muttered to myself. So I armed myself with courage and patience and waited until all the merchants had landed and were gathered together on shore. While they were talking and chattering about buying and selling, I went up to the captain and asked him, "My lord, do you know what kind of man this Sinbad the Seaman was?"

"I know nothing about him," he replied, "except that he was a man from Baghdad called Sinbad the Seaman, who disappeared while we lay anchored at the Rukh's island, and I have heard nothing of him since then."

Upon hearing this, I cried out, "Oh captain, I must tell you that I am Sinbad the Seaman and that when you cast anchor at the island, I landed with the rest of the merchants and the crew. After sitting down in a pleasant place by myself and eating some food, I became drowsy and fell asleep. When I awoke, the ship was gone, and nobody was around me. These goods are my goods, and these bales are my bales. For proof you only have to ask the merchants who fetch jewels from the Valley of Diamonds. They saw me there and will testify that I am the very same Sinbad the Seaman whom you lost. You see, I told them how you had forgotten me and left me sleeping on the island and about everything that had happened to me."

When the captain and the crew heard my words, some believed me and others did not. But soon one of the merchants, who had heard me mention the Valley of the Diamonds, came up to me and said to them, "Listen to what I have to say, good people. You remember when I told you about the miraculous event that happened when I and my friends cast slaughtered animals into the Valley of the Serpents and a man came attached to mine, you didn't believe me. In fact, you called me a liar. Do you remember?"

"Yes," they said. "You told us a tale like that, but there was no reason for us to believe you."

"Well," he resumed, "this is the very man who gave me diamonds of great value that are not to be found on the face of this earth, and he requited me by giving me more than I would have earned from my portion of meat. After that incident I accompanied him to Bassorah, where he took leave of us and went to his native city, while we returned to our own land. I am certain he is the same man, and he told us his name, Sinbad the Seaman, and how the ship had left him on the desert island. So you see that Allah has sent him here so that you could learn that my story was true. Moreover, these are his goods, for he told us about them when we first gathered together, and it is clear that he is a man who tells the truth."

Upon hearing the merchant's speech, the captain came up to me and looked at me closely. Then he said, "What were the marks on your bales?"

I indicated to him what they were and reminded him of some words that we had exchanged when I began the voyage in Bassorah. Consequently, he was convinced that I was indeed Sinbad the Seaman, and he embraced me and rejoiced that I was now safe. "By Allah," he said, "your story is truly marvelous, and your tale is wondrous. Praise be to Allah who has brought us together again and who has restored all your goods and gear to you!"

And Scheherazade noticed dawn was approaching and stopped telling her story. When the next night arrived, however, she received the king's permission to continue her tale and said,

While we were on that island, I was able to dispose of my merchandise to the best of my skill and made a large profit. As we continued our voyage, we bought and sold at several islands until we came to the land of Hind, where we bought cloves, ginger, and all sorts of spices. From there we sailed on to the land of Sind, where we also bought and sold. In these Indian seas I saw innumerable wonders, among them a fish like a cow that conceives its young and nurtures them like human beings. Bucklers are made from its skin. There were also fish like asses and camels and tortoises twenty feet wide. In addition I saw a bird that came out of a seashell and laid eggs and hatched her chicks on the surface of the water, never leaving the sea for land.

After spending some time in those waters, we set sail with a fair wind and the blessing of Almighty Allah, and after a prosperous voyage, arrived safe and sound at Bassorah. I dwelled there for a few days and then moved on to Baghdad, where I went at once to my house and greeted my family and friends. My earnings from this voyage were beyond calculation. So I gave alms and helped the widows and orphans as a gesture of thanksgiving. Then I began to feast and make merry with my companions and friends and forgot all the hardships I had suffered and the dangers I had faced while I was eating and drinking in such a joyous manner.

These, then, are the most admirable things I had sighted on my third voyage, and tomorrow I want you to come to me, and I shall tell you the adventures of my fourth voyage, which is even more wonderful than those you have already heard.

Then Sinbad the Seaman ordered that Sinbad thc Landsman be given a hundred dinars as usual and called for food. So they spread the tables, and the company ate the evening meal and went their ways, marveling at what they had heard. The porter, too, departed and took his gold to spend the night in his own house, where he wondered at what his namesake the seaman had told him. As soon as day broke and the morning showed its first light, he arose, said his dawn prayer, and went to the house of Sinbad the Seaman, who returned his greeting and received him with an open heart and cheerful mood. He made the porter sit with him until the rest of the company arrived, when he ordered the food to be spread before them. Then they ate and drank and made merry, whereupon Sinbad the Seaman related to them the story of

The Fourth Voyage of Sinbad the Seaman

After my return from my third voyage I soon forgot all my perils and hardships and began enjoying my friends and the comfort of repose. Then one day a company of merchants visited me and sat down and talked about foreign travel and trade until the old bad man within me yearned to go with them and enjoy the sights of strange countries. Indeed, I longed to meet and mix with all kinds of human beings and to trade and obtain profits. So I decided to travel with them, and after buying the necessary goods for a long voyage, more costly than ever before, I transported them from Baghdad to Bassorah, where I shipped out with the merchants, who were the major ones of the town.

With a favorable breeze and the best conditions we sailed from island to island and sea to sea until, one day, we encountered a nasty wind, and the captain cast out his anchors and brought the ship to a standstill, fearing the ship might founder in midocean. Then we all began to pray, but as we were doing this, a furious squall hit the ship and tore the sails to rags and tatters. The anchor cable split in two, the ship began to totter, and we were all thrown into the sea, goods and all. I kept myself afloat by swimming half the day and was about to give myself up for lost when the Almighty threw one of the planks of the ship in my way, and I and some of the other merchants scrambled onto it.

And Scheherazade noticed dawn was approaching and stopped telling her story. When the next night arrived, however, she received the king's permission to continue her tale and said,

Mounting the plank as we would a horse, we paddled with our feet in the sea and continued doing this day and night with the wind and waves helping us. On the second day, shortly before noon, the breeze became stronger, the sea wilder, and the rising waves cast us upon an island. We were practically dead from exhaustion, fear, cold, hunger, and thirst. After walking along the shore, we found an abundance of herbs and ate enough to strengthen our bodies and spirits. Then we lay down and slept right near the sea.

When morning arrived, we arose and walked all about the island until we caught sight of an inhabited house far away. So we headed toward it, and once we reached the door, a number of naked men suddenly came out, and without greeting us or saying a word, they seized us and carried us to their king, who signaled us to sit down. Once we did as he had commanded, they set food before us that we had never seen before in our lives. My companions ate it because of their hunger, but my stomach was repulsed, and I would not eat. Thanks to Allah, it was because I refused to eat that I am still alive now, for no sooner had my comrades tasted the food than they went crazy and their condition changed. They began to devour the food like madmen possessed of an evil spirit. Then the savages gave them cocoa nut oil to drink and anointed them with it. Immediately after drinking the oil, their eyes turned in their heads, and they began eating greedily, which was not their custom. When I saw this, I was confounded and concerned for them, and of course, I was worried about myself, for I was afraid of these naked people. So I watched them closely, and it was not long before I discovered them to be a tribe of Magian cannibals, whose king was an ogre. Any people who came to their country, or any people whom they caught in their valleys or on their roads, they brought to this king, fed them that food, and anointed them with that oil. Thereupon, their stomachs dilated so that they would eat a vast amount, and they would lose their minds and their power of thought and become idiots. The naked people would continue to stuff them with cocoa nut oil and food until they became fat and gross, whereupon the naked people would slaughter them by cutting their throats and roasting them for the king, who would eat them. But the savages themselves ate only raw human flesh.

When I saw what was happening, I became terribly concerned about myself and my comrades, who had now become so stupefied that they did not know what was happening to them, and the naked folk put one savage in charge of them. Every day he led them out to graze in a pasture like cattle, and they wandered among the trees and rested at will until they became very fat. As for me, I wasted away and became sickly from fear and hunger, and my flesh shriveled on my bones. When the savages saw this, they left me alone and paid no attention to me so that I was practically forgotten. So one day I gave them the slip and made for the distant beach, and there I spotted a very old man seated on a high place near the water. When I looked at him, I realized it was the herdsman in charge of leading my friends to pasture, and with him were many others like him. As soon as he saw me, he knew that I was in my right mind and not affected like the rest of those of whom he was in charge. So he signaled to me from afar as if to say, "Turn back and take the right-hand road, for that will lead you into the king's highway."

So I turned back, as he had ordered, and followed the right-hand road, running out of fear and walking to catch my breath, until I was out of the old man's sight. By this time, the sun had gone down, and darkness set in. So I sat down to rest and would have slept, but sleep did not come to me that night because of my fear, famine, and fatigue. When the night was half gone, I rose and walked on until day broke in all its beauty, and the sun rose over the heads of the lofty hills and across the low plains. Since I was hungry and thirsty, I ate my fill of herbs and grass that grew on the island and kept my body alive. After settling my stomach, I set out again and traveled all that day and the next night, stopping my hunger with roots and herbs. After walking seven days and seven nights, I caught sight of a faint object in the distance on the morning of the eighth day. So I made toward it, though my heart quaked because of all that I had suffered. Fortunately, it was a company of men gathering pepper grains, and as soon as they saw me, they rushed up to me and surrounded me on all sides. "Who are you?" they asked. "How did you get here?"

"Friends, I am a poor stranger," I replied, and I began telling them all about the hardships and perils I had suffered.

* * *

And Scheherazade noticed dawn was approaching and stopped telling her story. When the next night arrived, however, she received the king's permission to continue her tale and said,

The men were astounded by my story and shared the happiness of my safe deliverance from the naked savages. "By Allah," they said, "it's wonderful! But how did you manage to escape from these blacks who swarm the island and devour everyone who falls into their clutches? Nobody is safe from them, and it's impossible to get away from them."

After I told them what had happened to my companions and how I was fortunate to avoid their fate, they made me sit by them until they had finished their work. Afterward they fetched me some good food, which I ate, and after we all rested awhile, we went aboard their ship and sailed to their home country, where they brought me before their king, who received me honorably and asked me all about myself. So I told him what had happened to me from the day I had left Baghdad, and he was astounded by my adventures. He and his courtiers requested me to sit down with them, and after the king called for food, I ate with him and thanked Almighty Allah for His blessings. Then I left the king and walked about the city, which was filled with many people and had a prosperous air to it. There were numerous market streets with food shops and merchandise and plenty of buyers and sellers. So I rejoiced at having reached such a pleasant place and enjoyed myself after having been worn out. Soon I made friends with the townsfolk, and it was not long before I became more honored and favored by them and their king than any of the chief men of the realm.

As I was dwelling there, it became apparent to me that all the citizens, rich and poor, rode fine horses, which were thoroughbreds and very expensive. Moreover, they did this without saddles and bridles. Since I was surprised by this, I asked the king, "How come you don't ride with a saddle? You would feel more comfortable with it and have more control over your horse."

"What is a saddle?" he asked. "I never saw or used such a thing in all my life."

"With your permission," I responded, "I'll make you a

saddle so that you can ride on it and see how comfortable it is."

"So be it," he said.

"I'll need some wood," I stated, and he had it brought to me. Then I sought a clever carpenter and showed him how to make the saddletree by sketching it in ink on the wood. Next I took wool, teased it, and turned it into felt. After covering the saddletree with leather, I stuffed it, polished it, and attached the girth and stirrup leathers. Then I fetched a blacksmith and described to him what the stirrups and bridle bit looked like. So he forged a fine pair of stirrups and a bit and filed them until they were smooth, whereupon he covered them with a tin alloy. I added silk fringes and bridle leathers to the bit. Then I had one of the best royal horses brought to me, and after saddling and bridling him, I led him to the king.

After thanking me, the king mounted and was extremely pleased by the saddle, and he rewarded me handsomely for my work. When the king's vizier saw the saddle, he asked me for one like it, and I made one for him. Furthermore, all the nobles and officers of state came to me for saddles. So I began making saddles (having taught the craft to the carpenter and the blacksmith) and selling them to all who desired one. After a while I amassed great wealth and was held in high esteem by the king and his courtiers.

I continued living like this, until one day as I was sitting with the king he said to me, "I want you to know that you have become as dear to us as a brother, and we hold you in such high regard and affection that we cannot part with you or bear to let you leave our city. Therefore, I want you to obey me in a certain matter, and I won't have you refuse me."

"Oh king," I answered, "what is it you desire of me? Far be it from me to refuse you in anything, for I am indebted to you for many favors and kindness. Praise be to Allah, I have become one of your servants."

"I intend to marry you to a fair, clever, and pleasant wife who is as wealthy as she is beautiful," he declared. "Then you will be naturalized and make your home with us and lodge in my palace. I expect that you will obey and not oppose my plans."

When I heard these words, I was ashamed and held my

peace. Since I was rather bashful, I could not answer him.

"Why don't you reply to me, my son?" the king asked.

"My master," I said, "your word is my command."

So he summoned the kazi and witnesses and married me right away to a lady of noble ancestry and high pedigree. She was wealthy, the flower of an ancient race, remarkably beautiful and graceful, and she owned many farms, estates, and houses.

And Scheherazade noticed dawn was approaching and stopped telling her story. When the next night arrived, however, she received the king's permission to continue her tale and said,

Aside from marrying me to this choice wife, the king also gave me a large splendid house with slaves and officers, and he provided me with an allowance and pay. So I became a man of ease and contentment and forgot all my troubles and hardships. I loved my wife with great affection, and she loved me no less. We were as one and lived in the utmost comfort of life and in its happiness. And I said to myself, "When I return to my native land, I shall take her with me." But whatever fate ordains for a man, he cannot resist, and nobody knows what awaits him.

While we were living like this for some time, a neighbor of mine lost his wife, and hearing the cry of the mourners, I went to console him and found him in a very bad way, full of troubles and weary of soul and mind. I tried to console and comfort him, saying, "Don't mourn for your wife, for she has now found the mercy of Allah. The Lord will surely give you a better wife in her stead, and your name will be great, and your life will be long."

But he wept bitter tears and replied, "How can I marry another wife, and how will Allah be able to replace her with a woman who is better when I have but one day left to live?"

"Oh my brother," I said, "come to your senses, and stop announcing your forthcoming death, for you are healthy and in good shape."

"I swear by your life, my friend," he replied, "tomorrow you will lose me, and you will never see me again until the day of resurrection."

"How so?"

"The very day they bury my wife," he stated, "they are going to bury me in the same tomb. This is our custom. If the wife dies first, the husband is buried alive with her, and in like manner, if the husband dies first, the wife is buried alive with him so that neither may enjoy life after losing his or her mate."

"By Allah," I cried, "this is a most vile and lewd custom. No one should ever be forced to endure it!"

In the meantime, most of the people in the town came in and began consoling the neighbor. Soon they laid the dead woman out, as was their wont, and set her on a bier. Then they carried her and her husband outside the city until they came to a place in the side of the mountain at the end of the island by the sea. Here they lifted a great rock and uncovered the mouth of a stone pit leading down into a vast underground cavern that ran beneath the mountain. Into this pit they threw the corpse, and then after tying a rope of palm fibers under the husband's armpits, they let him down into the cavern and with him a great pitcher of fresh water and seven scones. When he arrived at the bottom, he detached himself from the rope, and they drew it up. Finally, they stopped the mouth of the pit with the great stone and returned to the city, leaving my friend in the cavern with his dead wife.

When I saw this, I said to myself, "By Allah, it's more bitter to die this way than to be the first!" And I went to the king and said to him, "My lord, why do you bury the living with the dead?"

"You must realize that it has been the custom of our forebears and our former kings from time immemorial," he responded. "If the husband dies first, the wife must be buried with him, and likewise if the wife dies first, so we do not sever them, alive or dead."

"What if the wife of a foreigner like myself should die among you," I asked, "would you deal with him as you've just dealt with my neighbor?"

"We would certainly do the same exact thing," he stated.

When I heard this, my gallbladder almost burst because of my terrible dismay and the concern I had for myself. I was dazed. I felt as if I were in a vile dungeon and hated their society. Now I went about in fear that my wife might die before me and they would bury me alive with her. However, after a while I comforted myself and said, "Fortunately, I'll probably die before her or shall have returned to my own land before she dies. Nobody knows what will happen first or last."

Then I pursued various projects to divert myself from thinking about this custom and its consequences. But it was not long before my wife became sick, was forced to stay in bed, and then died. As was their wont, the king and the rest of the townsfolk came to offer condolences to me and the family and to console us for her loss, not to mention to console me about my fate. Then the women washed her, and after arraying her in the richest raiment, golden ornaments, necklaces, and jewelry, they laid her on the bier and carried her to the mountain, where they lifted the cover of the pit and threw her in. Immediately thereafter all my friends and acquaintances and my wife's relatives came to me and bid me farewell, while I cried out, "Almighty Allah never made it lawful to bury live people with the dead! I am a foreigner, not one of your kind, and I cannot tolerate your custom. If I had known about it, I would never have wedded among you!"

They listened to me but paid no attention to my words. Instead, they seized me and bound me by force and let me down into the cavern with a large pitcher of fresh water and seven cakes of bread as was their custom. When I arrived at the bottom, they called out to me to detach myself, but I refused to do so. Consequently, they threw the rope down on top of me and closed the mouth of the cavern with the large rock.

And Scheherazade noticed dawn was approaching and stopped telling her story. When the next night arrived, however, she received the king's permission to continue her tale and said,

Now I looked around me and found myself in a vast cave full of dead bodies that exuded a loathsome smell, and the air was heavy with the groans of the dying. Then I began to blame myself for doing what I had done and said, "By Allah, I deserve all that has happened to me and everything that will happen to me! What curse compelled me to get married in that city? By Allah, I've often said, I tend to escape one catastrophe only to fall into a worse one. What an abominable death to die! If only heaven had granted me a decent death so I could have been washed and shrouded like a man and Moslem! If only I had been drowned at sea or perished in the mountains! It would be better than dying this miserable death!"

I kept blaming my own folly and greed of gain for landing me in that black hole, where I could not tell day from night. Then I threw myself down on the bones of the dead and lay there, imploring Allah's help, and in the depths of my despair, I invoked death, which did not come to me. Finally, the fire of hunger burned my stomach and thirst set my throat aflame, forcing me to sit up and feel for the bread. After eating a morsel, I swallowed a mouthful of water. It was the worst night I had ever experienced, and I got up and began exploring the cavern. I found that it extended a long way with small caves on its sides, and its floor was strewn with dead bodies and rotten bones that had lain there from olden times. So I made myself a place in a small cave of the cavern far from the corpses that had recently been thrown down there, and I finally fell asleep.

I remained in the cavern this way until my provisions started giving out, even though I ate only once a day and drank very little out of fear that my victuals would run out before I died. "Eat little and drink little," I said to myself. "The Lord will deliver you!"

One day, as I sat there pondering what I should do when my bread and water were exhausted, the stone that covered the opening was suddenly lifted, and light streamed down upon me. "I wonder what the matter is," I said. "Most likely they've brought another corpse." Then I spotted people standing at the mouth of the pit, and they soon let down a dead man and a live woman, weeping and bemoaning her fate. With her came a more ample supply of bread and water than usual. I looked at her and saw that she was a beautiful woman, but she did not see me. Meanwhile the people above closed up the opening and went away.

Then I took the leg bone of a dead woman, approached

her, and hit her on the head with it. She uttered a cry and fell down in a swoon. I hit her two more times until she was dead. Thereupon, I took her bread and water and found plenty of rich ornaments, jewels, necklaces, and gold on her, for it was their custom to bury their women in their finery. I carried the victuals to my sleeping place in the cavern side and ate and drank just enough to keep me alive, since I did not want to perish of hunger and thirst. So I managed to keep on living by killing all the folk they let down into the cavern and taking their provisions of meat and drink. Then one day, as I was sleeping, I was awakened by something scratching and burrowing among the bodies in the corner of the cave. "What can this be?" I said to myself. Fearing wolves or hyenas, I grabbed a leg bone, stood up, and went toward the noise. As soon as the thing was aware of me, it fled further into the cavern, and I realized it was a wild beast. Nevertheless, I followed it to the far end of the cavern until I saw a point of light no bigger than a star that seemed to appear and disappear. So I headed for it, and as I drew near, it grew larger and brighter, and I was sure that it was a crevice in the rock leading to open country. "There must be some reason for this opening," I said to myself. "Either it's the mouth of a second pit like the one through which they let me down, or else it's a natural crack in the rocks."

As I approached the light, I kept wondering what it might be, and fortunately it turned out to come from a breach in the back side of the mountain that the wild beasts had enlarged by burrowing in order to enter and devour the dead and to go back and forth as they wished. When I saw this, my spirits revived and hope came back to me that I would live when I had thought I was surely going to die. So I went on as if in a dream and scrambled through the breach to find myself on the slope of a high mountain overlooking the sea. Moreover, this part of the mountain was cut off from the city and the people could not gain access to it. After praising the Lord for my deliverance, I returned through the crack to the cavern and brought out all the food and water I had saved and donned some of the dead folk's clothes over my own. After that I gathered together all the necklaces of jewels and pearls, the trinkets of gold and silver set with precious stones, and other valuables that I found on the corpses. Then I made them into bundles with the grave-clothes of the dead and carried them back out to the mountain facing the seashore, where I intended to wait for some passing ship, hoping that Allah might provide me with relief. I visited the cavern daily, and as often as I found people buried there, I killed them all, men and women. It made no difference to me. Then I took their provisions and valuables and transported them to my seashore abode, where I waited a long time.

And Scheherazade noticed dawn was approaching and stopped telling her story. When the next night arrived, however, she received the king's permission to continue her tale and said,

One day, as I was gazing at the ocean, I caught sight of a ship in the midst of the clashing sea swollen with huge waves. So I took a piece of white shroud I had with me and, tying it to a staff, I ran along the seashore, making signals with it and calling to the people in the ship, until they spotted me. As a result, they sent a boat to fetch me, and when it drew near, the crew called out to me, "Who are you, and how did you get to this mountain? We've never seen anyone on it before in our lives."

"I'm a gentleman and a merchant," I answered, "and I was shipwrecked. I managed to save myself on one of the planks of the ship with some of my goods. With the blessing of the Almighty and my own strength I managed to land my gear in this place, where I've been waiting for some passing ship to rescue me."

So they took me into their boat together with the bundles I had made of the jewels and valuables from the cavern and rowed back with me to the ship, where the captain asked me, "How did you get to that mountain? I've sailed these seas many years and passed the city and the mountain many times, but I never saw anything on that side of the mountain except wild beasts and birds, for you can't get to that side from the city."

I repeated the story that I had told the sailors and did not reveal anything that had happened to me in the city and the cavern for fear there might be some islanders on the ship. Then I took out some of the best pearls I had with me and offered them to the captain. "My lord," I said, "you have rescued me from the mountain, and since I do not have money handy, I would like you to take this from me as a token of my gratitude for your kindness and good deed."

But he refused to accept the pearls and said, "When we find a shipwrecked man on the seashore or on an island, we pick him up and give him something to eat and drink, and if he is naked, we give him clothes. But we don't take anything from him. In fact, when we reach a safe port, we set him ashore with a present of our own money and treat him with kindness for the love of Allah the Most High."

So I prayed that he would have a long life and rejoiced that I had escaped, trusting that I would overcome my stress and forget my past mishaps, for every time I remembered being let down into the cave with my dead wife I shuddered in horror.

In the meantime we continued our voyage and sailed from island to island and sea to sea until we arrived at the Island of the Bell, and six days later we reached the island Kala, near the land of Hind. This place is governed by a powerful king, and the people produce excellent camphor and an abundance of the Indian rattan. There is also a lead mine on the island. After our visit we moved on to Bassorah, where I stayed a few days, and then went to Baghdad, where I returned to my home with a great deal of pleasure. Soon I gathered together with my family and friends, who rejoiced in my safe return. I put away all the goods that I had brought with me in my storehouses and gave alms to fakirs and beggars and clothes to widows and orphans. Then I indulged myself in pleasure and enjoyment, returning to my old merry mode of life.

Such, then, were the marvelous adventures of my fourth voyage, and tomorrow, if you will kindly come to me, I shall tell you what happened to me during my fifth voyage, which was even more unique and more extraordinary than all those I had undertaken before this one. And you, my brother Sinbad the Landsman, will have supper with me as you have been accustomed to.

* * *

J. LOUIS RHEAD

After the table was spread, the guests ate the evening meal, and then Sinbad gave the porter a hundred dinars as usual, whereupon the guests went their ways, glad at heart and marveling at the tales they had heard, for each story was more extraordinary than the one before it. The porter Sinbad spent the night in his own house in joy, good cheer, and wonderment. As soon as morning arrived and the sun shone, he said his dawn prayer and returned to the house of Sinbad the Seaman, who welcomed him and asked him to sit with him until the rest of the company arrived. When all the guests were assembled, they all ate, drank, made merry, and talked. Then, at one point, their host began the narrative of

The Fifth Voyage of Sinbad the Seaman

After I had been on shore awhile and had forgotten all the perils and sufferings I had endured, I was again seized by the longing to travel and see foreign countries and islands. Therefore, I bought costly merchandise suited to my purpose, and after making it into bales, I traveled to Bassorah, where I walked along the docks of the river until I found a fine large ship that had been recently built and was outfitted for sea. Since the ship pleased me, I bought it and had my merchandise placed on board. Then I hired a master and a crew and placed them in charge of my slaves and servants, who were to be their inspectors. A number of merchants brought their merchandise as well and paid me freight and passage money. Then, after reciting the Fatihah, we set sail and looked forward to a prosperous voyage and a great deal of profit.

We sailed from city to city, island to island, and sea to sea, viewing the cities and countries that we passed and selling and buying all over until one day we came to a great uninhabited island. It appeared desolate and deserted and had an immense white dome half buried in the sands. The merchants landed to examine this dome, leaving me on the ship, and when they drew near it, they discovered that it was a huge Rukh's egg. However, not knowing what it was, they began to beat it with stones and soon broke it open. A good deal of water ran out of it, and they could see a young Rukh inside. So they pulled it out of the shell, cut its throat, and took a lot of meat. Now I was on the ship and was unaware of what they had done, but soon one of my passengers came up to me and said, "My lord, come and look at the egg that we thought was a dome."

So I looked and saw the merchants beating it with stones and called out to them, "Stop, stop! Don't touch the egg, or the bird Rukh will come out and attack our ship and destroy us!"

But they paid no attention to me and continued hitting the egg. Then, suddenly the day grew dark, and the sun was covered as though some great cloud had passed over the firmament. When we raised our eyes, however, we saw that what we had taken for a cloud was the Rukh poised between us and the sun, and it was his wings that had darkened the day. When he came and saw his egg broken, he uttered a loud cry, whereupon his mate came flying up to him, and they both began circling the ship, crying out at us with shrieks louder than thunder.

I called to the captain and crew, "Put out to sea! Let's flee, otherwise we'll all be destroyed!"

So the merchants came on board, and we cast off and hastened away from the island, hoping to gain the open sea. When the Rukhs saw this, they flew off, and we set full sail intending to get out of their country. But soon the two reappeared and were flying after us, each carrying in its claws a huge boulder that it had carried from the mountains. As soon as the male Rukh was directly over us, he let the rock in his claws fall on top of us, but the captain turned the ship so that the rock missed it by inches. However, it plunged into the waves with such violence that the ship pitched high and then sank into the trough of the sea, and we soon saw the bottom of the ocean. Then the female Rukh let her rock fall, and it was bigger than that of her mate. As destiny would have it, the rock fell on the poop of the ship and crushed it. The rudder broke into twenty pieces, whereupon the vessel foundered, and everyone and everything were cast into the sea. As for me, I struggled for sweet life until Almighty Allah threw in my way one of the planks of the ship, to which I clung. Once I got on top of it, I paddled with my feet toward an island close to where the ship had gone down. The winds and waves carried me until, thanks to Allah, they cast me on shore, where I was half dead with hunger and thirst. More like a corpse than a live man, I lay on the beach awhile until I began to revive and recover my spirits. Then I began to walk around the island, which seemed to me to be one of the gardens of paradise. There were many trees that bore ripe yellow fruit. The streams were clear and bright. The beautiful flowers had a wonderful scent. The birds warbled with delight in praise of the Lord. So I ate my fill of the fruit and quenched my thirst with the water of the streams, giving thanks to the Almighty.

And Scheherazade noticed that dawn was approaching and stopped telling her story. When the next night arrived, however, she received the king's permission to continue her tale and said,

When night descended, I lay down and was dead tired because of my trials and tribulations and fright. So I slept soundly through the night, and when morning came, I arose and walked about under the trees until I came to the channel of a draw-well fed by a spring of running water. Sitting next to the well was a venerable old man, who had a waist cloth tied around him made of the fiber of palm fronds. I thought to myself that this sheikh was probably one of those who was wrecked in the ship and had made his way to this island. So I approached him and greeted him, and he returned my salaam by signs but did not speak.

"Uncle," I said, "why are you sitting here?"

He shook his head and moaned and signaled to me with his hand as if to say, "Take me on your shoulders and carry me to the other side of the channel." I thought I should be kind to him and did what he desired because he might be a paralytic and my good deed would win me a reward in Heaven. So I carried him on my back to the place to which he pointed and said to him, "You may get off now."

But he would not get off my back and wound his legs around my neck. I looked at them and seeing that they were rough and black like a buffalo's hide, I was frightened and tried to cast him off. However, he clung to me and gripped my neck with his legs until I almost choked. The world grew black, and I fell to the ground senseless, as if I were dead. But he still kept his seat and, raising his legs, he drummed with his heels and beat my back and shoulders harder than palm rods, forcing me to rise because of the excessive pain. Then he signaled to me with his hand to carry him here and there among the trees that bore the best fruit. And if I refused to do his bidding or loitered, he beat me with his feet more harshly, and it felt worse than being beaten with whips. Whenever he felt like it, he signaled with his hand, and I was compelled to carry him about the island like a captive slave. Indeed, he bepissed and besmirched my shoulders and back, for he stayed on them day and night. Whenever he wished to sleep, he wound his legs around my neck and leaned back and slept awhile, then arose and beat me, whereupon I sprang up in haste, unable to refuse him because of the pain he inflicted on me. Of course, I blamed myself and repented sorely for having taken pity on him. I continued in this condition and became exhausted beyond description until I said to myself, "I did him a favor, and he has repaid me with vile treatment. By Allah, I'll never help any man again as long as I live!"

Time and again I beseeched the Lord to let me die because of my exhaustion and misery. And I continued to live a long time in such a condition until, one day, I arrived with him at a place where there was an abundance of gourds, many of which were dry. So I took a large dry gourd, cut open the head, scooped out the inside, and cleaned it. After this I gathered grapes from a vine which grew nearby and squeezed them into the gourd until it was full of juice. Then I stopped up the mouth and set it in the sun, where I left it for some days until it became strong wine. Every day I used to drink from it to comfort and sustain me under the burden of carrying that obstinate fiend. Whenever I drank myself drunk, I forgot my troubles and took new heart.

One day he saw me drinking and signaled to me with his hand as if to say, "What is that?"

"It is an excellent cordial that cheers the heart and revives your spirits," I answered, and since the wine had gone to my head, I ran and danced with him among the trees, clapping my hands, singing, and having fun. I staggered under him on purpose, and when he saw this, he signaled to me to give him the gourd so that he might drink some wine. So I fearfully gave him the wine, and he drained the gourd and cast it on the ground, whereupon he grew frolicsome and began to clap his hands and do a jig back and forth on my shoulders. Meanwhile he relieved himself so copiously that my clothes were drenched with his piss. Soon, however, the fume of the wine rose to his head, and he became helplessly drunk. His side muscles and limbs relaxed, and he swayed back and forth on my back. When I saw that he had lost his senses in his drunken stupor, I put my hand to his legs, loosened them from my neck, stooped down to the ground, and threw him at full length.

And Scheherazade noticed that the dawn was approaching and stopped telling her story. When the next night arrived, however, she received the king's permission to continue her tale and said,

Once the devil was off my shoulders, I was still afraid that he might shake off his drunkenness and do me some harm. So I picked up a large stone lying among the trees and smashed his head with all my might so that his skull was crushed. His flesh and blood became like pulp, and he died and received his just reward. With my heart at ease, I returned to my former place at the seashore and dwelled on that island many days, eating the fruit, drinking the water, and keeping a lookout for passing ships. Then one day just as I sitting on the beach, recalling all that had happened to me and wondering if Allah would keep me alive and restore my home, my friends, and my family to me, I spotted a ship heading for the island through the dashing sea and clashing waves. Soon it cast anchor, and the passengers landed. So I started walking in their direction, and when they saw me, they rushed up to me, gathered around me, and asked me how I had

happened to come to that island. In turn I told them all that had happened to me, and they were astounded.

"The man who rode on your shoulder is called the Sheikh al-Bahr or Old Man of the Sea," they said, "and nobody before you has ever felt his legs on his neck and come away alive. Those who died under him he ate. So praise be to Allah for your safety!"

Then they set some food before me, and I ate my fill. In addition, they gave me clothes with which I could cover my nakedness. Afterward they took me to the ship, and we sailed days and nights until fate brought us to a place called the City of Apes, built with lofty houses, all of which face the sea, and there was but a single gate studded and reinforced with iron nails. Now every night, as soon as it was dusk, the dwellers of this city used to come out of the gate, put out to sea in boats and ships, and spend the night on the waters in fear that the apes might come down and attack them from the mountains. Upon hearing this, I was greatly disturbed, because I recalled what the apes had done to me in the past. Nevertheless, I decided to land in the city to find some relaxation there. Unfortunately, the ship soon set sail without me, and I repented for having gone ashore. I began to remember my companions and what had happened to me with the apes, and as I sat down, I started crying and lamenting. Soon one of the townspeople came up to me and said, "My lord, you seem to be a stranger to these parts."

"Yes," I answered, "I am indeed a stranger, and a poor one, who came here in a ship which had cast anchor here. I landed to visit the town, but when I wanted to return to the ship, I found that they had sailed off without me."

"Come and embark with us," he replied, "for if you spend the night in the city, the apes will destroy you."

"As you wish," I replied, and I embarked right away with him in one of the boats. After leaving the shore, they anchored about a mile or so from the land and spent the night there. At daybreak they rowed back to the city, and after landing, each went about his business. This was what they did every night, for if anyone tarried in the town during nighttime the apes would attack him and slay him. As soon as it was day, the apes would leave the city, eat the fruit of the gardens, and return to the mountains, where they slept until nightfall, when they would once again come down upon the city.

Now this place was in the furthest part of the country of the blacks, and one of the strangest things that happened to me during my sojourn in the city took place in this way. One of the company with whom I spent the night in the boat asked me, "My lord, you are apparently a stranger to these parts. Do you have any craft that you practice?"

"By Allah," I answered, "I have no trade, nor do I know any craft, for I was a merchant and a man of money and substance. I had a ship of my own laden with a great number of goods and merchandise, but it foundered at sea, and all were drowned except me. I was fortunate to save myself on a plank which Allah had placed at my disposal."

After hearing this, he said, "Take this bag and fill it with pebbles from the beach. After that you're to join a group of townspeople, whom I shall tell about you. Do as they do, and you will see that you'll be able to find a way to return to your native land."

Then he carried me to the beach, where I filled my bag with large and small pebbles, and soon we saw a group of people coming from the town, each carrying a bag filled with pebbles like mine. He introduced me to the people and told them to take good care of me. "This man is a stranger," he said. "So take him with you and teach him how to gather so that he may obtain his daily bread, and you will earn your reward in heaven."

"You may trust us," they answered and bid me welcome. Then they took me to a spacious ravine full of lofty trees with trunks so smooth that it was impossible to climb them. Now, sleeping under these trees were numerous apes, and when they saw us, they rose and fled, swarming up among the branches. All at once my companions began to pelt them with what they had in their bags, and the apes began to pluck the fruit of the trees and cast them at the people. I looked at the fruit they threw at us and found them to be cocoa nuts. So I selected a large tree full of apes and began to pelt them with stones, and in return they pelted me with nuts, which I collected, as did the rest. Consequently, even before I could empty my bag of pebbles, I had gotten a huge amount of nuts, and as soon as my companions had gotten as many nuts as they could carry, we returned to the city, where we arrived late in the day. Then I went to the kind man who had brought me together with the nut gatherers and gave him all I had collected, thanking him for his kindness. But he would not accept them and said, "Sell them and make a profit." And soon he added, giving me the key to a closet in his house, "Store your nuts in this safe place. Go out every morning and gather the nuts as you've done today. Choose the worst to sell, and store the rest here. In this way you'll be able to save the best to pay for your return home."

"May Allah reward you," I answered and did what he advised. Every day I went with the cocoa-nut gatherers, who helped me find the best-stocked trees, and I continued doing this until I had stored a large quantity of excellent nuts along with a large sum of money that I had obtained from the nuts that I had sold. Soon I was able to live in ease and bought all I saw and liked. So I was able to enjoy my time in this city until one day, when I was standing on the beach, I saw a large ship steering through the heart of the sea toward the island. After the ship cast anchor near the shore, a company of merchants landed and began to buy and sell their goods for cocoa nuts and other commodities. Then I went to my friend and informed him about the arrival of the ship and how I wanted to return to my own country.

"It's for you to decide," he said.

So I thanked him for his generosity and took leave of him. Then I went to the captain of the ship, and we came to an agreement about the payment for my passage, and I had my cocoa nuts and other possessions brought aboard the ship.

And Scheherazade noticed that dawn was approaching and stopped telling her story. When the next night arrived, however, she received the king's permission to continue her tale and said,

That very same day the ship weighed anchor, and I left the City of Apes. We sailed from island to island and sea to sea, and wherever we stopped, I sold and traded with my cocoa nuts, and the Lord requited me with more than I had and even more than I had lost. Among other places, we came to an island that had an abundance of cloves, cinnamon, and pepper, and the people of that country told me that a large leaf grew by the side of each bunch of pepper, and this leaf shaded the pepper from the sun and protected it from the water in the wet season. But when the rain stopped, the leaf turned over and drooped down by the side of the bunch of pepper. During my visit to this island, I exchanged my cocoa nuts for a great deal of pepper, cloves, and cinnamon. From there we traveled to the island of Al-Usirat, known for its Comorin aloes wood. Afterward we moved on to another island, where the Chinese lign aloes grew. This wood is better than the Comorin, but the people of this island were more vulgar in their customs and religion than those of the other island, for they loved fornication and wine and did not know prayers or how to call to prayer.

Our next destination was the pearl fisheries, and I gave the divers some of my cocoa nuts and said to them, "Dive for my luck and lot!"

They did so and brought a large quantity of large and priceless pearls from the deep sea, and they said to me, "By Allah, master, you are blessed with luck!"

Then we sailed on until we arrived safely at Bassorah. After staying there a short time, I returned to Baghdad, where I went to my home and gathered my family and friends around me, and they all rejoiced at my safe return. After storing my goods and valuables, I distributed alms to the poor, gave clothes to the widows and orphans, and made presents to my relatives and comrades, for the Lord had requited me with four times the amount of the goods that I had lost. Soon thereafter I returned to my merry ways and forgot all that I had suffered because I had gained so much.

Such, then, is the history of my fifth voyage and its wonders.

Now, let us have supper, and tomorrow, come again, and I shall tell you what happened to me during my sixth voyage, for it was even more miraculous than this one.

Sinbad called for food, and the servants spread the table, and after they had eaten the evening meal, he had

Sinbad the porter given a hundred dinars, and the landsman returned home and lay down to sleep, marveling at all that he had heard. The next morning, as soon as it was daylight, he said his dawn prayer, and went to the house of Sinbad the Seaman and wished him a good day. The merchant asked him to take a seat and talked with him until the rest of the company arrived. Then the servants spread the table, and when they had had their good fill of food and drink and were in a merry mood, Sinbad the Seaman began to tell the narrative of

The Sixth Voyage of Sinbad the Seaman

Many days after my fifth voyage, while I was sitting and enjoying myself with my friends, a company of merchants arrived in Baghdad, and they came to me and told tales of travel and adventure. In addition, they talked about the great profits and the money that could be made, and my soul yearned for travel and trade. So compelled by fate and fortune I decided to undertake another voyage, and once again I had fine and costly merchandise bound up into bales and journeyed from Baghdad to Bassorah. There I found a large ship ready for sea and full of merchants and notables who were carrying costly goods with them. After I had my bales also brought on board, we left Bassorah in safety and in good spirits.

We traveled from place to place and from city to city, buying and selling and reaping profits. Wherever we went we also amused ourselves by observing the different sights of the countries where strange folk dwelt. And fortune smiled on us until one day, as we were sailing along, the captain suddenly uttered a great cry and cast his turban on the deck. Then he buffeted his face like a woman, plucked out his beard, and fell down in the middle of the ship almost fainting out of grief and rage. "Alas!" he cried. "My name will be ruined, and my poor children will become orphans!"

All the merchants and sailors rushed to his side and asked, "Master, what's the matter?" For the life of them, they could not understand what was going on.

Then the captain answered by saying, "I want you to know that we have wandered off course and left the sea that I know, and we are now in a sea that is unfamiliar to me. Unless Allah guarantees us some means of escape, we are all dead men! So pray to the Most High that the Lord deliver us from this predicament. I hope there is someone among you who is righteous and whose prayers the Lord will answer."

Then he got up and climbed the mast to see whether there was any way to escape from that strait. He would have unfurled the sails, but the winds increased, and the ship whirled around three times and was driven backward. Then the rudder broke, and the ship headed toward a cliff. Once he realized what was happening, the captain climbed down from the mast and said, "Only Allah can save us now, and nobody can prevent what fate has ordained! We have come to a place of sure destruction, and there is no way of escape for us, nor can any of us be saved!"

So we all began to weep about our fate and bid one another farewell, since we believed that our days had come to an end, and we had lost all hope of surviving. Indeed, shortly thereafter, the ship struck the cliff and broke up, and everything on board was plunged into the sea. Some of the merchants were drowned, and others tried their best to reach the shore and save themselves on the mountain. I was among this group, and when we got ashore, we found a large island, or rather peninsula, covered with the wreckage of crafts, goods, and instruments cast up by the sea from destroyed ships whose passengers had been drowned. In fact, the quantity of the different items was so huge that it was impossible to calculate how much was there.

In the meantime I began climbing the cliffs and headed inland until I came to a stream of fresh water that rose up at the foot of the mountains and disappeared in the earth under the range of hills on the opposite side. All the other passengers went over the mountains to the interior, and they dispersed here and there, startled by what they saw. Indeed, they became like madmen at the sight of the wealth and the treasures that were strewn on the shores. As for me, I looked down into the bed of the stream where I was and saw a huge number of rubies, royal pearls, jewels, and precious stones, which were like gravel in the bed of the rivulets that ran through the fields. Moreover, the sands sparkled and glittered with gems and precious metals, and we found an abundance of the finest lign aloes, both Chinese and Comorin. There was also a spring of crude ambergris that flowed like wax or gum over the banks of the streams because of the great heat of the sun. It ran all the way down to the seashore, where the monsters of the deep came up, swallowed it, and returned into the sea. However, it burned in their bellies, so they threw it up again, and it congealed on the surface of the water, causing its colors and qualities to change. Finally, the waves cast it ashore, and the travelers and merchants who could recognize it collected it and sold it. But as to the raw ambergris which was not swallowed, it flowed over the channel and congealed on the banks, and when the sun shone on it, it melted and gave off a musklike scent in the whole valley. When the sun stopped shining, however, it congealed again.

We continued to explore the island, admiring the wonderful works of Allah and the riches we found there, but we were very troubled by our predicament and by our prospects of surviving. Now, while on the beach we had picked up some small victuals from the wreck and shared them carefully, eating but once every day or two in fear that the food would run out and we would die miserably from famine and fright. Moreover, we were weak because of a colic that had been brought on by seasickness and a bad diet. Consequently my companions died one after the other until there was but a small group of us left. Each man that had died we washed and shrouded in some of the clothes and linen cast ashore by the tides. Soon thereafter the rest of my comrades perished one by one until I had buried the last of the group and dwelled alone on the island with very few provisions left, I who was accustomed to have so much. So I wept over myself and said, "If only I had died before my companions and they had washed and buried me! It would have been better than dying without being washed and buried! But only the Almighty Allah can decide what is best!"

And Scheherazade noticed that dawn was approaching and stopped telling her story. When the next night arrived, however, she received the king's permission to continue her tale and said,

The only thing left for me to do was to dig my own grave on the seashore, and I said to myself, "As soon as I feel that I'm growing weak and know that death is near, I'll throw myself into the grave and die there. Perhaps the wind will cause the sand to drift and cover me. This way I'll be buried." Then I began reproaching myself for being so foolish and having left my native land to travel again after all I had suffered during my first five voyages. I bemoaned my fate, especially since I had no need of money and could not spend what I had, nor even a half of it, during my life. However, after a while, it dawned on me that the stream must have an end as well as a beginning. In other words, there had to be an outlet somewhere, and I thought its course might lead to some inhabited place. So I decided to make a little boat big enough to sit in and launch it in the stream. "If I escape," I said, "I'll escape because of God's mercy. If I perish, it will be better to die in the river than here."

So after collecting some pieces of Chinese and Comorin aloes wood, I bound them together with ropes from the wreckage. Then I chose straight planks of even size from the broken parts of the ship and fixed them firmly on the aloes wood. In this way I was able to build a boat-raft a little narrower than the channel of the stream, and I tied it so tightly and firmly that it seemed to be nailed. Then I loaded it with the goods, precious metals, jewels, royal pearls, and the best of the crude and pure ambergris together with what I had collected on the island and what was left of the victuals and wild herbs. Finally, I lashed a piece of wood on both sides to serve as oars, and I launched the boat. As I drifted with the stream, I wondered what would happen to me. I continued drifting until I reached the place where the stream disappeared beneath the mountain. Then I had to row the boat into the place, which was intensely dark, and the current carried the raft with it down the underground channel. The thin stream carried me on through a narrow tunnel where the raft touched the sides, and my head rubbed against the roof. Since it was impossible to return from there, I blamed myself for having risked my life and said, "If this passage grows any narrower, the raft will hardly pass, and I'll inevitably perish miserably in this place."

I threw myself facedown on the raft because of the narrowness of the channel while the stream continued to carry me along, and I could not tell night from day because of the excessive gloom and the terror and fear of death that overwhelmed me. Such was my condition as the boat went down the channel, which began to grow wider and then narrower until the darkness caused me to fall asleep and I lay prone on the raft. I do not know how long I slept, and when I awoke, I found myself in the light of heaven, and upon opening my eyes, I saw that I was in a broad stream, and my raft was moored to an island in the midst of a number of Indians and Abyssinians. As soon as these blackamoors saw that I was awake, they come up to me and talked to me in their language. However, I did not understand what they said and thought that I was having a vision or dream in my delirious state. Nevertheless, I was delighted to have escaped from the river. Then, when they realized that I did not understand them and did not answer, one of them came forward and said to me in Arabic, "Peace be with you, my brother! Who are you, and how did you get here? How did you find this river, and what kind of land lies beyond those mountains? We have never encountered anyone who has come to us from that way."

"Peace be with you," I responded, "and may Allah bless you. Who are you, and what country is this?"

"We are farmers and tillers of the soil and came out to water our fields and plants. When we found you asleep on this raft, we grabbed hold of it and tied it to the shore, waiting for you to awake at your leisure. So tell us how you managed to come here."

"For Allah sake, my lord," I said, "could you give me something to eat before I speak, for I'm starving. After zi eat, you may ask me whatever you want."

So he quickly brought me some food, and I ate until I was refreshed. My fear was calmed by a good bellyful, and my life returned to me. Then I told them about my adventures from first to last, especially about my troubles in the narrow channel.

And Scheherazade noticed that dawn was approaching and stopped telling her story. When the next night arrived, however, she received the king's permission to continue her tale and said,

After I had finished my story, the Indians and Abyssinians discussed everything among themselves and said to one another, "We must definitely carry him with us and present him to our king so that he can relate his adventures." So they took me together with the raft boat and all the jewels, minerals, and merchandise and brought me to their king, who was the king of Sarandib. After welcoming me, he asked me about myself and my adventures through the man who spoke Arabic, and I repeated my story from beginning to end, whereupon he was most astounded and rejoiced at my escape. Afterward I arose and fetched some precious metals, jewels, ambergris, and lign aloes from the raft and presented them to the king, who accepted them and treated me with the utmost honor, assigning me living quarters in his own palace. So I consorted with the chief of the islanders, and they paid me the highest respect.

Now the island Sarandib lies under the equinoctial line, and it has a night and day both numbering twelve hours. It is eighty miles long and thirty miles wide. The width is bounded by a lofty mountain and a deep valley, and one can see the mountain from a distance of three days. This mountain contains various kinds of rubies and other minerals and all sorts of spice trees. The surface is covered with emery that is used to cut and fashion gems. There are diamonds in the rivers and pearls in the valleys. I climbed that mountain and had the pleasure of viewing its marvels, which are indescribable. Afterward I returned to the king, and soon all the travelers and merchants who came to the place asked me about the affairs of my native land and about the Caliph Harun al-Rashid and his rule. I told them all about him and why he was so renowned, and I praised him because of this.

In turn, I asked them about the manners and customs of their own countries and learned all that I desired.

One day the king himself asked me about the way and manner my country was governed, and I let him know all about the circumstances of the caliph's reign in the city of Baghdad and the justice of his rule. The king was greatly impressed by my account of the caliph's appointments and said, "By Allah, the caliph's laws are indeed wise, and the way he rules the land is praiseworthy. Your account has caused me to admire him deeply, and I would like to make him a present and send it via you."

"As you wish," I responded. "I'll bear your gift to him and inform him that you are his sincere admirer and true friend."

Then I lived with the king in great honor and high regard for a long time until one day, while I was sitting in his palace, I heard news of a company of merchants who were fitting out a ship for Bassorah, and I said to myself, "Now is an opportune time to travel home." So I rose without delay, kissed the king's hand, and told him about my desire to set out with the merchants, for I longed to be with my own people.

"You are your own master," he said, "but if you should like to stay with us, we would be delighted, for you made us very happy with your company."

"By Allah, my lord," I answered, "you have indeed overwhelmed me with your favors and kind deeds. But I miss my friends and family and native country."

When he heard this, he summoned the merchants in question and told them to take care of me, paying for my passage and freight. Then he bestowed on me great riches from his treasures and placed me in charge of a magnificent present for the Caliph Harun al-Rashid. In addition, he gave me a sealed letter and said, "Carry this to the Commander of the Faithful with your own hand, and give him many salutations from us."

"As you wish," I replied.

The letter was written on the skin of the khawi (which is yellow and finer than lamb parchment) with ink of ultramarine, and the contents were as follows: "Peace be with you from the king of Al-Hind, who possesses a thousand elephants and whose palace crenelles are gilded with a thousand jewels. At this time we are sending you a gift which, though it is a trifle, we hope you will accept. You are like a brother and sincere friend to us, and great is the love that we bear you in our heart. Therefore, be so kind as to send us a reply. The gift does not befit your dignity, but we beg you, oh brother, to accept it graciously. May peace be with you."

The present consisted of a large ruby cup that had its inside adorned with precious pearls; a bed covered with the skin of the serpent which swallows elephants, and this skin has spots as large as dinars, and whoever sits on it never gets sick; a hundred thousand miskals of Indian lign aloes; and a slave girl like a shining moon. After the king placed me in charge of all these things, I took leave of him and of all my friends and acquaintances of the island and embarked with the merchants. We sailed with a fair wind and soon arrived at Bassorah, where I spent a few days and nights obtaining equipment and packing up my bales. Then I went on to Baghdad, the House of Peace, where I sought an audience with the caliph and laid the king's presents before him. The caliph asked me where they came from, and I told him, "By Allah, I don't know the name of the city, nor do I know how to get there."

"Oh Sinbad," the caliph said, "is this true what the king has written?"

After kissing the ground, I answered, "My lord, I saw much more in his kingdom than he has written in his letter. For state processions a throne is set for him upon a huge elephant, eleven cubits high, and he sits upon this while his great lords and officers and guests stand in two rows on his right and his left. In front of him there is a man with a golden javelin, and behind another with a large gold mace that has an emerald head a span long and as thick as a man's thumb. And when the king mounts his horse, a thousand horsemen mount with him, and they are clad in gold brocade and silk. Wherever the king goes, he is preceded by a man who cries out, 'Here comes the king his majesty!' And this man continues to repeat his praises in words that I cannot remember, but at the end of his panegyric, he says, 'This is the king who owns a crown not even Solomon or the great rajah ever possessed.' Then he is silent, and the man behind him proclaims, 'He will die! Again I say he will die!' And the other adds, 'Praised be the perfection of the living who is not dead!' Moreover, because of his sense of justice, intelligence, and laws, there is no kazi in his city, and all his lieges determine what is right and wrong."

"How great this king is!" said the caliph. "His letter reveals this, and with regard to the mightiness of his realm, you have told us all about it, and you witnessed it with your own eyes. By Allah, he has been endowed with wisdom as well as with extensive power."

Then I told the caliph all that had happened to me during my last voyage, and he was most astounded and commanded his historians to record my story and store it in his treasuries for the edification of all who might come upon it. Then he conferred great honors on me, and I returned to my home, where I put all my goods and possessions in warehouses. Soon my friends came to me, and I distributed presents among my family and gave alms. Afterward I indulged myself in mirth and merry-making and forgot all that I had suffered.

Such then, my brothers, is the history of what happened to me during my sixth voyagc, and tomorrow I shall tell you about my seventh and last voyage, which is even more wondrous and marvelous than the first six.

Then he ordered the servants to set the table, and the company had supper with him. Afterward he gave the porter a hundred dinars as he was accustomed to do, and they all went their ways, marveling at the story they had just heard.

The next day Sinbad the Landsman rose, said the dawn prayer, and returned to his namesake's house. Once the company was fully assembled, his host began to relate

The Seventh Voyage of Sinbad the Seaman

After the return from my sixth voyage, which brought me a huge profit, I resumed my former life of enjoyment and merrymaking day and night. However, it was not long before my soul yearned once more to sail the seas, see foreign countries, enjoy the company of merchants, and hear new things. So I packed some precious goods in bales, and I went from Baghdad to Bassorah, where I found a ship ready for sea. There were a considerable number of merchants on this ship, with whom I became friends, and we set forth on our venture in health and safety. Indeed, we sailed with a fair wind until we came to a city called Madinat-al-Sin, but after we had left it and fared on in good cheer looking forward to our trade, a violent headwind sprang up, and a storm drenched us and our goods. So we covered the bales with our cloaks, garments, and canvas to prevent them from becoming spoiled by the rain, and we began praying to Allah and begging him to deliver us from the peril that threatened us. Now the captain arose, and tightening his belt, he tucked up his skirts and climbed to the masthead, from where he looked out to the right and left. Then he gazed at the passengers and crew and began to buffet his face and pluck out his beard. So we cried to him, "Captain, what's the matter?"

"Ask the Lord for deliverance!" he cried out. "Our predicament is hopeless, and it's time to take leave of one another. The wind is too powerful and has driven us into the uttermost of the seas of the world."

Then he came down from the masthead, opened his sea chest, and pulled out a bag of blue cotton, from which he took a powder like ashes. Next he put the ashes into a little saucer and wet them, and after waiting a short time, he smelt and tasted the concoction. Finally, he took a booklet out of the chest and read awhile and began weeping. "I want you all to know," he said, "that this book contains some frightening information! I'm afraid that I must tell you that nobody has ever escaped these waters alive. This ocean is called the Clime of the King and harbors the sepulcher of our Lord Solomon, son of David. There are also tremendous and fearful serpents here, and those ships that make their way to these waters will be swallowed up by a great whale, and so will everything on board the ship as well."

We were most astonished by our captain's words, and no sooner had he finished speaking than the ship was lifted out of the water and then tossed back. Immediately we started saying the death prayer and committed our souls to Allah. Soon we heard a terrible cry like loud thunder, causing us to become terror-struck and to give ourselves up for lost. Suddenly we saw a huge whale as large as a tall mountain, and we became wild with fright, wept, and got ready for death. We could do nothing but marvel at its vast size and gruesome looks. Yet this whale was nothing compared to the second monster that quickly made its appearance. So we bemoaned our fate, and as we were saying farewell to one another, a third whale, bigger than the first two, came up from the deep. Its appearance caused us to lose all our senses, and we were stupefied out of fear and horror.

The three whales began circling the ship, and the third and biggest opened its mouth to swallow us. Its jaws were wider than the gates of a city, and its throat was like a long valley. So we cried out to the Almighty for help, and all of a sudden a violent squall arose and smashed the ship, which was tossed out of the water and settled on a large reef, the haunt of sea monsters. It was there that the ship broke and fell apart into planks, causing everything on board to plunge into the sea. As for me, I tore off all my clothes but my gown and swam a little way until I came upon one of the ship's planks. I grabbed hold of the plank, hoisted myself onto it, and rode it like a horse while the winds and waters had their sport with me. The waves threw me up and down, and I was in a pitiful plight and suffered from fear, hunger, and thirst. Of course, I reproached myself for what I had done, and I said to myself, "Oh Sinbad, oh seaman, you are always suffering hardships and travails, but you won't renounce the sea. And whenever you say 'I renounce it,' you proceed to belie your renouncement. So you'll just have to endure your inflictions with patience, for truly you deserve everything that happens to you."

And Scherherazade noticed that dawn was approaching and stopped telling her story. When the next night arrived, however, she received the king's permission to continue her tale and said,

So I continued talking to myself and said, "All this has been decreed by Allah to turn me from my greed for gain, and indeed, it is only because of my greed that I've gotten into this predicament, for I have wealth galore." Then I regained my senses and said, "But truly, this time I repent to the Most High with utmost sincerity. I deplore my lust for gain and venture, and never again shall I speak or think about traveling on the high seas if I'm saved."

I continued to humble myself before Almighty Allah and bewail my fate, recalling my former condition of comfort, satisfaction, mirth, and joy. For two days I floated on the ocean in this manner until I came to a large island with many trees and streams. After landing I ate the fruit of the trees and drank water from the streams until I was refreshed. Gradually I regained my strength and spirits. Then I walked about and found a large river with fresh water and a strong current on the far side of the island. Then I recalled the boat-raft that I had made during my previous voyage, and I said to myself, "If I make another one, I might be fortunate enough to get out of this predicament. And if I escape, I vow to Allah Almighty never to travel again. And if I perish, I shall be at peace and shall no longer suffer from my trials and tribulations."

So I stood up and gathered together a large quantity of wood from the trees and twisted creepers and tree twigs into a kind of rope with which I bound the wood, and in this way I built a raft. After saying, "If I be saved, it will be because of God's grace," I embarked and let the current carry the raft. I sailed for three days and lay in the raft. I did not eat anything, and when I wanted something to drink, I took some water from the river. Gradually I became as weak and giddy as a chicken because of exhaustion, famine, and fear.

At the end of the third day I came to a high mountain under which the river ran. When I saw this, I feared for my life because I had suffered from the narrow channel on my previous voyage. I wanted to stop the raft and land on the mountainside, but the current overpowered me and drew the raft into the subterranean passage like an archway. So I gave myself up for lost and said, "My life is in the hands of the Almighty Allah!" However, after a little while the raft glided into open air, and I saw before me a wide valley into which the river fell with a noise like the rolling of thunder and the rushing of the wind. I held on to the raft for fear of falling off it while the waves tossed me right and left. The raft continued to descend with the current, and I was unable to stop it or turn it shoreward. Finally, however, the raft carried me to a large and grand city with many people and buildings. When the inhabitants of this city saw me on the raft carried by the current, they threw out ropes to me, but I did not have the strength to hold on to them. Then they tossed a net over the craft and pulled it ashore, whereupon I fell to the ground as if I were a dead man.

After a while a venerable old man came out of the crowd, threw some fine clothes over me to cover my nakedness, and welcomed me. Then he had me carried to the Hammam bath and brought me cordial sherbets and delicious perfumes. In addition, when I came out, he brought me to his house, where his people indulged me in a most generous manner. They seated me in a pleasant place and set rich food before me. After I ate my fill, I gave thanks to the Almighty for rescuing me. Thereupon the old man's pages fetched me hot water, and I washed my hands, and his slave girls brought me silken napkins with which I dried my hands and wiped my mouth.

Now the sheikh gave me an apartment in his house and commanded his pages and slave girls to attend me and look after my wants. They were assiduous in their service, and I lived in the guest chamber for three days, eating and drinking well and enjoying good aromas until life returned to me, my terrors subsided, my heart was calmed, and my mind was put at ease. On the fourth day the sheikh came to me and said, "You have brought cheer into our house with your company, and praise be to Allah for your rescue! Now, how would you like to come down with me to the beach and bazaar and sell your goods? There you can buy whatever you need to trade. I have ordered my servants to remove your stocks in trade from the sea, and they have piled them on the shore."

I was silent awhile and said to myself, "What do his words mean? What goods do I have?"

Then he said, "My son, don't be disturbed or so cautious. Just come with me to the market, and if you receive a good offer for your goods, take it. But if you're not satisfied by the offers, you may store them in my warehouse until you find the right occasion to sell them."

So I thought about my situation and said to myself, "Do what he says and see what the goods are." And I said to him, "As you wish. I cannot refuse you, for Allah's blessing is on everything you do."

Consequently he led me to the market street, where I found that he had taken in pieces of my raft that were made of sandalwood. Then I heard the broker offering them for sale.

And Scheherazade noticed that dawn was approaching and stopped telling her story. When the next night arrived, however, she received the king's permission to continue her tale and said,

Soon the merchants came and began bidding for the wood against one another until its price reached a thousand dinars. When they stopped bidding, my host said to me. "Listen, my son, this is the current price of your goods in hard times. Do you want to sell them for this price, or shall I have them stored in my warehouse until the prices rise?"

"My lord," I answered, "the business is in your hands. Do as you think best."

"Will you sell the wood to me for a hundred gold pieces over and above what the merchants have bid?" he asked.

"Yes," I said. "The goods are yours."

So he ordered his servants to transport the wood to his warehouse, and after bringing me back to his house, he offered me a seat and counted out the purchase money to me. Next he put the money in bags, placed them in a secret place, locked them with an iron padlock, and gave me the key. Some days after this the sheikh said to me, "My son, I have something to propose to you, and I hope you will do my bidding."

"What is it?" I asked.

"I am a very old man and have no son," he stated. "But I have a pleasant, young daughter endowed with wealth and beauty. Now I would like to marry her to you so that you may live with her in our country, and I shall make you master of all I possess, for I am an old man, and you will take my place."

I was silent out of shame and did not respond, whereupon he continued, "Please do as I desire, my son, for I only wish what is best for you, and if you do as I say, you will have my daughter at once and be like a son to me. If you want to trade and travel to your native land, no one will hinder you, and your property will be at your sole disposal. So, do as you desire."

"By Allah, my lord," I replied, "you have become like a father to me, and I am a stranger and have undergone many hardships. Because of all the stress, I have lost my capacity to judge and think. Therefore, it is up to you to decide what I should do."

As a result of what I said, he sent his servants for the kazi and the witnesses and married me to his daughter. Following the marriage there was a noble feast and grand festival. When I went in to see my wife, I found her perfectly beautiful and lovely and graceful. She was clad in rich raiment and covered profusely with ornaments, necklaces, and other trinkets of gold and silver and precious stones worth a mint of money, a price nobody could pay. She pleased me, and we loved each other, and I lived with her until her father was taken to the mercy of Allah Almighty. So we shrouded him and buried him, and I inherited his entire property and all his servants and slaves. Moreover, the merchants requested that I assume his position as their sheikh and their chief. Now I was to have this rank.

When I became better acquainted with the people of the city, I found that at the beginning of each month the men were transformed into birds and sprouted wings. Then they flew to the upper regions of the firmament, and nobody remained in the city except the women and the children. So I said to myself, "When the first of the month comes, I'll ask one of them to carry me to their destination." Consequently, when the time came for them to change their forms, I went to one of the inhabitants and said to him, "May Allah bless you! Carry me with you so that I may be able to enjoy myself with the rest of you and then return."

"This cannot be done," he replied, but I persisted and pleaded with him until he finally consented. Then I left in his company without telling my wife, friends, or servants, and he took me on his back and flew up with me so high in the air that I heard the angels glorifying God in the heavenly dome. I was so astounded that I exclaimed, "Praised be Allah! Extolled be the perfection of Allah!" No sooner had I finished uttering Allah's praises than a fire came shooting out of heaven and all but consumed the company, whereupon they fled and descended, heaping curses on me and casting me down on a high mountain. Then they went away, exceedingly angry with me, and left me there alone. Finding myself in such plight, I repented what I had done and reproached myself for having undertaken something I was not suited to do. "Almighty Allah," I said, "no sooner am I rescued from one predicament than I get into one that is worse!" And I was bemoaning my fate when suddenly two young men who looked like moons came walking by, each using a golden rod as a staff. So I approached and greeted them. "May Allah bless you," I said. "Who are you, and what are you?"

"We are servants of the Most High Allah and live in this mountain," they replied. Then they gave me a golden rod they had with them and went their way, leaving me behind. I walked on along the mountain ridge and steadied myself with the staff. I was wondering about the two youths when all at once a serpent came forth from under the mountain. It had a man in its jaws which it had swallowed down to his navel, and he was crying out, "Whoever saves me, Allah will deliver from all adversity!"

And Scheherazade noticed that dawn was approaching and stopped telling her story. When the next night arrived, however, she received the king's permission to continue her tale and said,

* * *

So I went up to the serpent and hit it on the head with the golden staff, causing it to spit the man from its mouth. Then I smashed the serpent a second time, and it turned and fled. Now the man came up to me and said, "Since you have rescued me from the serpent, I shall never leave you, and you will be my comrade on this mountain."

"You're welcome," I answered, and so we continued walking along the mountain until we joined a group of people, and I noticed that the very man who had carried me and cast me down was among them. So I went up to him, excused myself politely for my behavior, and said, "But, comrade, what you did was not the way friends should treat friends."

"It was you who almost destroyed us by glorifying God on my back," he responded.

"Pardon me," I answered. "I didn't know that this was the wrong thing to do. But if you take me with you now, I swear not to say a word about the matter."

So he relented and consented to carry me with him on the express condition that as long as I was on his back, I was to abstain from glorifying God. Then I gave the golden rod to the man whom I had rescued from the serpent and bade him farewell, and my friend took me on his back and flew with me as before until he brought me to the city and set me down in my own house. My wife came to meet me and rejoiced that I was safe. "Beware of going out with those men again," she said. "You should never associate with them, for they are brethren of the devils and don't know how to mention the name of Allah Almighty. Nor do they worship Him."

"And how did your father deal with them?" I asked.

"My father did not associate with them, nor did he do what they do. And now that he is dead, I think that you had better sell all that we have. Then you can buy merchandise with the profits and journey to your own country and people. And since my mother and father are dead, I would like you to take me with you, for I don't want to stay in this city any longer."

So I sold all the sheikh's property piecemeal and looked for someone who might be traveling to Bassorah. While I was doing this, I heard about a group of merchants who wanted to make the voyage but could not find a ship. Consequently, they bought wood and built a large ship for themselves, and I booked passage with them. Then we embarked, I and my wife, with all our goods, leaving our houses and domains. We journeyed from island to island and from sea to sea with a fair wind until we arrived at Bassorah safe and sound. I did not stay there this time. Instead, I transferred all my goods to another vessel and set out right away for Baghdad, where I arrived safely. Then I went to my home, gathered my family and friends around me, and stored my goods in my warehouses.

It turned out that I had been away from Baghdad for twenty-seven years, and my people had given up all hope of ever seeing me again. So when they heard about my return, they gave me a great and joyous welcome, and I told them all that had happened to me, and they were most astounded. Then I swore that I would never travel again, neither by land or sea, for my last and seventh voyage had more than fulfilled my longing for adventure and travel. And I thanked the Lord and blessed Him for having restored me to my kith and kin and country and home.

"Therefore, think about all this, oh Sinbad the Landsman," continued Sinbad the Seaman, "think about the sufferings I have undergone and what perils and hardships I have endured before reaching my present state."

"May Allah bless you, my lord!" answered Sinbad the Landsman. "Pardon me the wrong I did you by envying your wealth."

And Sinbad the Seaman and Sinbad the Landsman continued to be friends and to enjoy all the comforts and pleasures of life until there came to them the Destroyer of delight and the Sunderer of friendship and the Caterer for cemeteries. And glory be to the Living One who does not die!

Conclusion: The Marriage of King Shahryar and Scheherazade

Now, during this time, Scheherazade had given birth to three sons, and when she had finished telling the tale of Sinbad, she rose to her feet and kissed the ground before the king.

"Your majesty," she said, "I am your wife, and for many nights and years I have entertained you with stories of people from long ago and have also provided you with lessons of admonition. May I then be so bold as to ask a favor of your highness?"

"Ask, oh Scheherazade," he replied, "and your request will be granted."

Thereupon she called out to the nurses and the eunuchs, "Bring me my children!"

So they quickly brought them to her, and there were three sons, one walking, one crawling, and one sucking. She took them, and after setting them down before the king, she again kissed the ground and said, "Oh king, these are your children, and I request that you release me from the doom of death as a dole to these infants, for if you kill me, they will become motherless, and you will find nobody among all the women in your realm to raise them as they should be raised."

When the king heard this, he wept, drew the boys to his bosom, and said, "By Allah, oh Scheherazade, I pardoned you before these children were born, for I found you chaste, pure, ingenuous, and pious! May Allah bless you and your father and mother and their root and branch! May Allah be my witness that I exempt you from anything that can harm you."

So she kissed his hands and feet and rejoiced immensely, saying, "May the Lord grant you a long life and increase your dignity and majesty! You were amazed by that which you experienced on the part of women. Yet, the kings of the Chosroës suffered greater misfortunes before you, and indeed, I have told you about what happened to caliphs and kings and others with their women. But telling all these tales can be exhausting, and listening can be tedious, and what I have told is sufficient warning for the man with good sense and also sufficient admonishment for the wise."

Then she stopped speaking, and after King Shahryar heard her words and profited from all that she had said, he summoned his powers of reason, cleansed his heart, became more understanding again, and turned to Allah Almighty, saying to himself, "Since the kings of the Chosroës suffered more than I have, I shall never stop blaming myself for the past as long as I live. As for Scheherazade, there is nobody like her in all the world. So praise be to Him who appointed her as the means for saving His creatures from oppression and slaughter!"

Then he arose from his seance and kissed her head, whereupon she and her sister, Dunazade, rejoiced with immense delight. When the morning came, the king went and sat down on his throne. Then he summoned the lords of his land, who all came in and kissed the ground before him. He singled out his vizier, Scheherazade's father, with special favor and bestowed on him a splendid robe of honor, treated him with utmost kindness, and said, "May Allah protect you, for you have given me your noble daughter for my wife, and she has been the means of my repenting that I have slain the daughters of my folk. Indeed, I have found her pure and pious, chaste and ingenuous, and Allah has granted me three sons through her, and may He be praised for such benevolence."

Then he bestowed robes of honor upon his viziers, emirs, and chief officers, and he told them what had happened between him and Scheherazade, how he had turned from his former ways and repented what he had done, and how he intended to wed Scheherazade and draw up the marriage contract with her. When those who were present heard this, they kissed the ground before him and blessed him and his betrothed, Scheherazade, and the vizier thanked her. Then King Shahryar brought this sitting to an end to everyone's satisfaction, whereupon the people went to their homes, and the news was spread that the king intended to marry the vizier's daughter Scheherazade. Then he proceeded to prepare for the wedding, and soon he sent for his brother, King Shah Zaman.

When his brother approached his city, King Shahryar rode out to meet him with his troops. Furthermore, they decorated the city in the most splendid fashion and sprayed scents from censers and burned aloes wood and other perfumes in all the markets and thoroughfares. They also rubbed themselves with saffron, while the drums beat and the flutes and pipes sounded, and mimes and mountebanks played and displayed their art, and the king lavished them with gifts and money. Indeed, it was a day to be remembered.

When they came to the palace, King Shahryar commanded his servants to spread the tables with roasted meats, all kinds of viands, and sweetmeats, and he ordered the crier to announce to the folk that they should come to the divan and eat and drink and that he wanted this to be a means of reconciliation between him and them. So, high and low, great and small, came up to him, and they spent the next seven days and nights eating and drinking with him. Then the king withdrew into his chamber with his brother and told him about everything that had happened between him and the vizier's daughter Scheherazade during the past three years, and he related what he had heard from her, all the proverbs, parables, chronicles, pleasantries, quips, jests, stories, anecdotes, dialogues, histories, and verses.

King Shah Zaman was greatly astounded and said, "After hearing this, my brother, I'd be glad to have her younger sister as my wife so we two may become brothers-german to sisters-german, and they would be sisters to us in the same way. Ever since the misfortune that I experienced and that led you to discover your own misfortune, I have taken no delight in women. Like you I lay with a woman every night during the past three years and put her to death the next morning. But now I desire to marry your wife's sister, Dunazade."

When King Shahryar heard his brother's words, he rejoiced with immense pleasure. So he arose right away, went to his wife, Scheherazade, and told her what his brother had proposed, and she answered, "Your majesty, we shall consent only on one condition, that he set up his residence here, for I cannot bear to be parted from my sister for more than an hour. We were raised together and cannot endure separation from one another. If he accepts this pact, she will be his wife."

King Shahryar returned to his brother and informed him about what Scheherazade had said, and he replied, "Indeed, this was what I also intended, for I never want to be parted from you anymore. As for my kingdom, Allah Almighty shall bestow it on whomever He chooses, for I have no longer a desire to be king."

When King Shahryar heard his brother's words, he was full of tremendous joy and said, "Truly, this has also been my wish, my brother. Praise be to Allah, who has brought about this union between us."

Then he sent for the kazis, the witnesses, captains, and notables, and they married the two brothers to the two sisters. After the contracts were written out, the two kings bestowed silk and satin robes of honor on all those who were present, while the city was decorated and the celebrations recommenced. The king commanded each emir, vizier, chamberlain, and nabob to decorate the palace, and the people of the city were ecstatic because of the good signs for future happiness and contentment. King Shahryar also ordered sheep to be slaughtered, kitchens to be set up, and banquets to be arranged, and he fed all who came, high and low. In addition, he gave alms to the poor and needy and was benevolent to great and small. Then the eunuchs went forth so that they could perfume the Hammam bath for the brides. They sprayed it with rose water, willow-flower water, and pods of musk, and they fumigated it with Kakili eagle wood and ambergris. Then Scheherazade and her sister, Dunazade, entered, and they cleansed their heads and clipped their hair. After they came out of the Hammam bath, they donned raiment and ornaments such as men were accustomed to prepare for the kings of the Chosroës, and among Scheherazade's apparel was a dress lined with gold and embroidered with images of birds and beasts. And the two sisters put on dazzling necklaces of priceless jewels so that they looked stunning and were more radiant than the sun and the moon. They lit the bright wax candles in a golden candelabra, but their faces were brighter than the candles. Their eyes were sharper than unsheathed swords, the lashes of their eyelids bewitched all hearts. Their cheeks were rosy red. Their necks and figures swayed gracefully. Their eyes fluttered like those of the gazelle.

After the slave girls came to meet them with instruments of music, the kings entered the Hammam bath, and when they came out, they sat down on a couch lined with pearls and gems. Then the two sisters came up to them and stood between their hands, bending and leaning from side to side in their beauty and loveliness as if they were moons. Soon Scheherazade was brought forward and displayed in a red dress, whereupon King Shahryar arose to look at her, and all present, men and women, were captivated. Then they attired Dunazade in a dress of blue brocade, and she looked like the radiant full moon. After they displayed her in this first drcss before King Shah Zaman, he rejoiced in her and almost swooned away because of his love and amorous desire for her. Indeed, his passion overwhelmed him.

Then they returned to Scheherazade and displayed her in her second dress of incomparable splendor and veiled her face with her hair like a chin veil. Moreover, they let down her locks, and she was astonishingly beautiful. After that they displayed Dunazade in her second, third, and fourth dresses, and she paced forward like the rising sun, and she swayed to and fro in insolent beauty. Next they displayed Scheherazade in her third, fourth, and fifth dresses, and she was perfectly lovely and graceful. Then they returned to Dunazade and displayed her in the fifth and six dresses. In the last one she was so lovely that she surpassed all the beautiful women of the four quarters of the world and outshone the full moon at rising tide with the brightness of her countenance. Then they displayed Scheherazade in her sixth and seventh dresses, and she came forward swaying from side to side and moved so coquettishly that she ravished the minds and hearts of all present and bewitched their eyes. She shook her sides and swayed her haunches, then put her hair on sword hilt and went up to King Shahryar, who embraced her as a hospitable host embraces a guest and threatened her in her ear with the taking of the sword. She was then followed in the same way by Dunazade, and when they put an end to the display, the king bestowed robes of honor on all who were present and sent the brides to their own apartments. Thereafter, Scheherazade went to King Shahryar, and Dunazade to King Shah Zaman, and each king enjoyed the company of his beloved consort, and the hearts of the people were comforted.

The next morning the vizier went to the two kings and kissed the ground before them. Thereupon, they thanked him and showed him their benevolence. Then they went forth and sat down on the royal couches, while all the viziers, emirs, grandees, and nobles presented themselves and kissed the ground. King Shahryar ordered robes of honor and gifts for them, and they prayed for long life and prosperity for the king and his brother. After that the two monarchs appointed their father-in-law to be viceroy in Samarcar and assigned him five of the chief emirs to accompany him and serve him to the best of their capabilities. The minister kissed the ground and prayed that they would have long lives. Then he went to his daughters, while the eunuchs and ushers walked before him, and he began saying his farewell. They kissed his hands, celebrated his appointment to kingship, and bestowed great treasures on him.

After that he set out on his journey and traveled many days and nights until he drew near Samarcar, where the people went out to meet him and rejoiced greatly in his arrival. So he entered the city, and they decorated all the houses, and it was a day to be remembered. When he sat down on the throne of his kingship, the viziers, grandees, and emirs of Samarcar paid him homage and prayed that he would be guaranteed justice, victory, and long life. So he bestowed robes of honor on them and treated them with respect, and they declared him sultan over them.

As soon as his father-in-law had departed for Samarcar, King Shahryar summoned the grandees of his realm and made them a stupendous banquet with all kinds of delicious meats and exquisite sweetmeats. He also bestowed robes of honor on them, rewarded them, and divided his kingdom between himself and his brother in their presence, whereby they rejoiced. Then each king ruled a day in turn, and they lived in harmony with each other, while the two sisters continued living harmoniously as well in the love of Allah. The people and the provinces remained peaceful, and the preachers prayed for them from the pulpits. Their fine reputation was spread abroad, and travelers brought news about them to foreign lands.

In due time King Shahryar summoned chroniclers and copyists and ordered them to write down all that had happened to him with his wife from first to last. So they wrote this book and called it *The Stories of the Thousand and One Nights*. The entire book consisted of thirty volumes, and the king stored them in his treasury. Thereafter, the two brothers continued to live with their wives in great pleasure and solace, especially since Almighty Allah had changed their grief into joy. Indeed, they continued enjoying life until the Destroyer of delights and the Severer of societies and the Desolator of dwelling places came upon them. After their departure they were succeeded by a sage ruler, who was just, wise, and accomplished and loved tales and legends, especially those which chronicled the deeds of kings and sultans. It was in King Shahryar's treasury that he found these marvelous stories and wondrous histories contained in thirty volumes. So he began reading the first volume, then a second, and a third, and each book astounded and delighted him more than the one that preceded it, and he kept reading until he finished all thirty. Since he admired everything that was recounted and described in the volumes, all the customs, anecdotes, moral examples, and reminiscences, he ordered his clerks to copy them and spread them throughout the world. As a consequence, the tales became famous, and the people called them *The Marvels and Wonders of the Thousand and One Nights*. This is all that we know about the origins of this book, and Allah is omniscient. So glory be to Him, whom the tides of time cannot waste away, nor does chance or change affect His sway. And peace be upon the Lord's Chosen One among His creatures, our Lord Mohammed, the Prince of humankind, through whom we send our prayers to our Lord for a good and divine

FINIS.

Afterword

No other work of oriental literature has had such a profound influence on the western world as *The Thousand and One Nights*. Translated first into French between 1704 and 1717 by Antoine Galland (1646–1715) a gifted orientalist, the *Nights* spread quickly throughout Europe and then to North America. The amazing success of the *Nights* was due largely to the remarkable literary style of Galland's work, which was essentially an adaptation of an Arabic manuscript of Syrian origins and oral tales that he recorded in Paris from a Manonite of Aleppo named Youhenna Diab or Hanna. In addition, the enormous European interest and curiosity about the Orient stimulated by trade and travel reports contributed to the popularity of the *Nights*. At first the tales were famous chiefly among the literate classes, who had direct access to the different English, German, Italian, and Spanish translations of Galland's work. However, because of their exotic appeal, there were many cheap and bowdlerized editions of the *Nights* in the eighteenth century that enabled the tales to be diffused among the common people and become part of their oral tradition. Moreover, they were also sanitized and adapted for children, so that by the end of the nineteenth century, the *Arabian Nights* had become a household name in most middle-class families in English-speaking countries, were an important source of knowledge about Arabic culture for intellectuals, and were known by word of mouth among the great majority of the people.

The development of the *Nights* from the secular oriental imagination of the Middle Ages into a classical work for western readers is a fascinating one. The tales in the collection can be traced to three ancient oral cultures, Indian, Persian, and Arab, and they probably circulated in the vernacular hundreds of years before they were written down some time between the ninth and fourteenth centuries. The apparent model for the literary versions of the tales was a Persian book entitled *Hazar Afsanah* ("A Thousand Tales"), translated into Arabic in the ninth century, for it provided the framework story of a caliph who, for three years, slays a new wife each night after taking her maidenhead, and who is finally diverted from this cruel custom by a vizier's daughter, assisted by her slave girl.

During the next seven centuries, various storytellers, scribes, and scholars began to record the tales from this collection and others and to shape them either independently or within the framework of the Scheherazade/Shahryar narrative. The tellers and authors of the tales were anonymous, and their styles and language differed greatly; the only common distinguishing feature was that they were written in a colloquial and somewhat vulgar idiom. By the fifteenth century there were three distinct layers that could be detected in the collection of those tales that came to form the nucleus of what became known as *The Thousand and One Nights*: (1) Persian tales that had some Indian elements and had been adapted into Arabic by the tenth century; (2) tales recorded in Baghdad between the tenth and twelfth centuries; and (3) stories written down in Egypt between the eleventh and fourteenth centuries. By the nineteenth century, the time of Richard Burton's unexpurgated translation, there were four "authoritative" Arabic editions, more than a dozen manuscripts in Arabic, and the Galland work, all of which one could draw from and include as part of the tradition of the *Nights*. The important Arabic editions are as follows:

Calcutta I, 1814 –18, 2 vols. (also called ed. Shirwanee)
Bulak, 1835, 2 vols. (also called the Cairo Edition)
Calcutta II, 1839 –42, 4 vols. (also called ed. Macnaghten)
Breslau, 1825 –38, 8 vols., ed. M. Habicht

* * *

Although Burton and John Payne relied on the Calcutta II and Breslau editions for their translations, neither these two nor the other editions can be considered canonical or definitive. There was never a so-called finished text by an identifiable author or editor. In fact, there were never 1,001 nights or stories, and the title was originally *One Thousand Nights*. When and why the tales came to be called *The Thousand and One Nights* is unclear. The change in the title may stem from the fact that an odd number in Arabic culture is associated with luck and fortune, and it also indicates an exceedingly large number. The editions vary with regard to contents and style, and though there is a common nucleus, there are often different versions of the same tale. Nevertheless, together the various editions along with the manuscripts and Galland can be considered to constitute what has become accepted in the West as *The Thousand and One Nights*.

As already mentioned, the tales of the *Nights* have been published in all western languages either separately or in collections of different kinds ever since the eighteenth century. However, as Burton himself remarked—and without trying to sound like a purist—"the *Nights* are nothing without the nights." That is, the Scheherazade framework is essential for the collection, and Scheherazade sets the tone for the employment of the narratives, even though they were probably created by different authors: it is she who provides the *raison d'être* for the tales, the driving impulse, and without comprehending why she was "invented," the *Nights* cannot be understood.

Given the patriarchal nature of Arabic culture, it would seem strange that Scheherazade assumed the key role in the *Nights*. Yet a woman exercised more power in Moslem culture during the Middle Ages in Baghdad and Cairo than is commonly known. Not only did she receive a dowry when she married and share in the disposition of the property with her husband, but she also was the absolute ruler of the home, children, and slaves. In particular, she was responsible for the children's early education, choice of faith, marriage, and profession. Perhaps most important, sexual initiation was a major part of her responsibility. In short, the wife was in charge of civilizing the children of a family more than the husband, and if we consider that the *Nights* are primarily concerned with the acquisition of manners and mores, it is clear why Scheherazade should exercise such a pivotal role in the collection: not only does she curc Shahryar's madness, ostensibly caused by another woman (perhaps even his mother, as some psychologically minded critics have suggested), but she also produces an entertaining manual for listeners who will not survive or become humane without learning the Moslem social code of that time.

The listeners are the fictitious Shahryar and Dunazade and the implicit readers of the texts, then and now. That is, the fictitious Scheherazade has a threefold purpose in telling her tale.

First, she wants to reeducate Shahryar and return him to the world of civilization and humanity. His reaction to his wife's betrayal is so extreme and his wound so deep that he has apparently been rcacting to some traumatic experience suffered during his childhood. In other words, he may have been abused by his mother or other women during his youth, and Scheherazade's narrative is the means through which he can regain trust in women and come to see that they have many different sides to them.

Second, Scheherazade obviously wants to relate all her wisdom through the tales to her other major auditor, her younger sister, Dunazade, so that Dunazade will know how to fend for herself in the years to come. Like Scheherazade, Dunazade has witnessed the three-year reign of terror by Shahryar, but unlike Scheherazade, who is a most accomplished scholar and confident woman, she does not have the means to contend with the caliph and his autocratic rule. Through listening to her sister's tales as the representative of other young Moslem virgins, she will be prepared to cope with men like Shahryar and to turn a male-social code to her advantage. In fact, Scheherazade teaches Dunazade how to plot and narrate her own destiny to achieve an autonomous voice, which receives due respect from Shahryar at the conclusion of all the tales.

Third, aside from educating her sister and Shahryar, the two fictitious listeners, Scheherazade's function as storyteller is to socialize the Moslem readers of her time and all future readers, who may be unaware of Moslem custom and law. That is, once her plot was invented, allowing the incorporation of different narratives, the anonymous editors of the *Nights* consistently and purposely chose a core of forty-two tales (most of them included in the present collection) that reappeared in the four different Arabic editions and Galland's work. Without disregarding the entertaining and humorous aspects of these stories, they are primarily *lessons* in etiquette, aesthetics, decorum, religion, government, history, and sex. Together they represent a compendium of the religious beliefs and superstitions of the time, and they also convey the aspirations and wishes of a strong middle class, for most of the tales concern merchants and artisans, who, like Sinbad and Judar, continually take risks to make their fortune. Since they are daring and adventurous, they can only survive through cunning, faith in Allah, and mastery of words. That is, there is an artistic side to them. Like Scheherazade, most of the protagonists are creative types who save themselves and fulfill their destiny because they can weave the threads of their lives together in narratives that bring their desires in harmony with divine and social laws. Narration is raised to an art *par excellence*, for the nights are paradoxically moments of light, epiphanies, through which the listeners gain insight into the mysteries and predicaments that might otherwise overwhelm them and keep them in darkness.

In the present collection, four of the major tales, "The Tale of the Merchant and the Jinnee," "The Fisherman and the Jinnee," "The Tale of the Three Apples," and "The Hunchback's Tale," parallel the framework narrative of Scheherazade in the sense that the narrator tells tales that often give rise to other narratives, all with the purpose of saving innocent lives. It is through the intervention of the word that life is maintained; his/story (embraced in this instance by her/story, i.e., Scheherazade's narrative) makes us aware of the past while guaranteeing a qualitatively better life. The words provide justice, recognize what is just, celebrate the just and humane cause. Moreover, we learn to see the meaning of the struggle between the sexes, races, and classes in a different light. In "The Tale of the Merchant and the Jinnee," the three sheikhs tell narratives of magical transformation that depict women both as benefactors and malefactors and argue against despotism and killing as a punishment. All three stories support the philosophical position assumed by Scheherazade, who represents the voice of sanity and mercy. However, Scheherazade's sanity does not preclude punishment by death, if the case warrants it. For instance, "The Fisherman and the Jinnee" contains stories in which mercy does not help. King Yunan and the wife of the enchanted prince are so outrageously destructive and perverse that there is no hope for them, and they must be eliminated. This lesson is something that the jinnee learns as well at the very beginning of the adventure through the kindness and narrative intervention of the fisherman. Still, the primary concern of all the major tales is survival through artistic narration that is convincingly wondrous if not miraculous. For example, "The Tale of the Three Apples" includes stories that save lives and a major one about Nur al-Din and his son that relates the trials and tribulations of a family in need of a marvelous reconciliation. Finally, "The Hunchback's Tale" brings together a Christian broker, a Jewish doctor, a Moslem steward, and a tailor, who must all "sing" for their lives, while the barber talks just for the sake of telling tall tales. His love of narrative is a love of himself. Yet all his tales and the others in "The Hunchback's Tale" are in a sense "miraculous" because they lead to the restoration of the hunchback's life. The function of narration assumes a holy aspect, and the various storytellers are astounded by the providential happenings and coincidences of their own plots and actions. Life becomes a wonder through their narratives that enable them to survive the threat of death.

While these major tales indicate the philosophical disposition of the entire collection of *Nights*, the other tales are exemplary forms of different genres, some with lessons commensurate with Scheherazade's task of educating Shahryar and Dunazade, others with representations of the conditions and mores of medieval oriental culture in the broadest sense. "The Ebony Horse" and "Julnar the Mermaid" are remarkable fairy tales that make use of numerous folklore motifs and are based on the traditional plot of the young prince compelled to undergo arduous tasks before he is allowed to marry the princess of his choice. "Prince Behram and the Princess Al-Datma" is a delightful example of one of the early folk versions of *The Taming of the Shrew* that found its German expression later in the Grimms' "King Thrushbeard." Whereas a haughty woman is put in her place here, "The Wily Dalilah" is a hilarious anecdote about a crafty woman and her daughter who put an entire city of men in their place. Like "The Tale About the Thief of Alexandria and the Chief of Police," it mocks the judicial system in Egypt and expresses sympathy with those who dare to break the law, especially when the law itself is ridiculous. There is also a subversive quality to the fables and parables contained in "The Hedgehog and the Pigeons," whereas such tales as "Aladdin and the Magic Lamp," "Ali Baba and the Forty Thieves," "The Tale of Judar and His Brothers," and "Sinbad the Seaman and Sinbad the Landsman" are much more serious in the themes centered on humility. All four are fairy tales that draw their material from Egyptian, Persian, and Greek oral traditions and celebrate the rise of the mercantile classes. At the very least, the dreams of the merchant classes are fulfilled. Aladdin is the son of a poor tailor, who exemplifes the rags-to-riches theme. Ali Baba is a merchant's son, who squanders his inheritance but regains his status through the help of providence and the slave girl Morgiana. Although Judar is poisoned in the end by his evil brothers, he epitomizes the humble merchant, whose goodness and perseverence enables him to become a great caliph. Interestingly, Sinbad vacillates between hubris and humility. Of course, it is his devotion to Allah that saves him in the end, and he becomes as wealthy as the caliph of Baghdad.

The constant appeal to Allah in all the tales indicates that the characters have little faith in the temporal order, which is either unjust or breaks down. Despite the long period of gestation and the different authors/editors, the tales are consistent in the way they derive their force from the tension between individual desire and social law. As Burton recognized, despite the fantastical elements the tales tell life as it is, and they expose hypocrisy, deceit, and, most of all, despotism. In fact, in the figure of Scheherazade, they empower the oppressed, who fulfill their deepest desires in ways they had thought were unimaginable. Yet everything is imaginable in the *Nights*, and it is no doubt the miraculous realization of the unimaginable in the tales that still draws readers to the *Nights* today.

Glossary

Abbas uncle of Mohammed; died 653. He was a wealthy merchant and chief supporter of Islam; his descendants founded the Abbasid dynasty of caliphs (750–1258).

abu father of

bastinado beating, punishment; also used to make someone confess a crime

bint daughter of

Chosroëus, Khosru king of Persia (531–79); he was the greatest of the Sassanid monarchs. Revered as a just but despotic ruler, he stimulated commerce, expanded the Persian empire, and reformed the taxation system.

Copt a descendant of the ancient Egyptians, also a member of the traditional monophysite Christian church originating in Egypt

dervish a member of a Moslem order who takes vows of poverty and austerity

divan a royal court where a council is held, or a large reception room

emir chieftain or military commander, a title given to descendants of Mohammed through his daughter Fatima

fakih doctor of law and religion

Fatihah the opening chapter of the Koran

Ghusl ablution complete ablution, washing of hands

gobbo a hunchback

Hammam bath bath for convalescence and relaxation, a necessity and a luxury

Iblis a cherub, who was at first cherished by Allah but then cursed and expelled from Allah's company. He is associated with the diabolus or despairer.

ibn son of

ifrit, ifritah masculine and feminine forms of jinnee, who are frequently evil

Jinn collective name for jinnees (masculine) and Jinniyahs (feminine)

khan a place of lodging, "hotel," caravanserai

kasidah ode, elegy

kazi chief justice, judge in religious matters, the great legal authority of a country

lign aloes the soft resinous wood of an East Indian tree used for making Nadd, a perfume

Lisam veil mouth band

mameluke white slave trained to arms

marid jinnee

nabob viceroy, govenor, or man of great wealth

olema the learned in the law

santon a European designation for a monk or hermit among the Mohammedans

sawik parched corn

sheikh an old man, elder, chief

shroff banker, money changer

syce a groom

vizier minister

Wuldan Ghilman, the beautiful youths of paradise

Wuzu ablution a kind of ablution necessary before joining in prayers

Bibliography

Major English Translations

Burton, Richard F. *The Book of the Thousand Nights and a Night. A Plain and Literal Translation of the Arabian Nights Entertainment*. 10 vols. Benares: Kamashastra Society, 1885–86.

———. *Supplemental Nights to the Book of the Thousand Nights and a Night, with Notes Anthropological and Explanatory*. 6 vols. Stoke Newington: Kamashastra Society, 1886–88.

Lane, Edward William. *A New Translation of the Tales of a Thousand and One Nights; Known in England as the Arabian Nights' Entertainments*. London: Charles Knight & Co., 1838–40.

Payne, John. *The Book of the Thousand Nights and One Night*. 9 vols. London: Villon Society, 1882–84.

———. *Tales from the Arabic of the Breslau and Calcutta Editions of the Book of the Thousand and One Nights*. 3 vols. London: Villon Society, 1884.

———. *Alaeddin and the Enchanted Lamp; Zein ul Asnam and the King of the Jinn*. London: Villon Society, 1889.

Secondary Literature

Ali, Muhsin Jassim. *Scheherazade in England: A Study of Nineteenth-Century English Criticism of the Arabian Nights*. Washington, D.C.: Three Continents Press, 1981.

Bencheikh, Jamel Eddine. *Les Mille et une Nuits ou La parole prisonnière*. Paris: Gallimard, 1988.

Burton, Richard F. "Terminal Essay" in *The Book of the Thousand Nights and a Night. A Plain and Literal Translation of the Arabian Nights Entertainment*. Vols. 5/6. New York: Heritage Press, 1934. pp. 3653–3870.

Caracciolo, Peter L., ed. *The Arabian Nights in English Literature: Studies in the Reception of The Thousand and One Nights into British Culture*. New York: St. Martin's Press, 1988.

Clinton, Jerome W. "Madness and Cure in the 1001 Nights." *Studia Islamica* 61 (1985): 107–25.

Conant, Martha Pike. *The Oriental Tale in England in the Eighteenth Century*. New York: Columbia UP, 1908.

Gerhardt, Mia A. *The Art of Story-Telling: A Literary Study of the Thousand and One Nights*. Leiden: Brill, 1963.

Ghazoul, Ferial J. *The Arabian Nights: A Structural Analysis*. Cairo: Cairo Associated Institution for the Study and Presentation of Arab Values, 1980.

Grossman, Judith. "Infidelity and Fiction: The Discovery of Women's Subjectivity in the *Arabian Nights*." *Georgia Review* 34 (1980): 113–26.

Kabbani, Rana. *Europe's Myths of the Orient*. New York: Macmillan, 1986.

Kelen, Jacqueline. *Les nuits de Schéhérazade*. Paris: Albin Michel, 1986.

Lahy-Hollebecque, Marie. *Le féminisme de Schéhérazade*. Paris: Radot, 1927.

Macdonald, D. B. "A Bibliographical and Literary Study of the First Appearance of the Arabian Nights in Europe." *Literary Quarterly* 2 (1932): 387–420.

Saadawi, Nawal El. *The Hidden Face of Eve*. London: Zed Press, 1980.